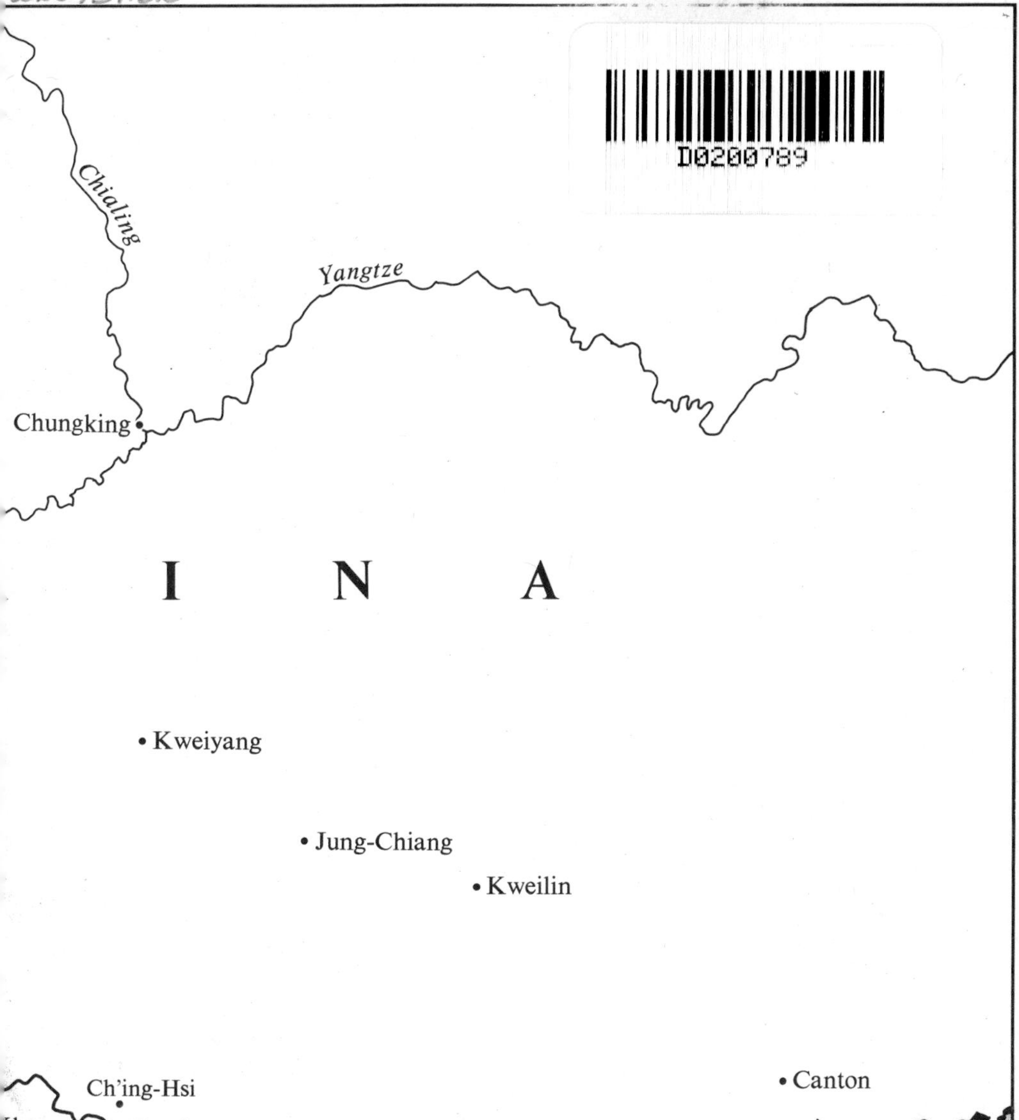
Chialing
Yangtze
Chungking
I N A
Kweiyang
Jung-Chiang
Kweilin

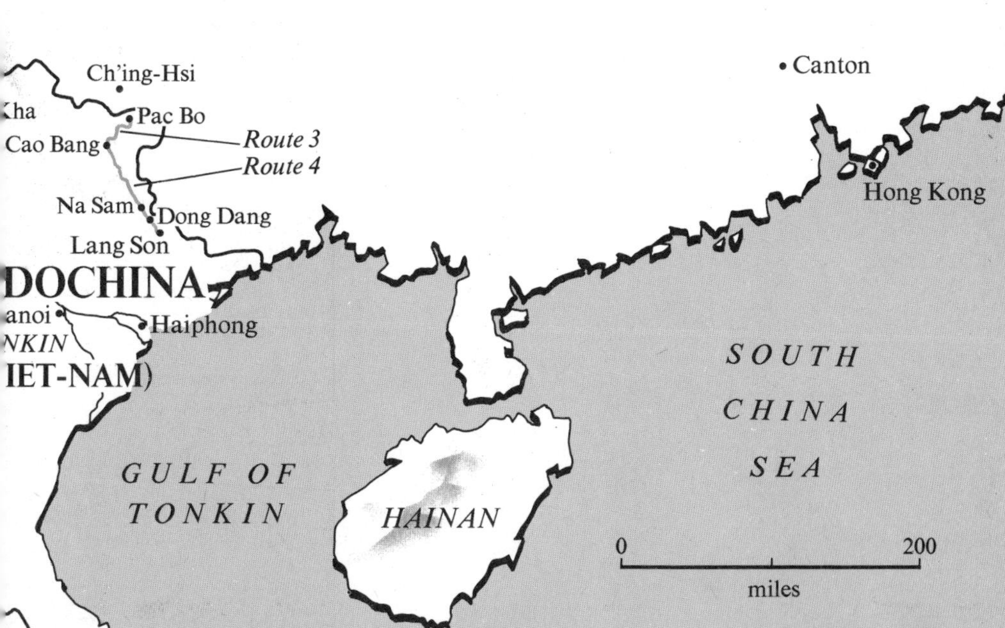
Canton
Ch'ing-Hsi
Pac Bo
Cao Bang
Route 3
Route 4
Na Sam
Dong Dang
Lang Son
DOCHINA
anoi
Haiphong
NKIN
IET-NAM)
Hong Kong
SOUTH
CHINA
SEA
GULF OF
TONKIN
HAINAN
0
200
miles

A Dirty Distant War

Other books by E. M. Nathanson

FICTION

The Latecomers
The Dirty Dozen

NON-FICTION

It Gave Everybody Something To Do
(collaboration)

A Dirty

E. M. Nathanson

Distant War

VIKING

VIKING
Viking Penguin Inc., 40 West 23rd Street,
New York, New York 10010, U.S.A.
Penguin Books Ltd, 27 Wrights Lane, London W8 5TZ
(Publishing & Editorial), and Harmondsworth, Middlesex,
England (Distribution & Warehouse)
Penguin Books Australia Ltd, Ringwood,
Victoria, Australia
Penguin Books Canada Limited, 2801 John Street,
Markham, Ontario, Canada L3R 1B4
Penguin Books (N.Z.) Ltd, 182–190 Wairau Road,
Auckland 10, New Zealand

First published in 1987 by Viking Penguin Inc.
Published simultaneously in Canada

LIBRARY OF CONGRESS CATALOGING IN PUBLICATION DATA
Nathanson, E. M., 1928–
A dirty distant war.
I. Title.
PS3564.A85D57 1987 813′.54 86-45845
ISBN 0-670-80334-0

Printed in the United States of America by
Haddon Craftsmen, Scranton, Pennsylvania
Set in Linotron Times Roman
Designed by Ann Gold
Maps by Paul Pugliese, General Cartography Inc.

TO ELIZABETH

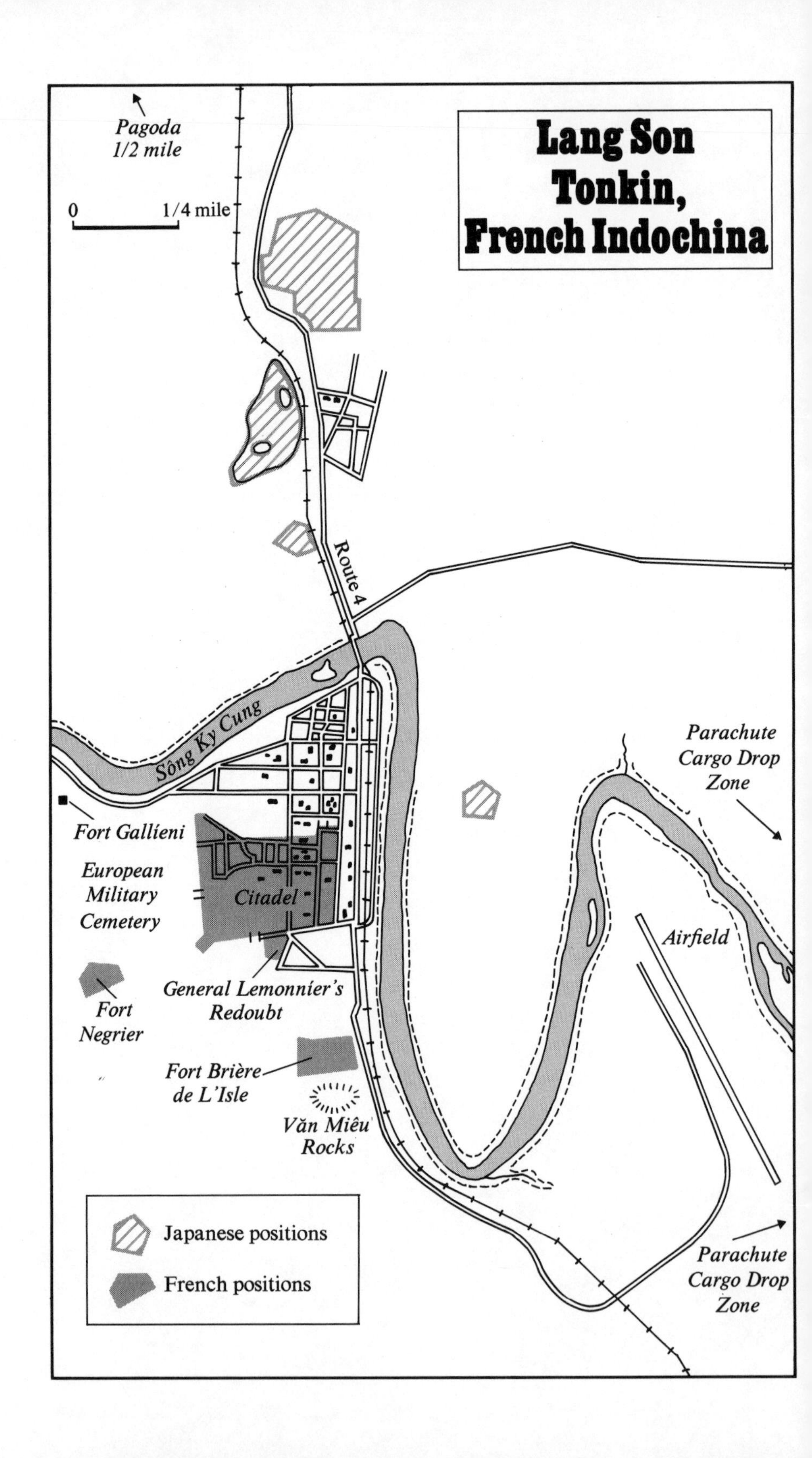
Lang Son
Tonkin,
French Indochina
Pagoda
1/2 mile
0
1/4 mile
Route 4
Sông Ky Cung
Fort Galliéni
European
Military
Cemetery
Citadel
General Lemonnier's
Redoubt
Fort
Negrier
Fort Brière
de L'Isle
Văn Miêu
Rocks
Parachute
Cargo Drop
Zone
Airfield
Parachute
Cargo Drop
Zone
Japanese positions
French positions

AUTHOR'S NOTE

There were real persons in military and civilian roles like these in Burma, China and Indochina in those years. Some appear here under their own names because they were public figures, their histories recorded, some with conflicting views. The fictional characters have their own histories.

The possibility of these things having happened exists within the known facts of what did happen. What interests me is the moment before Apocalypse, who was there, what was said and done, what might have happened otherwise. The story is fiction, but if I have portrayed true persons, living, dead or imaginary, it is exactly what I intended.

E.M.N.

. . . Besides, there is no king, be his cause never so spotless, if it come to the arbitrament of swords, can try it out with all unspotted soldiers.

—William Shakespeare

Henry V

PART I

Treachery in Transit

Chapter 1

John Reisman caught the sharp glint of sunlight off the Salween and hand-signaled the pilot to take him in. The C-46 began its steep corkscrew descent. Sitting in the co-pilot's seat, Major Reisman compared the reality of the terrain he saw with what the maps said should be there. He hoped the young pilot at the controls knew what he was doing and that the aircraft held together. They were flying south of the worst part of it, but the mountains and jungles across the Hump, the main Himalayan air route from India to China, were strewn with the wreckage of aircraft like this and the skeletons of the men who'd flown in them.

The Salween River lay deep in the undulating layers of hills and mountains, and it cleaved an endless green wilderness. To one side, from where they'd come, lay Burma. To the other was China. But there was no certainty about the frontier. The best maps allowed for "disputed territory." Reisman held two maps on his lap now, one a Burmese battle map printed on silk. It laid claim to land which

Chinese cartographers marked on their own maps as part of their province of Yunnan. The other map Reisman studied was a standard-issue flight map used by the U.S. Army Air Corps for the China-Burma-India theater. He didn't trust that one alone. There had been too many incidents in Europe and elsewhere when OSS men, depending on standard maps and the uncertain judgments of pilots and navigators, had been dumped out of planes to be captured or killed miles from critical drop points. There also had been times when carefully laid battle plans had been blown to hell because entire brigades had been parachuted to disaster in the wrong landing zone by bad intelligence, technical error and lousy navigation. Below the aircraft in which Reisman flew, there were still very active units of General Tanaka's 18th Division; troops who, having escaped encirclement by American, British and Chinese forces under Stilwell to the north and west, were fighting in the jungles and mountains of Burma, attacking and defending in strength as they withdrew to the east toward China and to the southeast toward Thailand.

The Burmese battle map had been a good find for Reisman when his plane had put down in Myitkyina. The town and its vital airfield had been only recently taken back from the Japs in brutal, slogging jungle campaigns by American Brigadier General Frank Merrill's Marauders and British Major General Orde Wingate's Chindits, soldiers aptly named after the fierce stone lions that guarded Burmese temples. Reisman's C-46 had landed in Myitkyina to refuel and so he could pry out the newest intelligence regarding the bizarre mission he'd been assigned. Presumably, until he had landed in Calcutta a couple of days before, he had been merely a passenger in transit between London and Chungking for more normal reassignment. Though normal could hardly be the word to describe the dirty jobs that Major Reisman (his exalted new rank less than a month old) had always been given since he had joined the Office of Strategic Services three years earlier, when it was first organized.

Nevertheless, because OSS Base Headquarters in Grosvenor Square (and good old Max Armbruster at Special Operations in Baker Street) did value his talents so highly, they were sometimes unexpectedly kind to him, tolerant of his idiosyncrasies. He'd had only one request before leaving London for reassignment to the Far East, where hundreds of General Donovan's "wild men" were being sent now that their very special and personal methods for problem solving, their propensities for nose-thumbing independence, their occasional penchant for trouble with the brass of all nations and their unorthodox military *modus operandi* were no longer much needed or wanted in the European theater. The thrust of the war there now was the massive pressing back, by the book, of the Nazi armies and the swift liberation of German-occupied territories. Free-lancers of Reisman's stripe were hardly tolerated any more.

His request had been to spend two days, just two days and the night in between, in a Paris that was at last free of the stink of Germans, the obscenity of Nazis and their signs and symbols, and free of the sight of the uniforms and faces of the Wehrmacht and Waffen-SS that he hated with such gut-churning rage. Paris had been liberated only days before. Max Armbruster, a full colonel now himself (though in Reisman's fond opinion still the college professor he had been before the war), had presented Reisman with his new gold leaves and had arranged to humor him with the two-day leave in Paris.

"I've told them at Base that you intend to brush up on your fluency in Chinese while you are there," Max had said dryly.

"Chinese? In Paris? How droll. My knowledge of Chinese was minimal at best when I was there," Reisman had said. "And you managed to wing that past them? You really do deserve those new eagles of yours."

"We owe you, Johnny. They owe you. I owe you. For Operation Amnesty and the job you did at the château in Rennes."

"Ancient history. All of three months ago," Reisman had said. "I didn't think memories lasted in brass heads. Besides, it wasn't me. I was just along for the ride. It was the men. Those poor benighted sons-of-bitches." He had started out hating them and had come to love them. Well, perhaps not all of them.

"The Dirty Dozen," Armbruster had intoned, in a postmortem benediction, shaking his head. "An experiment—but never again. How are your casualties doing?"

"The ones in hospital are coming along okay. I visited them a few days ago. The ones the Germans captured we still don't know about. The dead ones are fine, I suppose," he had added coldly. "Depending upon their particular persuasion. But we won't know about that till we get there, will we?"

Colonel Armbruster had looked away uncomfortably. Then he had made room for Reisman on a courier plane. In free Paris, the reality and fantasy of which Reisman had fought and killed for during many years, and many times had almost died for, he had walked and walked and walked through the streets, hardly pausing to rest or sleep. He had crossed the bridges over the Seine to the core of the ancient city, the Ile de la Cité and Ile St. Louis, and marveled that all was still there and whole as he remembered it. He had wined and dined in any restaurant that still boasted a menu. On the Boulevard St. Germain, in the Deux Magots, he had looked for Sartre and de Beauvoir, whom he had sometimes talked to there before the war, but he did not see them. Instead he had met a woman drunk on the wine of liberation, and, because he spoke French and had a certain manner about him, she said, a passion and sadness that blended like a piquant sauce, and he was not just one of the thousands of *les Américains* who poured through the city those days and nights, she had shared the wine of liberation and more with him in the night, and it had been very good for each of them. Perhaps they would meet again.

Then, wanting to fill his heart and soul with the possibility of something long absent, he had gone alone to a mass within the gargoyle-protected cathedral of Notre Dame, as a listener and observer, not a communicant; and afterward, feeling only a pleasant mellowness rather than the ennoblement and new grace he wanted, he had climbed the hill of Montmartre to the gleaming white basilica of Sacré Coeur to try again at a second mass for that which was said to be spiritual, universal and eternal.

He had not felt it, but he had felt good hearing again the Latin liturgy, the soaring voices in praise of all that was heaven, and drawing to himself the murmurs of thankful voices in French. Afterward he had even wondered, now that he had honored the religious tradition of his long dead Italian mother, if—in deference to Aaron Reisman, alive and well in Chicago—he should seek out the possibility of a synagogue still standing and newly functioning in Paris. But he had not done that. He would do it another time in another place. He thought perhaps he had given enough to God that day. It was time to render unto Caesar again. There was the courier plane to catch back to London. He had promised Max he would be there on time, to be briefed further, if there was anything, about his transfer to the Far East, and to depart without further delay on the long flight to Chungking.

In Calcutta, when he had been ordered into this unexpected and unwanted crisis mission that he was now on (*their crisis, not mine,* he had bitched to himself), he had been briefed in a vague way by the local bureaucrats. Then they had given him a C-46 for his own solitary employment, thereby verifying the high-level importance of the crisis, and had sent him on his way to Myitkyina. Once there, Reisman had traded a leather-sheathed hip flask he'd bought at Harrods to a Chindit sergeant-major to get the Burmese map, but it had been worth it. Leather would have rotted in the jungle anyway, and the silver flask would have burned black with his sweat. The map had probably been done just before the war by British army surveyors working one side of the frontier with Kachin and Shan tribesmen and the other side with units of whatever local warlord had been allied at that particular moment with Chiang Kai-shek's Kuomintang. The Burmese map was more concerned with close things that a soldier would find on the ground rather than the dense, flat bird's-eye view caught by an aerial photograph in a quick fly-by.

If Orde Wingate—whom he had admired and had met when Wingate had been a major in Palestine years earlier—had still been alive, Reisman might have welcomed the intrusion on his journey to Chungking and the side trip to Myitkyina, on the chance of seeing him again. But Wingate, an extraordinary man who had been as much a mystic and philosopher as he had been a most unorthodox soldier, had been killed in the crash of a B-25 a few months earlier. "A bright flame was extinguished," Winston Churchill had said in tribute. A terrible waste, Reisman had thought—and thought again now as his C-46 banked perilously into the gorges above the Salween.

There was no helping the flight pattern, though. Going in very low was the only way he would be able to spot Captain Bradford and his Kachin raiders or at least find the place where it was believed they would have to cross the Salween to go on into China. In Myitkyina they didn't want Bradford to do that. Nor did they want it in Calcutta, London, Washington or Chungking. Particularly not in Chiang Kai-shek's Chungking. Major Reisman had been sent in alone to stop it. He had insisted, therefore, that he sit in the co-pilot's seat of the C-46 and do the final navigating himself. He wanted to be very sure of where he jumped.

Last time, over familiar French countryside near Rennes, he'd had twelve finely honed killers with him and the loyal, courageous Sergeant Clyde Bowren who had come as a stowaway. "I've worked just as hard as these sons-of-bitches," Bowren had said when Reisman had discovered him aboard after they were airborne and over the English Channel, "and I'll be damned if I'm gonna let them think they can do anything I can't." Bowren had done magnificently, as had the others; he had survived the battle at the Château de la Vilaine, though he had been wounded and was now in a hospital in England recuperating.

This time, for Reisman, in these next minutes, parachuting alone into alien, menacing terrain, he would trust no one but himself—which had always been his way before anyway.

Chapter 2

The horsemen came down the steep trail to the river and Lincoln Bradford, who rode at the head of the column, saw ahead the place where they would be able to cross the Salween. He eased his mount to one side and halted in the dappled heat and sunlight that pressed through the dense canopy of thin-trunked trees. He lifted his dark, battered Anzac hat and wiped sweat from his forehead with his sleeve. He had let his blond hair grow thick these last months of fighting and riding. His head was wet and matted. His khakis, too, were soaked and dirty. Except for his lighter coloring and foreigner's face he might have passed for one of the dark, intense Kachins whom he waved past him toward the water.

Bradford commanded, alone—on his own authority—eight hundred tribesmen, a battalion of vengeance-bent Kachins from mountain villages high up north, east and south of Myitkyina, some from further west toward India. Only one in four of the *hypenlas*—the soldiers—rode the horses at any one time, but they took turns. The other *hypenlas* who were on foot, and the mules of the pack train, were precisely placed between troops of horsemen, moving forward in easy, loping marching order. The rear guard of the column was so far back in the trees on the winding descent to the river that it would not pass this point for another ten minutes.

With his Kachin lieutenants, Bradford had planned a faster moving, harder hitting and more secure operation than if they had gone in only on foot—though the Kachin *hypenlas* were more used to moving on foot. They could hike as much as fifty miles a day over jungle and hill trails. Pack animals were familiar to them from their lives as traders, caravan porters, transporters of goods from here to there, particularly opium. Poppies were among the crops cultivated in the terraced fields of their home villages, especially on the limestone outcroppings where the soil was most suitable. The farmers did the initial processing into opium, but used little of it themselves. It had actually been made illegal in Burma, though that had nothing to do with why the Kachins disdained addiction. It was just a good cash crop, that's all. For generations almost all of the stuff had been carried out to China, Thailand, French Indochina and the British colonies. What was not used there was transshipped to feed pleasures and addictions elsewhere in the world as morphine, opium or heroin.

Lincoln Bradford had learned a great deal in his time out here. Brahmin-born in Boston, educated at all the right prep schools and in the Ivy League college of his family's choice, he'd had a much more practical, sometimes painful and rather existentialist education since being dropped into Burma two years earlier.

None of his fellow OSS officers had wanted any part of his current operation, nor had they believed he would dare to go ahead with it. They remembered the trouble—generated first by a furious Chiang Kai-shek in Chungking—that had come after the last raid like it. The American OSS men involved in that one had been summarily sacked and shipped out.

"Who the hell do you think you are—Lawrence of Arabia?" one of the British officers from Special Office Executive had said to him when he'd gotten wind of something going on.

"Wouldn't think of it," Bradford had lied. With his own OSS people, those few he'd approached, the best he'd been able to do was get them to swear to keep their mouths shut.

Most of these Kachins had been away from their home villages for many months, had been in the action at Myitkyina, had clawed and slithered their way 6,100 feet up and over the Kumon Range during rains, fighting with Merrill's Marauders to help capture the airfield and then the town. Whatever village they were from, they all were fiercely Kachin, caring little for anything called Burma. Each of these *hypenlas* had been enraged and motivated to go on this personal, unofficial mission by the news that Chinese Kuomintang soldiers crossing into Burma had looted and destroyed nine of their villages.

Early in the war it had been the Japanese, bent on swift, brutal subjugation of the Kachins, who had come rampaging into peaceful villages to kill and torture men, women and children. They had burned to the ground *bashas* containing the living families and the honored spirits and implements of the long dead ancestors. They had raped and slaughtered women and girls. They had cut off the balls and penises of Kachin boys so that there would be no seed for the future and they had left those of the boys who survived to live on in agony as a warning to other villages. They had desecrated holy places, looted what amused them, destroyed ripening fields, carried off animals they could use, killed others. They had left behind only desolation where once there had been happy, closely knit families and societies. But in villages that had not been attacked, the Kachins had reached out to aid survivors who had fled to the bush. The tribal structure had survived, bonded together throughout hill valleys and high mountains from India to China.

Thousands of young Kachins had volunteered to become *hypenlas*. They had been trained, equipped and led mainly by men of the American OSS, men like Lincoln Bradford. They had quickly become shrewd, formidable and victorious fighters against the Japanese.

Now there had been these new, totally unexpected and treacherous depredations against their people. To know that they had been done, not by Japanese, but by Chinese; to know that Kuomintang soldiers, supposedly their allies, had attacked and looted Kachin villages, was reason for even greater rage and for a sureness of retaliation by battle-hardened veterans, *hypenlas* who demanded vengeance and knew how to exact it. Those from the looted villages had gone home to see the destruction, to bury murdered family and friends. Then they had raised the others who had come together in this battalion.

The *hypenlas* wore a variety of parts of khaki and olive drab uniforms, but the same good jungle boots made in the U.S.A. How they wore their uniforms and which parts, Bradford left up to them. Some wore heavy shirts or collarless sweaters. Some had their shirt-sleeves rolled up, some down. Some were in sweat-stained T-shirts or undershirts. In their variety of headgear they also showed their individuality, from simple G.I. field caps to soft, floppy fatigue hats to once fancy bush hats that in shape and decoration still retained some small semblance of the aspiring gallant.

Most carried arms similar to Bradford's—a carbine, a Kachin *dah* and bayonet, grenades and a .45 caliber sidearm. Many wore M-1 rifles on their shoulders instead of carbines. Twenty of them carried B.A.R.s and forty riders cradled M-3 submachine guns in their laps. Some of the men wore ammunition bandoliers criss-crossing their chests like Mexican banditos. They were more than just well armed for this mission. Bradford had seen to that with grim determination and a certain amount of chicanery.

There were eighteen mules in the pack train, spaced in groups of three at six places in the line of march. Extra ammunition, food and supplies were distributed among the animals. Broken down and tied to some of them were ten 60 mm mortars and a goodly supply of rounds to go with them. The *hypenlas* were skilled at assembling them swiftly and putting them into action, as they also were with the ten machine guns in the pack train. The *pièces de résistance,* though, were the four 70 mm pack mountain guns that had been captured many weeks earlier from the Japanese, plus a couple of hundred rounds to go with them. The Japs had actually broken down cannons like that and carried them into battle by hand. The Kachins could have done that too, but the wheels and carriages and barrels were bound to some of the pack animals.

Among the mounts—Bradford rode one of them—were dark, sleek cavalry horses captured when the Japs had been forced to retreat from their failed drive into India against Imphal and Kohima. The others were Tibetan and Mongolian ponies that had been "diverted" a few at a time from shipments bought in the far north by the Sino-American Horse Purchasing Bureau and brought into Burma by Chinese regiments that had finally made it into action with Stilwell's armies. During many months of comings and goings with his *hypenlas,* Bradford had seen to it that some of these animals had wound up in Kachin villages and he had taught them much about horsemanship, which he had learned himself under more elegant circumstances in horsy communities of the American eastern seaboard.

The sleek Japanese cavalry horses and the squat, strong Tibetan and Mongolian ponies descended slowly past Bradford, moving two and three abreast. Some of the men took his gesture with his hat as a salute and they broke their brooding silence with acknowledgments. Some called out a friendly, *"Bo!"* Others a more respectful, "*U Bo . . .*" And a few honored him with, *"Thugyi!"*—making his head and chest swell to be addressed as "great man."

Bradford's rank in the OSS was indeed that of a *Bo,* a captain. Though that was often also the title claimed by brigands. Perhaps what they were up to now would be thought of by his superiors as brigandry, but he didn't think so, nor did his men. He nodded and smiled at them as they went past, some on horse, some on foot, some with the pack mules.

"Wait at the riverbank! Stay under cover!" he called out.

Most of them spoke some English and he had learned a little of the Kachin language. Those who didn't understand English would have his orders translated by those who did. Many of the men he knew personally; he had trained them in arms and soldiery and had led them into combat against the Japs. How ludicrous, if not insane, he thought, that he was now leading them against the Chinese. Yet a lesson had to be taught and the point of it delivered all the way to Chungking.

The Kachins would wait for him below, he knew. They would follow his orders precisely. Not only because of their loyalty and respect for him, but also because among Bradford's chief lieutenants in this battalion were three village *duwas,* hereditary chiefs from whom the *hypenlas* sought counsel and to whom they paid heed. San Thau and Ba Chit had already moved past Bradford, one riding, the other hiking strongly, and they would be waiting in the last screen of trees at the bottom of the trail. The third *duwa,* Ne Tin, would be with the troop of horse guarding the rear of the column.

There were also four *umas* in the battalion. Ah Yin, Yow Khi, Sinwa Rip and Baw San were the youngest sons of *duwas,* though none of their fathers were with Bradford's raiders. In Kachin society it was the youngest son, not the eldest, who would one day inherit his father's role as headman. Therefore the other *hypenlas* respected and deferred to such aristocratic lineage.

Both the *duwas* and the *umas* looked to Bradford in matters of weapons, horses and battle plans, but he deferred to them in purely Kachin matters. He acquiesced in all strictures of social propriety and took care not to intrude upon, and in fact to pay heed and homage to, the Kachins' concerns for and relationships with the spirit world of *nats, bum nats* and *Ga Shadup,* all of which guided and guarded their lives.

When the last section of the pack train, just preceding Ne Tin's horsemen, came up to Captain Bradford, he called out a loud and teasing greeting to Baw San: "How's it going, little *maung?*"

Baw San stuck out his tongue and then laughed. He no longer liked being thought of or addressed as a *maung,* a little brother, an inferior, and he considered the term somewhat derogatory, though it was said with affection, not only by Captain Bradford but by all among the raiders who knew and liked him.

Baw San's status was somewhat different from that of the other *umas*. In theory he might already have become the *duwa* of his village—except that there was no more village. It was one of those obliterated three years back by the Japanese. Baw San's father, mother, brothers, sisters and many other relations and friends had been killed. He had escaped their fate only because he had been away on the day of the attack, having been sent by his father on an errand to a distant, more isolated Kachin village.

The wonder of Baw San, the joy of his presence to Linc Bradford, was that for a boy who had experienced as much horror as he had, he had a surprisingly cheerful disposition, with a ready smile and friendly, though demandingly inquisitive, conversation.

"I want the point when we cross the river," he called out in Kachin, "and one of those fast Jap horses. I'm going all the way to Chungking to cut off Chiang Kai-shek's head. You follow me if you can keep up."

"Chungking is many weeks away, little *maung,* even for a Kachin," said Bradford. "The Chinese would find us and kill us long before we even got to Kunming, and that is a lot closer."

"Nobody will kill me or kill you," Baw San shouted out. "*Ga Shadup* would not permit it. We still have much to do."

Baw San had been with him two years. He was Bradford's protégé; Bradford considered him almost more of a mascot than a soldier. On the march or in combat, the captain always tried to place Baw San in the position of least danger, though the boy, like everyone else well armed and competent in the use of his weapons, did not at all appreciate being treated like a child. He had pointed out a number of times to his mentor that he was now almost seventeen and should be assigned the same responsibilities and dangers as any other *hypenla.*

Baw San moved on down the trail in charge of the last section of pack mules. The dismantled parts of one of the Jap cannons, a mortar and a machine gun, plus crated ammunition, jounced lightly against the animals' flanks. The last of the horsemen, led by Ne Tin, came abreast of Captain Bradford. Ne Tin was older than most of the other *hypenlas,* with eyes deep set and narrowed as if always squinting against the sun. Creases had begun to etch themselves on the tawny skin of his cheeks and forehead. It was his preference to wear a Kachin turban wound around his head rather than a military hat. "The enemy will always know who I am," he had told Bradford. "I am not American or English or Burmese. I am Kachin." There was a fierce look about him and he had been in many battles, had cut off many heads until convinced that ears would suffice for the tally of enemies killed.

Captain Bradford wheeled his mount and followed the battalion down to the bank of the Salween River.

Chapter 3

A half hour later, the first stage of the crossing had begun and a few of the *hypenlas* were already on the China side. Most of the battalion was still screened behind the canopy of trees. Animals were grazing on what they could find, some eating fodder cut for them by the Kachins, and they were led in groups of ten to the riverbank to drink.

The raiders were at a place where the water was not deep or swift and could almost be forded a hundred yards to the opposite bank. But Captain Bradford had sent across a few strong young swimmers. They had dived naked into the stream, wearing the lead ends of spliced and knotted ropes around their shoulders. The ropes were now bound to trees on both banks, marking four lanes of passage through the river and providing a small margin of safety, something to grab onto for any who got into trouble.

The first troop of horsemen, led by Ne Tin, had started across, when the startling sound of an aircraft grew and filled the gorge with its roar.

Before trying to see what the plane was, Captain Bradford shouted in Kachin, "Out of the water! Take cover!"

The horsemen wheeled in the water and their mounts started to swim and splash back to the Burma side. The animals drinking at the stream were prodded back up into the trees. Each *hypenla* found a place to disappear under the green canopy. But the ropes were still out there plainly, tied from bank to bank, for anyone to spot from the air.

The roar of the airplane's engines grew deafening as Bradford looked up and saw it. It was a twin-engine C-46 Commando, one of the "Ol' Dumbos" that had been flying the Hump to Kunming and Chungking from bases in Assam for two years, strewing the 15,000-foot Santsung range with aluminum plating and bones. Bradford's first thought was that this plane, so much further to the south than usual, might be lost, though the weather was clear. Then he thought, as the plane came even lower, that it might be in some kind of trouble or out of fuel and about to pancake into the Salween.

Looking around quickly at the disposition of the men, he was horrified to see that a few of the *hypenlas* had dashed for the .30 caliber machine guns and were setting them up and pointing the barrels skyward.

"No! Hold your fire!" he screamed out, hoping they could hear him above the roar of the aircraft.

Baw San dashed up to one of the machine guns and kicked it over. Hadn't these foolish ones been taught the same important things that he had—the configuration and recognition of friendly aircraft and those that belonged to the Japanese?

"It's an American plane!" Baw San yelled angrily. "See the white star in the blue circle. It's a C-46."

Captain Bradford saw the wings waggle in a friendly signal as the plane flew directly overhead. Then it climbed, banked and came around higher on another pass.

Suddenly there was another object in the sky, a body dangling from a parachute, slowly descending toward the river. Bradford admired the skill of the man working the shroud lines, controlling his descent so that he would neither get hung up in a tree nor dumped into the water.

Baw San stared upward and marveled at the green-clad figure and white canopy drifting so effortlessly from the sky. *"Hla . . . hla . . ."* he murmured. Beautiful . . . beautiful.

The chutist landed about seventy-five yards up the bank from where Bradford stood watching him. When he touched down, his boots were in the shallows on the Burma side and only the canopy itself got soaked. He detached the parachute quickly and began to haul it out. Some of the Kachins, Baw San among them, rushed to help. Trotting up closer to him, Captain Bradford saw that the man was an American officer, a major in full combat gear and packs, armed with a carbine, short bayonet, grenades and a .45 automatic. He also realized that there was something familiar about the chutist, although his helmet and chinstrap covered much of his face.

As he removed his headgear, the man said, "You don't happen to have a spare Anzac hat like yours, do you, Linc? Very dashing."

Bradford stared with new astonishment and then growing joy when he knew for certain who it was who had just dropped from the sky.

"John Reisman! Johnny! What in the name of all the *bum nats* of Burma are you doing here?"

"Looking for you."

A broad and glowing smile spread over Bradford's face. He held his hand out to grip Reisman's, but that wasn't enough for what he felt. It was too common a greeting for so uncommon a meeting five or six thousand miles from where they'd last seen each other. He threw his arms around Reisman in a bear hug and even the most stoic of the Kachins smiled at this display of affection.

The warmth of the greeting was much more than Reisman had expected or wanted; though he thought now that perhaps it would make Linc easier to deal with, make him more amenable to the orders he had to give him. They had seen a lot of each other in London two years earlier, but one day Reisman had bid his friend a casual adieu, without telling him where he was going. One never did in their business. One just went. Information on a need-to-know basis. Was that when he had jumped into Italy the first time? Or was it one of his missions to the Maquis, helping the French underground set up their intelligence system and communications with London? In any event, Linc had been gone on his own adventure by the time Reisman had popped into London again.

"Oh? Away on business, I think," Max Armbruster of Special Operations had responded when Reisman had inquired after his friend. "Where, did you say? I don't really know." He had waved his arm somewhere out *that* way. "To the east, I think. They just came and took him away one day. People who needed him more than I did."

But then, as Armbruster and he had chatted on amiably and inconsequentially that day, Max had every now and then taken to whistling, humming and then trying to sound like Nelson Eddy singing half-remembered lines from "On the Road to Mandalay." Reisman had thought he'd gotten the point. And so he had. For now here he and Linc were together only three hundred miles from that very Mandalay, presently occupied by the Japanese army in great strength.

Their camaraderie actually went back to the year before London, when they'd first met—under incognito names, ranks and histories—at an OSS training camp in the Catoctin Mountains of Maryland. There they'd played quite seriously at espionage and guerrilla warfare and had learned from the great Major Fairbairn himself all sorts of pretty and ugly ways to kill in close combat; from others they'd learned how to observe, see, listen and report, how to operate radios and an assortment of common and uncommon weapons, and how to blow up a man, a bridge, a train and a fair-sized headquarters building.

Bradford eased off the bear hug and stepped back still glowing with the astonishment and pleasure of the reunion. He laughed and shook his head. "Well, at least you didn't say, 'Dr. Livingstone, I presume.' That's something in your favor."

"No, that's been done already," said Reisman, smiling. He remembered how they used to talk a lot about men whose exploits had elevated them so far above the commonplace that their names were universally known. Lincoln Bradford had wanted to be one of them, but he wasn't quite sure in which direction to go. The war, of course, had presented him with an opportunity to do *something*. Reisman nodded around at the Kachins and said, "Perhaps something out of T. E. Lawrence rather than Sir Henry Stanley."

They had each known books and had talked about them, and Reisman had been pleased about that, because Linc Bradford was an educated man and Reisman had done it on his own and could almost keep up. They had known and seen and talked about movies, too; but Bradford had been way ahead of him on theater. They had found girls and gone together to plays in London because that was the thing to do. That they had found so much in common, so much to talk about and enjoy together, was really the wonder of it. Because John Reisman had come from a background so vastly different from

Lincoln Bradford's. There were no Boston Brahmins in Reisman's family. In fact there was probably no one on either side of the family who even knew what a Boston Brahmin was. Sometimes Reisman had wondered if it was an unconscious social climbing on his part that had caused him to enjoy Linc's company. This was, of course, after the incognito aspect had been dispensed with and they came to know each other's true names, ranks and histories—though Reisman had kept much of his own history to himself, merely enjoying listening to Bradford's. At other times, Reisman had realized that it was perhaps their similar fascination with the war, its adventures, dangers and excitements, that had been the thing that he and Linc Bradford held in common.

"Maybe I ought to salute you and report in," said Linc, glancing enviously at the gold leaves on Reisman's collar. He did salute, with a very graceful and formal movement of his arm and hand. "Anyhow . . . *kaja-ee,* Major."

"Kaja-lo," Reisman replied.

Bradford actually looked startled to hear Reisman respond to the polite Kachin greeting. "I see you've learned a thing or two," he acknowledged.

"I usually do before I go in somewhere. You know that, Linc."

Bradford nodded. Yes, he did know that. And suddenly it worried him. "Why are you here, John? How did you know where to find me? From the look of you, you don't seem to be on vacation."

"I'm here with orders for you, Linc," Reisman answered firmly.

"And those are?"

"You are to turn your people around and go back to your base at Ngumla. You are not to cross the Salween. You are definitely not to do what *they* think you're going to do in China."

Bradford stared at him angrily a moment, then said, "Let's go sit down somewhere and seek knowledge." He waved an arm toward the treeline. "Perhaps under a banyan tree, if we are fortunate, as the Gautama Buddha did so long ago."

"Sure, Captain," said Reisman. "But as of this moment I'm relieving you of command of this battalion. I'm taking over. Recall your men from the other side."

"Not yet," said Bradford defiantly. "Let's palaver. I've listened to you. Now you listen to me."

Ne Tin, Baw San and the other Kachins close by were able to catch the drift of the exchange if not the subtleties. They at least understood that there was a dispute in progress and that the American officer who had just parachuted down to them did not want them to go on their raid into China. The news traveled swiftly through the battalion and there was much angry muttering and threatening looks toward John Reisman.

Bradford spoke to Ne Tin in Kachin. "Tell the men we will pause here to rest for a short while," he said. "Tell them to continue to feed and water the horses and mules. Tell them they may eat and drink now if they are hungry. We will not stop for it later. We will have to make up for this lost time."

"Then we will go ahead, despite what this man says?" Ne Tin commented with expectation.

"Yes. Bring San Thau and Ba Chit, also the *umas*. We need to talk to this officer. He too is a *duwa* and a brave and skillful *hypenla,* but he does not have the knowledge that we have. We must explain things to him."

Reisman didn't like not understanding what was being said. He felt very vulnerable. The Kachin boy standing nearby still looked at him in a friendly, even admiring, way. But the older one, the one Linc had just talked to, had a cruel and angry look about him when he glanced at Reisman. When he had jumped into Italy and France he had spoken their languages and could sniff out friend from enemy. He even knew enough Kraut to fake it, as he'd had to do in the attack at Rennes back in June. Only four months ago. Is that all it was? It seemed an eon away. How he wished a few of the Dirty Dozen were with him now.

The Kachins went about their business, whatever Linc had told them. He led Reisman to a flat, shaded spot just inside the tree line where he'd tied his horse. He stomped around in the ground cover a few moments and slashed at vines and low, matted growth.

"Snakes . . . leeches . . . mites . . . all kinds of things out here that like to make a meal of a man," Bradford explained. "On the other side of the mountain, in the jungle where we're used to operating, there are tigers to worry about as well as Japs. There are elephants that get very angry indeed if they even think you're invading their territory. There are big deadly cobras and small deadly kraits whose bite will do the job in about twenty minutes. There are all kinds of bugs, vermin, mosquitoes, insects and tiny microscopic things on the land and in the water that will give you any and all of those exotic diseases in the tropical medicine books, including just plain malaria or blackwater fever."

"Sounds like a well-stocked zoo," Reisman commented dryly.

"A beautiful, hellish country," said Bradford, dropping to the ground with his back against a tree. He gestured to Reisman to sit. "Quite safe."

Reisman unstrapped his packs and sat on one of them. From the other he took a field cap with a major's gold leaf pinned to it, put it on, and stowed the helmet he'd worn on the jump.

"Hungry, John?" asked Bradford solicitously.

"Yes. Thank you. I've brought some Ks and Cs with me, if you're short."

"No need for that. The Kachins are very hospitable people. At home they love to give feasts, but even on the trail these men do fine things with rice, vegetables and chicken. There's good stuff to eat in the jungle too, stuff that would turn your stomach if you weren't traveling light and mean and needing the food. Something we do quite often. This time, however, we brought along our own picnic supplies."

Reisman could see cook fires going and soon a bowl of food and a cup of tea were brought to him by the Kachin boy, who was introduced to him as Baw San. Despite the formal introduction of his guest as Major John Reisman, the boy addressed him as, "*Duwa* John." The food was hot with curry, not among Reisman's favorite cuisines, but he managed about half of it. The tea was strong and excellent, probably from one of the British plantations high up in the hills of Assam.

Seven of the Kachins came to sit on the ground with Reisman and Bradford, eating with them, and he realized that they made up a council of war. Linc introduced them each with respect and warmth. Ne Tin was the fellow wearing the turban who had been giving Reisman the ugly looks. He, San Thau and Ba Chit were *duwas,* Linc explained between bites of food, village headmen who were also his lieutenants and combat-wise guerrillas against the Japanese. The younger ones—Ah Yin, Yow Khi, Sinwa Rip and Baw San—were *umas,* heirs-apparent in an aristocratic lineage and, by that right, ranked high in the battalion. Something comparable to staff sergeants, Reisman surmised. They were also combat-hardened soldiers. In any event, these were the men in command of the *hypenlas,* though Reisman had seen right off that the youngest *uma,* Baw San, seemed to occupy a lesser status.

"Now, Johnny, let me tell you what we're up to and why," Linc said.

"I know what you're up to," Reisman replied, "and my orders are to prevent it."

"Listen to me, goddammit!" Bradford demanded.

The Kachins sat in silent tension, their feelings contained, their dark eyes watching first one white man, then the other.

"Go ahead, Captain," Reisman said, stressing the *captain.* He hated to pull rank, but that was why the army gave it, so that one man could tell another—or eight hundred others in this case—what to do, and be within his rights in giving the order, even if wrong decisions might have been made above him.

"Many of the men in this battalion have just had their villages looted and destroyed by Chinese—not Japs. While they were off with me fighting Japs behind the lines, doing a tough, dirty job for Stilwell and Merrill, for Wingate and the British, and for Chiang Kai-shek's inept—"

"I know that, Linc," Reisman interrupted. He wanted to ease what he had to do by being gracious, by paying a compliment where it was due. "I've heard it said that without the officers and men of your detachment, without your agents in the field, without the thousands of Kachin *hypenlas* who fought with us and the British and the Chinese, we never would have retaken north Burma, never would have made it to Myitkyina."

"Okay, you know that. You understand. Good. But while they were out in the jungles and mountains killing Japs with the OSS and our allies, their families and friends were murdered by treacherous bastards who are supposed to be on our side."

"Bandits," said Reisman. It was what he had been told to say, the excuse that had been transmitted from Chungking to Calcutta to him, probably with frantic agreement in Washington and London by bureaucrats unable or unwilling to disagree with the Chiang Kai-shek government in matters such as this.

"Who the hell are *you* working for?" Bradford now asked in a most suspicious way. "That sounds like the usual lying crap from the Gimo himself, or his buddy General Tai Li."

"Chiang Kai-shek and I don't travel in the same circles. The other fellow I never heard of."

"You sure will if you work out here a while," said Linc. "Tai Li is the Heinrich Himmler of China. The head of their Secret Service—the Chinese Gestapo. He's the Inquisitor-General of China, just like Torquemada was in Spain. Keeper of the Kuomintang faith, protector of his little friend, the Gimo, and conniver at anything that turns a profit for himself."

"I don't know what in hell you're talking about, Linc."

The Kachins were silent, observant. In the near distance were the sounds of the *hypenlas* talking and the occasional braying and neighing of their animals. Over it all was the gurgling and splashing of the river and sometimes a bit of soft wind in the trees, ever so slightly relieving the heat of the day. Except for the talk of mayhem, they might well have been a group of friends on a picnic to the mountains.

"Then I'll try to explain it to you," said Bradford. "The Chinese and the Kachins have been fighting for hundreds of years. They hate each other. But the attacks on the Kachin villages had nothing to do with politics as you know it, or nationalism. It has nothing to do with Chinese or Burmese or Kachins."

"What does it have to do with?"

"Poppies."

"You mean schoolboy shit like, 'In Flanders Fields the poppies grow between the crosses row on row . . .'?"

"Opium," said Bradford. "Those Chinese soldiers were under orders to get opium and they got it. They were sent in to loot the stuff instead of having to buy it at the far end of a trade route that's been going for a long, long time. The Kachins and other hill tribes like the Shan and the Meo over in French Indochina raise the poppies just like farmers back home raise corn and wheat. It's truck-garden stuff, though. Not much of it. They cultivate and process the poppies for the opium gum they get to ooze out of the pods. They keep a little of it for their own use, but most of it goes out on those trade caravans. It's a hell of a lot cheaper to steal it at the source."

Reisman shook his head. "The American Legion would be down on you if they heard you talking about poppies like that."

Bradford looked at him in disbelief. "You *can't* be that innocent!"

"No. I know about poppies and opium," said Reisman with a smile. "I even smoked a few pipes when I was in China some years back. I didn't know anything about what you're telling me, though, about the growing and the trading and the stealing."

"Those 'bandits' weren't bandits, Johnny. They were Kuomintang regulars. Which I know doesn't say much for them anyway. They're a sorry lot."

"Who were they, *exactly,* Linc? Do you know or are you just playing guessing games? If you do know, maybe we can get them another way, a legal way, through channels. It's too serious a business to start shooting up our allies because some of them misbehaved."

"Misbehaved? That's a curious choice of a word, Major," said Bradford caustically. "They were either the troops of Marshal Lung-Yün or whoever the *tuchun* is who holds power in Yunnan province this side of Kunming. The people in the villages were able to describe the uniforms, insignias and armbands."

"What's a *tuchun?*"

"A warlord. But that's a loose translation. In style they run all the way from Jesse James to Pancho Villa to Genghis Khan. Or even Chiang Kai-shek."

"How does Marshal Lung-Yün rate on your scale?"

"High up. Big man in the opium trade and hijacking American Lend-Lease war matériel. His primary allegiance is to himself, then to Tai Li and Chiang Kai-shek. The opium was probably to feed into Tai Li's network. There's an enormous amount of profit in it, particularly if you don't pay for it in the first place."

"Where do you expect to find these guys . . . these bandits you're going after?" Whether they were bandits or soldiers made no difference to Reisman. He was sympathetic to what Linc had told him, but he still had to stop the operation. If he could find a flaw in the plan, maybe that would be enough to dissuade the Kachins and turn the battalion around.

"They're in garrisons in Caojian and Yongping."

"Let me see your map."

Bradford unfolded it and Reisman was glad to see that it was one of the good silk ones with well-defined topography, roads, trails, waterways and special features.

"That's all of fifty and seventy-five miles from here. You expect to get in, hit them both and get out in one piece?" he challenged.

"No. Just Caojian," Bradford said, putting his finger on that spot on the map. "We're going to teach them a lesson and then beat it the hell out of there. We're going to blast the fuckers with artillery we took from the Japs they should have been fighting. When the 70 mms start knocking down their walls they might even think we *are* Japs and take off like they did during most of the war. If we hit them at Yongping too, we'd have another river to cross—the Lancang. That would slow us up—give their friends a place to catch us on the way back."

"Glad you noticed that. You make a hell of a field general, Linc," Reisman said sarcastically.

"I've done okay. Are you with us?"

Reisman shook his head and pointed to three other Chinese towns closer to the border than the target. "Have you considered, Captain, that there are Chinese regiments here at Tengchong, Baoshan and Lushui. Even if you get past their scouts and patrols—"

"The Chinese don't scout or patrol," Bradford interrupted. "They mostly sit on their duffs in garrison. When Stilwell finally got them to come over into Burma and help fight the Japs, it was the Kachins who did the scouting for them, just like we did for the U.S. Army and every Allied force that operates here."

Reisman had no idea if there were any Chinese regiments at those three towns or not, but they were closer to the Burmese border and it seemed logical. "If I may go on, Captain," he said brusquely. "Once the signal goes out from Caojian as to who you are and which way you're heading home, there's going to be massive deployment of Chinese troops at your rear. What you're doing, Linc, is leading your troops into a trap that will snap shut on them. You're going to lose a lot of good men. Maybe the whole battalion. Maybe yourself. It's not worth it . . . this tit-for-tat stuff."

"It is to the Kachins. They seek simple retribution and punishment for terrible crimes committed against them. That's why they're so good at killing Japanese, and the Shans, too, when they cross paths. That's an old mountain feud, sort of like the Hatfields and the 'Coys back home."

"Your plan is faulty, Linc. Your way in is too open and exposed. Look, even I found you."

"Ah, but you're a specialist at this sort of work, Johnny," said Bradford, smiling. "I would have expected you to find me. You're like that fellow they sent off with the message to García a couple of generations back in another war. Though I have wondered how you expected to survive in this hellish country and how you expected to get out if you hadn't found us . . . if we'd crossed already."

"I bought a round-trip ticket," said Reisman. "There are a couple of old flying strips within forty miles over on the other side of the mountains you just crossed. Just simple little runways the English put in years ago. They're pretty well hidden. I'll bet you don't even know about them. There are light planes due in there at designated hours to look for me and pick me up."

"I know about one at Htawgaw. I've had the pleasure of using it myself on occasion."

"That's one of them," Reisman went on. "I was to work my way back to either of them, depending on enemy activity, if I couldn't find you."

"The area is still crawling with Japs, you know," said Bradford.

"Then why don't we go fight them instead of the Chinese?" Reisman pressed.

"I've already told you why. We're going after them to teach them a very badly needed lesson, so that they will never try to do anything like they did again. Now, you're welcome to join us, John, but I won't think harshly of you if you decide to leave. You can say that you missed me at the crossing, and I'll swear to it if anybody asks."

"The pilot who dropped me already knows we made contact, and my orders are to turn you around, Linc," said Reisman softly. "Your entire plan is foolhardy."

"From a military or political point of view?" Bradford asked pointedly.

"Both. It won't work. Give it up. Your way back will be closed before you get there."

Bradford spoke in Kachin to his council of war. There was a brief discussion and then what seemed, to Reisman, to be a vote in which all concurred.

To Reisman, Bradford said, "Then we either kill you, tie you to a tree out here and let you rot—or you come along with us as a prisoner under guard."

Reisman became aware, in that moment, of someone standing behind him. He turned and saw that it was Ne Tin, the angry *duwa* who wore the turban. Somehow he had managed noiselessly to slip around in back. He held an M-3 submachine gun angled down at Reisman. The safety, the little hatch cover on top, was open.

"Now, very slowly," said Bradford, "put all your weapons out here on the ground where we can see them, John. We'll have to frisk you, of course. Spares in the boots and heels . . . that sort of thing, which we learned together."

Reisman handed his carbine over to Bradford. Then he undid his gun belt with the holstered .45 and the sheathed bayonet. Last were the grenades off his pack straps.

"Not much choice, is there?" he said. "I guess I'll just come along and see what happens."

Chapter 4

There was a valley and another range of mountains to cross before they would come to Caojian on the eastern slope. Reisman was placed under the personal guard of Baw San and both were always kept in the middle of the line of march. The boy held his carbine at the ready rather than slung over his shoulder. He tried to look very seriously, even threateningly, at his prisoner, but failed to maintain the harsh expression consistently. Sometimes he smiled at Reisman and spoke a few words in English—questions such as, "Where did you come from?" and, "How does it feel to float in the air, descend like a bird, as you did?" and, rushing on, "Some of the *hypenlas* have done this, but I have not."

Reisman answered the boy in a friendly, instructive way each time. Baw San looked pleased, but then remembering his role he would become grim-faced again. When it was Baw San's turn to ride one of the horses, Reisman rode one beside him. He found that amusing, for horses were creatures he knew little about and had hardly ever had occasion to ride—though he remembered wistfully a time in Palestine when he had ridden beside a *sabra* girl through the fields and vineyards of a *kibbutz* in Galilee and up into the bordering hills. They had both carried rifles, for there had been danger there, adding a certain zest to the point of the ride, which—though it was supposed to have been merely an educational tour for his enlightenment—had been romance for each of them. Her name was Galya—a black-haired, suntanned, vivacious *sabra* who had sprung joyously from the earth of that land; whose bold, bare legs gripped hard the flanks of the sorrel stallion she rode: who laughed at Reisman's awkwardness even on the gentle mare she had selected for him; and then whose eyes and lips and body had taken him passionately, triumphantly, in a dry river wadi in the hills.

Reisman looked over at Baw San and wished that it were Galya riding there beside him again. "What are you doing in such a place?" she would have said to him. "We need men like you in *Eretz Yisroel.*" That was what she had said to him back then. She had tried to keep him there, but he had stayed only a while and moved on, as he had stayed only a while in other lands and aboard the ships he had worked during those years. Sometimes, too, he had been a soldier in those other lands; other times a sojourner or simply a tourist. Amateur and mercenary soldiering had already begun to win out over the sea when the war had caught him up and hardened and honed him as a professional.

The battalion marched and rode through the night without stopping. The Kachins were used to long, silent treks on narrow trails through darkness. If any Chinese were to discover them, they were to try to bluff their way through by explaining in Chinese, "*Megwa bing* . . . American soldier." Their G.I. uniforms, varied as they were, and their American arms and equipment gave the story some credence, and they were indeed known officially as American-Kachin Rangers, though their modest pay as *hypenlas* came to them mostly in Indian paper rupees.

By dawn they were out of the narrow valley and well up into the next range of hills, on the other side of which was Caojian. By dawn, too, Reisman felt more sympathetic to, if not yet empathetic with the Kachins' need for blood vengeance against the Chinese who had attacked their villages. In the hours of the march, through the day and the night, he and Baw San had spoken and he had come to appreciate the basic good humor of the youth in the face of terrible adversity, and his integrity and the merit of his concerns and those of his tribesmen.

Baw San had told him what the Japanese had done to his village and others. "But they are new enemies from far away and when we get rid of them they will be gone for good and leave us alone. It is our friendly neighbors, the Chinese," Baw San said sarcastically, "who have been our enemies many times, and they too must be punished."

"Do you want to know what I think?" Reisman asked.

They were off the horses now, walking close together in the darkness, climbing upward, the scouts finding their own trail through growth not nearly as heavy as that on their own jungled hillsides. "Yes, I do, *Duwa* John," said the boy.

"This attack that you will make will be just as treacherous and dishonorable as that by the Chinese," said Reisman. "It will not make it right. It will just heat up the old feud."

"It is they who have heated it up," declared Baw San. "*Not* to retaliate would be dishonorable."

The youth's voice was more high in tone than low, but varied with his mood and what he was saying. There was an affecting pacing to the rhythm of his words that made Reisman listen closely. "You speak English well," he told Baw San. "Where did you learn it?"

"Some from the British before the war. Mostly from the *Bo . . . Duwa* Lincoln, and from the other American soldiers. *Duwa* Lincoln is also the name of one of your famous presidents. I know many things about your country. *Duwa* Lincoln has promised that I will go to school there after the war."

Duwa Lincoln himself came up to Reisman when the battalion finally stopped to rest soon after daylight. "I wish that you were with us on this, Johnny," he said.

Reisman looked at him a moment and felt the excitement of the coming action generated in the man's voice, the slightly wild expression on his face, and the vibrations of tightly held force emanating from his body—all of which infected Reisman with a touch of the same heady feeling.

"I might, Linc," he said, not surprising himself as much as he did Bradford. "I might, if I knew what your order of battle was—in detail. No hit-or-miss crap. I mean a detailed plan."

Bradford, dismounted, held the reins of his horse. He glanced back down the full length of the column and then to the front, as if counting heads. They had halted in a high meadow, the column holding their long, dispersed positions. No bunching. No easy massed target for unexpected mortars or artillery. Scouts had already gone ahead and returned to report that the pass through to the eastern slope was just ahead, a little higher up, and there was no one in the way.

But the *Bo* answered too casually. "We'll go in fast, do as much damage as we can, knock down and blow up their installations, kill as many of the offending bastards as get in our way, and get out fast."

"In broad daylight?"

"What do you mean?"

"I suggest, Captain, that you don't strike until long after dark and your bandits have gone to bed for the night." Reisman looked up ahead toward the pass. Rays of sunlight from the other side were defining granite outcroppings, stands of trees and sparse ground cover beyond the meadow. "You go through there now with eight hundred men, a couple of hundred horses and a bunch of mules and you're going to be on stage in the spotlight, even if the locals aren't expecting you. You've apparently got the tactical advantage of surprise now—which surprises the hell out of me—but I'd cover my bets if I were you."

Baw San and the other Kachins nearby listened to the exchange with the mounting interest of men whose fates were being decided by others. Among these men was Ba Chit, one of the *duwas*. He was a short, wiry man about thirty years old, with a faint mustache above his lips and traces of beard on his cheeks. He wore a stained bush hat with a rakish fold in the brim and a small plume of feathers in the band. Ba Chit came closer to the two American officers, so that he could hear better and understand better the new things that Reisman was saying.

"I bet no one in your group has ever even been in Caojian," said Reisman, shaking his head. He dropped his packs onto the ground and sat on them. Bradford, Baw San, Ba Chit and a few of the *hypenlas* also dropped to the ground near him; and now Reisman appeared to be in charge of a council of war. "I'll bet you haven't any idea whether the Kuomintang troops there are massed behind concrete walls and heavy guns in a fort, or whether they're stacked in two-bit wooden barracks, or living with the farmers' daughters, or camped out in a field in shelter halves. You probably don't know how many there are, what weapons they have, how much ammo, the extent of their supplies and communications—or whether to turn left or right to find the town and the soldiers once you go through that pass."

"The town is to the left," replied Bradford, smiling. He sensed that Reisman would be with him now. "The scouts could see it from the ridgeline. As for the rest of it—you're right. We'll just have to find out when we get there." He paused a few moments, looked around at the Kachins as if asking their permission for what he said next, and then spoke again to Reisman. "Unless you have some ideas you'd like to share with us. Maybe I've gotten stale in the jungle. We're used to a fast hit-and-run type of close combat on our own turf and terms. Perhaps, Major Reisman, you might suggest something more sophisticated."

Reisman thought a moment and then smiled with the memory of something that had always served him well. "Yes. The manual was written thousands of years ago," he said enigmatically. He had discovered it on a coaling ship bound for Australia when he had been a young seaman. He had read through every book, magazine and newspaper aboard until there was nothing left but a Bible. There in the Book of Numbers he had learned the foundation and basic instructions for all of military intelligence. He had read the words again from time to time over the years, fascinated by their simplicity and logic for him as a soldier, especially on a mission behind the lines into enemy territory. He remembered them well.

"Moses sent men to spy out the land of Canaan," said Reisman. "You, Captain Bradford, should send men to spy out the layout of Caojian."

Bradford looked at him with a smile of approval. "I never imagined that you might cite chapter and verse."

"Chapter thirteen of the Book of Numbers, verse seventeen, more or less and so on," Reisman remembered with a touch of élan. He took a deep breath and hoped he had it right. "Moses said, 'Go up into the mountain and see the land, what it is, and the people that dwelleth therein, whether they be strong or weak, few or many; and what the land is that they dwell in, whether it be good or bad; and what cities they be that they dwell in, whether in tents or in strongholds.' Sounds like a primer for the OSS, doesn't it—and damned good advice for you."

Among the Kachins there were many who knew the local Chinese dialect. They all volunteered, but only four were chosen to go. They changed into the shabbiest and least military-looking costumes they could put together from the motley contributions of the battalion. They were dirtied up, shown how to hobble and grovel and made to look like the beggars who infested the gates and streets of every village and city in China. In facial appearance they could pass, for the Kachins had come down from the north through Yunnan generations earlier and the racial similarities overlapped.

The four were from among the older *hypenlas* in the battalion, for it was thought that it would be easier for them to pass. They were to be under the command of the *duwa* Ne Tin, but they were to operate alone, slip in and out of Caojian individually and never come together where they could be seen. Ne Tin scowled when Reisman ordered him to remove his turban, but he understood the necessity for it.

Reisman asked no one's permission, but took immediate charge of the details of planning. "I will ride with you into the pass and then we'll scout the other side on foot from the ridgeline." To Bradford he said, "I want four other *hypenlas* with B.A.R.s and M-3s to ride with us. They are to hide in the pass, take care of the horses, stay ready to cover us, and act as couriers back to you—whatever is necessary while the spies reconnoiter."

"I must go with you. My orders are to guard you, *Duwa* John," Baw San spoke up eagerly.

Reisman looked toward Bradford in a gesture of silent deferral.

"Okay, you go with him, Baw San," said Linc, though there was no enthusiasm for it in his voice. Then he smiled encouragingly. "Just don't go riding off to Chungking, little *maung*."

As the reconnaissance party was about to mount their horses, Bradford handed back to Reisman all his weapons. "I trust you, John, and I don't want you going up there naked. My conscience would bother me if anything happened and you were defenseless." To Baw San, Linc said, "I relieve you of responsibility for him. Follow his orders."

Far up in the pass, almost through to the other side, they left the horses with the four *hypenlas* who were to find cover there among the outcroppings and brush. Reisman took Baw San with him and the four men who were to go into Caojian. Though Ne Tin and the others understood and spoke some English, there were things that they missed or couldn't explain sufficiently except in their own tongue. The boy was the most fluent in English and he needed him as translator. He also felt a curious need to keep him close by, to see that nothing bad happened to him.

From the ridgeline above the town, Reisman had a distant view of a good road coming down from the north, disappearing into the maze of tight streets, crumbling walls and closely built houses, and then leaving the maze at the south gate. Through field glasses, he saw tile-roofed structures of mud, stucco and, here and there, stone and wood. There were no outstanding features, no pagodas or temples immediately in sight. It seemed just a simple, spare hill town, a sprawl of ugly buildings that had grown there in a wild place for no special reason except that it might have been a way stop for nomadic tribesmen and traders' caravans. He could see telegraph poles and wires strung out along the road north and south. If there was a radio transmitter in the town, it would be at the garrison. But he was unable to pick that out.

With Baw San translating whenever necessary, Reisman explained exactly what they needed to find out in the town: "I want the exact location of the troops and the layout of the buildings they use. How many are there and how well trained are they? If there's a fort or barracks, do they lock it up at night? What are the gates and walls like? Exactly where and what do we have to go through to get to the garrison? Is there a radio transmitter? The telegraph lines we can cut easily on the road, but where do they keep the radio? Is there a central armory or munitions dump that we can blow? Most important maybe is to find out if these are the same men who attacked your villages."

Ne Tin shrugged angrily. "Now it is no difference. We have come to teach a lesson to all the Chinese army—and we will do it."

The four men left the ridgeline individually, fifteen minutes apart, following specifically assigned routes. Through the field glasses, Reisman watched them descend through the high, rough terrain to the first buildings and streets. Occasionally he passed the glasses to Baw San who thanked him for allowing him to follow the progress of his friends. Two of the men went to the north, one to the south, and Ne Tin, the last to leave, descended far down the hillside to dart across the north-south road, bypass the town and clamber up again into the middle of Caojian as if he had been traveling all along from the east. He would go to the marketplace first, he had said, for that was where one might begin to learn certain things of interest and importance.

There was nothing for Reisman and Baw San to do now for many hours except to wait and to keep watch on the hillsides and the town and road far below. Occasionally there was traffic on the road, some of it military in trucks and jeeps or with horses and mules. Most of it was civilian. People trudged along on foot, some led cargo-laden mules, some pushed wheelbarrows, some carried their wares in pails on long balance poles on their shoulders.

There was life down there and Reisman did not feel the same blood lust that Captain Bradford and the Kachins did toward the people and soldiers of this place, the same blood lust that he had felt toward the Nazis and Fascists of Europe and was prepared to transfer to the Japanese. He felt no reason to harm the life down there and yet he knew that, if all went well, he would go down there in the night with the others and bring destruction and death. He would do it, though the cause was not his, because the doing itself had become his way of life.

The first three scouts returned from Caojian just after nightfall. Reisman had instructed them to wait until then just in case anyone in the town had taken particular notice of them and decided to track them. Each of them brought details of the location of the garrison. They were in a large walled fort on the northeast side, surrounded by the narrow streets and houses of the town itself. The walls appeared to be thick and wide, with walkways and gun slits on top, but they were actually hollow stucco façades that allowed for troop movement on the ground inside the walls as well as on top. There were huge double doors of thick wood hung in the middle of each of the four walls. One of these gateways had been open during the day, casually guarded by two sentinels permitting easy access, and with much coming and going of vendors and peddlers. One of the Kachins had taken an untended wheelbarrow of vegetables in the marketplace and had wheeled it into the interior of the fort. He reported that there was a large parade ground, wooden barracks, mud-walled barracks, tents and a few solid cement structures, one of which was the armory. He'd also caught sight of a radio transmission antenna on the roof of one of the wooden barracks and surmised that the signal room was in the building below it.

There were about fifteen hundred soldiers stationed there, a reserve regiment that was part of Marshal Lung-Yün's army, as Linc Bradford had thought. They were well armed and had been among the units intensively trained by American instructors in a base at Kunming earlier in the year. However, each of these three scouts felt that there was an overall unguarded feeling to the place, with not the slightest concern about an attack from outside. The Kachin who had gotten inside had seen some soldiers drilling, but many who were just lounging around. There were no emplaced artillery, mortars or machine guns.

Listening to the men report in English to him and, when that was inadequate, in their own language to Baw San, who translated, Reisman was impressed by the precision of their military observations and the information they had gleaned from conversations with people and soldiers in Caojian. He complimented each of them—perhaps a bit too condescendingly. One of them muttered something darkly in Kachin to Baw San.

"What did he say?" Reisman asked.

Baw San's eyes looked away in embarrassment. "He said, 'What the hell did you expect? We've been doing this very thing with the Japs all these years. We're *hypenlas,* not children!' "

Reisman nodded, accepting the retort as justified. Perhaps there had been just a little of "the white man's burden" in his attitude. It was something he would have to get rid of fast.

They waited a long time after darkness had fallen for Ne Tin to return. Then, just about when they had given up on him and were about to leave, Reisman heard a gentle footfall behind them in a direction from which they did not expect him and suddenly there was Ne Tin moving down on them swiftly, a glow of satisfaction on his usually scowling face.

From a little bag tucked into his waist beneath his shirt he took two small blobs of something and held them toward Reisman in his hand. At the same moment he had raised his shirt, Reisman had caught a glimpse of the *dah* Ne Tin had managed to conceal there. In the darkness, Reisman was able to just make out the bloody bits of flesh on Ne Tin's palm.

Ears! The son-of-a-bitch had cut off somebody's ears and was displaying them now proudly to Reisman.

"You goddamned idiot!" Reisman muttered at him. To Baw San he said hastily, "Translate for me." Then turning back to Ne Tin, "I suppose you left the body out somewhere it could be found and raise the alarm!"

"No, I did not," Ne Tin insisted.

In English, Kachin and sign language to all of the group, he assured them that he had taken care to hide the body of the Chinese officer he had waylaid and killed outside the walls of the fort.

Reisman stared at Ne Tin in silent disapproval and tried not to show his feeling of revulsion. He too had killed men, often, but he had never done a thing like this.

"Now that you have been there and have seen what it is, do you think we can attack successfully and get out without heavy losses?" he asked.

"Yes," Ne Tin answered emphatically.

The blood lust on his face was undiminished.

"All right. Let's go back and tell the others," said Reisman.

Chapter 5

If the Kachins knew anything they knew how to keep silent in movement on the trail and out of sight as they waited in the darkness of the high meadow for friend or foe. Reisman and his nine-man patrol were already past the point elements and riding close to the middle of the hidden column when the *hypenlas* of the battalion rose from cover all around them.

"I was beginning to worry about you," Linc Bradford said, running up to Reisman. "Do we go in?"

"You forget why I'm here, Linc," Reisman answered evasively. He still didn't want to approve of what they were doing, though he couldn't prevent them from doing it. Other than that, he would help them bring it off well. "It's your party. Listen to what your scouts have to say and you make the decision."

Bradford summoned his council of war again and they sat together on the ground and listened to the reports of the four scouts who had been in Caojian. There was a quarter moon in the sky, giving some light to the meadow and the men and animals who had left cover. The temperature had dropped considerably since the daytime and many *hypenlas* had put on sweaters and jackets.

Ne Tin, cheerfully displaying his bloody trophy, was the envy of all the others. Though Reisman was glad to hear Bradford ask the man the same challenging question that he had asked Ne Tin earlier. Would the body be found and the garrison placed on alert? Ne Tin insisted that he had covered it well in a hillside gully away from the fort.

Bradford held a notebook and pencil in his lap and, as each of the scouts reported, he was able to draw a diagram of the town, the approaches to the garrison, and the fort itself. Baw San hunkered down close to him, illuminating the page with a small flashlight. Then, on a separate page, Bradford drew a diagram of just the fort and its interior buildings. He showed the sketches to Ne Tin and the other three scouts, to confirm or amend the details. When he was satisfied that the diagrams were as accurate as he could make them, including estimates of distances and elevations, he studied them a few moments in silence, then asked his council, "Do we go in or not?"

They were unanimous in their decision to attack. Bradford looked toward Reisman. "What do you think, Major?"

What Reisman thought was not what he said. He knew that it would be futile, perhaps even fatal now, to tell them again to turn around and leave. He saw the rightness of the Kachins being there to do what they had to do, but he still thought that Linc was out of his head for leading them there, and he himself was insane for helping them, instead of hauling out to one of the tiny secret airstrips back on the Burma side where the OSS liaison planes would be looking for him.

"If you're going to do it," said Reisman, "you'd better do it right."

"Will you help?" Bradford asked.

It was more challenge than question. Reisman didn't respond immediately, yet there was really only one answer he could give. "Yes," he finally said. It was more than just a practical response for the situation that prevailed. It was the answer that satisfied the old and constant goad he felt to test his courage. "But we've got to determine now exactly what our objectives are, and every man in the battalion has got to understand that he cannot go beyond them. Not only do you have to secure your objectives but you've got to bring your battalion out safely. Don't waste the men for the sake of blood lust and don't let them waste themselves. There's going to be a lot of official trouble for you, no matter what happens. Me too I suppose. But if you do teach a proper and lasting lesson to the marauders your raid will have served a good purpose; and if you bring the battalion back in good shape it will go easier for you than if you had a lot of heavy, futile casualties."

"What do you consider a 'proper and lasting lesson'?" asked Linc.

"Take the fort, blow up their installations, their arms, munitions and communications—but do it with precision," said Reisman, looking around at the faces of each of the Kachin leaders. "Translate what I say to your men, Linc. I want to be sure they understand. Ne Tin has his ears, but that sort of thing isn't necessary. Doing what I suggest will instill the proper amount of respect and fear. Just to show them you can do worse, if necessary. Then you show them a certain amount of kindness—graciousness in victory, if you will. After all, they are our allies in the big picture. Don't go in there just to butcher as many Kuomintang soldiers as you can. That will only incite the powers that be in Chungking and elsewhere to a more furious sort of retaliation. It would lead to retribution upon retribution."

Bradford and Baw San translated for the other Kachins and then Linc came back with a question. "What do we do, take prisoners?" He softened his voice a bit, but there was no way to keep the others from hearing. "You know, the Kachins do terrible things to their captives. A clean death in battle would be better."

"No, we don't want any prisoners. That would just slow us up. We can design an attack that scares the shit out of them, but leaves the majority of the garrison a way to get out the other side of town."

It would be a completely different kind of operation than the Kachins were accustomed to, Bradford admitted as they worked out the order of battle. The *hypenlas* were masters of ambush techniques against the Japanese in the jungle; there they knew how to use the trees, vines and plants as allies, and there were trails that only they knew how to find. They had always tried to avoid being trapped in a town or becoming engaged in set-piece battles.

Bradford divided the battalion now into four raiding companies. Each of the *duwas* would command one and he the fourth. Each company had its own cannon, mortars and machine guns. Besides rifles, carbines, sidearms, *dahs* and grenades, each company also had its own complement of *hypenlas* with B.A.R.s and M-3 submachine guns, whose main assignment was to clear a path for the demolition teams with their packs of dynamite, *plastique,* fuses, caps, wire, timing devices and detonators, and to cover the demolitions men while they placed their charges.

The attack was set for midnight and was to be broken off two hours later, whether their objectives had been achieved or not. Each commander and many of the men wore wristwatches which they now synchronized.

"That will give us three or four hours of darkness to withdraw and keep our escape route from being discovered," Reisman said.

"Which company will you go in with?" Linc asked pointedly.

He didn't *have to* go in with any of them, Reisman knew. But did it require more guts or less for him to say that and stick by it, and then just stay up on the ridge and watch the operation he had designed succeed or fail?

He allowed a few moments of silence to prevail, during which he returned the challenging stares of Bradford and his Kachin lieutenants. Then he said, "I'll go into the fort with Ba Chit's men. I'll take two machine gun squads out the northern gate. That's the one we don't hit with artillery and mortars. If our psychology works, the Chinese will realize that's the only way out for them. We'll be firing at them from the other three sides. They'll open the northern gate themselves and take off through it. While the charges are being laid, we'll set up defensive positions, just in case the Chinese try to counterattack."

By 2300 hours, moving under the quarter moon and starlight, the horses were contained in a makeshift corral in the pass. Baw San and five of the *hypenlas,* despite vehement protests, were ordered to stay behind with them. The eighteen mules, laden with heavy weapons and ammunition, were brought through to the other side, to go down to positions chosen for the pack guns and mortars. Also five of the horses were led down for the raid, mainly to carry back any who were wounded.

Watches were synchronized again and Ne Tin's company left the ridgeline first. They were to cross the north-south road and come in from the east, as he had done earlier in the day. They would keep their cannon in reserve for defensive action if they were attacked, but they would set up their mortars and precisely at midnight begin lobbing rounds up the hill, over the civilian houses and into the fort. At the same moment, two of the pack guns sited above the town would be firing down their barrels at the heavy doors of the fort's western and eastern gates. The western gate would be blown from the outside in. Shells aimed at the eastern gate would cross the parade ground, strike the doors on the inside and blow them outward. Ne Tin's men would then swarm up through the town and into the fort through the eastern gate.

A two-man team from his company was detailed to cut the telegraph line to the north of Caojian one minute before the attack began. Another team from Ba Chit's company was to cut the line on the south, while Reisman, Ba Chit and the *hypenlas* positioned themselves close to the first buildings on the southern approaches. The mortars on three sides would try to knock out the radio transmitter, but they would be firing high, blind trajectories and only a lucky hit might get it in the opening barrages, Reisman realized.

Bradford's company left the ridgeline next, traversing down and north through the rough hill country on the west flank of the town. They would take up the northernmost positions. The first round from their cannon at midnight would be the signal for the attack to begin. No one was to fire before them. San Thau's company left the point of departure five minutes later, following in Bradford's path, to take up nearer positions on the southwest flank of the town. Reisman admired how quickly and silently the *hypenlas* disappeared from his view. Then he and Ba Chit's company, with four of the mules and two of the horses, descended in single file to positions just above the road, close in on the southern flank of Caojian. Their mortars were ready to fire by 2350 hours. Ba Chit stayed with them. Reisman and the assault platoons with B.A.R.s, M-3s, rifles and carbines moved a hundred yards closer to the first streets and buildings. The machine guns, superfluous for the moment, were left on the mules.

The town was silent and mostly dark. Lights shone through window slits of some buildings—probably oil lamps, Reisman thought—and were being extinguished here and there even as he watched through his field glasses. He hoped that the civilians would be sufficiently frightened by the assault to stay put and that there would be no casualties among them. The Kachins were under strict orders not to take heads or cut off ears, civilian or military. Reisman hoped, too, that there was more than just contempt in Linc Bradford's feeling that once the captured Japanese cannons opened up on the garrison they would think it was a massive Japanese attack and would flee the fort through the northern gate. His plan of assault had been based partly on the validity of that supposition.

He looked around him at the *hypenlas* and, close to them in the tiniest illumination from the heavens, he saw the eagerness for combat in their faces and in the way they held their bodies like runners waiting for the starting gun. One of the *umas,* Sinwa Rip, had insisted that he, not Reisman, take the point. Reisman moved up and down the platoon of crouching men, whispering what he had told them earlier: "Hold your fire as we move through the streets to the fort. Shoot only if you meet opposition. We must destroy only the fort, not the people of the town." There was low muttering among them, but they at least understood.

He glanced frequently to the radiant dial of his wristwatch and crouched again next to Sinwa Rip as the sweep hand came around to 2400 and the first boom of cannonfire roared from the hillside on the northwest flank of Caojian, to be followed in seconds by the multiple blasts of mortars and mountain guns deployed against the fort. He couldn't tell if the shells were landing where intended, but he heard the explosions in the direction of the fort and saw the bursts of flame illuminate the night.

From behind him came the plunk and whoosh of Ba Chit's mortars and he could almost feel the air part as the rounds arced overhead toward their target. Though he could not see or hear them, he could tell from the frequency of explosions in the direction of the fort that Ne Tin's mortars were lobbing rounds from below the town and the mortars of San Thau's and Bradford's companies were at work in the hills. Only the muzzle blasts of the cannons gave away the positions of the raiding parties.

The forward-assault platoons waited under the barrage, counting off the long five minutes before they could go. Then, while they still waited, Reisman turned to the sound and sight of a different explosion, this one in the hills above the town at the site where, for four minutes, the muzzle blasts of one of the mountain guns had been visible. The hillside there leaped with flames and smoke, but there was no more firing from the cannon. Either it had blown up or the Chinese garrison had scored a direct hit with answering fire from their own artillery or mortars; or it might even have been one courageous Kuomintang infantryman climbing up there swiftly and closely with grenades or a bazooka. The Kachins had begun to pay a price in casualties.

Reisman was about to say, "Let's go!" when Sinwa Rip rose, and the others, including Reisman, followed without words, pulling the mules with them. The assault platoons darted down to the road and moved swiftly to the first buildings and streets of the town. Behind them, the mortars would move up and continue the barrage another five minutes while the lead elements moved closer to the fort. The other companies would be doing the same.

The streets were empty and dark, narrow dirt tracks between the buildings. The *hypenlas* glided swiftly close to the walls, the point squads alternating as one group covered another across the open intersections. One of the scouts who had been in the town that day pointed the way. No one came out to meet them. No one fired a weapon. The only sounds of war were the continuing barrage of the mountain guns and mortars.

Reisman darted for a moment into the doorway of a two-story mud-walled dwelling and almost fell over a woman and three children huddled there in terror. The woman looked at him with eyes that went wide and white with pleading. He put his finger to his lips and motioned her and the children to go back inside. Then he moved on. The street opened up and ahead of them was the south wall of the fort and the closed doors of the gateway. Flames and smoke rose from many places behind the walls, indicating the accuracy of the Kachins' mortars and cannon.

The mules were brought up and Sinwa Rip and his *hypenlas* began to assemble the company's own pack gun. Almost unexpectedly now, the sharp cracks of rifle fire came down at them from gun slits on the battlement. The fusillade was not heavy—in fact, to Reisman, it seemed almost a half-hearted token defense. Then he saw Sinwa Rip's bush hat fly off. The young *uma* careened backward from the force of the bullet that struck him and his body splayed out on the ground near the cannon. Almost in the same moment another *hypenla* grabbed at his thigh, took one step and fell. Blood poured through his fingers as he tried to stanch the wound with his palm. His face contorted in pain, but he did not cry out. Men closer to him dragged him out of the line of fire and took cover among the nearest buildings.

Reisman ran to where Sinwa Rip lay and threw himself to the ground beside him. The bullet had torn open his skull, shattered its interior and killed him instantly. The rifle fire continued as Reisman examined the dead *uma.* Bullets pinged and whined around him and kicked up dirt. Behind him, one of the mules screamed in pain, bucked and kicked, then fell to the ground thrashing, bleeding its life away through a torn belly.

From the corners of nearby buildings, B.A.R. men stepped out for a few seconds in turns and sprayed the gun slits on the battlement.

The men with M-3s, less accurate, did the same to try to keep the Chinese riflemen from aiming and firing.

Reisman lifted his head slightly and shouted, "Machine guns!" He saw a few of the *hypenlas* begin to unload the .30 calibers from the other mules and set them up, and he damned himself for the stupidity and overconfidence that had not made him order them set up earlier. He rose quickly and dashed for the cover of a building just as the two machine guns went into action and began to chew chunks of stucco from the top of the battlement.

Ba Chit came up just then with the mortar men. When he saw Sinwa Rip's body lying alone out front near the partly assembled cannon his features contorted in fury and anguish. Reisman tapped his shoulder and pointed to the big gun. They both ran to it in a crouching, weaving path, covered by the machine-gunners and a constant fusillade from the smaller weapons. Two of the *hypenlas* came after them, lifted Sinwa Rip's body, and carried it back into a street away from the fighting.

As the cannon was wheeled and set and the barrel lowered to point-blank range, an ammunition chain of *hypenlas* had rounds moving to the breech. Ba Chit inserted the first round and fired. It went right through the thick wooden doors of the fort and exploded somewhere beyond. Reisman reset the fuses on the next shells and with five rounds they shattered open the south gateway.

Then Ba Chit signaled his men to stop firing, and in the next seconds the firing of heavy weapons from the western and eastern flanks of the town also ceased. Bradford's and San Thau's companies were moving down on the fort from the west, Ne Tin's company coming up from the east. All gunfire had ceased. There was only the sound of the dying mule, and then even its anguished braying and thrashing movements stilled at last and it lay there with open staring eyes.

"Now we go in, *Duwa* John," said Ba Chit.

"Watch for the others," Reisman warned. "Don't be so trigger happy that you start killing your own men coming in on the flanks. Do you understand?"

Ba Chit nodded and passed words of caution to his men. They left the cannon where it was and, in two files, dashed for the wall and then through the exploded doors into the open grounds of the fort. There was no more defensive fire from the Chinese. A few bodies in smoldering, dun-colored uniforms lay on the ground. They'd been caught and killed by exploding rounds.

Reisman glanced up at the parapet, searching out signs of movement. There was nothing. At the interior base of the wall he saw a doorway. Taking a squad of B.A.R. and M-3 men with him, he climbed a dark wooden stairway to the battlement. From a landing, it gave entry to both sides at the top of the wall. Silently, he signaled the men how to proceed. Gun barrels went through first, then a spray of rapid fire, then the men. There were two dead Chinese soldiers on one side of the battlement, another on the other side. They apparently had been killed in the firefight earlier. Reisman hoped one of them was the man who had killed Sinwa Rip.

They descended again to the open parade ground and Reisman saw the compound fill with exuberant Kachins pouring through the blasted gateways of the western and eastern walls. There was no gunfire. Only the crackle of flames eating up what had been wooden barracks. The mortars had done their jobs well. The top of the radio transmission tower lay in a tangle on the ground, its base sunk in the burning barracks on which it had been mounted. Mud-walled and stucco buildings lay in heaps of rubble; tent canvas was burning. A few low cement structures with iron doors still stood, and Reisman assumed at least one of them was the armory.

Linc Bradford burst through the mass of Kachins. His eyes were bright, his face grimy with sweat and dirt. "It worked," he shouted, awed and exulted by the actuality of it. "The north gate is open and the garrison is gone."

"I'll get the machine guns out there," Reisman said quickly. It was not a moment in which he could pause. He felt no need to celebrate what had been done. His blood still pounded, he was still impelled by the tensions of combat, the stink of cordite, the vivid sounds and sights of battle. "Sinwa Rip is dead," he said dully. "Another man wounded."

Bradford registered the news and the wild look of exultation on his face dimmed for a moment. "We lost three dead on the mountain gun," he said. "They got a mortar on us right away . . . or one of the Chinese got up there with grenades or a bazooka."

"You see to the demolitions," Reisman said. He pointed to the cement structures. "Might as well get them all. Heavy charges and long delays. We don't know what's in them, but I figure it's stuff that could kill us if we're too close. We want to be well on the way when it blows."

He took his machine gun squads out through the northern gate and set them up to enfilade the approach. The other companies did the same at the other gates. But no one moved out there, neither military nor civilian. The routed garrison never came back and the people of Caojian kept to their hovels, fearful to confront what was happening. It would be that way at least until daybreak, Reisman thought.

With their dead and wounded tied to the backs of horses, the battalion was again on the high ridge, moving toward the pass, when the timed charges went off far below. Reisman gazed back at the fireworks display of explosives, gunpowder, shells, grenades and bullets that had been stored in the armory. The sequential explosions grew louder as one cache ignited another, and underneath them, in counterpoint, he could hear the machine gun–like chatter of exploding bullets.

The full insanity of what they'd done struck him now with unexpected, caustic laughter. He shook his head and felt almost giddy with the frenzied derangement of it all. Not only had Chinese been killed by Kachin soldiers trained by Americans in Burma and India, but Kachins had been killed by Chinese soldiers trained by Americans in Kunming.

"You know who paid for all that shit we just blew up?" he demanded of Captain Bradford. "You did. I did. The American taxpayer did. This fuckin' war out here is crazy! Nobody's on the same side. And you better have a damn good story ready about how you had nothing to do with it and you've never met me in your life!"

In the meadow, Baw San and the other five who had stayed with the horses hailed the returning *hypenlas* with envious questions. The sight of the four dead and the wounded did not dismay them. With stoic fatalism, Baw San said, "In war it is to be expected, *Duwa* John." The dead young *uma,* Sinwa Rip, had not been much older than he.

There was little desire for rest on the trek back to the frontier. They were all eager to be home. By dawn they had descended from one range of mountains, crossed the valley and were well up into the second range, on the other side of which was Kachin country, some Shan villages, and mountains and jungles still infested with Jap troops. There was no fear of the Japanese. It was they, in retreat, who would try desperately to avoid battle with the Kachins.

The men ate rations on the move, and the few brief stops were mainly to rest, water and feed the horses and mules, and to change riders. By midday, the battalion was back at the crossing on the

Salween. The ropes had been left in place. Ne Tin, on horseback, led his company across and they were safely on the Burma side when the sound of an aircraft again filled the Salween gorge.

Linc Bradford was in midstream, riding one of the Japanese cavalry horses and urging his mount onward with what he hoped were soothing, inspiring phrases. The four lanes were filled with riders, waders and swimmers holding equipment high over their heads. Baw San was far back, pulling a train of pack-laden mules after him into the water. Reisman was still on the China side, waiting to cross with the rear guard of *hypenlas*. He looked up and saw the airplane and felt a curious sense of a scene being replayed in which he had been a participant two days earlier; only he had been in the sky then, looking down.

The plane came lower and lower in what seemed an attack dive, and Reisman saw that there were no identification markings on the plane. He thought that was strange. It was all mottled with camouflage colors, but there were no national insignia, squadron symbols or numbers.

Baw San looked up. "B-25!" he called out, smiling.

Just then some objects fell from the bay of the bomber and at the same time Reisman heard, in suspended disbelief, the harsh, rapid fire of a .50 caliber aerial gun and saw the moving barrel protruding from the tail turret as the plane swept down the gorge. He saw the water churned up by bullets, watched men fall bloody into the stream, animals rear up in panic and pain, and saw the first explosions of bombs erupting in plumes of water, men and animals.

The B-25 banked and turned sharply, made one more bombing and strafing pass—and was gone. Reisman threw off his arms and equipment and flung himself into the stream to give aid to the wounded and retrieve the dead. Dozens of the Kachins did the same from both sides of the river, carrying wounded and corpses to the Burmese side.

Reisman thrashed through the water to where he had last seen Baw San. He found him struggling against the current, sinking in a swirl of blood and water, his eyes staring uncomprehendingly, in a state of shock. When he carried him out to the river bank on the Burma side, he saw that shrapnel had chewed chunks of flesh from his arms and legs; he had a wound high up on the right side of his chest and was having trouble breathing. Reisman set the boy down tenderly on the ground. Two Kachins took over, ministering to Baw

San from G.I. first-aid kits, stanching the flow of blood, pouring sulfa powder into the wounds and wrapping them with bandages.

Reisman flung himself back into the Salween to help others. The need for action, to bring order out of the melee and give help to those who needed it, kept him from feeling the full fury and despair that finally struck him when he pressed through a ring of silent, grieving *hypenlas* and saw the bloody, lifeless body of their *Bo* on the ground. Ne Tin, who had carried him from the water, still kneeled there beside the body, covered with the captain's blood. Linc had been caught head on by .50 caliber bullets that had torn right through his belly, chest and skull.

Ne Tin's face contorted with sorrow and the rage of betrayal. He looked at Reisman, who kneeled beside him. "It happened this way another time," Ne Tin murmured. "Thirteen of my people were killed then, twenty hurt. But that time it was not intended. It was a mistake . . . and we understood. This time it was not a mistake."

Reisman held the *duwa's* gaze and nodded his agreement. Then he stood up and took charge of the battalion. Ne Tin, Ba Chit and San Thau deferred to his command. There were nine more dead, including Linc Bradford, to be wrapped in ponchos or shelter halves and tied to horses or mules. Seventeen more had been wounded. Most would be able to make it back to Ngumla, carried on litters or tied to the animals. A few of them, including Baw San, he would try to get out to a hospital by air once they crossed the remaining range and were able to get to one of the little flying strips.

Reisman crossed the river once more to retrieve what had been left on the China side; then they began the trek upward under the green canopy of mountain jungle. His mind wandered far afield. Having failed in his mission to stop Linc Bradford, he felt that he had been manipulated into contributing to his friend's death—not by chance but by powerful forces beyond his understanding and control. He vowed to find out what they were and deal with them in his own way. It came to him during the long march that eight months earlier he had been sent to a prison in England to witness an execution and that out of that had grown his Dirty Dozen. And the parallel struck him now that here again he had been sent in to participate in another execution—one that might as easily have killed *him*.

PART II
The Fortunes of Soldiers

Chapter 6

It seemed to John Reisman that he had lived another lifetime by the time he finally boarded the C-46 at Chabua to fly over the Hump from India to China.

A month earlier, he had hardly been aware of the word *Kachin*. But in these last weeks he had been an honored guest in some of their villages, had heard their storytellers, the *jaiwas,* sing his praises, memorialize the great *Bo* Lincoln, and enter into tribal lore the tale of what they all had done together, a tale that would be repeated by generation after generation of *jaiwas*.

What he had not expected was that when he went to see Baw San in the military hospital in Calcutta to assure himself that he was coming along fine, the boy would ask to go with him, to be assigned to whatever new mission he was given. Reisman had agreed. Baw San stirred memories in him of what he himself had been like at that age—eager for experience, for the adventures of what lay beyond the next hill and the next sea, yet a little fearful (more fearful, perhaps, of being afraid and doing the wrong thing) and wary of the strange ways and the cruelties and abuse of others. Though he would always have all of the Kachins as *family,* Baw San had no immediate family. In a way, Reisman felt that he should now be the mentor that Linc Bradford had been for a couple of years, and maybe even help Baw San to get an education in the States after the war, as Linc had wanted to do.

Baw San, one arm still bandaged and in a sling, sat next to him on the long aluminum bucket seat against the wall of the plane. They had put on parachutes before takeoff and Baw San had listened eagerly as Reisman explained what to do if they had to use them. On either side of them and across the baggage- and cargo-filled aisle sat other transient military and civilian personnel, Americans and Chinese. No one looked cheerful. Every passenger and crewman who flew over the Hump knew too well the terrible mortality rate of this particular route of the Air Transport Command. The unarmed planes were prey to Jap fighters and to engines and systems that failed under the rigors of a flight they weren't built to handle. The high noise level of the two engines, unmuffled by the luxury of any interior soundproofing, made conversation difficult. Some had brought books, magazines and newspapers in which to immerse themselves during the 500-mile flight to Kunming. Both Reisman and Baw San studied English–Chinese basic texts he'd obtained for them at the OSS way station in the British tea country of northern Assam, where they'd had to lay over for a few days waiting for clearance to enter China.

That extra delay in the Assam holding area had puzzled Reisman. For if he wasn't wanted in Chungking, why had Colonel Waingrove, OSS Chief China, sent for him in the first place? Waingrove was a man he knew and respected. Reisman suspected that Baw San might have been the problem—although, before they had left Calcutta for Assam, he had taken the precaution of having records compiled for one Corporal Charlie Bawsan, born in San Francisco of Chinese-Burmese parents, who was to be detached from his duties with the American-Kachin Rangers and go on special duty as a translator and guerrilla specialist with Major Reisman. He had added ten years to the boy's age, just in case anyone were to doubt the proficiency of a seventeen-year-old. If challenged on it, he could always say that Baw San just looked a lot younger than his years, or that the birth date was an error. Reisman also wanted Baw San to have further medical attention in Chungking. It was the capital of the Nationalist government and he figured there ought to be some good civilian and military doctors around and some hospital facilities there.

They had safely crossed the Santsung range of the Himalayas and were about 8,000 feet up on the descent to Kunming when Reisman caught the first whiff of an overpowering and foul aroma that he thought might be familiar but was totally unexpected.

He caught the arm of a crewman making his bouncing way down the baggage-strewn aisle like a drunken broken field runner. "What's that stink?" he shouted above the scream of the engines.

The young sergeant smiled. "That's China!" he answered. "You'll get used to it after a while. I don't even smell it any more."

Of course that's what it was, Reisman remembered. Night soil, day soil, dung, manure, excrement, human and animal ordure, feces—shit! In China not a speck of it was wasted. The residue of one agricultural cycle was the fertilizer for the next. It had not been apparent in the mountains around Caojian, but he remembered back more than seven years when Nanking had been the capital before the Japanese captured it, and he had ventured far inland from there to get the feel of rural China . . . streams of people and animals, caravans on the roads, and farmers' boys with four-pronged forks and baskets picking up the droppings of animals and humans, all very precious. He had thought it strange then, as he did now, that in a country where human life was held so cheap, shit should be held so precious. But that the stink of it should reach 8,000 feet into the air and penetrate the aluminum tube of the aircraft—that was the astonishment of it!

They put down on the plateau of Kunming in mid-morning, flying over terraced fields of russet and green. A young army lieutenant, holding a clipboard, came aboard and advised personnel going on to Chungking to stay in their seats, while the Kunming passengers were to debark in the order of rank. Oh God, thought Reisman—chicken shit even in so simple a procedure as getting off an airplane.

He twisted around to glance through a window. He couldn't see much on his side. Just runways, tents and parked aircraft. Planes going out and coming in. Many were painted in camouflage patterns of green and brown. His gaze fixed on a B-25 and he felt the fury rise in his guts. Was *that* the one? It carried wing and fuselage insignia, but that meant nothing. The massacre in the Salween gorge had taken place a month ago; paint could go off and on in a few hours. He heard his name called and he turned to the debarkation officer.

"Major Reisman, would you please step outside for a few minutes."

He slipped out of the chute packs and left the plane, glad for the opportunity to stretch and move around. The side of the airfield he saw now was about the same as the other side, except for a few low, tile-roofed, stucco buildings, one of them the operations office. No big hangars or terminal buildings. Mechanics worked on planes in the open. The entire installation could be packed up and moved in a hurry if the Japs came on again in force.

A man's voice, familiar but not yet identifiable, called out to him from the shadow under the wing of another C-46 parked off the runway about forty yards away. "Over here, John."

The figure stayed back in the shadow and Reisman did not see who it was until he got there. When he did, he felt the elation he always felt when he unexpectedly came upon an old comrade after a long separation. It was almost a replay of the scene with Linc Bradford, except that in that reunion it had been Linc who had been surprised.

Reisman held out his hand and smiled. "Hello, Sam," he said warmly. "Who threw you out? Tito or Mihailovic?"

The last Reisman had heard, Sam Kilgore had been running around up in the mountains of Yugoslavia supplying arms to partisan groups and trying to get Tito and Mihailovic to fight together against the Nazis instead of slitting each other's throats.

Sam shook his hand firmly and there was a moment's glow of reciprocal pleasure on his face. "I got stale with both of those guys," he answered, "so London pulled me out and let somebody else take a crack at it."

Reisman saw now the silver leaves of a lieutenant colonel on Sam's shoulders. He stepped back and threw him a snappy salute. "Goddamn . . . last time I saw you, you were only a captain," he said.

Sam shrugged and tried to make his rank sound casual and unimportant. "Well, I made major while I was still in the Balkans. Now they gave me a new job and this is what the T.O. called for, so they bumped me up again."

Kilgore was a chunky man, a little taller than Reisman, freckle-faced, sandy-haired, boyish in appearance. But the exterior was deceptive. Reisman knew him to be tough, cunning, determinedly well schooled, and with considerable political savvy.

When they'd first met in London, he had joked about Sam's family name. "That's a hell of an apt name for a guy in your business. Kill! Gore!"

"No more than yours," Sam had told him, laughing. "A *Reisman* is a mercenary in German. I understand you were mixed up in a few little wars before we got into this one."

They had developed an easy friendship. Though they had never served together in the field, chance had brought them together a number of times between missions, they had kept track of each other and respected each other as soldiers.

"What's the new job? Are you stationed here or just passing through?" Reisman asked.

"I'm based in Kunming," Sam replied, "but they've got me running teams here and there."

"Where?" Reisman pressed.

"North and south."

Reisman scanned a map in his head. North would still be China, maybe up into Shensi province where the Communists had their stronghold at Yenan; or maybe up into Jap-held Manchuria or a peek at what the Russkies were doing over the line in Siberia. South would be a different story entirely—down into French Indochina, where the Vichy French still governed nervously under the harsh control of Japanese occupation forces; or maybe into Thailand, though that was more likely to be a British operation.

"Am I going to be working with you?"

"Don't know, Johnny."

Behind them, fuel was being pumped into Reisman's C-46 and a ground crew was swarming over the engines, fuselage, wing and tail assemblies and undercarriage, looking, testing and adjusting. Constant maintenance was needed on these workhorses and Reisman was glad to see his was getting it.

"Who is this Charlie Bawsan who's traveling with you?" Kilgore asked casually.

"He was with Detachment 101 over in Burma. Hell of a good man," answered Reisman with a straight face. "I figure I can use him on any assignment I get out here. He's a real eager beaver. Speaks a lot of the local lingos."

"If his MOS is that good how come he's only a corporal?"

Reisman stared off into space and improvised. "Charlie feels more comfortable as an enlisted man. Likes it down there with the real people. Want to meet him?"

Kilgore looked toward the plane. "No. I'll take your word for it. I'm not even supposed to be here talking to you, but I saw your names on the manifest and I came out to the field on my own, just for old time's sake. I want you to know there's a lot of crap waiting for you in Chungking—so be careful."

"What kind of crap?" Reisman demanded, feeling a surge of anger.

"About what happened up on the border."

"What did happen, Sam?" Reisman challenged.

"I hear rumors."

"Maybe you've heard who ordered one of our bombers out to kill Linc Bradford and his men." Reisman turned around and looked out over the airfield. "Is that B-25 out there now, Sam? I'd sure like to find the guy who drove it and the guy at the gun."

"Nobody knows anything about a B-25," Kilgore stated firmly.

"There are eight hundred Kachin Rangers who do," Reisman flung back at him.

"A lot of the men here in Kunming think *you* are responsible for what happened to Linc," Kilgore stated coldly.

The suggestion was so outrageous that Reisman could only stare at him in angry disbelief. Controlling his rage, he said, "If I'd done a thing like that, Sam, my head would be mounted on a pole in Ngumla instead of listening to this bullshit from you."

Kilgore held his gaze, then said, "Okay . . . I'm not one of the ones who thought so. Now just listen to me for a minute. Here's the way it works out here—"

Their voices competed with the roar and scream of aircraft engines. Reisman often had to strain to hear and shout to be heard.

"The action, the kind you like, all emanates from here in Kunming," Kilgore said. "The politics and bullshit are in Chungking. The boss wants you there just long enough to look you over and chew your ass out."

"You mean General Donovan?"

"No. He comes through from time to time, but he's not around now and he has nothing to do with this."

"You mean Colonel Waingrove then. He sent for me more than a month ago."

"Waingrove isn't there any more. He was canned and shipped out a few weeks ago. He wouldn't play the game the way the Kuomintang gang wanted him to. There's a navy commodore named Pelham Ludlow heading up OSS China."

"That figures," said Reisman, shaking his head. "When you need a plumber, send a shoemaker."

"It's politics, that's all," shouted Kilgore. "Washington shits every time Chungking has a bellyache, and they had a big one when Waingrove tried to run OSS China without clearing everything with them first. Ludlow is a smooth character who has friends in high places. In fact there aren't any higher. Besides OSS, he's also our top man in an outfit called the Sino-American Cooperative Organization. You know about them?"

"Max Armbruster briefed me in London. He said their main function seemed to be to keep OSS agents from operating."

"That's right. It's a real funny situation and you're gonna have to do some figuring out for yourself when you get up there. As our man in SACO, Ludlow is our chief intelligence link to Chiang Kai-shek's government. That means he tells them everything and they don't tell him a fuckin' thing that doesn't serve their own ends. Every American agent, every intelligence plan and special operation is supposed to be cleared through him. Despite the fact that the Chinese don't like to socialize much with foreign devils, Ludlow has become an asshole buddy of General Tai Li. I don't think Ludlow goes to the can without Tai Li giving the okay on it." Kilgore stared at Reisman and said, "You know who he is, don't you?"

Reisman had stiffened at mention of the name. Linc Bradford had spoken it to him the first time. "You mean the opium dealer?" he probed.

Kilgore laughed. "Everybody's an opium dealer in China. Other than that, if anybody can be said to run China on a day to day basis it's probably Tai Li."

"What's his actual job . . . his position in the government?"

"Head of the Secret Service. But he does a lot more than that."

"So I'm told."

"He's the Chinese equivalent of State, War, Justice and probably all the rest of Roosevelt's cabinet rolled into one."

"Linc Bradford knew about him," Reisman said. "The way I understand it, Tai Li is in charge of seeing that everybody kisses ass in the one true way—or they get burned at the stake."

Kilgore stared at him appraisingly. "Still the homely philosopher, I see." He held out his hand again and Reisman took it. "Be careful what you do and say up there, Johnny," Kilgore said. "Eventually I'll see you back down here, I guess—and we'll go to work."

"Doing what?"

Kilgore shrugged. "Who knows? There'll be something."

Chapter 7

Chungking lay bleak, weary and pounded upon its hills. Broken masonry, rubble and closely packed buildings cowered tier upon tier, black, gray and dirty in the dust-laden sunlight of mid-afternoon. Below the city ran the muddy waters of the two rivers converging into one.

Reisman had only a partial view through a small window as the C-46 banked to come in. Was Katherine still down there somewhere, he wondered, alive and well? That alone would make the journey to Chungking worthwhile, perhaps joyous. It was two years since he'd had any word from her—though that shouldn't be considered strange or worrisome, considering the times in which they lived, the besieged place where she was, and his own frequent change of what could hardly be called an address.

He had never been to Chungking before, but he knew, from her letters and from news reports and pictures, of the horrendous punishment the city and its inhabitants had suffered in the years just after the capital had been moved there in 1938. Japanese bomber squadrons had followed with impunity and had begun to pulverize the ancient city. Surviving buildings had simply been camouflaged with black paint. Now, though the raids had been stopped by American fighter planes, there was still no color to the city except in the sampans and steamers on the Yangtze and Chialing rivers, or the color that was reflected onto it from the lowering sun upon these great arteries which brought life's blood to and from the wartime heart of China.

Reisman thought of Katherine Harris with affection, and then with a stirring in his loins when he remembered the hesitant, then tender, then passionate discoveries she had first made with him. They had met in Nanking, when the capital had been there and Japanese armies were pressing toward it from Shanghai on the east and Peking on the north, and the Chinese were making an unexpectedly strong stand. The U.S. had been determinedly neutral then, though sympathies were with the invaded country. Reisman had signed off his ship in occupied Shanghai and the Japanese had been courteous, correct and seemingly uninterested in an American seaman on the beach and playing tourist. He had managed to slip out of the city and sail up the Yangtze on a trading junk, thinking that he might become a soldier again and offer his services to the Chinese. Ultimately he had decided not to, for he discovered that there was no such thing as a democratic China that he could fight for; there were only mistrustful factions that warred against each other as much as against the Japanese. But while discovering that—and his education had come partly from what she taught him about China—he had met Katherine.

He had been twenty-three then and she twenty-nine—a tall, slender, pale woman with auburn hair and a gentle, sweet warmth that had made him at first think that she was offering him more than she really was and was much more experienced in matters of amour than she really was. Actually, she had been quite innocent, a woman who till then had forgone intimacy under the strictures of social propriety and churchly thou-shalt-nots, though the passion and desire, the great outreaching that was her nature, had always been there, sublimated to other endeavors. Katherine was a teacher and translator who had been born in China of missionary parents, had gone to the States with them, and then had returned to China on her own because she missed the people and places of her childhood and they needed her. When the government had fled from Nanking, a few months after

Reisman had left China, Katherine had gone with them to Chungking and had written to him a few times. He had replied. As far as he knew, she would still be there.

The flight to Chungking from Kunming, for Reisman, Baw San and their fellow passengers, had been less anxiety-ridden than the flight over the Hump. There had been no towering Himalayas reaching up to snatch at the C-46, and the airspace was well guarded by fighters from General Chennault's 14th Air Force. On the field, Reisman saw some of the P-40s, their noses painted to make them look like hungry sharks. Many of the planes and the men who flew them were veterans of the American Volunteer Group, Chennault's Flying Tigers, who three years earlier had begun to turn the air war around for China.

Yet the capital and all of the interior of China was still under a state of siege, sometimes active, sometimes dormant. Coastal China belonged to the Japanese. But the U.S. Air Corps helped keep them at bay. Four hundred miles to the east and southeast of Chungking—at Hengyang, Kweilin, Liuchow and elsewhere—Americans had even managed to establish and defend advance bases from which fighters rose to intercept Japanese marauders. But those bases, Reisman knew, were extremely vulnerable if the Japs ever decided to move against them in strength on the ground. The one at Lingling had already been captured. Chinese divisions in the interior were numerically larger, but they were poorly armed and trained, hardly ever committed to combat, and were led by warlords who hoarded American war matériel for their own status, or as insurance against other warlords, or in apprehension of the Communist army to the north under Mao Tse-tung. The defensive integrity of the Nationalist armies was tenuous and uncertain. There was constant worry—as high up as General Stilwell himself, though denied by Chiang Kai-shek—that one day the Japanese would smash through them, capture the air bases and go all the way to Chungking and Kunming.

Walking beside Reisman to the reception building, Baw San looked around warily as he balanced his duffel bag with one arm. He leaned close and spoke in a tense whisper: "Chiang Kai-shek lives here?"

Reisman sensed what was running through the boy's head. The young Kachin considered himself behind enemy lines, just as he had when they crossed the Salween to Caojian. "Yes," Reisman answered with a reassuring smile. "But if you leave him alone I think he'll do the same for you."

Even before evacuating him by light plane from the flying strip at Htawgaw, Reisman had told Baw San that he must never reveal the true circumstances of his wounds, that he was to say he had been wounded during a Ranger action against the Japanese in Burma. Then, while waiting in Assam, he also had cautioned him against getting into any seemingly friendly, idle conversation there or in China that might reveal anything about himself. He was to play dumb and refer questions to Reisman.

After his unexpected meeting with Sam Kilgore at the airfield in Kunming, Reisman had cautioned Baw San again. "It's going to take us a while just to figure out who is working for whom," he had warned.

His suspicions were aroused immediately after they checked in at reception. There was a jeep and driver waiting for them.

"Sergeant Liu," said the driver, saluting Reisman and looking curiously at Baw San. "The deputy director sends you his compliments and welcomes you to Chungking. He expects you immediately for a briefing in his office."

Liu was taller and chunkier than the average Chinese, and he wore a .45 sidearm. He was in his early thirties, dressed in the dingy khaki of the Kuomintang army; he spoke English with an American accent. Something about his movements, as he helped them to stow duffels and bags, told Reisman that the man knew judo and karate and would handle himself well in unarmed close combat. He was not just a driver.

Baw San climbed into the back of the jeep and settled in amid their baggage. Reisman took the seat beside the driver.

"Who is the deputy director and what is he deputy director of?" he asked.

Sergeant Liu stopped smiling and looked at him narrowly. "Commodore Ludlow of the Sino-American Cooperative Organization."

"He's the deputy?"

"General Tai Li is the director."

Sergeant Liu's loyalties in the sub-rosa intelligence wars seemed apparent.

"My orders are to report to the commanding officer of the Office of Strategic Services," Reisman told him.

"Same guy, same place," Liu said cheerfully. "Happy Valley."

Reisman looked at the man amiably. "Sounds nice. What is it?" he asked as the jeep began to move. He remembered with what striking simplicity, frequently elegant lyricism and occasional farce the Chinese devised the ideographs of their cities, mountains, parks and temples. The one for Chungking also meant *repeated good luck,* and he certainly hoped that would prove to be true.

"It's the headquarters and home of General Tai Li. He has made it possible for many of our friends to work happily, peacefully and productively there."

Happy Valley, Reisman thought, was obviously devised by a man with a cynical sense of humor. Sergeant Liu steered the jeep onto the airfield's runway, which now became the road that went to the clustered hills of Chungking a short distance away.

"I want you to take us first to the American military hospital," said Reisman. "My corporal needs to see a doctor."

"But the commodore instructed me to—"

"First the hospital, Sergeant," Reisman ordered. "I'll take the responsibility."

"Yes, sir," muttered Liu without conviction.

In the back seat, Baw San stared with great interest at sampans and steamers on the Yangtze, near which the road ran; then at the thickening traffic of pedestrians, carts pulled and pushed, coolies carrying heavy loads on balanced shoulder poles, rickshas, horse carriages and noxious alcohol-fueled and coke-burning busses. Sergeant Liu turned his head occasionally and tried to engage Baw San in conversation in both English and Chinese, but the boy kept looking elsewhere and remained silent. The jeep's progress was impeded by the noisy mass of humans, animals and crude machines. Liu added to the din with constant use of the horn.

The pungent night-soil smell of China that had assailed Reisman's nostrils above Kunming was still apparent here on the ground in Chungking, but it competed now with vehicle exhausts, the rank smells of the river, the stink of sewage and garbage in the streets and alleys and the aroma of foods being cooked at roadside stands. Wide stone stairways descended to riverfront landings crowded with sampans delivering and taking on people, cargo and foodstuffs. There was an endless transfer of the goods of life. Narrower stairways climbed winding paths up the hillsides through tiers of shops and housing. Amid the rubble, new bamboo and mud-brick buildings were under construction in bombed out areas. Files of coolies, vendors and peddlers trod up and down the stairs and roads carrying on their backs and in their arms the commerce of the city. Men and women carried pails of water home from the river for cooking and washing. In the red sandstone cliffs, Reisman caught glimpses of the caves and tunnels where the people had burrowed for shelter from the bombing, where thousands had died, and where many still made their homes.

The military hospital that Liu drove them to turned out to be much less of a facility than Reisman had hoped for. It was tucked away from obvious target sites in the newer, less congested western section of the city. There were a few emergency beds, but it was more an outpatient clinic, first-aid and pro station than a fully staffed and equipped hospital. It was under the command of an older navy doctor who was a lieutenant commander, and he had two medical corpsmen working for him.

"There are much better facilities in Kunming," Dr. Briggs told Reisman as he undid Baw San's bandages. "More troops there. No navy, of course, but your Training Command is there, and lots of Air Corps coming through, often with casualties."

"We were there this morning," Reisman said. "Maybe the corporal should have gone into the hospital there."

"No. Whoever patched him up did a good job. He can stay here a day or two if he'd like, but he doesn't need hospitalization any more. I'll show him a few exercises to get the arm moving right again. Then maybe a couple of weeks of recuperation time. There's a big recuperation center in Kunming on Lake Tien Chih. Nice place to visit. Good climate."

Reisman liked the man immediately. While Briggs dressed Baw San's wounds with medication and changed the bandages he chatted on amiably. He had been in the navy as a doctor since the first war, he said, some of that time in China on the coast and along the rivers with American gunboats operating out of the treaty ports. He had retired before the new war, but after Pearl Harbor he had volunteered for active duty, and had been swept up eagerly and sent here.

"Now I take care of the diplomatic people, visiting firemen, journalists . . . our own military, of course . . . and a few Chinese and foreigners who are *persona non grata* types and can't get help anywhere else. Any of our own people who are really sick or badly injured we fly out. This is a lousy place to practice medicine," he said with a sigh. "Supplies are stolen or commandeered in transit and wind up on the black market or in some powerful bastard's private hoard. Even the relief stuff given by our people at home and the official Lend-Lease hardly gets through to the people who desperately need it. There are quite a few Chinese businessmen, bureaucrats and warlords getting richer and fatter off the war and the people's suffering." Briggs looked at Baw San closely. "You're pretty young to be in the army, aren't you, son?"

Baw San looked at Reisman for permission to speak and saw him nod. "I'm twenty-seven," he said.

Briggs peered at him foxily over the top of his glasses. "The hell you say."

"It's right there in his service records, Commander," said Reisman.

The doctor glanced over the folder Baw San had carried with him, glanced back at the boy and said, "Yes, so it is. Born in *San Francisco.* Now *there's* a town I really like."

"It's been many years since I've been there, sir," said Baw San. "My parents took me back to Burma when I was very young. I don't remember a thing."

Dr. Briggs looked at Reisman, winked, then back to the young Kachin. "Well, then, I'll tell you about it, son—just in case you have to answer any questions."

Reisman felt confident that he was leaving Baw San in good hands. Perhaps this was part of *repeated good luck.* "I'll be in to see you late tomorrow, Corporal," he said formally, and left.

Outside, sunlight was fading and fog rolling in. He remembered Katherine writing that Chungking was often as oppressed by fog as London or San Francisco. As he waited in the jeep, Sergeant Liu's expression was far from inscrutable—it was impatient, even angry. He didn't bother with the military courtesies. "You've been a half hour," he muttered. "Ludlow is really gonna be pissed off."

"Tough shit," said Reisman. "Just shut up and drive."

Liu's body stiffened and he gave Reisman a look of hatred, but drove on in tense silence. They took one of the few roads that permitted vehicles to climb up the crowded hillsides. It was dense with the same variety of foot, animal and wheeled traffic as the road below. They squeezed through alleys jammed with ragged children, ancient women on bound feet, and streams of plodding, antlike coolies. The foggy air was fetid with the smells of garbage, sewage and cooking food.

The road leveled briefly to a little wooded area where Liu stopped the jeep at a gate in a black-painted wall. Two Chinese soldiers with tommy guns eyed the jeep and its occupants, exchanged words with Liu, then unlocked the gate to admit them to an interior compound. It was quite a different world behind the high wall. There was an unexpected serenity among gardens and arbors. Liu parked the jeep in a motor court that contained other jeeps, trucks and staff cars. Silently, in ill humor, he led Reisman under an archway, along a path, up a short stairway, past gardens, fountains and statuary to a two-story cement building with a curled tile roof. It was one of several buildings of one and two stories set amidst the gardens of the walled estate. Nothing looked new, everything looked old, but Reisman couldn't tell if the place had been there for years and years or had recently been built in a bombed-out area. Walls and roofs were covered with peeling, gray-flecked black paint. Here and there he also spotted concrete-arched, steel-doored entries to bomb shelters tunneled into the hillside. There had been a pleasing, aesthetic attempt to screen them with waist-high scented shrubs and young pine trees.

A Chinese officer sat stiffly at a desk in a small reception lobby. Liu reported to him, then went on through and climbed a stairway to an upper floor. Reisman started to follow, but was halted by the officer. He waited an hour, sitting in an uncomfortable bamboo chair; then a U.S. Navy yeoman came downstairs.

The yeoman took a deep breath, looked somewhere beyond Reisman's head, through a window and said, "The commodore instructs me to tell you that since you did not consider your appointment with him important enough to keep it promptly he will not be able to see you until 1100 tomorrow."

Reisman squelched a surge of anger. The yeoman was just following orders. "Am I to stay here tonight?" Reisman asked.

"There were no instructions, sir."

"Where do transients usually stay? Is there a bachelor officers' quarters around somewhere?"

Reisman became aware that the Chinese officer behind the desk was eavesdropping on the conversation, absorbing it all with an expression of slight amusement. No doubt one of Tai Li's men on the SACO staff. Where was the general himself? Reisman wondered. And where did they keep OSS men who he could be sure were OSS men? Or were there such men whom he could trust in all of China?

"There's a BOQ near the airfield, but I don't think you want to go out there again, Major," said the yeoman. "There are a few hotels in the city and some Chinese inns. Perhaps you might make your own arrangements."

"And put in for per diem?"

"I suppose so, sir, since you are here on official business. It won't cost very much, though. We're getting about one hundred and eighty Chinese dollars for one of ours now."

"Well, my treat then," Reisman said, standing up. "Which hotel do you recommend?"

"The Chungking Hotel. It's right downtown and it has a good restaurant and bar. I know that some of our visiting congressmen and newspapermen have stayed there. But stay away from the building across the street from the hotel."

"Why?"

"That's where the Commies put out their newspaper, the *New China Daily*. Chou En-lai and some of the Reds from Yenan are there. The Generalissimo allows them to do that. He's real democratic about it. But he doesn't want any Americans talking to them. Those are also Commodore Ludlow's standing orders."

Reisman knew that there was a tenuous understanding, of sorts, if not an actual working truce, between the Nationalist government and the Communist opposition. It had been strenuously urged on both sides by Washington in an effort to get the war going against the Japanese.

"How do I get to the hotel?" he asked.

"Walk, I suppose, or maybe you can find a ricksha out on the road somewhere," the yeoman said, looking away in some embarrassment. "They don't usually wait around up here like they do other places. There's not much call for them. But you might find one passing on the road."

Reisman understood that he'd just been treated like a nonentity, with the yeoman merely conveying at secondhand Commodore Ludlow's petulant putdown. He left the building without another word and walked through the gardens to the motor court. There he found a jeep with the key in the ignition. He transferred his duffel bag and air force–style flight pack to it from the jeep that he'd arrived in. He wished Liu had left the key so that he could have taken that one. His combat gear was in the large duffel, including his carbine—broken down, cleaned, oiled and wrapped. The flight pack contained a coat, additional uniforms, both O.D. and lightweight khaki, changes of underclothes, shirts, shoes and personal gear. He wore his .45 on a gunbelt that cinched the bottom of his short-waisted O.D. "Ike" jacket. Only now, transferring his baggage, did it strike him how stupid it had been for him to leave all his gear untended in the open jeep, and he resolved never to do it again. Simple theft in these theoretically secure grounds had not occurred to him earlier, and now, though there was no sign of anybody having touched his stuff, it seemed feasible that some unknown and unfriendly "friend" would have had the chance to tamper and snoop, if not simply steal.

Driving to the gate, Reisman hit the horn once lightly to alert the Chinese guards on the outside. They swung open the gate and he left Happy Valley by the same way he'd been driven in.

Chapter 8

The light was fading and the streets and walkways were emptying fast. Night was no time to be wandering around Chungking alone. The inhabitants found sanctuary in their hovels in the hills and caves or down on the river in floating sampans where generations were born, lived and died. Except for a few downtown hotels, restaurants and nightspots frequented by the military, foreigners and Chinese entrepreneurs and hustlers, the night in Chungking belonged to bandits, police, military patrols, agents and spies. There was fog, but not so bad that Reisman couldn't see where he was going.

He remembered that Katherine lived in a house on a hill called Hongyancun, overlooking the Chialing River just a half mile or so before it continued to the south and its confluence with the Yangtze. She had written him picturesque letters about it and said that she sometimes felt as if she were on the bow of a ship stuck out into the stream. At least that had been her address when she last had written to him, and he had that address in his wallet. Her mail had been going out through the American embassy and he'd been writing her care of there. They would probably know where she was, but the embassy was across the Yangtze, where all the embassies were, and he didn't want to be ferried over there in a sampan at this hour just to inquire. In any event, he wanted to scout out the Chungking Hotel first. Perhaps they'd be able to have a decent dinner there later.

Most of the vehicles nosed up to the curb at the hotel were military, plus a few old civilian Buicks and Fords. Reisman parked, lifted the jeep's hood, removed the rotor from the distributor, and put it in his pocket with the key. Carrying his duffel and bag he entered the drab, crowded lobby. The room clerk was a white-haired Chinese in a dark business suit who spoke English with a clipped British accent. A refugee from Hong Kong, Reisman surmised. When the clerk quoted how many hundreds of Chinese dollars it would cost to stay the night Reisman was momentarily stunned until he remembered how little that meant in American money.

A young porter, small and thin, took the baggage and escorted him to a room on the second floor. Reisman kept wanting to take the duffel back, to ease the carrier's job, but he had learned long ago that such a gesture would be considered insulting, a threat to both pride and rice bowl. The porter's eyes went wide and he bowed graciously when he saw the size of the tip Reisman gave him.

The room was high-ceilinged, painted a dull gray, illuminated by a bare bulb near the bed and another near the washstand. On the wall were three framed photographs in rotogravure colors: Sun Yat-sen, Chiang Kai-shek, and Franklin D. Roosevelt. On another wall was a Chinese silk scroll, a pastoral scene in muted colors. Reisman was amused by the thought that this was likely a room to which American guests were directed, and he wondered if there were British rooms that substituted Churchill for Roosevelt, or even French rooms that substituted de Gaulle or one of the other contending French leaders, for there were Frenchmen operating in Free China, too, working to get back into their colony to the south.

Heavy drapes were drawn at the window. When the porter left, Reisman parted them and looked out a moment onto a side alley. Then he stowed his duffel bag in the closet, hung up some uniforms, and repacked his flight pack lightly with a change of clothes, his carbine and some ammunition clips. He didn't know where he'd spend the night, but he hoped it wouldn't be here. Though he didn't know what the local custom was for an officer theoretically off duty, he continued to wear his gunbelt and .45.

The sound of music came to him as he walked across the lobby to look into the restaurant. It sounded like a version of something familiar and popular . . . "Moonlight Serenade"? . . . Glenn Miller and his band? Entering the restaurant, he saw the musicians up on a slightly raised bandstand against one wall. The restaurant was filled with both military and civilians. It was either very good, Reisman decided, or it was the only place in Chungking to eat out safely and well. The uniforms were from many countries and service branches, but mostly American. The non-Chinese civilians were probably from the various embassies, plus visiting delegations and journalists. There were a lot of women, some in uniform, but mostly Chinese glamour girls wearing gorgeous clinging gowns of silk slit provocatively high up the thigh. People were dancing, but the band certainly wasn't the big draw of the place. Except for the drummer—an American soldier happily glazed into his own private world—the others were reading their sheets carefully, playing without verve, as if they couldn't quite understand what they were doing there.

Reisman knew the feeling. Coming from where he had, having done and seen the things he had—not just on this last mission but on all of them—the incongruity of all of this, of men and women at their pleasures—dining, drinking, listening to music, enjoying entertainment, dancing, feeling happy and unafraid, tumbling passionately with each other afterward in safe places blessed or unblessed—always struck him with clashing force.

He turned away from the restaurant and walked into the large, separate barroom. Wood-paneled and mirrored, it reminded him of some of the better London cocktail lounges. He wondered if this building had been bombed and rebuilt or if it had managed to escape the devastation that had destroyed much of the older, poorer, more congested parts of the city. In London, too, the Nazis had dropped most of their bomb loads on the poorer working-class districts. Perhaps the tactic of both Nazis and Japs had been to terrorize and destroy the broad base of the nations, the salt of the earth, and leave the leaders isolated and without help. The tactic had not worked there or here.

The barroom contained the same sort of military and civilian crowd as the restaurant, with a democratic mixture of officers and enlisted men, though they were not necessarily drinking together. Through an archway he could still see and hear the band. They'd segued into "In the Mood."

Reisman sat at the bar next to a master sergeant, a talkative, bibulous ground-crew chief from 14th Air Force. "Just get in, sir?" he asked, eyeing the flight bag. Reisman nodded. The sergeant had been around Chungking for a couple of years and knew the city very well, and Reisman very soon knew exactly how to drive up to Katherine's place. He also knew about the dance band, which he'd been mildly curious about. "Four White Russians who've been on the run since 1918," related the sergeant. "A couple of German refugees from Berlin who just beat it out of Shanghai ahead of the Japs. They've been on the run since 'thirty-seven or 'eight. The drummer's an Italian kid from Brooklyn. Works for me out at the field. If he didn't have this and some regular poontang they'd have shipped him out on a Section Eight long ago. Me, too, I guess. I don't play no instrument. I just sit here and drink and listen and then go over to my steady shack for some R and R. I take care of her, she takes care of me—till I go home. It's a nice arrangement and it hardly costs anything."

It struck Reisman suddenly that there was something else important that he did want to talk to this man about and it wasn't his sex life. "You know pretty much what flies in and out of here, don't you, Sergeant?"

"Sure do, Major."

"Have you ever seen a B-25 painted in camouflage, but without any identification numbers, squadron markings or national insignia?"

The sergeant thought a moment, then shook his head. "Can't say that I have. It's usually 14th and 10th Air Force planes coming through here and they're pretty well marked."

In the other room, the band came out of "Tuxedo Junction." There was a fanfare, an introduction and a polite clapping.

"Here comes the shantootsie," said the sergeant.

Reisman looked through the archway and saw an ample blonde woman in a stunning white gown, breasts quivering as if about to burst from her décolletage.

"Now *she's* some kind of a Rooshin countess or something like that," the crew chief went on with enthusiasm.

It was probably so, thought Reisman. Aristocracy anyway, if not exactly a countess. In his experience of the world, curious twists of fate had always made themselves apparent to him and here tonight he was witnessing another one. China between the wars had filled with remnants of Russian aristocracy. They had come seeking temporary haven, which circumstances had made permanent. After them, in the late '30s, had come German Jews who had fled east instead of west and had been unable to get across the Pacific. So here tonight both types of refugees found themselves trapped in an anomaly, playing and singing strange American music in the interior of China.

"I been tryin' to get into her pants for two years, but she won't fuck around with nothin' less than a major," the sergeant rattled on. He looked at Reisman's leaves and said, "Hey, how'd you like an introduction? She's a personal friend. You might be able to get somewhere with her."

"No thanks, Sergeant," said Reisman. "I'm booked for the night. Allow me to buy you a drink." He left a couple of extra dollars on the bar, picked up his bag and left. Behind him he heard the Russian "shantootsie" doing a splendidly accented version of "Don't Sit Under the Apple Tree with Anyone Else but Me."

He felt how little any of this had to do with his life. Momentarily diverting perhaps, if incongruous, and maybe he would bring Katherine back here to the restaurant if she wanted to come, but it was as alien to him now as if he had been in Tokyo listening to a *samisen* concert. Then it struck him how very wishful and presumptuous his thinking was about Katherine. He didn't even know if she was still in Chungking, if she was free of entanglements, if she would want to do anything with him except say hello.

Outside, Reisman remembered what Commodore Ludlow's yeoman had said about the forbidden building across the street. He saw some lighted windows and wondered if Chou En-lai and other members of the circumscribed Chinese Communist Party were actually there now putting out the *New China Daily*. The wily Chiang Kai-shek had once been allied with them, had used them and then turned on them and slaughtered thousands. It was a wonder any had survived. And not only survived but thrived to force a loose alliance again. Not that he thought the Reds were any nobler or could be trusted any more than their enemies. He had seen their own brand of treachery and brutality at work at first hand when he'd fought for the Republic in Spain. They had confused what he had thought, in his youthful naïveté, was a righteous cause, and they had given him even more reason to be mistrustful of fanatical true believers of any political or religious stripe.

He put the rotor back into the distributor, got the jeep going and drove toward Hongyancun. There was a low ceiling that obscured the night sky, but the ground fog wasn't bad. He became aware just then of another jeep following about fifty yards behind him. He slowed, it came closer and he saw the big white MP lettering. He wondered then if there was an alarm out on him for taking the jeep. He pulled to the side, parked, took out Katherine's address and looked at it under the dash light. The MP jeep pulled alongside, a spotlight was shone on him and a voice called out, "Everything all right, Major?"

"Yes, thank you. Just checking an address."

They turned the spotlight off and drove on. As he continued to wind his way upward on Hongyancun, they came back down the hill and passed him. He had the feeling that they would continue to do that until they knew where he had lighted. He parked a number of times and, using a flashlight, checked numbers painted on walls, doors and gateways before he found Katherine's address. He pulled the jeep in tight against what was apparently the wall of an interior courtyard and removed the rotor again. With a feeling of both elation and trepidation, he carried his bag with him down a few stairs along a side alley to a heavy wooden door. The street was quiet, empty of traffic and pedestrians, and when he knocked he wished it didn't sound so loud and imperious. Still, no one came to the door. Then he saw the handle of a bell pull, drew on it a few times and heard the clang of it across the interior court.

He heard a shuffling of feet on the other side of the door; then a peephole was opened and an old woman spoke to him in Chinese. He shone his flashlight on himself to reassure her and said, in English, "I'm looking for Katherine Harris. My name is John Reisman."

He heard the sharp intake of breath and then she spoke again in Chinese. Reisman drew a blank at first, but then finally understood that she was saying that Miss Harris was sick—very sick. He groped for a few words in the Mandarin he'd been relearning, though he knew how unintelligible they might sound to a woman here in Szechuan. "Please go tell her I am here," he said.

"I tell . . . I tell," said the woman in English, and Reisman felt a sense of accomplishment that they could communicate in a pidgin of both languages.

She was gone for a few minutes and then she was back at the door, unbolting it as fast as her hands could move and repeating over and over, in English, "Welcome . . . welcome . . . Miss Harris very happy . . . very happy."

Reisman entered the small courtyard and waited for her to secure the door again. He tried to help, but she waved him away, sliding heavy bars through iron slots. Dim light came through an open door and an upstairs window onto the walkway and garden. The woman beckoned him after her, moving with quick little steps, and led him into the foyer of the house. It was illuminated by a ceiling bulb that cast dim light into a living room where he could make out a few pieces of heavy upholstered furniture, chests, tables—but no Katherine.

"Upstairs—upstairs," the old woman said in both Chinese and English. She was smiling but there were tears in her eyes, and Reisman sensed that something was terribly wrong, that "sick" meant more than sick.

He dropped his bag and bounded up the flight of stairs. There were two closed doors on either side of the landing and an open one, softly illuminated, straight ahead. That would be the room that jutted out toward the river, he thought, Katherine's room. He entered it and there was an immediate heaviness to the air, the aroma of a sickroom—and something more. He saw first an oil lamp reflected in the undraped, closed glass doors that gave onto the rooftop garden. Through the glass, beyond the deck, were the lights of ferries on the Chialing. Reisman glanced to the left where the lamp burned on a small table beside a chair, but Katherine's voice came to him from the right, from the shadowed bed that he turned to when he heard her speak.

"When Su'lin spoke your name I knew that God had heard at least one of my prayers," she said.

She was a figure propped up on big brocaded pillows against the headboard. He still could not really see *her,* except that her arms stretched out toward him and the sleeves of her robe slid down along her very white, thin arms to bunch at her elbows. When he came close and saw her, Reisman had to force himself instantaneously not to let the shock show in his expression. One side of her face was disfigured, jaw smashed, lips torn, teeth gone. In smiling the joy she felt, as she was doing now, she looked grotesque. Reisman sat on the bed, took her in his arms and hugged her close. She clung to him with desperate strength.

"I hoped that you, of all people, might come back to China," she whispered fiercely. "There was no one left whom I could trust—no one who had the means and the courage to see things through."

Reisman drew away from her, made himself look directly at her so that she would accept his looking and feel at peace with it, and then he moved close to her again with his lips to gently kiss her mouth, her cheek, her eyes and hair. She looked so thin and wasted, felt so light in his arms. The woman he had held close in Nanking had been tall and strong, long-legged and slender, vivacious in spirit and then passionate and giving in love.

"Oh how many, many times I've thought of you holding me like this, John . . . yearned for you," she murmured against his ear now. "My soldier of fortune." It was how she had teased him then . . . *My soldier of fortune.*

"What happened to you?" he asked.

"Tai Li," she answered.

It was the fourth time Reisman had heard that name. First Linc Bradford, then Sam Kilgore, then Sergeant Liu, now Katherine Harris. Each time it had been in connection with something threatening, powerful, tragic and pervasively evil.

"I want to know about it," he said. "All of it. In detail."

Katherine sank deeper into the pillows but held tightly to his hand. The heavy, cloying aroma Reisman had first smelled upon entering the room was still in the air. It was not unpleasant. A spicy scent, redolent mostly of cinnamon. He could almost identify it, but not quite.

"I would rather remember the night you first seduced me," Katherine said with a sigh.

"I think it was you who seduced me. After all, I was just a tad of a lad."

"I don't think you were ever a tad of a lad, John Reisman."

"Tell me what happened to you," he said again.

She shut her eyes, breathed deeply and seemed about to begin when suddenly she grimaced as if something sharp had pierced her.

"Are you in pain?" he asked anxiously.

She nodded, tapped lightly on the blanket above her stomach, ribs and heart. "Those men did a good job on me," she said. "Now I know what it feels like to want to kill. The furies I contain, thinking of vengeance."

Imagining what might have happened to her, Reisman felt a surge of fury himself. Let her tell it in her own way, he thought. "Do you take anything . . . for the pain?" he asked.

She smiled a bitter little smile, turning the disfigured side to the darkness on the other side of her bed. "Yes. But not yet . . . soon. One must bear it a while and not overdo."

"Are you strong enough to talk?"

"Yes. First what happened. Then why. Two months ago I was walking home alone at night when two men . . . Chinese . . . attacked me and beat me into unconsciousness."

"Bandits?"

"No. It was me they wanted, not just some passerby to rob. They were waiting for me in an alley not far from here. They could have killed me, but that might have caused more trouble than could be handled in high places. It was to teach me a lesson so that I would stop what I was doing."

"What was that?"

"Helping to gather evidence of treachery, spying and collusion with the Japanese in high places."

Reisman was startled that she would even be involved with anything like that. As far as he knew, she had been a teacher in missions and schools and had done extra work as a translator, sometimes for American agencies, sometimes for business companies or individuals.

"But you haven't been involved in intelligence work, have you?" he asked.

"Officially, no. But I had met Colonel Waingrove and he asked me to help. There was need for someone inconspicuous, someone with a good cover to find out certain things, and there was need for a translator to verify certain documents." She became animated and pushed herself up from the pillows toward him. "You have no idea what's going on, John. I'm not just speaking about the treachery and venality of the *tuchuns,* or the trading that goes on across the lines with the Japanese, at great profit to Chinese bureaucrats and businessmen."

She was speaking with difficulty now, expending her energy in a burst to get it all out. "I'm talking about operational spying—signalers to bring Jap bombers on target, military secrets traded for favors and gold, operatives betrayed, agents murdered, battles lost, soldiers killed. Do you know that right here in Chungking there is a colonel of the Japanese Secret Police, the Kempitai, operating under the protection of certain members of Chiang Kai-shek's government?"

"Perhaps he is a double agent?" Reisman suggested.

"But in whose favor?" she demanded angrily. "In Kweilin there is a Japanese directional transmitter operating with impunity under somebody's protection, and more damned spies per square mile than anywhere. When Chennault loses fighters, *there* are some of the reasons why. The Japs know when they take off and where they're going to be. And there's more! So much more, John, that it's almost impossible to believe! The Kempitai has infiltrated Chinese embassies in India, Singapore and elsewhere. Chinese traitors are transmitting information to them. Some of Colonel Waingrove's officers and operatives found trails leading to the most wealthy, politically influential Chinese and the highest circles of the Kuomintang."

"Is that why he was canned?"

"Yes. To avoid embarrassment to an ally. Isn't that absurd? What about the deaths and maiming of thousands of our allies!"

Katherine fell back onto the pillows gasping and in obvious pain. She let go his hand, drained of strength.

"Including you now," Reisman said grimly, feeling a helpless fury. He looked at her pain-racked, wasted body and disfigured face and wanted to take her in his arms again. "Is this why Colonel Waingrove sent for me?" he asked. "Because of you."

"Yes . . . partly." She spoke so weakly now that he had to lean closer to hear, and he took one of her hands in both of his. "He wanted to even before I was attacked. He knew you, of course, and we talked about you. He needed help. But London said you were busy. Off fighting Nazis somewhere."

"Yes, I was," said Reisman, remembering where he had been and with whom and what they had done.

"We were forced to submit our evidence only through SACO—the Sino-American Cooperative Organization," Katherine went on softly. "Do you know about *that* lunacy?"

"Yes, I do."

"It made its way up to Tai Li. Instead of action against the enemy, there was a whirlwind against us. Colonel Waingrove was sacked and replaced by that treacherous fool Ludlow. He is an intimate friend of Tai Li's, and he would just as soon see the entire OSS network dismantled. Within days after the change, some of Waingrove's best men in the field disappeared or were killed. What was done to me was a punishment and warning."

She twisted her body and moaned and Reisman said, angrily, "Why aren't you in a hospital? Why are you here suffering alone?"

"I'm not alone. Su'lin takes care of me. She's been with me since Nanking."

"It's not only your face . . . you've been smashed up inside, haven't you?"

She whispered the list of it and he could feel the pain as if he had taken the blows himself: ruptured spleen, kidneys damaged, ribs broken, one of them pierced a lung. "I managed to stay alive through the worst of the bombings—and then this," she said with a bitter laugh. The laugh turned to a cry of pain.

"Listen," Reisman said. "I met a doctor named Briggs. He's in the navy on duty here. Maybe I can have him come around and take a look at you."

"Ken Briggs! He's a wonderful man. If not for him I'd be dead already. It was he who took care of me right after the attack. He still comes around regularly."

"Why the devil didn't he put you in the hospital or have you flown home?"

"This *is* my home, John. As long as I am here in Chungking I am an indictment of Tai Li and a threat to the corruption, venality and treachery that goes on day and night against the people of China and the people of the United States."

She was a martyr, not a threat, Reisman thought to himself, and nobody cared about martyrs—or even found out about them—until years and years later.

"What does Briggs say the prognosis is?"

"The damage is permanent and regressive. I have only one solace now. It relieves the pain." She struggled up from the pillows and leaned toward a table on the other side of her bed. "Come around here, my love. You can help. Join me if you'd like. I know you won't be shocked."

Reisman walked around the bed and slid along the dark wall to the table. He saw the spirit lamp and matches, the lovely porcelain jar, the chopsticks, the long-stemmed pipe with the tiny bowl. No, he didn't feel shock. Only sorrow. He looked at Katherine and they gazed into each other's eyes with the wistfulness and comfort of old love and new understanding.

"Will you light the lamp for me?" she asked.

He did so, adjusted the wick, and sat down on the edge of the bed. Then, with the chopsticks, he lifted a tiny glob of opium from the jar and placed it in the pipe's bowl.

"A little more," she said, touching his shoulder and leaning to kiss his cheek.

He added another tiny portion of opium and held the bowl over the flame of the spirit lamp. When the dark, gluelike lumps began to bubble, he handed the pipe to Katherine.

"You do that very well," she said, staring into his eyes just before she inhaled. "As you do other things—which we must regretfully forgo."

She took two deep drags and handed him the pipe.

"For this too I must thank Tai Li," Katherine said, her voice now a purr.

Reisman didn't speak. He was drawing, slowly, letting the smoke drift through the chambers of his head and throat and body; then he drew again and gave her back the pipe.

"He sends it to you?"

She answered before placing the stem between her lips again. "No. He controls the trade. Sees to it that there's just enough of the stuff around to fill the demand, at a good price for him. For many Chinese it is the only joy and abandonment they've ever known. It has been that way for generations, to the profit of men like Tai Li—and also many foreigners. The British were in it for a long time. The French too. Americans are rather new at the game. The Communists, I know, would stop the trade entirely. They're Puritans. Very conservative. They're right, of course, as far as this stuff is concerned. It's a soporific. Wonderful dream stuff for girls like me who have nothing else."

She sucked twice more and the pipe was done. She placed it in a tray on the table and lay back against the pillows.

"What's the word in Chinese?" Reisman asked. "I knew it once."

"Ta-yen," she answered dreamily. "The big smoke."

"Ta-yen," he repeated. Then he stood up and walked to the glass doors that gave onto the roof garden and saw below in the near distance the lights of the river poking through drifts of fog. He didn't want to sleep yet, to give in to the big smoke. Its spicy aroma, burnt cinnamon, filled the room. It was what he had smelled before but had not quite been able to identify. Now it stirred other memories: *"Fire of rum, blaze of cider, ignited by sticks of cinnamon!"* Tessie Simmons . . . Marston-Tyne . . . *They are hangin' Danny Deever, you must mark 'im to 'is place* . . . Rushing from the prison afterward, drinking in to the bones the cleansing rain as he dashed through the sleeping village to the Butcher's Arms . . . Tess bending over him with her steaming mug of cure-all and then enveloping and exalting him with her sweet, loving young self, with softness, beauty and the passion of life to squeeze gross death from his mind and body.

It was what he had wanted from Katherine Harris this night. He turned and went toward the bed, remembering how it had been once with her, the rapture they had given each other without *Ta-yen.* She was asleep now, gone to the land of the big smoke, at peace with whatever dreams and hopes were left for her. Perhaps one day he would inflict retribution for the terrible things that had been done to her.

He went downstairs and found Su'lin. She had prepared a supper for him and he thanked her and ate it. He stayed the night there on a couch in the living room and when he woke in the morning he found that she had covered him with a blanket while he slept.

Chapter 9

"You are a troublemaker, Reisman," said Commodore Pelham Ludlow. "You failed to keep an appointment with your commanding officer; you took a vehicle without authorization from the SACO motor pool; you have been associating with persons you should not be associating with. All of this in less than twenty-four hours in Chungking."

He had an articulate, mid-timbre voice, but every now and then a consonant would slur and a vowel would go off pitch as if he were thinking and speaking in an uncertain Chinese dialect. He also spoke briskly, as if he had more important things to do.

Reisman looked directly at him while taking the tongue-lashing, but Ludlow glanced away frequently to points of other interest in the room. He was a thin, nervous man in a double-breasted navy-blue uniform with gold buttons on the jacket and the wide band and star of his rank gleaming on each cuff. He also had the disconcerting habit of frequently sliding and twisting his swivel chair and casting worried glances over his shoulder through the window onto the grounds of the Happy Valley compound, as if trying to throw off the aim of a sniper drawing a bead on him. In between his erratic glances and movements he sat up stiffly behind his desk and cast severe glances at Reisman.

The handsome Chinese desk was lacquered black, had ivory inlays and was devoid of the clutter of command work, except for the commodore's stiff-crowned hat placed neatly to his far right and the open folder centered before him that contained the service records and some of the prior history of John Reisman. The topmost sheet was apparently a record of his activities and infractions since arriving in Chungking.

The large room where Reisman stood before the deputy director of SACO, who was also currently OSS Chief, China, was furnished and decorated in a heavy Chinese fashion, comfortable and elegant. It seemed more the conference chamber of a wealthy businessman or high-level government official. The padded swivel chair was the only item in the room that resembled familiar military office equipment, though the yeoman's anteroom looked more businesslike, with a plain desk, cabinets, typewriter, mimeograph, papers, manuals and shelves of books in English and Chinese.

Reisman stood before the commodore's desk at a relaxed attention, waiting for Ludlow to tell him to be at ease or to invite him to sit. But the man seemed determined to keep him braced like an academy undergrad called before a captain's mast. So far, it was a rather petulant tirade, intended perhaps to establish the hierarchy of rank.

"The Harris woman is off limits to anyone under my command," Ludlow stated. "Just as much off limits as Mao Tse-tung and Chou En-lai or any other Commie."

Reisman felt a hot surge of rage and had all he could do to keep himself from reaching across the desk and beginning the process of retribution for Katherine. But in the next instant his own experience of command in the heat of combat made him *think* rather than *feel,* and he forced his body and features to remain immobile. He had no indication yet of what Ludlow might know or not know—of the extent of his incrimination, if any, in what had been done to Katherine. And to Linc Bradford.

Most of all, Reisman knew that he now had to be the tactician and diplomat. He had to suppress his feelings, modulate his words and play to the egotism of this man. The fortunes of war had made the naval officer his nominal superior, and Ludlow could decree, by whim or design, the duties and paths that would be open to him or closed.

"With all due respect, sir, I'm sorry to hear you say that," Reisman said softly. "Miss Harris would be too. She is the daughter of Christian missionaries and a practicing Methodist. She was practicing, that is, until she was attacked and seriously injured by unknown assailants. I assumed, sir, that you might have heard about that."

Ludlow's face softened into a pious mask. "Yes, I heard about the bandits. It's really too bad—but she should not have been out wandering the streets alone at night, engaged in God knows what. In any event, Major, it would be better for you not to be associated with her in any way. The government here has a very unfavorable file on her. They consider her a dangerous thinker. It's a wonder she hasn't been expelled."

Reisman forced himself to try again for an equanimity he didn't feel and to observe the military protocols and courtesies with a properly deferential voice. "Miss Harris is an old friend, sir. And, again with all due respect to you, I would be remiss in observing the simplest of courtesies if I didn't look in on her while I'm here in Chungking. I'd had no idea of what had happened to her. She's in a bad way and I feel I have to visit and do what I can to cheer her up."

The commodore stared at him appraisingly. "There are a few other things that concern me about you, Major Reisman."

"Yes, sir?"

Ludlow riffled through some pages of Reisman's service records. "There are, of course, commendations for excellent performance of duty . . . even indications that there would have been citations for gallantry if you were in any other branch but this . . . ahh . . . silent service, so to speak. But there are also indications that you sometimes overextend yourself, go beyond the boundaries of your mission *and* your authority, and take uncalled-for risks."

"I was taught to go for targets of opportunity when they present themselves, sir. I believe that the tradition of the navy also allows an officer on the line in combat to use initiative, to do a certain amount of thinking for himself."

"True . . . yes . . . so it does."

"Where I've made mistakes, Commodore, I've tried to learn from them and not repeat them."

Ludlow leaned across his desk. "Then why in hell didn't you stop that idiot Bradford?" he demanded. "Do you realize the trouble your incompetence has caused! Chiang Kai-shek is furious! Here—read this!"

From beneath Reisman's service file, he yanked out a separate document and handed it across the desk. Reisman read it. It was a duplicate—not a carbon copy but a separately prepared duplicate—of an official letter from Chiang Kai-shek to the American ambassador. The letter was in both Chinese and English, written on the fine stationery of the president of the republic and bearing his personal identifying chop. The Chinese text was in a fine calligraphy; the English text was typed and ran on to a second page.

"An astounding document, sir, and I feel privileged that you've shared it with me," said Reisman insouciantly. "But I have no idea what it means."

"What it means is that Chiang is demanding twenty-five million dollars in reparations from the United States for the lives and property those goddamn Commies destroyed!"

The commodore was making it a little easier than Reisman had thought he might. Before saying anything more, Reisman went over quickly in his mind what he had said to Sam Kilgore at the airfield in Kunming. He remembered demanding whether Sam knew about the B-25 that had bombed and strafed them. But then Sam had either lied or had given him all he knew, which was nothing. Apparently the official position was that there never had been a B-25 and that the murder of Linc Bradford and the Kachins never had taken place—though they knew damned well and were outraged, as the Gimo's letter stated, that *somebody* had destroyed the fort at Caojian. On their side of it, however, it seemed to Reisman, they could only continue to speculate on what had really happened. Except for the instigators and perpetrators of the treacherous attack during the return crossing, nobody at Ludlow's level, or even Sam Kilgore's, could ever prove anything. The Kachins would keep their own counsel and deal with it in their own way if they ever could.

So be it, Reisman decided. He would play Commodore Ludlow's game as far as it took him.

"What Commies? I don't know what you're talking about, sir. I don't know what the Gimo—the Generalissimo—is talking about."

Ludlow stared at him with an expression that veered between anger, doubt, astonishment and confusion. Then he decided on another tack, or perhaps just remembered the simple courtesies. "Please pull up a chair and make yourself comfortable, Major. I believe that might help."

Reisman brought a side chair close and sat down. "Thank you, sir."

Ludlow looked through the window behind him once more, then swiveled back to Reisman. "Now, Major, the way I understand it is that you were given the use of a C-46 from Calcutta to Myitkyina to the Chinese border and ordered in to stop this fellow Bradford and his natives from crossing the frontier."

"That's correct, sir."

"The pilot reported that he saw Bradford and his men crossing the Salween and that you parachuted from the aircraft."

"That is partly correct, sir. The pilot and I both saw a large detachment of people down in the gorge—and made certain assumptions. I did indeed jump from the plane, and subsequently wished that I hadn't."

Ludlow leaned across the desk eagerly. "Why not? What happened down there?"

"Well, while I was still descending toward the river I realized what a terrible mistake I'd made. I looked back up and there was the C-46 climbing away and then gone—no help there!—and below me I saw, instead of Bradford and the Kachins, a goddamned bunch of Chinese bandits! I tell you, sir, I was scared stiff! They could have shot me up right there and then. But I guess they were as curious as I was scared, because they all just stood there watching me. I started climbing those shroud lines and maneuvering that chute so that I landed about half a mile away from them up in the hills on the Burma side. It's a wonder I didn't get hung up in a tree, but I spotted a little clearing, took aim at it and made it down there okay."

Ludlow stared at him with pursed lips. "How did you know they were Chinese bandits, Major, and not Bradford and his Kachins?"

"Their uniforms, sir. They were wearing Kuomintang army uniforms and I figured they were the same bunch of bandits I'd been told about in Calcutta and Myitkyina. The bunch that were done up like regular Kuomintang soldiers when they crossed the frontier and raided those Kachin villages in Burma."

Commodore Ludlow opened his mouth to speak, but then changed his mind. His eyes glanced away again to another part of the room. His expression was one of confusion tinged with doubt. Reisman thought the orchestration had gone quite well. There was even room for a coda, so he carried his story forward to where he might eventually link it up logically with subsequent events that the deputy director of SACO would have received information about.

"I've been in some tight spots, Commodore," he said, "but that was one of the worst. When I realized who those guys were I just took off through those woods like a big-assed bird and hid out till I was sure they'd gone back to China."

Ludlow now looked at him with the expression of a man who had maneuvered his opponent into a trap and was about to snap it shut. His voice was a rebuke.

"Major Reisman. My information, on excellent authority, is that when you came out of the jungle in Burma and made contact with Allied units over there . . ."

"That was Detachment 101, OSS, sir. An extraordinary bunch of men who . . ."

"I *know* who they were, Reisman," said the commodore irritably. "Please allow me to go on. When you came out of the jungle you were not alone. You were with a group of natives, many of them wounded, some dead, and you had with you the body of the late Captain Bradford."

The casual, bantering tone dropped from Reisman's voice, and he wasn't faking the cold, hard tone that replaced it. "That's right, sir. Linc had been killed by the time I caught up with him. I spent a couple of days slipping through the bush, dodging Japs, looking for him and his men, working my way back toward that little flying strip at Htawgaw which was one of my rendezvous points to be taken out. I was lucky the Kachins found me before the Japs did. Without them I might never have made it."

"And where did you find Captain Bradford?"

"Not far from Htawgaw, sir. He was dead and his men were carrying him out. That's their custom, sir. Apparently they had run into a heavy concentration of Japs, and Captain Bradford had been killed outright, along with many of his men. There were a lot of wounded too."

"And they never went over into China?"

"Nobody told me anything about it."

Ludlow picked up the Chiang Kai-shek letter again. "How would you explain this, then?"

"I wouldn't—Commodore."

Ludlow bracketed him with the most direct gaze he'd used yet. "I'll tell you something, Major. You may very well never have run into them in time to stop it, but Bradford and his natives were seen crossing the river back into Burma the day after this outrage the Generalissimo has written about to the ambassador."

"Seen by whom, sir?" Reisman asked. Ludlow had baited a trap and then stepped into it himself. He knew something, whether he had been connected with its doing or not.

"Why should that interest you, Major?"

"Curiosity, sir. Satisfying it is the reason the United States government pays me a salary."

The commodore swiveled his chair and stared out the window onto the gardens and paths. He continued to look out as he spoke. "I'm curious too, Major. I understand they are mostly Reds over there in Burma. Is that correct?"

"No, sir. If you are referring to the indigenous people, it seemed to me they have no interest in that kind of politics as long as they're left alone to live their lives in peace in their villages."

Ludlow swiveled back to face Reisman. " 'Indigenous people'? That sounds like those highfalutin words that Franklin Roosevelt uses because he doesn't think *native* sounds nice."

It seemed to Reisman that the commodore had spoken Roosevelt's name with a certain hauteur. "I've never had the honor of speaking to the president," Reisman said, "but I'm familiar with his policy of freedom for all the indigenous peoples of Asia after the war."

"I've spoken to him . . . listened to him . . . a few times, Reisman. A difficult man . . . *but* the commander-in-chief—so one pays attention. Do you agree with his policy?"

"Of course, sir. That's how the United States of America came to be. The Revolutionary War and all that. We're an anticolonial nation, sir, and that's the way it should be."

Ludlow smiled for the first time during the interview. But it was not a friendly smile, nor without guile. Actually, he made a little snort of derision. "That's what the Commies say, too. You're not some kind of a Red agent, are you, Major?"

The smile, Reisman supposed, was to negate any umbrage he might rightfully take and to imply that the remark was just a little joke between the two of them. Yet the commodore had more to add, with rather pointed intent. He turned to another page in Reisman's file. "It says here that you fought in Spain—on the wrong side."

"On the losing side, sir."

"The side with the Commies."

"It wasn't a Communist war, sir. It was a war to preserve a democratic republic. The Fascists and Nazis destroyed it. The same people we've been fighting in Europe."

Ludlow stared at the pages below him, scanning lines he knew were there. "All this traveling before the war, Major. Mexico . . . the Caribbean . . . Spain . . . Palestine . . . China . . . in and out of Europe all the time. It's as if you were working for somebody—a courier of some sort."

"I was mostly a seaman, sir. Ships go places."

"A mercenary too, it seems."

"I had some experience at it. It's what interested OSS."

"And you speak a few languages."

"That was also of interest."

"French. Italian. Spanish. German. Chinese."

"I'm far from fluent in all of them, sir."

Reisman felt now that besides Ludlow's clumsy attempts at wily interrogation and the apparent satisfaction he seemed to get out of exercising the power of a petty tyrant, he was also checking him out for something specific he had in mind. Such as a new mission.

"You sound more like a brain, Reisman, a professor, than the thug that the rest of your record makes you appear to be."

"I take that as a compliment, sir."

"Just an observation, Major. Generally, your organization seems to be comprised of a mélange of doddering old professors, young snotnoses, wealthy dilettantes, refugees, Commies, psychos and renegades of one sort or another."

Generally speaking, Reisman couldn't argue with the man. He had met all of those types. But he had also met and worked with some of the most extraordinary, brilliant and courageous of men. He noted that Ludlow had said "your" organization, thereby ludicrously distancing himself from the organization and the personnel he theoretically headed up in China.

"Where are all these *Wunderkinder* kept, Commodore?" Reisman inquired with as much naïveté as he could muster. "I mean, exactly where is the OSS headquarters? Where is the work done? Where are the men and women who staff the office? I was brought here yesterday by Sergeant Liu, but except for yourself and your yeoman and the Chinese officer at the desk downstairs, I haven't seen any sign of anything like the base and branches we had in London."

"It's here in Happy Valley, in another building. There's not much of an operation here in Chungking. Mostly Research and Analysis. SACO is the primary intelligence facility here, Major. Everything must proceed from, be approved by and return to the Sino-American Cooperative Organization, even when OSS personnel are the operatives. Do you understand me, Major?"

"Yes, sir." He understood it, of course, but he had no intention of abiding by it. "Will I have the pleasure of meeting the general while I'm here?"

"Which general?"

"Tai Li. He's the Director of SACO, isn't he—in addition to his other duties? I've heard so much about him and I would be honored to meet him."

"If you've heard about him, Major, that means that either he or his subordinates are not doing their jobs properly. Forget what you've heard. As far as you or anybody else are concerned, the man and his office don't exist."

"Does Happy Valley exist?"

"Only for those who need to know of it."

"I surmise you have some sort of operation in mind for me then?"

"*I* didn't send for you."

How long was the game going to go on? Reisman wondered. "Colonel Waingrove did, and he must have had something in mind. Didn't he brief you during the change of command?"

"Waingrove was ordered out rather hurriedly."

"That's what Katherine Harris told me. Did you know that she was helping him out—doing some research?"

"No, I wasn't aware of that, Major. I certainly wouldn't have employed her on anything sensitive. Which leads me to another matter." He looked down at a sheet in Reisman's file again. "I believe that this Charlie Bawsan you brought with you was born in your documents section in Calcutta. I could have cut him off the flight from Assam, but it interested me to see what you were up to. I know he's at Briggs's clinic now, but what was your reason for bringing him into China?"

"The man will be very useful to us in operations, Commodore. I'm used to selecting and working with men I train myself. That way we get to trust one another and we work well together. In the corporal's case, he also has been teaching me. He is a Ranger with two years of hard fighting experience against the Japs. He's a bit of a linguist too, a good man for intelligence work."

"He's rather young for all that, isn't he?"

"He's older than he looks, sir."

For Reisman, it seemed the right moment to introduce a related matter and to try to maneuver Ludlow to where he would be amenable to it. He had been feeling a growing need for comrades close to him whom he could trust. "There are some other men I'll want to send for just as soon as—"

"Out of Burma?"

"No, sir. England. Just as soon as I'm given my assignment and can assess the personnel requirements." He would never order them here. His intention always had been to scout out the situation first, to find out what his new assignment would be, and only then to give Bowren and the others a choice whether to join him or not. Now he felt he should begin the process. It might take days or weeks. Or they might not ever want to volunteer for anything again.

Ludlow was studying him again, seemingly trying to make up his mind about something. "Well, I suppose now that you're out here we *will* have to find something for you to do, won't we?"

Reisman didn't really believe it was all that casual. He felt that there had been something in mind all along. Perhaps even something that Colonel Waingrove had planned for him, other than pursuing treachery in high places with Katherine Harris—a matter he was certain that Ludlow and Tai Li would not want pursued. If there was something specific in the works for him he thought it would most likely be a mission that would get him out of Chungking.

"Who are these men you want to bring in?" Ludlow asked.

"Specialists, sir. Espionage . . . intelligence . . . guerrilla tactics . . . the works."

"Americans?"

"Oh, yes. Men who've gone in behind the lines with me in Europe. Men I'd trust with my life. They were with me just a few months ago."

"What sort of an operation was that?"

"I'm sorry, sir. I'm not permitted . . ."

If he were really to know who they were, what they had done, Reisman was certain that Commodore Pelham Ludlow would never let them get over the Hump.

The man bristled slightly, but gave the militarily most acceptable response: "Yes, of course." He allowed a few decorous moments to pass, swiveled to glance out the window once more and then went into what appeared to be his closing remarks. "As long as we do understand each other now, Major Reisman, I think you might go on down to Kunming in a day or two, whatever works out conveniently for you, and report to Lieutenant Colonel Kilgore at the OSS base there. He'll have further word for you. He will also handle personnel matters for you. We clear all entries from here, but few of you operations types are ever invited up to Chungking."

"I feel honored then, Commodore," Reisman said.

He stood up, saluted and walked briskly out to the motor pool. He left the Happy Valley compound hardly any wiser about what it all meant than he had been when he first reported there the day before. He drove out again in the borrowed jeep he'd never gotten permission to use.

Chapter 10

At the Chungking Hotel, Reisman gathered up his things from the room he'd never used, paid his bill and checked out. Then he drove back toward Hongyancun. Katherine was expecting him. "I promise to stay awake and alert. At least until night," she had said. "That is when the really bad time comes."

She wasn't a heavy user yet, she had said. She smoked the opium less for the escapist fantasies it allowed her to indulge in than to dull the pain and soothe anxieties. With a different kind of agony she could break whatever addiction was there. Yet there was no reason to, she felt, and he agreed. There was nothing of substance or hope yet to replace the therapy, except for some standard painkiller that Dr. Briggs had brought her.

Glancing at the rearview mirror frequently after making a number of true and false turns through the thick press of motley vehicles and pedestrians, Reisman confirmed that there was a tail behind him. Two Chinese, in a military staff car, but not wearing uniforms themselves. Probably from SACO. He found it more amusing than ominous. What skulduggery did Ludlow think he was up to? But perhaps it was not Ludlow himself who was having him followed. It certainly was a different kind of war out here. He had already had enough examples of proof that one's friends and allies were not necessarily one's real friends and allies. He had never had to be concerned about this sort of thing before except when he had been behind enemy lines.

Su'lin answered his ring at the gate with smiles, bows and chatter in two languages. Katherine insisted on coming downstairs under her own power. She refused Reisman's offer to carry her and he was glad. If she was in pain she managed to contain it very well. She had even put on a bright dress, poignantly too large for her now, but she said she could no longer bear the nightgowns and robes that had been her drab uniform for two months.

He held the chair for her at the dining table in the living room. Coquettishly, she said, "I think your presence inspires me, John. I'm looking forward to better things." He leaned down and kissed the undamaged side of her face and then her lips when she twisted around for it. He managed not to see the disfigured features and thin, wasted body.

Su'lin had prepared a feast for them. They had gone through times of very short rations, Katherine explained, but now fresh produce, meat and fowl were readily available, though the inflation was terrible. Despite her not being able to work now, they were still able to get along. She had some savings and a small continuing income from the missionary society and other past employers who felt a sense of obligation to her. Su'lin had learned to cook the highly spiced cuisine of Szechuan. There were cold noodles in chili sauce, hot dumplings, twice-cooked pork and some fiery side dishes. Proudly, Su'lin announced each main dish by its local name: "*Dan dan mien . . . caho shou . . . huiguo rou.*" She poured some of the local white wine, left them with a steaming pot of tea, and went off into another part of the house.

They toasted each other, fell to with their chopsticks and talked between mouthfuls. Reisman told about his meeting with Ludlow.

"He is nothing but a flunky," she said. "He does everything General Tai Li tells him to do." She helped herself to more food, closed her eyes, sighed and said, "My God, this is good. I haven't enjoyed food so much in two months."

"Have you met him?"

"The general? Yes. I've met both of them. Tai Li is the one to be dreaded, to be constantly on guard against. He is a ruthless man, powerful beyond belief. More powerful than Chiang Kai-shek in practical, day-to-day ways, though he serves Chiang faithfully with fanatical dedication. He once even joined the Communist Party for Chiang—to spy on them—that was back in the twenties. Then, when Chiang gave the word—in 1927, I think it was—Tai Li turned on his Red comrades and butchered them by the thousands with the help of Chiang's soldiers and the murdering gangsters of the Green Gang. They're an underworld society, still powerful today. Nothing of a criminal nature happens without their approval and without their sharing in the profits. That goes for politics and business too. Today—this very minute—Tai Li controls a network of tens of thousands, maybe hundreds of thousands, of agents. Not only in China and Asia. Officially he's the director of something called the Bureau of Investigation and Statistics."

"*And* the Sino-American Cooperative Organization," Reisman added.

"Yes . . . and that gives him effective control of all Allied intelligence operatives, including your OSS, in China and throughout Asia. But his tentacles reach into every country and city in the world with a Chinese community—the United States, too! In Washington and New York and San Francisco, his spies and agents are at work to promulgate whatever holy writ Chiang Kai-shek and the Kuomintang have decreed. They stop at nothing, including kidnapping and murder."

"With that kind of covert power, how come the Chinese aren't winning the war?"

"Because they're divided among themselves, fighting each other more than the common enemy. And those in control—Chiang, Tai Li, the *tuchuns*—don't really want to fight the Japanese, despite all their slogans, posters, lip service and phony news reports of great victories. They're conserving their armies, hoarding war matériel. They want others to do the fighting for them. They want the Americans and the Japanese to wear themselves out and then just leave China. Chiang and Tai Li expect to win by default. Colonel Waingrove gathered evidence of actual incidents of sabotage against the American war effort here and secret deals with the Japanese. The Kempitai, the Japanese Secret Service, is perhaps as wily. But it's not so all-pervasive; and their military forces are superior, if not so numerous."

Reisman told her about Linc Bradford, about the Kachins' retaliatory raid into China, and the bomber attack that had killed Linc and his men. "Do you think Tai Li has the power to order something like that?" he asked.

"Unquestionably. With or without American cooperation. He has the political and military control. He has vast resources of money, men and equipment. He issues orders and terrible things are done—even if only as a lesson to be taught—so that no American would dare to try an action like that again."

Katherine spoke with such passion and fury, Reisman wondered whether in her helplessness and frustration—and because of her personal injuries—that she might be obsessed and blowing things out of all proportion. But he didn't think so. "How naïve we are, we Americans," he said softly. He turned a porcelain teacup slowly in his hands, admiring its blue design. Warmth and aroma rose from the brew. "Boy scouts and girl scouts . . . so innocent. Innocent at home . . . innocent in Europe with its simpler war and clearer goals. This out here is all so overwhelmingly big and powerful, so complex, so Machiavellian. To what end? To serve what purpose?"

She drank more wine and said, "Man's greed. Man's pleasures."

"Opium?"

Katherine shrugged. "Could be. It has been a powerful and basic impetus and motivation for what is done out here for a hundred and fifty years and more. Growing and processing it, transporting it, selling and consuming it. Fortunes have been made. Wars have been fought. Warlords and nations have risen and fallen because of it."

Reisman looked across the table at her in the waning afternoon light. "You're part of it now," he said. "Would you steal and kill for it?"

Katherine sat upright and stared at him. "No, my love, I don't think so. Perhaps—but I don't think so. But I know that I could kill for other reasons," she added defiantly.

He told her he would be flying to Kunming the next day and a look of sadness crossed her face.

"I was hoping they would keep you here," she said. "What will you do there?"

"I don't know, but the commodore obviously has something in mind. I'm to report to Sam Kilgore. He's a light colonel. A good man. Someone I've known a long time."

"Will you be staying here again tonight?"

"No."

"I wish I could make it more attractive for you."

He got up, kneeled beside her chair, took her head gently in his hands and kissed her. "It's not that," he said softly. "I remember all the beautiful things between us."

She touched his cheek. "So do I, my love. So do I. If I had the capacity to feel that now I would use it on you."

When he left an hour later, Katherine walked slowly to the courtyard gate with him, leaning on his arm. She was tired, the animation gone from her face and voice; she was undoubtedly in pain, Reisman thought. She hugged him, kissed his lips and said, "Be careful. And send me a picture postcard."

"I won't lose touch," he promised.

Su'lin came out onto the path to wave her own goodbye and to be there if Katherine needed her to get back into the house.

At the clinic, Reisman found Baw San studying anatomical charts in a medical corpsman's handbook. He no longer wore a sling. Even as they talked he moved his arm in the slow exercise patterns Dr. Briggs had taught him to restore his wounded arm and shoulder to full use.

"Do you think I could learn to be a doctor in the United States?" he asked eagerly.

"Sure, I think you could," Reisman said.

"That's a bright and diligent lad," Lieutenant-Commander Briggs stated. "I think he can be anything he wants to be."

"Got a few minutes, Doc?" Reisman asked. "I have some questions."

Briggs brought him into the little room he used as private office and sleeping quarters. His desk was against one wall. He turned the chair for Reisman and sat down on the edge of the cot. Reisman set his duffel and flight pack next to the desk.

"Moving on?" Briggs asked.

"Yes. The corporal and I are flying out to Kunming early in the morning. I'd like to stay here tonight, if that's all right."

"Sure. There are an extra couple of beds out there. Help yourself. I wish I were going with you to Kunming. Care for a drink?"

"Yes, thank you."

Briggs took a bottle and a couple of glasses from a cabinet. "This is good stuff. Real scotch. Not any of your local *ching pao* juice. Pilot friend of mine brought it in for me." He poured two generous drinks, handed one to Reisman and raised his glass. "To the end of the war," he toasted, sitting down on the cot again. "And who knows when that might be? Leaving this great capital city would be no great hardship for me or any of the military and diplomatic personnel stationed here. Chungking and its weather are both oppressive. The rigid social, military and political controls are stifling. It is the capital of Free China—yet nobody is truly free here. Your new CO sent a man sniffing around yesterday after you left Charlie Bawsan here. I told him to bug off."

Reisman said, "A couple of them have been following me around all over town. They're probably up the street now waiting. Dull work."

"Why follow you?"

"They're not sure which side I'm on—which leads me to what I want to talk to you about." Reisman took another appreciative sip of the whisky. "It is good stuff. Very smooth. I want to thank you for the help you've been giving Katherine Harris. She's an old friend. I went to see her yesterday and again today. I'd had no idea what had been done to her, so it came as a shock."

"A lovely, courageous woman," said Briggs. "I'd met her a few times before it happened. I'd gladly forget my Hippocratic oath and cut off the balls of the men who attacked her. There's little I can do to help her here. I've told her to go home. Perhaps corrective surgery, proper treatment, rest without stress would do it. She won't go, though. She says her home is China."

"What's the prognosis?"

"Bad and likely to get worse."

"She's told me why it was done and who is responsible. What do you know about it?"

Briggs drained the last bit of whisky from his glass. "Only what she's told me, which is probably the same she told you. Tai Li and his *Gestapo,* which makes us—we in the American military, the American government—culpable too, because we give Chiang and Tai Li and the whole damned Kuomintang gang aid and approval. A year ago, Tai Li's gunmen used pistols and silencers provided by U.S. Naval Intelligence to assassinate important members of a democratic opposition to Chiang Kai-shek. Not Japs, not Communists, but distinguished men in Chinese cultural, literary and educational circles."

"How did you find that out?"

"An ordnance man I was treating for a bad case of conscience. He supplied the weapons, not knowing how they were to be used.

You see, Major, whatever Katherine knows, there's nothing she can do about it. They did just enough damage to her to put her out of action. They got rid of Colonel Waingrove. They'd get rid of you—have you transferred or kill you—if you started making trouble for them."

Reisman felt his adrenaline begin to surge as he perceived the enormity of the challenge. It was, curiously and familiarly, a heady and delicious feeling: one that he had experienced many times in his life, had sought out actively and had never turned away from when it came to him. "Then whatever I do will have to be done very subtly, won't it?" he remarked. So subtly, he thought, that they—whoever *they* were—would not even feel the knife going in.

Chapter 11

There was a warm welcoming grin on Sam Kilgore's face and he gave the thumbs up sign to Reisman and Baw San, as if greeting a team returning in triumph from a hazardous mission. The morning was sunny and dry up there on the high plateau, the air a lot clearer than in Chungking. To the north, east and west, beyond the airfield, beyond the terraced farms and night soil smells, high mountains ringed Kunming. To the southwest lay the big Lake Tien Chih. Sam Kilgore stood astride the walkway outside the small reception building; husky, beaming and neat in his crisp suntans, he looked like Tom Sawyer grown up.

After salutes, introductions and hand-pumping, Sam pointed to where he'd left the jeep and told Baw San to stow his duffel there; but he held Reisman back for a private word. "So that's your Corporal Charlie Bawsan! Twenty-seven years old? Born in San Francisco?"

"Sam, don't knock it. Baw San has fought and killed more Japs than you'll ever see. He knows more about jungle warfare and guerrilla fighting than either of us will ever learn. He knows how to deal with the citizens of this inscrutable East, and what he doesn't know he'll learn a lot faster than we will. Meanwhile, he needs a little R and R. I've got a letter here from his doctor. He needs a week or two."

"How about you?"

"I'm reporting for duty. Ludlow said you'd have something for me."

Sam picked up Reisman's duffel and they started toward the jeep. "What did you think of him?"

"We got along." He had no intention of discussing OSS Chief, China, until he knew how close the commodore and the lieutenant colonel were on a personal and professional level.

Kilgore turned to see that Baw San was settled in with the luggage, then started the jeep and drove away from the airfield. "How's your *parlez-vous* these days?" he asked Reisman.

"Serviceable. You're not sending me back to France, are you, for chrissake?"

"No. There's someone I want you to meet who's quite fluent in it. Also speaks English, Chinese and a bunch of other languages."

"Who is he?"

"Later," Sam shouted above the grind of the jeep engine and the wind.

They entered the town pressed within the stream of humans, animals and machines that seemed endemic to Chinese cities. The stream narrowed and slowed as they approached a massive stone arch. It was painted with gilded Chinese lettering and the roof was crowned by two curving tiers of tiles. Before reaching the arch, they drove past a wall covered with a gigantic painting in bright colors and slogans in black ideographs. The picture had the ingenuousness of an American comic strip, but with a Chinese cast to it: a peasant and water buffalo were plowing a field; in a bubble cloud behind the farmer was the smaller figure of a soldier charging the enemy with fixed bayonet.

Reisman called over his shoulder, "What does it say, Corporal?" He knew what it said, but he was playing to Sam Kilgore as an audience and he thought Baw San could do it.

They were moving slowly enough so that Baw San was able to

piece together the big, simple characters. "At the front, fight to protect our country," he sang out in mimicking tones of command. "In the rear, work to raise food."

"That's pretty good," Reisman said, beaming.

"Could you have done it?" Sam challenged.

"Sure."

Baw San leaned over the back of the seat. "The picture helped," he admitted with a big smile.

Sam's laugh boomed under the archway. "Do you want the travelogue?" he asked.

"Enchanté!" Reisman said. *"Wǒ yaǒ! Xìe xìe."* Glad to. That would be nice.

In a cheerful singsong voice, Lieutenant Colonel Kilgore launched into his lecture. "You have just passed beneath the famous arch of Pi Chih—named, logically enough, after the mountain of the same name which the arch faces in the middle distance."

"The mountain of the jade chicken?" Reisman tentatively translated.

"What?"

"There's something in Chinese mythology about a jade chicken."

"Of course there is. Everybody knows that," Sam said with a glance of amused rebuke. "To go on: down the street is the equally famous arch of Chin Ma—named for the mountain that *it* faces."

"The mountain of the golden horse?"

"As I was about to say, Major; also out of ancient Chinese mythology." Sam waved grandly at the crowded street through which they were slowly threading their way. "Thus we have the two names combined into Chin Pi Lu, the main street of Kunming. You can trade, buy or steal almost anything in your heart's desire on this street, gentlemen, or in one of the foul, narrow, twisting alleys and lanes that peel off to your left and right."

Reisman nodded with a feigned expression of wisdom. Baw San stared at everything with fresh excitement. Enjoying his role, Kilgore continued his carny barker's spiel past wooden buildings, mud-brick buildings, crowded balconies with laundry hanging out, power poles and telephone poles with wires and cables strung between them, small shops, streetside food vendors, blaring radios, U.S. soldiers, Chinese soldiers, French Indochinese soldiers, masses of civilian Chinese wearing black, blue or white pajama-like garments, men and women bearing balanced loads of produce, cement and whatnot hanging off long poles on their shoulders, rickshas, ponies, mules, water buffaloes, military jeeps, trucks and cars, and a variety of ingenious civilian vehicles powered by assorted fuels and animals.

"End of the two-bit tour, Johnny," he said finally, turning off Chin Pi Lu onto another road and heading away from the congestion. "Just a small introductory taste of the old city." There were new commercial and government buildings elsewhere, he explained, in tall, Western-style architecture, and also a vast, very different part of Kunming life that was lived entirely on the long canal connecting the city to Lake Tien Chih. "I'm sure you'll catch all that on your own," he concluded.

They drove past a lineup of rickshas waiting like a rank of taxis along a mud-brick wall, then were admitted through a gateway into a military compound. "Home," said Kilgore. "OSS headquarters . . . barracks, offices, mess hall . . . Plans and Training . . . Research and Analysis . . . Special Operations . . . Secret Intelligence. You want it—we've got it or we'll get it for you."

Within the compound were a number of two-story brown wooden buildings, a few one-story mud-brick barracks and some squad tents. Sam parked the jeep on the dirt road beside one of the two-story buildings. They entered a large room on the first floor where enlisted personnel were at work at desks, typewriters and file cabinets. There were also some Chinese in the room who Reisman took to be field agents. Kilgore caught the attention of a young tech sergeant wearing steel-rimmed glasses. He got up from his desk and came toward them.

"I want you to get in touch with that gentleman we've had on hold for a couple of weeks," said Sam. "You know the one I mean?"

"Yes, sir."

"Ask him to be here at 1300 for a meeting."

After lunch in the OSS mess hall, Baw San had been sent off with a jeep and driver to Lake Tien Chih. He hadn't really wanted the extra leave, he had protested, nor did he like leaving *Duwa* John alone in a new and uncertain situation. But Reisman had assured him that he would be called back to active duty very shortly and that his only orders for the next week or two were to rest, and maybe also to learn to read and pronounce in Mandarin at least fifty new Chinese ideographs.

Reisman stowed his gear in a footlocker and closet next to the bunk he'd been assigned in the one-story, mud-brick structure that was the BOQ. Then he walked back to Operations and upstairs to Sam Kilgore's office, a room furnished with a desk, phone, swivel chair, file and a couple of side chairs. A man was sitting in one of them talking to Kilgore; he stood up in a gesture of courtesy as Reisman came through the doorway. He looked to be Chinese, a short, thin man in his early fifties with receding black hair austerely trimmed and a sparse mustache and wispy goatee. He had the look of an ascetic mandarin or scholar, though there quickly appeared on his wan features a radiant look of anticipation. He wore a rumpled pajama suit of the sort in which one might disappear among the millions of others dressed similarly in China.

Sam introduced them: "Mr. Tong Van So, Major John Reisman."

"On m'a dit que vous parlez français, Monsieur Commandant," said Tong Van So.

"Oui, monsieur," Reisman replied. *"Avec plaisir."* And he went on to explain in French that he really was not commandant of anything in particular and that commandant in English had a meaning different from that of major.

As if it were the most pressing of topics, requiring immediate elaboration, the two men went on discussing in French the subtle differences in the meaning of words and translations, while Kilgore, whose French was rudimentary, listened mostly in ignorance. Finally, in irritation, he said, *"En anglais, s'il vous plaît, messieurs.* What in hell are you jabbering about, Johnny?"

"He commends me for my knowledge of the language, though he says I speak it more with the accent and idiom of a thug on the Marseilles waterfront than an intellectual in a Parisian literary salon. That and other highbrow stuff you wouldn't be interested in, Sam. I told him he was absolutely correct."

Kilgore laughed.

Tong Van So said, in English, "I didn't mean to offend you, sir."

"I'm not offended," Reisman insisted. "I commend you on your superior fluency. It is a surprising talent for a Chinese."

Tong Van So smiled. "I am not Chinese, though it would be best to continue that impression."

"He is an Annamite from French Indochina," Sam explained.

Tong Van So saw fit to elaborate on that. "Annam, it is true, is the territory of my birth. But Annam is only one territory of my country. It is even more than one of your states in America," he said pedantically, as if he were lecturing to a freshman class in geography. "Our ancient and traditional name for our country is Viet-Nam. In our north, closest to China, is Tonkin. In our middle is Annam. In our south there is Cochin. To the west there is also Laos and Cambodia, but they are different countries. We are none of us French, nor are we so-called Indochinese. That, *mes amis,* is a European conceit."

Kilgore waited with an impatient little smile on his face. When Tong Van So was finished, Sam continued: "The Japs are in control down there and that's why Tong Van So is here talking to us. We're going to help each other get rid of them. He's got a network we can use, but he needs stuff from us. I want you to work with him, Johnny. One of my predecessors gave him six revolvers and some rounds and said, 'Go get 'em, boys!' But they need more help than that and we're authorized to give it to them now."

"By Ludlow?" Reisman asked, surprised by that possibility.

"By Washington. I don't think the commodore is personally for it, but he's going along. That probably means that Tai Li told him to follow through for a while and see what happens. He and the Gimo like it when other people do their fighting for them, but they keep track of everything that's going on." He glanced around the room, scanning walls, window, ceiling and objects as if looking for something. "I don't think there are any listening devices or a tap on the telephone, but it wouldn't surprise me if they're aware of our meeting here this very moment. There's a private little war going on that's separate from the big one. Tai Li has got his sneaks and spooks everywhere. They try to see everything that's done, hear everything that's said and log every contact that's made. They probably have a few spies right here in our own outfit."

Reisman didn't like Kilgore's air of apparent unconcern about that. "Why the hell don't you find out who they are and get rid of them?" he demanded truculently.

"That would give offense to our hosts," Sam replied wryly.

Tong Van So leaned toward Reisman and spoke gently. "One must not act . . . uh . . . how do you say . . . in English, *monsieur—précipitamment?*"

"Precipitately," said Reisman.

"*Oui* . . . with too much haste in anger. You must learn to live with the continuing presence of these spies and try to be just a little bit more clever. I have been doing it for a very long time."

Reisman wondered if he meant with the Japanese or Tai Li's spy network or both of them—and more? "What do I call you?" he asked. "Mr. So?"

Tong Van So laughed and said, "In my country the family name is given first. Formally, it would be Mr. Tong. But since we are to be comrades, just call me Tong. That's okay."

"I'm John."

"Très bien! . . ." He gave it the French pronunciation, *"Jean."*

They stared silently at each other a few moments, each deferring to the other the possibility of opening the dialogue. But Kilgore pressed into the silence and it was just as well, for Reisman had a vast ignorance regarding French Indochina and what might be happening there.

"Tong and his people have been doing some escape-and-evasion work for us, helping flyboys who bail out or crash down there," Sam explained. "They've also been providing intelligence on the deployment of Japanese forces, supply routes, communications, the lot. Air Corps has hit Hanoi, Saigon and military installations on the Red River and other targets."

"Is there active ground fighting going on there now?" Reisman asked.

Tong began to give much more than a military briefing. It was a geopolitical lecture in English with Oriental accents, sprinkled with Americanisms and French phrases.

"No, *Jean,* I am sorry to say that there is no real war of liberation going on now in my country. Not even a little war . . . what you call a guerrilla war. Viet-Nam is occupied and controlled by two enemies who are collaborators against us and against you Americans. The French are left over from the Vichy government—which, of course, no longer exists now in France since your armies chased the Germans out. These fascist colonists—*colons,* as we call them—have not received the message that they are finished. They work closely with the imperialist Japanese."

Reisman bristled slightly. "I've never been to your country," he admitted. "But I must tell you, *Monsieur* Tong, that I have a great affection for France and its people and I've just come from there. Their defeat four years ago and the whole Vichy business and their collaboration with the Nazis and Japs was a tragedy that I shared. Now I rejoice in our victory. Things will be different in France, and in Indochina too."

Tong looked at him with an enigmatic little smile. "I see that you and I, *Jean,* will have much philosophy to talk about. It is very complicated in my country. It is like a big pot in which many ingredients bubble."

"A cauldron?"

"*Oui,* a cauldron—in which many factions simmer and contend with each other but nothing is ever cooked to completion or satisfaction."

"And you intend to heat the cauldron up further?"

"Yes."

"To what end?"

"To free my country."

"From whom?"

"The Japs immediately. The French later, preferably through negotiation."

Kilgore spoke up. "That seems to square with directives we're getting from Washington, John. They don't want the French back in there. Not as a colonial power. Those that live there will have to open it up into a democratic country and take their chances. The British don't like that, of course. They're worried about their own empire out here. But the Chinese are willing."

"Of course they are," Tong said gravely. "They would like to take us over again, but we don't want them either. The last time the Chinese came they stayed for a thousand years. We want to control our own lives and destinies."

"If we help you now," Reisman asked, "whom do we help you against?"

"The common enemy—the Japanese."

"What do you do about the French?"

"Nothing. If they leave us alone we will leave them alone. The Japs let them keep their military forces and weapons, their police and civil administration—which is in the hands of the admirals and generals, anyway."

"Do *you* have an army?" Reisman asked.

"An *army?*" Tong echoed, his voice rising into a bitter laugh. "No. Men and women who will fight to free our country? Yes. With your help perhaps we will become an army—a small one." He became the passionate orator again. "Do you remember what it says, *Jean,* in your Constitution? 'We, the people . . . in order to form a more perfect union . . .' It is one of my favorite documents in all history. It is what I intend also for my people."

"That's politics, Tong. That's not our business now," Sam Kilgore put in. "We'll settle for a couple of good battalions, John, like they have over in Burma."

There were a lot more than that over there, Reisman knew, and they'd be hard to equal. "What kind of help do you need, Tong?" he asked.

"Everything. Weapons—all kinds—ammunition, field equipment, communications, uniforms. And instructors to train my people."

"Do you have an organization of some sort?"

"Yes."

Reisman waited, but the man volunteered nothing more. "What is it? Does it have a name?"

"Viet-Nam Doc-Lap Dong Minh Hoi."

"What is it in English?"

Tong pursed his lips, raised his head slightly and closed his eyes for a few moments as if better to examine the words in the seclusion of his mind. He squeezed them out slowly, one by one: "Revolutionary . . . League . . . for . . . the . . . Independence . . . of . . . Viet-Nam."

"What's its politics?"

"A united front," Tong responded expansively. "All kinds. We are all nationalists. Democrats, socialists, businessmen, monarchists, communists, conservatives—all together to free our country."

"And *your* politics?"

"I am a nationalist. I want all occupying powers to go in peace. Beyond that I am open to fresh ideas from anywhere."

Reisman looked around the small office and felt the constraints and inhibitions of its confining walls; then he looked back to the slight, austere figure of Tong Van So, animated by the passion of what he'd been saying. From his own experiences in behind-the-lines operations in France and Italy, Reisman was sensitive to the nuances of political antagonisms among guerrillas, as Sam Kilgore was from his operations in Yugoslavia. No matter what Tong Van So's personal politics were, Reisman realized that the man was an astute politician. He'd covered most bases in his "united front" except for splinter groups like syndicalists and Trotskyites.

"Well, let's get started, Tong," said Reisman, standing up. He felt that they would do better together away from Kilgore. "I've got some ideas, but I'm wide open to yours."

Tong asked brightly, "Do you know the city of Kunming, *Jean,* and the surrounding countryside of Yunnan?"

"No, I've just arrived."

"Then perhaps you will permit me to escort you? There are some points of interest—some sights. I would like first for you to come with me to where I am staying. You will usually find me there, or you will be able to contact me through one of the people I will introduce to you."

Chapter 12

Tong Van So settled into the passenger seat of the jeep with the look of a man whose fortunes had begun to improve. He surveyed the road and its traffic serenely.

"Shall we speak in English or French?" he asked Reisman.

"Whichever you prefer."

"English. I need the practice. If necessary, French. I understand from the colonel that you also speak Chinese."

"Very little. Perhaps you can teach me more—and a few basic phrases in your own language. If we are to work together it will be useful."

Tong gave him directions to the house where he was staying. "I am honored that you accepted my invitation," he said.

"Business and pleasure," Reisman acknowledged.

"An old custom of the East."

They had to speak loudly above the engine and traffic noise, but they felt immediately comfortable with each other.

"How did you get out here to the base?" Reisman asked as they sped away from the compound.

"Ricksha. If you will look in your mirror you will see the man trotting furiously after us now. One of Tai Li's agents, perhaps? He was idling in the street outside my house when I needed transportation."

Reisman spotted the ricksha man, then saw him stop when an old black Buick pulled ahead and took up the tail. "Do you want to lose them?" he asked.

"It makes no difference. Not at this stage. Curiously enough, I believe that for the time being they approve of our working together, although they will continue to spy on us. The Chinese are a people hard to understand. They are as likely to hinder us as to help us—and each for the very same reasons."

"They are also divided and confused by the Communist issue. Which side are you on, Tong?"

Reisman glanced for a second from the road to his companion's face and saw nothing but equanimity on it as Tong responded: "Whichever side helps my people."

His expression changed a few minutes later, however, as they moved slowly east with the heavy traffic on Chin Pi Lu. They passed a group of French officers and Indochinese troops walking along the sidewalk past the storefronts, vendors and peddlers, talking animatedly. The black Buick, containing what they suspected were two of Tai Li's agents, was still following discreetly about fifty yards behind the jeep. But that irritated Reisman more than it did Tong. What disturbed Tong was the sight of the French. He turned his head away from them and hid himself further with a movement of his arm.

"It is doubtful that any of them would know me," he said, "but it is best that none of them ever see me."

"They're your countrymen, aren't they?"

"They are French officers and some Viet-Namese who serve in their army. There is a French mission here in Kunming, but even they are divided in loyalties—some still to Pétain and his defeated Vichy fascists, some to the Free French and de Gaulle, some to other generals and politicians. My presence here—my association with you—must be kept secret from all of them. For now we must have nothing to do with any of them."

Reisman felt inner conflict but refrained from comment as they drove along in the noisy tide of humans, animals and machines. Tong

Van So guided him: "On your right you will come to the stand of a peanut vendor, a Miao tribeswoman surrounded by three or four little children . . . just beyond her you will see the place of a public scribe . . . turn there into the side street and follow it as it winds."

They drove down a squalid, narrow, twisting street and then alleys foul with the refuse and ordure of a city without plumbing or a sewer and sanitation system. Reisman wrinkled his nose. "Pungent," he said.

"China," said Tong Van So.

"Is your country better?"

"In the cities, yes. In the countryside, no."

The twisting lane narrowed and Reisman drove carefully and slowly to avoid striking anyone or coming up against a building. He spoke without looking at Tong. "This organization you have down there. What did you call it?"

"*Viet-Nam Doc-Lap Dong Minh Hoi.* Let us refer to it in English as the League."

"Okay. How many members in the League?"

"There are many thousands, but not so that you could count them on a list. We are not tightly structured yet. Our strength is not yet great in numbers but in the power of the idea of *Doc-Lap*—independence—which all agree upon. Our leaders know each other and each knows his portion of the network."

"How do you fit into it? Are you some sort of ambassador?"

Tong smiled and said, "I had the honor to be elected by my colleagues as their leader."

"President?"

"Not as grand as that. A chairman. Someone to hold the League together, to direct the disparate elements of its membership, to act in its name as I am doing now in China. It is my duty now to be spokesman for my colleagues to you and your comrades and representatives from the United States of America."

"I don't represent the United States of America, Tong. I'm just a soldier taking orders."

"But with leeway to act on his own initiative, I think."

"Yes. There are limits, of course, but that's the way we operate in our outfit. We're told to get a job done, we figure out the best way to do it, the company store tries to give us the help we need. Sometimes they do, sometimes they don't. Sometimes we make it, sometimes we don't."

"But usually *you* do."

"I guess so. I'm driving you around Kunming, which is my reward for surviving, I suppose. Do you know Kunming well?"

"Yes. It has been necessary for me to come here from time to time during the past few years—sometimes for a short visit, other times for a lengthy stay."

"And this time?"

"I hope it will be a short visit and you will soon be able to cross the border with me. Park there, please, just beyond where the old woman is sitting in the doorway."

Reisman drove the jeep tight up alongside a wall, leaving enough room for another vehicle to get by. The old woman stared at the vehicle with a look of anxiety. Most pedestrians made sure to keep their distance from it, though they cast nervous glances. They still didn't understand these things, the black magic that made them work. There were those, however, who understood too well, and Reisman continued to take precautions against them. When he raised the hood and pulled the rotor, Tong Van So nodded approvingly.

"An act of charity," he said. "A thief who gets away with such a magnificent devil machine can retire for life. If he is caught, however, he will forfeit considerably more than the jeep. Perhaps the life that he wished to live in comfort."

The black Buick went past. Its two Chinese occupants, dressed in dark business suits, pretended to be oblivious to the jeep they had been following.

"Surprise!" Reisman called after them as they continued around a turn in the street.

Tong Van So shook his head. "It would be best that you do not let them know that you know that they know."

"Did Confucius say that?" Reisman taunted.

"Perhaps. I am not a Confucian," Tong replied with dignity, "though I approve of many of their traditional principles of ethics and morality. However, not as much of their politics, which leads to the rigidity of the mandarin class."

In a side alley, Tong unlocked a heavy wood door with a key and they entered a small, bare courtyard on the other side of the wall where the jeep was parked. The ground was of hard-packed earth, with a narrow path of cobblestones leading to a two-story building. There were no trees or plants in the garden. The house was old and in need of paint and repairs.

"We rent these quarters," said Tong Van So. "Our needs are simple. A place to sleep, to meet, to do our work."

A young man, who must have heard them in the courtyard, opened the narrow door to the house. He was slender, of medium height, with thick black hair that fell over his forehead. His coloring and features, particularly the eyes and nose, were of the same racial strain as Tong Van So, but he did not look like him. There was an almost feminine allure to his thick brows, long lashes, high cheekbones and gently hollowed cheeks. Yet his dark eyes were those of a man of zeal and strength, focused on some distant place, as if they'd beheld the burning bush and still contained the image. He greeted Tong with an enthusiastic burst of words in a language Reisman took to be Viet-Namese. It had the tonal aspects of a Chinese dialect but was different enough from the Mandarin Reisman knew so that it was unintelligible to him. Tong responded in a cheerful voice, apparently making reference to the guest he had brought.

Then he switched to English to make the introduction: "My associate, Mr. Tran Van Thi . . . who is called Thi. This is Major *Jean* Reisman."

Tran Van Thi extended his hand and spoke a few words of welcome in English. It was accented like Tong's, with sounds of both France and the Orient. The three men entered the house and turned into a sitting room furnished plainly with a couch, two upholstered chairs, a few small end tables and lamps and, against the window, a large table and chairs. The window looked out into the bare courtyard. The table was covered with papers, books, pens and a typewriter. A woman sat there writing. Hearing them enter, she turned and stood up to face them, greeting Tong with a warm and lilting flow of Viet-Namese.

"And this is Mai," said Tong in English. "Nguyen Thi Mai, who is secretary for our delegation and without whose tireless work and radiant spirit we mere men would often be lost in despair and confusion."

Reisman stared at her, half lost already, and felt good just in the looking. She was young and lovely and glowed under the flattering compliments Tong Van So paid her, as if the hand that gestured toward her held a royal scepter. Her radiance illuminated the shabby room. Reisman let his eyes roam over her, taking in individual features: jet-black hair gathered in a chignon at the nape of her neck, almond eyes that answered his stare boldly, a smile of great warmth that showed teeth of the brightest white against dark, full lips and skin the color of a golden summer tan. She was not wearing the pajama suit or long, prim dress he might have expected of a delegation secretary of the *Viet-Nam Doc-Lap Dong Minh Hoi*. Rather, she was dressed in a short khaki skirt that showed strong bare legs to fine advantage, and a white shirt with sleeves bloused to her elbows. On her feet were the same sort of strap sandals the men wore. She looked like a vibrant, athletic woman used to an outdoor life. She might have been an American college girl out on the campus on a warm day, or a girl from a *kibbutz* dressed for a social summer evening after a hard day in the fields.

"I'm John Reisman," he said, and she came to him, gave him her hand and repeated his name.

She was the only one of the three who gave "John" its proper English pronunciation. Her touch, just the hand held in his for a few long moments, had an unexpected feeling of intimacy rather than the formality he had expected. In answer to his query she told him she had learned English when she had lived in Hong Kong with her family before the war. They were from Hanoi, but her father's work had often required traveling and living abroad, even in Europe. Like her colleagues, she said she also knew French, Chinese and what she called *quốc ngữ*. When Reisman looked puzzled, she explained that it was the Romanized national script that the French had decreed must be used in her country instead of the old *chữ nho* ideographs, which she had also studied.

"That makes you a scholar," Reisman complimented.

"I was educated to be a teacher," Mai said. "When I am at home I still do that sometimes. I am glad that you are here to help us."

In another moment, Reisman realized that their dialogue had become a tête-à-tête isolating them intimately from the others. He caught the beaming look that Tong Van So bestowed on her—and then realized that it was on him too. A look of approval, fostering the possibility of something between them. He looked toward Thi and detected no note of disapproval to indicate that Mai was anything more than co-worker, perhaps surrogate sister-mother-daughter to the men of the house.

She left the room to prepare some refreshment. Tong asked Thi to show Reisman around the house while he read some letters Mai had got ready for him to sign. They passed a small kitchen where Mai was setting a kettle to boil on a charcoal stove and she turned to smile at Reisman again. Down a short corridor were two bedrooms, one of them Tong's, the other Mai's. Up a flight of stairs were a number of other sleeping rooms, one for Thi, the others for countrymen who came there from time to time. There were no bathrooms or toilets; they used chamberpots or commodes. Water for washing and cooking, boiled for drinking, was brought from the canal, purchased from water bearers who carried pails to them on balance poles.

"But this is really quite civilized compared to what we are used to at home," said Thi, and he went on like that in a tone of superiority. "There we have made our headquarters in the caves and forests while we build our forces. You Americans, of course, are not used to living and fighting like that. Your army is richly fed, housed in comfort, supplied with the best of arms and equipment. Everything must be sanitized and just right for you."

Reisman was more amused than slighted by the commentary, and he didn't bother to dispute Thi. The merits of suffering and deprivation were relative and arguable, sometimes useful, and he had been there often enough to understand them but not to wallow in them.

They went back to the sitting room and Mai brought tea and rice cakes. Reisman tried to pin down Tong as to exactly what their military plans and capacity against the Japs might be, but both Tong and Thi spoke only in the broader terms of geopolitics. Mai said nothing but listened attentively, sometimes writing notes on a pad. She shared the couch with Reisman while the others sat facing them, and when he was able to get a look at her notepad he saw that the script was totally unknown to him. It was apparently the *quốc ngữ* she had mentioned earlier. After a while, Tong allowed the younger man to do much of the lecturing, nodding his head from time to time in approval.

Reisman kept trying to pull the discussion back to practical matters. "How large are the Jap ground forces down there?" he asked.

"In actual numbers I am sorry to say we don't know," Thi answered. "They occupy Hanoi and Saigon and that is where their troops are seen mostly. But they also have strong garrisons throughout the country. Four years ago they made an accommodation with the French, allowing them to continue as administrators and go about their business, provided they do not interfere with Japanese war aims and economic plunder."

"And exactly what *is* the business of the French in Viet-Nam?" Reisman asked. He genuinely wanted to know, but he was also tweaked by their anti-French attitude.

"To play at being the ruling class," Thi lectured. "To grow rich and fat off the labor of our people and the resources of our land.

This is less possible now, of course, for the Japs are squeezing French profits very hard with taxes, quotas and restrictions. The Japs also fail to fulfill shipping agreements. They blame this on Allied sinking of ships and bombing of trains. Food and goods are scarce, inflation is rampant, the black market flourishes, peasants and workers starve to death. But the French survive, they remember the past and anticipate the future. They own the plantations that produce rubber, rice and agricultural products. They own the mines, forests, industries, banks, trading companies, the railroad, all transportation and shipping—except where the Japs have forced them out."

Reisman looked toward Tong Van So and said, "He sounds just like you."

"Of course he does," Tong acknowledged. "He is my pupil and I have taught him well . . . as he will teach others—perhaps you."

"In all of this enterprise," Thi went on, more angrily, "it is the men and women of Viet-Nam who are the slaves in the mines, factories and fields. A few are permitted to rise to slightly higher status. But they too become corrupt. They become landlords and moneylenders and prey upon their own people like vultures. Most are never able to improve their lot. Japanese aside for the moment, it is French planters, businessmen, managers and government functionaries who ride on our backs."

"There is the opium trade too. We must not forget that," Tong Van So spoke up bitterly. "Debilitating, immoral, dishonest. It is a French monopoly, along with alcohol, which they force on my countrymen."

There it was again, Reisman reflected. The money crop. Intertwined with politics, war and economics, the conduits of the opium trade crossed battle lines and national frontiers and left moral, religious and political righteousness unblemished. However, he thought he had grounds to contradict Tong.

"You can't blame that on the French," he said. "The poppies are raised up in the hills by your Meo. Over in Burma it's the Kachins and the Shans. The stuff was a trade item long before the French got here."

"They took it over by force and made it much worse," Tong declared. "It has been protected and perpetuated by the colonial administration, even while there are self-righteous outcries against it in Paris. The *colons* buy the crop and control the processing and selling of the opium in my country, just as the British did in all their colonies and in China in the last century."

Tran Van Thi added indignantly, "The imperialists made it easy for the poorest coolie in China to be an addict. He had nothing else. Every copper he ever earned was sucked from his bones and he became a slave to *ta-yen*. My countrymen, however, are stronger. Some use it, but we did not succumb en masse to *ta-yen* the way the Chinese did."

"Thi is correct," stated Tong Van So with sudden anger. "The French are corrupt and insidious! They have forced consumption quotas upon certain provinces and villages, and my poor people must pay for this opium whether they want it or not."

"If that is true," said Reisman, "then I too would fight against it. But these other things that you protest, about the economic and political life of your country—what if the French had never come? Would you have been happier? Your people better off?"

He wasn't quite sure why he was arguing this way. Two days earlier he had told Commodore Ludlow in Chungking that he agreed with President Roosevelt's policy of freedom for the indigenous peoples of Asia. Tong and his protégé, however, sounded too much like the sort of true believers who never allowed for truths other than their own.

"A debatable point," Tong replied. "Perhaps. Though if not the French it might have been the British or some other European country. Look at how you Westerners took advantage of China before the Japs threw you out. I'm speaking about your so-called international settlements and your treaty ports where the Japs are now. In my country, the Portuguese and the Dutch had trading posts four hundred years ago. The French came a little later, but they kept at us for hundreds of years—with Catholic missionaries, with merchants and soldiers—before we succumbed to the Protectorate Treaty in 1884. Perhaps we were still too weak from fighting the Chinese. As I told you and your colonel earlier, the last time the Chinese came they stayed a thousand years. But now we have the French and the Japanese. Forty thousand French *colons* under Japanese military control rule twenty-three million of my countrymen. If you will help us with the Japs that will help your country too, *non?*"

"What about the French?"

"We want to deal with them peacefully once we get rid of the Japs. We will deal with them as equals. After all, France is a civilized nation. She too has a history of revolution to bring freedom to her people. Violent revolution—which we would prefer not to have. We are, as it is, a country whose people are far from being united. We are ourselves of various ethnic strains, different religions and ways of life, a variety of languages."

"Then why should you be a nation?" Reisman challenged.

"Why should the United States of America be one nation, indivisible, with liberty and justice for all? That is all that we ask."

Tran Van Thi spoke up again, to fill the brooding moment of silence. He gave an ironic little laugh and said, "Our situation at home is even more complicated. So complicated that for a moment I forgot. There is even an emperor! Did you know that? We have our own Napoleon! Or perhaps more a Louis. He is a man much different from the many warrior kings we have had in my country during two thousand years of our history. Our Emperor Bao-Dai is merely a figurehead. He rules a nonexistent nation from the isolation and protection of a royal palace in Hué. He is a playboy! He sits on his throne at the pleasure of the Japs. He concerns himself only with money and women and the privileges of his position and all the modern luxuries he can acquire. While his people suffer, starve and die!"

"Sounds like the Louis who lost his head," Reisman muttered. He was bored with the politics and rhetoric, but he knew he'd have to get a good grip on it before he started letting them have guns from the company store.

Chapter 13

Late that afternoon, Reisman drove alone back to the base, picked up some of his things at the BOQ and drove back to the hovel where the Viet-Namese were staying.

"If I'm going over the border with you, we may as well get used to each other," he told them. "See who snores at night or talks in their sleep." He looked at Mai when he said that and she raised her head and answered his gaze without flinching.

He assumed he was followed each way by Tai Li's busy little men picking him up at different legs of the route, and even spotted the old black Buick waiting for him on the road near OSS headquarters. No wonder the Chinese weren't fighting and winning the war, he thought. Too many of them were employed as spies on each other and their allies. If each of Tai Li's agents was given a weapon and sent out to fight the Japanese there would have been five or six more divisions in the line.

For the evening meal they cleared the work papers from the table in the sitting room and sat together around it. Reisman noticed that each of them, even Tong, wandered back and forth to the kitchen and took part in the preparation and cooking. They did remarkably well considering the simple, charcoal-fueled equipment. The food was served with a festive air. There was a whole baked fish from the lake, bowls of rice, cubes of chicken done in a sweet sauce, a variety of vegetables, and even some wine. Reisman suspected that they did not usually dine so well and that this special meal was being laid on for him.

Tong raised his wine glass. "To the United States of America and President Roosevelt!" he toasted. He barely wet his lips with the wine and put his glass down, but urged Reisman to drink as much as he pleased, eat heartily and not to follow his poor example. "It is gratifying and right that we are now allies," he said fervently. "The United States was the first colonial nation to gain its independence through revolution. Eighty years ago we also looked to your country for aid. Our emperor then wrote to your President Lincoln proposing a pact of amity."

"What happened?" Reisman asked.

"Nothing. Mr. Lincoln, if I remember correctly, had other problems at the time."

Reisman steered the table talk away from politics and war. He wanted to know more about each of his new companions, particularly Tong Van So. But Tong was reluctant to talk about himself, and he deferred to the younger people. "It is they who are of interest," he said. "They are the fighters, the future of our country."

Tran Van Thi spoke about himself reluctantly. He seemed to want to emulate Tong's air of mystery, and yet he was compelled to acquiesce in his chief's urging.

"I am nothing and nobody," he said, but in a voice that was not humble enough for that. It was a proud and fervid little speech he gave. "I was born into a bourgeois family in Nghé An province, which is also the birthplace of our leader and teacher." He bowed his head toward Tong Van So. "I was subject early to the same forces and influences as he was, as were the patriots and fighters who preceded us. Perhaps breathing the same air, eating of the same earth, made me what I am."

"What is that?" Reisman asked. He was careful that the inflection of his voice made it a friendly, open question and not a challenge.

"A man who wants to see his country free from all foreign domination and influence," Thi answered.

"Your *raison d'être?*"

"Oui."

Reisman smiled. If Thi's reason for being was to totally dissociate his country and himself from all things French, including language and philosophy, he would find it difficult, perhaps even undesirable in the end.

"Tell him about Quôc-Hoc," said Tong.

Thi looked surprised. "Would such a thing be of interest to him?"

"Of course. In his country, it is also important what schools one goes to."

"It might be to some, but it isn't to me," Reisman said.

"For them, a form of intellectual snobbery," said Tong with a grin. "For you, *Jean,* the reverse: the arrogance of the man of action—or perhaps even the proletariat man, if that's what you might really be. Nevertheless, your leaders do tend to be educated at the same universities. The future leaders of our country go where, Thi?"

Tong sounded amusingly like a cheerleader exhorting the stands to give a cheer for the home team. But Thi became quite serious about it, and didn't even smile as he gave the old school pitch to Reisman.

"Lycée Quôc-Hoc. It is in Hué, the old capital, and it is the very best school in Viet-Nam. Not a university, by any means, or a college. Closer perhaps to one of your better high schools or preparatory schools."

"It was also my lycée," said Tong, trying to look comically haughty, but sounding pleased nevertheless. "Of course I was there more than thirty years before young Thi here."

"It is still the same," Thi declared.

"What makes it so special?" Reisman asked.

Tong Van So nodded to his protégé to answer.

"Our program there was not designed merely to turn us into imitation Frenchmen," Thi recited. "Quôc-Hoc gave us an education not only in the European subjects but also in classical Viet-Namese culture and language, which the ordinary lycées in our country do not have in their curriculum."

"It was after that, of course," said Tong, "that our young friend took the middle name he now uses with pride and distinction. However, I too adopted it in the same way, so it is another thing we share. In our language, *Van* means *cultured.*"

Thi looked slightly embarrassed at being the butt of his mentor's joshing, but he took it in good humor.

"And what about Mai?" asked Reisman, looking directly at her. "Isn't she going to tell me her life story?"

"Of course," she answered brightly. "I was born in Hanoi. I went to school there and in Hong Kong and even for a little while in both France and England. We are a Catholic family, but my early education, aside from religious observances, was probably more liberal than conservative. I live my life differently from my mother's generation and the traditional role of women in my country. Yet she and my father and my brothers and sister—there are four of us—always encouraged me. Maybe it was because we were all exposed to so much more of the world than most people in my country. My father is one of the few Viet-Namese who were promoted to positions of importance in the business world of the French. He is an executive of a company that controls many of the raw products our country exports. Thus he had reason to travel and live abroad and take us with him."

"Where is he now?"

"Hanoi. All of my family are there now except me."

"Does he know where you are?"

"He knows that I have gone to China. He is glad that I am away from the Japanese. But, to answer your next question—no, he does not know what I am doing here, who I am with, or that I am working for the freedom and independence of our country."

"Would he approve?"

She thought about that a few moments. "The goal, yes . . . the means, I'm not so sure. I think he would want to look into it personally."

After dinner, after everyone, including Reisman, had cleared the table and helped do the dishes, he asked Mai if she would take on her schoolteacher's role for a little while. He wanted her to give him his first lesson in Viet-Namese, to show him examples of the old and new forms of writing and explain the differences from the Chinese. Tong Van So and Tran Van Thi bid them good-night and retired to their rooms. Reisman and Mai sat side by side at the table under the light of an oil lamp. She placed sheets of writing paper, pens, brushes and ink before each of them.

"In the beginning—" said Mai.

Reisman grinned at her. "Sounds like you're starting the Bible."

She laughed and said, "Unintended. I had more than enough of that when I was a little girl. If I have any preference now it would be for one of our eastern religions."

"Fits the neighborhood better."

"How about, 'Once upon a time'?"

"I like that. It makes learning more fun. Tell me a story, teacher."

Mai looked at him with pretended severity. "I'll bet you were a little horror when you were in school. Let's get on with it, Major."

"John."

"Okay, John. Once upon a time when the Chinese first came to our country about two thousand years ago there was no written Viet-Namese language. There was a spoken language but no way to write down the sounds and ideas. So they took the Chinese ideographs for those words, changed them a little to make them distinctive from the Chinese characters, and in that way developed a written language. That's the script that became what we refer to today as *chữ nho*."

With a pen, Mai wrote the word *chữ nho* at the mid-top of the paper on the table in front of her. Under it she wrote: *(old Viet-Namese script)*. To the left she wrote: *Chinese ideographs*. To the right she wrote *quốc gnữ* and under it *(new Viet-Namese script)*. She turned to look at Reisman and his eyes moved up from her writing to her face.

Quickly, Mai continued, "*Chữ nho* is no longer the official script. It is more a scholar's language today, but it is the closest point of similarity between Chinese and Viet-Namese. Let us take, for example, the Viet-Namese word for heaven. The word is *tròi*. I'll write it for you in our present script, the *quốc gnữ,* which will be easier for you to pronounce because we now make use of the same Roman alphabet you use in English—with the addition, however, of these little diacritical marks, which indicate the correct pronunciation."

Under the *quốc gnữ* heading on the right side of her paper Mai wrote the word *tròi* and pronounced it again. "Think of a time then when there was no way to write down that sound. There was the concept of heaven, the Viet-Namese spoken word for heaven—*tròi*—but no way to write it or read it in a Viet-Namese language. Then . . . *voilà!* along come the Chinese, who have a written symbol, an ideograph, that means heaven. I will write that for you here on the left in the Chinese ideograph column." She brushed onto the paper, with quick, light strokes, the Chinese character that meant heaven. "That word in Chinese, in the Mandarin dialect, is pronounced—"

"*Thiên,*" Reisman said quickly.

She darted a pleased look at him and said, "Very good. But the early Viet-Namese had no desire to change their word for heaven to the Chinese word for heaven. What they did instead was to combine the Chinese ideograph for heaven with another Chinese character that means *over, up* or *above*." She drew the new character next to the Chinese character for heaven.

"Shang," said Reisman.

"Correct. The early Viet-Namese took those two characters, put them together in one ideograph and created their own way of writing *tròi*." She demonstrated for him by doing the brushwork right there on the paper under the middle heading of *chũ nho. "Comprenez-vous, Monsieur Commandant?"*

"Très bien, mademoiselle. Je comprends. Veuillez l'écrire davantage."

Mai obliged him by demonstrating the writing of a number of other words in Chinese, old Viet-Namese and new Viet-Namese. She had Reisman duplicate all the words and ideographs on the paper she had provided for him and commended him on his facility even though he inadvertently left out a couple of the subtle diacritical marks in the *quốc gnũ*. They turned and stared into each other's eyes often during the lesson. Their hands touched, their arms and shoulders brushed together, for they were sitting quite close. Reisman felt the spark between them, but he resolved to do nothing about it unless there was an open and obvious invitation.

"I wouldn't even advise trying to learn the *chũ nho,*" Mai said at the end of the lesson. "Just understand that it exists and then let it be. If you are serious about learning, I would advise concentrating on the *quốc gnũ*. Many of our people, as you know already, also speak French, English or Chinese. You will be able to get along well in our country."

Reisman went around with Mai afterward, checking the outside and inside security of the house, making sure everything was locked. There was still nothing from her that could be construed as an invitation.

"Good night, John," she said finally and walked down the corridor to her room.

"Good night, Mai," he called after her and went upstairs to the cot that had been assigned to him.

Chapter 14

In the next days, John Reisman came to know and like Tong Van So, though the man continued to be mostly vague and exasperating about his past—except for a few areas in which they each were pleased to find common ground.

The war itself seemed far away as they explored the city of Kunming. They behaved like tourists, driving the jeep to another part of the city, then exploring on foot while they talked. Occasionally they became aware that they were being followed, but Tong prevailed on Reisman to ignore them. "When it is necessary to lose them we will," he said.

Walking around the city, reacting to its people, events and places, proved to be a stimulus to the real purpose of their companionship: sizing each other up. Tong was a most knowledgeable tour conductor. He led Reisman to streets that specialized in only one form of trade, such as banks, rickshas, flowers, or prostitutes. On the Street of Pigs they watched the auction of live animals, hugely fat from the countryside, brought to market cruelly trussed on carrying poles because they were too fat to walk. Tong was more interested, however, in talking about guns.

Although he continued to be obscure about the *Viet-Nam Doc-Lap Dong Minh Hoi* and the exact number and disposition of forces under his command, he was positive and consistent about one thing: he wanted what amounted to a complete arsenal to outfit what was apparently still a nonexistent guerrilla brigade. While the pig farmers chanted about pigs and prices, Tong talked about rifles, pistols, carbines, machine guns, rounds of ammunition, grenades, field equipment and radios; and he wanted American instructors to train his people.

"They are waiting for us in Tonkin even now, *Jean,*" he insisted. "We can put to good use all that you give us. It will not simply be hoarded, as the Kuomintang hoards what America gives them. I have seen their reserve munitions depots—at Liuchow and Kweilin, for example. Huge amounts of matériel."

"How did you manage that?"

Tong's expression was inscrutable again, covering up something he didn't want to talk about. "I was traveling," he said. "I lusted after that matériel the way some men lust for women."

"Are you married, Tong?" Reisman asked.

"No." He merely shook his head, without any real interest in the subject.

"Any family?"

"Viet-Nam Doc-Lap Dong Minh Hoi," he answered softly. "It is a large family."

Tong was as interested in the details of Reisman's life as Reisman was in his.

"What did you do before the war, *Jean?*"

"I was a seaman."

Tong stopped in mid-stride and turned to him with a new look of open joy on his face. The two men were walking along the bank of the moss-covered canal, watching the sampans, houseboats and junks that plied constantly between the city and Lake Tien Chih. The boats were heavily laden, particularly those on the voyage in with building materials, fuels, salt, produce and the families that lived and worked aboard. The larger boats carried passengers in both directions.

"You mean like those?" Tong exclaimed, laughing.

In the stream, small, lean boatmen poled their vessels along from the side decks while their wives operated the stern oar and their children directed the rudder. On days when the wind was good the boats moved under sails of reed or bamboo matting.

Reisman grinned at the joke. "No. Big steamships. Crossing the oceans."

Tong's smile grew even broader. "Me too," he said.

"You were a seaman?" Reisman asked, incredulous.

"A long time ago. Before the war."

"That's just a few years ago."

"The First War," said Tong.

It took Reisman a moment to get a grip on that. He imagined what the world had been like then, the types of ships that had been sailing the seas. Surprisingly, Tong didn't mind talking about that part of his life, though he had been reticent about his other history.

Tong apparently had sailed on a number of tours at sea, in between which he had worked at a variety of jobs in France and England. He had started as a mess boy aboard a French ship from Haiphong to Marseilles, then had sailed to other ports in the Mediterranean and to Africa. He had gone ashore often and had come to know a little about other countries and cultures, much more than most men from his native land. He had gone to sea again in the first couple of years of World War I when deadly attacks by German U-boats had made experienced seamen in great demand for the dangerous voyage across the Atlantic. Tong apparently had been in New York and Boston and other ports along the East Coast and Gulf Coast of the United States. He made light of that, but he seemed to know of these places, their people and problems, from firsthand experience. Perhaps that was when he had first become enamored of the Declaration of Independence and the Constitution and learned something of the lives of the great American presidents, their philosophies and speeches, for he sometimes made reference to them. He seemed to favor Washington, Lincoln and Franklin Roosevelt, though he also spoke wistfully of Wilson's Fourteen Points for world peace and what a tragedy that they had never been carried out.

One morning, along the canal, Tong gripped Reisman's shoulder and said excitedly, "Look there! The fishing birds!"

Half a dozen big black cormorants perched on the bow gunwales of a slowly moving sampan. Small brass rings were fastened at the base of their necks. Their eyes searched the water hungrily. Then, spotting fish, two of them dived into the canal and disappeared beneath the surface. They each returned to the sampan and flapped aboard, choking on their catch, complaining that they were unable to swallow because of the brass rings. Their master swooped the birds up, turned them upside down and shook them over a basket to disgorge the live fish. The unhappy birds, still hungry, went back to their perches to repeat the process.

"The ring will be removed for the seventh fish," said Tong in a melancholy voice. "It is like we must do now with our Japanese and French masters. We are made to turn to them for our livelihood. We are kept captive. We are perhaps permitted to keep and eat the seventh fish, the seventh part of the rice we raise. But most of what we raise, most of what is dug from our ground, taken from our mines, forests and plantations, is sent elsewhere for the use and pleasure of others."

Reisman merely nodded to acknowledge that he had heard. But he had no mission to solve the internal economic and political problems of French Indochina—only to take action to defeat the Japanese.

They walked and talked in GI Street and in the Thieves Market, both of which drew their customers mainly from the American forces, and where almost anything could be bought, much of it shoddy, some of it stolen from someone else. On some streets the activity had nothing to do with trade, only with humanity at its most frightened and frightening levels. There was one for atonement where sinners crawled on their hands and knees praying to their god, and another street that was the gathering place for withered, misshapen beggars seeking alms.

One afternoon they stood together leaning against the railing of a stone bridge where Chin Pi Lu crossed the canal. Boats glided below them. The water mirrored the bridge, hanging vines, trees, blue sky, bright sun. It was a tranquil, picturesque setting on a warm and lovely day. Suddenly, Reisman became aware of a commotion in the water among a group of sampans about fifty yards away. He heard a man shouting, then screaming in desperation, and spotted him thrashing about helplessly in the canal. Other boatmen, within easy reach of him, were aware of his perilous predicament and were in fact gazing directly at him with some interest—but no one was moving to help.

"Christ, the guy is drowning!" Reisman exclaimed to Tong. He yelled down the canal to the sampan men, "Hey, give him a hand! Help him!"

None of the other boatmen moved to help, though only the length of an oar extended to the hapless victim would have done the job. Reisman shouted again, but no one paid attention. The struggling man disappeared beneath the surface, thrashed his way upward, and then vanished again. Reisman yanked off his garrison cap, thrust it at Tong, and started to pull off his jacket while at the same time he looked around for the quickest route down to the water short of diving off the bridge.

"No! *Arrêtez!*" ordered Tong, and Reisman felt the frail man's fingers close on his arm in a strong grip. "Do not interfere. It is their affair."

"Let go!" Reisman muttered, shaking off Tong's grip. But when he looked to the water again the man was gone. Except for the subdued voices of the other boatmen, it was silent where the solitary struggle had taken place minutes before.

Tong's face revealed no emotional involvement in what they had just witnessed. He seemed unmoved by the fact that right before their eyes and within their hearing—and maybe within their ability to have prevented it—another human being had just struggled desperately to live and had died. Where, Reisman wondered, was Tong's vaunted love for *the people* he always talked about, the poor and downtrodden? Was it absent because the man who drowned was just another Chinese water coolie and not one of his precious Viet-Namese?

"They believe that if you save a man's life you are responsible for him for as long as you both live," Tong explained calmly. He gestured toward the other sampans moving down the canal away from the death scene as if nothing had happened. "None of them wanted that burden. None would have been able to carry it . . . nor would you have."

"Their stupid beliefs are not mine," responded Reisman angrily.

The important thing had been to try to save an innocent and helpless man. He himself had killed men in battle with fewer qualms than those with which he had watched the boatman drown. The custom was more repugnant and inhuman to him than war. Nobody had even tried to fish out the body.

"Forgive my lack of compassion," said Tong. "The corpse will float to the surface somewhere and be found and taken away along with all the other corpses that are found in the streets and alleys each morning. There is so much death here in China—much of it anonymous, with no one to mourn."

▪ ▪

After the second day, Reisman transported provisions from the OSS commissary to feed the Viets and himself at their house. Sam Kilgore authorized it. They had to start the chain of supply somewhere, and food was an innocent enough beginning to establish the precedent that Tong's people were working with OSS. Reisman brought fresh meat, chicken, vegetables, milk, bread, butter, salt, sugar, coffee, tea, flour and anything else they needed. He let them do the cooking and noticed that Tong took on quite a bit of it himself and seemed to enjoy it.

On the fourth night Reisman brought them a field radio, a transmitter/receiver that worked off a hand-cranked generator when power lines and storage batteries were unavailable. He began right away to teach them how to use it, to take it apart, name and test the components and put it together again. They were all excited by its potential for keeping in touch with agents and relaying intelligence. The radio had a range of as much as 350 miles, depending on atmospheric conditions and how well the operator could place the antenna.

"How far is that in kilometers?" asked Tran Van Thi.

"More than five hundred and fifty."

Thi unfolded onto the table a map that covered both sides of the China–Indochina frontier from north of Kunming all the way to Hanoi and beyond to the South China Sea past Da Nang. He put his finger on Kunming and ran it south past Lake Tien Chih and in a straight line along the Red River into northern Tonkin province. He nodded to Tong Van So who looked quite happy.

"Magnifique!" said Thi. "It will enable us to maintain the kind of contact that now requires couriers, considerable time and great danger in the crossing. Can you obtain another one for us, *Jean?*"

"Probably. You want one for this house and one for down there . . . is that it?"

"Yes."

"Our OSS people communicate with us through the radio setup at the airfield. It's got a better range than this, coming and going. No reason why you can't get onto that network too—unless there are things you don't want us to know about."

"Of course not, *Jean,*" said Tong Van So quickly. "But our people expect us to be here, not at the airfield, and they might arrive at any hour of the day or night. Also, it is best that we try to continue to be inconspicuous in our dealings with you."

"A radio can be dangerous, too," Reisman warned. "Down in

Tonkin you've got to be sure the Japs don't get a fix on you with their locators. We had to worry about that with the Krauts in Europe. You can only stay on the air briefly and never at the same time each day. You have to work out a variable time schedule and identification codes. The Japs can get a fix on you, home right in and it's kaput—radio, personnel, the whole damn operation. The transmitter can help your network, but it can sure kill you in a hurry too if you're not careful."

For an hour that night, Mai gave Reisman another lesson in Viet-Namese. They were warm with each other, teasing and flirting with words, glances, and touching, as before; but again each retired to separate beds alone.

In the morning, though, Mai had a surprise for him. "I shall be your guide today," she said. "Mr. Tong has work to do here."

"How long is this tourist act going to continue before we get down to business and cross the border?"

"Are you ready for that?" she asked in surprise. "Ready to supply all our needs?"

"Not quite."

"Nor are we. A messenger will come, telling us the way has been prepared. Then, if you are ready, we will go."

She directed him to drive out of the city toward Lake Tien Chih. She was dressed differently, in a longish padded blue jacket and blue pants so full at the bottom they looked like a skirt. She wore a plain dark cotton scarf over her hair. On her feet were sturdier shoes of fabric uppers and leather soles and heels. Her costume would let her disappear into any crowd of poor, modestly dressed Chinese women.

"Today we will climb *Hsi Shan,*" she said, "and visit the Temples of the Western Cloud."

"West Mountain?"

"Yes. It is a mountain of religious pilgrimage. Very dramatic. Many beautiful sacred temples that were built one thousand years ago."

Reisman gassed up the jeep at OSS base and he and Mai drove southwest out of Kunming around the lake to the foot of the steep, rocky *Hsi Shan*. Even there they were already 6,500 feet above sea level, about a thousand feet higher than the city. He parked in a field with other vehicles and took his usual security measures to prevent theft; then they joined the long column of men, women and children climbing the winding footpath and steps carved into the mountainside. Another line of pilgrims was descending, and the two files touched and mingled on tight turns and narrow passes like columns of ants.

There was an inhospitable, barren look to the land through which they climbed. The steep slopes were strewn with boulders, rocks and seared brush. The sun was bright, the thin air temperate; clouds played in the sky, creating shadowed places; below was the deep blue of the lake, moving boats, and rice fields on the edge of the water. Reisman gazed along the shoreline and picked out a little peninsula on which there were some solid-looking buildings within a walled area. He thought that might be the R and R camp where Baw San was staying.

He pointed down and asked Mai, "Do you know that place?"

"Yes. It is the country house of Marshal Lung-Yün. He is the big *tuchun* in Yunnan."

Reisman remembered that Linc Bradford had told him about Lung-Yün.

"Right now it is used by your American army," Mai added.

"Looks nice. I have a friend who's staying there," said Reisman.

Above them they caught tantalizing glimpses of some of the Temples of the Western Cloud. The golden-roofed buildings were set upon knolls and niches in the mountain's contours, or hung precipitously along a jagged edge. Mai explained to him that some were Buddhist temples and some were Taoist, following the precepts of Lao-tzu, the Chinese philosopher who had lived in the sixth century B.C., just about the same time as the Gautama Buddha had lived in India. Followers of each were mutually tolerant, temples were cooperative, rites were often a blend.

Reisman and Mai climbed from one shrine to the next. Each gave access via stairs and path to the one above. There were more than twenty of them, each with its monks or soothsayers in attendance, each celebrating some sectarian devotion to benign Buddhas, fierce demons, lordly gods and holy saints. Each was also a palace of ornate art—painted statues, carvings, tile work and tablets. Reisman and Mai absorbed the sights, sounds and smells, but neither tried to be a participant or communicant as incense tapers were bought and burned, prayers chanted and fortunes told.

They paused to rest beside a garden pool near a temple, high on a wooded knoll. They gazed down the mountainside to the lake and all of the Kunming plateau.

Mai turned to him in the tranquil garden and said, fervently, "He is a very great man!"

The way she said it, Reisman knew that she wasn't speaking about Gautama Buddha or Lao-tzu. "Tong Van So?" he said.

"Yes."

"Are you his wife . . . his daughter . . . his girlfriend?" Reisman asked ingenuously, though he thought they had already told him the truth about those aspects of their lives.

"No, he has no one. Only our country. He has no emotion, time or energy for anything else. But I do love him, as all our people love him. There is so much you do not know about him. Who he is . . . what he is . . . what he has sacrificed . . . what he stands for."

"I've tried to get it out of him, but he won't talk, as you well know."

"There is a shyness, too."

Reisman frowned. "I'll bet. If you mean caginess, I'll go along with that."

"Perhaps I shouldn't tell you—but he has been in prison. The Kuomintang kept him in chains for eighteen months in one prison after another and he suffered very much. He almost died."

"Tai Li?"

"It was his hirelings who arrested Tong. Tai Li's power is felt everywhere."

Reisman remembered something Tong had said to him . . . about traveling. "Was he in Liuchow and Kweilin?"

"Yes, there too. They moved him on foot, wearing shackles, from city to city. He was chained to murderers and thieves—and perhaps to saints. But it was only his body that was in prison, not his mind. He wrote many beautiful poems. May I read you some?"

"Sure."

She took some pages from her jacket pocket, then looked around the garden and out at the wide plateau to the next range of mountains. "It is so lovely and peaceful here," she said. "It is a good time for you to hear these, and to think deeply about this man. The poems were written in classical Chinese, but I have translated them into English for you."

She read five short poems, each a less formal type of linked verse than haiku, evoking loneliness, yearning for freedom, bitter allusions and ironic, sometimes even humorous, comparisons.

"Here is my favorite of all," said Mai. "It is called 'Crushed Rice.'

The rice grain suffers under the blows of
the pestle;
But admire its whiteness once the ordeal
is over!
Thus it is with men in the world we
live in;
To be a man, one must suffer the blows
of misfortune."

Reisman reached out and took Mai's hand. "That's fine," he said. "It's not great poetry, but I understand his loneliness. I've felt things like that. Not so much now . . . more when I was younger."

Mai returned the pressure of his hand. "You have, I believe, experienced many horrible things, John. Too much war can burn tender feelings like that out of a man's heart and memories. That is the wonder of Tong Van So. He is a young man despite his years."

They stood up and climbed the path to the last of the Temples of the Western Cloud at the 8,000-foot level. Clouds of incense billowed around them as they moved onto the open, flat roof. Mai waved her arm grandly at the view. "Are you not impressed?" she asked.

"Very. Equal at least to the view from the Eiffel Tower or the Capitoline Hill in Rome."

Reisman put his arm around her and she leaned against him. "If only we could all learn to help each other instead of kill each other," she said in a wistful voice. "To love each other."

"With you it would certainly be a pleasure to try," he said.

Mai blushed and looked around to see if anyone was staring at them. Reisman removed his arm.

"I think we should descend from these heights," Mai said. "It does funny things to the head."

On the walk down the mountain she continued to study him. Nothing demure or reticent about the appraisal. Finally, she found the right words. "Thank you for what you said—about it being a pleasure to try . . . love . . . with me—but I don't think so. I must remember to be very careful what I teach you . . . and how I teach it."

Reisman twisted around and looked back up the mountain at what he could still see of the Temples of the Western Cloud. "Well, let's just leave it to the gods—okay?"

"Okay," Mai answered.

Chapter 15

In the early morning before dawn Reisman awakened in his cot upstairs at the Viets' house and for a delicious moment thought that he was in Paris. An aroma that could only be coming from a *boulangerie* wafted to his nostrils.

Barely awake, he drew on his trousers and shirt and went downstairs. There in the lamp-lit kitchen he found Tong Van So dusted with a light coating of flour, sliding a pan from the charcoal-fueled oven and closely inspecting the progress of a dozen croissants.

"Another few minutes," said Tong.

"I thought you were a politician, a philosopher—and maybe a soldier," said Reisman, leaning over the pan and sniffing with pleasure and admiration. "But you are really a baker."

Tong slid the pan back into the oven. "I will confess to you something, *Jean,* out of my dark and mysterious past," he said in good humor. "I do not, as you know, like to eat very much, nor drink. Certainly I do not have the desire for wine and food of a gourmand."

"Yet I notice how well you cook and how much of it you do yourself," Reisman complimented.

"*Merci beaucoup, monsieur!* That is my dark secret. Every once in a while I enjoy preparing something superb—for others to enjoy."

"This morning, croissants."

"This morning, croissants, which I too shall enjoy, for I have not had any for a very long time. The flour and butter you brought us has inspired me."

"But where did you learn to do this? They look and smell as good as any I ever had in Paris."

Tong Van So beamed. "When I was a young man—after the Lycée Quôc-Hoc and before I sailed the first time from Haiphong—I attended a cooking and baking school in Saigon. I could not earn an adequate living as a teacher—or as a politician or philosopher, for that matter," he added, laughing. "So it was necessary to learn a trade. My first job aboard ship was as a messboy."

"Messboys don't bake croissants like that. Not on the ships that I sailed on."

"Quite true, but that is only part of the story. When I tell you the rest you may not believe me. I find it hard to believe myself even now, looking back."

"Go ahead. Try me."

"In London, before the war—"

"First or Second?"

"First. I was employed for a while in the kitchens of the Carlton Hotel. There I had the extraordinary good fortune to come to the attention of the master himself, the greatest chef in the world at that time."

"Escoffier?" asked Reisman, incredulous.

"Escoffier."

"*Vraiment?*"

"*Oui.* He honored me with a position as pastry cook. And it was there that I learned to bake these croissants which we shall now have for our breakfast."

He slid the pan from the oven and placed it on a side counter to allow the pastries to cool. They glowed a lovely golden color and their smell made Reisman's taste buds tingle. He could not get over Tong's astonishing revelation. He basked in the pleasure of it and in anticipation of croissants à l'Escoffier by way of Tong Van So.

The sound of footsteps on the stairway made Reisman turn. A stranger stood in the entry to the kitchen—a Chinese or Viet wearing the dark blue cotton trousers and shirt jacket of a peasant. He appeared to be in his mid-forties or older, a man with wide shoulders and a wide chest, giving him a powerful look, though he was not tall. His features were strong and amiable, with the slightly leathery look of a man accustomed to the outdoors and to hard work; his hair was black, cropped short and touched with gray.

"This is Mr. Chin Li, who arrived in the night after you retired," said Tong in English. "We have been expecting him."

"From the south?" suggested Reisman.

Tong hesitated a moment, as if uncertain whether to reveal a fact. Then he went ahead. "No. Actually from the north. Chin is Chinese, not Viet-Namese. You can practice your Mandarin on him. He speaks neither English nor French." Tong spoke in Chinese to the new man. "This is the American officer who has been assigned to help us. Major John Reisman."

Chin held out his hand and Reisman took it. It was a strong hand, its skin thick and rough as he had expected, but there was warmth and friendship in the clasp. They spoke a few words in Mandarin and Chin was pleased and surprised that a foreigner had taken the time and trouble to learn some of his language. Reisman thought that if the man had indeed come "from the north," slipping in quietly in the night, it was more than likely that he had maneuvered himself secretly down from the communist enclave in Shensi Province. It seemed the most logical connection for Tong Van So in that direction.

Speaking Chinese, he asked innocently, "How are things in Yenan?"

Chin was not a man to be easily tricked, however. He cast a sharp look at Tong Van So and shrugged his big shoulders as if he hadn't understood the question.

Reisman went on with the same air of innocence. "Is Chou En-lai back yet? He was in Chungking when I was there last week. I almost got to meet him and regret that I didn't."

Tong looked at him severely and said, "You infer things that you should not, *Jean*."

The pleasant reverie of morning in the *boulangerie* with the happy, friendly baker was broken.

"I will stop inferring if you will always tell me the complete and unvarnished truth," Reisman snapped back at him. "I *infer* now that Chin Li is a soldier from Mao Tse-tung's Eighth Route Army at Yenan. I don't give a damn at this point about his politics or yours, Tong, and I certainly don't intend to blab to Tai Li or the Gimo about the company you keep—though with the type of scrutiny they've been putting on us it wouldn't surprise me if they know Chin is here. I don't even plan to tell the colonel. There are certain things in this business that one keeps to oneself."

And in the keeping, he thought, one lays the trap for others, to find out whether they have that knowledge and how they might have come by it. That went for Sam Kilgore too, and up the line to Commodore Pelham Ludlow.

Tong questioned Chin Li in Chinese. The man responded and shook his head. Tong said, "He is positive he arrived unobserved."

"How did he get in the locked courtyard door?"

"I left it unlocked for him when I took out the night soil and placed it on the street for the collector at just the hour Chin was expected."

Reisman had to smile at that. "Okay. I'll go upstairs and make my own contribution to Chinese agriculture—and make room for your croissants. What time is breakfast, *Monsieur* Escoffier?"

Tong bowed graciously. "Any time you wish, *Monsieur Commandant.*"

Reisman rejected even the slightest possibility of playing tourist again that day if anybody suggested it. He thought he probably knew Kunming now as well as he'd known Chicago before he'd fled from it fourteen years earlier as a boy of sixteen stoking coal on an ore ship on Lake Michigan.

He was eager to get on with his mission now, to cross the border into Tong Van So's cauldron of French Indochina and to make a personal assessment of the situation there. He took Tong aside after breakfast. The croissants, of course, had been a *succès fou*.

"I'm ready to go south with you now, Tong," he said. "How soon can we leave?"

They sat together in Tong's little bedroom, which had the spartan look of a monk's cell: a blanket-covered cot, a writing table and straight-backed wood chair, a lamp, a shelf of books and papers, a washbowl, water pitcher, chamberpot. On the wall was tacked a map of his homeland. An uncurtained window faced the wall around the property, just a few feet away.

Tong looked distressed and he shook his head. "We cannot just go to Viet-Nam like tourists, *Jean*. We must bring something of importance with us to establish credibility—mine as well as yours. Guns, ammunition, field equipment, radios. We have the one. It would be good to have a second one. We must bring matériel to demonstrate to my people that you mean business, that we are allies. I cannot return empty-handed."

"I'll start to take care of that today. We won't be empty-handed, but you're not going to get everything you want right away. I assume you've been waiting for Chin Li to get here to take him with you."

"Yes. That is correct." For the first time, he began to reveal more, as if it were the natural thing to do, and this pleased Reisman. "For the same reasons that you desire to see for yourself that we can work together against the Japanese, Chin Li must also make a report to his commanders in the north who would like to help us too."

"Then you've got the Reds, the Nationalists and the Americans all on your side," said Reisman in admiration. "That's pretty damn good politics, Tong."

"For now, each a possibility. Nothing more, nothing certain."

"I'm going in to the base," said Reisman. "I'll see you later. What do we need for transportation? Horses? Mules? Trucks? Walk? Small planes? How do we get in down there? Parachutes?"

Tong laughed. "I wish I had learned to do that, but I am afraid I am too old. It would be best to drive by truck from Kunming to a place near the border. From there we will walk."

"Where? What part of the border?"

"I will tell you later. Two trucks filled with arms and matériel would be a magnificent beginning. Your own drivers to a certain rendezvous point on the Chinese side. Our drivers will be waiting there to move the trucks to the place where we will unload, still on the China side, and then they will return the trucks to your men to take back to Kunming."

"How do we get the stuff across?"

"On foot. We have many feet and strong backs in my country. And trails that are known only to us."

"Who's going in this time?"

"All of us. You and I, Mai, Thi and Chin. Others will meet us."

Tong sounded like a commander now, a man who knew what he was doing—and Reisman liked that.

What he requested from the company store that morning was fairly standard infantry weaponry and ammunition, plus the second field radio. Lieutenant Colonel Kilgore approved the list he presented.

"They can't do very much damage with that, but it's a beginning," he said.

"I'd ask for a lot more, but I still haven't any idea what he's got down there in the way of personnel. It could be fifty or fifty thousand, and I wouldn't believe either figure unless I saw them in the flesh. We can part with this amount of stuff, though, and it won't be any great loss even if they never put it to any good use."

What he had asked for was twenty-five M-1 rifles and bayonets, twenty-five of the shorter-barreled carbines, twenty-five .45 caliber pistols, three B.A.R.s, three M-3 submachine guns, one hundred hand grenades plus twenty-five dummies for training, and two 60mm mortars, plus a moderate supply of ammunition to go with the guns. It was the same sort of weaponry the Kachins had put to such good use in Burma.

The two men were in Kilgore's office above the operations room as they talked, the same room in which Reisman had first met Tong Van So. He looked around and asked, "Did you ever really wipe this room for bugs, Sam?"

"Not with a microscope, but I think it's clean. Tai Li has his ways of finding things out anyway."

"We'll need a truck and driver for the trip down. I don't know exactly where we're going yet, but I estimate about four hundred miles round trip for the driver, so load extra fuel and fix the lights for blackout driving. I don't know if Tong plans to go in in broad daylight, but I don't."

"You can't take a vehicle over, you know. The French *colons* have the crossing points guarded and they're worse than the Japs. They'd grab the truck and guns, arrest everybody and turn you over to Hirohito's boys for amusement. Who's going in with you?"

"I'm keeping that to myself for now, Sam."

Kilgore gave him a strange look, then a shrug that said okay if that's the way he wanted to do it. "Let's get out of here and go to my place," he said. "There are other things I want to talk to you about."

"Your place? I thought you lived in the BOQ."

"I've got a cot there, just like you do, Johnny," said Sam with a wink, "but I don't *live* there."

They drove in Kilgore's jeep away from the congested bustling part of Kunming past Ta Kuan Lo municipal park to an area of good roads, fine houses and gardens on low hills. Sam unlocked the wood gate in a walled courtyard, drove through, locked the gate again and parked beside a charming house of wood and stone. It seemed more a pavilion than a house and, set on a rise, looked out toward Cui Hu, the lovely Green Lake, and its trees and gardens at the foot of Yuantong Hill.

"Obviously the high-rent district," said Reisman as he took in the flower garden, fruit trees and decorative pond. "Whose is it?"

"A business associate. I rent it from him." Sam unlocked the heavy, carved front door and strode in like the lord of the manor, calling out, "Betty Jane!"

"A business associate! I thought you were in the soldier business like me. We don't make enough money together to afford a place like this."

"It's the favorable exchange rate, Johnny. My friend lets me have it cheap."

The entry hall and rooms to either side were brightly lit by daylight that poured through windows framed by drapes of a cream-colored, textured fabric. But the light was as quickly absorbed by floors of dark, polished woods, rugs of deep hues and heavy furnishings of black lacquered wood and inlays and dark brocaded upholstery. It was not a light and airy house, despite its setting and possibilities, but it was a luxurious residence in the heavy style that Reisman had seen in more moneyed Chinese homes, and it particularly reminded him now of what he'd seen of Tai Li's Happy Valley in Chungking.

Lilting, fluting voices like birdsong came down a corridor from the back of the house, followed by two Chinese girls in long silk dresses. The girls were perhaps in their late teens, certainly no more than twenty, and they were strikingly lovely. They seemed alike and yet, if one looked closely, which Reisman certainly did, their faces were quite different, though each had thick, shiny black hair gathered to a jade clasp and combed out below the barrette to lie on one shoulder. Each girl's gown was slit provocatively high at one side. One was bright red, the other white with a black and gold dragon appliqué. Reisman became immediately intrigued by the positioning and apparent intent of the dragon. It was long and sinuous, curled diagonally over one shoulder and down her back, its tail wrapped part way around her waist to her navel, its fierce, open mouth spouting red tongues of flame that licked toward her pubis.

"This is Betty," said Kilgore, pointing to one, "and this is Jane. Though maybe it's the other way around. Anyway it hardly makes any difference. Betty Jane is easier for me than their Chinese names. Ladies, this is my buddy, Major Reisman, a famous soldier of good fortune."

They apparently didn't understand a word he had said, but they kept smiling and making little shy, graceful movements with their arms and bodies and chattering to each other with little birdlike sounds. Reisman, however, understood their words: that they were glad to see Colonel Sam at home and they liked the looks of his friend. Sam obviously was treating them well and they were quite happy.

When Reisman spoke to them in Mandarin Chinese they were delighted. But though he had understood some of their dialect he had to repeat things carefully for them now and then ask them, once they got the idea, to give him the right sounds in the Yunnan dialect. And soon they were great friends.

"Son-of-a-bitch," said Sam, laughing. "You're in my house five minutes and you take over my girls."

"You should learn to speak their language, Colonel," said Reisman.

"Oh, I do—I do. The only language that's really important. They each think I speak it quite well . . . particularly after a few drinks, a fine dinner and wine, and some lovely preliminaries. And they only cost me three bucks apiece."

"For the night?"

"Hell, no. Three bucks. Period. Semipermanent. I bought them when I came to Kunming and I'll sell them to somebody else when I leave. The GIs in the Training Command were doing it and I thought, what the hell, why shouldn't I? I got the best of the crop, though. Hardly been used. They take good care of me, I take good care of them. It works out. They'd be starving otherwise or out hustling their butts on the street getting into all kinds of trouble."

I take care of her, she takes care of me—till I go home. Someone else had used that phrase recently, Reisman remembered—the Air Corps sergeant at the bar in Chungking. Apparently it was the prevalent thing to do all over China. It filled a need on both sides. And not only in China. In England, France, North Africa, Italy and the Mediterranean, wherever the war had moved; and in the U.S. of A. and its territories, Australia and the islands of the Pacific. Wherever the transient armies stayed put for a while, the nesting instinct took possession of the men as well as the women. It was more than just getting laid. For him, in England, there had been Tess Simmons. But this business of *buying* offended him. It seemed so degrading. Particularly at three bucks.

Sam slyly demonstrated now, by ordering up drinks and lunch, that he did know how to speak some of the Yunnan dialect. Reisman had known him well enough, however, not to be too surprised. With his behind-the-lines operational experience and awareness, Sam was really too clever a man to allow himself to wander dumbly through his present assignment without knowing what some of the sounds, signs and symbols around him meant.

"Just a light lunch for now," he said after the girls glided from the room. "We've got a lot to talk about. I want you to stay for dinner. There's a cook out back working on something. Betty and Jane don't do that very well yet, though they're learning. You can stay the night—unless you've got something going somewhere else. There's plenty of room here—and there's Betty Jane."

"How kind of you," said Reisman with a phony British accent. He sounded as if he'd been invited for the weekend to a country home outside London but wasn't sure he wanted to accept. Then he realized that he really did disapprove. He didn't want anyone pimping for him. He didn't want to be vulnerable or obligated to Sam on so personal a level. He just plain didn't want to let himself go. "I prefer to find my own entertainment," he went on. "I don't like butting in on your territory or taking sloppy seconds."

"Christ, Johnny, you sound like M'Lord Smythe-Smythe-Smithers who's just been offended by a lout at his gentlemen's club. Don't be so damned stuffy."

"Let's talk about the operation, Sam," said Reisman. Kilgore nodded in resignation, waved him to a corner of the living room and they settled into heavily upholstered lounge chairs. "How much clout do you have with the chief?" Reisman asked.

"Donovan?"

"No. Ludlow."

"A little, I suppose. You may have noticed there are other officers here in Kunming senior to me," he said sarcastically. "I don't command the base. They just give me things to do and I do them, just like you."

Betty and Jane brought trays of whiskies, gin, soda, tonic, ice, sliced lemons and limes, cold beer and sandwiches and set them on a low table between the men. Where the hell did he get all the good booze, Reisman wondered? Most people had to settle for the notorious "air-raid juice"—*ching pao*. One of the girls poured a whisky and soda for Sam and pouted when Reisman declined one. Then they left. Reisman took a bottle of beer and a sandwich. His eyebrows went up when he realized that the beer was Japanese.

"Where in hell do you get something like this?" he asked. "I thought there was a war on and they were the enemy."

"Sure they are, but they make good beer. Probably learned it from the Krauts. Some of it gets captured or stolen."

"Or even traded?"

"Yeh, I suppose so. There's some of that going on across the lines, I understand."

Reisman decided to drop it. He poured the beer into a glass and drank. It was good. He began to eat a sandwich thick with Yunnan ham and American cheese and it too was good. There was a more important matter to pursue. "The way I see it," he said, "whatever I do down there in French Indochina, it starts out as a training operation—just like China Training Command has up here with the Gimo's raw recruits. Now, Tong could be pulling some funny business on us one way or the other, but I don't think he's got an outfit worth a shit down there. So, if it's a training job, I've got a bunch of men in mind I want over here from England right away to help me—but only if *they* want to come, mind you. This isn't one of those 'You, you and you volunteer' situations. They have to want to come. If they don't want to, I want them left alone. They've already been through a lot. These men know my *modus operandi* better than anybody."

"Are they OSS?"

"They were for a while earlier this year. I don't know their exact status at the moment. I'm sorry to be vague about it, Sam. There's one man who will know and be able to round them up for me if they're available. His name is Bowren—Sergeant Clyde Bowren."

"Give me the names, ranks, serial numbers, outfits and last known addresses and I'll get on it right away. They'll have to be cleared with Chungking before they come over the Hump, you know."

"That's why I asked you how much clout you had with Ludlow. When I was up there I told him I'd be putting in a request for these men, he said you'd handle it and he'd clear it from there. Didn't sound as if there'd be any problems."

"I don't see any either, Johnny," said Sam. "We all play ball with each other out here. That way we get where we want to be faster and happier." He finished his drink, then started on a sandwich and beer. Looking up slyly, he said, "There's something I want to talk to you about that's just between you and me."

"Sure, Sam."

"Keep your eyes open for opportunities down there."

"What kind?"

"Look, don't be stupid. You know what the hell I mean." He rubbed thumb and fingers together in the age-old gesture for money. "It's a new territory. Stuff to buy and sell. Over in Burma they got rubies and all kinds of precious gems, but the way I hear it the boys are doing nothing about it. Damn dumb." When he saw Reisman's disbelieving look, he said, "Have you ever noticed how many really rich guys we've got in this outfit? Now Ludlow, he's Navy, old Navy, and I'm surprised Donovan let him get the job—except that was politics and maybe Donovan had nothing to do with it. They had to make the Chinese happy. But have you ever noticed how many guys we've got in the outfit who are bankers, lawyers, stockbrokers, oil company executives, business magnates galore? They're out there protecting what they've got, exploring new territories, making new deals, and they've got nothing to worry about when it's over."

"I don't know anything about that, Sam," Reisman said brusquely. "The men I've known and worked with in OSS have mostly been extraordinary men putting their lives on the line to do a hell of a job—not guys out looking for business deals."

"Most of them, you're right. They've got it made anyway. But a lot of top-rankers who don't know their asses from their elbows have got power and swat only because they have wealth, family and social status in civilian life. And they've got them to go back to after the war. Me, I don't have that kind of background. As a matter of fact, how come a guy like you—poor family, no money, no background, no education . . . part Jew, part Guinea, part who-knows-what—how the hell did you make it in an outfit like this?"

Reisman had to smile at that and excuse Sam his GI right, his allotted share of bitching, though high-level in his case. "Just lucky, I guess, like the whore in Macao," said Reisman. "It's the ethnic blend of all those secret ingredients that does it, just like with you and millions of others in the U.S. of A."

Kilgore wasn't interested in philosophy or sociology, however. "Listen," he said, "don't you think Ludlow is on the take from Tai Li up there in Chungking?"

"Taking what, Sam?"

"How the hell do I know? Maybe it's the chop suey franchise for Szechuan after the war or a concession to drill for oil in Mongolia."

"Tai Li deals in opium. That much I know about."

"Tai Li deals in everything. It's all business, Johnny. The whole damn war is business."

"I'm not that cynical yet, Sam."

"Take what's happening right here in Kunming. It's booming. You've seen it yourself. Not that Old China bazaar stuff I drove you through when you arrived. I mean new six-story concrete buildings and industries, and new mines and power plants outside town. A man could make himself a bundle here with the right civilian contacts. I figure the same thing is possible down there in French Indochina. This business associate I mentioned—the one I rent this house from—he's interested in that sort of thing. Maybe you'll find something down there that we can sell to the Chinese up here, or the GIs."

"You mean like blood, Sam?" He let the bitterness of his sarcasm strike home before going on. "When you knock the rich and privileged you sound like a Commie. Then you turn around and sound like a two-bit hustler who wants to be a big-time capitalist. Whatever happened to God, Country and the Flag?" he chided with tongue in cheek and some good old rabble-rousing cynicism. "What about politics? We're here to save the world for democracy, remember?"

"Politics is just sorting out the shit of humans so we don't inundate each other, that's all," Kilgore answered without rancor. "Communism? Capitalism? There are men all around us and down in those jungles and mountains you're going into who've never heard of either one of them, but they would kill you for what they do believe in."

"Like opium?"

"Yes, like opium. But I'm thinking of other things. Listen, back in '42, before the Japs closed the Burma Road, the warlord who was running Kunming made a hell of a deal on rubber tires from Rangoon. He made it mandatory that every bus—even those little pony-powered jitneys—had to have rubber tires or go out of business. Everybody bought his tires and he made a fortune. That's the sort of thing I have in mind."

"I'm not a businessman, Sam. You've got the wrong fellow," Reisman told him sourly, trying to end the discussion. "I know nothing about business, never have, never will. I have no interest in it whatsoever."

"Well, think about it anyway," Kilgore said cheerily. "If you run into anything you think might be of interest just pass it along to me."

Late in the night the girl came to him as he knew she would, as he finally had hoped she would—for, by then, he was sated on the lieutenant colonel's good liquor, sumptuous food and fine wine and he felt an emptiness of spirit that spurred other yearnings of the flesh to fill it. With Kilgore grinning his blessings and winking approvingly at Reisman, she had been particularly attentive and teasingly affectionate to him at dinner, which the girls had served and shared. Whether she was Betty or Jane he didn't know and didn't care. She was the one in white with the dragon breathing fire at her vulva, and by the end of the meal and wine and the distant American music that Kilgore brought in on his short-wave radio—to which Reisman danced and hummed and held the Chinese girl close—he felt the heat too and wanted to slay the dragon and give his own fire to the fair maiden.

She came quietly into the bedroom where Reisman lay awake under a blanket, wearing his shorts and T-shirt. He had pulled open the drapes to feel a part of the garden and countryside in the soft glowing night, and moonlight illuminated the room. The girl closed the door, spoke a gentle greeting in Chinese, and glided to the bed. She saw that he was awake and she reached out a hand to him. He took it and drew her to him. Their lips touched, with but a moment's feeling out and hesitation, and then their mouths crushed against each other with the heat that had been building between them all evening, though Reisman still was thinking sufficiently to marvel that her ardor should be as passionate and demanding as his own; and still removed from himself, observing and analytical, as he tended to be, he spent another few moments thinking instead of feeling, another few moments wondering the why of it, what she might be feeling, how this could be—and then, knowing no answer and not really caring, he abandoned himself to feeling and tasting, feeding desire and swelling with joy. He helped her slide the dragon gown from her body, and the silken underthings she wore, and then she helped him out of his T-shirt and shorts and they kneeled pressing gently against each other on the bed, holding each other, sliding hands from heads to necks to shoulders, arms, breasts, waists, along each other's flanks and then, falling side by side, Reisman took the slim body in his arms and squashed his lips against her mouth and felt her tongue force his lips apart and probe its tip from surface to surface within his gasping mouth. Then she gave him back his mouth and he felt her tongue glide its way along his tingling flesh to his groin, where she lingered, played with him caressingly with fingers and hand, swirling tongue and sucking lips, while he slid his hand along her leg, cupped and kneaded her buttocks gently with his palm, then harder, feeling through his vibrating nerve endings her firm young flesh. He moved his hand down the curve of her flank, found the moist, warm lips and heard her own gasp of pleasure when his fingers penetrated.

They stayed like that a while, pleasuring each other—then another thought intruded, though he did not want to think. He thought that never was a man so weak and vulnerable as he was in these moments when, as a man, he was strongest. Then he gave way again to the demands of his body. All his senses were alive, as they were in battle, but he had no drive to conquer—only to feel, to share himself, to give and receive. The girl rose up along his body and he filled his eyes with the sight of her nakedness in the soft moonlight as her nubile body undulated around him. His nostrils filled with the aroma of her. He took one of her breasts, small and exquisite, into his mouth, tasted her delicious flesh and the powder or scent she had applied there, and he delighted in the feel of it responding; and then he tasted the other, her nipples rising hard to his ministrations.

They were children together for a time, discovering each other in delicious play that chased gross war and death from Reisman's mind. Yet each movement and touch—entwined and sheathed at last within the girl—drew him closer, teetering on the edge, to the unrefusable demand and conclusion of the ancient rhythms and rites of their game. He wanted it never to end—to keep tension, anticipation and exhilaration going, never to have that moment of final release and consummation that would return him to his thoughts.

In the quietness afterward, he covered both of them with the blanket and he thought to ask her name—her real name in Chinese. But then he decided not to. Better that she be just plain Betty Jane, one or the other. He thought now of Nguyen Thi Mai and wondered what *she* would be like as lover . . . and he remembered what Katherine had been like . . . and Tess at the Butcher's Arms.

Then he heard the bedroom door open and looked up to see Sam Kilgore's head pop around it and ask, "Hey, buddy, want to switch girls?"

The girl understood. She clung tightly to Reisman and whispered that she wanted to stay with *him*. He embraced her closer under the blanket, wrapping his legs and arms around her protectively. How adept—and perhaps loving—she had been for one so young. Still, she might have been experienced in this for years before Sam bought her.

Nevertheless, he replied, darkly, "No, I don't, Sam."

"For God's sake, Johnny, don't be so damned stuffy," said Kilgore.

Reisman mumbled a weary good night in his direction. Kilgore made a less than gracious sound. But he left.

Chapter 16

The next morning, while Sam went off to put together the arms and equipment for Tong Van So, Reisman sat at the lieutenant colonel's desk upstairs in the Special Operations building, writing messages he wanted to send to England.

"We'll transmit them to London and send the roster to Chungking at the same time for urgent and immediate clearance," Sam had told him.

"Urgent and immediate? That ought to take at least two or three weeks," Reisman had taunted lightly. "Probably longer."

Nevertheless, he was thankful for Kilgore's enthusiastic cooperation, and still filled with a certain *Gemütlichkeit* induced by the activities of the night before. He figured he'd need two or three weeks anyway to size up the situation south of the border and return to Kunming.

"If your men want the job, the way will be cleared for them right into Kunming airfield," Sam had assured him.

All Reisman knew for certain was that Clyde Bowren, Ken Sawyer and Joe Wladislaw had made it back to England from France before him and that they still had been there when he left for China. He had visited them in the hospital where they had been knitting up well from wounds suffered in the raid on the Château de la Vilaine or during the weeks afterward as the survivors of the battle, split up for the escape, had moved through the French countryside in the rear of the Nazi armies while working their way toward Allied lines on the Normandy coast.

What had happened to the other men who survived the raid itself he still did not know for certain, though five months had passed since their mission on the night before D-Day. Some, perhaps, were now prisoners of the Nazis instead of their own army. Others, he considered, might even still be in hiding in the French countryside, keeping out of the way of the fighting. For who among them, in the end, might not have grabbed the chance to sit out the rest of the war in anonymity and limbo? He had taught them to be wily, chameleonlike warriors, altering their guises as the need arose, changing from U.S. uniforms to German uniforms to civilian clothing as the foreground and background of their surroundings demanded, transforming behavior, personalities and even language for those who knew how. He had taught them how to use, as weapons both defensive and offensive, their innate intelligence, their rage, even their predilection for the tensions and conflicts that had got them into trouble in the first place and turned them into the Dirty Dozen.

He did know, though, who among them had been killed in the raid, either because he had seen it happen or had seen their corpses afterward, or because it had been confirmed in Major Stuart Kinder's intelligence reports and by Sergeant Bowren's statements. Reisman himself had come through the raid physically unscathed, but carrying with him the emotional intensity of the experience. In the days afterward, however, he had taken two minor flesh wounds in action while he, Bowren, Archer Maggot and Napoleon White had moved in zigzag patterns—forward, sideways, backward and forward again—along the roads and across the fields of Brittany and Normandy, with Reisman driving the big Nazi staff limousine they'd used to escape from the château. Both Bowren and White had been wounded. Bowren, more severely hurt, had drifted in and out of consciousness during that week. Reisman had been able to minister to him from the first-aid kits and with help from Frenchmen to whom he had revealed their identities. But he had become obsessed with bringing Bowren out safely.

The wounded Napoleon White also had been a problem, for there had been no way to pass off an American black as a German soldier, even though he spoke German and French better than the others, except for Reisman. Whenever they had been unable to avoid contact with German patrols they had identified Napoleon, wearing an airborne uniform, as a wounded parachutist they had taken prisoner and were bringing in for interrogation. Reisman's uniform and I.D. as a Nazi colonel had gotten them through.

In a nighttime firefight with a confused patrol of the German Seventh Army near Mortain, Reisman had been shot through the upper left arm; the bullet had cut through his flesh and out again without damaging the bone, and he had acknowledged the blessing of that rather than complain about the wound, for he'd had wounds like that in earlier wars and they healed up while one kept going. The second wound had been less severe. They had been dashing incautiously along a country road near Vire in the hour just after dawn, when an American fighter-bomber had swooped down with chattering guns on the blatant symbol of the Third Reich in which they were riding and had forced them into a ditch to escape; a tiny shard of a bomb had cut and seared the right side of Reisman's neck.

Days later, when Bowren had been picked up by American units at the farmhouse north of St. Lô where Reisman had just left him, the sergeant had reported his C.O. wounded. But Reisman already had started back toward Rennes, dressed like a French farmer, looking first for White and Maggot—who were no longer where he'd left them—and then for the others. His going back had also been reported by Bowren and noted in Kinder's report on Project Amnesty. Reisman had read the report in London weeks later, after he'd finally given up retrieving the rest of his team and had made it back to Allied lines alone.

In London, he was jubilant when he learned from Kinder, newly promoted to major, that Bowren, Sawyer and Wladislaw had made it out ahead of him. He had been glad, too, at the way Kinder had handled delicate matters of record and in the ways he had honored the men for what they had accomplished. On their records it had been noted that each of the Dirty Dozen had been returned to active duty in their former ranks as of June 5, 1944, the night they had jumped into France. Clyde Bowren had been promoted to staff sergeant and transferred from the Corps of Military Police to OSS London.

Now, preparing his messages for Bowren, Sawyer and Wladislaw, Reisman came to another rather delicate matter that Clyde in particular would have to handle on his own. Reisman did not want Kinder involved in any aspect of this new mission at all, because he would ask too many questions, then confuse and thwart arrangements with his good intentions. It was to be kept strictly secret from him. Orders would be cut and transportation arranged, but Bowren was to round up the men on his own. If any of the others had returned he was to go to see them and, if they were in good health physically and psychologically and gung ho for the job, he was to invite them to accompany him to China—provided, of course, that he too wanted to come. Reisman made that clear: it was a strictly voluntary assignment.

In the end, he included on the roster for Chungking the names of each of the men he knew had not been killed at Rennes.

Baw San was driven back to OSS base from Lake Tien Chih that afternoon.

"I thought you had forgotten me, *Duwa* John," he said, speaking in Mandarin. And then he quickly wrote and pronounced the fifty new Chinese ideographs he had memorized in the week he had been at the R and R camp.

Reisman complimented him and then asked, in English, "You don't happen to know how to speak Viet-Namese, do you?"

"No, but I will study it if you want me to," Baw San replied eagerly.

"How would you like to go south with me tomorrow? Just a reconnaissance. No action if we can avoid it."

He had thought the young Kachin would leap at the chance, but was surprised to hear him say, "There is something else I would rather do."

"What?"

"Go to jump school. I met a soldier at the recuperation center who told me there is a paratroop training center out in the valley not far from Kunming. He said they're training Chinese soldiers there, so I guess they ought to have room for one Kachin. I could even fake it as a Chinese if I had to."

Reisman understood his eagerness. Ever since he had floated down in front of him on the bank of the Salween River, Baw San had told him often how much he'd like to be able to do that himself.

"All right. I think that's a better idea for now," Reisman said, "till I get things sized up in Indochina. I'll ask the colonel to arrange it. You didn't happen to find out who owns that place on the lake, did you?"

"Marshal Lung-Yün," answered Baw San, pleased to relate this intelligence. "Friend of Tai Li . . . friend of Chiang Kai-shek . . . big big Chinese *tuchun*."

When he returned to the Viets' house that afternoon, after seeing Baw San off to jump school, Reisman told Tong Van So that the truck was loaded and ready for him and his group. One of the American noncoms from Special Operations would serve as round-trip driver. "We'll leave from the base any time you're ready," he said. "Tonight if you'd like."

"Only one truck, *Jean?*" said Tong petulantly.

"Yes. We're not outfitting a division yet."

"The second radio?"

"It's aboard."

"*Bien*. We can leave in the morning."

"Do you plan to cross in broad daylight?"

"We will know when we get there. Our people are waiting for us on this side of the border."

"The Japs and French are watching too."

"I'm aware of that, *Jean*. Please, in this matter you must allow me to be the commandant. Remember, it is my country, my border, my intelligence network."

"If we get too close in the daytime they'll know that somebody will be trying to cross. I've got the headlights fixed for blackout driving so we can move in close at night."

Tong gave him a shrewd little smile. "I am really surprised at a man like you being so cautious," he said, trying to shame him or bait him.

Reisman looked at him sharply. "In regard to you, your people and the places you're taking me, *Monsieur* Tong, you will find me to be doubly cautious."

Tong made a little pouting grimace, that little expression of displeasure which the French called a *moue*. Then, seeing Reisman's enjoyment of his discomfiture, he laughed and wagged his finger like a teacher scolding a naughty pupil. "Perhaps you are right," he said.

"Let us join Tran Van Thi and Nguyen Thi Mai. There are some things we must tell you about our cauldron before we leave."

It was more a political indoctrination, with the *Viet-Nam Doc-Lap Dong Minh Hoi* as the good guys and all other factions as the bad. They gathered around the large table in the living room. Tran Van Thi carried the burden of the lecture while Tong Van So sat back listening closely to see if his protégé missed any portion of the catechism. Mai—looking quite fetching this afternoon in a slightly more conservative version of what Betty Jane had worn the day before—sat at Reisman's side, digging out position papers and references from time to time as supportive evidence for Thi's lecture and adding her own few words. Chin Li, the guest from the north, listened and observed from the sofa, though he did not understand the English and French that was being used. Every now and then Tong or one of the others would say something to him in Chinese, just to keep him in the picture, and he would respond with apparent approval.

The substance of Tran Van Thi's lecture was mainly concerned with the current state of political, religious and cultural affairs in French Indochina and the history of various contending movements within the country. It seemed, to Reisman, to be a land torn by factionalism. Some factions, according to Thi, were just gangs of thieving, murderous bandits who preyed on everybody. Others claimed sanction from on high as originators of the one true word. Political philosophies ranged from nihilism to monarchy, from laissez-faire capitalism to social democracy to communism. There were factions with names that twisted the tongue and boggled the mind trying to keep them straight—bandits like the Binh Xuyen and religious sects like the Cao Dai and Hoa Hao.

Every group was a potential force in the political arena. However, they didn't just argue with one another; they often killed each other. In a way it reminded Reisman of Spain when he had fought there for the Republic during the civil war; even to the militant participation of the Catholic Church. Except that French Indochina sounded to him even more splintered and savage. The French and Japanese were the most obvious factions and easiest to understand, he thought, at least from a military point of view—which he kept insisting was all he was interested in.

"We're at war with the Japs and we'll help you get rid of them," Reisman reminded them. "Get this straight, though. I'm not an official. I don't make policy. I don't influence it in any way. I'm here to carry out orders, that's all. The fact that the present government in Washington is favorably inclined toward more freedom for you people is something to your advantage—but that's not the reason I'm here. I'm here because we want something back from you. We want our flyboys looked after when they come down in your country; we want a continuous flow of intelligence about Jap plans, movements and forces; and we want guerrilla action against them. We don't want you to take the guns and equipment we give you and use them to kill each other just because you have differences of political or religious opinion. And we don't want you to use the guns and equipment to murder French men, women and children or to kick out these people who are part and parcel of the country now. If anybody tried to do that to all the newcomers and foreigners in the U.S. there would only be a couple of tired old Indians around who wouldn't know where the light switch was."

"An amusing analogy," said Tong, though Reisman could tell he was not amused.

"Get out your maps now," Reisman told them. "I want to know exactly where we're going and the route we're taking to get there."

"Why?" demanded Tran Van Thi.

"So there are no surprises," Reisman snapped, bracketing him with a glare. "Why do you even challenge my question? My way of operating is to prepare in advance for as many contingencies as are likely to come up. A second reason, if you need one, is that the driver has to know, and a third reason is that the colonel wants to know. It's like filing a flight plan—so he knows where to start if he has to come looking for us."

"That is precisely why we do *not* wish to reveal these details now," interjected Tong. "We do not want such information to get into the wrong hands. We do not want anyone to come looking for us, to find our base in Tonkin."

"I understand that," said Reisman in exasperation. "But it's past time you trusted me completely."

"As you do me, of course," mocked Tong.

"We seem to be at an impasse, *monsieur,*" said Reisman, trying with some difficulty to be diplomatic and pleasant. "However, either you haul out your maps and show me where we will cross the frontier and where we're going from there—or that truck will never leave base. You want stuff from me, you play it straight with me, Tong. None of this inscrutable-East bullshit."

"Truly an impasse," agreed Tong. "I could lie to you, of course. Merely point the finger and say, Here, this is where we are going . . . but that would not be good, you would lose confidence in us. Perhaps if I tried to explain further . . . a matter of security. We risk revealing things to you which you will tell others, and which can be used against us. There is much treachery among the Chinese. Someone might betray not only our route but the location of our headquarters in Tonkin. We could be bombed from the air or even taken prisoner in a ground assault."

Reisman thought that over a moment. "Very well, Tong. Perhaps you're right about briefing others. The information will go to no one else. Especially not to the colonel. We will direct the driver as we travel. Since he will not cross the border with us, all he will be able to report is the route we took south."

"Agreed," said Tong cheerfully.

"We each risk something by trusting the other," Reisman continued, for he was all wound up with his argument now, and if he got it all out perhaps he would avoid the next one. "You, however, must risk a little bit more than you have. When you get right down to it, *monsieur,* I risk everything just by being here instead of Chicago."

Tong laughed. "Ah . . . I have never been in Chicago—but I understand it is a bad place . . . gangsters."

Reisman could not help laughing with him. Then Tong told Tran Van Thi to spread the map on the table.

Thi pointed out the various roads going south and southeast from Kunming. "This one is still the best for us," he said, moving his finger along a line that first cut east and then dropped south in the most direct path to the frontier about two hundred miles away. "Through Kaiyuan, Datunjie and Mengzie. It is not in such good repair as it was before the French closed the frontier, but it is still the best way for us. You Americans used to bring a lot of supplies up into China on that road when our country was still open to you. However, it is not as straight as it looks on the map. It is more like a treacherous snake when one is on it. Many twists and turns, high mountains and steep gorges."

Reisman examined the map closely. "Where do we cross the frontier?" he asked.

"Near Lao Cai," said Thi, pointing to it on the map. "Our scouts and many of our people will be waiting there to carry in the supplies we bring."

"And our ultimate destination?"

Thi hesitated and looked up at his leader for guidance. Tong Van So leaned over the chart and his finger circled the northeast corner of Tonkin province. "The area of Cao Bang," he said. "That is where we have established our base."

The route in was deceptive and a good one from a security point of view, Reisman saw. They might also be able to reach Cao Bang by driving east from Kunming, staying north of the border through the corner of Kwangsi province before crossing over—but that would more readily point the way to their ultimate destination if anyone was tracking them on the China side. And there was also a new danger to the east: the Japanese Eleventh Army was again on the move, fighting its way into Kwangsi province. They had already captured one of General Chennault's forward bases at Lingling. Anyone moving too far to the east was in danger of meeting the Japs fighting their way into western China.

That, Reisman knew, was the most important reason that OSS had assigned him to develop the relationship with Tong Van So and his *Viet-Nam Doc-Lap Dong Minh Hoi*. If they could start the kind of guerrilla war in Indochina that the Kachins had fought in Burma, it might force the Japs to move combat troops in from the north and ease the pressure on Chiang Kai-shek's armies.

"What do you think, *Jean?*" asked Tong.

What he thought was that he would have preferred an air drop—one quick, clean operation for personnel, arms and supplies. But that was out of the question now. "I think we should get out of Kunming before dawn and make sure none of Tai Li's spies are on our tail. South of Mengzie we should hole up out of sight in the hills for the rest of the day, then move to wherever your people are on the border after dark."

"That sounds quite reasonable," agreed Tong. "There is now only one more thing."

"What is that?"

The others in the room seemed to know what was coming, for they glanced back and forth between Tong Van So and John Reisman with expectant expressions. Even Chin Li seemed to be following closely the sense of what Tong was saying in English, if not the literal meaning of the words themselves.

"I intend, my friend, to take a new name," said Tong.

"Why?" asked Reisman.

"It is a custom among my people . . . to make the name suit the events."

Reisman pondered that a few moments with an expression of ingenuous interest. "I know about such a custom among other peoples," he acknowledged. He thought in particular about Samson Posey of the Dirty Dozen, the Ute Indian who had covered their withdrawal from the château at Rennes and was still listed as missing in action. Posey had told him about the name quests of Ute adolescents and how prevalent the custom was among the American tribes. "Is there something about Tong Van So that you wish to forget—or make others forget?" he asked.

Tong looked at him with the flicker of a smile, which was in itself sufficient as unspoken acknowledgment.

"What is the new name?" Reisman pressed.

"In your language," said Tong, "the name may be translated as He Who Enlightens. In my language it is pronounced Ho Chi Minh."

PART III

The Cauldron

Chapter 17

They were shadows first. Black upon black in the night. Except that their conical, pale straw hats made it apparent that somebody was there and subverted the possibility of total camouflage. To Reisman, the hats made them look like clusters of mushrooms rising suddenly on the ridgelines in the starlight of the night sky.

"Who are they? *Viet Minh?*" he asked Tran Van Thi, who stood nearest to him by the truck, watching the shadows take substance and come closer out of the brushwood hills.

Reisman had finally taken to using, as the others did, the shorter name for *Viet-Nam Doc-Lap Dong Minh Hoi*. He found the name more comfortable on his lips, much as he did the new name of Ho Chi Minh. A few times during the journey to the frontier he had mistakenly called him *Tong* and had been corrected with less and less forbearance; so he had repeated the name over and over to himself like a schoolboy doing blackboard exercises, until now in his mind and on his lips the man was Ho Chi Minh. Tong Van So no longer existed except in certain memories and records in China. Ho was out ahead there now, off to the side of the isolated dirt track where his driver had brought the truck; he and Nguyen Thi Mai were being surrounded and embraced by their people. The OSS sergeant who had driven them down from Kunming had been left some miles away, in the company of one of Ho's scouts, to wait for the return of his empty vehicle.

"They are *can slua tau,*" answered Tran Van Thi. " 'The people in black'—although their clothing is really a very dark blue, dyed with indigo. They are from the Nung, a hill tribe who live near our headquarters camp. They work with us as porters. The scouts are *Viet Minh,* and so are some of the other people, those who carry guns. See, they have brought similar clothing for Uncle Ho so that he will be like one of them, which pleases him and pleases them."

"He is your uncle?" Reisman asked.

"No, no, not actually. We use the word as a term of respect, and also of familiar endearment. They will have brought native clothing for us too."

"No, thanks. I'll keep my uniform."

The porters emptied the truck and took its cargo onto their backs or onto shoulder poles, or slung the heavier crates onto poles between two of them. As the loads were transferred, the porters and some of the Viet Minh guards moved off in single file into the brushwood hills and waited just out of sight for the rest of the caravan to form up.

Mai went into the emptied truck first to change in private. She was wearing a sweater over the skirt and blouse she had worn the first day Reisman had met her. Now she disappeared behind the canvas truck flaps for a few minutes. When she hopped down off the tailgate she looked like a woman about to go to work in a paddy field. The clothes she had removed and her personal kit were rolled into a blanket slung across her back. Then Ho Chi Minh, Tran Van Thi and Chin Li got into the truck to change. Ho and Chin came out dressed like *can slua tau,* carrying their other clothes and personal gear rolled in blankets tied across their backs. Thi, however, who had carried his own duffel down with him in the truck, came out wearing a lighter colored tunic, bloused pants, boots and a modified pith helmet; it was a military uniform like that which some of the Viet Minh wore. Thi quickly took possession of one of the new carbines and a .45 automatic and demonstrated his familiarity with them by loading clips in each, moving the first cartridge into the chamber and locking the weapons on safety before shouldering and holstering them.

"You look as if you're ready for business and know what you're doing," remarked Reisman. "What rank are you?"

"Nothing specific yet. That's unimportant in the Viet Minh. I've had a bit of training," Thi acknowledged. "But I'll defer to you on things of a military nature, if they should occur—which they shouldn't if our intelligence, our scouting and our line of march are correct."

Ho, who carried no weapon, came up to Reisman and said, "You are in good physical condition for a long march?"

"How long?"

"One hundred and fifty miles. The Nung will do it in three days and we must keep up with them. There will be halts for food and rest and to sleep, but it will be strenuous."

Reisman smiled at the fragile-looking man. "I think I can handle it, Uncle," he said. It would be like those forced marches with the Kachins; perhaps all the hill tribes of Asia had that same talent and capacity for arduous travel on foot, carrying heavy burdens over difficult terrain. "How do we keep clear of the Japs and the French?" he added.

"My scouts know the way. We will stop only in villages where we have friends."

That was not completely true, as Reisman was to see for himself in the next few days. There were approximately fifty men and women on the march: Nung porters, Viet Minh scouts and guards, and those who had come with Ho Chi Minh. The rendezvous and infiltration had been to the west of Lao Cai, so they had first to cross the big Red River, the Sông Hong, which ultimately poured its way southeast to Hanoi itself and then emptied into the Gulf of Tonkin. Sampans and rafts were waiting at prearranged rendezvous points to ferry them across in the night. And then again a while later, when they had to cross the narrower Sông Chay. Reisman commended Ho on the smooth coordination of contacts and movements so far.

"It will be harder now," Ho commented. "We will climb high again. Perhaps difficulties with some people northeast of Pa Kha. What I understand you Americans call 'Indian country.' "

It was an unexpected phrase, if what he meant was "dangerous country." How had he come to know an idiom like that? But at least Reisman had come to know that there was a lot to be unexpected about Ho Chi Minh.

The terrain through which they trekked was not thick, steaming jungle, as in the parts of Burma where he had been with the Kachins. It was more like the mountains in China when they had crossed the Salween, and like the brushwood and forested mountains and canyons through which they had driven on the way down from Kunming. Reisman, of course—wearing his American uniform, full field pack and combat gear, toting an M-3, .45 automatic, grenades and extra clips—stood out in the line of march as exactly what he was. There was no way for him to go native, nor did he want to. He was dependent on the Viet Minh for security, and ultimately on himself.

Thi, and sometimes Mai, marched close to him and performed the duties of host, escort and teacher. There was much to learn, so much more than they had ever told him during their geopolitical briefings in Kunming. Ho, Thi and Mai had filled his head with many of the confusions and fractions of Indochina, but they had never told him that it was also Indian country in the exact way that the U.S. once had been Indian country before it had become the U.S., when there had been Mohawks, Mohicans, Iroquois, Algonquins, Creeks, Seminoles, Sioux, Comanches, Apaches, Navajos, Zunis, Utes and hundreds of others—endless, diverse, fractious, in shifting alliances of war and peace.

Indochina was indeed Indian country, Reisman realized soon enough, but not only in the sense of danger that Ho Chi Minh had implied. It was tribal country. As they hiked east on trails through the hills, ravines and mountains, they passed through territories, hamlets and villages of the Lolo, the Man, the Tai, the Meo, the Tho, the Nung and others, while Tran Van Thi or Nguyen Thi Mai gave him the ethnographic rundown. They were none of them Viet-Namese; they were Lolo, Man, Tai, Meo, Tho, Nung and others—all separate, sometimes xenophobic, sometimes warring tribes. Most of them, Mai told him, disliked or hated the lowland Viet-Namese, to which majority group she, Ho and Thi belonged—though these same tribesmen were often cordial, even friendly and hospitable to them as individuals. Chin Li's identity, camouflaged in the costume of a *can slua tau,* was of necessity kept silently and secretly to themselves, for each of the tribes had old and ongoing animosities with Chinese of any political coloration.

Sometimes the villages they entered were only tiny clusters of three to eight dwellings made of planks, mud and thatch; sometimes they were larger groupings of twenty to thirty houses, a few more substantially built than others; some even with tile roofs that indicated the greater wealth and social position of their occupants. There was a wariness, though, upon entering some villages. Reisman could see it in the way the line of march slowed and armed scouts were sent off the trail to observe the activity in the village and come in on the flanks. It was good military procedure and he approved, but did one do that with "friends"? Sometimes they heard the banging of gongs or throbbing of drums up ahead of them, but were they sounds of welcome or warning?

"Alliances are always tenuous," Thi explained as they approached one village to the deep, reverberating clangor of brass gongs. "The Tho and the Meo, for example, are traditional enemies. West of the Sông Hong the Meo are mostly friendly to us in the Viet Minh—though they are also friendly to the French, who help them earn good money for their opium. But to the north and east of the Sông Hong and the Sông Chay the Meo often oppose us—perhaps because we are allied with the Tho, perhaps for other reasons of the moment."

Not one of the policymakers or brasshats in Washington, London, Chungking, Kunming or any other Allied headquarters had ever told Reisman about any of this. They had no idea, they were ignorant—or perhaps they didn't care! It did not fit into their sense of things. They were planning and ordering war on a global scale based on their own limited knowledge and fantasies, without knowing many of the parts of that globe, the people who lived there or the forces at work to confound them.

Fortunately, however, there were many hamlets and villages on their route where the marchers were greeted with more than courtesy and hospitality, and where Ho Chi Minh himself was greeted with homage and comradeship by village chiefs and their people.

It was late October now. In the high altitudes where they trekked, the corn, rice, vegetables, cereals and hemp harvests were long gathered, crops that had been grown on terraced fields cleared by slashing and burning patches of forest and irrigated by canals and bamboo pipes. It was the kind of cultivation, Thi remarked disparagingly, that depleted the land after a few years. Then the people moved on to new slash-and-burn sites, which they chose after proper consultation with and propitiation of the gods and spirits. The seeds of opium poppies were being planted in the same fields now, to be harvested in March, before the monsoons came. Ho Chi Minh gazed disconsolately at these fields and at the people working in them. But he kept to himself now his disapproval of the planting. He and his people had accepted food and lodging and it would have been more than unseemly—and perhaps dangerous—to insult their hosts with puritanical lectures about opium. Reisman knew about his hatred of the opium trade, but Ho was politician enough to keep his opinions to himself in these villages. He had no power to prevent it, nor could he offer any alternative way for the hill tribes to earn their living.

On the second night out they were guests in a Meo hamlet northeast of Pa Kha. It was there that Reisman began to learn and eventually see for himself that some of the Viet Minh's "friends" and "friendly villages" were gained through intimidation and terror.

Tran Van Thi could not keep his contempt for these people out of his voice. "Their language resembles the meowing of cats," he said, giving an imitation that made some of the Viet Minh laugh.

Mai gave him a severe look. "You cannot think or speak like that," she scolded, "if you expect them ever to join our cause, to be a united part of our country. You are too arrogant, Thi. They have not been fortunate enough to have your education and opportunities, but they are also people of this land we claim is ours, not Japanese or French."

Thi meowed again, wrinkling his nose afterward. "Perhaps that is why they are called Meo. But, unlike cats, who pride themselves on cleanliness, the Meo are unbelievably filthy. They believe it is unhealthy to bathe. Their houses are no better than pigsties."

The chief of the hamlet and a group of ten men, some young, some middle-aged, stood on the steep path entering the high woodland notch where their eight dwellings were clustered. Reisman, Ho and the Viet Minh scouts and guards stayed in the background and let the head porter of the Nung, who spoke Meo, palaver with the chief. The chief's name was Trang. He was a short, muscular, broad-shouldered man abouut forty years old. He wore baggy trousers, a waist-length jacket and turban, all made of homespun dyed black, and on his small feet he wore rattan sandals.

Trang greeted the people of the caravan with a dissembling smile on his face. His skin color was lighter than Reisman would have expected; his eyes were mongoloid, but the irises were a startling gray. His companions were also small, well-muscled men, dressed in similar clothes, with grim or nervous expressions on faces that ranged in color from that of Trang's to shades darker. A few had a little reddish-colored hair on their chin and upper lip, but no side whiskers.

Women and children were nowhere in sight, which was a sign that the visitors—or their hosts—were not yet to be trusted. The chief and his companions, men who belonged to the extended families of the hamlet, were obviously not happy to see the Nung and the Viet Minh stop there; but in the tradition of hospitality of the hill tribes Trang said he would turn over to his visitors his own dwelling, plus the guest house kept for that purpose.

Twilight was darkening to night. Pine torches were lit and placed in receptacles around the hamlet or held by the Meo. Some of the Nung and Viet Minh also lit torches so that they would not be at a disadvantage whatever might happen. All the buildings of the hamlet were long and low, where possible set directly on the ground, facing downhill, with rain ditches around them and stilts placed only where necessary to level the foundations. The people of the caravan split into two groups. Though there were young women with both the Nung and the Viet Minh, neither they nor the men were concerned with the problems and differences of sex.

Some of the armed Viet Minh went with the Nung porters who were assigned to the guest lodge. Reisman, Ho, Thi, Mai and the other Viet Minh were shown to Trang's house; it was a building over thirty feet long and fifteen wide, with a plank-and-thatch roof. There were two low doorways, one to the living area, an even lower one to the kitchen. The guests entered by the main doorway and everyone had to stoop to get through, passing under two wooden swords hanging on ropes.

"To keep evil spirits from entering," Mai explained softly to Reisman as he glanced up.

Reisman's nostrils filled immediately with the sooty, foul aromas of the interior. The floor was of beaten earth. There were plank partitions separating the main room, sleeping areas and kitchen. In the room where they were was an open fireplace with a blaze going; there was another open fireplace in the kitchen. Cast-iron lamps were burning. But there were no flues, no windows through which smoke might escape. It was as Thi had said: there was a layer of soot and dirt over the disarray of crude furniture, implements, possessions and people in the interior. Only toilet smells were absent. As Thi earlier had instructed Reisman, the people of all the hill tribes relieved themselves merely by wandering off into the brush, and he had only to do the same—though also to be careful where he stepped.

Trang and five of his men came into his house with their guests. The other men of the hamlet had gone to be hosts at the guest lodge. Trang paused for a few moments to make an obeisance at the simple family altar against the wall opposite the entrance. A bamboo cup on a table held sticks of incense, and he lit one and placed it in a holder. On the wall above the table were fastened some leaves, colorful strips of paper and some cock's plumes.

"They are offerings to the spirits of his ancestors," Mai explained to Reisman in a low, reverent voice. "Though I think maybe he is putting on a show for us."

Trang turned away from the altar and seated his visitors on low stools, benches and mats around a low table. Mai sat on the bench to Reisman's right, Thi to the left on a stool. Trang brought out earthenware jars, inserted bamboo drinking tubes and passed the jars around with ceremonial gestures and words. Reisman sipped a potent liquor made from corn. Ho Chi Minh barely wet his lips with the stuff, smiled diplomatically at Trang and passed the jug along. Mai, who nearly gagged on the liquor, told Reisman that it was an unusual honor for a woman to be served with the males in this way.

The uncertainty and tension eased a bit more when three Meo women entered the house to prepare the evening meal, and the sounds of children were heard playing outside. The women wore blouses, skirts, aprons, turbans and leggings, but their costumes were more stylish than their men's and were colorfully appliquéd and embroidered. Mai leaned close to Reisman and said, "I think this is very unusual, that they should allow their women to show themselves before strangers. Perhaps it is their way of saying they really do want to be friends."

Thi leaned over from the other side of Reisman and said, "Or a sly way to get us to trust them—to drop our guard."

"Yes, that too is possible," Mai agreed. Then she raised her brows in a comic look of awe and whispered, "I think that two or three of these women are married to Mr. Trang."

Reisman made a wry expression with his mouth, then grinned and said, "Must be a hell of a guy!"

"It is the custom, if one can afford it," said Mai. But Reisman could tell that she disapproved.

Dinner was rice, corn, vegetables and pork. They ate with chopsticks and wooden spoons, and drank water and more corn liquor. The serving of meat was in itself an honor, for Thi remarked that it was usually eaten only for festivals and special occasions. Ho insisted on paying for the food and drink that so large a group of unexpected guests there and in the visitors' lodge had consumed. Trang politely refused the required number of times and then accepted the Indochinese paper currency that was proffered. If it had been gold or silver, Ho was sure the man would have taken it more quickly.

Neither the chief's house nor the guest lodge were large enough to accommodate everyone in the caravan comfortably. For Reisman, and some of the others too, the thought of spending the night within the confines of the filthy, malodorous houses was unpleasant to contemplate. A nightwatch schedule was set. Many of the Nung and Viet Minh merely rolled up in blankets on the ground outside next to the campfires that were kept burning through the night—to dissuade intrusions by such exotic and unwanted wildlife as tigers and elephants, which were among the beasts inhabiting these same hills of northern Tonkin.

When they went outside again, Reisman offered Ho a cigarette. He took it and inhaled deeply. Reisman had noticed early on that smoking appeared to be Ho's only vice and that he much preferred American brands to the foul, stinging smokes of Chinese or other Asian manufacture. Thi and Mai smoked also, but not as heavily; they declined Reisman's cigarettes now, perhaps still suffocated by the smoke and smells of Trang's house. Reisman had made certain that there were plenty of American cigarettes in the truck.

It was almost incongruous, then, when Ho said, "We are lucky to have dined so well tonight in Viet-Nam. In other parts of Tonkin, in the lowlands in particular, there is much famine. My people are dying of starvation, thousands of them."

Reisman expected it was the prelude to another anti-French tirade. "Why?" he said. "These people up here seem to be doing all right under rather primitive conditions."

"Typhoons did terrible damage. Many dikes in the lowlands which protect the rice paddies and farms were destroyed. There was much flooding and loss of crops. The Japs and French have hoarded in their warehouses whatever food and rice they could find. Prices have soared beyond reach, yet they continue to speculate instead of allowing the Viet-Namese to eat. My people become weak and sick and die."

Was it true, Reisman wondered, or was it more of the same sort of propaganda Ho had been feeding him since they met? "Why didn't you report it in Kunming?" he asked. "We might have tried to organize some kind of food drop."

"Not until we crossed the frontier was I told how severe it had become," Ho answered.

Reisman nodded. "We'll let Kunming know, but not until we reach your headquarters. We're too vulnerable out here. I won't transmit yet, but let's go see what kind of traffic is on the radio. What I want to do tonight is show you how to eavesdrop on Jap and French transmissions. That's one way you can learn where enemy troops are, and where they're going. When you put different signals together you can figure out what's happening. Research and analysis, that's all it is. Then you figure out if you've got the strength to take action or should fade away for another day."

Ho smiled. "That is what we've been doing for many years, *Jean*. It is the fading-away part that I no longer like very much."

They got the rucksacks containing the radios from the Nung bearers who had been carrying them and took them to a clearing away from the houses. The separate hand-cranked generators for each transmitter-receiver were heavier than the radios themselves. A second man was needed to carry them and to turn the crank at a fast, constant rate in order to generate electricity while the operator was tuning, listening, speaking or working the key.

The second radio had a different purpose and capacity from the one Reisman had brought to the house in Kunming. Its range was not as far, but it could receive and transmit voice as well as Morse code. What OSS wanted in Indochina was another good listening post. Reisman set up both radios for demonstration purposes, though he intended only to listen and not transmit. He gave the ends of the long antennae to two of Ho's younger men and directed them to climb two trees and loop the antennae as high up as they would reach.

Chin Li, with apparent approval, observed all the activity with an occasional remark in Chinese to Ho. A couple of Viet Minhs got on the hand-cranks and soon had both receivers humming. Any of the Meo or Nung who tried to come close were ordered away. This was considered to be private and sacrosanct business.

Reisman swept the band on the longer-range Morse receiver. He found some clear transmissions, but nothing he could understand right away. He quickly wrote down on a pad some of the sequences of dots and dashes, but none of it made any sense to him. The signals were probably cryptograms, and he couldn't tell if they were French, Japanese, English or even Chinese. Without the decoding counterpart of the encoding cipher he would not have been able to translate the sounds into military intelligence anyway, even if he had known what language was being used. He passed the notepad around. Both Ho and Thi knew Morse, but they could not make anything out of the random signals either.

Reisman began working with the voice receiver and showed them how to search out and lock onto military frequencies used by the Japanese and French. Between waves of crackling static he began to pick up urgent voices in each language. He heard a French officer in Bac Quang giving route directions and orders of battle to a patrol in the field.

"Check the coordinates on your map, Thi," Reisman said with quickening interest. "This one sounds close enough to concern us."

The others in the group who understood French leaned close, and now they all clearly heard orders to intercept infiltrators from China trying to slip east through the mountains.

"That, in itself, is not unusual," said Thi softly, looking at his map. "There is always movement back and forth across the border and the military occupiers or the police pursue them. Sometimes escapees, sometimes those returning like us. More often traders and smugglers—contraband of one sort or another—or opium, which both the Japs and French understand, as long as the right people are paid."

Reisman made a gesture for silence as a transmission came on the air from the patrol's field radio back to its base headquarters, giving their location and status.

"Yes, they are close to us," said Thi, looking up from his map. "Less than fifteen miles away and moving in this direction. If they are coming here they could be here in four or five hours."

"Less than that, maybe," Reisman muttered.

He did not believe in chance—though he recognized that one had to take advantage of it where it existed. He did believe in the order of things. One made preparations for contingencies and conditions, one tried to stay a jump ahead or be skillful enough to parry an unexpected thrust. Tonight he was listening to the radio because it fit into the proper order of things to do; and because of that, perhaps he and his companions would gain a sharp edge on those *others* and thereby live through the following day.

Then a Japanese voice came on the same frequency. Ho understood some Japanese, but two men in his band of Viet Minh who were fluent in it listened carefully and translated into Viet-Namese. Ho in his turn translated into English for Reisman. The infiltrators were reported to be in a Meo village to the northeast of Nam Ric.

"That sounds like it could be us," said Reisman.

Now another voice in Japanese came on the air. This one was a transmission back to base from the patrol. It confirmed to a Japanese commander what had already been reported to the French commander.

"It is us," said Ho grimly. "The Japanese even know the name of the headman. The French gave it to them."

"Trang?"

"Yes. We are betrayed," Ho replied. There was a deep sadness in his voice and on his countenance that such a thing had been done—and now had to be dealt with. "They know we are here in this village. While he entertained us at dinner, Trang must have sent a man to the nearest French outpost."

What Reisman and Ho finally put together from the intercepted radio messages in the two languages was that there was a combined Japanese-French patrol of approximately twenty soldiers under joint command hiking west in the darkness along the same trail that Ho's group would travel at dawn. The patrol was under orders to arrest the infiltrators, to take them captive while they slept, if possible, or to kill them if they resisted.

"The Japanese no longer leave these matters entirely to the French," said Ho. "They trust them less and less, particularly since your liberation of Metropolitan France. They are afraid of an Allied landing here in collusion with the *colons;* perhaps a combined attack from the sea and from China. The French, however, are more concerned, as always, about Viet-Namese who want to throw off their yoke."

Ho paused a moment. The light of the pine torches illuminated his face as he stared at Reisman. "So, *mon commandant,* what would you do now?" There was a vivaciousness in his voice, a note of challenge. "Fade away or attack?"

"Ambush them," said Reisman.

"*Très bien*. It is exactly what I would do. And it is Trang and his men who will help us. They are very good at this sort of thing."

At first it was Ho Chi Minh himself who took command. He did not defer to Reisman or even ask questions, and Reisman had the opportunity to observe him in a military crisis—though, given the choice, he himself would just as soon have done without it. Then, after a little while, Reisman saw that it was Tran Van Thi who was conveying the actual instructions to the Viet Minh, the Nung and the Meo; Ho was now in charge of the operation's overall strategy, while Thi, the executive officer, saw that his orders were carried out.

Those of the Viet Minh who were to have had later watches were roused from their sleep and the new situation was explained to them. The men of the hamlet were rounded up and brought into Trang's house under heavy guard. The women and children were placed under guard in the guest lodge.

Crates of the new weapons and ammunition were opened and the contents distributed. Guns were cleaned and loaded. Most of the group, Reisman was glad to see, were familiar with the new weapons. Those who weren't turned to their companions or to him for quick instruction. He was also surprised to see that Mai also showed a certain familiarity with the handling of weapons. She cleaned and loaded a .45 automatic and tightened the belt and holster around her waist over her shapeless *can slua tau* jacket. Then she slipped a clip into a freshly cleaned carbine, checked the chamber and safety, and slung it over her shoulder.

"We, with Uncle Ho, are a cadre and we have been fortunate to have a certain amount of training," she explained when Reisman went to help her. "Though there is much that I am sure you can teach us—many who have had no training whom you will be able to help."

The four women of the group who had come to the border as scouts and guards were also well armed now. Along with Mai, their assignment was to stay in the village with the Nung porters to guard the remaining matériel.

"If it goes badly for us," Thi told Mai, "I will send someone in time to warn you. You and the Nung must then vanish from here. Our comrades"—he nodded to the other women—"know other ways to reach Cao Bang. It is your responsibility to see that what is left here of our new arms and matériel reaches our friends there."

The chief porter of the Nungs was told of the plans and agreed to them readily; he and his people had no wish to be involved in the events of the next few hours. Chin Li, however, the Chinese guest from the north, took charge of one of the B.A.R.s. He insisted that he was not there merely to observe but also to share the dangers of the attack with his comrades.

Reisman said, in Mandarin which he realized was inadequate, "I surmise that you know how to use this gun and that you will require no instruction."

Chin Li leaned forward with a quizzical expression on his face. The phrasing of the question had indeed been stilted, perhaps even rude, but he made allowances. Ho quickly leaped in to translate and Chin Li smiled. "Yes, I have had some experience," he said. Reisman understood that clearly.

Ho interposed his own explanation. "In his army, Mr. Chin holds a rank comparable to yours. He is a man of many years of experience and many battles."

When he entered the headman's house again, Ho did not reveal to Trang that he knew of his treachery. He merely stopped using the deferential tone of a guest to a host. Under the Viet Minh's guns, Trang and his ten men were made to cooperate in all that followed.

There were twenty men in Ho's attack group: Reisman, Ho, Thi, Chin and sixteen Viet Minh troops. They were enough to assure that the Meo would do what was wanted of them, and they had enough firepower to ambush the enemy patrol successfully or even to defeat them head on, if it came to that.

Before they left the hamlet, however, Thi tried to talk Ho into staying behind with the women and the porters. He spoke in Viet-Namese. "We cannot risk letting anything happen to you," he said anxiously.

Ho smiled at him indulgently, then rejected the suggestion sharply. "It is required now that I go where my troops and our friends are so willing to go. I risk the same as you do. I am neither irreplaceable nor infallible, Thi," he said with quiet determination.

What the Meo were particularly good at, Reisman learned in the next two hours, was setting snares and traps and making camouflaged *punji* pits. They were not allowed to take any weapons other than the poisoned spikes for the *punjis* and the crossbows, arrows, spring devices and lines used to make their deadly mantraps. Before taking Trang and his men down the trail from the hamlet, Thi warned them, speaking in a mixture of Viet-Namese and Meo, that if one of them dared to use any of these implements against the Viet Minh, made any hostile move or tried to escape, the entire group would be slaughtered and the Viet Minh would return to the hamlet and kill all the women and children also. When Mai grimly, almost nervously, translated these words for him, Reisman felt that it was no idle threat. He remembered the look of the fanatic he had perceived in Thi when he first met him in the arid garden of the house in Kunming.

The enemy patrol moved badly, as if they were unchallengeable masters of the land and the night. They chattered, cursed, laughed and let their equipment bounce and rattle. Reisman heard them coming a quarter mile away. He and four Viets were in cover on the hillside above the trail where the patrol would pass. The place selected for the ambuscade was about a mile east of the hamlet. Reisman and the four Viets were a hundred yards further on, where the trail first became much wider, opening into a glenlike pass that invited soldiers to halt for a rest or to bunch up to cross. Only after the Meo had set their snares and traps and made their camouflaged *punji* pits had he been asked for his advice regarding the disposition of troops and firepower.

He had suggested taking the Meo a short way off into the hills and tying and gagging them, which had been done. Then he had suggested a position for Chin and his B.A.R. and the other two B.A.R.s, which had met with Chin's approval; and where to locate the three men with the M-3 submachine guns and where to set up the skirmish line of riflemen.

His own assignment, with the four Viets, was to come down onto the trail behind the enemy patrol and block their escape. Now he watched their dim shapes pass through the darkness below him and move on toward the ambush. Then he signaled to his companions and the five of them silently descended and followed.

In two minutes, Reisman heard the first screams of fear and pain as men of the enemy patrol dropped through the mats and dirt hiding the *punji* pits and were impaled on the poisoned spikes; others were pierced at chest height by arrows sprung from crossbows they had triggered by jostling a bush or breaking a thin tendril bent across their path.

The Viet Minh held their fire for about fifteen seconds, time enough to let terror, confusion and panic take possession of the Japanese and French soldiers milling around. Reisman heard shouts and orders in both languages. Then the fusillade began, a murderous, relentless firing into the darkness where darker shapes and sounds of voices revealed frightened, disoriented targets.

Reisman and the four Viets darted forward, crouched low. They moved as close as they could to the point of ambush without coming into the crossfire of their own men. They hit the ground with their weapons aimed up the trail, but there was no need to fire; no one came toward them or fired in their direction.

It was over in minutes. There had been no time for the patrol to set up a defense, hardly time to do more than return a few ineffective answering shots. Then all movement and counterfire from the patrol ceased and Reisman heard Thi shout an order that silenced the Viet-

Namese guns too, making the sounds of the surviving enemy more audible: guttural yells, a voice or two of suicidal fury and hatred at the unknown, and moans and whimperings of pain.

It had been, once again, an execution, thought Reisman. He took no pride in it. He heard Thi's voice calling out in French for the survivors to throw down their weapons, raise their hands and stand if they were able to, then to move into the open glen where they could be seen. One of the Viets repeated the orders in Japanese. Five figures moved in the darkness, three standing up with arms raised in surrender, two crawling forward slowly, obviously wounded. Reisman started to move closer to get a better look at the enemy. But in the next instant, before he could intercede, two of the Viet Minh stepped to point-blank range of the prisoners and fired their submachine guns in short bursts. In seconds, five victims were sprawled torn, bleeding and dead at their executioners' feet.

Reisman went close and stared at the faces and uniforms of the newly dead. He was swept by feelings of anger and revulsion at the senseless carnage. Two were Japanese, two were native Indochinese in the uniforms of the colonial army, one was a middle-aged Frenchman whose uniform bore the insignia of a sergeant. It was toward him that Reisman felt closest. How many years of military service had he given, how many battles might he have fought, to finally come to this end?

Reisman turned in fury upon Ho Chi Minh, who came up silently from the background. "This is murder, not war," Reisman accused, in a voice filled with contempt.

"They have done worse to my people," replied Ho.

"Some of them *are* your people."

"That is the sad part," said Ho.

Their dialogue was interrupted by new gunfire. Reisman whirled around with his own M-3 at the ready, and saw then that more of the patrol, perhaps wounded and unconscious, perhaps trying to hide, had been slaughtered.

He felt suddenly drained of all the self-righteous anger and compassion he had been feeling. He walked away from Ho, gripping the M-3 so tightly that his hands ached. He stared around the ambush scene, moved slowly among all the other corpses the Viets now lifted and brought together, and was left only with a residue of bitter sadness. Why had he felt differently about this carnage from the way he had after what they had done at the château at Rennes—or, more recently, as an interloper in the attack on Caojian?

No, he protested to himself, Rennes had been different. That had been a motivated assault against evil that he hated, and it had been a battle against heavy odds, not a massacre. Here, in the wilderness of a country he did not even know, against soldiers he had not yet learned to hate, there was still no bloodlust; the cause was still not his, as it had not been at Caojian. The doing itself was his way of life.

He watched as the Viets scavenged the bodies and battleground for arms, ammunition and equipment. The patrol's field radio and generator was still in their rucksacks. The attack had been so swift and unexpected they had not had time to contact their base at Bac Quang.

Thi came up to Reisman. "Now you see yourself what we are capable of doing, Major," he said rapidly in an excited voice. "Ten Japs, a French lieutenant and sergeant and eight Viet-Namese traitors. A good night's work, *n'est-ce pas?*"

"*Au contraire*—a bad night's work," muttered Reisman. "You are a fool, Thi. It was overkill. No finesse. You would have been better off taking prisoners."

"What would we have done with them? They would have slowed us down, created problems."

"Interrogate them. Gather military intelligence. Find out more about your enemies. Be able to plan your operations with less risk. That's what you and your gentle Uncle Ho could have done with them," Reisman declared angrily. "It is what we prefer in our friends and allies. Not butchers! How do you plan to hide twenty corpses? Dead, they are a liability to you. They advertise your ignorance and savagery. A few of them left alive, treated well, would have given you a bargaining position for something or someone you might want." In a voice of controlled anger and filled with pointed irony, he added, "They might even have spoken well of your courage and cunning in battle, your humility in victory, your kindness and humanity. The kind of strength and respect Gandhi has earned in India."

Tran Van Thi was startled by Reisman's vehemence. He had expected the American to be pleased by simple victory.

"The Meo will bury the dead in places where they will not be found," he answered civilly. "We will get them right now and begin. They will do it willingly. They will cover up for us, as you Americans say, because they know it will go very badly for them with the French and Japs if their part in this is ever discovered."

"I suggest you get a couple of your men down the trail a few miles," Reisman told him. "I'm going back to the village to tune in the radio again. They'll be out looking for these guys in a few hours."

"We will move quickly," acknowledged Thi. "We will not have the luxury of sleep tonight."

Reisman took with him one of the Viets who was fluent in Japanese. Mai was very relieved to see them when they trotted back to the hamlet. She had heard the sounds of the battle, she told Reisman, and had been tempted to go forward to see what was happening, but had followed her orders and stayed there.

"It went too well," Reisman said shortly. "Twenty to nothing for our side. Let's get on the radio and see what else we can find out."

"Where are the others? Where is Uncle Ho?" she asked anxiously.

"Burying the dead. Hiding the evidence."

Mai looked confused by his caustic words and attitude. She had expected him to be pleased, or at least relieved. He didn't bother to explain. One of the Nung ran the antenna wire up into a tree while another got the generator going, and Reisman tuned in to the same frequency that had warned them of impending danger hours earlier.

A number of times he heard the Jap and French commanders in Bac Quang trying to raise their patrol. Then the officers must have retired and left radio operators to do the job for the rest of the night. The voices became different ones, less urgent and authoritative. Reisman moved to other frequencies to see if he could pick up anything of interest. Nothing. He went back to the Bac Quang frequency and noted that the transmissions were going out about every ten minutes. He was exhausted now, didn't give a damn if anybody else slept but knew that he needed to for at least a couple of hours or he would be worthless on the march the next day.

"Can you run this thing yourselves?" he asked Mai and the Viet who understood Japanese.

They said they could. Reisman pointed to the Nung who was turning the generator handle. "Better get someone to replace him soon. That's wearing work. I'm going to get some shuteye. I'll be ready to move out when your boys get back. We should try to be well on the way before daybreak."

He looked in on the Meo women and children in the guest lodge. Most of them were asleep but a few were awake and nervous. They threw him anxious, hateful glances. Two of the armed Viet Minh girls were guarding them while the other two slept.

"Tell them their men are all right," Reisman ordered one of the girls, speaking French.

She made the announcement in Viet-Namese and the Meo women must have understood, because it seemed to soothe them, especially the two or three whom Reisman recognized as Trang's wives. He walked to the headman's house where he'd stowed his blanket and the rest of his gear. Empty of people, with the cookfires barely going, the interior seemed less smelly and more appealing as a place to sleep. He found a sleeping mat, dragged it into a far corner and curled up in his blanket on top of it, facing the low main doorway, his .45 in his hand.

He fell asleep immediately and when he woke did not know at first if it had been only a few minutes or the two hours it actually was. There was a shout, a scream and then the sound of women keening. He threw off the blanket and aimed his pistol at the doorway. There was no one there. He holstered the pistol, grabbed his M-3 and moved quickly through the kitchen to the other low doorway. Bending down, he flattened himself against the wall and peered through the opening. The blackness of night had softened into the beginning grayness of dawn, though pine torches still burned outside. He saw the men, women and children of the hamlet standing together in a loose semi-circular formation, their backs toward him. Beyond them in another formation stood the Viet Minh and the Nung, and all of them were staring at something on the ground between the two groups. The keening continued, but there were no sounds of violence. Around the keening there was only a silence of fear and awe.

Reisman stooped low and went through the doorway to the outside. Still holding his submachine gun as if he were about to use it, he walked slowly and softly to a place where he could see around the Meo villagers to what they were staring at. What he saw there on the ground chilled him. The keening came from the three women of Trang's household, collapsed in the dirt with their weeping, terrified children around them. Close by was what remained of Trang himself.

His body was naked to the waist, belly down in the blood-soaked dirt. His bare arms were bound behind him above the elbows with rope that cut into his flesh. His head was almost severed from his neck; it was twisted, gaping away from him, connected only by thin bits of tendon and skin and soaked in gore that covered his chin, mouth and nose. His dead eyes were half open, as if he'd observed his own beheading with only partial curiosity. The sword that had been used to decapitate him—perhaps one of his own weapons—lay on the ground close to him, the blade wet with his blood.

Who had done this? Which of them had swung the sword through Trang's neck? Had one of the Viet Minh troops obediently carried out an order? Or had Thi, in his mania, done the deed himself? Not Uncle Ho. Of that he was certain. Ho might have given the order or permitted it to be given, but Reisman could not picture him as the actual executioner. He could not tell who it might have been now. The Nung stood together in one group, the Viet Minh in another, as if they and the Meo formed the sides of a military parade ground where a punishment had been meted out.

The bloodlust and murder he had participated in that night had almost inured Reisman to feeling. He stared at the scene as if it were something natural, to be expected in this place. He heard Ho Chi Minh speaking and looked toward him.

"There was a trial while you slept. We did not want to disturb you."

Reisman walked toward Ho, staring down again at the butchered Trang and then into the faces of Ho and the rest of the Viet Minh.

"What was he convicted of?" Reisman asked softly.

Tran Van Thi stepped forward as if to block an attack against his leader, and he took upon himself the onus of what had been done.

"Crimes against the people," he declared, his voice unwavering in its self-righteousness.

Reisman sought out the face of Nguyen Thi Mai among the Viet Minh. He saw her staring at the ground beside her feet, denying the horror a few yards away. He walked closer to her and she raised her eyes to him.

"Why so cruel?" he asked. "Why not just shoot him?"

Mai stared at him impassively now, unwilling to reveal in voice or manner whether she believed in what she was saying or not. "The punishment is more effective this way," she replied. "They believe that when the head is cut off the spirit escapes and is condemned to wander lost forever more. It is a more terrifying lesson for others."

Reisman turned away from her, shaking his head. He looked once more at the corpse and then toward Ho and Thi. "We'd better get the hell out of here fast," he muttered, "or we'll all wind up under a French guillotine. They will come looking for their patrol soon."

His words broke the morbid spell that held them. Thi shouted at the Nung and Viets to get ready to move out and the porters, guards and scouts immediately began taking up their cargo, packs and weapons. To Reisman, Thi said, "We will take a different trail to Cao Bang. It will be harder and take a little longer, but they will not find us."

Ho stepped closer to Reisman. "A Japanese spy," he declared, dismissing the corpse with disdain. "There will never be another one in this village again."

Reisman stared at the man coldly. Did Ho really dare to think he was that naïve? "He was no more a Jap spy—or even a French spy—than you are," he said defiantly. Trang and his people had merely wanted to be left alone. The label of spy was both too simplistic and too sophisticated. That Trang had sent word about the Viet Minh to the French, trying to ingratiate himself where he believed the power and his best interests lay, had been a fatal error in judgement.

"These people here—" Reisman began. He gestured to Trang's widows, weeping near his corpse in the dirt, and to the terrified villagers huddled together. "They will be justified now in telling the French and Japs everything that happened and who is responsible."

"If they do," said Ho, with a look of cunning satisfaction on his face, "then the French and Japs will see that it was the Meo who made the things that trapped and wounded their men before the bullets killed them. They will be very mad. They will take revenge on this village. Perhaps that will turn the other Meo villages and the other simple people to our cause."

"But it is you who executed Trang for trying to help the French and the Japs," Reisman said heatedly. "The people of the village will explain that. The French and Japs will see it for themselves."

"The people will not be believed. They never are," said Ho, with a distant look in his eyes.

Minutes later, the column cleared the hamlet, moving north instead of directly east; and Reisman knew that the cauldron he had helped to bubble again was one that would be almost inexplicable to the men who had tossed him into the pot.

Chapter 18

They entered the region of Cao Bang on the fourth day. Tran Van Thi fell back in the line of march and informed Reisman confidently, "We are in the liberated zone! The Viet Minh controls the villages here. We have replaced the colonial rule with our own," he said proudly, "and the people are at last free and happy."

In Kunming that would be surprising news, Reisman knew—as it would also likely be in Tokyo; and in Paris, London and Washington, where knowledge of what was happening in the mountains of Tonkin was almost nil and not considered of much importance. He wondered if even the ubiquitous spy network of Tai Li had carried this news to Chungking. He also wondered if it were true.

"What does that mean, Thi?" he demanded. He remembered too vividly how Trang had been replaced.

Thi ran on cheerfully like a chamber-of-commerce booster. "Their taxes are lower, their education better and their livelihoods more secure. They are able to keep much more of the food they grow, the things they make and the earnings of their labor."

"Ho told me a few days ago that your people were starving to death by the thousands," Reisman said.

"In the lowlands, because of the typhoon and because the French and Japs have locked up all the food in their warehouses. Here in Cao Bang everything is much better."

"What about security and defenses?"

"We are protected here. Unless the enemy moves in massive force, which they are not prepared to do, they would not dare to come here to attack us."

They trekked further east in the next few hours. Lookouts hailed them and joined the column. Reading his maps, the sun and his compass, Reisman saw that they were almost up at the Chinese border again, one hundred and fifty miles east of where they had crossed into Indochina. The area they were in had not been adequately surveyed. RELIEF DATA INCOMPLETE appeared frequently on the maps, as did the word KARST, the geological term for regions of limestone formations, sinks, ravines and underground streams. The wind blew softly at that season, neither warm nor cold; the air was clean, filled with the scent of trees and shrubs and the sound of birdsong.

In the late afternoon, near the village of Pac Bo, they reached the headquarters camp and training base of the Viet Minh set amid limestone caves and high jungle thickets. There were forests on the upper reaches, and freshwater streams running nearby, and the caves had been furnished as living quarters, workrooms, factories and meeting chambers. As a redoubt, it was a good choice.

Waiting for them in a small meadow were a reception committee and a company of about two hundred Viet Minh soldiers carrying a variety of arms, drawn up on parade for inspection, some in uniforms like Thi's, others in the indigo jackets and trousers of the *can slua tau.* Standing with others in front of the troops was a sad-looking little man in a baggy white suit and a Borsalino hat. To Reisman he looked too young and slight and insignificant to be anything but a curiously well-dressed civilian visitor, perhaps with some minor commercial or bureaucratic connection.

Ho Chi Minh, who was walking some thirty yards ahead of Reisman in the column, halted before the waiting committee and troops and shouted a greeting in Viet-Namese, to which they replied en masse. The man in the Borsalino hat embraced him and they spoke privately for a few moments. Then Ho turned to Reisman and Chin Li and extended his arm in a gesture that invited them forward.

Speaking French in a bantering tone, Ho introduced the man first to Reisman. "May I present to you Mr. Vo Nguyen Giap, commanding officer of our armed forces. We are not sure yet what his rank should be. Perhaps a corporal—perhaps a general. It depends, I suppose, on how well he does in the job."

Giap did not smile at the joke. He listened attentively as Ho continued, "Giap, you see, was educated to be a schoolteacher, as I was myself." Then, with a bit of a flourish, Ho said, "Major *Jean* Reisman of the United States Army."

Giap examined Reisman with eyes that were dark and sad and unwavering. The face was smooth and youthful, the mouth sensual, but his expression was one of great weariness and there was something ancient and all-knowing about his eyes.

"Would you care to inspect the troops?" he asked, speaking French. But without waiting for a reply he turned immediately to Chin Li. They spoke the Canton dialect to each other and seemed comfortable in it. From the little he was able to pick up Reisman gathered that they had met before and shared important memories.

Giap turned and snapped out commands to his troops, who came to attention and presented arms. Then he led Reisman, Chin Li and Ho up and down the ranks of soldiers. They were short, lean, hungry-looking men, and every now and then Reisman realized that the man he was glancing at was actually a girl. He took particular note of the international variety of weapons—everything from old U.S. Springfields and German Mausers through modern Jap, French, Chinese, German and American rifles, pistols and submachine guns. Some of them had no guns at all.

Reisman had come to the end of one rank and was about to turn down another when he caught sight of Nguyen Thi Mai moving away from the welcoming ceremony toward a man who had just come out of a thatched hut and was walking toward her with a big smile on his face. He was Asian, though Reisman would no longer presume to guess which nationality. He greeted Mai with an embrace, a kiss and—thinking they were unobserved—a caress of her hips and derrière that brought a quick smile to her face, and to Reisman it hinted of old and mutual past pleasure, perhaps to be resumed.

When the inspection was over and the troops dispersed, Mai and her friend started toward Reisman. They were still a short distance away when Tran Van Thi hurried up to them and spoke a few words. The other man listened courteously, looked toward Reisman and shrugged off whatever Thi said to him. Then, smiling confidently, he came over to Reisman with Mai, who looked a bit shy, though not worried.

He was tall for an Oriental, slender and handsome. There was an incongruous look about him. His clothes—gray flannel slacks, dark blue polo shirt, sweater, white bucks—seemed much more suited to an American country club or a garden party of British colonials than to a Viet Minh encampment in the mountains of Tonkin.

"This is—" began Mai.

But the man interrupted her quickly and loudly. "Haro!" he said.

Reisman wasn't sure he had heard right. "Haro?"

"You got it," said the man in unaccented American English. "Haro. Like in 'Haro, how are you?' " he added, mocking a Japanese accent.

"Is that short for Harold?"

"No. Just plain simple Haro—until we get to know each other better."

"You sound like an American."

"But I don't look like one?"

"I wasn't expecting one here."

Mai, nervously following the repartee, blurted out something strange to Reisman's ears. It sounded like "*Keee—*," then she strangled it in mid-vowel and said, "Haro, this is the American observer, Major Reisman—John Reisman."

They shook hands. Just a nice cordial clasp. Neither trying to demonstrate how strong he was. Haro was playing a game with him but wasn't winning any points—so Reisman, feeling no threat yet, was willing to let it go on until Haro or Mai either put him in the picture or explained the rules.

"Just think of me as one of the boys for now," said Haro, gesturing around to the Viets. "By the way, who won the USC–UCLA game this year?"

Reisman stared at him uncertainly. "I don't know."

Haro snapped his fingers in a damn-it motion, as if the football score was the most important piece of intelligence Reisman could have brought him from the outside world. "Hey, I ought to congratulate you, anyway. Your team made a touchdown a few days ago. You may not have heard about it while you were on the road."

"My team? I don't have any team."

"Sure you do. Army and Navy played on the same side for a

change last week. First-team stuff. Landed a whole damn army on Leyte. Beat the shit out of the Japs there. Next game is Luzon, I figure . . . all the way to Manila. What do you know about it, Johnny?"

That "Johnny" brought Reisman up sharply. He was not used to being called Johnny by anyone except old and close friends. "It's news to me," he said.

"Well, MacArthur said he'd be back, and it's no surprise to me. What brings you out this way anyway, Major?"

"Just a tourist. How about you?"

Mai, who had been looking from one to the other as the dialogue bounded back and forth, piped up, "Haro's an adviser!"

"About what?" asked Reisman.

"International relations," Haro answered.

"To whom?"

"I'm trying to keep Mr. Ho and his people out of trouble."

"Who are you with? State?"

"More of a free lance now, I think. My bosses don't agree on which way to go, so I'm just figuring things out for myself."

"Sounds like what I have to do sometimes. Though I think we're working at cross-purposes now. I want Ho to stir up trouble, not stay out of it."

"I figured that was what you were here for," said Haro in a tone of good-humored disapproval.

"Who *are* you working for, Haro?" Reisman pressed.

Haro wagged a cautionary finger and smiled. "My secret for now, Major. Information on a need-to-know basis. You *do* understand." He extended his hand again and Reisman shook it. Letting go, Haro said, "We will have lots to talk about, I'm sure, Major."

Reisman didn't know what to make of the man—except that he was not to be trusted. He was suddenly struck by what he both liked and didn't like about the man: he was too much like himself. That relaxed air of self-assurance and superiority . . . a bit too cocky, a tendency to hide tension, uncertainty, even anger, in badinage that gave one time to jockey for position and strength.

He was watching Mai and Haro walk across the field toward one of the thatch-roofed huts, wrapped in their conversation, when Thi came to take charge of him and give him a tour of the base before nightfall.

"Who is that man, Thi?" he asked.

"A friend of the Viet Minh."

"What kind of friend? From where? Doing what?"

"An adviser," Thi replied. "Beyond that there are things which it is better for you not to inquire about too closely for now. He is no danger to you, as you must not be to him."

Reisman got through to Kunming on the Morse transmitter that first night in Pac Bo. He ran the radio in the small bamboo-and-thatch hut—not far from Mai's—they had given him as his personal quarters. Two Viet radio trainees took turns on the generator for their first lesson. As arranged, an operator in the radio shack at Kunming airfield was standing by for his signal and acknowledged it. Reisman encoded his message to Sam Kilgore using a one-time cipher pad matched by an identical one in Kunming. He told Sam they had arrived safely but said nothing about the action along the trail. If there was a leak in the intelligence network, he reasoned, let that bit of dirty business be blamed on somebody else. He didn't want the Japs or any of the conflicting French splinter groups to be certain who was responsible for the ambush. It was the same attitude, he supposed, as the guy who had sent the unmarked bomber after Linc Bradford and the Kachins. In continued deference to Ho, Reisman did not tell Sam the location of the Viet base. He did report, however, what Ho had told him about famine in the lowlands of Tonkin. He also described the man calling himself Haro and asked Kilgore if he knew what agency he worked for.

Two nights later Kilgore replied that he didn't know who Haro was but that he might be a Chinese-American civilian named Jimmy Lum. Reisman remembered that during one of his early briefings in Kunming he had been told that one of the most effective intelligence networks in Indochina was run by a bunch of civilians—a Canadian, an American and a Chinese-American—all of whom used to work for an oil company in Saigon and had established contacts and listening posts throughout the country. Kilgore also signaled that the famine report had been relayed to higher Allied headquarters for possible action. He wanted Reisman to continue to report on the economic, social and political conditions he observed, as well as the military. Reisman couldn't help wondering if Sam was reminding him to keep an eye out for private trading opportunities or was ordering him into new areas of official business. In either case he didn't feel qualified.

Next day he began to train a class of ten Viets, three of them girls, in Morse code and in how to use the radio equipment—both what he had brought in from Kunming and the Jap stuff they had captured from the bushwhacked enemy patrol. Thi had selected for him only trainees who spoke French as well as Viet-Namese. A few of them also knew Japanese and would be able to monitor enemy broadcasts. Reisman met with them in his hut a couple of times a day. The rest of the time, while they were practicing their dah-dit-dahs on the key, he had free run of the camp.

Occasionally he crossed paths with Chin Li. They sometimes observed activities together or exchanged comments, but since they really weren't playing on the same team they remained independent. Reisman was tempted to ask if Chin knew anything about Haro, but doubted he would tell if he did. Haro seemed to have disappeared from camp after a few days, though before that he had noticed him slipping in and out of Mai's hut.

"Where is your friend?" he finally asked her.

"He went to Hanoi on business," she replied warily.

He wondered if she was mocking him. He used "on business" himself in reference to his missions. Haro—or Jimmy Lum, if that was who he really was—was apparently off on his own "business."

When he wasn't wandering around the camp on his own, Reisman was sometimes accompanied by Ho, Thi, Mai or Giap, who would explain some aspect of the routines and facilities, the training program, or the Viet Minh's ways and means of governing in the "liberated zone."

Giap spoke to him in French as they watched a demonstration put on for his benefit. In the forest, small, darting figures emerged from tunneled blinds that he had not seen; they fired old rifles and new submachine guns at cardboard targets towed along a trail and then moments later disappeared again into their dugouts without leaving a trace. Reisman admired how cleverly the Viets made use of natural assets and limited arms and matériel in moving, hiding and fighting, tactics he had already witnessed during their trek across northern Tonkin. It was Giap the former teacher, now the military commander, who had devised what and how to teach the raw recruits.

"We now have the capacity to turn out forty trained guerrilla fighters a week," he said proudly.

Reisman looked at him and smiled. "That doesn't go very far, does it? One well placed mortar round and you're liable to lose half your army."

Yet he began to feel a military man's empathy for them. They were doing something for themselves with whatever they had to work with. He and the men who came from England—if they volunteered to serve with him again—would have something to build on and be able to help them improve their training and expand their operations.

"If we lose half our army we will replace it from our people," Giap said with calm certainty. "The enemy cannot do that as easily. 'The enemy must fight his battles far from his home base for a long time. . . . We must further weaken him by drawing him into protracted campaigns. Once his initial dash is broken, it will be easier to destroy him.' Do you know who wrote that, Major?"

"Karl von Clausewitz?"

"No. His theories and practices of war would not work here. That was written by Marshal Tran Hung Dao six hundred and sixty years ago in his *Essential Summary of Military Arts.* It was he who defeated the Mongols during their third invasion of our country. We still study that book today, as we do the writings of our leader, Ho Chi Minh, and our contemporary in China, Mao Tse-tung."

Sometimes Giap strapped on a Colt .45, but he continued to dress like an underpaid schoolteacher or a tired commercial traveler—except for the Borsalino hat. That was grand, thought Reisman, and it became him; it did not have the cavalier dash of the Anzac and bush hats the Kachins in Burma had worn, but it had enough of the boulevardier about it to make Giap's usual demeanor slightly less sad and severe.

"He is actually a scholar, a man of great learning," Mai told Reisman one day as they stood together watching Giap run a new platoon through the basic manual of arms. "Mr. Giap also went to the same school as Uncle Ho. It was afterward, but before Thi was a student there. Then he studied at the University of Hanoi and received a degree in law and a doctorate in political economics."

"Where did he pick up the soldier business?" Reisman asked. "He's pretty good at it for a politician."

Mai looked uncertain about answering, but then said, "Friends."

"In China?"

"Yes. There were times when our people were able to train with the Kuomintang. They were a liberation movement then. They worked with many factions. Their common goal was to free China and all of Asia from foreign domination. Now we can no longer be certain about them."

"Why does Giap always look so angry and miserable? He never smiles."

"He has much to be angry about!" Mai snapped at him. "Terrible things were done to his family by the *colons.* They will pay for it one day."

Her tone of righteous indignation annoyed him. "As terrible as what you people did to Mr. Trang a few days ago?" he asked with mocking innocence. "Or the butchering of wounded soldiers who had surrendered?"

Mai's eyes flared at him, then they misted, but whether from rage or sorrow he couldn't tell. "His wife, baby son and sister-in-law were killed by the French!"

"Killed? Like Trang and the others?" he retorted, unswayed by her feelings.

"The infant died of neglect or starvation or disease—who knows?" she went on in a dull, tight voice. "Giap's wife, Minh Giang, died in prison in Hanoi. Her sister, Minh Khai, had her head cut off on a guillotine. That, perhaps—to answer your question—was like the traitor Trang."

"What had they done?"

She glared at him again. "The infant? Nothing except to be born the child of his parents. Minh Giang and Minh Khai had been active workers for *Doc-Lap.* There came a time of repression and arrests. Everybody was pursued by the Sûreté. Giap's family thought it was better to split up. He and others fled to China. The sisters found refuge in Vinh, where they were safe for a long time. Then they were captured, tried by a military court and found guilty of conspiracy."

Reisman wondered how true it was. Perhaps it was so, just as Mai had told it. But to pursue the matter of righteousness—righteous politics, righteous war, righteous cruelty and retribution—was futile. In the wars of his life, in these lands of Asia in particular, assaulted by the new yet steeped in the ancient, he had learned long ago and again these last two months that there was no cause, nation, soldier or civilian all unspotted who could pass judgment. Least of all himself.

He went often to Ho's gloomy cave. Stalactites formed by eons of limestone drippings hung like spears from the damp ceiling. The rough, pitted walls were dark and clammy. The only bright spot was the flag they had devised for the country they didn't have. It was draped down one sloping wall: one large gold star with five points on a red field. "Gold, not yellow!" Thi had corrected the first time

Reisman had seen one of the flags and referred to the colors. "I do not like the negative connotations of yellow."

The furnishings of the cave and Ho's personal possessions were spartan. A rattan suitcase contained his few clothes and belongings. His sleeping mat was laid over branches on a homemade bamboo cot. There was a sitting mat on a ledge of the wall and a map table in a prominent position. Close by was a charcoal stove used for both warmth and cooking, mostly for boiling water for tea. Meals were eaten in a communal dining hall made of bamboo and thatch. The food was mainly rice, corn and wild bananas.

In Ho's cave one day, Reisman told him and Giap, "You've got to standardize your weapons, limit the caliber of ammunition you need. I see everything from antiques to the latest submachine guns out there. You're shooting twenty-twos, thirties, thirty-eights and forty-fives. It complicates your supply problem."

Giap stared at him with a look that was almost disdainful. He had none of Ho's talent for diplomacy. "If your country will supply us, we will gladly standardize," he declared. "Until then we must use whatever we can buy, beg or steal."

"I'll ask for an air drop of more thirty-caliber guns and ammo," Reisman said.

"We need mortars and bazookas and lots of ammunition for them," Giap told him. He made it sound like an order rather than a request.

Reisman stared at the man's stoic, emotionless face and wondered what it would take to make him smile again. "Stir up enough diversionary action against the Japs down here and you'll have a better chance of getting them," he said.

"When we are strong enough," Ho said. "Until then we will not dissipate our forces in meaningless actions. We must use our resources carefully."

They talked against a background of rushing water. Outside the cave a stream wound its way around the mountain. Ho went there to bathe in the early morning no matter how cold it was. Like a worrying, doting uncle he urged the virtues of cleanliness on everyone else. When the weather was warm he wore khaki shorts, a long-sleeved white shirt and sandals. His legs were thin, tanned and sinewy. When physical labor was necessary, even the meanest of tasks, he liked to do his share, not only as an example but as exercise and conditioning for a body that had suffered over the years. That morning, conferring in the damp chill of his cave, he wore long tan cotton trousers and a tunic buttoned to his throat. Giap wore a similar high-collared jacket and trousers in a darker color. It was more like a military uniform than his usual rumpled suits. Reisman, in combat fatigues and a field jacket, carried his .45 on a gunbelt.

"Come look at this," said Ho.

He led Reisman to the map table. He was delighted by a new raised contour map that had been made in camp from data gathered by their own surveyors. It was a relief model of the northeastern portion of Tonkin that included the base at Pac Bo and extended across the frontier into the Chinese province of Kwangsi. Reisman saw that the cartographers had filled in all the places that on other maps were incomplete. These people knew the contours of their land intimately. They could move swiftly with confidence along its paths and find sanctuary in its secret places.

Ho pointed out to Reisman the routes they generally used to cross back and forth into China, much nearer than the westerly route they'd followed with him at Lao Cai. "We have agents in place here at Ch'ing-Hsi and Chiu Chou Chieh," Ho remarked, pointing to two small villages on the China side.

"Why did you make me walk one hundred and fifty miles, then?" Reisman asked.

"Security."

"From whom?"

Ho looked up from the map and shrugged. "Bandits," he said vaguely.

The border area was thick with them, Thi had told him, brigands who had only simple, venal goals and no conflicts or confusions about philosophies and politics. Some had allied themselves with the Viet Minh, some preyed on them and had to be bought off or fought. The Sûreté and the French colonial army lumped them all together.

"Perhaps Tai Li's spies," Ho suggested. "Maybe spies from your own OSS—unknown to you, of course. But mainly I felt that you, *mon commandant,* would not have approved of the easiest way in."

Ho had assessed him correctly. If Reisman had thought that crossing the frontier was going to be too simple he would have automatically assumed there was something wrong with the Viets' familiar route. Yet their journey had been arduous and deadly and might have been as fatal to them as it had to the enemy soldiers and Meo chieftain they had killed.

Ho worked constantly, Reisman observed. He was always protected by a screen of armed men; sometimes they were obvious, other times subtly dispersed. Like a chief of state, he received colleagues and emissaries from other parts of the country, even adversaries he was trying to win over. He studied, wrote, lectured, led political discussions, taught a variety of subjects—including reading and writing—to adults and children at the base and in nearby villages, and he gathered firewood when that had to be done and because he enjoyed the vigorous outdoor activity. Some days, dressed in his *can slua tau* clothes and accompanied by a cordon of armed guards, Ho toured the mountains personally delivering to the villagers copies of *Viet Lap,* the newspaper that he and his colleagues wrote and mimeographed in camp. Reisman went with him a few times and took along one of the radio teams he had begun to train, to let them practice sending and receiving transmissions with the other teams on duty at the base camp.

When he went out with Ho into the villages of the "liberated zone," Reisman asked a lot of nonmilitary questions which Ho and his aides seemed pleased to answer. He reported what he observed and was told via radio to Sam Kilgore, but he was aware that both could be faked by clever propagandists, which these people certainly were. They were only too glad to expose him to situations that would make them look good in the eyes of an American.

For two days during his second week in Pac Bo the Viets put on a series of meetings which they tried to pass off as part of their regular political process, but which he thought were laid on for his benefit. Men and women were escorted into the base and convened with Ho and his top aides in the camp's lecture hall, another of the simple utilitarian structures they had built there in their jungle redoubt. The meetings were conducted in Viet-Namese, and though Reisman was studying the language Thi still had to translate for him.

"These meetings are an example of our united front," Thi explained. "They demonstrate that people from all segments of our country approve our goals and participate in our programs."

"Who are the people?" asked Reisman.

"Members of our National Salvation Associations," explained Thi. "Each group puts forward its own special interests and concerns. Today we have scheduled meetings with the National Salvation Association of Landlords."

Reisman looked at him dubiously. "Landlords?"

"Yes. You have such things in your country, Uncle Ho tells me. Why should we not have it in ours?" Thi replied insouciantly. "After landlords, we will meet with the National Salvation Association of

Intellectuals and then the National Salvation Association of Women."

Reisman continued to stare at him skeptically, as if the man were making jokes. "Whatever became of plain old peasants and workers?" he said sarcastically.

"Ahh—they are tomorrow," responded Thi cheerfully, "and also students. However, you must understand that everything begins at the village level. That is the most important aspect of Viet-Namese social, political and economic life. True power—"

"How about Hanoi and Saigon? You wouldn't call those villages, would you?" Reisman interrupted. He never trusted Thi's chamber-of-commerce pitches.

"They too are represented, of course, and our industries as well. But we are mainly an agricultural society," Thi went on, "and the central government's mandate stops at the village gate. True power and responsibility rests within our hamlets and villages and flows outward."

"Then these are the village politicians?" Reisman suggested. "Back in Chicago we called them ward heelers."

"No. These are people who were elected to the provincial committees. The National Salvation Associations are constructed like a pyramid. Below the provincial committees are the village and district committees. Above them are the central executive committees with whom they are meeting here."

"Sounds as if you're all set up to take over the country once everybody else gets out of the way."

Thi looked pleased, as if a dull student had finally given the right answer. "It is more democratic, I think, than your United States of America."

"I doubt that," Reisman retorted. "We've had a lot more time to oil and grease the system. Are the Japs and French aware of all this?"

"In the rest of the country it is underground, a shadow government to the *colons*. It makes little difference to the Japs as long as nothing is done against them. Only in the liberated zone does it flourish openly. The French would arrest all these people and try them for treason."

"It is not the French we want you to fight, Thi. It is the Japs," Reisman reminded him.

He reported it all to Sam Kilgore during his next radio contact with Kunming, and he pressed the colonel about the arms and supply drops he had requested earlier. He knew that his reports would be evaluated and political decisions regarding them made elsewhere, by other men. But considering the urgent needs of China Command, with the Japs pushing inland again from the coast, Reisman thought he had enough evidence of a prospectively effective guerrilla organization. He wanted to help the Viets plan at least one small operation and train them to carry it out on their own before he risked bringing across the men he expected from England.

"They are on the way. Here in a week," Sam signaled to him.

He was standing by in the radio shack at Kunming airfield and only the time needed to encode, transmit and decode slowed down direct communication.

"How many?" Reisman asked.

"Don't know yet. Got a job for you and the Viets now."

The rest of Kilgore's message was about a flight crew that had crashed in the mountains of northern Tonkin after bombing Jap shipping in Haiphong harbor. Air Ground Aid Section of Chennault's 14th Air Force wanted Reisman and the Viets to find them before the Japs did.

Chapter 19

If they had not been out looking for the American airmen they might never have found the Frenchman and he might well have gotten clean away with his mission.

It was early afternoon. Reisman was in his hut, working with his signal group at taking the radios apart and putting them back together, when he heard a great hullabaloo outside. He looked out, and at first he thought it was one of the Americans who was being dragged bloody and half-conscious through the camp. When he saw one of the Viets kick the limp figure he charged into their midst, hit the kicker and momentarily startled the others with his fury.

"*Pháp quân!*" shouted the man he'd hit. "*Quân báo!*"

He started to unlimber his carbine and Reisman grabbed it away from him. The Viets were all shouting at him now: "*Pháp quân! Quân báo! Phản gián!*"

Mai suddenly appeared and he asked her, "What are they saying?"

"He's a French soldier. A spy."

Reisman stared more closely at the prisoner. He was a slender man of about thirty, with black, crew-cut hair spotted with blood. His head hung down, but he was trying to raise it. His face was lean to the point of gauntness, his dark eyes bulged slightly, his skin was very white. He wore jump boots and fatigues like Reisman's, except that the uniform was dirty, torn and bloodied. One of the Viets holding him was wearing the man's field jacket, which was much too big and made him look like a small boy playing soldier.

Reisman reached out a hand to finger the cloth of the jacket and the guerrilla drew back. "*Chiên lọi phãm!*" he declared.

"What's he say?" Reisman asked.

"War booty," Mai answered.

Another Viet placed his hand protectively over the holstered .45 at his waist and a third man carried an extra carbine, apparently also *chiẽn lọi phãm* taken from the captive. Staring at the prisoner again, Reisman saw the insignia of a French lieutenant and recognized the shoulder patch of Leclerc's Second Armored Division. He last had seen that emblem in Paris in August. They had been the first Allied troops through the Porte d'Orléans into the liberated city. The man also wore a U.S. Airborne combat badge and American and French ribbons.

"Whoever he is, he's not a spy," Reisman said quickly to Mai. "Tell them that. He is an Allied officer in uniform and is to be treated that way."

Mai translated. The Viet soldiers muttered darkly among themselves, but stood back while Reisman kneeled beside the prisoner lying on the ground.

"Ça va bien?" Reisman asked. *"Qui êtes-vous? Comment vous appelez-vous?"*

"Qui êtes-vous?" came the mumbled reply, as the man tried to focus on his questioner.

"John Reisman. I'm a U.S. Army major. Office of Strategic Services, Kunming. Who are you?" Reisman answered, still speaking French.

The man looked around anxiously at the Viets, then dropped his voice and spoke in colloquial English, but with a heavy accent.

"Belfontaine, Philippe, Lieutenant. I'm glad to see you. What are you doing with these bastards? I was on my way to Lang Son when they grabbed me."

"I'm here on duty as an observer," Reisman explained. "Where did *you* come from?"

Belfontaine looked around warily and went on quietly in English. "Calcutta. The British dropped me yesterday. I am from de Gaulle in Paris. There are things I must do—people to contact. We are allies. You must help me."

Reisman touched the division patch on the lieutenant's shirt. "I was there in August," he said.

"A glorious time," the Frenchman murmured, forcing a smile.

"Are you injured or wounded?" Reisman asked.

Belfontaine struggled to rise, wincing. Reisman helped him. Belfontaine nodded his head and flicked his eyes to encompass the watchful Viets. "*Salauds!* Fucking yellow little savages! They beat the shit out of me. Otherwise I am fine. No injuries. The jump was good. No wounds, except old ones. Nobody shot at me. Nobody knew I was here. I thought I was alone in the jungle. Then they jumped me!"

"Where are they taking you?"

"I don't know."

He asked Mai. She questioned the guards, then said, "To Uncle Ho."

He thought of what had happened to Trang and resolved that it would not happen again. He walked beside the limping prisoner as they led him across the camp. The guards left him alone this time, but other men and women clustered around them, jeering and cursing. Their hatred was palpable.

Tran Van Thi halted them at the mouth of the cave. Two of Ho's bodyguards took charge of the prisoner and frisked him roughly.

"*Thôi!*" Reisman commanded.

They looked up, even Thi, startled by his unexpected use of their language. He had wanted to say, "Leave him alone!" but didn't know how, so he had settled for "Stop!"

"This is not your affair," Thi told him.

"*Au contraire.* It is very much my affair." He insisted on speaking to Ho and Thi let him enter with the Frenchman.

Inside, he found Ho and some of his aides waiting expectantly. Five men were seated on wood blocks around a plank table. There was one empty place for the captive.

"The lieutenant is an Allied officer on official business," Reisman stated quietly. "He is to be treated with courtesy and respect." His eyes went to each of the men. He hardly knew their strange names. They were silent, serious men in their thirties and forties. Giap was not there.

Reisman fixed his gaze on Ho. "With this man it must not be like it was with Trang," he warned. "If the slightest harm comes to him I will withdraw all American and Allied assistance from you and your people."

Ho's eyebrows raised in innocent surprise. Though Reisman knew that the fate of one French lieutenant—or one American major, for that matter—would hardly influence high-level policy, he had at least given Ho something substantial to worry about. He put his hand on Belfontaine's arm and said, "*Bonne chance!* They are working with us against the Japs. Keep that in mind as you speak to them."

The man was nervous, but he mumbled, "*Merci,*" smiled weakly, and took the empty seat Ho indicated.

Reisman went back to his signal group and the radios. Two hours later, after he had dismissed them and was sitting tensely on the steps outside his hut, smoking a cigarette, Ho himself came to him and invited him to stroll.

"It is all right," Ho said. "Nothing will happen to your Frenchman."

They walked together in silence a few minutes. The sun slanted low through the trees and very soon would disappear over the mountain ridge. The late afternoon was cooling fast. Ho stopped near the stream, where he had a favorite flat boulder that was his outside "office." They sat down and Ho said, "He is a lucky man. If you had not been here he would have been tried, sentenced and shot."

"For being a Frenchman?"

"For being a spy."

"An officer in uniform is not a spy."

"He is a brave man and a fool. He would tell us nothing about why he parachuted into our country. Only some sentimental story about looking for his sister whom he has not seen in ten years. That is very commendable, *Jean,* but we believe he is here on a military mission for the new government in Paris. Perhaps you can find this out for us?"

"You want me to spy for *you,* is that it?"

"We want to know what the French are up to."

"OSS has given you arms and radios to find out what the Japs are up to, not the French. They will fall in line when we make our move."

Ho sighed and asked, "Have you met de Gaulle?"

Reisman smiled at the apparent naïveté of the question. "I don't travel in those circles," he answered.

"He has not been *le grand* Charles for long," said Ho. "He was only a colonel when the Germans attacked France."

"He was a brigadier when he escaped to England after Dunkirk," said Reisman. "Stubborn, difficult, determined—and I admire him."

Ho offered cigarettes and lit them with a zippo. "He has no vision and understanding beyond his own fantasy of France redeemed, of new French glory. He knows nothing about the rest of the world . . . about Asia . . . about Viet-Nam . . . about the struggling masses of humanity. He is a very tall man, I understand, and he looks only outward and upward, missing a great deal. He has spoken of a new political order for Indochina within the French community."

"What's wrong with that? It sounds like a good first step toward the independence you want."

"It is a euphemism. What you Americans call bullshit."

Reisman laughed. He was impressed, as always, by Ho's practical grasp of languages and politics.

"There was a conference in French Africa early this year regarding the future of all their colonies," Ho went on. "Despite the intentions of President Roosevelt and the American people, who I know are against colonialism, de Gaulle's delegates excluded any idea of autonomy and independence for any of their colonies, even in the most distant future. They have liberated France from the Nazis, but refuse to grant us freedom from their own fascists and imperialists. I think that this Lieutenant Belfontaine has come as an agent to fight against us. It is you Americans, not the French, who will finish off the Japs. The *colons* will conserve their resources and manpower to try to restore their empire. Just as Chiang Kai-shek saves his armies and the weapons you Americans give him to fight Mao Tse-tung, not the Japs."

"Turn the Frenchman over to me," said Reisman. "I will find out about these things."

"Agreed," said Ho.

Belfontaine's weapons, field jacket and personal gear were restored to him. His cuts and bruises were tended and he was fed. Then Reisman made room for him in his hut. He seemed a very intense man now, wary and stiff in manner, unsure of the prerogatives and courtesies of rank between them.

"Am I free to go, or am I merely paroled to you, Major?" he asked.

"First of all, forget the rank. There is little formality in the company I work for. Call me John and I'll call you Philippe or even Phil, if you don't object."

"No, of course not—*Jean*."

He too gave it the French pronunciation, and Reisman resigned himself to it. "I need you to work with me," he said. "That is my agreement with the Viets. Work with me for now and return with me to Kunming when I go. Otherwise they'll dump you across the border on your own and shoot you on sight if you try to get back in."

"Do you know who that man really is?" Philippe demanded in an outraged tone. He did not wait for an answer, but went on, "He is an agent of the Comintern! A Communist! His true name is Nguyen Ai-Quôc. He has been wanted by the police of many nations for the past twenty years!"

The accusation, true or not, did not startle Reisman as much as it seemed to shock and anger Belfontaine. Reisman even allowed for the fundamental truth of the allegation, having listened often enough to the political diatribes of Ho and his associates. It would make no difference, at this stage, to his mission, as long as the Viets fulfilled their end of any bargain struck. He had dealt with Communist guerrillas in the past in Europe, some of them effective allies, some not.

"How did you learn all this?" he asked.

"A dossier was put together for me before I left Paris. Information from the Sûreté, both in Paris and Hanoi. Information from the British, who once held him in Hong Kong. Information from our mission in Kunming. The Chinese Nationalists actually held him in jail more than a year. It is a wonder that they did not kill him."

"Maybe they decided he would be more useful to them alive," Reisman suggested. "Just as he finds them useful now."

"And as you find him, too?"

"Very much. But not you?"

"No. He is an enemy of France."

"There are more immediate enemies of France," said Reisman pointedly. "I've fought against them and continue to do so. It seems to me that you would do well to make this man and his comrades your friends and allies. Did you tell him what you know about him?"

"No. He might have shot me dead on the spot. How can you Americans deal with such a man?"

"Necessity. I must have your promise that you will cooperate."

Belfontaine was silent a few moments, then said a reluctant, "Yes."

"Why were you going to Lang Son?"

"To find my sister. Before the war she married a wealthy planter, a French colonial named Thibaut whom she met on holiday in Paris."

"Is that your home?"

"No. Far from it," said Philippe, a wistful note entering his voice. He was seated on the bench beside the radio table. Reisman sat on the edge of his bamboo cot. He offered a cigarette and they smoked. "How I would love a good cognac now," said Philippe.

"Sorry. No got," said Reisman, smiling. "You might have to wait until we get to Kunming." Sam Kilgore had some, he remembered.

"We used to visit Paris occasionally, but I could not live there happily, nor could Madeleine. We are country people. My family has a ranch in the Camargue. Do you know it?"

"I've been through there. In Provence. Marshland . . . horses . . . cattle . . . fighting bulls . . . Roman ruins."

Philippe brightened. "*Oui.* At home I am a *gardien,* a cowboy. But it has been a long time. Five years since I have been home. Ten years since Madeleine came out here with Thibaut. He was killed."

"The Japs?"

"Perhaps. But just as likely rebels like these. Madeleine was forced to abandon their plantation. There were a few letters. First she was in Hanoi, then Lang Son. There is a a fortress there, garrisoned by French forces. I must go there. You have to help me, *Jean*."

"Perhaps we can go together," said Reisman. "I will try to arrange it."

He doubted that the man had parachuted into Tonkin merely to locate his sister. He asked him about his army background and tried to make it sound merely one soldier's interest in another soldier's experiences. Philippe told him he had been in the war from the beginning. After Dunkirk and the French surrender in 1940 he had gotten away to England to join the Free French. They had moved him around a lot, building both his combat experience and his diplomatic skills as a liaison officer. He had taken jump training in England and then had been attached to various Allied airborne units that went into Tunisia, then Sicily. In Italy he had fought with the French Expeditionary Corps and then had been taken out of the line below Monte Cassino to return to England to train with Leclerc's division. The exultation of having helped to liberate Paris still burned within him.

"This too is France," Philippe said fervently, "as are Algeria, Morocco and Tunisia."

"You and I will not determine that," Reisman told him. "That's for after the war. Right now I have my orders to get these people to work with us against the Japs and take some of the pressure off China."

"I too have my orders, *Jean*."

Reisman examined the Frenchman's gaunt, pale face and saw in his eyes the glazed light of the committed zealot. Not unlike the look he had seen on the face of Tran Van Thi and Ho Chi Minh and others of the Viet Minh.

"Did de Gaulle really send you?"

"Yes. A great honor. He approved my mission and we spoke personally before I left. His aides tried to arrange my journey through you Americans, but I was refused clearance and transportation. The British understand these matters, however, and were very helpful."

Yes, they would be, thought Reisman with a touch of regret. In the beginning, both France and England had been concerned only about survival. Now they were more concerned about preserving and perpetuating their empires.

"Merely to visit your sister?" said Reisman sarcastically. "How considerate of them."

The color rose in Philippe's pale face. "That is only part of it, of course," he said defensively. "I am to assess the situation here and report back—to prepare the way for liberation, just as we did in France."

"Then we should be able to work together," Reisman told him. "You and I—and the Viets."

Philippe stared at him uncertainly. "I am obliged to you—perhaps for my life. But I must go to Lang Son and then Hanoi. Arrange it with these *salauds* and I will fight with you Americans against the Japs, just as you fought with us against the *Boches*. But I will not help the Communist rebels of Nguyen Ai-Quôc."

Reisman let it go at that. He knew, though, that he would not be able to trust the Frenchman completely . . . just as he could not trust Ho Chi Minh completely . . . or Lieutenant Colonel Sam Kilgore—or anyone.

He put Philippe on the generator that night when he got ready to transmit to Kunming. They were alone. He had dismissed the Viet radio class, much to Philippe's relief. The man was unable to adjust to being in the midst of people he considered enemies, and he seethed with barely suppressed anger and frustration.

"To whom do you want to report your status?" Reisman asked as he finished encoding his own messages with a one-time pad.

"No one," Philippe answered, beginning to turn the crank. "Please do not transmit anything to anyone about my arrival here."

Reisman stared at him warily. "Why not?"

"The French representatives in Kunming were not told about my mission, nor were the officers I must contact in Indochina."

"What are you doing—fighting your own private war?"

Philippe spoke louder, so that he would be heard above the noise of the generator. "There are factions who are opposed to de Gaulle. They would try to stop me. Perhaps even betray me to the Japanese."

Reisman bent over the Morse key. No one seemed to be on the same side anymore, he thought. "All right. I never met you," he said. But just before he started to tap the key he looked up again at Belfontaine, who was steadily turning the generator crank. "Whatever your mission is," he added, "don't ever try to do anything against me."

When he raised Kunming at the scheduled time, Sam Kilgore was again waiting in the airfield radio shack. There was an unexpected urgency in his signals:

"Japs got Kweilin yesterday. Heading for Liuchow. Another spearhead striking toward Kweiyang."

It was like listening to news reports during the darkest days of Axis conquests. If the Japs took Kweiyang, Reisman realized, it was conceivable that Kunming and Chungking would fall next. Despite their heavy losses in the Pacific and Burma, the Japs seemed bent on conquering all of China. Months earlier, they had started to move inland from their long held coastal enclaves. Sam's message meant that they were now driving into the interior of China with powerful blitzkrieg attacks. The Nationalist Chinese defenders were apparently collapsing and disappearing, letting the enemy rampage where they wanted. It was what General Stillwell had warned everybody about for years. It was the possibility that Chiang Kai-shek had denied could happen. It was what General Chennault had tried to prevent with air power alone. Now the Japs had rolled up his advance bases at Hengyang, Lingling, Kweilin and were moving on to Liuchow. It was also conceivable that they would roll across southern

China astride the border, join with their divisions in Indochina and form one solid occupied land mass.

"Imperative that you step up guerrilla operations down there," Kilgore radioed.

"Double my order with the company store," Reisman responded. "Add bazookas, machine guns, mortars, ammo. Specify date, time drop. Will give drop coordinates when you are ready."

Sam responded with, "Don't have stuff here. Trying to get it."

Reisman wondered how much truth there was to that; though he knew that every military command in China had been screaming for weapons, ammo and supplies for years. Everything still had to be flown over the Hump on a priority basis. The Burma–Ledo road would ease the problem, but it would not be completed for another few months, provided the Japs didn't cut it again.

"Any news of the flight crew?" Sam asked.

"Not yet. Viets out looking for them," Reisman answered.

The next signal puzzled Reisman for a few seconds. "Find any trade goods?" Sam asked.

Then Reisman remembered their talk about opium and business deals and he tapped out a firm "No" on the Morse key.

He ended the contact and went outside for a breath of the cool night air. He lit a cigarette and sat on the stairs. From inside, Philippe called out good night. It was after midnight and the camp was quiet. He looked toward Mai's hut and felt an unexpected yearning. He turned away and then looked back when a movement caught his eye. He saw a man in uniform slipping silently up the stairs. Haro is back, he thought, though he couldn't really see who it was at that distance in the dark.

Maybe it was the little peaked cap that did it, or the general silhouette of high boots and bloused pants, but he suddenly realized that the uniform was Japanese.

Chapter 20

He did not do anything for a few minutes. He merely sat there, smoking, staring into the night, listening to the sounds of animals in the jungle. He had no desire to barge in on anybody *in flagrante delicto*. If it was Haro—or Jimmy Lum—the man would be leaving Mai's hut to go to his own quarters in the minutes before dawn. That had been his habit in the past when Reisman had observed his comings and goings, to make it seem as if he had spent the night alone and avoid embarrassment to Mai.

Reisman considered setting up a private little alarm patterned after one of the Meo booby traps, a little trip-cord noisemaker like those the Viets practiced with to set off mines and grenades. A taut length of cotton or fine wire, or a tendril of tropical creeper artfully placed across a stair. Then he remembered what Thi had told him, that he and Haro were no danger to each other, and he decided that a confrontation, playful as it seemed, might be taken in the late, dark night as a threat. Instead he went to sleep, fully dressed, tuning himself to rise in the hour before daylight.

When he woke, Philippe was still sleeping soundly. Reisman looked out the open doorway. Ten minutes later he saw Haro leaving Mai's hut. He was dressed in his leisure costume and was carrying his uniform and boots. Reisman waited until Haro had vanished into the bush, then went quickly across the clearing and entered Mai's hut.

"Did you forget something, Kita?" her voice called out sleepily in French.

Reisman moved closer to her cot and spoke softly in English. "So that's his name."

Mai twisted around and sat up, startled. The blanket fell to her waist and he dimly saw bare shoulders and the sway of her breasts. He stared. She didn't bother to cover herself. "It's you," she said.

"Who is Kita?" he asked. He sounded like a lover betrayed, though it wasn't what he intended.

"That's really none of your business, Major," she answered, anger rising in her voice.

"In another time and place that might be so, but the man was wearing a Jap uniform when he came in here last night. I think it's time I was let in on the game. Who is he? Which side is he on?"

Mai saw him staring at her body and drew the blanket up to her neck.

A soft voice behind Reisman said, "I've been asking myself that same question for months now." He turned and saw Haro coming through the doorway, still carrying the Jap uniform and boots. "You saw me. I saw you. Tie score," Haro went on.

Reisman felt no threat in the man's voice or posture, merely a note of weariness, perhaps boredom. "Who are you?" Reisman asked.

Haro took a deep breath, stood at a mock stiff attention, and said in a clipped voice, "Shidehara . . . Kita . . . Colonel . . . Kempitai! At your service!" He bowed stiffly, juggling the stuff in his arms. He also tried clicking the heels of his bucks together like a German, but the bucks were too soft to make any noise. Haro looked down in chagrin and then smiled at the comedy of it all.

Reisman stared at him in disbelief. The man behaved as if he had seen too many American movies and was mistakenly trying to use the dialogue and action of a drawing-room comedy in a situation of high drama. "You wouldn't be Jimmy Lum, would you?" Reisman suggested.

"Good man. I've heard of him." Haro looked toward the cot. "Tell him, Mai."

She looked at Reisman over the edge of the blanket. "He really is Kita Shidehara. He is a colonel in the Kempitai."

Reisman looked from one to the other of them to see if they were joking. But they weren't. He felt suddenly both foolish and angry. "Then what are you doing messing around with him?" he demanded of Mai. "I thought they were the enemy." Then he turned to the man who had just identified himself as an officer in the Japanese secret service. "And what are you doing wandering loose around here, playing buddy-buddy with everybody? Why don't they lock you up or put a bullet in your head? Why don't you call your troops in on them?"

Kita shook his head. "Jeezus, buddy, but you're naïve," he said. "All that rah-rah stuff is for the peasants—for the *Lumpenproletariat.*" Then he dropped the comedy act and said, "Enough of this bullshit. We've got business to discuss and we may as well get started."

"Go ahead. Put me in the picture."

Kita looked past him to Mai. "Would you get up and make us some tea?" Then to Reisman, "Look away for a moment, Johnny, so the lady can get dressed."

The "business" that Kita Shidehara wanted to discuss was not nearly so astounding as the fact that it came from the mouth of a colonel of the Kempitai. It was, thought Reisman, comparable to sitting down to tea with the local Nazi gauleiter in any of the occupied countries where he had worked with the Resistance. Except that the colonel continued to sound more like an American Jimmy Lum than a Japanese Kita Shidehara. Mai had lit an oil lamp and brewed tea on a little charcoal stove. She took the one chair and the men sat on mats on the floor, drinking tea from small cups.

The news Kita conveyed was already stale. He told Reisman about the smashing new victories of the Japanese drive in China, and he gloated just a little bit about it: "Your Chinese team ain't doing too good. They've lost a lot of yardage. Maybe the coaching is lousy!"

Reisman shrugged. "Yeah. I heard about that."

"You know about the air crew that's down? Nine guys."

"Yes."

"Of course. Your radio," Kita said, snapping his fingers. "Here's something new to tell Kunming. The Japs have got three of them in jail in Hanoi. The Frenchies have got three hidden somewhere and are refusing to turn them over to the Japs. Trying to play nice guy, I guess—win a few points to look good with you guys. The other three flyboys are still wandering around out there in the hills and jungles. You ought to get Uncle Ho onto them."

"He is. So far he's netted one Frenchman. Tell me, Colonel—"

"Please, skip the rank, John," Kita said with a waving motion of his hand. "We're strictly informal around here."

"Are you an American? A Nisei?"

"Nope. Born and bred in Japan. Ever been there?"

"Briefly, a few years ago. Off a ship in Yokohama."

"Like it?"

"I got up to Tokyo. Hated it. It was like living in a rabbit warren."

"Anywhere else?"

"Yes. Some of it was beautiful . . . really grand and beautiful. It made me wonder how people of such exquisite sensibilities and taste could behave with such cruelty and savagery toward the rest of the world."

Kita drew back in mock horror. "If that was meant to insult me, forget it, kid." Reisman hadn't been called "kid" in a long time. He was thirty and he figured the colonel at maybe five to eight years older. "Anyway, it was easy," Kita continued. "We watched what you Westerners were up to, then just turned our samurai loose."

"Where did you learn to speak American?"

"I started with English at the Imperial Army Language School in Tokyo. They were sticklers for getting the idioms and colloquialisms right."

"I don't believe you, Kita," said Reisman. "You must have been in the States."

"I didn't say I hadn't."

"Nobody gets to speak a language like a native unless he lives among the natives."

"How about some more tea, Mai?" Kita asked, holding up his cup.

"That's American," said Reisman. "A Jap would wait politely until he was asked."

Mai poured tea for both of them, then turned off the lamp. The early morning light was sufficient. She sat down and continued to follow the conversation in fascination. Even she hadn't known this much about Kita.

"Okay. That's one of the things I learned in the States. How to be pushy."

"Is that where you developed your wise-guy sense of humor?" Reisman taunted. He was sure that Japanese propriety didn't permit such easygoing style. That was why they had gone so crazy, he figured. That, plus trying to ape one of the western countries they held in such contempt. Only they'd made a bad choice in Germany.

"Yeah, it stayed with me. Everything is so damned funny there that you have to laugh in order to live. I was lucky, I guess. The real me was able to come out."

"What were you doing there?"

"I was a spy. A student spy. Or a spy student. Depends how you look at it. Listen, none of this means anything now. We've got more important things to talk about."

"What have you got in mind?"

"Working together to help the Viets."

"Against whom?"

"The French."

"What about you Japs?"

"We'll be leaving." A new tone of irony sounded in his voice. "What's happening against the Chinks are easy, temporary victories, though it must be scaring the shit out of your boys in Kunming and Chungking. We're losing it elsewhere. I don't think the Co-Prosperity Sphere is going to make it in its current form. We're going to have to go back to the drawing board and rethink it."

"You want to give me a date on your departure?"

"When it's necessary. What we don't want is for the French to come back in here. Asia for the Asians and all that."

"It seems to me that they're here already and they've been here all along. You never kicked the French out."

"You're right. It was easier to let the ones who were here stay on and do the dirty work for us. We've been taking what we wanted and shipping it home. Any time we want to take care of the local Frenchies we've got the power to do it, just like that!" He snapped his fingers again.

A very American habit, thought Reisman. "If you expect to turn me around to work for you, you're badly mistaken," he said brusquely. "I'm a guest here and I've been asked to behave myself regarding you, so that's what I'm doing."

"I'm not asking you to betray your country, Major," Kita said indignantly.

"Then you want to betray yours."

"Of course not."

Reisman shook his head. "I still don't understand what you're up to, Colonel—or Kita, or Haro, or whatever your name is. You're on the wrong side in this war, remember?"

"A mere detail," said Kita. His voice was bright, his manner suave again. "The war has come to the point where you and I are pretty much on the same side in regard to the Viets. The Kempitai has been going it alone with them a long time and we're in pretty deep."

Reisman looked over at Mai and said, "Yeah, I guess you are."

She glared at him, but said nothing.

Kita went on, without humor. "That's not what I mean. We've got our own fight going with the Imperial Army here and the damn bureaucrats back in Tokyo. It's almost as bad as the fight you've got going between OSS, the army, navy and air corps, not to speak of the ones you've got going between Washington, Chungking and all your so-called allies."

"What do you know about that?"

"Everything there is to know," Kita said confidently. "We've got our people everywhere. I even know the paltry amount of arms you brought in with you for the Viets: twenty-five M-1s, twenty-five carbines, twenty-five—"

"Never mind!" snapped Reisman. "I know the laundry list." He looked over at Mai again. "I suppose you got it from the Viets."

"Nope. I knew it before you crossed the border. You guys ought to be ashamed of yourselves. Trying to buy love with a few little souvenirs when you've got all that good big stuff pouring out of your factories. It's just like your ancestors trading a few beads to the Indians for their birthright."

"My ancestors didn't know any Indians," Reisman answered lamely. He was trying to cover his confusion about the crazy duplicity of the war he was in now. How the hell did Shidehara know what weapons he had brought from Kunming? Where was the leak? Was it just the ordinary network of agents everywhere or was it closer to home—Kilgore, Ludlow, Tai Li? "Let's get back to you, Colonel," he said.

"Kita, please."

"Pick it up from where you were a student spy in the States."

"A real fun time." His happy-go-lucky expression changed for just a few moments, but Reisman caught it. Colonel Shidehara's handsome features tightened and darkened. Then he glanced toward Mai and gave her what might have been a look of apology for what he was about to say. "Not much American nookie available for a Jap, but I managed with your lower classes."

Reisman waited for more, but the man seemed to be brooding on unpleasant memories. "You didn't travel six thousand miles just to fuck American girls, did you, Kita?"

A barely perceptible flicker of new rage flared in the man's eyes. He forced his features into a grin. "No, my bosses sent me to USC to study America and Americans and learn how to talk right. Which often turned out to be wrong as far as correct English is concerned, if you follow my drift."

"Who were your bosses?"

"My superiors in the Kempitai. Their names are none of your business. I was already an officer in the army. The military is a tradition in my family. Patriotism, Bushido and all that. They needed somebody to work the territory. They had plans, as you know."

"Yeah, we found that out at Pearl Harbor," Reisman said crisply.

"Personally, I think that was a mistake."

"Where were you then?"

"Back in Tokyo getting prepped for another assignment. I told them, but nobody listened. I had a pretty good idea what you Americans would be able to do if you got mad enough, pulled together and started building a war machine. You had all the manpower and resources right there. I used to travel around a lot on school vacations. This was in the late '30s, right into early '41. I could see what was beginning to happen even then when you were cranking up to help your English friends. I was all over California and the northwest—over to Denver, Chicago, New York, Washington. Hell of a big country. I even took a week going through Texas. Why, that alone is probably bigger than all the Jap islands put together. I bought an old car and slept in it. There seemed to be some difference of opinion as to whether or not I was entitled to accommodations in some of the towns. Same thing all over the south before I got the car. Never knew if I was supposed to sit in the front or back of the bus."

It was when he remembered things like that—the racial and social insults and prejudices that he felt had been inflicted on him in the United States—that Colonel Shidehara's mask of jollity slipped a bit. Reisman continued to question him, trying to perceive falsity and truth, still not certain that the man was really who he said he was. Even though the mere declaration of it by Shidehara seemed to put them each in untenable positions. Unless they went for their guns, which Shidehara kept pointing out would be bad form, since they were both guests on more or less neutral ground; and he was willing to concede the relative neutrality of the Viet Minh's bastion, even though his country officially occupied Indochina under treaty with the French colonials and the former Vichy regime in Metropolitan France.

"Of course, the durability of that arrangement now seems to be under some dispute," he quipped. "Your flyboys have been raiding us with increasing determination, and we keep expecting your armada and landing ships to turn up any day in the Gulf of Tonkin. You don't happen to know anything about that, do you, Johnny?"

Reisman gulped his tea, then stared at Colonel Shidehara's eager, open expression. The general good humor of the man—whether fake or not—was infectious. So much so that Reisman had to keep reminding himself who he was, or claimed to be.

"No, I don't," Reisman replied, trying to sound as pleasant as possible. "At my level I wouldn't be made privy to that sort of information, anyway."

Assuming that it was his turn now in this polite way of exchange they'd fallen into, Reisman asked a few general questions about the operation of the Kempitai and was surprised at Kita's frankness. He pointed out the similarities in independent power and action between the Kempitai and the OSS. They were both always at odds with the regular services and their respective political bureaucracies. Differences of opinion regarding the direction of Japanese policy in Indochina and the extent of aid to Viet-Namese independence groups had now reached a critical stage, however.

"In Tokyo, and even among some factions in the army in Hanoi, they are worried about postwar retribution from the French," Kita said. "We in the Kempitai, however, believe that problem can be avoided by the exercise of just a little more courage and daring now, instead of timorousness and waffling."

"How?" Reisman asked.

"By enabling the native Viet-Namese to form their own sovereign government."

"In which case there would be no French colonial government to trouble you with retribution and reparations."

"Precisely," Kita acknowledged cheerily. "Certain ill-advised factions, however, have limited the extent of our activities with groups such as Mr. Ho's, and seek to curtail them even more. The Kempitai is therefore forced to go it alone in whatever ways we can manage. In a curious way, Johnny, you and I are on the same side now—and please check with Washington on this, don't take my word for it.

We're bringing independence to the Viets and keeping the French out."

Reisman could not help being amused. Yet he looked at him dubiously. "Are you free-lancing this thing yourself?" he demanded. "Or is your outfit behind you on it?"

Kita pondered that one carefully, then said, "Initiative—that's what it is, Major. No different from what you have to do—as you yourself pointed out the day you arrived."

"What exactly do you want from me, Colonel?" challenged Reisman.

"Hmmm . . . well, you've got your news about your flyboys. I'd get right on it if I were you. I'll help if I can."

"What do you require in return?"

"Nothing—for the moment. Just keep doing what you're doing—and don't sneak up on me some dark night."

There were sounds outside now, people moving, the men and women of the camp starting work for the day. Reisman glanced out. Philippe was standing uncertainly in the doorway of their hut. Then he ducked back inside as a squad of armed Viets marched past. In the dim morning light that entered Mai's hut, Reisman stared from the man to the woman and back again. He considered all that had been said and still could not place confidence in either of them. He was on a journey through a maze of contradictions, a passage that had begun the moment he parachuted from the C-46 over the Burma–China frontier. It was an existentialist maze in which *self* was paramount. At the Deux Magots in Boulevard St. Germain the philosophers of existentialism used to speak of things like that—and he agreed with them.

There was one personal thing he very much wanted to know. "You don't happen to know the identity of your man in Chungking, do you, Kita?" he asked lightly.

"Yes, I do."

Reisman waited for him to go on, but he didn't. "I'd sure like to know that one."

"I'd be reluctant to tell you that, Johnny. If you blew the whistle on him it would only confuse international relations. We're all getting along pretty smoothly now. He gets just enough out of the Chinks and they get just enough out of him to justify his position there. I'd like to meet your Frenchman now."

"I'll be asking you again, Colonel," Reisman said crisply. "Perhaps next time there will be enough reason for you to tell me. What do you know about the Frenchman?"

"Only what he told the Viets."

Reisman looked at Mai. She stared back at him without flinching. Of course. Even before he had mentioned the Frenchman so offhandedly, Mai had briefed Shidehara.

"All right," he said. "But see that there's no trouble between you. The man is under my protection."

They walked across the clearing to Reisman's hut. Just he and Kita. Kita made no attempt to conceal his identity, and Reisman saw a look of astonishment and anger cross Philippe's face when the introductions were made. It was a brief, uncomfortable meeting. Kita was the epitome of graciousness, Philippe rather testy. Kita merely exchanged pleasantries and then asked a few questions about the new Paris government's plans for Indochina. It was enough to make the French lieutenant clam up and glower silently at the Japanese colonel. No points for either of them, Reisman concluded.

Chapter 21

Reisman sought an audience with Ho Chi Minh in the cave immediately after the morning meal. Thi and Giap were there too.

"I want to go to Lang Son with the Frenchman," Reisman told them. "I'll need some of your people as guides and escort."

Neither Ho nor his colleagues paid much attention. They had apparently been discussing a matter that excited them more than the Frenchman and Lang Son.

"There is something else more important," said Ho.

"You'd better hear me out first," Reisman persisted.

He told them about the new Japanese drive into the interior of China.

"That is what we want to talk about," said Ho.

Reisman was surprised. "I only got it on the radio from Kunming last night. How did you—" Then he understood. "Your amusing Jap friend must have briefed you the minute he drifted in."

Ho realized the game was up, and he did not try to dissemble.

"Colonel Shidehara keeps me informed," he said. "He brought me news of the fall of Kweilin. Liuchow will be next, perhaps then Kweiyang. The loss of the forward fields of your General Chennault, whom I admire very much, is very bad. If the Japs capture Kunming and Chungking, the war could go on for years, even if you Americans captured their home islands. They are fanatics."

"Shidehara seems a reasonable sort," Reisman said lightly.

"Shidehara is different. We are lucky to have him work with us. His function is similar to yours."

"The hell it is! I'm here to kill Japs, not entertain them."

"You must learn to be more accommodating, *Jean*."

"As you were with the late Mr. Trang."

"As I am now with Lieutenant Belfontaine," Ho said irritably. "Enough of this. Kita told you what he knows about the American flyers?"

"Yes."

"There is more news this morning. One of the men was found by the Nung near the village of Na Sam. He is in good shape. They are taking care of him."

"How far is that?"

Ho beckoned him to the map table and pointed to Na Sam on the big relief model. "Here, approximately sixty miles south of us."

Reisman saw that the most direct route would be sixty miles forced marched along footpaths and cart tracks over mountains, down canyons, through jungle. He didn't want to spend two arduous days hiking there. But about fifteen miles below Na Sam, on the main north–south road, was the French fortress town where he wanted to go with Philippe.

"Do you know the man's name, rank and serial number?" he asked.

Thi read a note he took from his jacket pocket: "Filmore, Randolph, Technical Sergeant Fourth Class. He is a waist gunner and flight mechanic." He read off the numerals of Filmore's army serial number.

"I want a copy of that, Thi. I'll let Kunming know on the wireless. It will earn you people some points. I'll pick him up on the way to Lang Son."

"There is no need to trouble yourself, *Jean*," said Ho. "I will have the man brought here by the Nung. I have not said that you could go to Lang Son, and it would be better if you do not. There is something much more important that we want you to do. It must be done quickly if it is to be done at all."

Reisman did not take easily to having his freedom of action controlled by Ho Chi Minh and his Viets. But if they didn't want him to go to Lang Son with the Frenchman they could easily stop him. He didn't want to argue. There was another way to get them to acquiesce.

"What is it you want me to do?" he asked.

"Go up to Kwangsi and steal the munitions depot of General Chiang Fa-K'uei before the Japs get it," Ho replied, with a little smile, anticipating Reisman's look of astonishment. Giap and Thi stared at him.

"Just like that, huh?" Reisman retorted, snapping his fingers. Even as he did it, he thought, Damn, that's what Shidehara does. "You've got to be kidding!"

"There must be planning, personnel, vehicles, of course," Giap spoke up. "But you must act fast. It must be done!"

Reisman stared at them in disbelief. He had expected them to want something of him, something that he might agree to only if they would conduct him and Philippe to Lang Son. But what Ho wanted did not sound like a reasonable exchange, even if it were possible.

"I think you'd better tell me a little bit more," he said drily.

Ho beckoned him over to a wall where a map of China had been hung on the damp, gritty limestone. Yellow shading, hand drawn in crayon, indicated Japanese occupied territory, and fat yellow arrows showed the extent and direction of new Jap salients into the Chinese interior.

"Here," said Ho, touching his finger to the spot, "between Kweilin and Kweiyang, hidden in a canyon off the road, is the munitions cache of General Chiang Fa-K'uei, the *tuchun* of Kwangsi province."

"How do you know there is a munitions dump there?" Reisman demanded.

"I was there. I saw it myself," answered Ho.

Reisman remembered that "Tong Van So" had spoken of that before, one day when they were walking around Kunming. "How long ago were you there?" he pressed.

Ho raised his head and closed his eyes for a moment. "Nineteen forty-three . . . in the summer. One and a half years ago." He looked toward Giap and Thi and said, "My friends will remember that time, though they were not with me."

"How do you know that the guns are still there? Maybe Chiang Fa-K'uei's troops are finally making use of the stuff against the Japs."

"Perhaps, but it is not likely. I know the character of Chiang Fa-K'uei and the others like him. He will not use these guns for the purpose for which they were intended—huge caches of weapons and ammunition that were shipped at great cost from your United States, to be used in the fight against Japan. But perhaps you do not care," Ho taunted. "Your resources are limitless."

"Our transport isn't," retorted Reisman. "It all still has to be flown over the Hump from India and carried there from home by ships and planes."

In his excitement, Ho switched back and forth from English to French. "*Un gaspillage terrible! Quel dommage!* It is the wasteful hoarding of these armaments that gives these *tuchuns* their status and power against each other. That is their primary concern: to maintain their power against each other and against Chiang Kai-shek, who is their leader and master only as long as he can conserve his military strength to dominate the alliance of the Kuomintang. And they all live in fear that Mao Tse-tung's Eighth Route Army will come down upon them from the north."

"Will it?"

"I do not know."

"Let's ask Chin Li, your Chinese compatriot."

"Mr. Chin has gone home."

That surprised Reisman. "With assurances of fraternal support, I am sure. Perhaps they will even be able to spare you a gun or two. It was impolite of him not to say goodbye." Yet he felt neither slighted nor surprised, remembering Ho's constant advice to his own guerrillas during these weeks: *Stealth, continual stealth—arriving unexpectedly—leaving unnoticed.*

"Mr. Chin asked me to convey his good wishes to you," said Ho pleasantly.

"I'll bet he did."

Ho ignored the sarcasm and rambled on. "Chiang Kai-shek and all of the Kuomintang warlords have a greater fear of honest men like Mr. Chin than they do of the Japs who attacked your country, and with whom they have made certain accommodations."

"As you have!" Reisman charged.

"*Not* as I have!" retorted Ho angrily. "I do not have the same manpower and weapons that they have to fight *anyone!* But for those cowards to use their armaments against the Japs might mean that they would lose them. Even now Chiang Fa-K'uei is whining and wringing his hands like a miser about to lose his gold. Go up and take it from him, *Jean,* or the Japs will get it and shoot it back at you."

It was the sort of tantalizing and daring plan that Reisman relished. But he had to find out how much was true. "You saw this stuff yourself, huh?"

"It was not a fantasy, *Jean,*" Ho answered, and he looked past Reisman into another time and place, a pained expression on his countenance. "I was a prisoner of the Kuomintang Chinese. They marched me in chains from town to town, tied to others like a common criminal, wherever it pleased them to move me. On the day I saw Chiang Fa-K'uei's munitions hoard, I had already been a prisoner more than a year."

He had suffered much, he told Reisman. Sometimes he had been incarcerated with others in bare, cold, foul and vermin-ridden cells; other times he had been made to march day after day along the road, through heat and dirt, chained to other starving, thirsty, beaten, scabious, emaciated and staggering corpses.

"There was a time when we were told he had died," Tran Van Thi interjected. "The news shattered us all."

Vo Nguyen Giap, usually so stoic, added emotionally, "We have each faced terrible things—arrest and imprisonment, torture, loss of our families—but Uncle Ho suffered the worst."

"Why did they arrest you?" Reisman asked Ho.

He shrugged. "A mistake? *Qui sait?* They said I was a spy."

"For whom?"

Ho gave a bitter laugh. "For the French. Also for the Communists. A conflicting combination, *n'est-ce pas?*"

"Were you tried in a court?"

"You joke, *monsieur.*" He went on with his story of the arms cache. "It was perhaps mere chance that I saw it—what we say in my language is *thoi co,* a lucky circumstance. I was trudging along in a file of prisoners on the road between Kweilin and Kweiyang when Chiang Fa-K'uei himself came up in a staff car with his usual escort. It seems he was looking for me."

"You knew the man?"

"We had occasion to meet from time to time over the years. He had interrogated me himself at the time of my arrest. Actually, he is not such a bad fellow. That day on the road, in fact, he had come to grant my release. He had them remove my shackles and he took me into his car. We drove into the hills on a side road and were admitted by guards through a gate into a narrow pass that entered a small closed canyon. The hills rose steeply above us. There were caves there—perhaps man-made, I do not know—covered by iron grilles, with roadways climbing to the upper ones, and there were concrete buildings on the canyon floor and against the hillsides. There was a detachment of soldiers, there were civilian workers and barracks. I also saw heavy weapons emplacements covering the road and up on the hills. It was obviously a military facility of great importance. I recognized the place for what it was: a tremendous arsenal. Chiang Fa-K'uei took me into a little guard shack where we could talk in private."

"How much stuff was there?"

"Thousands of rifles, carbines, pistols and grenades. Machine guns, mortars and cannons, and millions of rounds of bullets, thousands of artillery rounds. We could go for years on what that fool has stored up and refuses to use. Once he realized that I was aware of what the place was, he told me himself what was there. He was trying to impress me with his importance and power."

"Were there trucks?"

"Just a few, and jeeps. Certainly not enough to move what was there. He must have been building it up for years, siphoning off what was doled out to him from your Lend-Lease."

"Then we would have to find our own transport," Reisman said.

Ho smiled. "Ah, you are interested."

"Of course I'm interested. Though I have no idea how it can be done or if it can be done. After all—without insult, even your personal intelligence is worthless today. Who knows what's there now, if anything? Maybe the Japs will get there first, anyway."

"That's why you must move swiftly!" Giap declared. "What we could do with all those weapons and ammunition! We would be not just guerrillas, we would be an army! We would start another front for you Americans and we would liberate our country at the same time!"

Reisman stared at them and shook his head. He understood their ambitious dreams but he was not fired by their fervor. He didn't believe in their capacity to carry off anything so grand, whether they had the Kwangsi warlord's arsenal or not.

"It's the beginning of an idea, that's all," he said. "I'll look into it—but only if you people help Lieutenant Belfontaine and me get to Lang Son first."

"There is no time for that!" Ho flared in agitation.

"That's the deal, Uncle," said Reisman coolly. "You people take us to Lang Son or you can go up into China after those guns yourself."

There were long moments of silence while they glared at him. Then Ho asked, with forced pleasantness, "How long will you delay there?"

"No more than two or three days. My superiors want me to do it and their appraisal of my mission here is dependent upon it," Reisman lied. "It will give me a chance to learn a little more about your country, get other points of view. That's the democratic way, you must remember."

Ho looked at him grimly. He obviously didn't want him wandering loose and unsupervised through Indochina, perhaps picking up anti–Viet Minh opinions. "Then what will you do about Chiang Fa-K'uei's arsenal?" he asked, his voice more plaintive.

Reisman tapped his temple. "I'm working on it already. Actually, by going to Lang Son first I'll be able to get back to Kunming and then up to the Kweilin-Kweiyang road a lot faster than if I started north from here today on foot." He strode over to the map table and they followed him. "There is an airfield at Lang Son and allies, friendly to me if not to you, particularly if I bring in Lieutenant Belfontaine—allies who might allow me to call in a small plane from Kunming."

He thought he could get Sam to send an L-5, a light plane that would hug the hills and canyons, come in low under Jap fighters and any air detection screen on the border. If the French cooperated and let the plane land and depart secretly he could bring the air corps sergeant to Kunming in a matter of hours instead of having to go through days or maybe weeks of a dangerous overland trek.

"That will be the easy part. Now how do we get quickly from here to Na Sam and Lang Son?" he asked, as though the matter of being given liberty to go there had been settled already. "I don't want to waste days in the bush just getting there. When you people need to move quickly, what do you do? Do you have vehicles stashed somewhere?"

"It will be arranged," said Ho with more enthusiasm than he had shown earlier. "I will escort you personally. It has been a long time since I have been in Lang Son and I too would like to visit it."

Reisman looked askance at him. He could not believe that Ho would voluntarily put his head in a noose like that. "That's very brave of you—or foolhardy. Will you go as Ho Chi Minh?"

Ho smiled. "You are beginning to understand these things, *Jean.*" Then with a wistful look to some distant past, he said, "If it is necessary to introduce me to anyone, you may call me Nguyen That Than, an old peasant from the province of Nghé An who has helped you to find your way. The Frenchman too must play our game, without any thought of betrayal, or it will be over for all of us. Him first."

"Nguyen That Than," Reisman repeated. "Does that name too have meaning?"

"It is the name that my father gave me when I was ten. It means, Nguyen Who Will Be Victorious."

"An interesting custom, this change of names to suit events," commented Reisman in a light, bantering tone. "There are men in Chicago who also change their names frequently. Their new names are called aliases and they are people who are often in trouble."

Ho appeciated the humor of that and he did not take offense. "Yes, I have read about that custom among your gangsters. Nevertheless, I prefer to think that the name my father gave me is prophetic."

"What were you called before that?"

Ho waved his hand in that now familiar gesture that decreed that something was of no importance. "What does it matter?" he said. "Are you compiling a dossier?"

"Merely curious," Reisman continued lightly. "I like to know as much as I can about a man when I place my life in his hands."

Still in good humor, Ho told him, "You have done very well with us so far. There is no reason why it should not continue."

Reisman dropped the repartee. "What about a vehicle?" he asked again, scrutinizing the raised contour map on the table. "A short hike out of the hills from Pac Bo and we can get onto this road here," he said, pointing.

"Route Three west to Cao Bang," Thi spoke up. "We avoided that coming in, as we did all main roads."

"If we first go there," said Reisman, following the road markers on the model, "we can connect at Cao Bang with what appears to be the main north–south road."

"Route Four," Thi identified.

"From there we can drive directly south to Na Sam and Lang

Son." Reisman looked up, challenging them again. "Or do the Viet Minh risk traveling on the main roads, whether on foot or in a vehicle?"

"Kita Shidehara will also go with us," answered Ho. "He will provide the transportation and a certain amount of official cover for us, provided we dress properly and are discreet. We must hope in the meanwhile that the Japanese begin to tire slightly and slow their advance in China."

"They will more likely run ahead of their supply lines," Reisman told him, staring again at the map of China on the wall of the limestone cave. He turned back after a thoughtful moment and looked directly at Ho Chi Minh. There was something about the man's story that bothered him. "What did Chiang Fa-K'uei want to talk to you about that day he took you to his arsenal?"

"The terms of my release. The arsenal was just *thoi co.* A place to talk. It was nearby."

"Why did he release you?" That was what Reisman really wanted to know.

Again Ho pursed his features into a questioning expression and raised his shoulders in a shrug.

"That won't do, Uncle," said Reisman. "What did he want in return?"

"To allow me to work to establish a unified and friendly front to his south. A country that will be friendly to the Kuomintang generally and to him personally."

"With economic and political advantages to him?" Reisman suggested.

"As he believes."

"And you remain on good terms with him?"

"It would seem so. But one never knows about the Chinese."

Chapter 22

The Viet Minh had many bicycles at Pac Bo, which they used as much to haul cargo as they did to pedal themselves along their narrow trails through the mountains and jungles. But what was even better was that Kita Shidehara used a motorcycle to get in and out of camp and kept a second one cached there for the Viets to use for fast courier work.

Ho sent Tran Van Thi to bring the Kempitai agent to the cave. When he had heard them out, he joined in their plan in a spirit of amused élan, as if they were all going on a happy outing to a tourist resort. Reisman was appalled that the Viets would openly reveal to a Japanese colonel that they intended to smuggle arms into the country. He still had trouble as to what stance to take toward Colonel Shidehara.

"You're not going to just sit by, are you," he challenged, "while we bring in weapons to attack your troops and destroy your installations?"

"We would expect—" Kita began. He paused. "I speak for those whose policy I am here to implement—and I do agree with it completely—we would expect judicious use of the matériel we allowed you to bring in."

"Against whom?"

"No one, until we gracefully retire from the scene."

"You're even more naïve than I am, Colonel. Will you provide trucks to move the stuff, if there is any?" He went to the wall map and jabbed at the place Ho had described between Kweilin, now in Jap hands, and Kweiyang far to the west, toward which they seemed to be heading. "If you came in from the east the Chinese would probably think you're part of the Jap army."

"No," replied Kita. "So would your people and they'd blow the shit out of us. Particularly your air force. Only people like you and I, and Mr. Ho, understand the subtleties of these sorts of arrangements."

Reisman thought that Sam Kilgore would understand also. And Tai Li and Chiang Kai-shek, who already had their dealings with the Japanese. Although those two would likely try to grab the arsenal for themselves. He wondered what Commodore Pelham Ludlow would think of it. Probably whatever Tai Li wanted.

"The French at Lang Son have trucks," Kita suggested. "Get them to help."

"Fat chance," said Reisman.

"Not if they think the stuff is for them."

"No, we must not let the French know anything about this business," Ho cautioned. "Not a word to Belfontaine. The purpose of our trip is simply to bring him safely to his people in Lang Son."

"Then he must stay there, not return to Kunming with me, as you said before," Reisman asserted.

Ho thought about that a moment. "You are right. We will have to let him stay in our country. If his superiors then allow your airplane to come in it will be because they want to reestablish their position as your allies after years of collaboration with the Japs. The only purpose of your flight, as you will tell them, is to return by the fastest and safest means to Kunming with the missing airman you were sent in to find. Is that not so, *mon commandant?*"

Ho paused, waiting for Reisman to pick up his cue on the story they were improvising. "Yes, of course, *mon commandant,*" Reisman responded with exaggerated courtesy.

"You were fortunate to locate him quickly at Na Sam," Ho continued. "Beyond that the French must not be told about your weeks with us, and certainly not one word about the arsenal of Chiang Fa-K'uei and what we plan to do with it. They would tighten and extend their security and make those Japanese who are not as sympathetic to us as Colonel Shidehara's people take aggressive action against us. The French would try to stop us from bringing in even one pistol, much less what I expect you will find in this munitions cache."

"How much stuff was there?" Reisman asked again. "I know what you said—thousands of this and thousands of that and millions of rounds of ammo—but let's bring it down to a practical level. How many trucks will be needed to move the stuff?"

"I don't know, *Jean.*"

"You know what we were able to bring down on the one six-by-six when we came in. It can hold two-and-a-half tons. Divide that into what you saw at the munitions dump."

Ho fixed his eyes on the wall map of China as if it might show him again what he once had seen on the road between Kweilin and Kweiyang. Finally he said, "I am unable to estimate. I was never permitted actually to see what was there." He turned to his aides and continued uncertainly, "Perhaps Giap, who knows about these things, can—"

"Twenty-five!" exclaimed Vo Nguyen Giap positively. "Bring us twenty-five truckloads of armaments and we will be very happy indeed, Major. Your trucks might also hook a few big guns and ammunition caissons behind them and tow them along."

"My trucks!" Reisman repeated, in admiration at Giap's facility for ready invention. "I don't have any trucks. All I'm doing is improvising—just like you."

"I'm sure you are good at that, *Jean,*" Ho complimented cheerfully.

Reisman stared at him. Then he said, "I'll send you a signal if there is an arsenal there. Moving it will be your responsibility, not mine." Ho shot him one of those how-could-you glances, but Reisman continued, "I will also try to put together a truck convoy, but you must not depend upon it. If I find the transport, so much the better. However, when I give you the signal I want you to send up fifty of your own men, armed and ready to fight—and they must bring with them the twenty-five trucks, if that's what you want. I don't care where you get them. Borrow them or steal them. I'll try to get what I can from the OSS motor pool, but I doubt that they're going to be willing to commit manpower and trucks for an operation like this. It will be your problem to move the stuff down here."

"But how are we to do that, *Jean*?" asked Ho plaintively.

"The same way you yourself move back and forth. You said you have agents in place at Ch'ing-Hsi, didn't you?"

"Yes," replied Ho regretfully.

"Then work through them. I'm sure there's a network moving out from there. Maybe not as big and powerful as Tai Li's network, but you've obviously got men and women in place, channels of communication and transport. Use them. Don't sit back now the way you accuse the Chinese and the *colons* of doing."

He stared at the China map on the wall, then went to the raised model on the table, where he was able to pick up in better detail the threads of roads and trails as they came to the frontier and crossed. Ho moved beside him and said, "We don't have the capability to operate on that scale deep inside China. Only if you bring the matériel to the border. There the Viet Minh will move it on bicycles, backs and legs."

"Why don't you bring the stuff in by water?" Reisman suggested. "Slowly and inconspicuously in sampans and junks. Here, for instance, on the Sông Hong. You can pick it up south of Kunming and sail right across the border at Lao Cai. You have access to rivercraft. Why not send them upstream as far as they can go? When they come back loaded you can take the stuff overland with porters just the way you did when we first came in."

"Traffic on the Sông Hong is too easily observed. Though your idea is good," replied Ho. He moved his hand eastward over the map table and darted it among the thin blue veins of streams and rivers. "Many smaller ones cross the border here. Some are not even named. They pass through unpopulated hill country."

"You could split up the shipment on the rivers, and still move some of it by land," Reisman continued. "It would give you a better chance to get it through. I'll also try again for an air drop."

"Very well," said Ho. "We must hope again for *thoi co*. What will you do if you can't fly out of Lang Son?"

"Go out the way you usually do."

"Then let us leave quickly."

Reisman and Kita left the cave together to go to their huts and prepare for the journey. "Why are you doing this, Kita?" Reisman asked as they walked through the camp. "Don't you have any loyalty to your country?"

"Of course I do. This is the best way I can help now. Fate has brought you and me to a field of common interest—for the time being, at least."

"Why should I trust you? How do I know that at any moment you won't revert to that crazy Bushido business and stick it to me, instead of this buddy-buddy act you're putting on?"

"It's not an act, Major," Kita said wearily. "I long ago came to the conclusion that Bushido is Bullshitto, whether it's the Japanese variety or American-style. Your government gives medals for it. There are few medals given to Japanese soldiers for bravery. It is expected of them—to fight fiercely and unquestioningly for emperor and country, to die rather than be defeated—and that's the way it is, kiddo. I'm trying to secure the future without adding too much damage to the present, both here and at home. I don't want the sort of destruction in Japan that we made in China and which your armies and air forces are now bringing to France, Italy and Germany. My business is intelligence. I'm using mine. You use yours."

Kita smiled and strode off briskly toward his hut, leaving Reisman staring after him, feeling only a little less wary and distrustful than before. It was the nature of his business to be distrustful, he supposed; it came with the territory and it had served him well so far. Though he sometimes wondered, as he did now, if he was overdoing it; if, in fact, it was the business of his nature rather than the nature of his business.

Philippe was waiting for him anxiously. "We go," Reisman said. "Right away. Get ready. Ho and the Jap are taking us. We'll stop on the way to pick up one of my airmen. They've found him not far from Lang Son."

"*Magnifique, Jean!* I shall not forget this!"

"We have to get our stories straight first."

"Stories?"

"Lies. *Mensonges.*"

"I do not understand."

"You must never reveal that you were captured by the Viet Minh and that you stayed here. You do not know that this place exists. You have never met Ho Chi Minh or any of the others. The man who will escort us to Lang Son is called Nguyen That Than, an old peasant whom we met on the road. I have given a pledge in your name and mine in exchange for a guarantee of safe passage."

"I see," said Philippe, looking at the ground somberly.

"You and I met by lucky chance in the mountains," Reisman went on. "We each jumped into Tonkin from separate departure places on separate missions. I am here from Air Ground Aid Section China to find the missing airmen. You are here for . . . whatever reasons you are here for, Philippe. We met Nguyen That Than and he helped us. Do you understand?"

The Frenchman looked up at him. "Yes, of course. It will be difficult. A matter of honor, but which way lies honor? What about the Jap?"

"He will tell you what he wants you to do. He is, of course, our chief escort and our protection. No matter what guise he takes he has safe passage from the Japs, the French and the Viets. Do you agree to abide by these terms, Philippe?"

Belfontaine gazed at him, torn by the conflict of needs and desires. At last he nodded. "I agree. Now I know what Pétain and the others in Vichy must have felt," he said sadly. "An accommodation."

Reisman tried to make him feel easier about it. "Don't be so hard on yourself, *mon ami.* This is neither heroism, collaboration nor betrayal. You merely keep your mouth shut and do what you planned to do when you jumped in. Go find your sister and make your contact for de Gaulle. Just leave Shidehara and Ho out of it."

They packed knapsacks and radio equipment, inspected carbines and pistols, and were about to leave when Nguyen Thi Mai, wearing her dark peasant's clothes, came to say goodbye. Belfontaine nodded to her, muttered a brusque adieu and went outside to leave them alone.

Mai grasped Reisman's hand and thanked him for all he had done. Impetuously, she stretched up her head to kiss his cheek. Then, even more unexpectedly, Reisman felt her lips slide to his mouth and kiss him with gentle warmth.

She drew away and smiled at him.

"What does that mean?" he asked, feeling again the pleasure and excitement of their first meeting.

"One never knows," Mai answered softly. "Perhaps only *bonne chance*—good luck!"

Just before they mounted the motorcycles to leave camp, Ho Chi Minh confronted Lieutenant Belfontaine with his own warning: "You must never tell anyone where you have been, or our names, or what you think you have learned here, or reveal the location of this place. You must agree—as a French officer and man of honor—to reveal nothing. Only that you met *Commandant* Reisman in the mountains after you parachuted and later you found kind people to help you to your destination."

Philippe stared at him tensely. "Are you Nguyen Ai-Quôc?" he blurted out.

"I have heard of that man," Ho answered in a quiet voice. "But my name is Ho Chi Minh, as my colleagues will tell you. Even that name I forbid you to reveal to anyone. For this journey I am Nguyen That Than. That is how you must think of me always, *monsieur*. Just an old peasant whom you met walking in the mountains."

Chapter 23

They left the Pac Bo base on a dirt track through the tangled growth of the high hills in the early afternoon. Their faces were half covered by goggles. Reisman drove one motorcycle, with Philippe sitting behind him. They wore field caps, fatigues and jackets without insignia. They carried carbines and pistols. Their knapsacks were strapped on as saddlebags. The radio and generator overhung the luggage carrier and made the machine long, heavy and awkward to handle. Reisman had insisted on taking one radio and had put operators in the guerrilla camp on twenty-four-hour alert with the equipment they had there.

Kita drove the lead motorcycle, with Ho as passenger. Ho was dressed for colder weather in a longer, heavier version of the traditional farmer's *cu-nao*. Kita wore his military uniform. In the Viet Minh liberated zone where they would travel the first couple of hours, they would be recognized and left alone by hidden guards and observers. Later in the journey, Kita was confident he would be able to get them through any unexpected Jap or French roadblocks. Reisman and Philippe would pass as French colonial officers on a field inspection trip.

It was about twenty miles south and west to Cao Bang, and they were there in less than an hour. Kita kept a Jap army truck there, under the protection of the Viet Minh, garaged in a separate little building that looked like just another farm storage shed in an area of such structures.

"You really know the neighborhood, I see," Reisman cracked as they switched vehicles.

"Been working it longer. My customers are my friends," Kita responded. "Here, give me a hand, will you?"

They ran a plank up into the truck bed and wheeled one of the motorcycles aboard, then shoved the plank in after it. "Just in case," said Kita. "Like a lifeboat."

There was a duffel bag in the back of the truck too, and a *can slua tau* costume on a hook. Colonel Shidehara came well prepared, Reisman observed. He left the second motorcycle in the garage, hidden under a pile of hemp sacks, and locked the door.

Kita drove, Ho sat in the middle and Reisman against the passenger door. Belfontaine sat back in the bed of the truck, close to the canvas flap window that gave onto the cab. Reisman wondered if the man, armed as he was, might dare try to take them prisoner and betray them in Lang Son. It was possible but he doubted it. Philippe surely had enough sense to realize that even after they reached the French fortress it would be Shidehara who would be in command if he chose to be. For he was still not only a theoretical ally of the French *colons* but, more importantly, a ranking officer of the occupying power. Though Reisman had no idea what Kita intended to say or do once they reached Lang Son, or if he intended to enter the town.

The road carved its way southeast, seeking passage parallel to streambeds and through high rifts and valleys that rose to three thousand feet and dropped below one thousand. It was a principal road with some secondary stretches—narrow, rutted, spewing up dirt and dust. There were forty-eight miles to travel between Cao Bang and Na Sam, where the downed American airman was. Lang Son was seventeen miles further.

Reisman examined the gray, chill sky that hinted at the possibility of rain.

Ho seemed to read his mind. "Perhaps a little drizzle from the northeast," he said. "But it will not be bad this time of the year. It is in summer and early fall we have big rains from the southwest. Monsoon and typhoon."

Traffic on the road was light. The terrain was thinly populated. Villages and hamlets were tucked away out of sight in folds of the hills and behind tangled growth. Occasionally Kita swung the truck out to pass oxcarts, handwagons, pedestrians, mule trains and ponies. Motor traffic was sparse, and there were hardly any military vehicles. Reisman commented on that.

"Nobody has much desire to stick their noses out up here in the Viet Minh zone," Kita said. "It's pretty much a stand-off. Everybody tries to stay in secure zones and mind their own business."

Ho waved his hand over a ridge on their right. "That way is Hanoi. It is much different there," he said wistfully. "There are hundreds of villages, millions of people struggling in the delta of the Sông Hong." He gestured to the jungle-grown hills on either side of the two-lane road. "Here there is not much to see. It is very simple, a primitive region of my country. There are not many people. There is much wilderness and the villages are isolated. Would it amuse you to go to Hanoi, *Jean*?"

Reisman kept his eyes on the road ahead. "It would amuse me, but there is no time to be a tourist, as you yourself have pointed out. I must pass it up, *monsieur*."

"It would almost be better for you to go there than to Lang Son," Ho added cryptically.

Reisman turned to look at the Viet leader. "Why?"

Ho smiled, to cover whatever he had really been thinking. Smoke from one of his frequent cigarettes rose against the windshield and made the cab stuffy. "It is a charming city. Broad, tree-lined boulevards, stately French architecture, cozy cafés."

"You make it sound like Paris," Kita Shidehara commented, turning his head to them for a moment and then back to the road.

"Have you been to Paris?" Reisman asked.

"Yes, a number of times," Kita replied. "I liked it very much. I like Hanoi too. Though it is perhaps too conservative. Not as much fun as Saigon."

"It is not so much Paris," Ho continued, "but at least a French city, with its French university, its Pasteur Institute, the magnificent Catholic cathedrals. Are you a Catholic, *Jean*?"

"Sometimes."

"I would not mind a visit there myself," Ho went on. "It has been a long time."

There was a wistful tone to Ho's reverie, yet Reisman could not help wondering if the man was mocking the French aspects of Hanoi rather than longing for them.

It was Colonel Shidehara, however, who confounded him even more. What did the man really want? What did he really know, and how much intelligence could be dug out of him? He was not a man who would be easily used or fooled. More likely the other way around. Reisman had already been led to imagine he was an operative from another U.S. branch, maybe a spook from the State Department or the man called Jimmy Lum. That the Kempitai officer hadn't taken advantage of that opening was perhaps a point in his favor. So, instead of trying to be cute or devious, Reisman decided to ask him some simple, direct questions. The answers, if he got any, would be of strategic importance in Kunming and Chungking.

"How much do you know about this new drive into China?" he asked.

Kita gave him an amused glance. *"Ichigo!"* he answered cryptically.

"What's that mean?"

"Number one. That's what they call it. It's a big operation. More than fifteen divisions."

"How far will they go?"

"Any place your team wants to stop them."

"What's that supposed to mean?"

"Exactly what it says. They've already achieved their primary objectives, but the Chinks keep fading away ahead of them and they keep going. Chiang got Stilwell fired because Stilwell kept telling him the truth and he didn't want to hear it. Now Wedemeyer is trying to get the Gimo to send in his best troops and ship guns and equipment to the front, but he still won't do it. It's not that he doesn't have the troops and the guns. He does. The Chinese gave a good account of themselves under Stilwell over in Burma once they got into it. They were well fed, well trained and equipped by you Americans in India—not the sick, starving peasant recruits who had been flown over the Hump to Ramgargh."

"We really ought to draft you to take over our side, Colonel," said Reisman wryly. "Where do you get all this information?"

Kita turned his head from the road for a moment and gave him a forbearing look. "It's what I do for a living. I'm supposed to know these things," he said. "Chiang's afraid to use those soldiers. Their officers are respected and effective. He's afraid they'll turn against him." Then he chuckled. "You know," he said softly, "at this stage all you really need to stop the Jap drive on Kunming and Chungking is to let them *think* you're bringing your first team into position to fight them."

Reisman started to scoff at that. "If that's all it takes—"

"No, there's another part to it," Kita interrupted. "The greater fear is that Chiang will shake hands again with Mao and this time they'll make it stick, and that the three million men Mao's supposed to have in the north will come rampaging down on us in the south and east. I had a few chances to talk to Chin Li at Pac Bo. If the rest of his people are anything like him then we've got real trouble and so has Chiang. And so have you Americans, if you're planning any mercantile mischief in China after the war."

"That's not my department," Reisman said distractedly.

He was still mulling over the first part of what Kita had said. The possibility of mounting a vast deception against the Japs in China intrigued him. It had been done in Europe prior to the Normandy invasion, and had worked beautifully against the Nazis. An entire phantom army had been set up in the south of England, complete with dummy installations, barracks, vehicles, and a constant and heavy stream of phony communications—all devised to fool Nazi spies and aerial observers into thinking that *that* was the big invasion army. The Germans had not believed that the Normandy landing was the real invasion until it had overwhelmed them.

Perhaps Kita was right—that all it would take to halt the new Jap drive toward Kunming and Chungking would be to get them to *think* that the Chinese were doing what everybody knew they had the capacity to do and what their American allies had been urging them to do.

It was the kind of stunt OSS would go for, even if China Command and the Kuomintang didn't.

Ho guided Kita off Route 4 near Na Sam and they ground up into the hills a couple of miles on a narrow dirt track to the Nung hamlet where the American air corps sergeant was being held. It was mid-afternoon, but an early gloom had settled into the woods and brush of the high saddles and ravines. The sky above was gray and drizzly, the track muddy and rutted. In heavy rains it would probably be a running quagmire, Reisman thought. They had to leave the truck and walk the last hundred yards. The settlement was built haphazardly on the edge of cultivated fields, about twenty houses and animal sheds with thatched roofs and walls made of crushed bamboo and mud.

Short, muscular men wearing indigo clothes gathered for their arrival. These too were *can slua tau* who sometimes worked as porters for the Viet Minh and were allied with them generally. Ho made proper obeisance to the headman, whom he knew. They spoke in Viet-Namese, Ho enunciating his tones with slow, heightened clarity, the Nung chief stumbling over some words but pleased to be able to communicate in what to him was a foreign tongue. Ho turned to Reisman to give the gist of the dialogue.

"Your man has ingratiated himself very well with these people," he said with a broad smile. "The chief says he would consider canceling the engagements of his daughters and would look with favor upon the American flyer to marry one or even both of his daughters."

"Does Filmore know about this?"

"Not yet. Among the Nung, the proposal is usually made from the father of the boy through an intermediary," Ho said impishly. "Perhaps you can serve as the father and I as the intermediary, once we find out the sergeant's wishes in the matter."

"I think not, Uncle. The man's booked for the duration plus six. They want him to go back to work."

While the headman escorted Ho and Reisman to the hut where Technical Sergeant Fourth Class Randolph Filmore was being entertained, Shidehara and Belfontaine stayed behind near the chief's house, exchanging smiles and grunts with the other tribesmen. Kita tried out some of his Viet-Namese, then some Chinese, but managed contact only with a few words of French, which made Philippe feel less nervous and alien.

Filmore the waist gunner was not happy to see Major Reisman come though the doorway of the crude shack. The interior was furnished with a few simple benches and tables, and mats were spread on the floor. The room was dim and foul-smelling, and a layer of soot from the cookfire covered everything.

The sergeant, still in his flight uniform, was lying on a mat, smoking a pipe of opium, attended by two nubile Nung maidens. The girls were intricately dressed in colorful embroidered layers of jacket, skirt, baggy pants and turban, and were liberally adorned with silver buttons, bracelets, necklaces and earrings. Filmore was drowsy from the pipe. The girls looked at him adoringly out of dark mongol eyes, their wide faces alight with chubby-cheeked smiles and nice white teeth. Food and drink were ready to be served.

"Do I have to go back, Major?" the sergeant whined when Reisman identified himself and told him he had come to rescue him and take him back to China. He didn't look as if he wanted to be rescued. "Next time around one of those Japs could kill me."

Reisman, who had expected the man to be bursting with joy and gratitude, could readily see the merit of his complaint. He decided that Filmore would respond better to guile than threats. Forcing a solemn expression onto his face, he said, "I think you ought to know, Sergeant, that the headman and I have already discussed your marriage to these ladies—as sort of an international gesture of goodwill. It's voluntary, of course, but if that's what you prefer I'll just see to the proper authorization."

Filmore rose from the mat with a sudden burst of energy. "I'll be coming right along, sir," he mumbled. He gathered his scanty gear together, shook hands formally with the now saddened girls, and tottered out, Ho holding him firmly and disapprovingly by the arm.

When he saw Colonel Shidehara, however, he drew back in fear and said, "What the hell's going on?"

"It's okay, Sergeant," Reisman assured him. "It's only a costume. He's part of the rescue party. Nothing to worry about."

Kita stared at Sergeant Filmore with a look that ran the gamut from hostility to disdain to pity. "I think—just in case we run into anyone—that you'd better find him an old *cu-nao* and one of those big straw hats," he said. Then, laughing, he went on, "Roll him around in the mud first to darken him up a bit."

When it was done and they'd taken away his uniform and Filmore looked as much like a native as he was ever going to look, Reisman was for getting on the road instantly. But Ho, listening to urgent words from the headman, told him it was necessary to delay the journey a little longer. The chief wanted Filmore, whom he'd grown fond of during these days, to visit the *p'u tao,* the Taoist priest of the hamlet, to go through the traditional ceremony for a man about to leave on a long trip. It would help to make his journey safer.

"I'm all for that. Let's do it," Reisman agreed readily. He too wanted whatever gods and spirits who inhabited the paths and places of his journeys to be on his side.

The headman led them to a dwelling slightly more substantial than the others, with a porch across the front. The *p'u tao* awaited them there. He was a robust, broad-shouldered man with thick eyebrows and a projecting brow, dressed in dark, baggy cotton trousers and jacket, topped by a turban more elaborate than the others. When they gathered before him he began to chant, shake a tambourine and turn intermittently to strike a gong. Then he addressed Filmore in a voice of great authority. The headman translated the *p'u tao*'s words into Viet-Namese for Ho, who in turn translated for Filmore.

"He wishes you good fortune on your journey and advises the following," Ho intoned somberly. "You must abandon the journey if you meet a man combing his hair . . . or if a woman is the first person you encounter . . . or if you hear the cry of a flying squirrel . . . or if a bird flies across your path . . . or if you see two birds or snakes mating . . . or if a spider descends in front of you."

Filmore listened entranced at first, but with growing uneasiness as the harbingers of bad fortune were enumerated. "Hell, Major," he mumbled, "we ain't never gonna get out of here at that rate."

Even as he listened, fragments of another folklore and sorcery rose in Reisman's memory: *a country lane in Somerset; Tess Simmons huddled close to him; a noisy magpie appearing before them on the branch of a tree. "Raise your hat and make the sign of the cross on your breast!" Tess had urged. "It's bad luck if you don't."* When he wouldn't, she had turned and spat three times over her left shoulder as another way to exorcise the malevolence of the bird. In the end he had raised his hat and made the sign of the cross anyway. And he had had good luck since.

Reisman came back from his reverie. "Doesn't seem to leave us much leeway, does it, Filmore? Tell you what. You keep your eyes and ears closed until we're in the truck and on the road. That way you won't know the difference."

The sergeant took him literally. He shook hands with the headman, bid farewell to the villagers, then plugged his fingers in his ears and closed his eyes tightly. Reisman held him by the arm and guided him out of the hamlet to the truck.

"I'll sit in the back with him," he told Philippe. "You go up front."

Belfontaine made a wry face, but went obediently to the passenger door. He would wait for the others to get in so that he would not be squeezed between the two men he considered enemies.

Shidehara and Ho took Reisman aside for a moment. Ho told him, "You must order your man not to say one word about Kita or me in Lang Son. You must impress on him the importance of this. Afterward, though, when he returns to China, it would be good if he told his superiors it was the Viet Minh who rescued him. I want General Chennault to know that we have been of service to him and will do much more. Perhaps one day he will return the favor. *Comprenez-vous?*"

Reisman smiled at him. *"Mais oui, mon commandant!"* he snapped exaggeratedly. They both understood quite well that the Viets were still only a probationary ally. "Are you two going into Lang Son with us?"

"Not with you," Kita replied. "We will go separately and observe things in our own way."

As the truck bounced back down the rutted track to the main highway, Reisman and Filmore were alone for the first time. The airman finally opened his eyes and unblocked his ears and stared around the musty gloom under the canvas. He scratched distrustfully at the unfamiliar *can slua tau* costume he wore, looked over his shoulder toward the driver's compartment, then leaned close and asked, "What happened to the other guys in my crew, Major?"

Reisman told him what he knew: that three had been captured by the Japs, three were being held by the French, and the others were missing. Then he told him where they were going and what the plan was, and drilled him on their cover story.

"The lieutenant and I were alone when we picked you up at the village," he warned. "You were never in this truck and you never set eyes on the driver or the man with him. We walked all the way to Lang Son. Got it, Sergeant?"

"Yes, sir."

"Good." Reisman leaned back against the truckbed stakes and smiled ingratiatingly. "What kind of a plane do you fly, Filmore?"

It was the same sort of question he had asked the crew chief at the bar in Chungking more than a month earlier, and he was asking it for the same reason.

"B-24, sir—this last mission. But I've flown others."

"Ever fly in a B-25?"

"Sure have, Major. Medium bomber . . . twin engine. Low-level stuff . . . bombing and strafing right down where a guy with a cap gun can get at you. Funny thing is, I never got shot down in one of those."

"You fellows ever have reason to paint out your squadron markings and I.D.?" Reisman asked casually.

"No, sir, but I seen one once."

"When was that?" Reisman tried not to change the tone of his voice, to sound anything more than casually interested.

Filmore warmed to the story. "A couple of months back when a slopehead crew slipped into Kunming late one night. They was passengers on a transport."

"Slopehead?"

"Yeah. You know . . . Chinee. Spoke some English with Texas accents. Funniest damn thing you ever heard. Trained there, I guess. Nice bunch of boys. Had a special job to do somewhere. Hush-hush. They came in quick-like from Chungking that night. We had to fix up a plane for them."

"What do you mean, 'fix up'?"

"Took all the markings off, like you said, like it come from the moon or Mars and didn't belong to nobody. Could've even been taken for a Jap, 'ceptin' it was a B-25."

Reisman closed his eyes. The memory of it was seared on his mind: *Baw San shouting, "B-25!" The aircraft diving low. All of them expecting the friendly waggle of wings. Then bombs falling, machine guns firing, Kachins dying all around him. And Linc Bradford killed.*

Sergeant Filmore had given it new substance. There had been a Chinese crew. Sent from Chungking. By whom? Reisman thought he knew. But he did not know what he might do with that knowledge, if anything. Perhaps *thoi co* would work for him too.

Chapter 24

Kita drove the truck slowly, for he didn't want to reach Lang Son until after dark. Occasionally he drove off the main road for a few minutes to poke into narrow tracks and assess the desirability of hiding places behind trees and brush.

At Dong Dang, the road and the town sat astride a dagger salient of the Chinese frontier. There was another French outpost there, controlling the border area, and the truck was stopped by colonial soldiers at a checkpoint. Reisman listened, with some admiration, to Kita's easy conversation with them in French and added his own cheerful "*Bonsoir!*" when one of the guards peeked into the back of the truck. Then they were on their way south again. It was seven miles to the outskirts of Lang Son and they moved slowly now in fast fading twilight.

The route descended from the hills onto high tableland. Three miles from Lang Son, Kita pulled off the road close to a stand of mangrove. He came around back and asked Reisman to help him roll the motorcycle out of the truck and hide it. The man was covering his bets, Reisman realized.

"Hiding the lifeboat?" he remarked as they muscled the machine into the thicket.

"That's right. Close enough to town so I can get to it if I have to," Kita acknowledged.

Back on the road, Reisman looked around in the last twilight and saw no obvious way he might recognize the place again. To the east and south the tableland opened out into featureless marsh and paddy land. There were hills behind them and to the west. Far to the east and south he could just make out the silhouettes of other hills and mountains against the night sky.

"How are you going to find this place again?" he asked.

"I have a good sense for this sort of thing," replied Kita. "Look there across the paddy. See the lights? The village of Na Tuot. It will be my guide, if necessary."

"What are you going to do with the truck?"

"Drive it in closer. I've got another place for it."

A mile and a half further along, with the lights of Lang Son visible ahead, Kita again took the truck off the highway—this time on a dirt road across dry tableland—for a couple of hundred yards before he stopped. Reisman heard new voices, peered out and saw two saffron-robed monks, one holding a lantern, the other swinging open a wood gate that gave onto the interior courtyard of a large pagoda. Kita drove across the yard into a shed opened by another monk.

"This is it, gentlemen," he called through the window from the cab. "We walk from here."

Reisman and Filmore slid the radio and generator rucksacks to the edge of the truckbed and jumped down. Philippe came around and lifted the generator onto his back. Reisman took the radio.

In the courtyard, Ho chatted amiably in Viet-Namese with the monks. He turned to Reisman. "They are friends," he explained. "They know how to maintain silence."

Kita climbed up into the back of the truck. When he jumped down again a few minutes later to help close and lock the shed door, he was wearing a *can slua tau* costume. Reisman watched him shuffle toward them in a slumped, weary posture, the worn peasant's sandals on his feet listlessly kicking up dirt. He seemed to have shrunk a few inches in height and his body moved all askew, as if it belonged to another man.

Ho looked at Kita with approval. "Very good," he said in Mandarin. "I see that you have read Sun Tzu on the subject of spies."

Kita smiled, stood slumped in an open-armed, submissive pose, and replied also in Mandarin. "The ordinary class of spies," he recited in a mocking humble tone. "What some call surviving spies, who bring back news from the enemy's camp."

They both looked at Reisman, who had understood their words, and switched to English for his benefit.

"Such a spy," quoted Ho, in an amused oratorical style, "should be a man of keen intellect, in outward appearance a fool, of shabby exterior, but with a will of iron."

Kita stood tall, thrust out his chest and chin in an exaggerated pose, and continued the words of Sun Tzu:

"He must be active, robust, endowed with physical strength and courage, thoroughly accustomed to all sorts of dirty work, able to endure hunger and cold and to put up with shame and ignominy."

"Sounds like my MOS," Reisman commented with a wry look.

"I thought you would appreciate that," said the Kempitai colonel, smiling. "The requirements were codified a long time ago and remain pretty much the same."

It intrigued Reisman that in Shidehara he had met "the enemy" face to face and found him to be a man much like himself: both cautious and bold, sometimes outrageous, contemptuous of form and authority; a man who thought things through and left as little to chance as possible; who spoke many languages; preferred mind over muscle to accomplish his ends; yet was likely highly skilled in military combat, though there had been no occasion to demonstrate it as yet.

"What's the drill now, Colonel?" he asked.

"We stay off the highway and slip into Lang Son as quietly as possible. You and your airman and your Frenchman present yourselves to the commander of the garrison at the fort, where I am sure they will not be pleased to see you. It will disrupt the sanctity of their nice, safe, dull routine."

"What about you and the uncle?"

"We will go a certain distance with you and then separate," Ho spoke up. "We have friends to visit."

To Reisman that meant that there were Viet Minh agents in the town, perhaps even in the fort itself. He was intrigued by the thought of the old peasant Nguyen That Than gathering the latest military, political and economic intelligence of the region to use in the plans and operations of Ho Chi Minh. Perhaps he would even inspire the locals with the presence of their leader, if they knew who their leader was.

"I want a rendezvous with you before dawn tomorrow—let us say at 0500," Reisman told them. "You know the territory. Pick a place and tell me how to get there."

Kita thought a moment, looked at Belfontaine and Filmore and then beckoned to Reisman and Ho to follow him out of earshot. "The less they know, the better," he whispered. "If the *colons* don't intern you right off the bat, meet us at the airfield, north end of the runway."

Reisman remembered details of the map table in Ho's cave. He would have to go there anyway to reconnoiter the field before bringing a plane in. "South of town, across the river," he said.

"You have been here before, *Jean*?" Ho asked in surprise.

"Your map, Uncle."

"Ah, of course. Very good. A military mind," said Ho. "We will cross the Sông Ky Cung together tonight by boat. There is a bridge, but it is guarded. The fort is also on the other side."

"Make it 0500 in the rice paddy at the north end of the strip," Reisman repeated. "If I'm not there, it means they've locked Filmore and me up."

"What would you like us to do then?" Kita asked brightly.

"Figure out some way to spring us. And Ho, you let Kunming know where we are."

They returned to the others and Kita spoke to Belfontaine in French. "A word of warning to you, Lieutenant, in addition to what we told you earlier about not betraying us. Be cautious with your countrymen. Don't give your hand away immediately."

Philippe bristled. *"Que voulez-vous dire?"* he demanded.

"You must be aware that whatever politics and plans you bring may not be acceptable to these people. Except where it conflicts with my government, the French here still run their military and civil affairs as collaborators with the Vichy government, which, of course, no longer exists now. Its laws and treaties are repudiated in Europe—but not here."

Philippe nodded. He could not quite bring himself to say thank you.

The five men left the pagoda and began walking toward the town on a footpath west of the highway. Kita took the point. Ho placed himself close to Reisman, bringing up the rear.

"I do not like Lang Son," Ho told him.

"Why?"

"It is a place of terrible violence and death," said Ho broodingly. "The air is thick with the spirits of martyred patriots and the ground reeks with their blood. Generation after generation of our people have had their massacres at Lang Son—uprisings, war, defeat and slaughter. Even the French suffered there at the hands of the Japanese when the Japs first came in 1940. And afterward my own people again."

Reisman sensed that this was what Ho had started to tell him earlier while they were still on the road to Na Sam, when he had suggested it might be better to go to Hanoi than Lang Son.

"Why there in particular?" asked Reisman.

Ho shrugged. "It is isolated, close to the Chinese border, a route for invaders to come and go. Perhaps it is like Jerusalem—in the way and coveted by enemies."

Reisman snorted. "No, Uncle, not at all like Jerusalem. That is a special conceit."

"You have been there?"

"Yes, long before the war . . . this war . . . I spent a little time there . . . as a tourist."

"As you are touring now in Viet-Nam, eh?"

"The circumstances were different."

They broke off the chatter as they scrambled up a railroad embankment and dropped down to the other side. Reisman was surprised by the reality of the tracks, the intimation of the possibility of normal, peaceful, civilized travel and commerce in this place, of a connection to other places.

"Do the trains run here?" he whispered.

"Not so often now," Ho answered. "Your air raids are successful. My agents have helped with intelligence. Many engines and cars have been blown up, bridges and track destroyed. The enemy is having great difficulty maintaining heavy transport. It will all have to be rebuilt after the war. I hope that the United States will help us."

Reisman kept his silence. The man had made a quantum leap to a time that might never arrive for either of them. The strength of his ego and confidence was astonishing. In the darkness it seemed to Reisman that they were moving beside paddy fields or marshland. The night was overcast, cold and drizzly. He hated not knowing exactly where he was, where he was going or what it would look like when he got there. He disliked being dependent upon the judgment and actions of others. In the near distance he caught sight of lighted places, silhouetted clusters of houses, large buildings, patterns of streets and crossroads. They took footpaths and tracks to avoid them. Their own footfalls and whispers were the only sounds Reisman could hear in the night. Then the mist thickened and they topped the earth-mounded levee that was the bank of the Sông Ky Cung. Ho left them there, walked toward some shacks built close to the levee, and came back a few minutes later with a man who took them across the river in a sampan.

In the darkness and mist, within the town and forming an enveloping barrier to part of it, the wall of the fort loomed above Reisman and his two companions as they made their way along a path that separated the citadel from paddies on the west. Their escort was gone now and they were on their own. Ho Chi Minh and Kita Shidehara had pointed the direction of their march and left them half an hour earlier atop the levee on the south side of the Sông Ky Cung.

The high wall of the fort was formidable, in an eighteenth- or nineteenth-century way. Reisman knew about places like this. Perhaps a Vauban, he thought, as he moved swiftly along its massive base. All over Europe, colonial America and the outposts of western empires in the Far East, similar strongholds had gone up in those centuries, based on the fortification designs of the great seventeenth-century French marshal and engineer. This one was doubtless here as much to keep the natives of the Lang Son region subjugated as it was to defend their land against invaders.

Reisman knew about places like this for the same reason he knew about Sun Tzu's ancient *Principles of War*. He had an intellectual as well as a practical interest in the arts, implements and making of war. Over the years he had read much of the military literature of the ages. Coming upon the fort like this, secretively in the night, gave him an unsettling reminder of the death and destruction he had helped wreak upon the Chinese stronghold of Caojian. He assumed that the citadel here was much larger, stronger and better manned, but he knew how useless it was in twentieth-century war, except as a place to quarter troops and store armaments—though there were those who might still put their faith in the strategic and tactical value of such a place.

He led Belfontaine and Filmore out of the paddies, rounded the southwest corner of the fort and saw ahead that the footpath joined a vehicle road leading to the lighted entry portal. He watched the activity there for a few minutes. The gateway doors were open. Two soldiers with slung rifles flanked the portal, scrutinizing vehicles and foot traffic; another soldier, wearing side arms—probably the corporal of the guard—was busy saluting, checking I.D.s and waving vehicles through. It was 1900 hours, still early enough in the evening for a fair number of vehicles, animals and pedestrians.

"You're in charge from here, Philippe," said Reisman softly. "You do the talking. We're just going to walk up to them as if we belong here. Two Frenchies and a local boy coming in from patrol. The radio makes it look even better."

"*Mon Dieu!* They will think we dropped from the moon."

"Just get us inside to the commandant's office with as little fuss as possible. We'll be lucky if Filmore's act holds up at the gate, but it doesn't make much difference at this point." He turned to Filmore and asked, "Do you speak French, Sergeant?"

"No, sir. Never did learn any."

Reisman switched to French. "I must remind you, Lieutenant, to keep in mind what Nguyen That Than and the Jap told you and to act accordingly."

"Of course. I gave my word," Philippe answered in an injured tone. *"Allons, commandant!"*

He started forward, but Reisman held him back. "*Attendez*. There is one other thing: you must also keep in mind that the most important part of this operation for me is to get these people to let me bring in a plane and fly out with the sergeant. I don't intend to get into politics, and I recommend that you don't either. Tell them you jumped in to find your sister and they'll think you're one hell of a guy. After we leave, you can tell them the rest. You'll learn soon enough who is for de Gaulle and who is against him."

Philippe looked at him glumly. "I have learned already, Major, that is unimportant here," he said. "I am more concerned now about Nguyen Ai-Quôc alias Ho Chi Minh alias Nguyen That Than and God knows how many other aliases. He is a Communist agent, Major. An enemy of France. And it is about him and the wily Jap that I am regretfully sworn to silence."

Reisman realized the man's moral turmoil and tried to make him feel better. "Philippe, there are things I haven't told you," he said in a conspiratorial voice. "You stumbled into the middle of a critical Allied intelligence operation involving double agents. You were carried along for your own safety. The reason we are here had nothing to do with you. Your silence now will contribute to the Allied cause and help end the war much quicker. Beyond that I can tell you nothing."

Belfontaine's face brightened somewhat. "I understand, Major," he said. "You will have no reason to worry. *Allons!*"

Reisman and Filmore followed the Frenchman as he marched confidently up to the lighted portal. There was some confusion on the part of the Indochinese soldiers, but Philippe demanded that the officer of the guard be summoned. The man who arrived on the double, accompanied by a squad of native soldiers, was a European lieutenant in dress uniform and képi. He looked at them warily, particularly Sergeant Filmore in his dark native costume and conical hat. Philippe did not even try for a phony story. He took his colonial counterpart aside, identified himself and his companions by name, rank and country and asked that they be allowed to report to the commandant immediately.

The officer's eyes widened. "From de Gaulle?" he gasped. Then his hand flew to his mouth and he looked around at his Indochinese troops, evidently hoping none had heard.

"From France," answered Philippe without emotion.

They waited in the gloomy tunnel of a corridor outside the commandant's office, still under the searching gaze of the escort troop, while a noncom went to find the ranking officer present in the fort that night. Two men arrived who identified themselves as Lieutenant Colonel Gauthier and Major Derrieu, second and third in command.

"Colonel Robert is away in Hanoi for a few days," explained Gauthier nervously.

He was a pale man of around forty-five, thick-bodied yet not fat, wearing crisp dress tans and jacket. He dismissed the officer of the guard and his armed detail, except for two he asked to stand duty in the corridor. Hesitantly, as if he were not certain he was correct in doing this, he brought Reisman, Filmore and Belfontaine into the commandant's office, removed his képi and smoothed his sparse black hair across his scalp in a self-conscious gesture.

Filmore took that as a signal to remove the conical straw hat that he had worn since leaving Na Sam. Gauthier stared at him and saw that the camouflage of dirt-darkened skin paled abruptly above his brow line.

"You are?" he asked.

Filmore looked puzzled. He did not understand the question in

French. Reisman prompted him in English and the sergeant gave his name, rank and serial number.

Gauthier, standing before the desk of the commandant, stared at Filmore as if willing him to go away. "You were shot down?"

Reisman translated and the airman responded, "Yes, sir."

Gauthier did not look at all happy to hear these first confirmations of the report that had summoned him here. He turned to Reisman and Belfontaine and said, "Identify yourselves. In French, if you please. I do not speak English."

Reisman nodded for Philippe to speak first. He identified himself as an officer of the French division that had helped liberate Paris and was even then fighting on the German border.

"But what are you doing here!" Gauthier exclaimed. He did not wait for an answer, but turned to Reisman and demanded, "And you?"

Reisman recited his name, rank and serial number and told the story they had made up: that he was with Air Ground Aid Section China and had jumped into Tonkin to locate and rescue Filmore and his fellow airmen.

The lieutenant colonel seemed at a loss for what to say next. He started to sit down behind the C.O.'s desk, then changed his mind, took a side chair and waved the others to chairs along the wall of the spartan, whitewashed room. "This is most unusual . . . highly irregular," he murmured.

Major Derrieu—a younger, more sinewy-looking man dressed in field fatigues, with brown hair cropped close and a lighted cigarette hanging from his lips—seemed more relaxed about dealing with the unexpected arrivals, even a little amused by Gauthier's discomfiture.

"Welcome to Indochina, gentlemen," he said with good humor.

Gauthier cast him a displeased look. Then he stared suspiciously at the radio and generator packs resting on the floor close to Reisman and Belfontaine. "You parachuted down wearing all this heavy radio equipment, Major?" he challenged.

"No, sir, the packs were dropped separately. I stashed them in the hills until I made contact with natives who helped carry the equipment and turned the generator when I radioed Kunming."

Major Derrieu's interest quickened at that. "You have communicated with Kunming from Tonkin?" he asked.

"Yes. A few times. I've kept them informed on my progress. They know I've found Sergeant Filmore and that we were hiking to Lang Son."

"Did you not also tell them about Lieutenant Belfontaine?" asked Derrieu.

"No. The lieutenant asked me not to. Information on a need-to-know basis. You are aware of that, of course, Major."

He had sized up Derrieu as more of a field-operations officer than Gauthier. It seemed logical that his duties might also be concerned with breaches of internal security on the frontier—which, strictly speaking, would have to include any unauthorized contacts beyond the border. Though perhaps he was also a man who was waiting for someone like Belfontaine to arrive with instructions from Paris.

Gauthier spoke up, as if to reassert his preeminence in the room. "How did you manage to meet each other out in the wilderness?" he asked. He leaned toward them in a friendly, put-yourself-at-ease pose, but the képi on his lap fell to the floor.

An amusing man, thought Reisman, one who probably had found position and home in a colonial sinecure. Better here, he supposed, than to have shared the debacle of events in France. He waited until Gauthier picked up the képi, dusted it and placed it on the C.O.'s desk behind him.

"Some people in the hills brought me to Lieutenant Belfontaine," Reisman related. "They heard about a stranger in a hamlet some miles away and thought he was one of the airmen I was sent in to find. It's amazing how quickly they pass news from village to village. When we were brought together, the lieutenant and I immediately decided to help each other. He wanted to reach Lang Son. I wanted to find the air crew that had gone down and get back to China the best way I could. We learned barely a day later that Sergeant Filmore was being sheltered in another hamlet, and we went there to collect him before coming here."

"Three of your air crewmen were captured by the Japanese," Gauthier informed them sadly.

Reisman pretended that he knew none of this. "What will happen to them?" he asked.

"I do not know. But three others were found by patrols of the colonial army and they are safe. They are interned, of course, but the French authorities in Hanoi have refused to turn them over to the Japs. There is much trouble."

"There are two more out there somewhere," Reisman said.

"We are aware of that," Major Derrieu put in. "Perhaps we will be able to find them first—if they are still alive." He stood up, then sat on the edge of the commandant's desk, facing them. "Would you be able to show me on the map exactly where you came down, Major?" he asked.

"I think not, Major," Reisman answered pleasantly.

"What about the hamlet where you were given shelter and those where you met Lieutenant Belfontaine and your sergeant?"

With the utmost cordiality, Reisman said, "We gave our word not to implicate any of them in any way. We are here now, not in a Jap prison, because they sheltered and guided us. We fully intend to keep our part of the bargain."

"Not one name . . . one village . . . one person?" Derrieu prompted.

"I think one old fellow was called Nguyen something or other," Reisman answered carefully.

"*Monsieur* . . . in this Godforsaken land everybody is called Nguyen something or other!" snapped Derrieu.

"He looked like a peasant, and he was very helpful."

"They all look like peasants. And they are as likely to slit your throat as help you. You, Belfontaine, can you provide answers to these questions?"

Philippe glanced at Reisman, then replied, "No, sir."

"Then perhaps you might be at liberty to tell me exactly how you arrived in Indochina, Lieutenant?" Derrieu demanded.

"By parachute, sir."

"From China?"

"No, sir. I was dropped by a British aircraft that flew from Calcutta."

Gauthier broke in again. "For what purpose, Belfontaine?"

"I had a leave coming. I asked to be allowed to come here—to find my sister."

"To find your sister!" Gauthier repeated, incredulous. "And who is she?"

"Madeleine Thibaut. My last letters from her were posted from Lang Son. Do you know her?"

Gauthier's expression changed to a warm smile. "You are the brother of Madeleine Thibaut?"

"Yes, sir. Do you know her?"

"Yes. She is indeed here in Lang Son," Gauthier said excitedly. "She has spoken of you. I also knew Roland very well, before—" His voice trailed off sadly. "Does she expect you?"

"No, sir. She has no idea. Neither did I. I thought I would be in Germany now. This trip was an unexpected opportunity."

"For what purpose?" Major Derrieu demanded.

"I just answered that, sir."

"Belfontaine!" said Derrieu, in a tone that announced his irritation. "I too have had the honor to meet Madame Thibaut and her late husband. She is a brave and beautiful woman. But I do not believe that the Provisional Government in Paris and the English flew you halfway around the world just to visit your sister."

Philippe persisted. "They asked me to observe conditions here and report back to them," he said, as if it were a matter of no great consequence.

"Conditions?" Derrieu muttered. "We are maintaining the presence of France in this little backwater of the world by kissing Japanese asses and by allowing the illusion of equality and fraternity to those Indochinese who will work with us, and killing or jailing those who won't."

Neither Reisman nor Belfontaine had expected so frank a declaration. Nor had Gauthier. He looked at Derrieu with dismay. "Come, come, Raoul, things are not that bad," he said.

Derrieu's bitter remarks, however, gave Philippe his chance to divulge more about the reason he had parachuted into Tonkin. He glanced at Reisman first, as if silently asking his permission, then informed the two colonial officers, "I come from de Gaulle personally. My orders are to help prepare for the full dominion of France in Indochina."

Gauthier looked shocked. He stared at Philippe in apprehensive silence. Derrieu took the remains of the cigarette from his mouth.

"What does he expect us to do, drive out the Japs?" he said.

Philippe shook his head. "That is only part of it—and first we must finish off the Boche."

"Then what does de Gaulle want of us now?" asked Gauthier anxiously.

"To plan . . . to prepare . . . to behave like soldiers again."

"What about guns, ammunition, supplies?" Derrieu pressed. "Our matériel is very limited."

Reisman felt hopeful. They were rising to the possibilities Philippe opened for them, and that was good for Reisman's purposes too.

"The English have agreed to supply our forces in Indochina by air drops," Philippe replied. "Our own planes are too far away and too few."

"What about you Americans?" Derrieu challenged, bracketing Reisman with a scornful look. "I have read the views of your president. He will not help us here. Why then did you come to Lang Son?"

"You have an air strip. I want to radio Kunming and have them send in a courier plane to fly the sergeant and me out."

"That is impossible," Gauthier blurted out in distress. "The Japanese will learn of it and take action against us. We have a treaty of cooperation with them, and to permit such a flight would violate it. They would consider it a hostile act."

Reisman did not speak the first thoughts that came to his mind. They were too explosive and would have defeated in anger what he felt might still be accomplished with tact and gentle coercion. "I understand your concern, Colonel," he said. "As an ally of France, though, I must ask this small favor of you. There will be minimal, if any, risk to your command."

"I cannot make such decisions myself," protested Gauthier. "It must await the return of Colonel Robert."

"When will that be?"

Gauthier shrugged. "A few days, a week. I do not know."

"No good. I will make radio contact tonight. The plane will come tomorrow or the next day."

"You presume too much!" Major Derrieu said angrily. "You cannot just come in here and expect to do as you please. You have no business here at all. Not when we also must hear the poor opinion your president has of us!"

Reisman turned on him in icy rage. "Then allow me to remind you, Derrieu—and you too, Colonel Gauthier—that tens of thousands of Americans have been killed and wounded in the liberation of your homeland. Damn what the president says and damn what all the presidents, kings and generals say. We have paid for this alliance in blood and I am here to collect a small portion of the debt."

Derrieu turned away, still bristling but humbled to silence. Gauthier looked deeply chagrined, uncertain how to respond. He seemed torn between his officially negative attitude and his own instinct. Then he said softly, "I will send word to Colonel Robert in Hanoi. Let him decide, or submit the matter to higher authorities."

Reisman forced himself to sound quietly reasonable. "With respect, sir, this is not a matter for international negotiation. The more people who know about it the less chance it will have to come off cleanly."

"I cannot give you permission," Gauthier murmured.

Philippe thrust himself into the middle of it. "Then do not give them permission, sir," he blurted out. "Just leave them alone to do it themselves. Only we in this room need know about it. I owe a debt to Major Reisman. Without him I would not be here alive. In the name of General de Gaulle I ask you to comply with his request."

Gauthier, in turmoil, stared at Philippe and Reisman, unable to decide. Then he turned to his second-in-command. "What do you think, Raoul?"

Derrieu squashed out his cigarette in an ashtray on the commandant's desk. He shrugged. If not eager, he seemed now at least willing to make amends. "In the name of de Gaulle—why not?" he said. "The others have not been of any help. Perhaps he will."

Gauthier nodded. He seemed relieved, as if the responsibility for a decision had been lifted from his shoulders. "All right. Do what you must do," he told Reisman. "Keep Derrieu and me informed. But officially we know nothing."

"Thank you, sir," Reisman said.

"Now let me send for Madame Thibaut," Gauthier said, smiling at Philippe. "It is time for a little joy around this place."

Chapter 25

There was an allure about her that drew Reisman immediately.

A lieutenant brought her to the commandant's office. She entered calmly, giving no indication that she expected to find there the brother she had not seen in ten years. Reisman assumed the escort had been instructed not to tell her; a cold-hearted ploy, he thought, though perhaps it was their way to test Philippe's story. All of Asia, after all, boiled with plots, spies and counterspies.

She was blonde, classically handsome rather than daintily pretty; young, perhaps thirty, yet with dark circles under the eyes and an air of wistfulness about her, as if she had not known happiness for a long time. She was dressed with the smart restraint of the girls he had seen in Paris just before the war—a lightweight brown coat, a green silk scarf tied loosely at the throat, low-heeled leather pumps—equipped for a cool, damp evening in November.

All the men stood up, but she didn't look around at first. She went directly to Lieutenant Colonel Gauthier, to whom she gave her hand, a smile and a warm greeting. Then she looked around at the other four men, greeted Derrieu, passed right over Philippe staring at her with bursting heart, and paused to gaze with more than passing interest at John Reisman. He watched her look away then, back to Philippe, saw her eyes widen and her face contort in the emotional shock of delayed recognition.

"Philippe?" she whispered. "Is it you?"

"Madeleine," he answered hoarsely.

They fell into each other's arms with tears and cries of joy. The others turned away shyly. Reisman envied Philippe his homecoming, though he and his sister embraced six thousand miles from France.

Madeleine took them home with her. She lived about half a mile outside the walls of the citadel in an area overlooking the Sông Ky Cung. She drove them in a rattling old army Citroën that Gauthier loaned her. She was still in shock, but it was a happy astonishment and her face was radiant. She kept turning from the wheel to gape through the darkness at the man sitting beside her as if to reassure herself that it was her brother

"Talk to me, Philippe! Tell me everything! Don't stop!" she pleaded.

They spoke of family, years of questions and answers compressed into these first minutes. Though Philippe had not been home in five years he had learned before leaving Paris that their parents were well. The region of their ranch had been liberated by Allied forces in a second invasion on the Mediterranean coast. Other relatives had not fared as well. Some killed in the war, both soldiers and civilians, men and women; others disappeared into Nazi captivity.

Reisman felt like an intruder into their family talk and private lives, but there was no way he could not listen. He was squeezed into the back of the small car with Filmore among radio packs, duffels and weapons. He found himself listening to the sound of Madeleine's voice and admiring her silhouette each time she turned her head toward her brother. He had been glad to accept her invitation, to get out from under the eyes and ears of the officers at the fort. He needed nothing from them. What he did now he would do better on his own, giving the French only enough information to make sure they stayed out of the way.

They arrived at the house in a few minutes. It was a bungalow located in an enclave of French residents. Madeleine had rented it after her husband's death, she told them, when it no longer had been possible for her to stay alone on their isolated plantation. She had not wanted to live in Hanoi under the eye of conquerors and bureaucrats. But neither had she wanted to abandon Indochina. She was determined to reclaim her lands after the war and make them prosper.

"There are no servants," she said as they climbed the porch and she unlocked the front door. "I trust no one any more. Only myself. I still do not know if Roland was killed by the Japs or the Viet Minh."

She frowned at Filmore, who was still wearing his *can slua tau* clothes. "Don't you have anything else to wear, sir?" she prodded in French.

Reisman interceded. "It was a little game we were playing, madame. I think the man would be very grateful for a place to bathe and change. I've got his uniform in my bag."

It was all too unexpectedly pleasant. The three men took turns luxuriating in a hot bath, then presented themselves in rumpled uniforms for a festive dinner Madeleine had rushed to prepare. Reisman had to remind himself that the war was out there, actually quite close. One wrong move and he could bring it on fast. There were a few hours yet before he was scheduled to make radio contact with Kunming. Contrary to what he had told Gauthier and Derrieu in the fort, OSS still had no idea that he had moved on from Pac Bo, picked up the airman, was now in Lang Son and eager to get back into China fast. So much had happened since he last "talked" to Sam Kilgore, yet only a night and a day had passed.

He was troubled by something else too. Ho Chi Minh and Tran Van Thi had lectured him about famine in the country, and he had reported that to Kunming—yet he had seen no evidence of it himself, neither in the places they had taken him nor here in Lang Son. He needed to balance the one-sided report he had been given and he needed to weigh the veracity of Ho and his people.

The dinner conversation until then had been cheerful and general, though Reisman had perceived that after her initial burst of sisterly spontaneity there was a certain cautiousness on Madeleine's part before speaking. She waited for Philippe or Reisman to introduce subjects, as if she were politely biding her time, assessing the men, even her brother, and waiting for the right moment to broach a matter of greater importance.

Reisman had been addressing her formally as "Madame Thibaut," until she said, "Please, Major. I am Madeleine."

"And I am John."

"Very well, *Jean*." She gave it the inevitable French pronunciation.

He found her to be an enormously attractive, intelligent and warm-spirited woman. The officers at the fort had called her brave and beautiful. Perhaps they meant that she was a woman of integrity, strength and independence, all necessary and admirable in a young widow.

Sitting at her good table in her comfortable home, dining on ham, vegetables, rice and fruit and drinking Portuguese wine from Macao, it seemed almost ludicrous, if not mean-spirited, to ask if she knew anything about reports that thousands of Indochinese were dying of hunger. But he did.

Madeleine put down her fork and stared at Reisman gravely. "Yes, I have heard about famine in parts of the country," she answered. "There have been typhoons, floods and loss of crops. Prices are very high, but here, as you see, we are more fortunate."

"Is anything being done to help those who are starving?"

"What do you mean, *Jean*?"

"Government aid."

"I do not think so. The war and the Japs have made it impossible. As did the Nazis in Europe. *Liberté, égalité* and *fraternité* have suffered."

"Would an Allied relief operation help? Food dropped at designated places in the countryside?"

"It would most likely fall into the wrong hands," she replied.

Reisman did not press the question of whose hands would be wrong. His business was war, not famine relief. The subject would be valid only if they could starve the Japs into submission, though he did not think that letting the people of the land starve to death was the way to military victory for either side.

Madeleine looked around the room as if concerned about being overheard. When she spoke again to Reisman it was in a hesitant voice. "I hope, Major . . . *Jean* . . . that you have come here to help us drive out the Japs and return this land to its rightful owners, the people who built it and made it fruitful."

"I am in Lang Son for only one reason," he answered. "To get out of Indochina with Sergeant Filmore as quickly as possible."

Madeleine looked at her brother with a worried expression. "And you, Philippe? I haven't asked you that question. Why have *you* come?"

"To find you, Madeleine."

She smiled, and there was affection and gratitude in her voice. "For this I thank you. But I believe there must be more."

He shrugged. "Nothing to concern yourself about, Madeleine. I am still on duty, subject to orders."

She gave him a severe look. "I beg to differ with you, dear brother. Neither France nor England—" She looked toward Reisman. "—nor the United States would have helped you get here if you did not have a more important mission."

"The United States did not help," Philippe said. "No . . . that is not quite correct. Major Reisman, who is a United States officer, helped me more than I can ever repay."

Madeleine stared at Reisman. She understood what her brother meant, though she had no awareness of the details. "Thank you," she said softly. She was thoughtful again, then at last spoke what she had on her mind. "Philippe, are you here as an agent of General Giraud or General de Gaulle?"

Philippe tried to make light of the question. "I did not think that you were concerned about politics, Madeleine."

She smiled at her brother, but Reisman saw a flash of anger in her warm brown eyes. It added to her allure, he thought. She looked very lovely in a burgundy dinner dress with décolletage that was just immodest enough to be deliciously tantalizing; and she wore an antique gold necklace from which hung a single large ruby in a filigree frame. In moments of ardent talk, such as now, she reached up and grasped the pendant lightly with her fingers as she leaned toward whomever she was addressing.

"You are remembering the woman I was, Philippe," she said sharply. "Just a snip of a girl really, but no longer. Anyone who lives in these times in this place must be concerned. Are you a Giraudist or a Gaullist?"

Her brother still tried to avoid a direct answer. "What difference does it make? At home there is still some enmity, but they are working together against the Vichyites and collaborators. It is all part of the democratic political process, that's all. In the end we will work together for the good of France and her empire."

"*This* is my home, Philippe! Not France—Indochina!" Madeleine replied. "And here it does make a difference. Here the enmity is very much alive. There are strong differences in political positions which still cannot be resolved by a simple election." She paused and thought over her next words carefully. "I must tell you something now, Philippe." She looked at Reisman and Filmore. "And you too, gentlemen. I do not think you would bring me harm, and perhaps you will bring us good. I am a Gaullist. I am an active member of the Resistance. I often go to Hanoi and other parts of the country as a courier, and I too am on duty, subject to orders. I have not taken up a gun yet, but I will do it if necessary."

Philippe stood up, walked to her chair, knelt down and took her in his arms. "We have come to the right house, Madeleine," he said joyfully.

She brought him the bottle of cognac he had been longing for. It was rare, she explained, and expensive, but still available from Chinese tradesmen.

Later, Reisman contrived to be alone with Madeleine on the veranda. He had suggested privately to Filmore that in order to ingratiate himself with his hostess he volunteer to do K.P. Philippe, in an apparent burst of fraternity, had insisted on helping—though Reisman thought that he was probably more interested in interrogating the American airman alone. Before going outside with Madeleine, Reisman had overheard Philippe plying Filmore with questions in heavily accented English that surely must have bemused the sergeant; they were seemingly innocent questions regarding American aims in Indochina, questions that not even the State Department could have answered. All Philippe would get would be 14th Air Force latrine rumors, but Reisman couldn't blame the man for trying. It was the same sort of futile probing that Ho Chi Minh and his people had subjected Reisman to since Kunming, in the hope that high level policy information might have filtered down to GI Joe in the field.

On the veranda, Reisman stared through the darkness across a road to the top of a levee. It was quiet on the fringe of the town. Lights showed from houses and on streets and occasional vehicles. Blackout regulations were apparently of little concern. Mist hung over the water, as it had earlier in the evening when he and his companions had crossed another turning of the Sông Ky Cung less than a mile to the west on the other side of the citadel. The levee blocked the view and he could not see if there were boat lights moving on the stream.

"I am overwhelmed by what has happened," Madeleine said softly, looking out into the darkness.

Reisman turned to her and smiled. He said, "Thank you for bringing us into your home."

They spoke easily in French as they had been doing all evening, for she did not know much English. In the house, however, her conversation had been influenced by the presence of her brother and Filmore. Now she seemed to want to say something that was more private, just between the two of them. Or was it, he wondered, only the attraction he felt toward her that was telling him that?

"It is a miracle that Philippe is here," she said fervently. "Thank you for helping him."

He wanted to find the right words. "It was a fortunate meeting. We helped each other," he ventured. "I appreciate your hospitality. It has been a long time since I dined so pleasantly in the company of a beautiful woman."

In the dark he couldn't tell if the remark pleased her or not. She said, "You speak French very well for an American."

"I've spent a lot of time there."

"Before the war?"

"Yes. During it also. I worked with the Resistance."

There was new excitement in her voice when she asked, "Is that why you are here?"

"Yes."

It was true, of course—but a different truth from the one she assumed. Working with the Viet Minh was not what she meant, nor would she have approved.

"How can I help?"

"How far are we from the airfield?"

"Two kilometers."

"I must go there very early in the morning."

"You are leaving so soon?" she asked, disappointed.

"No. Perhaps tomorrow night or the next. I want to see what the landing strip is like. What's the best way to go there without being seen?"

"On the river. I have a rowboat we can use."

He had heard the "we" and accepted it without comment. "I must be there before five," he told her.

"I will be ready. Is there anything else?"

He asked her if he could set up the radio in her house and transmit to Kunming. "There is a slight danger," he explained. "But even if the Japs intercept the signal they will not be able to decipher it and will not have enough time to get a fix on the transmitter."

She reached out and touched his arm. "Of course, *Jean,*" she said. "With gratitude."

▪ ▪

Reisman was able to work the transmitter-receiver alone, since it could be plugged into the house current. He set it up in the bedroom where he and Filmore were to spend the night. Then he encoded his messages with the one-time pad and was ready to transmit quickly when he got through to Sam Kilgore in the radio shack at Kunming airfield. He told him where he was, that Filmore was with him, that the other airmen were reported captured or missing, and that he wanted an L-5 to fly in to pick them up within the next thirty-six hours, as soon as he could check out the landing strip and the security of the area.

He waited for the ciphering process at the other end. The dah-dit-dah's came back in short bursts which, when decoded, gratefully acknowledged his report and approved the rescue flight. He was to pick the time, ensure security and arrange the landing signals. Sam and the pilot would take care of the rest. They were to communicate the following night to confirm the operation. Sam added that the Japanese armies were still driving west and south, but the flight path and escape route close to the border remained open.

Reisman tapped out one more query: "Men from England?"

The reply was, "Now in India."

At 0400, after only a few hours' sleep, he went out to the veranda and found Madeleine waiting for him. The early morning was black, cool and misty. He was both startled and amused by her appearance. She wore an indigo peasant's jacket over slacks and sweater. Her blonde hair was bound in a dark kerchief and on her feet were rubber boots. He could see all this by the light of the oil lantern she held in one hand. She also carried fishing tackle, a thermos and a small picnic basket. Reisman was dressed in fatigues, field jacket, boots and cap, and armed with carbine and pistol.

"One of us seems to be out of uniform," he said, grinning.

"You can hide under the tarpaulin in the boat if necessary."

He pointed to the fishing tackle. "Do people actually do that sort of thing around here at this hour?"

"Oh, yes. If I'm to be alone in the boat for a while, I must be doing something ordinary."

It was clever of her, he thought. But he did not want to forget that he was in a war zone, could be shot at if he ran into the wrong people, could be killed or captured by the Japanese or interned by the French. If anyone came at them now he didn't know whether he would shoot or hide. It was a strange war here, yet this part of it was not much different from his times behind the lines with partisans in Italy and the Maquis in France. His job had always been to seek out friends, as they had sought him, to help each other in alliance against the common enemy. He took the thermos and basket from her.

"*Allons*!" she said and they crossed the road, took a path that climbed over the levee, and came to a small dock where a few rowboats were tied. Madeleine undid the canvas cover on one. They got in and she rowed them smoothly out into the stream.

"Would you like me to do that?" he asked.

"No need. I'm fine."

They spoke barely above a whisper so that their voices would not carry. She was skillful and quiet at the oars. The Sông Ky Cung was about a hundred yards across, he estimated, and did not seem as busy a waterway as the rivers he had crossed weeks earlier when he first had come into Indochina; nor was it anything like the congested commercial arteries he knew in China. The stream went south for a kilometer and then bent sharply north. Sampans and boats were tied or anchored near shore, but he saw no boats moving through the darkness and no fishermen.

"Would you like coffee?" she whispered.

He looked at the radiant dial of his wristwatch. They were early. He had time. "Yes, thank you."

She stopped rowing, filled cups she took from the basket, and handed him a roll on a napkin. It reminded him of an early morning in Kunming many weeks back when someone else had surprised him with croissants. They drank the coffee and ate the rolls in silence for a few minutes while Madeleine let the boat drift with the current. Finally, she asked, "Are you meeting someone?"

"I have to check out the condition of the field for the pilot who will fly in," he told her.

"Why not wait until it is light?"

"Perhaps I will, once I'm ashore. You don't mind waiting, do you?"

"I like to fish. I find it very relaxing, whether one catches anything or not."

"I've never been a fisherman," he said. "Oh, I went with my father a time or two out on the lake when I was a boy, but that was it."

He told her about Chicago and Lake Michigan and a little about going to sea. She rowed and they came abreast of a small island in the stream. She took the boat between it and the eastern shore, pointed and said, "The end of the runway is over that way. You'll have to cross a paddy on the other side of the levee, but then you'll see it. Can I come with you? I can leave the boat. No one will take it."

"I have to go alone."

"Are you meeting someone?" she asked again.

He tried not to make his answer sound too brusque, but he told her, "I don't mean to offend you. You have been more than kind. But it's better for both of us if I say nothing."

"Sorry," she said softly. "I understand. I'll drop you off now. When you're ready to leave, just come down over the levee and I'll row in."

It was still very dark, but he saw Kita and Ho before they saw him, and he liked that. He had gone almost through the paddy to a road that paralleled the runway when he saw their darker silhouettes coming off the end of the road and dropping lower to the marshy ground. He moved noiselessly to within ten yards of them, then called out softly in pidgin Viet-Namese, *"Tôi dây, Chú."* He had wanted to say, "I am here, Uncle," but he had forgotten the "am."

"Ah, you are becoming quite fluent," Ho joked.

"How'd you make out, kid?" Kita asked.

The vernacular brought Reisman up short, as it always did, and he wondered again how the Jap colonel could possibly have learned to speak American like an American so well.

"There'll be a little puddle hopper coming in to take us out."

"When?" asked Ho.

Reisman stared down the long level stretch of darkness and saw glints of light in low sheds in the distance. Operations and radio would be down there somewhere. They looked quiet. At this end of the field there were no structures and no planes tied down.

"I think at this time tomorrow, just before dawn. What's the runway like?"

"Fair. Three quarters of a mile of grass and dirt," Kita answered.

Reisman would look it over himself once it got lighter to be sure the surface was good and there were no surprise obstacles, but there was enough room for the L-5 to land and take off without going near the operations end of the field.

"I'll want this end of the strip lit with flares or lanterns just before the plane comes in," he said. "Do you have people you can deploy?"

"Do you not trust the French to help you?" Ho prodded.

"I don't trust anybody," Reisman retorted. "You have more to lose, though, if this flight doesn't come off. Remember the arsenal of Chiang Fa-K'uei."

"I cannot forget it. My friends will be here with lanterns at the appointed hour."

"I want no trouble from them," Reisman told him. "No potshots against the French. They must remain invisible."

As for the French personnel at the airfield, he would request that Gauthier and Derrieu divert them by telling them that a secret "training operation" would be conducted for a few minutes in the early morning, an exercise that they were to disregard while it was underway and forget when it was over.

"Anything else?" asked Kita.

"Yes. What's the name of the Kempitai man in Chungking?"

Kita laughed. "You don't give up, do you? Why is it so important to you?"

"It's something personal," Reisman told him. He thought of Katherine Harris's disfigured face and broken body and the anger rose in him again.

"Perhaps we might make a trade one day," Kita said.

"What do you have in mind?"

"I'll think of something."

Reisman turned his attention to Ho Chi Minh. "Have you figured out how you're going to get your men and trucks up to the arsenal?"

"The men will leave Pac Bo the moment you signal us. The trucks we will 'borrow' in China. Do not fail us and we will not fail you."

Reisman smiled at him. "I thought that I could count on your resourcefulness, Uncle. Be here tomorrow at the same time and I will leave my radio and generator with you."

"Your carbine and pistol too?" Ho asked greedily.

"Sure. Secure the field and help me bring in the plane and they're yours," Reisman told him. He had already added his M-3 submachine gun to the arsenal at Pac Bo. There was no point in carrying the guns down twice. He could replace them in Kunming. He looked around and saw that the sky was just barely beginning to grow light. "Let's break up the party now," he said. "You leave first. I want to scout around just a little bit on my own."

Ho and Kita seemed relieved to get out of there. They left quickly, moving through the marshland beside the road until he could no longer see them. Then Reisman scouted along the embankment, popping up at intervals to view the road and the runway beyond it, to assure himself it was in good condition, that the area was not ringed by troops and guns, and that there was no dawn patrol of pursuit ships waiting over the field to shoot down the little L-5 the next morning. He scouted as far as the structures at the southeast end of the runway and then, satisfied, returned to the river and waved Madeleine in to pick him up. It was light now, though there was still mist on the water to help conceal them. Reisman took the oars and rowed them back quickly the two kilometers to her dock.

Later that morning, he and Philippe returned to the fort in the Citroën they'd borrowed the night before. Reisman found both Lieutenant Colonel Gauthier and Major Derrieu now eager to cooperate. They agreed to his plan to divert the airfield personnel for the time the L-5 would need to land, take Filmore and himself aboard and clear the area. But they wanted something in return: to be let in on secrets.

"Is it true that an American landing is planned soon?" Gauthier asked eagerly.

"I know nothing about it, Colonel," Reisman answered truthfully.

"So much of what we do here now is dependent upon that," Gauthier told him. "I ask you to take us into your confidence."

Reisman was suspicious of their change in attitude. Yesterday, Derrieu had spoken scornfully about President Roosevelt's unwillingness to help France retain Indochina. Today, Gauthier seemed to think American troops were on the way.

"There is nothing to tell you," Reisman said.

Derrieu crushed out his cigarette and said angrily, "Since August there have been rumors of this invasion—from the sea and from China."

"Perhaps there has been talk of such an operation," Reisman told them, "but I know nothing about it personally and I don't think there is anything like it under way now. They've got enough trouble with the Japs rampaging through China."

"We are nevertheless waiting and hoping," Derrieu continued bitterly, "but there is no end of conflicting loyalties among us. De Gaulle has declared war on Japan from Paris. Yet Admiral Decoux, our governor general in Hanoi, is forced to work with the Japs as if they were our friends and allies. He too is waiting and hoping, but he issues orders that continue to make us subservient to the monkeys. The army is powerless, the resources of Indochina are plundered by Tokyo at will—or bombed by you Americans and the British."

"On the other hand, there is Mordant," Gauthier broke in.

"Who is he?" Reisman asked.

They stared at him in disbelief. "You really do know nothing," Derrieu commented acidly. "He was commander of all French forces in Indochina."

Gauthier explained, "He is retired—but he is not retired, if you understand what I mean."

"No, I do not."

"He is the secret governor general—really above Decoux now—and the head of the Resistance."

"How secret?"

"Everybody knows about it," Derrieu declared scornfully.

"The Japs?"

"Yes. They are on to him, I am sure."

"You see, *monsieur*, the confusion is endless and profound," said Gauthier. "We no longer know what to do—as soldiers or Frenchmen. That is why we demand to know about American plans."

"If there are plans for Indochina, I know nothing about them, gentlemen," Reisman repeated.

Philippe, who had been silent until now, but was listening with great interest, spoke up. "No matter what the Americans plan, or the British or Chinese or Russians, I assure you, my friends, that General de Gaulle and the Provisional Government in Paris intend that France will retain her sovereignty here, just as before the war."

They were pleased to hear that again.

"You will be staying with your sister?" Gauthier asked.

"Yes. Is there any objection?"

"Of course not. I will issue papers to each of you now, identifying you as officers of the Colonial Army. Insignia will not be necessary. Continue to wear only your battle fatigues—which I assume is all you have—and I think you will pass muster with both our forces and the Japs, if you should run into any."

Major Derrieu had a concluding word. "Please do not leave the immediate area," he cautioned Philippe. "Colonel Robert will wish to speak with you personally upon his return—and you must be prepared to report the true purpose of your mission here."

Chapter 26

Pacing tensely through the afternoon, Reisman was eager for the night and the radio traffic with Kunming, and then the dawn and the plane that would take him out. Madeleine sensed his tension and restlessness.

"Is my company so unpleasant that you can't relax?" she teased.

He had just glanced at his watch again and then outside through the windows at the cloud-streaked sky. It was not raining and there were big patches of blue, but he was worried nevertheless about the weather in the night and early morning.

"No, of course not," he said. He turned away from the windows and watched her bring another pot of tea into the living room. "On the contrary, I'm glad to be alone with you," he added truthfully.

The teasing itself he welcomed, for it conveyed an intimacy that he wanted, though he wondered whether such a flirtation would offend Philippe, or even Madeleine—or his own sense of propriety.

Philippe had gone out to reconnoiter the city for his own purposes.

Sergeant Filmore was staying out of sight in the guest room to avoid anyone who might turn up unexpectedly. Madeleine had taken him a tray of food and then lunched tête-à-tête with Reisman.

"You don't have to entertain me," he had said gently.

"I want to," she had answered.

She had told him that she did not have to be anywhere else that day, so he had asked her about the day-to-day details of her life. She would have been at the fort, she had said, when not away on a courier assignment for the Resistance. She was training part-time at the hospital there, "In case I'm ever needed." Or she would have been doing volunteer work, helping to organize social, recreational and educational programs for the garrison. This gave her a good cover story when she had to travel around the country. Her late husband had left enough money to spare her any worries about earning a living.

The underground network of which she was a part was an exclusively French operation. She apparently knew nothing about the Viet Minh network except that it was rumored to exist. She considered them untrustworthy traitors, enemies of France. Reisman had not tried to disabuse her of that notion; nor did he tell her what he knew and had experienced.

Madeleine had commended him again on his easy, colloquial French. He remembered what "Tong Van So" had said about it when they first had met in Kunming, and he had laughed. "A man I know tells me I speak more like a thug in Marseilles than an intellectual in Paris," he had commented.

"Not at all," she had insisted. "That man sounds like a snob to me."

Watching her now in the dimming light of late afternoon, as she set the replenished tea tray down, he said, "If I appear ill at ease, it has nothing to do with you." Then he added, because he felt that she wanted him to, "Except for the usual reasons."

She looked at him directly, a little smile on her lips, an expression in her wide brown eyes that told him she had heard these things before and wanted to hear them again. "Oh? What are they?" she asked innocently.

"*Cherchez la femme* and all that. The normal girl-boy tensions."

He felt himself drawing closer to her, felt her arousing a part of his nature he usually kept forcefully damped, felt a burgeoning warmth in his loins stirred by her mere presence, awakening that same appetite and yearning which the Chinese girl in Kunming had stimulated and slaked but had not fulfilled.

"Ahh, *monsieur,* I didn't think you were vulnerable," Madeleine teased again.

"But I am."

She held his gaze a moment and then, suddenly skittish, changed the subject and mood of the moment. "Beer or cognac, if you'd rather?" she asked. "The beer is brewed locally with paddy. I went out and bought some at the Chinese this morning when you and Philippe were at the citadel. I even managed another bottle of cognac, but there's no whisky to be had for love or money. That's what you Americans drink, isn't it—whisky?"

"Your cognac is too precious," he said. "But I'd like to try the rice beer, if I may."

He watched her walk away to the kitchen and admired the lovely curve of her calves and the sway of her hips against her pleated skirt. It was a vivid green textured silk and above it she wore a long-sleeved white silk blouse with a demure neckline. He visualized her presiding over an elegant gathering in a great house, in which someone else went to the kitchen.

She brought a tall glass and a cool bottle of a beer called Phénix. "Did Philippe say when he would be back?" she asked as she filled the glass for him.

"No. Just gone out scouting around he said. Beer's nice and cool. How do you manage it?"

"Icebox. The Chinese make it and deliver it in blocks."

She poured fresh tea for herself. Reisman sipped the beer slowly. Just enough to take off the edge of tension—not enough to befuddle the brain and make him say or do things with her that would be better not. The brew had more bite to it than the American and European brands he was used to, but he liked it.

Madeleine stared off into remembered time and said, gently, "Poor Philippe. He has always felt that he had to work harder, be braver, to be accepted as a real Frenchman."

"Why?"

She shrugged and said, "We come from the Camargue . . . somewhat out of the center of things in France."

"Yes, he told me."

"It is a little like your Wild West, I believe. Ranches, cattle, cowboys . . . but a different wilderness of marshlands and water."

"I've been there."

"You know it, then!" she said excitedly.

"Not well. I spent a night at Arles once."

"And Les Saintes-Maries-de-la-Mer?"

"Missed it."

"But how could you? It is where the gypsies gather. My father used to take me to visit them when I was a little girl."

"I am glad he is well—and your mother. I heard Philippe telling you when we were in the car last night."

"Yes, thank you," she said. "They were wonderful parents. I have felt bad about being so far from them in these terrible times . . . not having seen them all these years. We would have gone home to visit—Roland and I . . . or even I alone. But then the war."

To make her feel better, perhaps also to share his own feelings of love and regret, Reisman told her about his father, Aaron, in Chicago, and his mother, Mary Donato, who had died long ago when he was very young. "There were a lot of relatives around on both sides of the family, and a lot of friends, but it was my father who raised me after that," he said. "We loved and respected each other, so it worked out okay. He took his responsibilities seriously and so did I. He had a more limited, traditional view of life, though. Mine quickly became pragmatic and I opened myself up more to the world. I left there fourteen years ago and I've only been back a few times since. I still love and respect him—and I write occasionally."

Madeleine spoke on in a mood of reverie, staring into the deepening shadows of the room. "Father taught us to love nature, wilderness and animals. He left Paris before we were born. He didn't want the life of commerce and finance that his family had been involved in. Mother loved him very much and she went willingly. They were young and could build something together. It is what Roland and I were doing here before he was killed."

She looked over at him and Reisman asked, "How did it happen, Madeleine?"

"They found him in his car in a ditch, shot to death. Two years ago. It could have been Japs or Annamites. He had left the estate to drive to Hanoi on business." She smiled with forced cheerfulness. "We were very happy for eight years. Even after the Japs came, we did not suffer as people did in France under the Nazis. There was very little fighting. Mostly accommodation—and hatred. Even the Annamites began to hate us more when they saw that we were powerless against the Japs. Nevertheless, we continued to improve our estate, even added to it, and we grew more crops. We wanted children, but we decided we would not have any until the war was over and we had won. The Annamites who worked for us were treated well and paid fairly. But the Japs commandeered more and more of what we produced. They forced us to accept less than it was worth. Roland had complained a number of times and he was on his way to a meeting in Hanoi when he was ambushed."

She spoke of it calmly, as if she were relating an event that had happened to someone else in another time and place; but Reisman, while he admired her fortitude, also sensed the depth of passion, the anger and loss that underlay it. He said nothing and listened with pleasure to the sound of her voice, glad that it was herself she wanted to reveal to him rather than Philippe.

"When I met Roland, we were both on vacation in Paris. He fell in love with my beauty—or so he told me," Madeleine said, smiling wistfully. "It was perhaps only what you have called 'the usual reasons . . . the normal boy-girl tensions.' I was enchanted by his sense of adventure, his stories of the Far East. He proposed to me and I invited him to the Camargue. Father and mother liked him very much. When I took Roland to visit the gypsies he told me that the people of Indochina were like gypsies. I accepted his proposal. Father was glad that I was going to an agricultural way of life. One day I will have it again!" she said vehemently.

"Who works your land now?" Reisman asked.

The reverie and softness were suddenly gone from her. "Japs took it over," she said. "Something about failure to meet production quotas and pay taxes. They have an arrangement with village chiefs who make peasants do the work and pay them less than we did." She put down her teacup and said, with a note of finality, "Enough of that, *Jean*. I will deal with it when we are free again. There are more important matters."

It struck him that when Madeleine said *free* it was not the same thing as when Ho Chi Minh said *free*. There was an enormous difference in perspective and it was not even a matter of who was right or wrong.

"Tell me about General Mordant," Reisman said abruptly.

Madeleine looked at him warily. "Do you wish to contact him?"

"No, I'm just curious."

"What have you heard?"

"That he is de Gaulle's man in Hanoi. Head of the Resistance."

"You know too much already, as, I am sure, does the Kempitai,"

Madeleine said caustically. "Mordant is running the Resistance as if he were still commander of the army and the Resistance were just another military operation. But it is not. It is in conflict with the present role of the army."

Reisman wanted to hug her, for he knew exactly what she meant and had been dealing with a similar problem for years. The clandestine services, such as OSS, were often in conflict with the entrenched military—which was why it made little sense to have a man like Commodore Pelham Ludlow in the linchpin job. "What is the role of your army here?" he asked.

"A very difficult one. They must appear to remain neutral, to survive intact for the moment of liberation, and only then to act—with help from the outside . . . which I continue to hope is the reason you are here."

"I'm here for other reasons," Reisman told her guiltily.

She looked at him closely in the shadowed room and said, "Whatever the reason, I am glad you are here. I am glad to have met you."

Reisman reached out a hand and she folded it in hers with warmth and tenderness. "I wish we were in Paris together . . . on vacation," he said. "I would know what to do there. Here I am not so sure."

"What do you mean?"

"About you."

She held his hand tightly and said, "We shall see."

Philippe returned from his reconnaissance of Lang Son and its environs. He looked very worried.

"Did you know there are Jap encampments north of the city?" he asked Reisman when they were alone for a few minutes in the living room.

The news startled Reisman. "No. I thought the French were guarding the border region. Why didn't Gauthier and Derrieu tell us yesterday?"

Philippe stared at him uneasily for a moment, then ventured a defense of his countrymen. "Perhaps it is nothing unusual to them. They assumed we knew and had taken great care in traveling with our guide. How else could we have managed to get through to the fort?" He unfolded a rough pencil sketch. "Here, I've drawn a map," he said. "They're grouped near this place called Ky Lua on the other side of the river within the last mile of the approach to Lang Son. There are at least three positions. Didn't those—" He lowered his voice and looked around the room and behind him, concerned lest even Madeleine get a hint about Nguyen That Than and Kita Shidehara. "Didn't those two tell you anything about this?"

Reisman stared at the sketch and said, "No." The Jap positions flanked both sides of Route 4. But they were south of the pagoda where they had left the truck and taken to the trails. They had walked right past the positions while he was chatting away with Ho Chi Minh as they made their way by tracks through the paddies and marshlands. "The son-of-a-bitch never said a word," Reisman muttered. Nor had Kita. Their little walk had been more dangerous than Reisman had imagined. Which was probably why Kita had stayed with them until they crossed the river. If a Jap patrol had spotted them he would have bullshitted them out of trouble.

"How did you learn this stuff?" Reisman asked.

"A simple walk through the countryside, *monsieur,*" said Philippe, smiling, "with a compass, a piece of paper and a pencil. Also my pass from Lieuteuant Colonel Gauthier."

"Did you actually see these Japs?"

"From the distance, *Jean*. The guards on the bridge were of the Colonial Army and they warned me to be careful. I moved after that like your Indians, from tree to tree and bush to bush."

Reisman grinned at him. "Have you ever seen an Indian, Philippe?" A vision of Samson Posey rose in his mind.

"Only in the cinema."

They all dined together again that evening and talked about cheerful, impersonal things, of times before the war and hopes for after it, speaking in both French and English so that Sergeant Filmore would not feel left out. Madeleine was radiant. She had changed into an oriental dress of royal blue silk, a sensuous sheath that molded itself to her body alluringly. The mandarin collar was braided with gold thread and on the dress were small gold dragons with fiery tongues that reminded Reisman of the Chinese girl in Sam Kilgore's house. He looked at her often. There was an exquisite undercurrent of tension between them. Or was he merely imagining all this, he wondered? He wished there were time for them, but there wasn't.

In the late night he raised Kunming on the radio again and received confirmation of the next day's flight. He specified the predawn hour, the landing approach, the grid coordinates of the runway and the frequency on which he would be transmitting a signal, using his field radio as a homing device. He would switch to voice transmission when the L-5 flew within range. The pilot would leave Kunming immediately, Sam told him, and stage at Ch'ing-Hsi in China, two hundred miles southeast of Kunming and a hundred miles north of Lang Son. He would put down there and wait for Reisman's signal to come on over.

Sam concluded the transmission with, "U.K. shipment due tomorrow."

To Reisman that meant that Sergeant Bowren and whomever he had rounded up of the Dirty Dozen were coming over the Hump at last. He felt excitement and anticipation. Events were moving again at the swift pace he relished. They took his mind off Madeleine and stilled the desire he felt, and he slept for a few hours, rousing himself and Filmore at 0300.

He found Madeleine alone in the kitchen preparing coffee and rolls. "I will go with you to bring back the boat," she said.

He touched her arm gently. "No. It will be better if you do not."

She nodded, continued to bustle about, then stopped and looked at him. Her voice caught as she asked, "Will you ever return?"

He answered, "Yes," before he could even think it through. For, unless his mission was changed, he would be back in Indochina within a few weeks. He knew the way now between Pac Bo and Lang Son and could negotiate it without the Viet Minh.

"I would like that very much," Madeleine said, looking into his eyes.

Reisman leaned toward her and she gave him her lips. He felt the gentle pressure of them on his mouth. "I will see you again soon, Madeleine," he said when he drew away. He wondered if he had been a fool not to try to sleep with her in the night.

As if she could read his thoughts, she said, "I did not sleep much." Then she laughed in a bittersweet way and turned away to pour him a cup of coffee. "When I was a girl I used to read romances in which the heroine suffered vague, undefined longings. I could not imagine what they were. Last night I felt like that innocent little girl again."

She handed him the cup. "Thank you," he said, and he meant it both for the coffee and what she had said.

Philippe and Sergeant Filmore joined them in a few moments for the coffee and rolls. Philippe said, "I will go with you—to be sure there is no trouble."

Reisman laughed, and glanced between brother and sister. He wondered if their offers of help had been made independently, or if they had colluded. He didn't think that Philippe would renege on what he had promised to keep secret, but Madeleine had been given no such restrictions. He believed, without thinking any less of her, that if she were to uncover his dealings with Ho Chi Minh and Kita Shidehara, she would report it all the way up to General Mordant, and would try to thwart him.

"No. I appreciate your offer," he said to Philippe, "as I appreciate yours, Madeleine. But the sergeant and I will go to the field alone. I'll leave the boat on the shore there. If it's found before you get it, just say that it was stolen. Wait until noon before you go out there. We ought to be long gone by then."

On the veranda, Reisman and Filmore strapped on their packs, weapons and radio equipment and said their goodbyes.

Philippe asked one favor. "If there is to be an invasion, tell your people that we will rise to help them," he said fervently. "Just as the Maquis did in France."

"I'll tell them," Reisman said. But he didn't think anyone was prepared to listen, or would do anything about it. The position of the French here was very different from what it had been in Europe.

Madeleine made a great show of kissing each of them on the cheek and wishing them, *"Bonne chance."* As she brushed past him, Reisman whispered, *"Au revoir . . . à bientôt."* Louder, to both of them, he ordered, "Stay here. Don't even follow us to the river. I know the way."

They were in place at the north end of the landing strip before Ho and Kita arrived. The predawn sky was black, with clouds scudding across and mist rising off the Sông Ky Cung. Hunkered down on the river side of the embankment, Filmore turned the generator crank and Reisman sent the takeoff signal on their agreed frequency to the L-5 pilot waiting at Ch'ing-Hsi. Acknowledgment came back and he signed off.

It was the pilot's game now. If he flew smart, rather than coming straight across the border he would hug the China side of the frontier as it twisted and thrust east and south through canyons, hills and floodplains. The heights were lower, the high terrain more level on the China side. Then he would bring the plane into the Lang Son sector low from the northeast over the floodplain to pick up the homing signal Reisman would begin transmitting in half an hour.

He saw dark silhouettes now sliding along both sides of the runway. Two of the figures detached themselves and came to where he and Filmore waited.

"Bonjour, messieurs!" Ho greeted them.

"These early hours are uncivilized," complained Kita. "Is your airplane coming?"

"He's on the way. Ought to be here in forty-five to fifty minutes," Reisman told him. Then he reached out and grasped Kita's arm. "Are your Japs coming?" he demanded.

"What in hell do you mean?" Kita asked sharply, jerking his arm loose.

"Why didn't you tell me about the Jap positions we passed coming in?"

Kita stared at him calmly. "Information on a need-to-know basis, Major. There was no need to worry you unduly, or make you too trigger-happy. I know about you gung-ho types."

"What if your people see the plane coming in?"

"They might," Kita acknowledged without apparent concern. "There is a small detachment stationed in the flats across the river, less than half a mile from us."

"What the hell are you trying to pull?" Reisman demanded angrily.

"They won't disturb us," Kita assured him. "If they notice the plane they'll think it's a Frenchman. And I sent the local Kempitai chief and his staff off on a tour of the border yesterday. Nothing to worry about from him."

"Local Kempitai chief!" Reisman exclaimed.

"We cover the territory quite well," Kita said cockily. "I wouldn't want you to meet this particular fellow anyway. I don't think he would approve of you or our little business arrangements."

Ho Chi Minh, who had been listening to this discussion with an air of amused forbearance, now interrupted. "Our friends are in place with lanterns," he said. "They will light them and set them along the edge of the runway when you are ready."

"Not until the plane is in close. I'll tell you when. The moment he touches down we'll start running for it. The whole operation shouldn't take more than two minutes. Then you kill the lights and get out of here fast."

"With your radio, generator and guns, *Jean,*" Ho reminded.

"Of course."

"When will you go to the arsenal of Chiang Fa-K'uei?" Ho pressed.

"I'll look into it immediately, as soon as I reach Kunming. But I won't go there until its existence is confirmed. I'll radio you tonight. You'll be in Pac Bo?"

"Yes. Fifty men under Tran Van Thi will leave immediately. A truck will meet them just beyond the border."

"One truck? Is that all you'll have?"

"The others will be waiting for them at various places as they travel north."

Reisman was impressed. If the arsenal was there on the Kweilin-Kweiyang road he would get it for them. How they planned to transport it was their own business, though he hoped they would heed his recommendations.

"You'll have Tai Li's men on your tail," he warned.

"Of course," Ho answered, "but we also have our ways of deception, *Jean*."

Reisman no longer doubted him. But Ho's proud revelation that they had the network and strength to carry out such an operation, the capacity to move a large shipment of arms secretly through China and across the border, also meant something else. He could hardly cry poor boy anymore, or deny operational help to the Allies, or to Reisman himself, in a time of need.

Half an hour later, Reisman started transmitting the homing signal. The L-5 pilot didn't really need it to find his way, but it was an extra navigational aid and it would reassure him that it was worth the risk to keep coming in, that his passengers were there and waiting. Sergeant Filmore turned the crank on the generator steadily, without complaint. Kita Shidehara squatted in the dirt near him, constantly scanning the night landscape and sky. His acute alertness to every possibility belied his pose of ennui. He and Ho wore the same dark peasant clothes that they had the day before.

"That thing sure makes a lot of noise," Kita complained. "You really ought to get your technical people to improve it. It's a good thing there aren't any Japs close by. I assume you arranged something with the French."

"Yes," Reisman assured him. Then he turned his attention to him fully. "By the way, you also speak Japanese, don't you, Colonel?" he asked archly.

"Of course."

"How do you say, in Japanese, 'Colonel Shidehara of the Kempitai in Hanoi sends regards'?"

Kita laughed. "To whom do you wish to deliver that message?" he asked with exaggerated grammar.

"Your man in Chungking."

"Then you do know who he is?"

He didn't, but the simple logic of an idea that had been growing in him made him say, "He's right there in Tai Li's Happy Valley, along with the other spooks."

Kita lost his smile. Reisman continued to improvise.

"Listen to me, Colonel," he went on. "What if there's an emergency—if I absolutely have to get a message through to you or Ho and every other channel is blocked?"

"Then you just continue the war without me," answered Kita wryly. "You're not going to get what you want from me without a substantial quid pro quo. I've got to be able to show the guys above me that the trade was worth it."

"What did you have in mind?"

"I really don't know, Johnny. Suggest something. A little horse-trading as we play the game is acceptable, but I'm reluctant to finger a man who is serving a function for both sides. Tai Li wouldn't let you take him out anyway."

"I told you it was personal."

"That makes it worse."

There had to be a way to extract a clue out of the man, Reisman thought. Then they heard the drone of the courier plane coming in and Reisman had to turn away from him. "Tell your men to light the lamps, Ho!" he ordered.

The Viet leader darted over the embankment, and in a few moments ten well-spaced lanterns glowed on either side of the runway, marking off about a hundred yards at the closest end. Ho was back just as Reisman went to voice transmission, talking the pilot in closer and lower until he said he could see the lamps and had a clear shot at the runway.

"Don't leave the plane!" Reisman told him. "Turn it around for takeoff, open the door, and we'll make a dash for you!"

"Roger . . . wilco," came the response.

They could see the plane now, silhouetted against the sky. Reisman ended the transmission, turned to Ho, and said, "The radio's all yours now, Uncle." He took off his carbine and pistol, handed them over also, and heard a grateful, *"Merci!"* Only then did it strike Reisman that he had something else he could trade to Kita Shidehara.

"Get ready to go, Sergeant," he said. "Soon as that plane touches down we run for it." He turned to Kita, took him firmly by the arm, startling him, and drew him out of earshot just as the colonel yanked his arm back angrily. "I don't need your translation. I can get it from anybody," said Reisman quickly. "I want the Kempitai agent in Happy Valley. You don't have to give me the name. Just a clue."

"What do I get in exchange?"

Reisman drew the one-time cipher pad from his pocket. "The code I've been using."

"You can change it like that!" Kita said, snapping his fingers.

"Take it or leave it!" Reisman told him, gazing toward the landing courier plane. "You've got about thirty seconds."

Colonel Shidehara used up five of them in hesitant silence. Then he said, "Go to a fellow named Chang Wen Ming who works there."

"Is he the agent?"

"No. But he can get word to him and him to me. That's what you said you wanted, wasn't it? An emergency contact. That's all you're going to get out of me, kid."

Reisman repeated, "Chang Wen Ming," and handed Kita the code pad. The L-5 touched down and Reisman and Filmore ran toward it. Behind him he heard Ho Chi Minh call out, *"Au revoir, mon ami!"* and he realized what sitting ducks they were. At any second, Japs, Viets or French could start shooting at them and they would have no means of defending themselves.

The plane braked and turned sharply back the way it had come, and the door flew open just as they reached it. Filmore was in first with Reisman after him, yanking the door tight and locked as the pilot started racing back down the runway to flying speed.

Then they were airborne and the pilot stuck his hand out and shouted, "Burt Webley!" without turning his head, keeping his eyes fixed on the dark rushing terrain. "One of you keep a sharp eye to port, the other to starboard. I'll take care of what's in front, and let's not talk till we get to Ch'ing-Hsi!"

PART IV

Apocalypse Poised

Chapter 27

His first sight of Kunming airfield and the high, cultivated plateau in the clear early morning light looked unexpectedly good to Reisman. The landscape, buildings and people seemed to him more civilized, less inconstant and threatening after his three weeks in the jungles and mountains of Tonkin.

Webley taxied the little L-5 in close to the reception building. There was Lieutenant Colonel Sam Kilgore standing out front with his thumb stuck up in the air again.

"Thanks for the ride, Burt," said Reisman when Webley cut the engine and they climbed out.

"Any time, John," answered the pilot jovially. "Just call in to the hack dispatcher when you need me."

They shook hands and Webley walked away to the operations shack. There was a team from 14th Air Force to take charge of Filmore. They had brought thanks to Reisman from General Chennault himself. Filmore repeated his gratitude and left with them.

Now there was just Sam Kilgore beaming at him like a proud scoutmaster. Sam ran through his own cheery speech. It seemed that the whole chain of OSS command from Kunming to Chungking was elated about the rescue of Filmore—because it validated their operations in Indochina—and they were very pleased with Reisman's reports about the Viet-Namese guerrillas and their military potential.

"I got a few ideas down there, Sam, that will make them even happier," Reisman told him as they got into the jeep. He was going to let him have it all at once on the ride in to OSS base. There was no time to waste, no time to feel his way along with subtleties. They had to get started immediately if his plans were going to work.

Kilgore drove away from the airport onto the familiar road into the city, which was visible in the near distance. He merged into the stream of motley vehicles, animals and people that always filled this road. Staring around and absorbing it all again, Reisman saw the bright sparkle of light off Lake Tien Chih across the plateau to the southwest and rising above it the steep, rocky *Hsi Shan* where he had climbed with Nguyen Thi Mai to the Temples of the Western Cloud.

"Go ahead," said Sam. "Right now you've got a lot of juice all the way to the top. They'll listen to you . . . probably do anything you want."

Reisman told him first the idea for the phantom armies and misleading radio traffic; though he didn't tell him the scheme had been suggested by an amusing, cynical comedian of a Kempitai colonel bent more on entertainment than mayhem.

"That's a hell of an idea," said Sam excitedly as they passed under the arch of Pi Chih and saw ahead of them all the hustle and bustle of the main commercial street of Kunming. "And it won't cost anybody a damn thing, even if it doesn't work."

"Just one of the codes, Sam." He told Kilgore a story that one of the Viets had planted the code pad where it would be found by Jap officers.

Kilgore still didn't get it. "Why'd you do that?"

"To validate the scheme. Transmit the most critical messages relevant to it using that cipher. Broadcast the rest in plain talk, like you're in a big hurry."

Sam turned his head away from the thick stream of traffic and grinned at him. "Damned clever, my boy! It fits right in with other things that are happening, which I'm sure the Nips are aware of. Ambassador Hurley has flown up to Yenan to try to bring Moose

Dung down here to make up with Mr. Shek. All that potential manpower ought to scare the shit out of the Nips!"

"You'll do it, then?"

They were talking loudly, to be heard above the jeep's engine and the street noise. Reisman leaned closer to him.

"I think the Chinese will like it very much," Sam said. "If they don't, however, we have the signal equipment and manpower to do it ourselves. No reason why we can't have it working in a couple of days. A network between Ramgargh, Chungking, Kunming and dummy corps and division headquarters moving into position—where?"

Remembering the other little errands he had to run, Reisman pictured the map in his mind's eye and said, "Set up your radio teams on a north-south line from fifty miles east of Kweiyang all the way south to the Indochina border. Make it look as if they're moving east fast. It's hill country, but there are enough roads in there to lose a few divisions."

"We can get the Psych War boys to write the dispatches—unless you want to do it yourself?" Sam ran on enthusiastically.

His C.O.'s confidence in what he could do with the plan immediately made Reisman wonder how high up his direct channels went. "No, there's something else I've got to get onto right away," he answered. "I think you'll like it."

Sam gave him a conspiratorial glance. "You ran into an opportunity down there," he said eagerly.

Reisman knew what he meant—the business opportunities and trade goods Sam had spoken about that night they'd spent partying in his fancy house before Reisman had gone south.

"Yeah . . . lots of opium down there," he answered glibly. Telling Sam that first would make the next part easier, he thought.

"Can you get hold of a steady, dependable supply?"

"I think so."

Sam turned the jeep off Chin Pi Lu onto the road that led to OSS base. "What do we need to trade for it?"

"Guns and ammo."

"That's hard."

"No, it isn't."

He told Sam what "Tong Van So" had disclosed to him about the arsenal of Chiang Fa-K'uei, though he said nothing about Tong's new *nom de guerre*. "It's supposed to be about halfway between Kweilin and Kweiyang, in a canyon off the main road."

"It doesn't surprise me," Sam said as they drove into the OSS compound. "Two other secret dumps like that have turned up right in the path of the Jap drive. We've got demolitions teams out now destroying them."

"What a terrible waste!" Reisman muttered, echoing Ho Chi Minh. "Why don't we try to save part of this one and use it for trade goods? That way you won't have to account for it."

Sam stopped the jeep next to the two-story barracks that contained his Special Operations office. "You shock me, Major," he said, grinning. "Trouble is, the Japs have got Kweilin and they're heading toward Kweiyang. They may have overrun the dump site by now, if it's there."

"Find out," said Reisman crisply. "If the stuff is there, I'll go in and get it myself. My men from England are due in today, aren't they?"

"Yes." Kilgore looked at his watch. "About 1700."

"I'll take them with me. Ought to be an easy refresher for them. You provide the transport. A jump plane for us and . . . let's say, twenty-five trucks to meet us there. More if you can get them."

They climbed the stairs to Kilgore's office on the second floor. "You're running a bit ahead, Johnny," he said. "Let's find out first if the stuff is there. No problem getting you a C-46, but you'll be lucky if I can round up twenty-five trucks. Might have to borrow them from the Chinese."

"They're ours to start with, aren't they? Just like the guns and munitions these big *tuchuns* sock away instead of using them against the Japs."

Sam sat down at his desk and swiveled his chair around to face him. "Okay, you made your point. Don't overdo it," he said. "I'll get onto this one too right away. We should know something by tonight. Now sit down and tell me what's happening down south."

Reisman expanded on everything he had already put into his radio dispatches about the military, political and economic condition of the Viet Minh. Then he added what he had learned in Lang Son about the French colonial situation, their military forces and the Resistance. As he had promised, he said nothing about Lieutenant Philippe Belfontaine and his mission from de Gaulle.

When Kilgore had finished debriefing him, he asked again about the opium.

"It's all over the place," Reisman declared with some exaggeration. "The hill tribes cultivate it just like in Burma. In fact, the

French encourage it. They're right in the middle of the buying and selling."

"How do you get hold of it?"

"I've made friends. The Viet Minh are against growing and using the stuff, but they need the tribes on their side, so they don't fight it. They'll work with us on the trade goods if we supply them with what they need to help us fight the Japs."

Hearing himself rattle on like this, Reisman really didn't know if he'd ever actually want to get involved in the trade, or whether the Viet Minh and the hill tribes would let him buy some of the stuff, or whether he'd just go right on bullshitting Kilgore as long as it served both their aspirations.

"Will they take Chinese money?" Sam asked.

Reisman laughed. "I wouldn't. If we were dealing with the Japs they'd take copper coins, but only to melt them down and use the copper in their factories."

Kilgore tilted his swivel chair back, stared thoughtfully at the ceiling a moment and then spoke with unexpected fervor: "No dealing with the Japs. I know and you know that some Chinese are doing it, but I draw the line there. I won't and you won't."

Reisman wondered if Kilgore really meant that, and what he would say if he knew about his dealings with Kita Shidehara of the Kempitai and Kita's help to the Viet Minh. It was not so different from the convoluted brokering that went on in China, as Katherine Harris had described it to him and his own observations had confirmed. Though he would never let his own secret transactions reach the point of treachery and betrayal. Nor did he think that Colonel Shidehara would on his side.

"I couldn't agree with you more, Sam," he said.

"What do you need from me then, to get you started?"

"Send me back well supplied from the laundry lists I've radioed up to you. For starters, Chiang Fa-K'uei's cache ought to take care of requirements nicely—if it's there, of course."

Kilgore let the spring of his swivel chair pop him back up again and he scrutinized Reisman closely. "You look as if you might need a bath, a meal, a bed and a change of clothes first," he said. "Want to go to my house?"

Reisman wondered if Betty and Jane were still in residence there. "No, thanks," he said. "I left some clothes at the BOQ last month. I'll go there. Is Corporal Bawsan still out at the jump school?"

"Yes. He ought to be finishing up about now."

"I'll pick him up, then meet my men at the field later. Do you know how many are coming?"

"No. All the names you gave me are cleared to come over the Hump from Assam, but I don't know how many actually made it there." Kilgore looked at his watch again. "I'd better get on the horn now and get these operations of yours going. I'm going to clear them with Chungking first. Let's meet back here at 2000 hours tonight. I ought to have something for you by then and we'll figure out the next steps."

Reisman started to get up, then dropped back into his chair again. "One more thing, Sam," he said.

"What is it?"

"That B-25 that killed Linc Bradford and his Kachins."

"I told you I never heard of it."

"I did. It had a Chinese crew that flew in here from Chungking on a transport, then took the bomber out."

"Where did you come up with that?"

"A guy that talked to them and saw the plane right here at Kunming airfield. How come you missed that one? You're supposed to know what's going on."

"Sounds like a guy that had too much to drink," said Kilgore evenly. He knew better than to ask who the guy was. "I'd forget about it if I were you. Even if it happened as you say, then it's Chinese business and they don't like anybody butting in . . . even their friends."

"So I've heard, Sam . . . so I've heard. I know it happened—and you probably know it happened—and I'm not forgetting about it."

Kilgore just stared after him as he went out the door, but he didn't say anything. Reisman wondered what his reaction would be if he told him he had a lead to the Kempitai agent in Kunming. He still didn't know what he would do with it, but that one he was keeping to himself.

He stood on the edge of the marked landing zone and stared up at the C-46 lazily droning across the clear sky. It was pleasantly cool out there on the Kunming plateau, hardly any breeze, a fine day for a jump. The scene was framed by mountains in the near distance.

Baw San didn't know he was there. When Reisman had called the parachute training center he had been told that the young Kachin was out with his class and was scheduled to make his fifth and qualifying jump in the early afternoon. He'd had more time for training during these past three weeks than Reisman had given the Dirty Dozen in England seven months earlier.

The jumpers came out in a stick, one after the other, just as they would in combat. Reisman estimated the altitude at about fifteen hundred feet above the plateau. He watched the canopies stream out, blossom and snap the jumpers into swaying, doll-like figures. He tried to pick out Baw San, but couldn't. Two months earlier it had been the Kachin on the ground, looking up with awe and delight while Reisman had floated down to their first meeting on the bank of the Salween River.

He finally picked out one particular figure, imagined that he was more relaxed and graceful than the others, that he was glorying in the experience, and guessed that it was Baw San. Reisman found himself murmuring instructions. "Legs together . . . don't fight the drop . . . don't try to climb back up . . . stay with it . . . legs together . . . feet together . . . easy hit . . . bend the knees to cushion the impact as you touch down . . . take a little roll . . . come up pulling in the lines and spilling air out of the chute."

The jumper didn't need his coaching. It was a textbook landing, right on the target panel. Reisman saw, with approval, how the man had tied down his carbine, grenades and heavy field packs so he wouldn't lose them or kill himself. Now he unsnapped and rolled the chute, saw who was staring at him, and ran toward Reisman shouting joyously, "*Duwa* John!"

They drove back to OSS base together in the jeep Reisman had borrowed from the motor pool. Baw San wore his parachutist's badge proudly and wondered why Reisman didn't wear one too.

"In my job it's better not to advertise," Reisman told him.

The boy started to unpin the badge and Reisman reached out a hand to stop him. "You deserve it. Wear it for now. I'm proud of you too."

Baw San was exuberant, pouring out every detail of his three weeks of intensive airborne training. "When I go home," he said, "I will jump from the sky into the village of the *duwa kaba,* the chief of chiefs of my district. I would want all the old *duwas* and young *umas* to see me, and all the Kachins of Detachment 101. They will know then that I'm no longer just a little *maung.*"

Reisman wondered if that was what Baw San really wanted. "Are you asking for leave now? You can have it if you want it."

"No, of course not, *Duwa* John. Not until the war is over. You helped my people . . . now I help you."

Reisman got Baw San settled into enlisted men's quarters in the compound, alerted the NCO in charge that there would be an unspecified number of men coming along later, and traded the jeep for a personnel carrier to drive alone to the airfield. A jeep, he hoped, would be too small to hold all the men coming back.

The plane came out of the last light of day to the west. Reisman stood just off the tarmac watching it, cushioning it down out of the sky to a safe landing.

Almost unconsciously, he realized now, he had been building a new Dirty Dozen with whom he had become enmeshed. A strange and disparate group: Baw San, Sam Kilgore, Ho Chi Minh, Nguyen Thi Mai, Tran Van Thi, Vo Nguyen Giap, Kita Shidehara, Philippe Belfontaine . . . perhaps even Madeleine Thibaut. Now he had some of the originals coming in and he felt both uneasiness and happy anticipation.

Seven was the largest possible number that Bowren might have rounded up—and that, he knew, was highly unlikely. Of the seven, five had still been missing in action when he had left England early in September: Napoleon White, Archer Maggot, Samson Posey, Luis Jimenez and Vernon Pinkley. Their faces and voices, even their quirks, rose in his mind's eye as he conjured them up. Only Ken Sawyer and Joseph Wladislaw had returned, wounded; as had Sgt. Clyde Bowren. He had seen each of them in hospitals in England, their wounds healing nicely, their spirits high. The other five of the Dirty Dozen—Myron Odell, Roscoe Lever, Calvin Smith, Glenn Gilpin and Victor Franko—had been killed.

Franko had been Reisman's only disappointment among them—though he understood the man and felt only sorrow not hatred when he thought of him. He still carried with him vividly the final scene as they had sped away from the château in one of the Nazi general's big open staff cars with Reisman at the wheel . . . Franko threatening him with a Schmeisser machine pistol, trying to force him to stop and surrender instead of breaking through the German roadblock. Sergeant Bowren had shot Franko dead.

Watching the transport land now, Reisman wondered at his motives in asking any of the survivors of that mission at Rennes to stick out his neck again in the Asian wars. Yet, by what right, or error of chance, might they have been sent back into combat somewhere else, to fight again and perhaps die, according to the whimsical needs of the army? He, at least, in his pride and arrogance, knew their capabilities and shortcomings, understood their true worth and valor, and would try to keep them out of the valley of the shadow of death.

The transport taxied close and stopped. The debarkation officer boarded and a few moments later the file of uniformed figures started down the ramp in order of rank. In the dim light, Reisman finally picked out Clyde Bowren. He wore winter O.D.s and had a duffel bag balanced on one shoulder and a flight pack gripped in one hand. He was a slim man of medium height, with a very youthful face, who moved with agile, sinewy grace. Behind him, similarly dressed and burdened, came Ken Sawyer and Joseph Wladislaw. Sawyer was a little taller, with broad shoulders and a big square jaw. Wladislaw was a little heavier; he had a husky body on a medium frame, and a full-fleshed, wide face with high cheekbones. He would be fat if the army didn't make him keep moving.

Reisman began to feel jubilation. He kept his eyes fixed on the aircraft's doorway, willing that there appear there the angry brown face of Napoleon White, and maybe close to him the flushed white face of Archer Maggot still baiting Napoleon, and then Luis Jimenez with his new look of dignity and bonhomie, and Vernon Pinkley who would have come along just because the others did, and the giant figure of Samson Posey—in Ute ceremonial dress if that was the way he wanted it.

But none of those five showed. Other soldiers debarked, but not them. Reisman broke the misty, other-world mood in which he had dwelled for a few moments. Bowren, Sawyer and Wladislaw were staring all around, taking their first look at China, but seeing little in the gathering darkness broken by airport lighting.

Joe Wladislaw spotted Reisman first. He broke into a big grin, nudged the others and pointed. The three of them burst out of the line moving toward the reception building. They trotted up to Reisman, dropped their bags and gave him a grand salute.

Wladislaw spoke first. He stood in a forced, formal attention, his husky frame rigid. He could barely get the words out for laughing: "Egg rolls, rumaki, egg foo yung, chicken chow mein, sweet sour shlimp, pork flied lice, moo-shu gai pan—and fortune cookies." He blurted the words out in a rapid stream, as if he had been containing them for 6,000 miles. But he couldn't hold his pose. His cheeks began to twitch, his eyes danced around looking for another resting place, and he turned aside laughing.

Reisman himself now couldn't keep a straight face as he returned their salutes. "Your Chinese vocabulary is pretty good, Joe," he said. "But your accent needs a little work." Then he cracked, burst out laughing and started pumping hands.

"You'll have to excuse him, Major," said Sergeant Bowren. "I told him we were going out for Chinese. That was in London. He's been working on that line all the way."

Reisman gazed at each of them in turn, filled with memories of their past and the wonder of their presence alive and well in China. Clyde Bowren now wore the rocker and three stripes of a staff sergeant. The raid at Rennes, and his wounds, had taken some of the youthfulness from his face; but he still had the kind of open, clean-cut features that inspired confidence. At twenty-seven, he was four years younger than Reisman and two or three years older than Wladislaw and Sawyer.

Wladislaw was still laughing, delighted with his own joke on the major and the fact that he'd pulled it off. Yet Reisman had remembered him as a dull-witted clod, seemingly without imagination, humor or daring. He had almost never smiled or tried to communicate beyond necessity during all those months of training at Stokes Manor.

"Don't worry, Joe. We'll get you a good meal pretty soon," Reisman assured him, trying to keep Wladislaw upright while shaking his hand.

Ken Sawyer glowed. "It's great to see you again, Major," he said ebulliently.

He looked less travel-worn than his companions, as if he had somehow managed, aboard the plane, to get ready for inspection. He was shaved, pressed and shining. The same parachutist's emblem and ETO campaign ribbons were resplendent on his O.D. jacket as on the others, and the corporal's stripes were back on his sleeve, the rank he'd held before his court-martial.

"Same here, Ken," answered Reisman with just as much fervor.

He remembered the first time he'd set eyes on Sawyer, the hangdog look of shame and defeat about him and the other Dirty Dozen. Bowren, an M.P. corporal then, had detested and distrusted most of the men. Now there seemed to be a genuine camaraderie between him and Wladislaw and Sawyer. Clyde was no longer just the tough, demanding sergeant driving his charges relentlessly through training.

"Any news about the others, Clyde?" Reisman asked at last.

The sergeant shook his head. "No, sir. I tried everything. Casualty control, POW lists, the OSS network on the continent. But I couldn't turn up anything. What you sees is what you gets."

Reisman still could not help but show his elation, though it was tempered. "Thanks for trying," he said. "I'm grateful that the three of you are here."

"You got something special for us, Major?" asked Wladislaw.

His tone was suddenly wary, no longer joking.

"Strictly volunteer—for each of you," Reisman said, looking from one to the other. "If you don't want to go, no hard feelings. You can sit around town eating chop suey until it's over. We'll have a briefing tonight, maybe go to work tomorrow. Nothing too fancy to start with. Let's get you through processing now, and then some chow."

He had only a few hours in which to get to know them again. Driving down Chin Pi Lu toward OSS base in the personnel carrier, he saw how excited they were by this new place, how they twisted and turned to take in all the exotic enticements of nighttime Kunming. Before the evening was over they would want to know where the girls were, though there would be no time for that tonight.

Baw San was waiting for them at their barracks, equally excited. Reisman had told him that he was to have new American buddies and that he was to look after them, to be their teacher in things they didn't know, their guide through the strange ways and languages of Asia and its peoples.

The young Kachin stood proudly inside the barracks entry, dressed in Class A suntans. He placed his palms together, bowed slightly, and greeted the new men: *"Kaja-ee!"*

Reisman copied Baw San's gesture with his hands and the bow and said, *"Kaja-lo!"*

Bowren, Wladislaw and Sawyer stared at him and the boy in bewilderment. Reisman made little prompting gestures until they got the idea. They dropped their baggage, placed their palms together, bowed and repeated after him: *"Kaja-lo!"*

"Is that Chinese, Major?" asked Wladislaw, pleased with himself.

"It's the language of the Kachins, Corporal Bawsan's tribe in Burma," Reisman explained. "He'll look after you and keep you out of trouble."

Instead of eating in the base mess hall, Reisman treated the four of them to dinner in a restaurant in the city. "I don't get much chance to spend money out here," he said. The purchasing power of the

American dollar, translated into Chinese money, actually embarrassed him. He knew what it meant: that too many Chinese were working too hard for too little.

The restaurant they went to was one of the few that had been cleared by the Medical Corps as fit for U.S. personnel to eat in. But when Wladislaw ordered certain dishes he was accustomed to getting in Chinese restaurants in Chicago—his hometown, too—he was upset to find out that they didn't know what he was talking about. Still, they found enough on the menu to fill their bellies pleasantly and for the new men to feel that they were at last eating Chinese food in China. The drinking was limited to one beer apiece and no one complained.

"We'll need clear heads later," Reisman cautioned.

The men got along well with Baw San. They pressed him to talk about his combat experiences against the Japanese in the Burmese mountains and jungles. He did so readily, but, as agreed, did not mention the action on the Salween River that almost had killed him. He explained away the Purple Heart ribbon on his chest with the same diffident story he had told in the military hospital in Calcutta and afterward. The men quickly realized that Baw San was the most seasoned soldier among them, except for Reisman.

For them Reisman was in a class apart. He had done things that none of them would ever want to do, and knew things that none of them would ever be asked to think about or would want to. They'd had the searing experience of their five months of service with him; beyond that they knew only some of his history. But that was enough to hold him in high regard, with some affection, and to follow him—though they were somewhat aloof, as if embarrassed, by what had gone between them before, by the awesome things they had already done under his command.

Each knew how the others had made it back to England after the raid—and they privately mourned the ones who had not. So they didn't talk about that. They spoke in general terms about the progress of the war in Europe, the Pacific and China. The three new arrivals were startled to learn that the Japs were still moving toward Kunming, where they sat dining comfortably and where nobody seemed very anxious. They had believed, as did most of the outside world, those fabricated stories of great Kuomintang victories over the Japanese.

"They're still three hundred and fifty miles away," Reisman told them. "And once they hear that you guys are here I think they'll turn and run the other way."

He really expected the Jap drive to stop one way or another, most likely because they were running ahead of their supply lines and winter was coming on. Or there was the possibility that the phantom army scheme would work. He didn't tell the men about that now, or about where he'd been for the last three weeks, or that he wanted them to go back there with him. He hadn't even told Baw San.

First there was the matter of the arsenal of General Chiang Fa-K'uei.

Chapter 28

"We've found it," said Lieutenant Colonel Kilgore, beaming at Reisman as he and his four men filed into the Special Operations office that night. "Your source was correct."

Points for Ho Chi Minh, thought Reisman.

The formalities of greetings and introductions were gotten through quickly. Kilgore made some attempt to ingratiate himself all around—and perhaps take some of the credit for making it possible—by saying how glad he was that Reisman now had serving with him some of the special personnel he had wanted. Then he pointed them to a group of chairs and stood next to his China operations map and a smaller aerial photo mounted on the wall. He started right in, directing his remarks only to Reisman, never asking if the four enlisted men in the room knew why they were there and what was going on—which they didn't.

"I should tell you first, John," said Kilgore, "that Chungking has gone for your other idea—the phantom armies—in a big way. The new radio network will be in place and operating in two or three days."

Reisman nodded. "That's fine, Sam."

He still hadn't told his men about it and didn't plan to, since they weren't going to be part of it. But he was very pleased and amazed that Kilgore had the juice to get something like that rolling so fast. He noted, though, that Sam had not said *who* in Chungking had gone for the scheme. It had to be an official or an organization with the power and resources to put it into swift effect. It could be Ludlow, OSS Chief China, or General Wedemeyer, who had replaced Stilwell as Commanding General China Theater, or General Chennault of the Air Corps, or Tai Li of the euphemistically named Bureau of Investigation and Statistics—or even Generalissimo Chiang Kai-shek himself. Or perhaps none of them, but rather some nameless officer or spook outfit in the overlapping, intertwined chains of command.

Since Kilgore had not thought it necessary to tell him who, Reisman thought it might be prudent not to ask. He also hoped that Sam had not disclosed the existence of the secret arsenal to anybody in Chungking who might be disposed to interfere with his plans.

"Do you have any idea how much stuff is there, John?" asked Sam, tapping the aerial photo.

All that Reisman could make out in the flat, dim light of the overhead fixture were the variegated tones of gray, white and black that were the convoluted folds of mountains, canyons, roads, valleys and plateaus, and a few clusters of buildings and streets that were towns. It was a high-altitude picture that revealed nothing of the subject under discussion.

"Tong Van So said there was quite a lot," he answered.

"A lot!" Sam's eyes rolled upward in emphasis. "Two of our agents out of Kweiyang went snooping around and found an incredible collection of stuff in a canyon near Jung-Chiang." He tapped a dark fold in the hills again. "There's supposed to be ten thousand tons in there!"

Reisman was astounded. A standard six-by-six truck held two and a half tons. That meant four thousand truckloads to completely evacuate the arsenal. And Vo Nguyen Giap in his exuberance had taken a wild guess at twenty-five.

"Just where Tong said it was," Reisman said, his voice falling off.

His four men looked at him somewhat suspiciously. It was time to put them in the picture, thought Reisman, since Sam evidently wasn't going to bother. Though Sergeant Bowren would be scrupulous in following orders and Baw San would be pleased to serve wherever he was asked, Reisman didn't think that any of the men, particularly Sawyer and Wladislaw, would accept being treated as unimportant little cogs in an unknown machine.

Joe Wladislaw spoke up before he could. "Hey, Colonel, we haven't any idea what you and the major are talking about!" he said. "If we're supposed to be part of some operation, I sure would like to know what it's all about."

Kilgore glanced somewhat irritatedly at him. To head off any argument, Reisman said hastily, "I didn't tell them earlier, Sam, because I didn't know if we were going. Want me to do it?"

"Please," answered Kilgore stiffly.

Reisman got up and stood next to him. He explained to the men the basic objective of what they were being asked to do: to evacuate as much as they could of a huge Chinese munitions dump and destroy the rest before the advancing Japanese army could capture it. He did not offer any of his own ideas about how the mission was to be undertaken. He wanted them to be part of the planning process. He also repeated his earlier offer that they were free to accept or reject the assignment, which brought a look of disapproval to Kilgore's face.

"Sounds like a simple enough job," commented Bowren. "How close are the Japs?"

Kilgore took over the briefing again. "The munitions dump is here, near the town of Jung-Chiang," he said, tapping the map. "Forward elements of the Japanese Eleventh Army are here." His hand didn't move very far.

"That's less than thirty miles," said Reisman staring at the map. "How fast are they moving? Do we have days or hours?"

"I don't know," Kilgore answered. "They've hooked their drive around to the southeast for the time being." He swooped his hand around the map to illustrate. "Mopping up on their flanks and consolidating their line. They seem more interested in moving on Liuchow now, but there's no way of knowing for sure. It's going to be at least two days before all your trucks can get there, so you can't go in before then."

Reisman wondered why Sam was so much keener on the operation now than he had been that morning—so enthusiastic, in fact, that he was running commendably ahead of him in the planning. Either he was motivated by the fearful prospect of so tremendous an arsenal falling into Jap hands, or somebody above him had told him to get cracking on it pronto.

"What about the trucks?" Reisman prompted, turning to face the men so that Sam would have to include all of them when he responded.

"There aren't enough in China to move that stuff out in a hurry," Kilgore said. "But I got you the twenty-five you asked for. Mostly Chinese drivers, but a few of our guys from the motor pool. Ten trucks have already left from here, and ten are driving down from Chungking."

An alarm went off in Reisman's head. This meant that people in Chungking now knew about the operation, people whom he might not be able to control. But he made no comment.

"I think they want a piece of the goods in return," Sam added casually. Reisman felt even more worried at this news. "And I rounded up five trucks in Kweiyang that will be waiting there for the others. They'll all make up a convoy there and move on to the dump near Jung-Chiang."

Reisman turned to study the map, estimating distances and times. The roads through the mountains were bad and driving time would be slow even if they kept going day and night. The ten trucks from Kunming, already on the road, had the longest trip, about 380 miles, and that was likely to take at least two days. The ten from Chungking had about fifty miles less to travel. Both convoys would have to gas up again in Kweiyang and carry extra fuel. The five trucks waiting in Kweiyang, where the full convoy would make up, were only about 120 miles from the munitions dump. However, once east of Kweiyang, Kilgore now told them, the convoy might have to face another problem, the result of what Kita Shidehara had called *Ichigo*.

"Hordes of Chinese—soldiers, officers, and their families, and civilians—are fleeing," he went on. "They're jammed into trains and clogging the roads on foot and in anything with wheels. They're passing through to the west of Jung-Chiang now and they've left an empty corridor behind them twenty to thirty miles deep."

Reisman stared at the corridor developing between the fleeing Chinese and the line of deepest enemy penetration. It ran all the way south to the Indochina border. From the frontier to Jung-Chiang was about 265 miles. The corridor would be a silent no man's land now, empty of people and war, filled only with terror. But this, Reisman now realized, would actually help the part of his mission that he had kept secret from Kilgore. Tran Van Thi and his fifty Viet guerrillas might be able to drive safely up that corridor—if they could somehow lay their hands on the trucks they needed—and they too could make the journey to the arsenal within two days. If the Japs didn't get there first.

"How about radios?" he asked Kilgore.

"The convoy leaders have them. You've got to be in the canyon before them, have the place secured, signal them to come in, and help them load and get out of there fast before you blow the rest of it. You will be designated as a demolitions team, but you will have written orders from the highest American and Chinese commanders to first remove what you can with the transport available."

As Kilgore spoke, Reisman watched the faces of his men and saw how intently they were absorbing the details. Their minds would work just as brightly and deviously as his and Sam's.

"Are the Chinks going to fight us?" asked Ken Sawyer.

"They haven't at the other dumps we've had to destroy," Kilgore answered. "Why should they? They're our allies, after all."

Reisman was not as certain about that. What neither he nor Kilgore could have explained, if they had been asked, was how so much war matériel had been siphoned off the main U.S. supply lines without anyone raising a stink. It was a question to which they'd probably never get a satisfactory answer, even if anyone had the gumption to challenge the Chinese hierarchy. Stilwell had been fired for doing just that. It had probably taken Chiang Fa-K'uei many years to build a hoard of ten thousand tons, years in which the stuff should have been shot at the Japs instead of being cached away to increase the personal power of one provincial Chinese warlord. The other two secret munitions dumps that Kilgore had mentioned that morning, which he had said were being destroyed, might have belonged to the same warlord or any of his rivals. Perhaps they had been kept secret even from Chiang Kai-shek and Tai Li, perhaps not. But while the Chinese government screamed for more help from the United States, this gigantic supply of guns and ammunition had never been used in the fight against Japan. Which was perhaps one of the reasons why Japan was still winning the war in China while losing it elsewhere.

Reisman went over to study the aerial photo. The canyon where the munitions were stored was just a dark slash that revealed nothing, but he could make out more of the road network in the area. "Come on up and take a look at this," he said to the men.

They gathered in a semicircle around him and Sam. "How are *we* going in, Major?" asked Wladislaw, examining the picture.

"Anybody got any ideas? Here's the target in here," Reisman answered, pointing to the dark slash that looked no different from any of the others, except for the road that clearly disappeared into it.

"Why don't we jump, *Duwa* John?" suggested Baw San excitedly. He pointed to an area of relatively level terrain a mile west of the canyon.

Wladislaw went to the operations map and said, "We could fly into Kweiyang and see if they've got any good Chinese restaurants there. Then drive out with the trucks."

"Too much time wasted on the road," Bowren countered, then realized Wladislaw was putting them on.

"They're giving us jump pay now. Might as well earn it," Sawyer said.

"Okay, an air drop," Reisman agreed. He and Kilgore exchanged glances, both knowing that it was how he had intended to go in all along. "It will give us time to work out the details, let the convoy get up close, and keep tabs on the Japs. I'm going out to the field now, Sam, to contact Tong on the radio. He'll be pleased." To the men he said, "You guys turn in now. We'll go to work in the morning."

Before they took off from Kunming in a C-46 two mornings later, Lieutenant Colonel Kilgore gave Reisman some last minute advice: "You're batting a thousand now, Johnny. Keep it up. Use diplomacy and tact—even deception. But don't make war on the Chinese, like Bradford did over on the Burma side." He gave Reisman the kind of accusing look that said he assumed more about Reisman's participation in that incident than he was saying or could prove.

Sam's use of baseball metaphor did not escape Reisman's notice. It reminded him of a certain colonel of the Kempitai who often spoke about "your team," as if the war was a game or a business.

The C-46 climbed above the terraced fields of the Kunming plateau and flew east at 11,000 feet. Unarmed transports didn't usually go very far in that direction without escorts. There was a flight of fighters upstairs somewhere, keeping track of them, maintaining radio silence, but ready to come to their help if they were attacked.

Reisman and his men had been outfitted with jump gear, chutes, weapons and field equipment from the company store. A new radio and generator, and demolitions equipment in cargo chutes, were on the plane to be dropped with them. The munitions dump itself held the explosives for its own destruction. Yet Reisman had to keep reminding himself that they were not on a combat mission. Intelligence had reported that the forward elements of the Japanese Eleventh Army had not advanced beyond where they had been two days earlier. In that time, the various sections of the truck convoy had joined up in Kweiyang and were on the road to Jung-Chiang. They had been radioed to halt two miles west of the access road into the munitions canyon and not to proceed further until they received the signal from Reisman. He estimated that the trucks would reach that position by the late afternoon.

For him, however, the main reason for the operation was to get a portion of Chiang Fa-K'uei's arsenal into the hands of the Viet guerrillas. Two nights earlier he had communicated with them in Pac Bo using a code they had devised together. He had told them about the route north between the Jap advance and Chinese retreat. Thi had signaled back that they were leaving immediately. Theirs would be the more tortuous and dangerous journey. They had to approach through the mountains from the southeast, as if escaping from the Jap drive, and they had to be at the arsenal at least two hours before Kilgore's convoy arrived from the west. Provided, of course, that they had actually gotten hold of the trucks they needed.

An hour and a quarter into the flight, Reisman felt the aircraft descending. He got up to go forward. He and his men were the only passengers. They had taken off their 'chutes, packs and weapons and were sprawled out along the bucket seats. The tech sergeant who served as flight mechanic and jumpmaster was seated against a bulkhead, reading *Yank* magazine. He gave a friendly wave as Reisman tottered past and poked his head into the cockpit.

"Where are we?" he shouted above the engine roar.

The co-pilot showed him on the chart. They were about sixty miles south of Kweiyang heading toward Jung-Chiang, still half an hour away from the drop point. The pilot had descended to a lower altitude because the mountains under their flight path were three to four thousand feet lower than the ones they'd had to clear near Kunming.

"We get to see more down here," the pilot yelled over his shoulder.

Reisman wanted that too. Now he could tell them the private things he wanted them to do—not part of the flight plan at all. They agreed. The pilot took the aircraft even lower, while Reisman and the co-pilot alternately studied the map and watched the ground. Soon they could pick out the streams of refugees along the roads west of Jung-Chiang and twice they caught sight of jam-packed trains creeping through lonely canyons and passes with refugees piled on top of cars and clinging perilously to the sides. Then Reisman spotted the truck convoy moving against the refugee stream, which flowed around the sides of the trucks like a malevolent tide. The trucks were right on schedule and the aircraft flew on ahead of them.

The pilot picked up the course of the Tu-liu River, then by-passed their intended drop point near the munitions canyon, as Reisman had asked. They overflew Jung-Chiang and went thirty miles east until they spotted the closest Jap forces and Reisman could confirm that they were halted in bivouacs and towns, no longer advancing on their way out from captured Kweilin. Though their aircraft, flying in the bright light of early afternoon, must surely have been spotted, there was no gunfire from the ground and no sign of enemy fighters in the air. The Japanese either felt very secure in this sector and had no interest in one lone C-46 straying close to their lines, or they were wary of such obvious bait.

Satisfied that the Japs were unlikely to thrust closer to Jung-Chiang in the next few hours, Reisman now had the pilot fly a search pattern over the empty corridor south, then west, picking up and following for many minutes at a time the secondary roads that wound up and down through the dry brown mountains. He made a game of matching the actual look of the land below him to the chart depicting it.

Two roads from the south came together at a town called T'a-p'ing, then went on as one road toward Jung-Chiang. Here Reisman spotted a motley grouping of vehicles moving north. It was a most unmilitary-looking convoy of old and new trucks of various sizes and automobiles and buses of assorted age and shape. Reisman counted seventeen vehicles in the caravan. They looked like a fleet of refugee conveyances that had banded together to cross hostile country, as indeed they were. He felt certain it was Tran Van Thi and his Viet-Namese now driving below him.

"Come around and wigwag them," he told the pilot.

The C-46 circled back, flew over the convoy again and gave its friendly sign of recognition. A few heads popped out of the vehicles to stare upward, and arms were waved in acknowledgment.

It was 1315 hours when Reisman went out the door of the C-46 above the patch of level terrain he had first seen on the aerial photo in Sam Kilgore's office. The weather was clear and they'd had no trouble finding the drop point. The canopy popped open above him with a loud crack. He felt himself seized and snapped in the familiar sequence and then the pleasure of floating down, taking control of the lines and bringing himself to earth close to the spot he had selected.

The others followed and the cargo chutes were pushed out after them. Reisman watched the aircraft make one more pass to check on their condition, then wigwag its wings and fly off toward Kunming. The five men gathered up radio, generator and demolitions packs, left the parachutes behind and quickly found the access road into the munitions canyon. Reisman had discarded any notion of slipping over the ridge and taking from behind anyone who was on duty there. It might have led to senseless shooting; he could still hear Kilgore saying, "Don't make war on the Chinese!" A direct and purposeful approach on the road, with authorization papers in hand, seemed the best way to gain the confidence of whatever guards were there.

The roadway curved through low, rocky hills and dry brushland. Then, at a narrow pass ahead, Reisman saw the fence blocking the road and the gatehouse, just as Ho Chi Minh had described them to him only five days earlier. Two startled Chinese soldiers came out of the gatehouse and pointed their rifles at the approaching party. They wore forage caps and the high-necked, dun-colored, shapeless uniforms of the ordinary Kuomintang soldier. Reisman and his men kept their weapons slung and were careful not to make any hostile gestures.

"Megwa bing!" he called out. "American soldier!"

The guards' wary, frightened expressions changed to smiles, and they lowered their rifles. Reisman asked in Chinese to see their commanding officer. One of them ran off to get him while the other let them inside the fenced area. Staring around, Reisman saw what Ho had seen a year and a half earlier when he had been a prisoner. Beyond the narrow defile that gave entry, the canyon opened up to a couple of hundred yards wide across its middle, then narrowed down and closed at the other end. The hillsides rose more steeply further back. The ridges were cleared, strung with barbed-wire coils and crowned with a few concrete bunkers and gun emplacements covered by camouflage nets. On the floor of the canyon were three wood barracks, a few sheds and five low concrete structures he took to be explosives stores. Roadways climbed the face of the hillsides to storage caves covered by iron grilles. There were a few trucks, jeeps, trailers and carts in sight, and a staff car, a Ford sedan, parked close to one of the barracks. Reisman could see there was little in the way of transport that he could commandeer to help evacuate the place, but he also saw an easier way to keep what he couldn't remove from falling into Jap hands.

Looking down the main interior road, he saw the gate guard and two other soldiers come out of a barracks and stride toward him. In the lead was a young officer wearing a visored hat and a more tailored tunic nipped in by a Sam Browne belt and holstered sidearm.

He saluted Reisman and said, "I'm Captain Kung, aide to General Chiang Fa-K'uei of the Fourth War Area. How may I help you?"

His English was crisp and clear and he seemed pleased to show it off, but his manner was formal rather than friendly. Reisman gave his name and rank in English and then spoke a few words of greeting in Mandarin and explained his business there. He handed Captain Kung his written orders covering the evacuation and destruction of the arsenal.

Kung's face darkened and he handed back the paper. "This is not possible," he said. "The matériel here is the property of General Chiang Fa-K'uei and no one else. It is his responsibility and his alone to see to its disposition."

Reisman decided to be diplomatic. "That's fine," he said, "as long as he gets it out of here or destroys it all before the Japs arrive."

"We don't have enough trucks to move this much tonnage."

"That's an understatement, Captain," snapped Reisman, unable to keep the impatience out of his voice. "I've got some on the way, but they'll be able to take only a tiny fraction of it. The rest will have to be blown up. We're going to start setting the charges immediately and have them ready to go when we clear out."

The captain scrutinized Reisman and his men closely, taking particular note of the assortment of weapons and grenades they carried, and the radio and generator. "You look more like an infantry patrol than a demolitions team," he said.

"You've read the orders," Reisman told him. "Please start loading the vehicles you have available. Take anything you want. I want you and all personnel in the canyon to be clear of the area in two hours. Where you go is your own business. We'll take care of the rest."

Captain Kung looked as though he was neither used to hearing such orders nor to acting so quickly on anything. "I think, Major, that you had better speak to the general yourself," he finally said.

"The general is here?" Reisman asked in astonishment.

Kung almost smiled at what he assumed to be the arrogant American's discomfiture. "Yes. We have been trying to devise some way to save our stores," he said. "Perhaps you can help. Please come with me. Your men may wait here at the gate."

Reisman tried, not very successfully, to sound diplomatic and deferential. "Captain Kung, may I present Sergeant Bowren, Corporal Bawsan, Corporal Sawyer and Private Wladislaw." They all acknowledged his introduction with a snappy salute that required Kung to return it. "They will not be able to wait here at the gate, Captain," Reisman continued calmly. "You will take me to General Chiang and then you will personally escort my men around your installation so that they may make an inventory of the contents before our trucks get here."

There were a few moments of tense silence while Kung pondered this and stared from one to the other. Reisman saw that some gesture was needed to help him save face in the eyes of his men. Bowing slightly to the Chinese officer, he said slowly, in the best Mandarin he could manage, "My men would be honored to learn from your own lips the superior system of storage you use here. I would be grateful for any assistance you can give us. I am certain that General Chiang will approve when he learns of our mission."

Captain Kung smiled at Reisman and his men for the first time and invited them to follow him.

The man who sat before him behind a writing table in the plain barracks room proved to be quite different from Reisman's mental image of a *tuchun*.

"I have been expecting you," said Chiang Fa-K'uei after the introductions had been made and Kung had left them alone. He had gone out, with the warlord's approval, to take Reisman's men on an inspection of the munitions dump. The general spoke in a soft, pleasant, thickly accented voice. "You must excuse my poor English. Not as good as Captain Kung, who studied and trained in your country."

The *tuchun* was a slender man of about fifty, with fine, well-shaped features and the long, thin, waxed mustache of a guardsman and a bristly shaven skull. He held in his hand a long, thin brush poised over a sheet of graceful ideographs; close by was a porcelain enamel inkpot.

Reisman went through the formalities, speaking in Mandarin and apologizing for his own linguistic shortcomings. That done, he asked, "Who told you we were coming?"

Chiang Fa-K'uei invited him to sit in a chair across the table from him. He put aside his brush and ink and studied the written orders Reisman placed before him. "I was not informed of your coming," he said, continuing to speak in more than adequate English. "However, news of the demolition of Chinese war matériel elsewhere reached me at my headquarters."

"An astonishing amount of matériel, General," Reisman put in, trying to sound naïve and uncritical. "Even more than what's here."

Chiang Fa-K'uei sighed with understanding and smiled gently. Reisman had expected some crude brute of a tyrant. This man did not fit the image. "I have been trying to think of some way to save what is here," Chiang said in a voice of reason.

Reisman told him that trucks were on the way. Remembering the rag-tag Viet-Namese convoy he'd spotted from the air, he added, "Buses, cars, trailers . . . anything my people were able to round up. I request that you leave the matter to us now, General. You've seen our orders and know what we have to do."

"That would be such a great waste," Chiang objected gently.

"The waste was before now, when all this stuff wasn't put to good use against the Japs," Reisman retorted, abandoning tact.

Chiang Fa-K'uei smiled at him with the look of a man who had found the secret of some kind of inner peace despite living in a land rent by war. "The use of this matériel is unimportant," he put forth softly. "Like a great but unspendable treasure, it is only the possession of it that is important; the threat that it implies—the power that it conveys to the possessor."

The warlord's English was getting better all the time, Reisman noted, though its content was ridiculous. He felt a surge of anger at this blatant confirmation of all the rumors he had heard about the power plays of the *tuchuns*. It went against everything Reisman's experience had taught him and in which he believed. Yet he knew that he had to keep talking, try to be a diplomat, try to ingratiate himself with Chiang and bring him around.

"It is beyond my competence to understand, General," Reisman said with deference. "Though an old friend of yours did try to explain this philosophy to me. He told me that you might think this way."

"Who is that?"

"Tong Van So."

The general sighed. "An interesting man. Where did you meet him?"

"Kunming. He is doing some work there for one of our information agencies."

"Be very careful of him," warned Chiang. "I like him. He is a clever and dedicated man, but he is a Communist and a French spy."

"There is a certain contradiction in that," Reisman said dryly.

"That is part of his cleverness. He will do anything, anything at all, to accomplish what he thinks is best for his people. He was in custody here for a long time."

"Why?"

"Certain officials did not approve of his activities in China."

"Tai Li?"

Chiang seemed startled to hear the name from Reisman's lips. "Yes, him too. However, I took an interest in Mr. Tong and thought that he could be of some assistance to us."

"I understand that he is."

"Well, it was you Americans who wanted him released," declared Chiang. "Any problems will be yours, not mine."

Reisman wondered how true that was. He knew that Chiang, like Ho Chi Minh, would say or do anything to accomplish his own ends. "Your advice is well taken, sir. I'll tell the people who have to deal with Tong," he said in his most diplomatic voice. It was intriguing, though not particularly enlightening, to hear the warlord's comments on Ho; but Reisman had to get to the point and convince Chiang to clear out and, before the two convoys arrived, to let them use the remaining hours of daylight to select the arms, ammunition and supplies that could be saved and start planting the charges around the canyon and running the wires out to a safe distance. "I suggest, General," he said, "that you now order your men to load your vehicles with whatever you want to take with you and leave here immediately."

The *tuchun* gave him that serene philosopher's look again. "I have another plan, Major," he said, touching the sheet of paper before him. "Do you read Japanese?"

"No, sir. I might be able to figure out a few characters, but I don't really read or speak it," Reisman replied.

"Pity. I thought you might be able to suggest something else in my letter."

"What is it?"

"I'm writing to General Yokoyama."

"Who's he?"

"Lieutenant General Isamu Yokoyama, commander of the Japanese Eleventh Army, which threatens us at the moment."

Reisman stared at him warily. "What's in the letter?"

"I'm asking him for payment in gold for the contents of this arsenal. Captain Kung, who is fluent in Japanese, will carry the letter through the lines to Kweilin for me."

Reisman's wariness turned to astonishment. It was the most unexpected and convincing evidence of duplicity. "That's insanity, if not treachery, General. You can't be serious," he said angrily, no longer concerned with tact. "We didn't ship all this shit over here for you to make a profit on it."

Chiang Fa-K'uei smiled benignly. "No, no, you misunderstand," he insisted gently. "Be practical, Major. This is a way of keeping everything intact right here. It would be a crime to waste it. I've told Yokoyama he must either buy it or I will destroy it."

"And you want him to use this stuff to slaughter Chinese and American troops?"

"Of course not. It's quite possible the Japanese will never even come this far. They haven't moved in days."

"You'll give them excellent reason to with your letter. What's to keep them from just barging in here and taking everything?" Reisman demanded. "There's nothing between you and them now but space."

"I haven't told Yokoyama where the matériel is located. I will not do so until he replies that he wishes to negotiate."

"He can squeeze it out of Captain Kung."

"He would not do that. This is a matter between gentlemen who understand these things. We do not behave that way."

Reisman laughed derisively.

"Also," Chiang continued, "the negotiations may never go beyond this first exchange. Perhaps you have not heard. There are new Chinese armies on the way. We have overheard their radio messages at my headquarters. They are coming from Burma and India, strong, healthy, well trained and equipped by you Americans."

Reisman did not want to disenchant him. If the wily warlord believed, then perhaps the Japs too believed. He was gratified that the phantom-army ploy was actually in operation. "How does Tai Li fit into this?" he demanded. "Is he getting his cut?"

"Tai Li knows nothing about this arsenal."

"That's unlikely," Reisman scoffed. "He has his spies everywhere."

Chiang Fa-K'uei examined Reisman's official orders again. They were written in both English and Chinese and signed, as Sam Kilgore had promised, by American and Chinese commanders high enough in rank to impress the warlord. "Perhaps now he does know," Chiang conceded halfheartedly. He shrugged off the thought. Then, vigorously, he said, "However, my proposition to General Yokoyama has nothing to do with Tai Li or anyone else. In making it, I am being neither cynical, mercenary, nor traitorous—only pragmatic. Yokoyama will accept my offer only if he intends to advance his troops to this area, which our new armies will now be able to prevent."

"In which case you will take the gold and run, and cheat him," said Reisman.

"Of course not. I told you we do not do things in that way at our level," declared the *tuchun*, as if he were speaking to a difficult student. "The gold will be only a form of collateral in case it is necessary for us to retreat from here. When we return I will have the gold to buy it all back. Then I will have these weapons again to fight the Reds when they finally come down from the north, as I fear they will."

Now it was Reisman who sighed. As far as he was concerned, if the Japs got hold of the hardware in this canyon they would use it to kill Chinese and Americans and it would help them to continue their onslaught all the way to Kunming and Chungking.

"Are there really ten thousand tons of arms and war matériel stored here?" he asked.

"Oh, yes. Your intelligence is quite good," Chiang said brightly. "An excellent inventory: rifles, pistols, carbines, submachine guns, machine guns, grenades, bazookas, mines, Bangalore torpedoes and demolitions packs—even some artillery—and ammunition for all of it. Plus many drums of gasoline and a variety of other military equipment and supplies. Also mortars. Very important."

It was incredible and infuriating to think of destroying most of that. There might be enough there to persuade both the Viets and the French to start a new front in the south. But there was no way to move all of it. What couldn't be taken away by the two convoys would have to be destroyed, regardless of Chiang Fa-K'uei's wishes.

"How many men do you have in the canyon, General?" he asked in exasperation.

"About thirty, I believe."

Reisman's initial assessment of the place, when he had glanced around outside, had been that he and his men could set charges to destroy the stuff in the five low concrete armories, the sheds and barracks; the entrances to the caves could be closed and hidden by explosives placed to bury them in rockfalls, and the narrow pass into the canyon could be blocked by charges that would fill it with landslides. Maybe Chiang's men would help. The explosions would set the hills on fire. They would have to be well on the way out of the immediate area before he detonated the first charge.

He stood up and leaned over the writing table, his hands pressed firmly on its top. "General Chiang," he said in a calm and reasonable voice, "we've got to start placing explosives and wiring this place now, without any further delay."

Chiang Fa-K'uei smiled up at him serenely. "We've already done all that, Major," he said with an air of satisfaction. "The explosives and detonators were installed from the beginning. The facility was designed to be destroyed quickly if ever circumstances warranted, as they seem to now. Your men will confirm this when they've completed their inspection. Captain Kung will point it out to them, of course, if they don't observe it themselves."

Reisman was surprised by such contradictory foresight, but he was glad for it. "You've saved us time and work then, General," he said. "Now you must start moving. Load your vehicles with whatever you can carry—and go. I want you and your men out of the canyon in an hour."

A look of anger rose in Chiang Fa-K'uei's face. "And if I refuse, Major? You are heavily outnumbered, you realize."

Reisman looked at his watch and began to improvise. "At this very moment, General, Fourteenth Air Force has bombers heading in this direction. If they don't get a radio signal from me calling them off, they will come in and do the best job they can on this place from the air. It will not be as precise and effective a job as we can do here on the ground, but it will suffice."

Chiang Fa-K'uei stared at him in astonishment that turned quickly to alarm. "You are mad!" he exclaimed.

"Damn right I am."

"They will kill all of us!"

"All you have to do is leave, General, and let us go about our work."

The warlord's no longer serene features worked through a range of frustration, anger and fear, never quite making it back to the mask of the inscrutable philosopher. "I don't intend to be a martyr," he finally said calmly. "It would be as pointless to fight you people as the Japanese."

With that remark, Reisman threw away any remaining deference toward the man. It went swiftly after that. Chiang was unhappily showing him the master storage roster and the schematic for the in-place demolitions when Captain Kung returned with the men from their inspection of the arsenal. Bowren confirmed what Reisman had learned about what was stored there and that the entire canyon had already been wired to blow.

"Very clever—and we're right in the middle of it," Bowren told him in an anxious voice. "The leads are concealed and the dynamite is hidden among the other stuff in the buildings and caves. Whatever doesn't blow will be buried."

Reisman showed him on the schematic how the wires all came together at a control box in the gatehouse. All they had to do was connect new leads to the terminals and unreel wire far down the access road to their own exploders.

In the next hour, Reisman stayed close to Chiang Fa-K'uei while the *tuchun,* dressed now in a finely tailored but unadorned brown tunic, reluctantly supervised the hurried evacuation. Reisman still didn't trust the man. To keep up the deception that an aerial strike was imminent he kept looking anxiously at his watch, staring up into the clear mid-afternoon sky above the hills, and urging the Chinese to greater haste.

He told Wladislaw and Sawyer to set up the radio and generator in plain sight where Chiang's men were loading the vehicles. Baw San connected a long extension to the antenna wire and carried it up to the ridge for better transmission and reception. The Chinese troops loaded their personal gear and then filled three six-by-six trucks, two jeeps and attached trailers, and the general's staff car with selected items from the arsenal. They could take very little and still left barely enough room for themselves to squeeze onto the vehicles. Three artillery pieces were hitched to the trucks.

Chiang Fa-K'uei dashed about frantically giving and countermanding orders, trying to choose among all the guns and matériel, practically wringing his hands in despair, just as Ho Chi Minh had said he would. Reisman tried to help him choose the basics. From time to time he went to the radio and, while one of the men cranked the generator, he mumbled inaudibly and mysteriously into the microphone and came away shaking his head, muttering anxiously, "Can't reach them yet."

None of his men knew what he was talking about, but Chiang Fa-K'uei did. When the warlord and his soldiers were at last jammed into their vehicles and ready to depart, Reisman bent his head close to Chiang at the passenger window of his sedan. Captain Kung was at the wheel and an ordinary soldier had been allowed the privilege of being squeezed in between the two officers. The soldier sat there stiff and bug-eyed, his rifle poking up between his legs. Crates of guns and ammo extended over the back of the front seat, forcing the occupants to bend forward uncomfortably.

"Where will you go, General?" Reisman asked, trying to sound casual and friendly.

"That is not your business, Major!" Chiang replied petulantly.

"I might want to get some of this stuff returned to you," Reisman offered. "Depends on how many trucks get here." He looked skyward again and at his watch and shook his head. "If they make it in time."

Chiang Fa-K'uei's expression softened slightly. "That is different," he said. "If you are able to accomplish it, I will see that you are rewarded, Major. My headquarters is near Tu-Yun."

Reisman took a map from his field jacket and unfolded it close to the warlord. "Please show me, " he said.

Chiang Fa-K'uei tapped his finger at the place. Reisman was glad to see that he and the men would be able to comfortably by-pass Tu-Yun during their journey back to Kunming. "Have a good trip, General," he said, stepping back and saluting.

The *tuchun* made a half-hearted response, Kung started the car and they led their little caravan out of the canyon.

Alone with his men, Reisman finally revealed to them that there were to be two separate convoys and pledged them to secrecy regarding the first one.

He heard the Viet-Namese convoy on the access road a half hour later, just as he was coming down from the storage caves after completing his own inspection of the demolitions system. It seemed to him that, if it worked as intended, the placement and sequence of the charges was sufficient to accomplish most of what had to be done. The only addition would be to place demolitions in the hillsides above the narrow access road so as to cause avalanches that would close the road behind them after they left.

When he first caught sight of the figures getting out of the motley array of trucks, buses and cars, Reisman was startled. A contingent of armed Chinese soldiers appeared to be guarding a hapless group of civilian men and women.

Then he heard a familiar voice call out, "Major Reisman!"

It was Tran Van Thi, dressed like a Kuomintang captain. He

looked as if he might have waylaid Captain Kung and stolen his hat, jacket and Sam Browne belt and gun.

"Is it true . . . as Uncle Ho said?" Thi asked anxiously.

"Yes. There's so much stuff here," Reisman replied, "it will make you sick just to think of what you have to leave behind."

Thi's dark eyes glowed and his usually serious face broke into a fleeting smile. "We could not obtain twenty-five trucks," he apologized. "I am very sorry. We did the best we could."

Reisman was gratified that they had made it at all. He could now see the deception they had prepared in case they ran into any doubting Chinese. A third of them were dressed in Kuomintang uniforms; the rest, men and women, looked like refugees forced to flee with the soldiers from the enemy drive. If the Japs had caught them, though, they would have been finished.

"You did well, Thi," Reisman said. "We've got to work fast now. I'll tell you which cave or building to drive your vehicles to, and what to take. No arguments. Just load up fast and get the hell out of here. Are you returning by the same route?"

"Part of the way south. Then we have a plan to split up."

"I don't even want to know about it," Reisman said. "Whatever you do when you leave here is your responsibility. But I can only give you a little more than an hour to load up and leave. There's a Chinese convoy out on the road to the west, waiting for my signal to come in. That's my cover for being here. If any of you get caught on the way home, you must never tell anybody where you got the stuff. Agreed?"

"Gladly. *Allons, Jean!*"

It was 1545 and the day was still bright and clear when they started to load. The fifty Viets worked swiftly and efficiently with Reisman and his men during the next hour. He steered them to the most useful weapons and ammunition for guerrilla action: M-1 rifles, carbines, submachine guns, grenades, land mines and demolitions packs. Thi stared covetously at the pistols and at the heavier machine guns, both of which Reisman excluded, though he allowed four B.A.R.s. He did not think pistols were the most effective weapons for guerrilla operations, and machine guns would displace lighter, more mobile weapons in the limited transport. He did include, however, five 60 mm mortars with 200 rounds and three bazookas with 50 rounds. Much of the stuff was still packed in crates, the guns smeared with cosmoline. There was also an unexpected bonanza of basic medical supplies.

By 1650 there was no more room in the vehicles. "You get caught with all this stuff now—by Japs or Chinese—you've had it," Reisman warned Thi as they inspected the line of vehicles ready to move out. "You won't even be able to use any of it to defend yourselves."

"We are prepared," said Thi. "When will you return to Pac Bo?"

"Depends on my orders. Soon, I expect," Reisman replied. *"Bonne chance!"*

Thi shook his hand warmly and took the wheel of the point vehicle, a six-by-six with Chinese unit designations on it. Reisman watched the caravan drive away down the access road. They would turn east for a short distance toward the Japanese lines, then south through what he hoped was still an empty no man's land. He got on the radio immediately, raised the leader of the Chinese convoy waiting for his signal two miles to the west, and told him to come in.

The leader turned out to be an American OSS lieutenant who spoke Chinese. From what Reisman could get out of him, he was merely serving as a delivery boy for Lieutenant Colonel Kilgore. He knew nothing about any other aspect of the mission. He had with him four American and six Chinese drivers from the Kunming motor pool, and each truck had one Chinese soldier riding shotgun. Everybody doubled now as loaders, and Reisman ran them through the same procedure as he had the Viets.

While the trucks were being filled he sent Bowren, Wladislaw, Sawyer and Baw San up on the hillsides beyond the front gate to plant the explosives that would create the avalanches to block the road. It was twilight when they scrambled back down, unreeling wire behind them. The loading was finished by then and the convoy was ready to move out.

"What about the rest of the stuff?" the lieutenant asked.

When Reisman told him he was going to blow it all up, the man shook his head. "Stupid damn waste," he muttered.

"It's going to make an awful bang," Reisman told him. The high explosives, artillery rounds, gasoline and ammunition in the caves and blockhouses would take everything else with them. "I'm sending three of my men out with you now. Wait for me at the place where I contacted you on the radio. Signal me when you get there, and keep listening for me after that, just in case I need you. I'll bring up the last truck after I set off the charges."

The truck he was keeping had a radio powered off the battery and engine and had been loaded only with hardware, no explosives. He took his men aside and told them what he had to do. "I need one of you to stay with me and drive the truck out while I work the exploders," he said.

They all volunteered. He picked Joe Wladislaw, maybe because he remembered that Wladislaw had been a truck driver in civilian life, maybe because he was so surprised that Wladislaw had volunteered.

The convoy pulled out slowly, leaving plenty of space between each vehicle, their headlights cutting the new darkness. Wladislaw parked the last truck fifty yards down the road with the engine running and the radio on. Reisman set to work in the gatehouse where all the demolitions system circuits from the caves and blockhouses came together in a terminal box. He had three drums of double cable and three exploders they had brought in with them. With new leads, he spliced, crimped and taped the ends of each cable onto a number of circuits so that the cable would feed current from an exploder to more than one circuit simultaneously. Then he unreeled the cables to the back of the truck, to be hooked up to the exploders. He did the same thing with the spools of cable that the men earlier had run down from the explosives buried up on the hillsides.

He had to prop up a flashlight in the truck so that he could see to work; finally he brought the light close to double-check his connections. He heard the crackle of static on the open radio in the truck's cab. Then the lieutenant's distant voice. Then Wladislaw calling out, "They're there and waiting, Major!"

"When I tell you to, put her in gear and start rolling slowly," Reisman shouted to him from the back of the truck. "When you hear the first bang, hit the gas and get the hell out of here."

He was going to use all three exploders, each capable of generating enough current for a number of circuits in rotation. When he'd snaked out fifty more yards of cable off each drum, he picked up the first exploder, shouted "Go!" to Wladislaw, and activated the handle. He was half prepared for a great joke on the part of Chiang Fa-K'uei and was almost surprised when he heard the first explosions in the caves. Then, as Wladislaw accelerated the truck, Reisman quickly picked up and fired the second and third exploders before he ran out of cable and they were yanked out onto the road.

As they sped away, one explosion after another destroyed the munitions dump behind them and part of the hillside slowly rolled down to close the gap. The noise was horrendous and the concussions rushed at Reisman and made him grab onto the side of the truck for support. Fire and smoke and pieces of things leaped above the ridgelines. He thought of the great expenditure of lives, labor, time and money that had brought all that matériel from the United States to China. He was transfixed by the receding scene. He had never before caused so great an explosion of elements on the face of the earth. Neither the château at Rennes with the Dirty Dozen, nor the fort at Caojian with Linc Bradford and the Kachins, nor anything he had ever caused to happen. He remembered the words he'd shouted at Linc as they'd climbed into the hills above Caojian: *You know who paid for all that shit we just blew up? You did. I did. The American taxpayer did. This fuckin' war out here is crazy!*

He felt the same way again. Could Chiang Fa-K'uei's way really have been any worse? He didn't think so.

Seven minutes later, Wladislaw eased the truck to a halt behind the waiting convoy. Reisman leaped to the ground over the tailgate—and found himself staring into the gun barrels of five Kuomintang soldiers aiming rifles at him from both sides of the road.

Chapter 29

There was no way to fight back in the first moments of the ambush. There were at least a hundred heavily armed Kuomintang soldiers in the capturing force—a middle-aged captain, a couple of lieutenants, assorted NCOs and troops. The captain behaved with courtesy but refused to say anything except to warn them not to resist or try to escape. Everybody was disarmed, and Reisman and his four men were separated from the others and placed, with two guards per prisoner, in one of their captors' trucks.

"Shit, we been hijacked!" Wladislaw said angrily when the convoy started moving again.

He glared through the darkness at Reisman sitting on the bed of the truck across from him, as if holding him responsible for the turn of events. All eight Chinese guards turned their heads toward Wladislaw, wary of the foreigner's anger.

"Cool it, Joseph," Reisman cautioned in a pleasant voice. "You're making our hosts nervous. Just go along with them for a while."

"I thought these guys were on our side," Sawyer muttered.

Reisman tried to soothe him and reassure the others, though both Baw San and Bowren, at least, were following his lead calmly. "They are on our side," he said. "Remember that war game in England last spring, Ken?"

"Yeah?"

"Think of it that way and nobody will get hurt."

He still couldn't explain to them what was really happening, though somebody with great authority had obviously given much importance to intercepting them. Their captors had traveled in their own jeeps, personnel carriers and trucks, had known exactly where to find them and had taken up excellent positions to capture them without any trouble. He had thought at first of Chiang Fa-K'uei, but dismissed that possibility as unlikely.

Speaking in Chinese in his most ingratiating manner, Reisman tried to worm some bit of information out of the soldiers riding in the truck with them, but they were stone-faced. For a long time, Reisman and his men sat slumped silent and disconsolate against the truck stakes. The oily-smelling roof canvas was tied down all around except at the tailgate, where the flaps were open. He could peer past the guards into the darkness and see the narrow, unpaved road that rose and fell and twisted between the hills. The vehicle went slowly, seldom more than twenty or twenty-five miles an hour, Reisman estimated, maybe thirty in brief spurts. There was one long stretch of road where the convoy had to force its way slowly through a mass of refugees still moving westward in the darkness.

In the middle of the night, after about six hours on the road, they halted at a military installation in what must have been Kweiyang. Reisman and his men were ordered out of the truck onto a barricaded street set amid barracks, sheds and storage yards. He could see the OSS lieutenant, his four American drivers and all the rest of the convoy personnel milling around close to their trucks nearby, guarded by dozens of soldiers. A moment later, the Kuomintang captain in charge of the ambush party strode over to demand the manifest on the contents of each truck.

"There isn't any," Reisman told him truthfully.

The captain glared at him and turned away, but Reisman stopped him and demanded to be allowed to contact OSS base in Kunming to inform them of his whereabouts.

The captain refused.

"How about letting us in on the game then?" Reisman pressed.

"It is not a game," the captain replied curtly. He spoke a few words in Chinese to the impassive guards, then strode back toward the long line of trucks laden with arms and munitions.

"Any man that concerned about our taking a piss can't be all bad," Reisman translated for the men.

They were taken under guard to a nearby latrine to relieve themselves. When they came out, they passed within sight of the OSS lieutenant and his drivers waiting their turn. Reisman started toward him but his way was immediately blocked by his guards. The lieutenant managed a wave of his hand and a shrug of his shoulders to disassociate himself from what was happening. In the near distance, Reisman could see the Chinese captain and three of his men moving from truck to truck making a quick survey of contents. Then some worker-soldiers who had been rousted out of their barracks helped rearrange some of the cargo between vehicles. There was no lighting in the street except for hand-held lanterns, so they worked by the glare of the various vehicles' headlights.

When the captain had everything rearranged to his satisfaction, he issued new orders, and shortly afterward long lines of worker-soldiers appeared out of one of the storage yards carrying five-gallon jerry cans to top off all the gas tanks and replace the empty reserves. Weapons were returned to the OSS lieutenant, his drivers and the Chinese soldiers who had driven out with them riding shotgun. Then they climbed aboard ten of the trucks and, waved on their way by the captain, drove away westward, without so much as a by-your-leave to Reisman.

"Where are they going?" he asked, watching the last truck disappear into the night just as the captain came up to him.

"Kunming."

Reisman was surprised to get an answer out of him at last. "And us?" he demanded.

The captain ignored the question. "Get them into the truck," he ordered the guards.

"Where are we going?" Reisman repeated.

The captain smiled for the first time. "Chungking," he said.

The journey took all of that night and most of the next day. It was not a great distance between Kweiyang and Chungking—210 miles, Reisman had estimated—but the convoy, with its cargo of war matériel, moved slowly; the roads were poor, rising, falling and twisting through hilly terrain. Reisman and his men often dozed in their rocking, bouncing truck—as did the guards—waking with a start to rediscover where they were. There were a few rest stops and exhausted drivers were replaced. Reisman and his men were given one meal at midday, the same simple rice, vegetables and tea as the Chinese soldiers. Wladislaw decided he didn't like Chinese food after all.

"This is what I get for breaking Rule One!" he griped.

"What's that, Joe?" asked Reisman.

They had been permitted to get out of the truck. Their food had been spooned out into their own mess kits and they were bunched together, sitting, squatting and standing by the side of the road, always under the watchful gaze of the guards. Their American uniforms—garrison caps, field jackets, combat fatigues and good jump boots—set them apart from the Chinese soldiers in their drab, high-necked uniforms and old-fashioned leggings. Wladislaw was staring out to the strange rocky hills all around them, speaking to no one in particular. Reisman thought his wide, high cheekbones made him look almost oriental in the setting they were in.

"Never volunteer for nothin', no how, no way," Wladislaw muttered.

Bowren looked at him in irritation. "Listening to your bitching makes me feel right at home, Joe," he said, only half in jest.

Baw San looked at Wladislaw disapprovingly. "Listen to *Duwa* John," he advised from his squatting position, "and all will be well."

When, a few minutes later, Baw San whispered to him about escape, Reisman shook his head. It did not seem the thing to try to do yet.

It was the rush of the great Yangtze River seen out the back of the truck in the late afternoon that made Reisman realize they were very close to Chungking. That and the thickening procession of pedestrians, animals, carts and struggling vehicles of every description moving toward the congested riverside hills that were the wartime refuge of the Kuomintang government of China.

At the military depot to which they were taken on the southern side of the city, their captors turned them over to another contingent of Kuomintang officers and troops. Reisman and the men watched from an open compound as their own weapons and equipment, including the radio and generator, were carried from one of the trucks and sequestered in a guarded barracks. This suggested the possibility of deliverance. But then the hijackers drove off with all the vehicles, salvaged guns and munitions, and the rest of the personnel of the convoy.

"We seem to have done somebody else's dirty work for them," Bowren commented acerbically. Usually reticent and uncomplaining, he was angry now. "I give up, Major. What in hell is it all about?"

Reisman caught the accusing tone in Clyde's voice, so very unexpected. He realized now that Bowren, Wladislaw and Sawyer might think that they were being used as patsies in some bizarre scheme. Remembering the raid at Rennes, they would have reason to. Only Baw San wouldn't.

"Just ride with it for a while, Clyde," Reisman said, trying to be reassuring. "Patience is a way of life out here—and things eventually come clear."

Their new guards treated them with more courtesy, but Reisman was again refused permission to contact his base in Kunming or the OSS office right there in Chungking. A smiling young Nationalist lieutenant showed them to a primitive shower and gave them towels and soap. When Reisman asked for their knapsacks so that they could also shave and change socks, shorts and T-shirts, the packs were brought immediately, though they were watched closely to be sure that they had no hidden weapons.

It was getting dark and they had just finished washing up when a familiar Chinese NCO—tall, chunky, glowering and wearing a .45—came through the door of the barracks where they were being held. It was Sergeant Liu, who had picked up Reisman and Baw San at the airport many weeks earlier when they first came over the Hump, and had then driven Reisman to the Sino-American Cooperative Organization office at Happy Valley.

"Boss wants to see you," Liu said to Reisman with no salute or hint of deference.

His manner seemed even more antagonistic than at their first meeting. Since the three stripes he wore couldn't explain his attitude—not when set against major's leaves—Reisman assumed it must be the advantageous and prejudicial secrets the man carried about with him and the omnipotent people he worked for that let him think he could get away with that sort of behavior; or else it was merely a natural aspect of the man's character, a racial contempt of the same kind suffered in reverse by many Americans.

For the moment, though, Reisman didn't care what the man's problem was. He was glad to see him and greeted Sergeant Liu with a disarming smile. The simple fact of the man's arrival gave Reisman reason to believe that one of his earliest suspicions about the operation, even before they had left Kunming, was justified. But he would not give Liu the satisfaction of asking him questions that he would likely refuse to answer. Those answers, Reisman surmised, would soon be forthcoming at SACO headquarters.

"We're ready to go, Sergeant," he said.

Liu looked briefly at Bowren, Wladislaw and Sawyer, and a moment longer at Baw San, as if still trying to figure out what the young Kachin was doing in China.

"Only you, Major, not your troops," Liu declared.

"They go with me," Reisman insisted. "I will not leave them behind."

"They're not invited."

"Then arrange it. Tell your boss if they don't come, I don't."

Reisman thought he caught just the slightest twitch of Liu's right hand toward his holster, and he instantly shifted his own stance so that he could chop the pistol out of his hand if he drew it. But Liu changed his mind before executing his move. Bristling with anger, Liu turned on his heel and left the barracks muttering, "I'll find out."

Baw San stared after him with an expression of dislike. "I remember that one, *Duwa* John," he said darkly.

"Snotty son-of-a-bitch, ain't he!" commented Wladislaw.

Reisman wondered if he had pushed too far with the SACO errand boy. The opportunity to hear from the lips of Commodore Pelham Ludlow, Deputy Director SACO and OSS Chief China, all the whys and wherefores of this Chinese labyrinth, was more than he had hoped for. More importantly, a visit to Happy Valley might let him pursue his own objectives. Perhaps *thoi co* would allow him to locate Chang Wen Ming, whose name he had bartered out of Kita Shidehara, and then enable him to track down the Kempitai agent protected there in Chungking—and most of all to find and punish the men who had beaten and maimed Katherine Harris.

When Liu returned ten minutes later, he delivered his message woodenly: "The boss says it's okay. Permission granted. Let's go."

"Not quite yet, Sergeant," Reisman said. "Our arms, equipment and wireless must go with us."

He expected to be refused again, but Liu's new instructions apparently allowed him more leeway. "Okay. Permission granted," he said. He seemed to enjoy that phrase, as if he were personally dispensing largesse. "I'll get them to give you back all your stuff. Let's just get the hell out of here. The boss is waiting."

The same smiling young Nationalist lieutenant who had presided over their showers now supervised the return of their weapons, ammunition and grenades. He looked slightly alarmed, however, when Reisman immediately ordered the men to inspect the barrels and chambers of the potent array of carbines, pistols and submachine guns, and to lock and load all of them with full magazines.

"There's no need for that," Sergeant Liu protested.

"Of course not," agreed Reisman, smiling. "Let's go."

There were too many passengers now, however, and too much equipment to fit comfortably into Liu's jeep. He had to borrow another vehicle from the local motor pool. Reisman steered him to a personnel carrier that had a canvas roof and sides. He took the wheel and his four men stowed all the gear and slid up onto the benches close to the driver's compartment.

"Follow right behind me," Liu called out harshly as he climbed into his jeep.

"Sure thing," Reisman answered cheerfully. He figured it wasn't every day the SACO driver got to order an American officer around and he let him enjoy himself because it fit right in with his own plans.

Fog lay upon Chungking now in the night, heightening fears, mysteries and dangers, driving its war-weary citizens and refugees to their sanctuaries. Japanese bombings had long since been halted—and a night like this would have given respite, in any event—but, to Reisman, the city seemed hunkered down, peering tensely over its shoulder, waiting for the next blow.

The curbside in front of the Chungking Hotel held the usual variety of military and civilian vehicles. Across the street, the lights of the *New China Daily* glowed dimly in the gloom. Reisman followed close enough behind Liu's jeep to give mutual assurance that they were both there, but not so close that Liu could observe and try to prevent what he intended to do. They were driving in the newer, western part of the city now.

"Baw San!" Reisman called into the back of the carrier. "Do you think you can find Dr. Briggs's clinic?"

"I think so, *Duwa* John. Do you want me to guide you?"

"No, I want you to take the men there."

Easing back from the jeep ahead of him, he also glanced in the rearview mirror to be certain they were not being followed. He explained to the men that he did not want them to accompany him to Happy Valley. He wanted them to wait for him with Lieutenant Commander Briggs, a naval officer he trusted.

"We're in the general area now," he said, peering through the fog. "I'll slow down in a minute. Get ready to go. Take everything—my stuff too, and the radio and generator."

He slowed the personnel carrier until he could no longer see Liu's jeep. Then he told the men to go. They slipped off the back of the carrier and disappeared quickly. Ten minutes later, when he parked next to Liu on the grounds of Happy Valley, he was alone, and when Liu became aware of it, staring into the back of the empty vehicle, Reisman was particularly pleased by the look of stupefaction on his face.

"Where are the others?" the sergeant demanded.

"Must have been hijacked," replied Reisman casually. "Happens all the time out here, you know."

Liu stared at him with the loathing of a man adding to a long list of grievances. He did not speak, but beckoned Reisman after him with an imperious gesture and led him out of the car park, along the walkways through the fog-shrouded gardens. He did not take him to the same building where he had met with Commodore Ludlow more than a month earlier. Reisman tensed when the sergeant bypassed that building and moved deeper into the gloom. He walked half a step behind him, watching the man's gun hand, wary of sudden martial movements, for his first feelings about Liu—that the man was much more than just a driver—had been reinforced during this last hour.

They proceeded along the path, up a stone stairway, under another arch, and then turned right. Cascading fountains and ominous-looking statuary loomed out of the dark mist. Two of the statues became real soldiers with submachine guns blocking the entrance to another two-story building with a curled tile roof. Liu spoke and one of the soldiers opened the carved door behind him and stood aside. They crossed the threshold into an elegant, softly lit reception hall, where a Kuomintang captain rose from behind an ebony desk and two more soldiers with submachine guns guarded an interior door.

The door was immediately opened for Liu by one of the guards and the captain spoke deferentially to him as he strode past. Reisman started to follow him, but the guards blocked his way and the captain, speaking in Chinese, ordered him to remove his pistol and leave it there. When he handed over his holster and belt, the captain pointed to a bench along one wall and said, rudely, in English, "Wait!" Surely someone of great consequence held court in this building, Reisman thought. It was beginning to dawn on him who it might be.

Liu came out in a few minutes, a smug look on his face. "General Tai Li will see you now," he said, as if pronouncing sentence.

Reisman felt excitement surge through him. To actually be brought face to face with the boogeyman himself, the notorious head of the secret police, was more than he could have expected. That Liu had such free-wheeling access to Tai Li also suggested, as Reisman had begun to suspect, that the sergeant's Kuomintang rank and role were merely a convenient cover for his real role and duties, whatever they were.

As he stood up and brushed past him, he wondered if Liu could be one of the Green Gang thugs he had heard about from Katherine Harris and others: the underworld gang of Shanghai bully boys who, many years earlier, had been brought into Tai Li's Bureau of Investigation and Statistics.

Reisman went through the doorway opened for him by one of the guards. The room he entered was like Ludlow's chamber elsewhere on the Happy Valley grounds, not a working office but a luxuriously decorated drawing room in which to entertain and hold conferences. It was very large and finely furnished in the heavy Chinese fashion. A dining table in the middle distance was set at one end for two, though it might have seated as many as twenty in the high-backed, upholstered chairs placed around it.

For a few moments there was no one else in the room, then a figure materialized out of a corridor at the far side. He was a stocky man of middle height, about fifty years old, wearing a simple, high-necked military uniform, finely tailored but unadorned. There was a bull-like look of strength about him, nothing of the aesthete. His features were broad and chubby, his hair thick and black. He came forward with a politician's smile on his face and Reisman had his usual uncertainty about whether or not one saluted a general—anybody's general—in less than formal circumstances. Tai Li stuck his hand out to shake, thereby solving the problem.

"I have been looking forward to meeting you, Major," he said. He spoke English quite well, with a singsong quality. Then he wagged a cautionary finger and scolded gently. "You are a man of rebellious spirit who does not follow orders scrupulously."

Reisman was not going to let him get away with that. "In my organization, General," he responded, "that is an asset, not a liability. Unexpected circumstances require improvisation."

Tai Li stared at him in surprise. He was evidently not accustomed to a snappy comeback. "Yes . . . so I have been told," he observed dourly. He motioned Reisman to a couch and sat in a wing chair facing him. Between them was a low table on which stood a decanter and wineglasses. "I am indebted to you, Major," he said in a hearty voice, switching to Mandarin.

Reisman responded in Mandarin, as if this were a test he had to pass: "What for, sir?"

"Discovering the arsenal of Chiang Fa-K'uei."

Reisman continued in Mandarin, though a wincing look on Tai Li's face confirmed his linguistic inadequacies.

"It was not me personally, General," Reisman said. "It was an OSS operation. We were able to put together some intelligence from various sources and act on it. There were also two other dumps."

Tai Li continued the sparring game, switching back to English. "You are too modest, Major Reisman. I understand that the intelligence on which you acted came mainly from you. Even I did not know that Chiang Fa-K'uei had managed to acquire so much war matériel."

"I find that hard to believe, sir," Reisman ventured, also speaking English again. "It is said that you know everything."

Tai Li laughed and said, "Alas, that is not true. We try, but we do not always succeed." He poured pale wine into two glasses. "Which is one of the reasons I wished to speak with you."

Reisman waited for him to go on, but he didn't. Instead, he handed Reisman a filled glass, raised his own with a convivial look and, with a cry of *"Gam-pei!"* tossed it off neatly. Reisman hesitated. Bottoms up, indeed. He sipped instead. It was a strong, thick wine, with a kick almost like whisky.

"Orange-blossom wine!" exclaimed Tai Li with satisfaction. "Have another."

"No, thank you, sir. It's very good, but I'd rather not."

The director of SACO had no such reservations. He poured himself another, as if he had been waiting much too thirstily for this hour, and downed it with another *"Gam-pei!"* He looked at Reisman with what might have been construed as an affectionate smile and said, "Now to business. I want you to work for me."

Reisman took another little sip of the orange-blossom wine and hung on to his glass. He was certain that Tai Li would fill it the moment he placed it on the table. "That is very flattering, sir," he said. "But, as you know, I already have a job."

"This will not be official," said Tai Li with a conspiratorial glance. "It will be only between us. No one else. You will continue in your duties for American intelligence as before. From time to time you will pass along information to me through my agents—or even come to see me directly, if you prefer, as you are doing now."

"General, I didn't prefer," Reisman said, with a half-smile. "I was hijacked and kidnapped."

"Perhaps it seemed that way," offered Tai Li apologetically. "But, nevertheless, you are here at my invitation. Come, we will have dinner."

He stood up and led Reisman to the long dining table. Tai Li sat at the head and pressed a button, which immediately brought two servants with steaming bowls of soup. The meal went on for more than two hours—a sumptuous variety of delicacies that included pork, fish, duck, rice, vegetables, fruits and wines. Reisman was hungry and he ate his fill, though the opulence of the occasion gave him pause. He wondered how many millions in China went hungry that night while he dined with one of the men accountable for their condition.

They sparred all through the dinner, while Tai Li continued to try to inveigle him into becoming a double agent. The general laid on a heavy dose of charm and Reisman had to keep reminding himself that this was the same *bête noire* of rumor and experience; the same monster whom Katherine Harris held responsible for the attack upon her; the same ubiquitous power whose name he first had heard in evil context from Linc Bradford in Burma; the same insidious director of the Bureau of Investigation and Statistics, hated and feared by the people of China—even the warlords; the same omnipotent, treacherous director of the Sino-American Cooperative Organization who was responsible for thwarting OSS operations against the Japanese and killing OSS operatives; the same secret policeman and evil manipulator of whom both Kita Shidehara and Ho Chi Minh were wary and probably envious.

Tai Li seemed to be genuinely enjoying himself, eating and drinking prodigious quantities without any apparent dulling of his senses or of the sharpness of his thinking and clarity of his speech. He knew a great deal about many things and he revealed what he wanted to in his own good time, always for his own purposes. At one point he declared condescendingly that Reisman's knowledge of Chinese was confused by too many dialects and hardly adequate for the important matters they had to discuss.

"Speak only English!" he commanded.

"How did you learn to speak it so well?" Reisman asked ingratiatingly.

"Necessity," replied Tai Li. "I have studied very hard and practiced diligently, as have many others in our government. Your country, after all, is our main supporter."

"Then why, may I ask, isn't the favor returned?" Reisman blurted out, not giving a damn if he offended the man or not.

"You are misinformed," said Tai Li sharply. "My government is extremely cooperative with the government of the United States and always open to new ideas. Even now we have implemented an American idea that found great favor with us. Do you know about our new armies rushing into position in the east to defeat the Japanese?"

"Yes, sir, I've heard a rumor about them. I hope it's true."

Tai Li made a great show of looking all around and behind him, as if concerned about eavesdroppers. "Phantoms," he divulged in a lowered voice. "The cleverness of it—so unexpected from you Americans. A few men, a few radios, a game of wits. It sounds more like the scheme of an Oriental."

And so it is, thought Reisman, remembering Kita Shidehara. "We used it in England against the Nazis and it worked," he said.

"Perhaps, but you westerners do not have the tradition of espionage and military intelligence that we do," Tai Li declared. "No subtlety, no finesse—which is why we prefer not to have you involved in intelligence activities here in China. Your guns and equipment are one thing, but your political and military interference are quite another."

Reisman felt his anger rise at such arrogance. "Is that why you had Colonel Waingrove fired?"

"Waingrove? Who is that?"

"The American colonel who had Ludlow's job a few months back. He was the man who originally requested my transfer to China."

"Oh, him. I hardly knew he existed."

"How about Katherine Harris?"

Tai Li's expression did not change. It was one of concentrated interest without any sign of recognition. "I do not know who that person is," he said.

"An American woman. She has met you—perhaps at a diplomatic function."

"Perhaps, if she said so. I do not attend many. My work is best served by remaining unseen and unknown. Who is this woman?"

"A devoted friend of China. The daughter of missionaries. A teacher and translator."

Tai Li shrugged. "Admirable," he said, "but what has she to do with me?"

"She was brutally assaulted one night in the street near her home, about three months ago."

"Bandits," said Tai Li, shaking his head. "We try, but we have not yet been able to get rid of them. Bandits and Communists, they are our scourge."

"And the Japanese?"

"Easier to deal with."

"How about the Burmese? The Kachins in particular?"

Tai Li looked bemused, as if unable to understand why the question had been asked. "They are our allies against the Japanese," he answered cautiously.

"Then why do Kuomintang troops attack their villages?"

Tai Li's face seemed to be fighting any open display of the emotions that Reisman's temerity provoked. "That is a lie," he said. "You should not believe rumors."

"How about the rumor that Kachins crossed the border to retaliate?"

Tai Li's eyes could no longer hide his anger. "I did not invite you here to discuss these matters, Major," he said brusquely.

"Or the rumor that an OSS captain and many Kachin rangers were killed by one of your bombers while crossing the Salween River?"

Tai Li glared at him now, no longer willing to play the innocent. "That is not a rumor, Major," he pronounced coldly. "It was a lesson."

Reisman smiled, but felt no joy. "At last we understand each other clearly, General," he said.

"Then you will work for me, as I have asked?" pressed Tai Li.

"No."

"I will make it worth your while."

"I'm sure you would, but the answer is still no."

The general stared at him calculatingly. "You are a Communist agent," he declared.

"Don't be ridiculous," Reisman retorted, abandoning all semblance of tact. "If I were, I would leap at your offer."

"Why do you associate with Tong Van So? He and his friends are all Communists."

"I'm following orders, General." He remembered something

Katherine had told him and, without even weighing it, he let it fly. "The same as you did twenty years ago when you joined the Communist Party."

That caught the secret police director off guard. "Perhaps we understand each other too well, Major," he said menacingly.

"I don't make up policy, and you damn well know that," Reisman continued attacking. "All we care about now is that Tong is a guerrilla leader helping us fight the Japs."

"I haven't heard of any such fighting in Indochina, Major," retorted Tai Li.

He was right, of course, and Reisman found himself arguing weakly, "They're training . . . building their strength and supplies."

Tai Li reared back and laughed derisively. "Yes, of course. I know all about the great help you have given them—twenty-five rifles and bayonets, twenty-five carbines and pistols, three B.A.R.s, three of this and three of that, and some bullets and grenades, of course. Do you want me to go on? It's not very much."

"I know the laundry list, General," Reisman acknowledged curtly. He remembered he had said the same words to Kita Shidehara a month earlier when the Kempitai colonel had belittled the same arms shipment he had taken south by truck with the Viets. Though there was more reason to expect that Tai Li, the master spy of China, would know about it, Reisman wondered if the two men subscribed to the same source of information in Kunming. "Do you want us to give them more?" he threw in as a taunting afterthought.

He didn't really expect the answer he got. "Yes. For the time being it might be useful," answered Tai Li, filling both their glasses again. "However, I must be consulted about every gun and cartridge that is sent in. There must be controls and compensations for us—" he hesitated a moment, pondering a tactful euphemism that would not obscure his real meaning, "—if only of a private nature."

Here it comes, thought Reisman. Tai Li the wheeler-dealer businessman. "Could you be more specific?" he asked, picking up his glass and touching it to his lips. He had managed all during the meal to fall far behind his host in the amount of wine consumed—though Tai Li seemed none the worse for having drunk so much.

"I am not so much interested in public statements of commitments and loyalties on the part of Mr. Tong and his people, but rather in demonstrations of private loyalties."

"For example?"

"Trade. I want him to provide me with certain things of value."

Reisman decided to be naïve. "Oh, they've been very good about that, General. Helping our downed flyers, relaying military intelligence and target information."

"Opium," said Tai Li softly. He gazed at Reisman with an expression of forbearance.

"I don't know anything about that sort of thing, General," Reisman responded, meeting his gaze directly.

Tai Li's broad, chubby features contorted with impatience. Now, thought Reisman, was the moment when the Director of SACO and master of Happy Valley might be expected to let him have it: *Don't think you have gotten away with that other clever business. I know that you helped the Viet-Namese to steal seventeen truckloads of guns and war matériel fom Chiang Fa-K'uei's arsenal! You must now do what I require of you or you will be very severely punished!*

Instead, Tai Li fixed a little smile on his face. "I see," he said wearily. "Perhaps . . . maybe . . ." He opened his mouth again to say more, but then changed his mind. "I think it would be best to have somebody else enlighten you."

Reisman breathed a little easier. All during the evening, he had been expecting the master spy of China to reveal that he actually knew about the second convoy at Jung-Chiang. Apparently he did not know, for if he had he surely would have flung it in his face by now and gloated over his omnipotence and cleverness. Perhaps they had gotten clean away with it—though with the number of operatives Tai Li controlled one could never be sure—and provided, too, that the weapons and war matériel arrived at their destination and were put to good use against the Japs. Tai Li hadn't learned about it, he surmised, because the boldness of the plan itself had been beyond his stodgy imagination. Reisman was almost tempted now to ask some seemingly innocuous question about Chang Wen Ming, whose name he had wangled out of Kita Shidehara—but he thought better of it, for he realized he was dancing on the narrow edge of hubris and to give Tai Li any hint of his interest in the man would be foolhardy. He vowed to himself, though, that he would give the master spy further lessons so subtle and skillfully executed that he would never know they had been delivered.

"Who did you have in mind to enlighten me, General?" he asked brightly. "Who could possibly know as much about these matters as you?"

Tai Li pushed his chair back from the table, announcing a conclusion to the dinner as far as he was concerned. "Your commanding officer is in complete agreement with my policies," he said emphatically. "You wait here, Major. He will deal with you as he has dealt with others for me."

On that ominous note Tai Li stood up. Without another word, he walked out of sight behind Reisman's chair and left the room via the corridor by which he had entered two hours earlier. Reisman twisted around to watch him go, then turned back to brace himself to deal with Commodore Pelham Ludlow.

A few minutes later, he heard someone coming down the corridor, and from behind him came a different voice, a very familiar one.

"Johnny . . . Johnny . . . Johnny . . . you have offended Herr Director mightily."

Chapter 30

Reisman turned and looked into the smiling scoutmaster face of Lieutenant Colonel Sam Kilgore—and in that instant so many things fell into place.

"Hello, Sam," he said ruefully. "I really wish it had been Ludlow. It was a lot easier to hate *him.*"

Kilgore walked around the head of the table, made as if to take the chair Tai Li had vacated, then moved on and sat down directly opposite Reisman. There was about five feet of table between them. "No reason to hate anyone," he said. "The commodore does what he's supposed to do for Tai Li, and he knows nothing about what I do. It works out nicely that way."

"He's the surface villain—the easy mark," said Reisman bitterly. "I owe him an apology for the things I've been thinking about him. You're the treacherous, conniving son-of-a-bitch who gets people hijacked, kidnapped and killed."

Kilgore looked surprised. "I hadn't heard that anyone was killed."

"Linc Bradford—about two months back. Remember that, Sam?"

"Sure I do."

"You must have been responsible for the B-25 that killed him and his men."

There was a tense silence. Then Kilgore said, "Responsible? No." He reached for the wineglass that Tai Li had been using and ran a napkin around the inside and the rim.

"Then you had guilty knowledge," Reisman said accusingly.

"Guilty? No." Kilgore poured himself some wine, drank it and shook his head. "I've been trying to get him to switch to whisky and gin, but I don't seem to have much influence."

"Knowledge, then. You must have been part of it. You found out where they were crossing the Salween from the same OSS people in Calcutta who sent me out to stop him."

"Bradford brought it on himself."

"But you were part of the scheme that killed him—and might have killed me."

"You were with him then," said Kilgore, confirming an old suspicion.

"Oh, yes, I was with him. And you fingered us, Sam. You arranged the unmarked B-25 and the Chinese crew that Tai Li sent you. Without your help, Linc and his Kachins would have made it safely back across the river."

Kilgore seemed remarkably unconcerned. "Maybe, maybe not. If you were there, you'd know better than anybody else what happened." He looked down at the empty wineglass as he twirled it around in his hands, then raised his eyes to Reisman again. "I figured you were probably with him, the way you were carrying on about it. But you gave Ludlow some bullshit about finding Bradford dead in the jungle."

Images of the carnage on the river that day rose in fury in Reisman's mind and for a moment his body tensed as if to lunge across the table at Kilgore. But he held himself back, allowed himself to be caught up in cathartic banter. "That's the nature of the job, Sam," he said laconically. "You've got to move fast on your feet and know how to bullshit all sides."

"I wouldn't file a report on any of this if I were you," Kilgore admonished. "You'll wind up in jail or in front of a firing squad for what you and Bradford did to the Chinese."

He was probably right, thought Reisman. "You'd do the same thing to me if Tai Li told you to, wouldn't you?" he charged.

Kilgore's long silence was sufficient acknowledgment. Reisman had more reason now to trust Kita Shidehara than he did Sam Kilgore. "Did you send those goons after Katherine Harris?" he demanded.

Sam looked at him quizzically. "I don't know her. Who is she?"

This time Reisman sensed that he was telling the truth. "Another of Tai Li's victims."

"Tell me about it."

"No. But if I ever found out you were connected in any way with what happened to her, I wouldn't write up a report on it, Sam. I'd kill you."

It was Kilgore's turn to get angry. "I could have your ass shipped out of China for a remark like that, buddy," he snapped.

"Go ahead. You'll be doing us both a favor."

Kilgore studied him a few moments and then shook his head. "I think not, my friend. We still need you here. If you won't work for Tai Li, at least you're still working for me, and that's the way I intend to keep it."

"What are you dealing in, Sam—opium? Gold? Guns?"

"All of them—and services and information—whatever Tai Li wants," Kilgore replied. "I take care of him, he takes care of me. The payoff is liquid and untraceable. Come in with me, Johnny. There's more than enough for both of us."

"Why are you doing it, Sam?"

"I worry a little about me after the war," Kilgore answered matter-of-factly. "I'm not a career man—or a banker, or a lawyer, or a business big shot, the way most of the rest of the company top brass is. I got where I am by being better than they are. When the shooting stops, I intend to be richer."

"No politics? No passions? No loyalties?" asked Reisman.

"Nope. I told you once that politics is just sorting out the shit of *Homo sapiens* so we don't inundate each other. I intend to be rich enough after this war is over so that I don't have to smell or step in anyone else's shit."

Reisman's head was filled with vengeful thoughts that he would not have allowed himself to consider before. Now that matters were out in the open, he felt almost relieved. He restrained himself from introducing the name of Chang Wen Ming, for he had a new idea of how to make use of his secret contact to the Kempitai. In the past months, horrible things had been done for other people's reasons of expedience. Now it was his turn. He did not accept lightly the role of pawn in this game of byzantine politics that was being pursued to feed the greed and pleasures of others. He was determined to rejoin his men that night and put into action immediately a private plan of retribution.

"What happens now, Sam?" he demanded. He would fight his way out of this place with his bare hands if necessary.

"We simply go on as before," said Kilgore with a cynical smile. "You can go back to Indochina with your men if you want to. I assume you know where they are. They seem to be AWOL at the moment. If you go yapping to anybody about me without hard evidence—and I've made sure there isn't any—you'll have to answer for what you and Bradford and those Kachins did to the Chinese at Caojian two months ago. Either that or they'll ship you home on a Section Eight."

"Does Ludlow know about any of this?"

"No. He doesn't even know you're in Chungking, and that's the way we're going to keep it."

That fit in nicely with Reisman's plans. "Okay, get me out of here clean. You don't know I'm here, I don't know you're here. I'll take the personnel carrier I came in. No tails. I'll just disappear into the fog. My men and I will see you in Kunming in about a week. You give us what we need down there and we'll go in to Tonkin again."

"And continue to look for business opportunities?" asked Kilgore, smiling broadly.

"Sure. Why not?" replied Reisman glibly. Kilgore knew his feelings were contrary to that. He had made himself very clear before he had left for Tonkin the first time. But if Sam preferred to believe otherwise, Reisman wasn't going to try to change his mind.

When he reached the medical clinic, he found Dr. Briggs poring over a map of the city with Bowren, Sawyer, Wladislaw and Baw San. They were relieved to see him.

"These fellows of yours were planning a rescue operation if you didn't turn up by morning," said the doctor.

Reisman was touched by their concern. He even felt a little guilty at having dined so well at Happy Valley. "Did you guys get any chow?" he asked.

"The commander took care of us very nicely," Bowren said.

"All I want now," Sawyer put in, "is a place to sack out for the night."

"Yeh," added Wladislaw, "it's been a rough couple of days. If you got any more funny stuff for us, save it till morning, will you, Major?"

"Sure," agreed Reisman. "If you promise not to pee in his beds maybe the doc will let you sleep in the ward."

Briggs laughed and said, "Help yourselves, gentlemen."

Baw San, who knew the facility from his previous stay there, led the way down the corridor to the ward.

"How is Katherine?" Reisman asked when he and Briggs were alone together in the little room the doctor used as private office and sleeping quarters.

"About the same. I still look in on her regularly. She has good days and bad."

He gestured to the desk chair, then took his good scotch and two glasses from the cabinet.

"Do you think she has the strength to go out for a few hours tomorrow night?" Reisman asked.

Dr. Briggs handed him a glass and poured. "If it's really important, I think she could go out in a car or ricksha," he said. "Your visits last month were a big help. They strengthened her will, if not her body." He poured a drink for himself, sat down on his cot and raised the glass. "Nice to see you back here, John."

Reisman raised his glass to the naval officer. "It was good of you to look after my men. I appreciate it."

They each took a sip, savoring the good scotch whisky. "A fine antidote to what I've been drinking tonight," Reisman said with appreciation.

"Business or pleasure?"

"Business. No pleasure at all."

"I gather you've had an adventure or two since last we met."

"Yes," Reisman acknowledged. He studied the lined, weary face of the old naval doctor. "I have to take you into my confidence about something," he finally added.

Briggs stared back at him a few moments, then said, "I could tell you to forget it, keep your own secrets, but that would be like refusing a man treatment for a bad wound, Major. Confidentiality goes with my business, so if you have something to unburden, go ahead. I'll listen."

"I'll go at it slowly and build to the point," said Reisman. "I want advice from you and I want you to yank me back if you think I'm going off the deep end."

"Agreed."

"The line of work I'm in requires me to be devious, but since coming back to Asia I've had to learn to be even more so," Reisman told him. "I have an idea . . . the beginnings of a plan to smoke out the bastards who beat Katherine half to death. We may get the same men or we may get others close to them, but it will strike at their network and let them know they can't get away with that sort of thing with impunity."

"Whatever it is, count me in," said Briggs. "I've been leading too sedentary a life. No excitement."

"Your part in it can only be advisory," Reisman cautioned. "You can turn me in as a dangerous nut—or tell me it can work and how to make it better."

"Go ahead."

"You know Commodore Ludlow, don't you?"

"Oh, yes. A stiff-necked, self-important prick. He hasn't had a good idea of his own since he graduated from the Academy."

"How about Tai Li?"

"I've seen him at official receptions a couple of times, but I've never talked to him. He hates foreigners and rarely sees any, except for Ludlow and the highest-ranking emissaries."

"I suppose I should feel honored, then," Reisman commented wryly. "I had an unexpected invitation to dine with him tonight. That's where I've been."

Dr. Briggs was taken aback. "You travel in strange circles, Major. If anyone is responsible for the attack on Katherine, directly or indirectly, it's that son-of-a-bitch. I doubt that Ludlow would suborn violence against an American woman or would have approved if he'd known it was planned."

"Ludlow thinks it was bandits. At least that's what he told me last month. Tai Li denied any connection with it when I brought it up."

"You do live dangerously, don't you?"

"Have you heard of a man named Chang Wen Ming who works for him and Ludlow at Happy Valley?"

"No. Who is he?"

"I have reason to believe he's a connection to the Kempitai."

"That's the sort of thing that Katherine told me she and Colonel Waingrove were looking into."

"Let us suppose, then—" said Reisman. "First, let us suppose that you are Ludlow. You receive a hand-carried letter tomorrow morning from Katherine Harris that denounces Chang Wen Ming—whose treachery may or may not be known to you or to Tai Li."

"More likely known to Tai Li and protected by him," Briggs commented. "It could have been his reason for sending his men to attack Katherine."

"Get back to Ludlow," Reisman urged. "Try to think and feel as he does. The letter from Katherine says that she will come to his office tomorrow evening to give him the evidence. What would you do?"

The naval officer answered without hesitation: "Leave word at the gate that she was to be turned away and sent packing. She was not to be admitted under any circumstances. I would consider her a crazy meddler. Then I would call in Chang Wen Ming—"

"If there is such a man, and if you know him," Reisman interrupted.

"Yes. I would call him in for a private chat and ask him, 'Do you know this woman?' And, of course, if he knew anything or not he would deny it."

"Now suppose that you are Tai Li in the same circumstances," Reisman continued. "You receive a very literate letter written in faultless Chinese from an American woman who is, at the very least, *persona non grata.* It denounces Chang Wen Ming and informs you that she will bring the evidence tomorrow evening. What would you do, General?"

"I would think about it, but I would certainly not respond to the woman myself," answered Briggs confidently. "Nor would I deign to send any notice to the gate. I am too high and mighty to give such a trifling person and matter any consideration in the eyes of my subordinates. However, I would send for whoever is—or might be—Chang Wen Ming, and ask him the same question: 'Do you know this woman?' The purpose of the question would not be to elicit an answer, but to sound an alarm."

"And if that person had guilty knowledge," said Reisman, picking up the thread, "not only of who the writer of the letter is, but also of how she had been punished—then he would assume that she was now well enough to make trouble again, and he would see to it immediately that she was silenced, either by himself or others. She would likely be attacked again somewhere on the way home. Maybe the same spot where they got her before. Does that make sense in Chinese?"

"In English too," said Dr. Briggs, "except that you want her to be a decoy."

"Only if she is willing."

▪ ▪

In the morning, Reisman, Baw San and Dr. Briggs started out together in Briggs's jeep toward Hongyancun, the section of the city where Katherine lived. They stopped along the way at various ranks of rickshas until Briggs selected one pulled by a wiry youth who had some resemblance to Baw San. The doctor then continued the journey to Katherine's house in the ricksha while Reisman and Baw San took a circuitous route in the jeep. It was Dr. Briggs who opened the garden door to them when they arrived. The ricksha was standing just inside the wall.

"The boy is in the kitchen," Briggs said. "He has accepted our proposal. Su'lin is feeding him."

Reisman entered the house and started upstairs with Baw San a step behind him, when he heard his name called from the living room. He turned and saw Katherine sitting on a sofa, wearing one of those conservative wool suits he remembered her wearing in Nanking years back. She stood up as he bounded down toward her. She did indeed look stronger.

Without embarrassment or restraint before Ken Briggs and Baw San, she wrapped her arms around his neck and kissed him full on the lips. "It's so good to see you again, John," she said softly, as she drew away.

Reisman held on to one of her hands, turned and introduced Corporal Charlie Bawsan, who responded with great deference, the placing of palms together, the bow, the murmur of *"Kaja-ee, Daw."*

Katherine looked puzzled. "That's not Chinese," she said.

"No, ma'am. It is a Kachin greeting to a lady," explained Baw San.

"Do you speak any Chinese?" she asked in Mandarin.

"I am learning," Baw San replied in the same dialect.

"Welcome to my humble home," Katherine continued.

Baw San smiled, bowed again and thanked her.

Katherine let go of Reisman's hand, waved them all to couches and chairs and sat down again. "Dr. Briggs tells me you have a plan," she said eagerly.

"It's a way to get back at the people who hurt you."

"Tai Li?"

"Not him personally, but through people who work for him. We may get the same men who beat you, we may get others, we may get nothing. But I think we have an opportunity to pay them back for what they did to you."

"Go ahead."

"It's a dangerous plan, particularly for you, and if you don't want to go ahead with it—if you don't think you have the strength for it—we'll drop it and I'll figure out something else."

"Tell me what you want me to do, John," Katherine said with calm determination. "You should know that danger doesn't faze me."

"Okay. First: when you were working with Colonel Waingrove, did you ever have suspicions about a man named Chang Wen Ming who is somebody at Happy Valley?"

"Yes. We never met him, though it might have been a secret name for someone we did know. And we never learned what his official function there is. But that name cropped up a number of times in references to the Kempitai."

It was confirmation enough. Reisman told her his plan. She agreed to it readily, indifferent to her great personal danger. Indeed, Reisman could almost see the energy surge through her as she saw her chance to rise up from her sickbed and make real the vengeful fantasies of her opium dreams.

Katherine then sat down and wrote two letters: one in English to Commodore Pelham Ludlow, the other in Chinese to General Tai Li. They read:

Dear Sir,

I have not been well or I would have come to see you sooner. I have information regarding Chang Wen Ming. He is a Kempitai spy. I will bring evidence of this to your headquarters at seven this evening.

The ricksha boy was paid handsomely for the use of his conveyance, his clothes and his silence. Baw San set himself between the poles and trotted off toward Happy Valley with Su'lin as his passenger, carrying Katherine's letters and grandly giving instructions. Dr. Briggs stayed behind with Katherine.

Reisman followed the ricksha on foot. Patches and swirls of white fog fused by the morning sun still lay here and there upon the hillside streets and alleys of the city. The light was harsh upon the eyes, the air heavy with smells of decay. The streets and walkways were dense with coolies, animals and conveyances hurrying about the business of the city. Ahead of him the roadway flattened out beside the little wooded area and the long, black-painted wall. The ricksha stopped at the gate where two Chinese soldiers stood with tommy guns held ready at waist level. Reisman stayed back and let the stream of pedestrian traffic flow around him. He saw an officer summoned from inside the gate of the Happy Valley compound. He watched Su'lin hand the letters to the officer and observed the payment of the bribe to speed them on their way. He also observed Corporal Sawyer and Private Wladislaw passing the gate as planned, gawking around like G.I. tourists.

When the transaction at the gate was completed, Baw San began the return trip with Su'lin. He smiled and winked as he trotted past Reisman, pulling the ricksha behind him. Sawyer and Wladislaw disappeared with the stream of pedestrians at the top of the road. Reisman followed the ricksha, again looking for places along the route where attackers might lie in wait for Katherine in the night. Five minutes later, Sergeant Bowren drove down the hill at the wheel of the personnel carrier, with Sawyer and Wladislaw in the back. He stopped to pick up Reisman and they trailed the ricksha back to Katherine's house and watched it taken inside the garden wall again. Along the way, each man continued to check the route carefully and identify the most likely places for an ambush, particularly the alley where Katherine had been attacked three months earlier. They retraced the route three more times, until they knew it thoroughly and each man had patrolled on foot the part of the route that was to be his responsibility that night.

When Reisman gave her the revolver to carry as a precaution, Katherine stared down calmly at the cold blue steel in her hands. It was a navy-issue Smith & Wesson .38 that he had borrowed from Dr. Briggs—just in case.

"Have you ever fired one before?" Reisman asked.

"No," Katherine answered.

"Do you think you can if you have to?"

"Yes."

They were sitting in the lamplit living room, ready to leave in a few minutes. She looked up at him and then at Dr. Briggs, looking rather formal and concerned in his dark blue navy uniform, and at Baw San wearing the ricksha boy's shabby clothes. "I have no fear," she assured them. "This is what I want to do. Even if they accost me, I know that you or one of your men will be close by."

Reisman took the loaded revolver, removed the cartridges and showed her how to draw back the hammer—with her left hand if her right thumb wasn't strong enough—and how to aim and squeeze. She took the empty gun and repeated the firing procedure.

"I should have learned this long ago," she said ruefully.

When he was satisfied that she had the idea, Reisman reloaded the revolver and extended it toward her, holding it by the barrel so that she could take the grip in her hand. "What's the first thing you do at a sign of trouble?" he challenged.

"Pull the hammer back two clicks," she answered confidently, repeating his earlier instruction. "I'm torn between hoping I have to and hoping I don't."

Reisman stood up, smiled reassuringly, and said, "Well, let's go out now and see if they've taken the bait."

He felt as Katherine did—wanting it to happen, worried that it might. There was no backing off now, though. They had set things in motion that had to be played out.

Su'lin opened the garden door. Dr. Briggs went out first, climbed into his jeep and drove off. He had insisted on being allowed to take part and so was to drive ahead on the route to Happy Valley, make certain that Bowren, Sawyer and Wladislaw were in their positions, and then return when he was sure the ricksha had reached its destination. Then he would park the jeep in the same place against the garden wall and patrol the streets and alleys around Katherine's house on foot. He carried a .45 automatic in his coat pocket.

Reisman helped Katherine into the ricksha and tucked a robe over her lap. She slipped her hand under it, holding the .38. He kissed her and mumbled "Good luck!" Su'lin touched Katherine's arm and murmured blessings. Then she opened the garden door and Baw San pulled the ricksha out into the street. Reisman followed immediately.

New fog had settled in, partly obscuring buildings, vehicles and pedestrians. Reisman matched his pace to Baw San's. He carried a carbine slung over his left shoulder, his right hand rested on the butt of his .45, his eyes scanned left and right and tried to see ahead of the ricksha. As he passed their positions, Bowren, Sawyer and Wladislaw each stepped out from cover and silently acknowledged their presence. In half an hour, the ricksha stopped before the gate of Happy Valley and Reisman halted in an advantageous position across the road. Within moments, he saw Ken Briggs driving his jeep slowly up the street past the ricksha, as if he were looking for an address. Then he passed out of sight into the gloom.

A Chinese officer who had been waiting outside the gate, flanked by the two duty guards, stepped forward and spoke to Katherine.

Reisman couldn't make out the words. Only in that moment did it occur to him that they had made no provision for what to do if she was actually admitted to the compound. He had a sudden sinking feeling—then saw, with relief, that Katherine was being turned away. Baw San picked up the ricksha poles and started to retrace the route just taken. The headlights of Briggs's jeep illuminated the scene as he came back down the hill, swung around them, and drove on.

Reisman fell in behind the ricksha again, concentrating acutely on every movement and sound around them. The thick, foul, sweating traffic of daytime Chungking had vanished with the damp, cloying night. Few vehicles or pedestrians passed in the narrow twisting streets and lanes. Shops were shuttered. Ahead of him in the fog, Sawyer, Wladislaw and Bowren were scrutinizing the shadows of the night. As first the ricksha and then Reisman passed each of them, the men fell in twenty yards behind, keeping pace, forming a screen at the rear, moving closer to Katherine's house, where Briggs was now patrolling. Reisman matched the sound of his footfalls to the trotting pace of Baw San, eager for something to happen.

Twenty-five tense and uneventful minutes passed. When they were safely past the spot most likely to be dangerous—the alley where Katherine had been ambushed before and where Bowren was now on guard—Reisman began to feel almost foolish, having planned so carefully for nothing.

It was then, scant minutes from home, that two Chinese in coolie clothes leaped from cover to block Baw San's path. They displayed no weapons, but jumped on Baw San as he shouted "Bandits!" in Chinese and tried to run around them, still pulling the ricksha.

Reisman raced forward, drawing his automatic, seeing the attackers pummel Baw San and bring him to the ground. The melee covered his movements. There was no sound from Katherine. Baw San went into his cowering-for-mercy act and Reisman darted around the ricksha, aiming at the closest attacker. He resisted the urge to pull the trigger, got in near enough to kick the ass of one of the men bending over Baw San, and shouted in Chinese for the attackers to stand still and raise their hands.

The man he had kicked turned around and Reisman stared into the familiar, contempt-filled face of Sergeant Liu. He glanced at the gun, then looked into Reisman's eyes.

"You're supposed to be on the way to Kunming, you nosy son-of-a-bitch!" he spat out.

Before Reisman could reply, two things distracted him. Baw San sprang up from his cowering position and, using his feet and fists in a flurry of graceful, powerful blows, sent the second attacker reeling back toward the cab of the ricksha. At the same time, the sound of running feet made Reisman turn his head. It was Bowren and the others, not more attackers.

"Stand back! Don't shoot!" he shouted to them. He wanted Liu alive.

In that instant Liu smashed the .45 from his hand with a judo chop and made a flying leap after it. Reisman still had the carbine, but he gave only a fraction of a second's thought to bringing it around from his shoulder and firing. Instead, he dropped it and threw himself after Liu, landing hard on his back. Liu heaved upward, rolled away from the gun, and was on his feet before Reisman could get a grip on him. The pistol and carbine lay on the ground, but Reisman blocked the way.

From the corner of his eye he caught sight of Baw San and the second attacker, who had his hands in the air in surrender at last. Katherine, invisible in the blackness of the cab, had still not uttered a word. But Reisman couldn't really see everything that was going on out there just a few feet away. He had to concentrate on Sergeant Liu. He almost expected him to pluck a weapon from beneath his wide coolie jacket. But if he had—and Liu must have recognized that himself—he would have been shot down instantly by the men now aiming guns at him, including Dr. Briggs who had just rushed up.

Liu took a classic judo stance and began to circle, dart forward and leap back, his arms in constant motion, his fingers tensed together, his hands rigid and ready to strike. "When I take you, Major, we're even," he called out. "Everybody goes home. Right?"

Reisman didn't answer. He followed and anticipated every movement of his antagonist. It was like a dance between them now. A personal thing. He was enjoying himself. All the others had passed out of his immediate awareness, even Katherine.

Then Liu, eager, saw his first opening and attacked. Reisman met the hard edge of the man's hand with his forearm, darted aside and chopped down at Liu's neck with the same arm while the man's momentum carried him past. The blow angered Liu and he rebounded fast, smashing through Reisman's defense with a flurry of jabs and chops, fooling him with feints and spins. Reisman took the jarring blows to head and body, was goaded and sharpened by the pain. The sergeant did not go unpunished. Reisman knew where to find his opponent's points of imbalance and weakness, how to use his strength and momentum against him. Each time Liu struck, there was a fractional opening of his own defense and Reisman hammered and jabbed through it. It was his head that Liu protected most strongly at first, so Reisman worked over his body. He rammed three fingers stiff as daggers into Liu's belly, chopped his kidney as he doubled over, and hammered him gasping to the roadway, rolling out for a moment's respite.

Reisman darted quick glances through the foggy darkness of their arena. He had lost track of time, but little more than two minutes had passed. The faintest light from a street crossing touched the scene and he saw the rapt faces of the watchers. Bowren, Sawyer, Wladislaw, Briggs and Baw San were caught up in the fierce, choreographed offense and defense of the hand-to-hand combat. And there was something not quite right about that, thought Reisman.

Liu came at him again. He was good and quick and when he found Reisman's head unprotected he hit him twice hard enough to send him sprawling. But when he dove after Reisman to try to finish him off on the ground, Reisman had his knees bent and his feet up and caught Liu on a catapult that spun him through the air to a hard, bouncing landing. But again Liu came up, whirled and was ready to go at it again—this time with a knife in his hand, yanked from under his jacket.

Briggs shouted a warning.

Reisman yelled, "Don't interfere! Stay back!" He wanted to take Liu or kill him with his bare hands.

Then it struck him what worried him about the others: nobody was watching the second attacker. He glanced again through the foggy night and saw the man standing with his hands raised—but he was not watching the fight, he was measuring the vigilance of the others, backing his way closer to the front of the ricksha cab.

"Watch the other guy!" Reisman yelled.

He saw the man dart his hand inside his jacket, draw out a pistol—and in the same instant sensed Sergeant Liu coming at him with the knife and turned to meet him. Liu moved left foot forward, left arm extended to block and feint, the dagger held back in his right hand close to his hip, ready to stab. Torn by anxiety for what was about to happen behind him, Reisman stooped low, as if to get under the knife, then rose suddenly, raising his left arm and opening himself to a thrust. Liu lunged and Reisman, having invited it, twisted away from it and chopped his left hand down onto Liu's knife arm, impelling him further off balance, positioning him to meet the next blow.

A single shot exploded, startling Liu, freezing him into vulnerability for the length of the reverberating sound—just as Reisman swung the flat hardened edge of his right hand upward in a hammer blow under his nose, striking diagonally toward the ears. He felt the bones break as they drove upward into Liu's brain. Blood spurted from his nostrils and ears and he dropped to the ground, lifeless.

A second shot and a third cracked out, and Reisman's body braced for the smash of bullets. When they didn't come, he looked up, chest heaving from the fury of the fight, gasping for breath. Then he thought—Katherine! It was as if all time had become transfixed . . . yet only seconds had elapsed since the other Chinese attacker had drawn his pistol . . . seconds less since Sergeant Liu had made his fatal move.

Reisman turned in fear toward the ricksha. Wladislaw and Sawyer were blocking his view. They were staring in awe from the dead man to him. Inanely . . . delaying time and denying new reality . . . he remembered that he had frightened them back in England when he had taught them to do things like this . . . and he saw that he had frightened them again now in the doing. Now they too turned toward the ricksha. Events had happened all too quickly for everything to be taken in at once. With a flood of relief, Reisman saw Katherine struggling from the cab, the .38 held limply at her side. Lying athwart the ricksha poles, his pistol on the ground beside him, was her would-be killer, whose last move had been to aim blindly into the dark cab. But before he could pull the trigger she had shot him—and Bowren and Briggs, now bending over her assailant with their .45's in their hands, had caught the man twice more as he fell.

Reisman looked quickly around. The melee . . . the shots . . . the quick, stark reality of assault and death in the Chungking night had brought no one else to the scene. If the sounds had disturbed anyone behind their shutters and mud walls, no one had dared to come out. But he knew they had better clear the area fast. There were police and military patrols to worry about, and the salutary lesson of this night's work would be delivered only if who and what, cause and effect, were kept secret and secure from the probing of others.

He took the gun from Katherine's hand. "I want you to look at them," he said.

She did not hesitate, understanding that he too wanted confirmation and vindication as much as she did. She stared at the upturned face of the man she had shot, nodded recognition, then walked over to the corpse of Sergeant Liu and nodded again. She looked at Reisman with grim satisfaction.

"I told you I would kill for the right reasons," she said without emotion. "These two are the ones who attacked me three months ago."

Lieutenant Commander Briggs came up and put his arm around her. "Get into the ricksha," he said. "Baw San and I will take you home."

She did as he asked, walking with surprising strength. Reisman watched her go and wondered if it would hit her hard later. He sent Bowren to bring up the personnel carrier hidden nearby, then examined the two bodies under a flashlight held by Sawyer. He wondered if either of them was the man called Chang Wen Ming. He searched their bogus clothes, discovered Liu also had a pistol, which he took, and found I.D.s on each of them for the secret police and SACO, which he also took. But nothing with the name of the Kempitai contact.

They cleared the street swiftly after that. Bowren brought up the personnel carrier and the corpses were lifted in. They drove out of the city beyond the airport to an isolated area and dumped the corpses into the Yangtze River. It was a popular method of disposal, Reisman knew. The bodies would float along with the numberless, nameless others whose fates had brought them to the great mother of China waters. Perhaps they would be fished out, perhaps not.

Driving back to Katherine's house, he thought with satisfaction that Tai Li himself might now learn how diabolically clever an American opponent could be. Except that total success, he realized, would mean that neither the director of SACO, nor any of his secret policemen, nor the Japanese Kempitai, nor the American OSS would ever find out what had happened.

And that would be better.

Chapter 31

"I want you to go home," said Reisman.

"I am home," Katherine replied, drawing contentedly on the opium pipe he had prepared for her.

They were in her room again. Katherine was propped up in bed against the brocade pillows in the dim lamplight, just as she had been that first night he had come there more than a month earlier.

"Boston," he insisted.

He knew she still had family there, could get medical help and, with new hope, might break the opium habit. He did not accept the gloomy prognosis he had heard from both her and Ken Briggs the month before. Her uncommon valor and strength tonight had been sufficient evidence to the contrary.

He waited for Katherine to respond; but she had gone already to the land of *Ta-yen,* lost in the false comfort and dreams of the big smoke. He had refused any for himself. Even without it, an ennui descended upon him, a weariness of spirit. The night's work had drained him, but still it was necessary to remain on guard.

When he had returned here with his men at 2230 hours, after completing their macabre visit to the river, he had set two-man, four-hour watches in the garden to see them through the night.

"I thought the Chinks were on our side, Major," Wladislaw had grumbled.

It was the same refrain he had heard from Sawyer two days earlier when they had been kidnapped with their cargo after leaving Chiang Fa-K'uei's arsenal. Though Reisman knew even more now about the powerful, manipulative forces that moved people and armies around—usually for reasons quite different from what he, his men and most Americans assumed—there was still no way for him to explain simply and adequately the convoluted treachery of the war in China and French Indochina.

And he was playing the game himself now.

"Anyone tries to break in here—kill him!" he had ordered. "Quietly, if you can."

They had sent the ricksha boy off with his conveyance, his clothes, more money, and dark threats of arrest by the agents of Tai Li if he divulged one word of where he had been. The boy had been terrified—but the cruel threat itself would serve to protect both him and them.

As a further precaution, Lieutenant Commander Briggs had driven their personnel carrier to a hiding place, taking Baw San with him for protection. Then they had slipped back to Katherine's house on foot and Briggs had returned to his clinic in his jeep. Through all these comings and goings they had kept a lookout for a tail, but had finally concluded that there really was no one else out there looking for them.

The night passed without further incident. Dr. Briggs returned in the morning and brought rations for the men. He also brought a concurring opinion that Katherine had to leave Chungking.

"We have to get her out of China now," he said to Reisman. "There's no delaying it. I've been worrying all night."

"Same here. But she says she won't go," Reisman told him.

They went up to her together. There was a depressing heaviness to her bedroom in the gray morning light—and the lingering smell of the opium. Katherine, dressed in a navy blue wool suit, was sitting in a chair near the glass doors that gave onto the small rooftop terrace where a few struggling plants were set about in pots and boxes. Her breakfast was sitting beside her on a small table. She held a teacup in her hand and was staring through the glass doors toward the boat traffic on the Chialing, the view still partially obscured by fog.

"I was just thinking how nice it would be to be out of doors again in the warm sunshine . . . if there were any," she said wistfully. "We'll probably have to wait until spring, though."

"Katherine . . . we have to make plans for you to leave," said Briggs firmly.

She looked at him with a sad, drained expression. "Did last night really happen?" she asked. "I've been trying to come to terms with it—the violence and killing. I think it's easier to be a victim."

"It happened," Reisman said impatiently. She had made him remember his own anguish the first time he had killed a man. He had been only a boy then in Chicago and it too had been in self-defense. "You've had your vengeance now," he continued, "but you're still in danger. You've got to get out." He knew about that too. It had been the high probability of ruthless reprisal from a dead hoodlum's cronies that had sent him to sea stoking coal on an oreship fourteen years back.

"I'm not going to be forced out," she replied adamantly. "I'm not going to run. It's what they want."

"I think they'd rather see you dead now," Reisman told her bluntly. Then, softer, "I've got to leave here with the men in a day or two and go to Kunming. What will you do then against Tai Li and his operatives?"

Katherine looked at him blankly and shook her head.

"There is nothing more that you can do here to help China or help yourself," Reisman said insistently. "Go home and get well and you can do both."

Katherine looked up at him, struggling with her emotions. Finally she said, "I will not go without Su'lin."

"Of course not," Dr. Briggs spoke up quickly. "It can be arranged."

"But how?" Katherine argued, seemingly satisfied that nothing could or would be done. "It takes time. Transit visas and passports and all the other official nonsense. A U.S. visa for Su'lin. Travel arrangements for the two of us might be refused."

"It can't be done officially," Reisman agreed. "All the wrong people would find out about it."

"I was thinking the same thing." Briggs said. "However, there's a better way."

He told them he would try to make private arrangements with one of his pilot friends in the Air Transport Command, to fly them secretly out of Chungking to Kunming and then over the Hump to India. "It's been done before," he said. "In India he would arrange for you to continue the journey to the States. If you're lucky you'll get a pilot and plane going all the way."

Reisman looked to Katherine for a response, but all she said was, "I'll consider it."

However, the idea appealed to Reisman for another reason. "See if you can get him to squeeze the rest of us aboard," he said to Briggs. "We'll go as far as Kunming."

He had never liked the prospect of having to drive there. It would mean many days of struggling through the primitive, mountainous back country of western Szechuan and northern Yunnan in a personnel carrier on dubious loan from the Chinese army. Nor had he wanted to stir up officialdom by trying to arrange a flight through regular channels.

"I think it can be done, John," said Briggs. "I'll go to work on it immediately and prepare whatever travel documents are necessary."

Late that night, Reisman woke to the sense that something was not right. He had been sleeping fully dressed on a couch in Katherine's living room. He swung his booted feet to the floor, picked up his M-3 and moved to the bottom of the stairway, listening. Katherine and Su'lin, he assumed, were still in their separate rooms upstairs. Bowren and Wladislaw had come off watch and had gone to sleep in the third room up there. It was quiet in that direction and he turned his attention outside. Baw San and Sawyer were in the garden on the 2400 to 0400 watch.

He heard scuffling sounds from there and darted through the front door. It was very dark. No stars or moon. Some fog. He saw the black shapes of the few small trees, the bordering hedges and the mass of the high surrounding wall. But no people, no sounds, not even the two men who were supposed to be there. Then from behind a hedge on his right came a familiar voice in a whisper: "Sorry to disturb you, *Duwa* John."

Reisman walked close to Baw San and saw the Kachin *dah* in his hand and a wild, sweaty look on his face. He was cleaning the knife with a piece of cloth that looked as if it had been ripped off someone's clothes. A moment later, Sawyer came up behind Reisman, moving so silently that he never heard him until he spoke from about five feet away. "Hope the noise didn't wake you, Major," he said with a nervous tremor in his voice. "We tried to do it quiet, like you said." There was a bloody trench knife in his hand and he seemed to be futilely looking for a way to clean it.

"What in hell have you two been up to?" Reisman demanded in a low, harsh voice.

They took him behind a hedge and showed him the crumpled bodies of two more Chinese in coolie clothes. Reisman shone a flashlight on them and saw with what brutal efficiency the knifework had been done. It was as if the two from the night before had risen from the river and come back.

"I heard them trying to force the door," Sawyer explained in that same soft, tight voice. "When they came over the wall we were right there waiting for them. Poor bastards never saw us."

When Reisman showed Katherine the bodies the next morning, she turned away and gagged. But after that there was no more denying that she and Su'lin had to leave.

Lieutenant Commander Briggs arrived at 1100 hours. Before he could tell his news, Reisman showed him the new problem they had hidden in the garden. The I.D.s and weapons he had taken from the dead men left no doubt that they were two more of Tai Li's men.

"You'd better burn the papers along with what you got from the others," Briggs advised. "I know you'd like to make a case out of it somehow—blow things up here—but it won't work, John. Burn the papers and we'll dump the corpses and weapons in the river tonight on the way to the airfield."

"You've arranged it?" Reisman said with relief.

"Yes. You and your men and Katherine and Su'lin can fly out tonight, depending on the weather. It would be best if we left no evidence of what happened here."

Briggs told him that a C-46 would be waiting for them on the tarmac some distance away from the airfield buildings, ready for takeoff. They were to by-pass the operations office and go directly aboard. Briggs would prepare a special passenger manifest and medical evacuation orders for each of them, just in case they were needed.

"Have there been any spooks following you, or outside watching the house?" Reisman asked.

"Tai Li's men? I don't think so."

Reisman pondered that a few moments. "You'd know about it if they were," he said. "They're not very good at it. Too heavy-footed and obvious."

Nevertheless, logic warned him to be cautious, to expect that Katherine and anyone connected to her would be under surveillance. Beyond that, though, he would not predict—or be hobbled by—what the Bureau of Investigation and Statistics might do or how Tai Li might account for the disappearance of Sergeant Liu and the other three operatives.

"I think you ought to have everybody ready to leave at 1930," said Briggs. "That will give us enough time to take care of our little errand on the river and make our rendezvous at the field. I really don't think that Tai Li or Ludlow would consider that we might be up to something like this."

"You'll bring the personnel carrier? Your jeep won't do."

"Yes, of course. I'll get rid of it after you've gone."

They went into the house then to tell Katherine, Su'lin and the men.

The loud, grinding, familiar noise of the aircraft engines were curiously satisfying to Reisman. The power and movement were a form of catharsis for him. No one had bothered to put on parachutes. There was an aura of fatalism about his companions in the plane.

Katherine, sitting next to him on the long aluminum bucket seat, sometimes smiled when he glanced at her, other times her eyes were closed and she was lost in her thoughts. Talking was difficult because of the engine noise. Su'lin was sitting on the other side of Katherine, bundled up against cold and fear. She had never flown before. Baw San, who was sitting on her other side, had made himself her friend and protector.

Katherine looked as if she had been wounded in combat—and in a way she had been. Ken Briggs had given her sedatives and painkillers to take along, but she had to be careful about how she used them. This first leg of the journey was only a short flight of two hours, but ahead of her was a dangerous, arduous trip across Asia, the Middle East, Africa and the Atlantic Ocean, a journey that could take a week or more and exhaust whatever strength she had bravely mustered. She and Su'lin had been able to take very little of their clothes and possessions with them. Briggs had promised to look after the rest, and Katherine had vowed to return.

In the dim illumination of the plane's interior, Reisman studied the faces of his men and thought again of that other night, less than six months earlier, when Bowren, Sawyer, Wladislaw and the other ten had flown with him through the night in an aircraft like this and parachuted to the château at Rennes. They'd had no choice then about where they were going and what they had to do. But this afternoon he had given them the chance to determine their own fates. He had gathered them together in the living room at Katherine's house and put before them a proposal he had been mulling over for days.

He was troubled, he had told them, by the unexpected confusion and danger he had led them into since he had brought them to China. He had leveled with them that it might get worse. Then he had revealed a little bit about their pending assignment to Indochina and in particular that they would be operating behind enemy lines.

"Theoretically among friends," he had said, "but we will never be certain who is the enemy and who the ally."

He had told them frankly that it was his belief that the rest of their tour in Asia would be even more confusing and treacherous than what they had experienced so far. Then he had startled them by saying, "I'm giving you the option to stay on the plane when it stops in Kunming."

Baw San had shaken his head almost angrily, and Sergeant Bowren had started to protest. Reisman had suggested that the Kachin fly over the Hump to India and from there make his way home to Burma. Bowren, Wladislaw and Sawyer could escort Katherine and Su'lin all the way back to the States. He would see that proper orders were waiting for them in Calcutta.

"I want you to think about it right up to the time the plane touches down in Kunming," he had said.

It was still night when they landed on the lighted runway on the high plateau. Each of his men stood up and prepared to debark as if he had never given them the option not to. It struck Reisman that his proposal to them might have been more for his own benefit than theirs. The thought of any of them being hurt or killed because of a decision by him weighed heavily on him. He functioned better as a loner.

That settled, he turned to Katherine. "Well, one good thing came out of my coming to China," he said. "You're in better shape than when I arrived—and you're going home." He embraced and kissed her.

Katherine held tightly to him for a few moments, then said, "Go quickly now, or I will change my mind. I will write to you as soon as I reach Boston. You had better reply or I will come back to look for you."

"Give it a few months," he said. "I'll be out of touch."

"I understand," she said softly. "I'm rather Chinese about time now. Fatalistic."

The others were milling about in the semidarkness of the cabin, preparing to debark. He kissed her once more, then embraced Su'lin because she was sitting there beaming at him and it seemed to him that she wanted him to. Behind him, the men stepped up to the women one by one, hugged and kissed each of them as if they were family, and then followed Reisman from the C-46.

They waited there at the field until the aircraft was inspected, fueled and airborne again into the night. Then they borrowed a jeep and drove to the OSS compound, where a surprised and very sleepy charge of quarters assigned them to cots in the transients' barracks.

In mid-morning, Reisman went alone to the two-story barracks that was the headquarters of Special Operations. He climbed the stairs to the second floor, preparing himself to deal with Sam Kilgore. Despite the enmity and mistrust he felt toward him now, he expected Kilgore to make good on his promise that he could return to Indochina with the men.

When he entered the office, however, instead of the lieutenant colonel he was startled to see a familiar figure in the dark blue uniform of the U.S. Navy. Commodore Pelham Ludlow, OSS Chief China and deputy director of SACO, was beaming at him with unusual friendliness.

"Major, how pleased I am to see you again!" exclaimed the commodore jovially. "I was afraid we would miss each other."

"What are you doing here, sir?" asked Reisman politely.

"On the way to Washington for conferences."

"Where's Sam . . . the colonel?"

"In Chungking. The Chinese wanted to talk to him. Are you aware of this extraordinary idea he came up with—about the phantom armies?"

"I believe he mentioned it, sir. I thought it was quite interesting. Worth a try."

"Well, we've tried it, Major Reisman—and it's working! The Jap divisions that have been moving on Kweiyang—and, God knows,

Chungking and Kunming would have been next!—have actually halted their advance and pulled back slightly."

"I think they'd have run ahead of their supply lines by now, sir."

"Well, perhaps, Major—but give the man credit where credit is due. That's what I believe. Colonel Kilgore has commended you, by the way, for your excellent work down south."

"He has?"

"Oh, yes. In glowing terms."

"Thank you, Commodore."

"General Chennault is grateful, too. For the air crewman you brought back."

"The reason I'm here, sir, is to make arrangements to go down there again. That team I was telling you about—the men from England—they're here now and we'll be ready to go in a day or two. I want to jump in this time and take some extra guns and supplies with us."

"Anything you need, Major. Both Chungking and Washington still want a second front down there. The goddamn Russkies aren't going to do anything up north, so it's up to us to take the pressure off the Generalissimo."

"I'm certainly going to try, sir. Give us the weapons and supplies and I think the people down there will be able to do a lot more than they have."

Ludlow chewed that over a moment. "Too bad we can't work directly with the French," he said. "I certainly would prefer that. But orders are orders."

"Yes, sir."

"By the way . . . are you still in touch with that Harris woman?"

"Not recently, sir."

"I received a strange letter from her a few days ago. I ignored it. Didn't think it was even worth a response," said Ludlow crisply. "But General Tai Li was asking about her just before I flew down here. Seemed very solicitous about her health. He'd heard from her too. I think the poor woman is losing her mind."

"It's the war, sir. Does that to people."

"Well, while I'm in Washington I'll see what can be done about bringing her home. She's refused in the past, you know."

"I think, sir, that she might go if you include her housekeeper."

"That's an idea, Major. Perhaps I can arrange something for both of them."

Reisman wondered if the man truly did not know that Katherine and Su'lin had already left China. It suggested to him the possibility that the Kuomintang secret police didn't know either; and that Tai Li had neither discovered the fate of Sergeant Liu and the other three agents nor had any knowledge of Reisman's involvement.

"When are you leaving, Commodore?" he asked.

"Later today."

"Before you leave, sir—since Colonel Kilgore is away—would you authorize our supply people to deliver the items I need?"

"Glad to. Do you have a requisition ready?"

"Not yet. I'm working on it, Commodore."

"Well, I'll just tell them to give you what you need. How's that?"

"Fine, sir. We'll need a transport too."

"Of course. I'll arrange it with air support," Ludlow said with a proprietary air. "Good luck down there, Major, and keep in touch."

Reisman thanked him, saluted and left. He hoped the man knew how to follow through on the requisitions. It would make things a little easier than if he tried to do it himself.

"The only reason I didn't take up your offer to fly home, Major," said Joe Wladislaw that afternoon, "is I wanna keep checking out the Chink restaurants here. That one you took us to last week—just so-so. Maybe there's a really great one, huh?"

Reisman glanced at Wladislaw in the rearview mirror. He and the four men were driving down crowded Chin Pi Lu in a jeep from the OSS motor pool, heading toward the house where "Tong Van So" and his Viet companions had been living when Reisman first met them.

"We're not supposed to eat away from the base," Reisman shouted above the engine and street noises. "Except in places the medics have checked out."

"Shit, Major, you sound like my mother," Wladislaw muttered.

Reisman was taken aback, but he didn't feel the anger a remark like that might have spurred in him six months earlier. He turned off Chin Pi Lu into the narrow, twisting streets and alleys and parked the jeep against the familiar courtyard wall of the Viets' house. He had no idea if anyone was there, but it had been five days since the raid on Chiang Fa-K'uei's arsenal and he wanted to make contact with Pac Bo, find out if the stuff had gotten through and make arrangements for himself and the men to go in.

The heavy wood door to the garden was locked. He yanked the bell pull and a few minutes passed before the peephole opened and an eye peered out at him. Then the door was opened and he was surprised to see a smiling Tran Van Thi standing there. Thi greeted him like an old friend and welcomed Reisman's four men warmly. He was occupying the house with another man and a girl who had been in Reisman's radio training class at Pac Bo.

In the sitting room, as Reisman greeted them in both Viet-Namese and French, his men—even Baw San—were properly impressed. The room was just as it had been the month before. The large table near the window was still covered with papers, books and a typewriter, as if Nguyen Thi Mai was still working there and Tong Van So was about to come in to sign some letters.

"Are you making good contact with your base?" Reisman asked the radio girl in French.

"Yes, Major. We spoke on the key last night," she replied. Then, slyly, "We have our own code now."

"Which you intend to keep secret from me?"

"Those are my orders."

Tran Van Thi's eyes arched upward and he mumbled, "Security."

Reisman approved. He would get the code if he really needed it. "You will send messages for me, won't you?"

"Of course," replied the girl.

She took on the role of hostess, invited their guests to sit, and went to the kitchen to prepare tea.

"Wouldn't mind something a little stronger," muttered Wladislaw.

"We'll get our own later, Joe," Reisman said in a tone of mock severity. "Be a good boy and don't embarrass your mother in company."

Bowren and Sawyer burst out laughing, and Wladislaw joined them. Baw San and the Viets didn't get the joke and stared at the Americans in puzzlement.

"An army joke," Reisman tried to explain as they all sat down.

Tran Van Thi smiled politely. He took a chair from the table and brought it close to where Reisman had sat down in one of the two easy chairs. The second Viet-Namese man was trying to exchange pleasantries with the Americans, but he was speaking in French and Viet-Namese and they were speaking in English and nobody was getting through. Baw San tried Kachin without success, but then he and the Viet found some common ground in basic, faltering Mandarin.

Reisman and Thi got their own separate conversation going. "Why have you come here?" Thi asked.

"More importantly, what are *you* doing here?" Reisman responded. "I expected you to be in Tonkin by now. What did you do with your convoy? I sure hope they're not parked in downtown Kunming."

Now it was Thi's turn to laugh. "No, of course not."

He explained that the weapons, ammunition and supplies in the bootleg convoy had been split up into many small segments after they had traveled halfway back to the border. Some of the stuff had been transferred to sampans and barges on various waterways, as Reisman had suggested. Some had been transferred to other vehicles, to carts and onto the backs of porters. The shipment had been dispersed in many ways, taking different routes south and west, eventually to be smuggled across the frontier. Some of it was temporarily cached in secret depots in China.

"Some of it may have crossed the border by now," Thi said, "but a lot will still be in transit. It may take many weeks to arrive. However, there is no hurry."

Reisman looked at him sharply. "Yes, there is," he insisted. "I've got orders to get you people moving. We took this risk so that you would start fighting Japs—not sit on your butts up in the woods."

"We will, of course," Thi responded defensively. "But not until Uncle Ho decides that we are ready. We need to have more of our men and women armed and well trained."

Reisman gestured to his four men seated across the room with Thi's companion. "These men will be going in with me in the next day or two," he said. "We'll give you all the help we can. Some of the additional stuff we liberated from Chiang Fa-K'uei is here in Kunming. I'm going to try to get hold of it and drop it in with us by air."

That night, Reisman was surprised at how well the radio operator had learned her job after so little training and experience. She wasn't fast on the key or in deciphering, but neither was the operator at the other end in Pac Bo, 250 miles away. They were more concerned about the accuracy of their messages. The girl had carefully encoded what Reisman wanted to transmit and was ready when she went on the air.

Ho Chi Minh came to sit beside the radio operator in Pac Bo and was able to respond right away, though the encoding and decoding took time. Reisman told Ho he wanted to jump in two nights later and drop cargo chutes, but was concerned about revealing the location of the mountain redoubt to the pilot who would fly them in. Ho signaled back that Tran Van Thi could show him on the map a good landing zone about twenty miles west of the base. He would have people waiting there to help. He also reported that some of the new arms had begun to arrive and he was very grateful. Reisman's closing message was that he would signal again the following night with additional details.

Later in the sitting room of the Viets' house, Reisman's entire group studied the map of Indochina with Tran Van Thi. Thi pointed to a wide rift in the massif northwest of the town of Cao Bang. It was a valley with yet another river, the Sông Bang Giang, slicing through it.

"This is the place Uncle Ho means," he said.

"What is the terrain like?" Reisman asked.

"There are rice paddies and fields on either side of the river. You might get wet, but you will not have to worry about the Japs and French. It is within our liberated zone."

"We could also drown," observed Reisman caustically, "and lose the cargo chutes." He studied the map more acutely and pointed to an area north of the river. "The ground should be firmer here near this brushline, just before the elevation starts to rise again. Do you know the place, Thi?"

"Yes, you are right, Major," said Thi, chagrined. "We will tell Uncle Ho to light the signals there. He will be very pleased that you are bringing instructors this time."

Staring at the map, trying to sound out the names of towns and hamlets, Corporal Sawyer burst out laughing. "What kind of a crazy country is this?" he commented derisively. "Every other town sounds like 'Go Fuck a Duck'!"

"It's their language," said Reisman. "The sounds don't mean the same thing as in English."

"Here's one that sounds like Ding Dong Dang!" Sergeant Bowren commented.

"So it does," murmured Reisman.

He saw that Tran Van Thi, who understood both the English and the ridicule very well, was now quietly seething with anger and embarrassment. It occurred to Reisman that the rank and file of Americans might not do very well in Indochina. There was no affinity for the language, the people or the culture.

Chapter 32

Dropping from the night sky, Reisman saw below him again the mushroom clusters of conical straw hats and the black-upon-black shadows, bobbing and darting in the dancing flares of the fire beacons. Five bonfires, acrid with kerosene and the smoke of rotted jungle cuttings, marked the perimeter of the drop zone. In the air around him and above him he confirmed the chutes of his four men and the cargo packs descending tight to the target. It was a good drop.

On the ground they were greeted as heroes. Armed men and women, wearing simple high-necked military uniforms and pith helmets camouflaged with branches, surrounded them and helped with the chutes. Others wearing the indigo *cu-naos* of peasants and porters went after the cargo. There were about fifty in the welcoming party.

Their leader came close and Reisman was surprised to see who it was. "I almost didn't recognize you without your Borsalino hat," he joked in French.

Vo Nguyen Giap gave a rare smile. He too was wearing a military uniform and pith helmet. "You have done many good things, Major," he said. "I am glad you are back with us safely."

It seemed to Reisman as if he had been gone for months, yet only ten days had passed since he and Sergeant Filmore had been airlifted from Lang Son.

"Is the area secure?" he asked.

"Yes. Between here and the base all is peaceful," Giap replied. "But we hear of troop movements elsewhere. Uncle Ho is waiting. He will tell you."

Reisman stared around at the faces of the other Viet Minh who were fussing over his men and bringing the cargo and chutes to a collection point for loading on backs, poles and bicycles. They were as fascinated by the young Kachin tribesman from Burma as they were by the new Americans. Baw San spoke to them in Kachin and other hill dialects and finally found a few words they had in common. Reisman looked for Nguyen Thi Mai and Kita Shidehara, but they were not there.

The forced march to Pac Bo over mountain trails was arduous. They hiked, with little rest, from before dawn to late morning. When they reached the base camp, Ho Chi Minh lavished praise on Reisman and his men. He acted the doting uncle solicitous of the welfare of his guests.

"I will confer with you later on important new military matters," he said, "but first I am sure that you would like to clean up . . . perhaps eat a light meal and then rest for a few hours."

Nguyen Thi Mai, who stood with Ho and the group that had welcomed them in the central compound, stepped forward and embraced Reisman with unexpected warmth. She wore a dark, shapeless pajama suit, but he felt, unexpectedly, the same physical attraction to her as when he had first met her in Kunming.

"Where is Colonel Shidehara?" he asked, trying to distance himself from her.

"Away," she answered with pointed disinterest.

"On business?"

She smiled. "Yes . . . on business."

Reisman felt there was something newly coy and flirtatious about her that did not ring true.

Ho proudly showed them the primitive showers and new, enclosed outhouses that had been constructed in the camp in the days before their arrival, built according to the field sanitation principles of a U.S. Army manual newly obtained by his agents in China.

"We are honored, Uncle," Reisman acknowledged glibly.

Ho, Mai and the entourage that had escorted them on their tour of the camp left them alone after showing them to their quarters. Reisman was assigned his old hut, not far from Mai's. He left his packs and carbine there, and the new radio and generator, and went to the larger hut that his four men were sharing nearby. He had kept his .45 automatic and a trench knife with him and told the men never to go about the camp without at least those two weapons. They would also be issued M-3 submachine guns and grenades from the cargo packs that had been dropped with them.

Baw San seemed fairly content with the rustic thatched shack in which they were to live, but Reisman could see that the others were not, as they tried to stow their gear where there was no place to put it and make up their bedrolls on bamboo and vine pallets.

"Officers' quarters any better, Major?" chided Wladislaw.

"The same—only much smaller."

"Hope the roof doesn't leak," Sawyer muttered, staring up at the thatch.

Sergeant Bowren kept his silence, which was tantamount to his agreeing with them.

"You guys weren't expecting the Waldorf, were you?" Reisman joked. "This is a guerrilla camp. The boss man and a lot of the others live in caves. The rest have huts like this or nothing at all. They think we Americans are soft. We're going to show them otherwise."

"I'm a Kachin," Baw San reminded him.

Wladislaw kidded Reisman about the cozy way he had been greeted by Mai. He and Sawyer made ribald comments about the availability of the other young women they had seen in the camp.

"What *is* the fraternization policy, Major?" asked Sergeant Bowren. "Just so I know whether to keep these studs in line or not."

Reisman muddled over that. The company rule was that an OSS operative was not supposed to bed down with anyone during a mission, no matter whose side she appeared to be on. But he had a feeling he wouldn't be observing the rule strictly himself.

"I don't have any policy," he finally told them, "except common sense and discretion. Don't let a hard-on get you into trouble like some of the guys we did time with back in England."

Baw San cautioned them. "In my country," he said, "girls are very friendly if you observe our traditions with respect. Here, I do not know."

"I think you'll find the girls here are more interested in your guns, your military intelligence and your politics than they are in your cocks," Reisman told them.

Yet, that evening they were surprised by a feast given in their honor in the communal dining hall, cheerfully illuminated by oil lamps and candles. Ho Chi Minh described it as their belated Thanksgiving Day dinner. "I know all about your customs in America," he said, putting on his best public-relations face.

Reisman and his men were separated and seated among the Viets at different tables—to foster new friendships, Ho said. Mai sat next to Reisman at a table shared with ten other men and women, some dressed in better clothes than those usually seen around camp. Ho arbitrarily selected a place to sit elsewhere in the bamboo-and-thatch hall.

The meal was heavy on the staples of rice, corn and bananas, but there was also chicken and pork and liquor, beer and wine. The Viets had dipped deeply into their food stocks to impress the Americans, and there was much toasting and drinking. Ho gave a speech in which he praised the history and traditions of the United States. Reisman realized how much the Viet leader was playing to the new men to earn their friendship and loyalty.

It also became apparent to him that evening that he was wrong about the women of the Viet Minh. Beginning with Mai. She fussed over him and kept his glass filled with wine. She was wearing an extremely attractive outfit consisting of a gaily colored long dress split way up the sides, with white satin trousers underneath. Reisman eyed her with more and more interest as the evening wore on. At one point, he discovered himself running his hand along the fabric of her costume, enjoying the feel of her flesh underneath it. He felt quite warm and mellow.

"What is this called?" he asked.

"Aó dài," she murmured against his cheek.

"Of course . . . long coat . . . how could I forget? . . . very beautiful."

He looked around the dining hall and saw that Bowren, Wladislaw, Sawyer and Baw San were being fussed over in the same way by other Viet Minh girls; the language differences didn't seem to be a barrier. He was suspicious of the women's motives, and Mai's in particular, but he decided to just relax and let things go on. Something strange was happening in his head and body. He was not sure exactly what. He had not had that much to drink. Then he became aware that Mai had not been pouring her wine from the same carafe as his. He challenged her to drink from his glass, but she refused.

Unbidden and unwanted, a feeling of raw lust suddenly rose in Reisman. It was a strange sensation, devoid of tenderness, filled with an emotion akin to violence.

"What's in the wine?" he demanded.

Mai smiled at him with a look of dominance. "A stimulant," she whispered in his ear.

"What kind?"

"A love potion. An aphrodisiac."

"Why?"

"For pleasure."

"With whom?"

"Anyone who pleases you."

"What about you?"

"Perhaps."

"You're Shidehara's girl."

"I'm nobody's girl."

"Did Ho put you up to this?"

"He will be pleased if you are pleased."

Reisman raised his wineglass to her lips, his brain and loins confused with anger and lust. "Drink some," he ordered through gritted teeth, tilting and forcing the glass against her mouth.

She pushed it away and some of the liquid ran down her chin and splashed onto her dress.

Reisman glanced around the dining hall and observed that his men seemed happy enough with their new friends. All the Viets were in their own celebratory mood and no one was paying any special attention to him and Mai. Pretending to be caught up in the sensual, free-wheeling mood of the party, he wrapped an arm around her waist and grasped her right wrist to her side in a hurting grip. He picked up the wine carafe with his left hand, rose from the table and dragged Mai with him. "Let's go see if it works!" he muttered.

She started to pull away and Reisman said, menacingly, "Come along nicely or I'll break your goddamn wrist!" He was furious with her for tricking him and angry with himself for letting down his guard. He propelled her outside with him, not caring if anybody saw them or not. Alone with her on the path, he forced some of the liquid down her throat. When he was certain she had swallowed it, he taunted her, "Okay now, Miss Innocence, your place or mine?"

"Neither one if you don't behave yourself."

Reisman gave an ugly, derisive laugh—and hearing his words he could hardly believe it was him. "Behave? I thought the reason you put that shit in my wine was so I wouldn't behave!"

He felt himself losing control, and that in itself incited him to new, confused fury. He forced another mouthful of the drugged wine down her throat. She pulled away for a moment, but he was still holding tightly to her wrist. Then, unexpectedly, she took the carafe from him and drank the rest of it.

"Let's see if you're a better lover than the Jap!" Mai challenged.

The taunt neither goaded him nor stopped him. He had no need to prove anything to her, but only to ride out and assuage the powerful tensions induced by the aphrodisiac. Yet her words had sharpened his perceptions. If Kita was "the Jap" to her, then it could not have been affection, love or libido that made her Kita's *fille de joie*. Nor would any of these reasons have required her to put a love potion in Reisman's wine. What she was doing, he realized, was for reasons more blatant and less personal—the expedience of political opportunism. It had nothing to do with him as a man, just as the ache he felt now had nothing to do with caring for Mai or any other woman.

"You're on, *tovarich*!" he mocked—for, besides the aphrodisiac now also working in her own body, he was certain it was the sly business of the comrades that had motivated her.

His *"tovarich"* brought a cunning little smile of acknowledgment to her face. But did she think that she was giving him an official reward for services rendered? Or did she—did they?—want something from him that he might not ordinarily give unless made helpless before her? She didn't want him strong, she wanted him weak, and at the moment she was winning the game. If not for the drug inflaming his brain and his balls he would have dumped her in that instant.

"Your place!" he mouthed angrily, and yanked her after him along the path, oblivious to anything but the lust she had tricked him into experiencing.

But he was no longer certain whether he was pulling her or Mai was running freely ahead. They raced up the stairs to the platform of her hut, banged closed the flimsy door and tore at each other in the darkness. No words, no tenderness, no concerns. Only the fervid animal cries and moans of passion rising in their throats and the sounds of their naked bodies thrashing and smacking against each other.

It was not a joyous coupling for Reisman. It was a wild, fevered but disappointing rutting—for, in the doing, the alluring Mai was less adept than Reisman's occasional wantings and fantasies had envisioned. He did not presume to attribute her present gropings and thrashings to anything but the demands of the aphrodisiac and the Viet Minh. She had no imagination in this regard, no lyric fantasies. In moments of respite it became ludicrously apparent why she was debauching with him. She plied him—goading, cajoling, whining, taunting—with those same questions the Viets had pressed him with in the past: What were the plans of the United States government and its military forces for the land and people of Indochina?

Reisman alternately laughed and muttered and said that he knew nothing. But she didn't believe him, she cried out. He had done so much for her and her people already, surely he could give her the answers to these questions. But the only answers he gave her were variations on what they were doing.

As the effect of the aphrodisiac wore off, Mai began to bore him. He wondered if his men were undergoing similar blandishments and questioning elsewhere in the camp. But what difference did it make? They knew nothing. He hoped they were enjoying themselves.

His fantasies drifted off to other women. The exquisite Chinese girl in Kunming. No politics there. Just pleasure. Tess Simmons in the inn at Marston-Tyne. A dear and lovely girl who touched him deeply on levels beyond sex. Madeleine Thibaut in Lang Son. Mystery there. Admiration. Strong attraction and affection between them. He would have preferred to be with her, he knew, and never again with Nguyen Thi Mai.

Close to dawn, he was thoroughly sated, felt unclean, used and abused. He dressed and slipped back to his own hut, wondering if anyone had observed his coming and going, as he used to observe Kita Shidehara's. He suspected also that Kita took this sort of thing more lightly than he did.

Ho Chi Minh wore a knowing little grin on his face when Reisman entered his cave later that morning after looking in on his men. They had all experienced the same sort of night—even Baw San, who had seemed oblivious and uninitiated in these matters—and they all had obviously enjoyed it without worrying too much about reasons and consequences.

"Did you sleep well?" asked Ho solicitously.

Reisman's gaze traveled from him to Vo Nguyen Giap, to two other aides, each examining him with some amusement, perhaps expecting some confirmation of whatever Mai might already have told them about her futile frenetic dalliance with him.

"Okay," Reisman responded, as if the night had been uneventful. He would be as inscrutable as caricature purported all Asians to be. He was immediately all business. "What's this new military situation you spoke about?"

"First we must thank you again for the gifts from Chiang Fa-K'uei and those you brought with you yesterday," said Ho.

"Is the stuff from the arsenal coming in okay?"

"Some is here already," Giap told him. "The rest is still in transit. Our transport system is slow but secure. There is no hurry."

It was what Tran Van Thi had told him in Kunming, and it drew the same response: "*Au contraire, mon Général!* My orders are to get you people operational immediately. We don't have any time to waste. I've brought you four good instructors, all combat veterans who have fought beside me. We'll help you train and plan, but we want action so that the Japs have to redeploy troops and equipment to another front here in Indochina."

"They are doing it now," Ho said, startling him. "That is what we must talk about. Both the French and the Japs are moving troops to new locations."

"Together?" Reisman asked in disbelief.

"Not necessarily together in a combined operation," Giap spoke up. "It is as if they are doing a dance. One moves and then the other."

"Or like a game of chess," Ho suggested. "Which is, of course, a game of war. It is not clear, however, who intends to attack whom—or if perhaps they have a third party in mind."

"Such as you?"

"We would be pleased to accommodate them," Giap blurted out.

"No, we would not!" Ho declared hurriedly.

He cast a nervous look of reprimand at Giap, and Reisman perceived that this was an ongoing conflict between them: the military leader eager to test his men and means in battle, and the political leader who felt compelled to exercise caution and guile, to wait for the right time and place to strike.

"We do not know what it means," continued Ho. "Maybe an invasion of China by the French and Japs in alliance. It would be very easy for them to reach Kunming from the south."

"What in hell would the French want with China!" Reisman exclaimed.

"The same as they want here in Viet-Nam. The same as they and other European countries have had in their territorial concessions in China. Profit."

"That's ridiculous," Reisman declared. "They'd never make it up to Kunming anyway. The Chinese have brought crack divisions over from Burma and India to defend Kunming and Chungking."

"A fantasy," said Ho, smiling. "I know about this scheme that you and Kita worked up. You gave him the code for that very reason . . . so the Japs would listen to radio messages that make it seem real. But you've never used that code again for anything else."

Reisman smiled. "I have further news for you—and for him when he turns up. The idea was so good that the Chinese have actually started to fly real troops over. It's no longer just a phantom army. They'll be in place and fully operational within a couple of weeks."

"It's about time those fools did something right," Giap said derisively. "If only we had their resources—we would show them something."

"What does Colonel Shidehara have to say about the troop movements?" Reisman asked.

"He is away in Hanoi trying to find out," said Ho. "But we are not dependent only upon him for our intelligence. Our own network has gathered information about developments that threaten our united front against the enemy."

Ho reported that both the French and Japs were secretly and separately recruiting military and paramilitary forces from the native population. The French were avoiding the Annamese but were finding supporters among the more savage mountain tribes who were willing to fight against both the Japs and the Viet Minh. The Japs, on the other hand, were organizing and training Viet-Namese nationalists, religious fanatics and gangsters who were willing to fight against both the French and Viet Minh.

"Kita has confirmed what the Japs are doing," Ho went on. "It is another Kempitai operation, but one over which he has no authority. They want to make so many warring factions in my country that no one will be able to govern. The French, however, want to restore their empire. They will use gullible and unsophisticated minorities to help them, and those who grow and sell opium, and those who exploit the labor and suffering of their own people."

"Are they planning to attack the Japs?" Reisman asked.

If they were, then surely it would influence the operational strategies of his bosses in Kunming and Chungking, maybe alter the policy of their bosses in Washington and even the directives of the president himself.

"I would like to know the answer to that," said Ho. "Perhaps you will go to Lang Son for us and try to find out? I do not think they have the strength to do it. If they act prematurely it will be a disaster."

It was the opening Reisman wanted, to go to Lang Son for his own reasons, but he didn't want to seem too eager. Nor did he believe in Ho's seeming concern for the welfare of the French.

"I must begin the training program immediately," he insisted. "That's why I came back. That's why they let me bring in these four good men."

"Yes, of course, *Jean.* But perhaps you can leave tomorrow?" Ho urged. "We will give you whatever transport and escort you require."

"Let's try for tomorrow night," Reisman told him.

They started the new training program that afternoon in one of the camp's bamboo-and-thatch lecture halls. Reisman began with a general lecture to a cadre of forty squad leaders who—working under Baw San, Bowren, Wladislaw and Sawyer—would later teach weapons and tactics to their own nine-man squads.

To Reisman's chagrin, it was Nguyen Thi Mai who stood on the platform with him to serve as translator. But she gave no hint in voice or manner of what had gone on between them the night before, and he was pleased to see that she did her job superbly and was completely familiar with the weapons he demonstrated. He limited his first lecture to the M-1 rifle and .30 caliber carbine, because they had more of those than anything else. The Viets—both men and women—were very quick to learn. They stripped and assembled the pieces and learned the names of parts in English. Reisman and his men in their turn learned them in Viet-Namese.

Afterward, Reisman gave a chalkboard lecture on tactics. *"Chiẽn pháp,"* he said, pleased that he had learned the Viet-Namese word for tactics from Giap and could surprise Mai with it. Then, in a pidgin of English, French and Viet-Namese, he got a laugh from his audience and ingratiated himself with them by telling them that he would not presume to try to teach the technique of hiding and appearing to men and women who were already masters of the art: "What you call *ãn hiên* and we in America call peekaboo."

That night, as he was about to go to sleep, Mai came to his hut and started to undress. Reisman stopped her with words about his terrible fatigue and depletion of resources, words that amused her more than hurt her, though she returned to her quarters pouting.

Chapter 33

In the morning, the training group, instructors and translator were back in the lecture hall working with pistols, submachine guns and bazookas. In the afternoon they went into the field to work on squad tactics. The program was off to a good start. Reisman felt he could leave for a while. Sergeant Bowren and his men would take charge of the training and coordinate it with Giap's program.

He left Pac Bo that night, taking with him Baw San, two radio operators and two of Giap's best guerrillas. He estimated three nights for the trek to Long Son. They would rest in the daytime, except where circumstances and terrain urged them on. Though he was concerned that he might be wasting time going that distance on foot, it was probably the most secure way to travel. He also wanted to test himself on their footpaths, to see the extent of their network of trails and tracks and how fast a Viet Minh attack group might be expected to move. He planned to arrive at the pagoda near Lang

Son before midnight on the third night. He would leave Baw San and the Viets there and go into Lang Son alone for two days.

At 0200 on the third night he was at Madeleine's door. The city around him was dark and silent. He had taken a skiff and crossed the Sông Ky Cung at the same spot where he had crossed with the others two weeks earlier. Then he had skirted all around the citadel and the southern flank of the town to reach her house near another bend of the river. He had decided against just walking across the bridge, which would have brought him closer to the house; for, though he was dressed in the same fatigue uniform as a soldier in the Colonial Army might wear, and was carrying the papers Lieutenant Colonel Gauthier had given him on his first visit, he had not wanted to alert anyone else to his presence.

Madeleine, frightened from her sleep by his tapping, dressed in a nightgown and robe, greeted him joyously when she heard his voice calling softly through the door on the veranda.

"I hoped, but I dared not believe," she said.

They embraced and kissed passionately, like ardent lovers long separated. Reisman held her away from him, overwhelmed and grateful for the feelings she stirred in him. She made him feel as if he had come home.

"Is Philippe still here?" he asked.

"No. I am alone. He is away," she told him in an animated voice, her face flushed.

She rushed on to relate that Colonel Robert had returned to the fort from Hanoi a few days after Reisman had flown to China; Philippe had conferred with him privately and had been provided with a wardrobe of Colonial Army uniforms, a vehicle and driver, and official orders requiring him to travel to military units throughout the country. As she spoke, Madeleine led Reisman by the hand toward the kitchen, pausing to turn on lamps, chattering away with nervous vivaciousness . . . "Coffee?" . . . not waiting for a reply, moving automatically, speaking in rushes that put off that which he knew was uppermost now in their hearts and minds.

"Philippe is going everywhere to make contacts and assess our strength," she said excitedly. "To Hanoi and Saigon and the outlying districts of Annam and Cochin. He will not return for two or three weeks. Coffee?" she repeated when they were standing before the stove. "How long will you stay this time?"

Reisman drew her close to him again, wrapped her in his arms and kissed her tenderly. "Two days," he said when his lips were free again. "You must arrange for me to see Colonel Robert."

"Is that why you have come?"

"Partly," he said and signaled the rest by pressing his lips against hers again. He felt exhilaration, passion, tenderness, and the rightness of being there with her. "I don't want coffee. Thank you."

"Yes, of course . . . it is late . . . or early . . . however one looks at it. You must be tired. Do you want to sleep?"

"Sleep, no. Bed, yes," he said softly.

Madeleine stared into his eyes and nodded. Without a word, she grasped his hand and led him to her bedroom, not bothering to turn on lamps now. Yet they could see each other in the nebulous light that filtered into the room from elsewhere. Madeleine let go his hand and turned to face him near the bed, standing still with her arms at her side, breathing gently, seeking his eyes with her own, searching out his features.

"I have been very lonely since Roland died," she whispered.

But still she did not move—and though he knew she felt desire and affection for him, as he surely did for her, Reisman perceived in her words and stance a fear of being awkward, a tremulousness; not an uncertainty of wanting, but of how to give and how she would be received.

He moved the step between them, took her face in his hands, and touched his lips to hers so softly and tenderly that she would know he felt her fragile mood. They stayed like that for many moments, until Madeleine leaned away with a sigh. "It has been too long since I felt like this," she whispered. "I had almost forgotten."

Reisman felt a twinge of guilt about his night with Nguyen Thi Mai. But he spoke the truth when he said to Madeleine, "It's good to be with you again. I've thought of you often."

He kissed her again in the same gentle way, until it was she who pressed their tantalizing, feathery touch into something more demanding of his mouth and hands. He undid the tie of her robe and pushed the cloth from her shoulders. It fell away behind her. Her nightgown was pale and chaste. She stood with her arms at her sides, waiting, watching his face, letting him show her the way. He held her at the hips and she arched back a little, making him grip her harder so that she wouldn't fall.

"I began to feel this way when you were here before . . . but I held myself back," she said very softly.

"I was trying to be a gentleman."

"You were too good at it. I am so glad you are back." She smiled a wonderfully inviting smile, edged with shyness. "Perhaps this time you will fail."

"At being a gentleman?"

"Yes."

He felt the pleasure of her flesh beneath the coarse cotton fabric, and a welling of tenderness in his heart that told him again that the feelings he had for her were more than just the normal boy-girl tensions they had joked about two weeks before. There was an allure of spirit as well as flesh, an embodiment of the best of life and love that there had ever been for him and the promise of what yet might be.

Madeleine raised her arms and he slid the gown up over her breasts and head and dropped it onto the robe. The whiteness of her body glowed for him, seeming to draw to herself all the scant, transient light that entered the dark room. She stood immobile, her disarrayed hair falling back upon her shoulders. He was transfixed by the lovely fullness of breasts, hips and limbs sculpted out of the darkness. She watched him with a softer look, inviting the admiration of his gaze.

Finally, he had to touch her, to feel the reality of her flesh against him; so he wrapped his arms around her naked body and held her tightly to him, until he heard her whisper at his ear, for the first time in English, "I want so much to love you, *Jean.*"

"And I you," he murmured.

He stepped away from her and undressed with swiftly pounding heart, startled to find himself still wearing his gunbelt there in her bedroom, fumbling with his boots, yanking off his socks, shucking shorts and T-shirt, and then it was Madeleine, still standing, watching him grow naked, who wrapped her arms around his body and held him tightly to her, who stretched her head up to press her mouth against his and dart in her tongue with a sound of pleasure.

He picked her up, carried her to the bed still rumpled from her interrupted sleep, and stretched himself out beside her. He felt an exultant stirring in his loins. A joyous abandonment. He stopped thinking. Only feeling. And made love to her. And she to him.

Hours later near dawn, still folded together in a half sleep, Reisman opened his eyes just as Madeleine raised up on her elbow and exclaimed, "*Mon Dieu!* How did you get here? I never asked."

"I jumped northwest of here up in the hills, then hiked down," he answered vaguely.

Madeleine pressed against him and shivered. "You could have been caught or killed this time, *Jean,*" she murmured against his chest. "The Japs have brought in many more troops. You must not use the airfield again, if that's what you intend. One sees them going about now in the bend across the river."

"In Kunming," he lied, "I was told that both Japs and French are deploying troops in new positions. That's one of the reasons they sent me back. To find out. Do you know what's happening, Madeleine?"

"We are preparing," she whispered. "That is all I know. We are preparing to throw out the monkeys. Colonel Robert will tell you what is necessary for you to know. Surely you—you Americans—will help."

"Will Robert come here? I should stay out of sight until he agrees to cooperate and arrange a cover for me, like he did for Philippe."

"I will go to him this morning," Madeleine said. "I have his confidence. He appreciates clandestine activities better than his superiors do."

She left at 0730 to walk the half mile to French headquarters. Within an hour she was driven back by Major Derrieu, who brought Reisman a khaki Colonial Army uniform.

"An extra one of mine on loan," he said, "until we can have the quartermaster work up something for you. Colonel Robert would like you to come to his office."

To Reisman this meant tentative acceptance. Yet he knew the conflicts inherent in such an implied alliance. He could work with the French Colonials only in limited ways, and he dared not let them know that his main assignment was to Ho Chi Minh.

When he had changed into Derrieu's uniform, complete with blue garrison cap embroidered with golden anchors, and reentered the living room, Derrieu exclaimed, "Now you are a *marsouin!*"

"Marsouin?" Reisman repeated. *"Qu'est-ce c'est que ça?"*

Madeleine laughed. She tried to explain in English. "How do you say . . . a fish . . . a big fish . . . ?" Her arms spread very wide.

"A whale? . . . a shark?"

"No, no . . . like a whale, but much smaller."

"A porpoise?"

"Oui," she said in a mélange of French and English. "It is the *sobriquet* of the soldiers of *La Coloniale.*"

"Ah, the nickname," Reisman acknowledged. He smoothed the fabric of the uniform and nodded to Derrieu. "Nice fit. Thanks."

In an impulsive gesture, Madeleine kissed him goodbye and said she would expect him for dinner. Outside, Major Derrieu grinned and remarked, "You are a fast worker, *monsieur*. I have known that beautiful woman for a few years and have been fortunate to be permitted to shake her hand."

"It must be the uniform," Reisman joked as they climbed into the familiar old Citroën.

The layout and environs of Lang Son were more important to him now than they had been on his first visit. While they drove toward French headquarters, he observed with a mapmaker's acuity the features of the land and the city. The road from Madeleine's house ran with the natural contours and elevations of river, marshland, paddies and heights, and flowed into the small, attractive city's ordered pattern of boulevards, avenues and streets laid out in a modified grid. The architecture was a mixture of rural Chinese, provincial French and frontier utilitarian, set against the lush green vegetation of a high flood plain.

Derrieu complied with his request to drive past and identify for him all the key buildings and facilities in the closely built center of the town. He readily answered questions about military installations, principal public buildings, streets and population. Approximately 100,000 people lived in the immediate area. Two percent were French, a small number were from other European countries, and there were many Chinese tradespeople. The native population was mainly Tonkinese, Annamese and Nung, though Reisman noticed that Derrieu had a conversational tendency to lump them all together without distinction as "Annamites." He wondered if, in his own limited secret experience, he might already have learned more about the ethnic divisions and tribal rivalries of Indochina than the French Colonials had.

He was expecting finally to be taken into the fort itself, to what he had thought was the commandant's office, where he had met with Derrieu and Gauthier two weeks earlier, but was surprised to find out now that French headquarters and various other key buildings of the military establishment and civilian bureaucracy were not all within the walled citadel, but were located on the streets nearby, particularly on Boulevard Gallieni, the main street, named after a field marshal.

"How large is the garrison?" Reisman asked as they drove for the second time past the citadel on Avenue Clamorgan.

"Approximately twenty-four hundred . . . officers, NCOs and troops. Mostly Colonial Army . . . some Legionnaires . . . a mixture of different types . . . French professionals, Senegalese, Indians and nationalized Indochinese."

"How many French?"

"About five hundred, I would say. Officers, of course, and many NCOs and troops."

"And the Japs?"

"They outnumber us here now two to one and I think that there will soon be many more. They are increasing their strength all the time. They began to violate their transit agreements with us as soon as they were signed four years ago. Their armaments too are very modern. Half of ours are from the nineteen fourteen–eighteen war."

Derrieu was surprisingly frank, but at last he asked Reisman why he had not probed like this on his first visit.

"All I wanted then was to get out fast and in one piece."

"Why have you come back, Major?"

"I'm on assignment with Air Ground Aid Section to continue to look for our airmen . . . and to gather any intelligence that will be of use to the Allies."

"Are you planning an attack this time?"

"No. Are you?"

"Against whom?"

Reisman was scrutinizing the east wall of the citadel on their left, five hundred or more yards long. Across the avenue from it, on their right, were the military hospital, the commissariat and the artillery park. He remembered what Ho Chi Minh had suggested, outlandish as it was. "China—in league with the Japs," he said.

Major Derrieu turned his head from the road and looked at him angrily. "Don't be absurd! We have problems enough of our own."

"Then against the Japs—or even against certain native groups?" Reisman probed.

"There are no plans," Derrieu responded wearily. "Only fantasies and hopes . . . one of which is that you Americans and the British will send us more guns and supplies and then land in force from the sea. But I do not think your president would allow that."

"Mr. Roosevelt does not consult me," Reisman said dryly.

Just ahead of them, filling the top of the avenue, was the white, two-story building Derrieu had identified on their first pass as the Kempitai station. Reisman felt again the anger and frustration and the touch of cautionary fear that he had felt often in Nazi-occupied France, staring at buildings that housed the Gestapo and watching the popinjays of the Waffen SS go by.

The streets of Lang Son were not as heavily traveled at this early hour as in Kunming and Chungking, but there was just as much variety. Of the motor vehicles in sight, many were military, some Japanese. He saw French officers on horseback, troops and civilians walking, and men and women in pedicabs and cyclos. Bicycles were much in evidence, used by natives and Europeans. There were also many oxcarts heavily loaded with fruits and vegetables and other cargo. Some native men and women carried goods on poles, like in China. Then something startling caught his eyes and he was enchanted by it.

"That's a sight!" he exclaimed.

Ahead of them were two elephants with riders on their backs moving ponderously along the public thoroughfare.

"Hill tribesmen," explained Derrieu, "come to town on market day."

For the second time, he turned right on Rue des Tailleurs. They passed the Hotel Taiwa—"Where our little yellow friends take their amusement," Derrieu muttered—then turned right onto Boulevard Gallieni. They had driven this way earlier to give Reisman his survey of the city. Ahead of them on the left was the big, whitewashed Residency where the top civilian administrator of the region lived and worked. It was an imposing two-story building with a large portico and gated entry to a courtyard. Down the boulevard on that side were other important buildings: the Hotel of the Three Field Marshals, which was the officers' mess; the Foreign Legion unit, which Derrieu had explained was a command separate from the Colonial Army; the Customs House; and at the bottom of the boulevard the handsome French Catholic Church. On the opposite side of the street going south were the artillery park, the commissariat and the military hospital, all a block deep and flanking the eastern wall of the citadel on Avenue Clamorgan on their other sides.

Derrieu did not continue south this time. Just before reaching the Residency, he turned right onto Avenue Folie de Joux and then crossed the street into the car park of the *Subdivision Militaire,* the French Colonial Army headquarters. It was a two-story building of white-washed brick. A sentinel in white dress uniform saluted and admitted them to the interior.

▪ ▪

Three men were waiting eagerly for Reisman as he and Major Derrieu entered the military commander's large office on the second floor. One was Colonel Robert, a craggy-faced man in his late forties with close-cropped gray hair. He wore the open-necked khaki uniform of the Colonial Army, with embroidered gold epaulets of rank on his shoulders and the golden anchor of the *marsouin* on one shirt pocket, making him look more like a naval officer to Reisman.

The second man, wearing a white suit, was the Resident, M. Auphelle. He was a tall, slender man with white hair who wore glasses. The third man was Lieutenant Colonel Gauthier, who was now beaming at Reisman with approval.

Each man greeted him with an enthusiasm that stirred Reisman's heart with memories of men who had received him like this on missions behind German lines in France. Though Auphelle was the highest authority in Lang Son, he deferred in a calm, aristocratic manner to Colonel Robert.

"I understand from Lieutenant Belfontaine that you were in Paris during the days of liberation," said Robert.

"I was lucky," Reisman responded diffidently.

"I envy you . . . to be there fighting, instead of—" Robert hesitated a moment, almost in embarrassment—"instead of what we have had to do here."

Responding politely, Reisman said, "It will happen here soon," and a moment later, seeing their eager, excited faces, realized that he should have said nothing, that he was playing to them as an audience he wished to influence, feeding them lines they desperately wanted to hear, acting a role he had no authority to perform and in which he was unlikely to be supported by his superiors.

"We here are the highest officials in Lang Son," the colonel said earnestly. "What news have you brought us? We think as one, and you are free to speak. When and where is the attack planned?"

"What attack?"

"Surely that is why you are here this time!"

"I am here for the same reason as before," Reisman told him. "To try to locate and rescue the rest of the air crew that went down—and to stand by in the hills to help others."

Robert looked crestfallen. "There is no change in that matter," he stated, as if offering evidence before a tribunal. "My government has refused to place in Japanese hands the three Americans we are protecting. The Japs have imprisoned three. You rescued one. There has been no word of any others."

"Two are still missing, and it's my job to keep trying to find out what happened to them."

Robert looked at him doubtfully. "And that is the only reason you have parachuted into Indochina again?"

Reisman realized he had to give them a bit more, for credibility. "They have asked me also to try to gather as much military intelligence as I can about the Japs. From any source—you people here and the natives up in the hills."

"We are already providing such information," Robert insisted. "On this frontier, Major Derrieu is in charge of this work. Our Military Statistical Bureau in Hanoi collects and collates military intelligence and sends it on to the Free French Military Mission in Chungking. Aren't you aware of that, Major?"

"No, sir, I am not. I'm based in Kunming. Maybe your people don't talk to our people."

It was not a maybe, it was a fact. In the Asian cauldron as Reisman had experienced it so far, each military and intelligence branch went its own way and did whatever its own narrow, sometimes arcane policies directed—perhaps at the behest of some larger ethnic or political entity, or for some specious noble cause or economic advantage.

"Who are your 'people,' Major?" asked M. Auphelle pleasantly. "Your military unit?"

Reisman hedged, for he didn't want to open up a whole new kettle of fish about what he was really doing in Indochina. "I'm on detached service with AGAS. Air Ground Aid Section of 14th Air Force," he replied.

"And when you are not so 'detached,' *monsieur*?" pressed Major Derrieu. "What is your military unit?"

Reisman responded with ready insouciance, "OSS," as if the thought of a cover story had never occurred to him. After all, Philippe had known he was OSS since that first day in the Viet Minh camp, and Madeleine knew he was there to work with the Resistance, though she did not know anything more specific. Each of them might already have revealed that fact.

"I thought so," said Derrieu.

Reisman prepared to take some flak, though he really didn't know what the man's self-satisfied comment meant. He wondered if Philippe had divulged anything more. But he doubted it. For if these men knew anything about his assignment to the Viet Minh they would not be treating him with such friendliness and respect.

Colonel Robert's patience, however, seemed to be waning. "May I remind you, Major, that it was you who asked for this interview," he said bluntly. "You have revealed yourself to us either because you have something important to tell us or because you want something from us. What is it? Why have you come to Lang Son?"

Why *had* he come? Reisman wondered. Was it for Madeleine? Partly. Was it to follow up the rumors he'd heard from Ho Chi Minh about troop deployments? Also partly. But he could not declare either of these reasons to the highest notables in Lang Son. And there was yet another, crazier reason—one that he certainly couldn't talk about. He had the preposterous idea that he could be the means of bringing together the guerrillas of Ho Chi Minh and the forces of the Colonial Army to drive out the Japanese and unite a new nation.

Shades of T. E. Lawrence. Worse—shades of Lincoln Bradford, lately dead in Burma. But the deceptive response he gave was a ploy from the *modus operandi* of Kita Shidehara.

"What I tell you must be kept in absolute secrecy," he said softly, with a properly grim expression. They all leaned forward in their seats, eager anticipation returning to their faces. "I must have your word on this," he continued, "for I'm here representing only certain people in OSS—not the U.S. Army or government."

The other men looked to each other and then to M. Auphelle. "Agreed," said the Resident.

"As you know," Reisman went on, "we are not authorized to provide aid to French forces in Indochina, except in very specific circumstances where you might be fighting the Japs and taking the pressure off us up in China."

Robert looked at him distrustfully. "We are not fighting the Japs at all," he said defensively. "You know that and the entire world knows about the agreements we were compelled to sign with them and which we are forced to abide by, even when they do not. What are you driving at in this complicated way, Major?"

"We've learned in Kunming, through our own independent sources, that you are conscripting natives and redeploying units."

"That is really not your business, Major," declared the colonel sharply. "But it does no harm to confirm for you that we have many nationalized, loyal Annamese in the Colonial Army and the militia. We are in the process now of organizing volunteers from the Thô and Meo tribes into paramilitary forces."

Reisman hoped he sounded as simplistic and naïve as he was trying to sound. "And the Japs are doing the same thing," he muttered.

"Building up their own forces and training favored native groups. Who is going to attack whom first?"

There was a nervous silence in the room. Then Colonel Robert said, "We cannot do anything without outside help. We have neither the troops, the guns, nor the matériel."

That was Reisman's cue. He said, "I was asked privately, by certain OSS people who knew I was returning here for AGAS, to find out what kind of limited, unofficial help we can give you."

There was a collective sigh in the room.

"*Mon Dieu,* we were hoping for something like this!" Gauthier blurted out.

Colonel Robert's doubtful expression changed to a smile. "It does take you a while to get to the point, doesn't it, Major?"

"Caution, sir. Just feeling my way along like I do in the field," Reisman told him. "Like I said, I don't speak officially for my outfit or the army. They don't know a thing about this in Chungking or Washington. You've got to keep it secret from your people too—in Hanoi, Chungking, Paris or anywhere—otherwise we call it off."

M. Auphelle, the pragmatic civil servant, asked the appropriate question. "What do you want in return, Major?"

"Feed me whatever you know on the Japs and let me wander around the countryside quiet-like. I don't want anybody with me. I'll check in here from time to time and I'll convey your needs to the people in Kunming, who will attempt to drop the stuff. Whatever is at the top of your list—guns, ammo, supplies. We know the British have been doing this from Calcutta and we figure it's time we did our share."

Colonel Robert rose from his desk and beckoned Reisman over to a wall map of the Lang Son sector. "You cannot use the airfield now. Too dangerous. That's not the way we've been doing it, in any event." He moved his finger a mile and a half east of the airfield across yet another bend in the Sông Ky Cung, to a place beyond the paddies and marshland just where the foothills of the highlands began. "We have had very good luck with airdrops here from the British. I would like to see a sample delivery from you people. We will place our radio facilities at your service, since you apparently didn't bring your own this time. Ask for a drop tonight or tomorrow night. Will that do?"

"All I can do is try."

▪ ▪

Waiting in their communications room that night, Reisman felt a certain perverse pleasure in being on the spot. He had gone over and over it again in his mind during a distracted evening with Madeleine, unable to take her into his confidence. The operative word was greed. Or, as Sam Kilgore had described it, *business.*

Using a sheet from his new one-time code pad, he raised Kunming on the key and was relieved to learn that Kilgore was back. He hated having to deal with him, but the man was still his immediate superior and he needed him to make the scheme work. Kilgore would back him up on unorthodox operations if he thought it would benefit him personally and professionally. Reisman told them to bring him to the radio shack. Extremely urgent. He signed off for half an hour, then made contact again.

The first words he deciphered from Kilgore were a hearty greeting, with not the slightest hint of the treacherous secrets and bad blood between them. It was like dealing with a viper—but in this instance that was an advantage.

In a coded exchange of dah-dit-dahs, he finessed Kilgore into believing that he was out in the field with a new native group he had contacted. They were eager to work as guerrillas against the Japs, but needed an immediate demonstration that Reisman could do for them what he said he could. To sweeten the pot, he told Sam the new group had an enormous cache of the kind of trade goods he was interested in—opium. He said he had made a deal to take their opium for guns and ammo, but it was imperative that he prove his reliability to them by producing an arms drop the following night.

When Kilgore asked how the opium would be delivered, Reisman knew he had him hooked. "I'll stash it with Tong," he replied. "Deliver later."

A few moments later, Kilgore signaled approval and asked what items should be dropped, what time and where.

Three platoons went out the following night. One, under Major Derrieu, was there to protect the drop zone from intruders; the second team, under Lieutenant Colonel Gauthier, was assigned to create a diversionary action if needed; the third team, which Reisman and Colonel Robert accompanied, lit the signals. They used big cooking pots filled with sand and gasoline, which could easily be extinguished with blankets if they were interrupted.

A Liberator bomber came over the hills at 0100 and dropped cargo chutes with fine accuracy. The recovery went very well. Reisman even recognized some of the cargo he had liberated from Chiang Fa-K'uei. A most fitting use for it, he thought; closer to his heart than supplying Ho Chi Minh.

Afterward, a very pleased Colonel Robert gave him leave to depart, and assurance that he would be welcome in Lang Son anytime. He went quickly to Madeleine's house and bade her a fond adieu, promising to return in a couple of weeks. He slipped out of Lang Son the same way he had entered it three nights earlier.

By 0230 he was across the Sông Ky Cung and headed through the paddies to the pagoda beyond the Jap positions where he had left Baw San and the Viets. Within an hour he was entering the silent grounds.

In the doorway of the monks' quarters, he saw a saffron-robed figure stir out of the darkness, rise from a squatting position and glide toward him with a begging bowl in his hand. He was a very young man with a shaven head who made a gesture of obeisance and walked on.

Then from behind him Reisman heard laughter and a familiar voice exclaimed in accented English, "It is good to see you again, *Duwa* John! I have been very worried."

It was Baw San. "You see, I have fooled even you," said the boy with delight.

Reisman stared at him in astonishment as Baw San explained how he had accompanied one of the monks on a walk through the Japanese encampments to spy on them. Reisman chastised him for endangering himself.

"I could not just sit here, *Duwa* John," Baw San said earnestly. "The knowledge of them so near . . . they murdered my family and destroyed my village. They are lucky that I did not kill any of them. Perhaps I have learned how to be a careful spy from you."

Reisman continued to stare at his disguise in wonder and admiration. "I didn't know that you spoke Japanese," he said.

"I understand a little, but it was not necessary to speak," Baw San explained. "My companion told those who tried to question me that I had taken a vow of silence. I listened well, however."

"What did you hear, Corporal Bawsan?" Reisman asked, smiling.

"Some of those soldiers just came down here from China. An advance party of the Jap 37th Division. They are all experienced fighting men, not occupation troops. More are coming down later."

Reisman commended him. This bit of intelligence fit the pattern of what he had learned in Lang Son and what Ho Chi Minh had told him. But it still didn't tell him who was going to do what to whom. The Japs to the French? The French to the Japs? Either one of them or both of them to the Viets?

"Wake up the others," he told Baw San, "and let's get on the road."

Chapter 34

They were even more cautious on the return trek to Pac Bo, having confirmed the increased number of Jap troops in the region and knowing that they and the French were redeploying in Tonkin and making use of new paramilitaries. The two Viet Minh scouts were masters of their craft, finding one-man trails where Reisman would not have thought they existed, moving with "stealth . . . continual stealth . . . arriving unexpectedly . . . leaving unnoticed."

Except for the radio. His operators contacted their base twice each 24 hours, as they had been doing since they left, using the key and code for transmission, rather than voice. There were three radios at the Viet Minh camp now, one kept tuned to their wavelength, the others eavesdropping on the Japs and French, ready to alert the patrol to danger.

At dawn of the fourth day they were met on the trail by Sergeant Bowren, Joe Wladislaw, Ken Sawyer and a squad of guerrillas. His men greeted Reisman like parents who had waited up for a teenager out too late on a Saturday night: glad to see him home, but peeved that they had come to the point of worrying.

"Didn't want you to get lost so close to home," Bowren muttered.

"Thanks, Clyde," Reisman acknowledged, touched by their concern.

They called him "sir" less since their reunion, he had noticed, and treated him with the respect and camaraderie of shared experience rather than deference to rank. They made him feel a little guilty now for having left them alone for eight days in a country they neither liked, understood, nor trusted—and for having enjoyed himself in Lang Son.

Hiking beside him, Bowren said softly, "I wish to hell I spoke their lingo, Major. I just don't trust them."

"Anything happen?"

"A lot. First off, there's another American in camp, a Chinese-American civilian. He says he knows you."

"Jimmy Lum?"

"Yeah, that's his name. He's a funny guy. He came right out and told us he's a spy."

"He is," Reisman said, certain that it was Kita Shidehara.

"He's been asking a lot of questions, but I told Wladislaw and Sawyer to keep their lips buttoned up till you got back."

"Good. Anything else?"

"I don't think you're gonna like it," Bowren continued apologetically.

He reported that in addition to the training program, they had gone out on a couple of test forays planned by Vo Nguyen Giap against isolated enemy outposts.

"Jap outposts?"

"I'm afraid one of them was French. But me and the boys didn't know that till we got there," Bowren told him disconsolately. "They beat us off. Surprised us with bigger firepower and more men than Giap thought were there. There were some Viets killed and wounded. We laid back when we realized who we were shooting at. It didn't seem right."

The news angered Reisman. "You did the right thing, Clyde. That isn't our fight. We've got to stay out of it."

"We'd rather go with you next time, Major."

"You're not supposed to stick your neck out anywhere, either with me or with them," Reisman told him emphatically. "You're on a training assignment here, not to get shot at."

As they entered the Viet Minh redoubt, Bowren looked around cautiously and spoke very softly. "I think these guys are a bunch of con men, Major. Except for the raw recruits, they need our kind of training about as much as you do. I think they're just after the guns and ammo and supplies. I may know a few more weapons than they do, but they already know more about jungle fighting than I'll ever learn."

Reisman moved back along the line and talked to Wladislaw and Sawyer separately. They told him they felt very strange there, stranger than they had ever felt in Europe. They didn't like working with the Viets.

"I thought you had a girlfriend keeping you happy, Joe," Reisman kidded Wladislaw.

"It was a one-night stand, Major. She was the one came after me that first night, just like yours. She ain't much interested any more in what I'm interested in—you know, just plain old R and R. She talks a little Frog and a little English and keeps pestering me with questions I don't know nothing about and wouldn't tell her if I did."

Reisman left the men at their hut and went immediately to Ho Chi Minh's cave. Ho was in good spirits, but Reisman cut him short and tore into him for sneaking in an attack against a French outpost while he was away and endangering the lives of his men.

"Une erreur terrible!" Ho exclaimed. "When I heard about it I too was truly distraught. Until only the week before, that place in the forest that they attacked was indeed a Jap position. Not until the moment of attack did our forces learn that the Japs had abandoned it. It was an outpost of no real military value, and the French had occupied it secretly. It is an example, *Jean,* of what I have told you. Each of them is moving their troops here and there for reasons that we still do not understand. I have reprimanded Giap for his mistake."

Reisman did not believe his elaborate tale. "If you did bawl him out it was for failing to win," he declared.

"My thesis entirely," Ho acknowledged glibly. "Do nothing until you are prepared. It will not happen again, I assure you. What have you learned in Lang Son?"

Reisman went over to the big relief map table and started to tell him about the increased Jap troop strength outside the city, but then saw that the positions were already marked.

Seeing where Reisman was pointing, Ho said quickly, "Colonel Shidehara is back!"

"Then my trip was redundant," Reisman snapped. "A dangerous

waste of time, other than a pleasant little vacation with my friends." He didn't really feel that way, but he thought that a display of petulance was called for in the game Ho was playing. "Apparently Kita brought you the same intelligence that I bring," he accused.

"But he was not able to learn as much about the *colons* as you," Ho pressed. "I am most eager to hear your report."

Reisman had no intention of saying anything about the activities of the French, and certainly not about the arms drop he had arranged for Lang Son. "I agree with the assessment you made before I left," he told Ho. "They don't have the strength to attack anyone—maybe not even to defend themselves."

"Perhaps that is what they would have you believe," Ho said pensively. "Just as the Japs would have you believe that they are very powerful, to frighten everybody into doing what they want them to do. They are arrogant and cruel, and they are thieves who take goods and services without proper payment. They are up to something, those two," he added darkly, "and it worries me very much. I do not trust either of them, and I do not forgive either of them for what happened in Lang Son in 1940."

"What was that?" asked Reisman. He remembered how morbid Ho had been the day they first went there together.

"In September 1940," Ho related in a melancholy voice, "Viet-Namese patriots, trusting the Japs, came across the border with them from China when they fought the French for a few days. But when they made their accommodation, the Japs abandoned our patriots and the French slaughtered those they could catch. Others escaped back to China. It was a tragedy."

"Yet you trust Kita Shidehara," Reisman challenged.

"He is useful. For his own reasons."

"Everybody seems to have his own reasons out here," Reisman commented cynically.

"What are yours, *Jean*?"

"To get out of here as quickly as possible, as whole as possible."

"You are not interested in our country? Or in politics?"

"Not in the least," Reisman declared positively.

"Then why did your government send you here?"

Reisman was about to reply with the simple, mundane truth—*Because I was available, I speak French and I know how to fight dirty*—when he realized that Ho was leading him into another dialectical bullshit session.

"*They* didn't send me, Uncle," Reisman reminded him pointedly.

"It was *you* who invited me—after you led Lieutenant Colonel Kilgore into believing you intended to fight the Japs."

"We provide military intelligence . . . very good stuff."

"Agreed."

"We saved your American flyer and we will save more."

"Commendable."

"We have made some attacks against the Japs."

"Not enough."

Ho was silent. He stared at Reisman gravely, as if suddenly bored or offended by the repartee. Then he said, "You and your men have almost doubled our capacity to train new soldiers, and for this we are very grateful. But we cannot commit every one of them to immediate, futile action. It could decimate us. This has happened in years past and I vowed that I would not let it happen again. Also, we still do not have sufficient weapons. Though, with much gratitude to you and your company, we now have many more than before."

"When?" asked Reisman. "When will you be ready to move out in strength? What if we need you desperately for a critical mission? What if I personally need your troops for something, because there are no others?"

"Not before six months. We will need six more months. By June of next year we will be ready."

"I'm going to report that to Kunming," said Reisman, "and let them decide if they want us to continue as we are."

He left Ho's cave and headed for his hut. He needed a few hours of sleep. Baw San was probably asleep already, while Bowren, Wladislaw and Sawyer were supposed to be off drilling the newest weekly class of Viet guerrillas. So he was startled to see them sitting on the steps of their quarters with Kita Shidehara. Moving closer, he overheard the Kempitai colonel regaling the men with a story of his former happy life in San Francisco.

Wladislaw spotted him. "Hey, Major, here's Jimmy Lum."

Kita was his usual antic, bright, witty self. He said, "Your Corporal Bawsan and I have just been going over familiar places back home. He doesn't seem to remember as much as I do."

"I've been looking for you—Jimmy," said Reisman sourly.

"And I you."

"Let's take a walk."

They strolled to the stream and settled down on the big boulder that Ho sometimes used as his outside office.

"That's quite an act you've got going, Colonel."

"Are you going to give me away?"

"No. I think it's better that they don't know," Reisman replied. Then he added in a calm voice, "But I warn you—never do anything to hurt any of them."

Kita looked at him with an unflinching gaze. "I would prefer not to," he said, no longer wisecracking. "And that includes you."

There was a surprising solemnity in his voice.

"What can you tell me about our confused little world down here?" Reisman asked.

"It was better when my side was winning it . . . when we were in charge of things and could make them stick," Kita answered.

"Yeah, I know. Everybody loves a winner and likes to be one," Reisman snapped, thinking Kita was being flip again. "You had your turn—now ours is coming up."

But Kita was not in a mood for light banter. Staring pensively into the rushing stream, he said, "I loved the cleverness of what we were able to do here in Indochina. Very little violence. Nothing like the rape of Nanking . . . the savagery in the Philippines and Singapore . . . all of which I deplored when I heard about it. Cleverness is one thing, brutality another." He snapped his fingers in that familiar gesture and turned away from the stream, just remembering something. "That's why I loved that crazy scheme I came up with about the phantom army. I must congratulate you—you did it and it worked."

"The Chinese liked it so much they've been sending real troops."

Kita laughed. "Yes, I've heard. But *Ichigo* had halted already, gone into winter quarters. It's all feinting and parrying now. Not many get hurt. No great armies slaughtering each other senselessly. And, fortunately for my side, the Great Gimo and the Red Menace still won't get together, I hear. They never will, you know, with that absurd ambassador of yours trying to get them to love one another. He's a walking insult—with his dirty jokes, his Indian war whoops and 'Mr. Shek' and 'Moose Dung.' "

Reisman stared at him searchingly, not without some admiration. "How do you find out all these things, Kita?"

"I told you. It goes with the territory."

Kita's manner was even more exaggerated and vivacious than usual. Reisman realized he was going on and on about one thing to cover up something else. He had come to know the man, to like him—almost to trust him.

"What are you trying to tell me without actually telling me?" he asked. "If you know what's going on in China so well, you must know what's going on down here."

Kita's cheerful features dropped into melancholy. "I don't know," he answered, "and that is the problem. When I was in Hanoi I could sense something going on, but nobody would admit to knowing what it was. I even slipped up to Lang Son and looked in on the local Kempitai chief to see if I could learn anything. Troops coming in, natives being trained—but that's all."

"I was there too."

"So I learned when I got here. Wonder what we might have said if we'd run into each other?"

"Ought to plan for that if there are others around. I don't know you, you don't know me. That's probably best."

"I suppose so. Anyway, they explain away the increased troop strength by telling me that they're afraid—of the French, the Americans, the Chinese, the British—everybody."

"I think they are mostly afraid of the terrible things that they have done to others," said Reisman, careful not to say *you.* "And of the retribution that is coming."

Kita forced a smile onto his face again. "Well, the game isn't over yet," he said. "What did you learn from the French?"

Reisman considered saying nothing, but then realized that the truth, or at least part of it, could not harm them. "They too are frightened," he said. "Of the Japanese, the Chinese—and perhaps even of the Americans, though mainly they are displeased with us."

"And what do they say about the Viet-Namese—the Annamites, as they call them?"

"Very little. A minor annoyance."

Kita smiled with satisfaction. "Well, keep me posted, and I'll do the same."

It was colder in the highlands that winter than any of the natives could remember, but for the Americans it was almost pleasant, certainly nothing like the snowy cold they had known at home and in Europe. When the men heard about the big Nazi counteroffensive in the Ardennes, the terrible Battle of the Bulge raging there, they figured they were better off where they were. Though for Reisman it was an uneasy time.

In his radio messages Sam Kilgore agreed to settle for the thousand guerrillas Ho had promised for June and instructed Reisman to continue to train the Viets, use their intelligence network—and explore new *opportunities*. He knew the sort of opportunities Kilgore had in mind. Daily life settled into a routine of training, preparation, anticipation of something about to happen—and frustration that not much did.

Nguyen Thi Mai's attitude toward Reisman returned to what it had been before—friendly, respectful, argumentative, but spiced with a wistful touch of warmth. Kita Shidehara, apparently unaware of her one-night stand with Reisman, or perhaps indifferent to it, continued to slip into her hut when he was in camp.

Reisman thought often about Lang Son and Madeleine and resisted longer than he wanted to the urge to go there again. He felt it would be as if he were awarding himself a pass to town without allowing his men the same. Not that Lang Son could ever be a place of rest and recreation for them. It was in fact a place of great danger for all of them.

The Viets in the guerrilla camp, encouraged by Ho Chi Minh, tried to make a holiday atmosphere for them during Christmas and New Year's. It was appreciated, but felt more dismal than joyous. It was not until mid-January that Reisman finally rationalized that it was time to return to Lang Son on another intelligence-gathering mission. He found out that Colonel Shidehara was going there to stay just one night and he asked if he could travel with him.

"Glad for the company, John," Kita responded with alacrity. "Perhaps we can compare notes afterward and try to figure out who's planning to do what to whom."

They left the Viet Minh base in mid-afternoon. Reisman rode out of the hills behind Kita on one of the motorcycles. He wore his working fatigues and weapons for this first part of the journey and carried a Colonial Army uniform rolled into his pack, along with the I.D.s and transit papers Colonel Robert had issued him last time. Kita wore casual civilian clothes—no weapons—and carried his uniform in a saddle bag. They changed in the shed in Cao Bang where Kita kept his truck.

Staring at the transformation in his traveling companion after he had put on his military uniform, Reisman asked, "How come the Japanese Imperial Army or the Kempitai doesn't spring for a gun for you?"

He realized that he had never seen the man carrying any kind of weapon.

Kita tapped his temple and smiled. "Don't need one in my line of work," he retorted. "That's for gung-ho types like you."

He was being a smart-ass again, thought Reisman, and he supposed he would have to listen to him as the price of his ticket to Lang Son. But as they drove southeast on Route 4, Kita became more somber and introspective. He sent up a few trial philosophical balloons that revealed a less than buoyant frame of mind.

"Perhaps there is nothing left now but personal pleasure, private desire . . . no more collective will," he sighed at one point.

"There is no such thing . . . never has been," Reisman replied. "Any idea is always the idea of one man adopted by others. I think part of your confusion is that you had your mind opened by your years in the States. It wasn't as bad as you make it out to be. You learned a lot and felt the clean breath of freedom—even among a people tainted by petty prejudices."

"I wish you people had just let us stay in charge out here," Kita said reasonably. "Somebody has to be in charge, and the Co-Prosperity Sphere idea is a good one."

"Pearl Harbor," muttered Reisman.

"Pity," said Kita, sighing again. "There is no going back, is there?" He lifted his right hand from the steering wheel and snapped his fingers. "By the way, did you ever try to contact Chang Wen Ming?"

"No. I haven't been in Chungking since I first got out here."

"Hmmm," murmured Kita. "I'm told that he's not there any more. Thought you might know something."

"No." But it made Reisman wonder again if Chang Wen Ming had been one of Tai Li's agents they had killed and dumped in the Yangtze. And he wondered too if Kita knew he was lying.

It was dark when they crossed the Sông Ky Cung. On Rue Unal, just over the bridge into the city, Kita asked, "Where shall I drop you?"

"Where are you going?"

"Hotel Taiwa."

"Convenient to the Kempitai station."

Kita glanced at him with a wry look. "You're really quite good," he acknowledged.

Between the cinema and the prison he turned right onto Rue des Japonaises. There was a line of soldiers and civilians queueing up to buy tickets. "Drop me right here," said Reisman.

Kita completed the turn and stopped. "Going to the movies?"

"An amusing thought." Reisman actually found himself wondering what was playing, but he couldn't see the posters from where he was.

"Where will you be staying?" Kita asked with genuine concern.

"I have a friend."

"Ah . . . *cherchez la femme!* I thought so."

"Where shall I meet you tomorrow?" Reisman asked.

"You wouldn't want to come to the Kempitai station at one P.M., would you?"

Reisman smiled. "I wouldn't want to push it. How about outside the railroad station on Rue Gouttenègre? That's right across the tracks from the—"

"I know—the church. See you there. Thirteen hundred hours."

Watching him drive away, Reisman wondered what Kita would say if he knew that the main reason he was visiting Lang Son was to spend the night with Madeleine Thibaut. Ho Chi Minh, of course, had urged both of them to go there to snoop around and see what the Japs and French had been up to during the past six weeks. Except for the obvious presence of the military, everything looked peaceful and civilized.

He slipped around to the front of the cinema and saw on the posters that two oldies were being shown: a French movie, *Mayerling,* starring Danielle Darrieux and Charles Boyer, which he had seen in Paris before the war; and *King Kong,* which he had seen in New York many years earlier in between transatlantic voyages. The soldiers and civilians lined up at the box office were surrounded by an army of ice-cream vendors wearing thermos boxes.

There was a war on somewhere, but not here.

It was Lieutenant Philippe Belfontaine who came out to the veranda when Reisman knocked.

When he saw who it was, he opened his arms wide as if to clasp Reisman to his bosom, then settled for a hearty handshake and grasping of the shoulders. His face was joyous. "We were just talking about you, *Jean*!" He called out, "Madeleine! Come see who is here!"

In the instant before falling into his arms, Madeleine pulled back enough to make her actions more discreet in the presence of her brother: a hug, a kiss on the cheeks, a holding at arms' length for inspection, and then a second hearty embrace and kiss.

Reisman and Philippe were alone for a few minutes while Madeleine went out to the kitchen to stretch dinner for one more guest. Philippe thanked him for the arms drop. "When I returned and learned about it I was very surprised. Does that mean your government's policy has changed?"

"No. It was just something I was able to arrange privately."

"Can you do it again?"

"I can only try. No guarantees."

"To other parts of Indochina?"

"I can request it."

Philippe told him about his travels through the country to assess French readiness. Units in Tonkin, Annam and Cochinchina were eager to coordinate an internal uprising against the Japs with the expected Allied invasion from the sea or China. "Surely you are here with important news this time?" he said hopefully.

"There is no news about invasion plans," Reisman told him.

"Then what are you doing in Tonkin?"

"Same as before. To help our grounded birds. Beyond that, to watch, listen and report. I came down out of the hills because I was bored and needed a change."

Philippe turned his disappointment into a challenge. "Then you must report to your superiors that the morale of the Colonial Army and the French Foreign Legion is superb; that our training and state of readiness throughout the country is improving each day; and that if our arms and supplies matched our morale we would go it alone."

Reisman doubted that. It seemed to him that Philippe was becoming a victim of his own wishful thinking and propaganda. Once again, Reisman felt the tantalizing call to serve as ministering angel. "You don't have to go it alone," he said. "There are the people of this land."

What was the allure, he wondered, in serving as go-between and savior? Was it the danger of it? The impossibility? Yet he was tempted to transform his reason for being in Indochina into something never intended by the people and forces that had sent him there.

"We already have many in the Colonial Army and militias," Philippe said.

"You know damn well what I mean!"

Philippe accepted the challenge unwillingly. "Yes . . . Nguyen Ai-Quôc and his renegades. I have wiped them from my mind, as you requested. That is sufficient to the debt I owe you, and the promise to them. But I am happy to tell you also that I am less concerned about them one way or the other now that I have discussed the matter—in general terms, not specific names and places—with military authorities and civilian underground leaders throughout the country. They have tried their little attacks and have been soundly beaten. One day the army—without any assistance from me—will clean them out once and for all. Or the Japs will do it. It makes no difference."

"You are making a great mistake, Philippe," Reisman told him. "You and the rest of the colonial establishment."

Madeleine called them to dinner then, and they tried to keep the conversation away from the war. Instead, Reisman told them something more about his boyhood in Chicago and his years at sea, and they told him about growing up at home in the Camargue. In the night, he slipped into Madeleine's bedroom and banished everything else from his mind. In the morning, he suspected that Philippe knew and approved.

For Reisman and his men in the Tonkin mountains, operations in January and February settled into a routine of training guerrillas, helping them plan an occasional raid against Jap transportation and communications, gathering military intelligence, standing ready to help AGAS if there were any more downed flyers, and maintaining radio contact with Kunming. The Japs and French continued to build strength and redeploy troops in shadowboxing maneuvers.

The big news early in February from Lieutenant Colonel Kilgore—who was getting more and more anxious about when he was going to receive his trade goods—was that the first American truck convoy, loaded with new war matériel, had just driven all the way from India to Kunming on the finally completed Burma–Ledo Road, which had been renamed the Stilwell Road. No longer was the perilous air route over the Hump the only way to get guns and supplies into China from the western Allies. Reisman wondered if the main war now would pass by this backwater in the south and make whatever they did there unimportant in the overall plan to defeat the Japanese Empire.

From regular news broadcasts on Armed Forces Radio Network, he learned—with a certain wistfulness—that Allied armies had broken through the Siegfried Line and were fighting on German soil. In the Pacific, the brutal island-hopping war against the Japs was moving relentlessly closer to Tokyo. In the Philippines, the "next game" that Kita Shidehara had predicted so flippantly, back in October, was now on. The battle for Leyte Island was over. The American invasion of the main island of Luzon and the drive toward Manila was on. Particularly pleasing to Baw San was the news that Allied armies were fighting their way south and east from liberated northern Burma, driving ahead of them and cutting up the remaining Jap forces and sweeping them forever from his homeland.

Though in China and Indochina the Japs still remained strongly in control, the general trend of the war news was very depressing to Kita Shidehara. He sought out Reisman for private talks and Hamlet-like monologues.

"Somebody has to be in charge . . . there has to be order," he declared. "Whether it is us or somebody else . . . as long as it works well and not too many people get hurt. I'm afraid of what's happening now . . . chaos is looming."

Yet the man surely was responsible for at least some part of what was to come, Reisman thought. Was he preparing for some sort of Japanese *Götterdämmerung*? *Hara-kiri*? No, Kita was too clever and urbane a man for that. One day he said, "If the Americans come in and it is all over here for people like me—would you help me? Have I earned any points? Would you help me just plain get away? Maybe home to Japan . . . maybe up here to stay with someone like Ho . . . maybe somewhere else I've never been before, where I can just disappear—and live pleasantly, of course."

Reisman thought it over. "Yes . . . I would," he said. "As long as you had done nothing terrible, I would."

How strange, he realized, that he'd never seen a cruel or violent act on Kita's part, nor heard a violent thought. Though the man's cohorts, despite their much heralded interests in tea ceremonies, flower arranging, exquisite arts and crafts, had a penchant for the most cruel and savage behavior toward other people.

It was early in February before Reisman managed to get Kita to drive into Lang Son again. He didn't want to spend the time hiking down as he had in December, and the drive there posing as a French officer in the company of the Kempitai colonel seemed the most secure procedure despite its obvious dangers.

In the town, they separated as before. Reisman refused to tell Kita where he would be staying. Kita said he would be at the Hotel Taiwa. They planned to remain in Lang Son two nights this time, and arranged to meet for the return to Pac Bo at 1300 on the third day.

Reisman strolled through the evening streets filled with colonial military and civilians. He saw few Japanese, for the direction he was heading was not their part of town. Making certain he was not followed, he arrived at Madeleine's house within the hour. She herself opened the door and peered out warily. Her appearance in the dim light—sad, tired, vulnerable—brightened in the instant of recognition and she gave a cry of joy as they embraced and kissed. When Reisman apologized for always turning up like this unannounced, she touched her fingers to his lips and silenced him.

"C'est la guerre?" she whispered, and put a little question mark at the end to make it their private joke.

Philippe was also at home and he greeted Reisman warmly. "At last!" he said, teasing his sister and implying his approval. "Her sadness was beginning to depress me."

From each of them Reisman learned that they and every Frenchman with whom they came in contact had been telling each other new rumors about an imminent Allied invasion. They still believed that he had something to do with it.

"Where do you get these stories?" he demanded of Philippe. "You are exciting false hopes and making the Japs very nervous about your own activities."

"It is not a rumor, it is the truth," Philippe insisted. "I myself have been informed by the Far Eastern French Liaison Section in Calcutta."

Reisman did not believe the rumors. Yet he realized it was possible that he had been kept in the dark intentionally by his superiors.

Philippe said, "Colonel Robert and Resident Auphelle have told me that I must bring you to them immediately you return. Will you come now?"

"Of course."

There was no phone, so Philippe went out first to arrange the meeting. Reisman and Madeleine had just about enough time alone together to build up a good head of steam between them—and no time to do anything about it—when Philippe returned to drive Reisman to French headquarters.

"They are delighted to receive you," he said. "They are coming there from their homes especially to see you. There is also someone else very important whom you will meet."

When they entered the familiar large office on the second floor of the headquarters building, the Resident and the colonel were waiting with a tall, ascetic-looking soldier wearing a huge old revolver at his waist.

Colonel Robert made the introductions. "May I present my superior, General Emile Lemonnier, commander of the Third Brigade of the Tonkin Division of the Colonial Army. General Lemonnier is military commander of the entire region."

Reisman felt that a salute was called for, and he stood to attention and executed one sharply. Lemonnier returned it and then extended his hand in a warm welcome.

"We meet . . . but we do not meet, Major," he said with a wink. "I am here secretly on inspection, which I do from time to time. If the sons of Nippon learn of my presence here they will invite me to dinner . . . a reciprocal military courtesy which I would prefer to forgo."

Reisman was struck by the absurdity of such a formal duty. He had never even considered that such social proprieties were part of the game. He wondered what the table talk would be like—the lies they would have to tell each other pleasantly, the truths they would have to cover up. Which the cat and which the mouse?

Usually leery of anyone of that rank, Reisman found himself unexpectedly charmed and relaxed in the presence of the general. "Sounds as if it would be hard on the digestion, sir," he commented.

Lemonnier and Auphelle laughed. As the highest rankers, they set the tone. Then the others followed. The general thanked him for the arms drop in January. "It was necessary for Robert to tell me, so that I would understand better our capabilities here, but nothing has been reported to Hanoi or anywhere, as you requested. I understand that you deny any knowledge of an imminent Allied invasion, which, you must know, we are preparing for. May I ask you why you have come to Lang Son again? Perhaps another air drop?"

Improvising for the requirements of the moment, Reisman acknowledged the possibility of an air drop. He certainly could not tell the general he had come to Lang Son to make love to Madeleine Thibaut and snoop around for Ho Chi Minh.

"If I may use your radio again, sir, I would like to try for another one," he said. "My orders are to make sure always that the delivery will not fall into the wrong hands—which is why I am here. Please understand also that it can be only a small shipment and must be kept secret. Otherwise our friends in Kunming will get into trouble."

"Agreed," said the general. "One other thing troubles me, however. What else are your orders for these very private operations in Indochina? Where do you come from before you appear here on your bountiful visits? Where do you disappear to when you leave? It is, as you must know, more than just curiosity with us, or any narrow concern with violations of territorial security. Our concern is more for the matter of whom you are in touch with in the highlands and the nature of the military intelligence you are conveying to your superiors."

Reisman gave his usual response, but admitted this time that he had a team. "I've got three Americans and a Kachin Ranger up there in the hills. We mostly do escape and evasion for our downed flyers, plus we listen to what's going on. We've been lucky to find natives to help us, but we've got to protect them. All I can tell you is that we're all working together to get the Japs out of Indochina and China."

There was silence for a few tense moments. Then the general said, "You do not think it is important for us to know always where you are—for your safety?"

"No, sir, it is not. There is one favor I'd like to ask, however." It was an idea that had been growing in his mind, though he had never mentioned it to his men. "I want to bring them down here in a few weeks and fly them out from your airstrip."

"It is very dangerous now," Colonel Robert spoke up. "The Japs watch everything more closely."

"You use the airfield, don't you?"

"Yes. Liaison planes are sometimes based there."

"Do the Japs personally check every flight in and out?"

"No."

"Then we can work it out."

"I think you ought to wait until sometime after Tet," Colonel Robert suggested.

"What's that?" Reisman asked.

"The lunar New Year they celebrate here. It's a religious and social holiday. There are often portents of things to come. It falls late this year, toward the end of this month."

"Then I'll plan to be here with my men early in March," Reisman told them. "I'd better get to your signal room now, and see if the company store can deliver tomorrow night."

"May I suggest, Major," said Colonel Robert, "that this time you throw in a few mortars and machine guns—bazookas would be nice—and plenty of ammunition for everything. Our armaments generally are rather antiquated here."

Reisman contacted the radio shack at Kunming airfield and had Sam Kilgore brought in. He went on the air again after half an hour and, using the one-time pad, told Kilgore he was back with the natives who had all the opium and he needed another arms drop the following night. The lieutenant colonel signaled that he would comply, but added that he was eager to get his hands on the trade goods soon.

Reisman told him he had a plan in mind for early March delivery.

That night, Madeleine, passionate in her lovemaking, revealed the depth of her feelings for Reisman. "It is absurd, I know," she whispered. "I look for you constantly . . . always expect you . . . though we make no promises."

He rose up on his elbow and smoothed the long blonde hair back from her face. "How would you like to get out of here in a few weeks? Return to France by way of China?"

"With you?"

"As far as Kunming, anyway. I might be able to bring in a C-46 this time . . . or more than one L-5. I have the feeling things are going to explode down here soon. I want you somewhere safe."

"No, *Jean.* I must be here to take possession of my land again. I will not run away."

She drew his head down and pulled him tighter. His lips moved against her breasts as he told her his fantasies . . . Paris together . . . travel after the war . . . the States . . . all of the world . . .

Chapter 35

There was a festive air about the guerrilla camp that week of Tet. Peach-blossom branches and decorations appeared in the caves and bamboo-thatch structures. The training schedule was lightened. Some were given leave to go home for the holiday. Reisman and his men made a futile attempt to share the festival spirit.

"It is a time of rebirth," Mai explained. "Like Easter. People dress up, go home to their villages, visit their families, honor their ancestors. It is a time for settling debts and conflicts . . . for prayer and good wishes."

Reisman was with Ho, Giap and the Viet Minh executive when they listened to the broadcast of a New Year's message to his people from the Emperor Bao Dai. Reisman had almost forgotten that there was such a personage. The speech was in Viet-Namese and he could understand only part of it. Mai translated for him while Ho and his colleagues muttered imprecations at what they heard:

"France has suffered greatly to restore herself. This restoration is the forerunner of a period of peace and prosperity, through which all countries living under the protectorate of France will profit . . . We eagerly thank Admiral Jean Decoux, who is piloting the Indochinese ship through the world storm. Thanks to him, Indochina is enjoying conditions of peace and security."

When the speech was concluded, Reisman felt a sense of embarrassment for all of them. He shook his head and asked, rhetorically, "Where do they keep *him* locked up?"

Mai missed the humor of the remark and answered him seriously. "Usually in his palace at Hué, in Annam. The French have only let him come to Tonkin once in the last twelve years. He has never been to Cochinchina, though he married a girl from there."

"He sounds as if somebody wound him up and handed him the speech," commented Reisman. "It's all so obviously untrue, it can't be taken seriously."

"But in the rest of the world they will not know that," Vo Nguyen Giap spoke up angrily. "Maybe even in your country they will believe him."

"I don't think anybody in the U.S. knows what's going on here—or gives a damn!" Reisman told them.

With surprising gentleness, Ho Chi Minh said, "You must understand, *Jean,* that our so-called emperor has no political power at all, only a certain formal authority to which many in our country still give reverence. He is more French than Viet-Namese, having been raised and educated in France. I must say in his favor that he did try to introduce a few modern reforms into the government, but it has hardly made any difference in the lives of our people. I have never met him, but he is probably a nice enough young man. I feel sorry for him."

"Sorry! The man is a dilettante and a fool!" scoffed Giap. "His only noticeable duties are ceremonies we can do without, such as honoring the royal dead. He is a leech and a traitor. He debauches in wasteful, undeserved luxury while his people are enslaved, starved, arrested and killed. All he does is play tennis and golf, go hunting and wenching and driving expensive cars."

Reisman wondered what the Japanese thought of the speech. There had been a glaring lack of reference to the reality of their ever-threatening presence in Indochina. It seemed to him that they must have been consulted before allowing it to be broadcast—and must have approved it. Perhaps they were pleased by the lulling effect it might have on the French.

A few days after Tet, Reisman brought Ho Chi Minh a radio message he had ostensibly decoded late the night before from Lieutenant Colonel Kilgore. It ordered him to return with his men to Kunming as soon as possible. His superiors wanted a firsthand report on their operations in Indochina in order to assess how much further they might want to go with the mission.

Ho was depressed by the new orders. "You will give them a good report about us?" he prompted.

"Of course," Reisman assured him.

Kilgore's actual message had been an anxious query about the opium Reisman was supposedly piling up in "Mr. Tong's" camp, and requests to know how and when he planned to send the stuff across the border. Reisman had replied that he would bring it out himself and would advise him soon about how he was to help.

"I am very sorry to see you go, *Jean,*" said Ho sadly.

"We'll keep in touch by radio," Reisman told him. "I'll urge OSS to continue to drop you arms and supplies. I imagine they will either send me back or send in a new team."

"How will you cross the border—by foot to Ch'ing-Hsi? We will send a strong escort with you."

"No, we're going to fly out of Lang Son. It worked well last time."

"Very dangerous now."

"So is crossing the border—and this way is quicker. I'll ask Colonel Shidehara to drive us down in his truck. I think he'll be glad to see us go."

"No, he will not," Ho said. "He respects you and likes you. He has told me this."

"Then he will help," said Reisman confidently.

Two days later in the early afternoon, watching Reisman in his Colonial Army uniform and "Jimmy Lum" in his Japanese uniform load up the two motorcycles, Joe Wladislaw muttered nervously, "Jeez, you both look like spies now! Reminds me of old times!"

Reisman knew what he meant. He and the Dirty Dozen had parachuted into France in June wearing German army uniforms. He wondered what Wladislaw would say if he knew that "Jimmy Lum" was really Colonel Shidehara and came by his uniform legitimately. He had told none of the men about Kita; it seemed safer that way.

However, he had seen a look of hatred cross Baw San's face when Kita joined them wearing what they were told was a cover costume for the operation.

Reisman strapped a radio onto the luggage carrier. Backpacks containing his clothing, equipment and a few hand grenades were strapped on as saddlebags. His carbine and M-3 submachine gun were rolled into a poncho tied across the handlebars for quick access. He wore a holstered .45 and knife. Kita carried the generator and his personal duffel strapped to his motorcycle and, for once, was wearing a holstered pistol. Sergeant Bowren, Wladislaw, Sawyer and Baw San wore full field packs with all their clothing and gear and carried the same weapons as Reisman.

The plan was for him and Kita to drive the motorcycles along the footpaths and tracks as they had done before, down to Route 3 and then to Cao Bang where Kita's truck was hidden. Behind them, the men, accompanied by a Viet Minh escort, were to hike out as far as the village of Quang Uyen, to which Reisman and Kita would double back to pick them up in the truck. Viet Minh scouts and trail watchers all the way to Cao Bang had been alerted and would see that they passed through safely.

Except for a few private goodbyes—to Ho, to Giap and to Nguyen Thi Mai—there was little notice taken of their departure from camp. "Arrive unexpectedly . . . leave unnoticed," Reisman had reminded Ho when he had suggested a more ceremonial farewell.

In the farm shed at Cao Bang, Kita and Reisman loaded the truck with sacks of rice, corn, vegetables and three live pigs in crates, leaving space in the middle for the four men they would pick up. Kita had prepared an official cargo manifest in both Japanese and French, stating that he had purchased these agricultural products for the kitchen of the Kempitai in Lang Son. As usual, they stowed a motorcycle aboard near the tailgate and covered it with a tarpaulin.

Toward twilight they rendezvoused with Bowren, Wladislaw, Sawyer and Baw San west of Quang Uyen where a footpath came down out of the hills to Route 3. The truck was partly unloaded, the men climbed into the middle and first produce, then the snorting, squealing pigs and the motorcycle, were replaced, blocking the view of the interior from anyone who might peer into the back.

By the time they got back to the junction with Route 4 and headed south to Lang Son it was dark, which was what they preferred for this trip. At both French and Japanese checkpoints along the way and at the bridge over the Sông Ky Cung, the Kempitai colonel and French officer driving with him were familiar figures and were passed through quickly. They had stopped earlier to hide Kita's motorcycle in the brush off the road near Na Tuot.

On Rue des Japonaises, next to the cinema, Kita parked the truck and got out. Reisman slid over to take the wheel. Over his shoulder he called out softly to the men in back, "We're almost there. Hang on and keep quiet." To Kita, who came around to the driver's window, he said, "I'll park it here in about two hours, with the key under the front seat."

"Don't wait for me then. Get out of here fast," Kita said tensely. "If anything goes wrong, we've never met."

"Are you going to be at the Taiwa?"

"Yes. A few days, anyway."

"Thanks for all your help."

Kita stared at him sadly, then forced a smile. "You can buy me a drink after the war, my friend. It shouldn't be too long now. *Au revoir!*"

Carrying his duffel, he walked quickly across Boulevard Gallieni toward the Hotel Taiwa. Reisman turned left on the boulevard and took it all the way through town, then around the military hospital to the southern gate of the citadel on Avenue Clamorgan. Using his Colonial Army I.D., he was admitted. But before driving through the portal, he asked the sergeant of the guard to summon either Lieutenant Colonel Gauthier or Major Derrieu. It was Derrieu who arrived on the double and greeted him in astonishment.

"I've brought my own rations this time," Reisman said, dropping the tailgate and displaying the pigs, rice and vegetables.

Derrieu examined the interior with suspicion. "Perhaps we should take this to the commissariat across the street."

"Not yet."

"Your men? Have they come with you?"

Reisman called out loudly, "Everybody okay in there, Clyde? It's all right now. We're safe."

Bowren's voice boomed out, "Except for the stink, everything's just fine."

Derrieu and a detail of troops quickly removed the pigs and sacks and welcomed Reisman's men. There was little other activity in the interior compound; few troops were in evidence. The high walls of the citadel loomed above them. The empty parade ground stretched away into the darkness. Lights glowed from the windows of barracks and sheds.

"Can you find quarters for them here for a few days?" Reisman asked.

"Easily. They have a choice this week of at least eight hundred beds," Derrieu replied in a cynical voice. "Two *bataillons* of the Tonkinese *Tirailleurs* are away on maneuvers."

That startled Reisman. "Away! I thought your garrison was undermanned to start with. Outnumbered two to one by the Japs, you told me. And worried about what they were up to. It's a hell of a time to be playing war games!"

He could not help but think of the *Kriegsspiel* at Rennes where he and the Dirty Dozen had caught the Nazi generals by surprise.

"The odds are even better now," said Derrieu grimly. "Five or six to one . . . plus they have a great superiority in artillery and armor. Actually, we don't have any real tanks, what we have is a motorized detachment of the 5th Foreign Legion Regiment with a few Bren gun carriers from the First World War and some old half-tracked vehicles. Our total strength here is down to little more than fifteen hundred—officers, NCOs and troops. Our Nipponese guests meanwhile have moved in what appears to be an entire new division across the river."

Remembering what Baw San had learned in his monk's guise almost three months earlier, Reisman said, "That must be the 37th Division. They've been moving down from China."

Derrieu glanced at him sharply. "That's what you people wanted, isn't it? To take the pressure off the Chinese? I commend you on your intelligence network, Major."

"And I commend you people on your ability to slip two *bataillons* of sharpshooters past my observers. The Japs may be up to something, but I think you people are also. This is no time to be depleting your forces on some kind of phony maneuvers. Where have they gone?"

Major Derrieu would not rise to the bait. He replied with a wave of his arms in the vaguest terms: "To the north . . . to the west . . . away from the coast and the population centers. They will have room to maneuver in any eventuality." Then, as if suddenly just seeing it, he inquired, "May I ask you, *monsieur,* how you managed to obtain a Jap truck and your load of farm goods?"

"I stole it." Reisman glanced at his watch. It was 2100. "You keep the comestibles and look after my men. I've got an errand to run. Think you can set up a meeting with Colonel Robert in two hours?"

Derrieu threw up his hands in exasperation. Reisman hadn't answered his question, but he accepted in good grace what he had been given. "Of course. He will be pleased that you are here. General Lemonnier is also here again secretly. I am sure that he and Resident Auphelle will wish to see you." He too glanced at his watch. "Shall we say at 2300 at headquarters?"

Reisman left the radio, his packs and weapons, except for his sidearm, with his men. He drove the empty truck back to Rue des Japonaises and left it there without incident. Near the cinema he hired a pedicab to take him to the vicinity of Madeleine's house. The driver seemed unduly nervous. Reisman paid him with Indochinese money he had carried since Kunming, and the man kept looking around and seemed unusually anxious to depart. Only when the pedicab had gone and Reisman was sure he was not being followed, did he walk the short distance to Madeleine's house.

She and Philippe were both there. Madeleine, no longer concerned about discretion in the presence of her brother, embraced and kissed Reisman, but their exultation lasted only a moment. Reisman perceived an air of tension about them similar to the nervousness of the pedicab driver.

Philippe blurted out, "Have you heard what's happening?"

"Not the invasion again, please!" Reisman scoffed.

Philippe glared at him, but what he said next was chilling. "We've had an alert that the Japs will attack us, sometime between the eighth and tenth."

The anger and certainty in Philippe's voice cut through Reisman's attempt at derision and he felt a surge of adrenaline in his gut. Had he blundered by bringing his four men into a trap?

"Today's the eighth . . . ," he uttered tensely.

Yet he had seen nothing on the road, in the town or in the citadel to indicate either that the Japs were marshaling their forces for an immediate attack or that the French were aware of it and were preparing their defenses.

"I've just been with Major Derrieu at the citadel," he said. "He reported nothing. In fact, he told me that two *bataillons* of the *Tirailleurs* have been sent off somewhere on maneuvers."

Madeleine spoke up in anguish. "They are fools! Orders from Hanoi. Admiral Decoux and General Aymé and their clique do not take the warning seriously. The military disregards the civilian Resistance. Many in the Resistance will not obey General Mordant, whom de Gaulle has appointed to lead the Underground. There is no cooperation and no coordination. There is no secrecy. The Japs know everything. If they attack now we are lost."

"Only General Sabattier has gone on alert so far," Philippe broke in. "He has left Hanoi, without permission, to join his troops at his field headquarters."

"Where are you getting your intelligence?" Reisman demanded.

"I have a radio now here in the room where you had yours, *Jean,*" Philippe told him. "It is one of the sets your people dropped to us last time. I am in touch with our own network. The tip-off has come now from a high-ranking Annamite official in Hanoi who is a secret agent for our French Liaison Section in Calcutta."

"That's the same outfit that's been stirring everybody up about an invasion all these months, isn't it?" Reisman said disparagingly.

"This warning is not from Calcutta. It is from one of our key men in Hanoi."

"We have heard it also here in Lang Son," Madeleine declared in exasperation. "From friendly Annamites and Chinese tradesmen. They have seen the signs and they are very worried."

The awesome potentiality of what they were saying got through to him. "I'm on my way to French headquarters for a meeting. I'll find out more there," Reisman told them. "I've brought four of my men down from the hills just now, damn it. I'm going to try to bring in a plane from Kunming again and fly them out. I want you to come with us, Madeleine."

She stared at him in distress and then replied angrily, "How can you leave at a time like this? I have already told you I will not go. That is still my answer."

Reisman understood her courage and stubbornness, but also the futility of it. "If the Japs do attack here, there is little that we can do to stop them. I don't intend to have my men slaughtered for my mistake in bringing them here. As it is, I don't know if a plane will come—or get in and out safely. I can only try. I'd like to use your radio now."

Philippe turned to his sister. "It would be better if you went with him," he said. "It would be very bad if the Japs took you prisoner. This façade of gentility they present to us here is not their usual character in war. They are capable of terrible things."

"Then they must not be permitted to conquer us," Madeleine replied bitingly.

▪ ▪

Using the radio in their house, Reisman got through to Lieutenant Colonel Kilgore in Kunming. He signaled in code that he had brought the opium and wanted to be airlifted out in a C-46 from the Lang Son airstrip at dawn. Kilgore suggested a small liaison plane again. Reisman replied that his four men were coming out with him and the trade goods alone were too big for an L-5.

"Three L-5s or one C-46," he insisted.

Kilgore advised him to make contact the following night.

"Can't wait that long!" Reisman tapped out. He could almost feel his hands tightening around the man's throat. "Rumors here of imminent Jap attack."

Kilgore's response was even more infuriating. "No such info here. Against whom? Where?"

"Against the French. Here and throughout the country. Suggest you alert China Command and air groups for urgent support on signal."

"Contact tomorrow night," Kilgore repeated. "Best tentative pickup dawn tenth."

Chapter 36

There was none of the activity at French headquarters that Reisman had come to expect on the eve of a great battle. The only thing unusual was the late hour of the briefing that had brought General Lemonnier, Colonel Robert, Resident Auphelle and ten other officers from their homes and quarters to Robert's operations room in the building on Folie de Joux and Boulevard Gallieni.

They were waiting for him when he arrived with Philippe, who drove him there in the Renault he had been using for the last three months. Lemonnier greeted Reisman warmly, rising from his chair at the large conference table. Reisman saluted, then shook the general's extended hand and the hands of others who rose to greet him. Derrieu and Gauthier were there. Others were introduced. The mood was calm but there was an undercurrent of tension and uncertainty.

"I assume that you are here to fly out again," said Colonel Robert.

"Yes, sir."

"We cannot guarantee the security of the airfield. You have come at a very ominous and precarious time."

"It is after Tet, as you suggested."

"The signs and portents are not what I had hoped," Robert replied grimly. "What intelligence do you have on the Japs?"

Reisman glanced with disapproval at Major Derrieu, who had told him nothing earlier. "Only what I learned from Lieutenant Belfontaine and Madame Thibaut—that an attack is expected."

"Rumored, Major," corrected the colonel. "You and your men saw nothing on the way here?"

"No, sir."

"I understand from Derrieu that you came in a Jap truck. I admire your audacity . . . *courage sans peur.* Would you like to tell me how this was possible?"

"No, sir. I would like to confine my remarks to the reason I am here and then get out of your way."

Resident Auphelle, the highest authority in Lang Son, spoke up. "Major, we do not question your personal alliance with us. You have certainly given evidence of this by your arms drops. However, we must ask: If the Japanese attack us, will your country—your forces in China—come to our assistance?"

All eyes in the room turned on him, and Reisman had never felt so much on the spot. "I do not know, sir," he replied. "I do not formulate policy or give orders in that regard. I merely follow orders. I can only transmit your request in such an event and urge that my superiors comply with it."

"And if you were still here with us during an attack?" asked General Lemonnier.

Reisman smiled. "Then I would urge them even harder. Though I don't believe that would have much effect. I'm not even certain they will send a plane for my men and me. I have to contact Kunming again tomorrow night for confirmation."

Colonel Robert and General Lemonnier exchanged glances, then looked to Resident Auphelle, who nodded his approval for them to continue.

"Let us begin with your request, Major," said the colonel. "I will explain the problem to you and you must make the decision. I will also try to explain to you our situation here, so that you will convey it to your people in Kunming and Chungking, either by radio or in person."

Robert stood up and beckoned Reisman to a large wall map of

the Lang Son sector. He pointed to a spot across the Sông Ky Cung from the airfield, a site in the paddies and marshland enveloped on the west, south and east by a deep bend in the meandering river.

"The Jap position closest to the field is here . . . about eight hundred meters from the end of the runway," he said.

"Half a mile . . . with the river between," Reisman acknowledged.

"We must assume that they watch activities at the field, though I have no way of knowing how diligent they are," continued the colonel. "They would like us to believe, of course, that they are all-knowing and all-powerful."

"Are you willing to give us covering fire there, if necessary?" Reisman asked. "Just till we load, take off and get out of range, or if the plane is fired on as it comes in. Last time we were off the ground again in about two minutes from the time the plane touched down."

"Only if there is a prior attack upon us, Major," General Lemonnier called out from the table. "We have heard that General Sabattier has gone on alert, but we have had no such orders from the Governor General or the Commander-in-Chief. Quite the contrary. Our standing orders are to try to maintain the status quo. We do not wish to provoke them . . . only to defend ourselves, if necessary. We don't want to start a war just to cover your escape."

Reisman understood the general's need to be cautious, poised as he was on the edge of apocalypse. He asked, "What if there is only an assault against *us,* but no overt attack against you people?"

"That will be a difficult decision to make," answered the general. "Perhaps one that might best be left to the commander closest to the scene in the event such a thing happens."

Philippe, seated at the table next to Gauthier, broke in. "Sir . . . I would like that assignment. One weapons platoon with some heavy—"

"Lieutenant," Colonel Robert interrupted, "I don't believe General Lemonnier was calling for volunteers."

The general rose from the conference table and strode to the wall map. The holster of the big old revolver he wore slapped against his thigh. "What I mean," he said, jabbing a spot with his finger, "is that the commander here at Fort Brière de l'Isle will be in a better position to judge."

Only now did Reisman see clearly on the map that to the south and west of Lang Son there were three other fortified positions manned by the French, each within half a mile of the main citadel. There were also three large Jap installations marked north of the city across the Sông Ky Cung on either side of Route 4, plus the Jap position located within the bend of the river closest to the airfield.

"At the field itself, if I remember correctly," Lemonnier continued, moving his hand around on the map, "we have only the two Hotchkiss machine guns for antiaircraft defense." He moved his hand across the river to the Jap position. "They won't do you much good if an assault comes from here. Major Boery . . . you are in command at Fort Brière de l'Isle, are you not?" he asked, turning to the officers at the table.

A short, brawny man rose and said, "Yes, sir. Second *bataillon* of Third Regiment *Tirailleurs*. We are in good shape there with emplacements of the new 13.2 mm heavy machine guns Hanoi sent us. Also a battery of four 90 mm guns from the Fourth Regiment Artillery. Plus a small group of retired Legionnaires on call."

The general turned aside to Reisman for a moment and commented, "Would you believe, Major, that among them are Germans and Dutchmen, caught here by the war? Loyal Legionnaires to the core. Thoroughly courageous and dependable."

"Yes, I would believe it, sir," Reisman responded easily. "I've found there are as likely to be strange, unexpected friends in this war out here as there are unexpected enemies."

General Lemonnier pondered that a moment and then seemed to understand the complexities implied in Reisman's remark. "Ah, but to distinguish one from the other, that is always the difficulty," he said with a philosophical sigh. "For example, here we are discussing the possibility of imminent war with the sons of Nippon and yet Resident Auphelle, Colonel Robert and four of his staff are invited by Colonel Shizume to dine with him and a group of his officers tomorrow evening at the Hotel Taiwa. Would you call that friendly or unfriendly? Fortunately, they don't know I'm here or I too would be invited. To refuse would be considered by them to be a slap in the face and would only exacerbate the tensions between us."

The disclosure set off an alarm in Reisman's head. *Remember Pearl Harbor,* he thought to himself.

The general turned back to Major Boery and asked, "If they attack our American friends at the flying field, what would your response be?"

"I wouldn't wait for an attack, sir," Boery responded immediately.

"I'd send a weapons platoon along with them, as Lieutenant Belfontaine suggested—just in case. Then if there is any shooting at all from the Japs, sir, whether it is directed at us or the Americans, I think we will be justified in turning our guns on them."

General Lemonnier looked at Reisman. "Will that be satisfactory, Major?"

"Very much, sir."

"Knowing the great danger that exists, do you still wish to summon an aircraft?"

"Yes."

"Very well. Colonel Robert, please continue," the general said, returning to his seat at the table.

With Reisman standing opposite him at the map, Colonel Robert briefed him—and, more important, the officers of his command—on the disposition and condition of French and Japanese forces in Lang Son. Curiously enough, the citadel itself—bounded by thirteen-foot-high walls of brick, mud and stucco that ran about five hundred yards on four sides—was not the strongest French position, though the largest number of men were stationed within it.

The best defensive position was Fort Brière de l'Isle, less than half a mile south of the citadel, with concrete outworks facing the city, many small barracks set amidst dense vegetation, and behind it a group of hills, the Văn Miêu Rocks, rising to about 900 feet. To the west of the citadel and slightly north was the small Fort Gallieni, an uncompleted position manned by one platoon. To the southwest of the citadel was Fort Négrier, an outpost encampment with very little in the way of defensive works, manned by one platoon, an artillery battery and some retired Legionnaires.

Pointing across the Sông Ky Cung, Colonel Robert indicated the fixed positions and encampments of the Japanese. "Here there are three infantry regiments, reinforced by two artillery battalions and an armored battalion," he said. Addressing himself particularly to Reisman, he elaborated. "This Jap superiority in numbers is even greater than simply matching unit for unit. As you may be aware, Major, a French *bataillon* and regiment have less than half the personnel of those of other armies. The Japs therefore appear to outnumber us in the Lang Son area by about five or six to one.

"As for small and medium arms and ammunition," he continued, "we are in somewhat better shape than we were a few months ago, thanks to the armaments your OSS has dropped to us and thanks also to the Sten guns and other equipment our British friends have dropped here and elsewhere in the country. However, as you see, we are still heavily outnumbered in men and equipment."

"How about air support?" Reisman asked.

"Probably none whatsoever. Except for small flying fields such as ours, the Japs control all the airports. Our own combat aircraft hardly exist. In all of Indochina we might have fifteen old fighter planes and a few obsolete bombers." The colonel tapped the map. "Fix these positions in your mind, Major. Better still, we will provide you a copy of this map. If there is an attack, we will need immediate help from you Americans. Air-to-ground support. Pinpoint strafing and bombing. You have been bombing Indochina for some time anyway—their facilities *and* ours. Here you would have a new opportunity to contribute to their ultimate defeat. Tell that to your superiors in Kunming and Chungking."

"I will, sir," Reisman replied. Then, with as much tact as he could muster, he said, "I do have one question, though."

"What is that?"

"Why, under present conditions, have two *bataillons* left Lang Son on some sort of maneuvers?"

"Orders, Major. I'm simply following orders from my superiors, just as you do."

"But not on the eve of an attack, sir—if there is really going to be one."

Reisman saw anger rise in the colonel's face and knew he had overstepped himself. He glanced to the men at the table and saw there a suspended, uncomfortable silence, as if they all shared the same secret.

General Lemonnier called out, "Your assessment is correct, Major, but events have changed swiftly. Let us hope that they will not overtake us." Then, with a smile and a gentle note of challenge, he said, "I must assume that you have had considerable experience in the field."

"Yes, sir, I have."

"Then, may I ask, if you were the commanding general in the present situation, how would you begin this moment to handle it?"

"Are your two *bataillons* north of the bridge or somewhere to the south?"

"They are north and west."

"Then I would order them back here immediately. Instruct them to cross the river somewhere on the flanks by whatever means available, even if they have to swim. And I would get a demolitions team out there immediately to blow the bridge over the Sông Ky Cung, which the Japs have got to use to get at you."

There was again a nervous silence in the room. Finally the general responded. "Good advice . . . but our hands are tied," he said without sarcasm or reproach. "In Hanoi they want the two *bataillons* to be doing what they are doing now and I do not have the authority to recall them. As for the bridge . . . if we blow it up, then surely the sons of Nippon will take it as an act of war."

Yes they would, thought Reisman. And they might even cancel—though he hadn't the heart to taunt these men with such a reproach—they might even cancel the invitation to dinner tomorrow night!

Resident Auphelle spoke up: "Major, I have but one demand to make of you. I ask, in the name of the old and enduring alliance between the United States and France, that when you radio to Kunming you apprise them of the dangerous situation here and urge them to prepare immediately for tactical air support if it becomes necessary."

"I already have, sir," Reisman told him. "I did that earlier tonight when I contacted them."

When the briefing concluded, Reisman had Philippe drop him at the citadel so he could stay the night with his men rather than return with Philippe to Madeleine's house. Each had a transmitter-receiver now that could reach the other by voice. They agreed on a wavelength and times to contact each other. When not using the sets for other purposes they would keep tuned to each other.

Reisman and his men took over one of the barracks of the absent Tonkinese *Tirailleurs* and set up their radio there, plugged into the electrical mains. They each took a one-hour watch on the radio while the others slept, and the night passed without incident. There was still no general alert, no manning of the ramparts. In the morning the garrison in the citadel went about its daily routine as if there were no imminent threat of battle.

Major Derrieu came by the barracks to invite Reisman to breakfast in the officers' mess, located in the Hotel of the Three Marshals on Boulevard Gallieni. "Your sergeant and your men will be very welcome in the NCO's mess on Rue Gouttenègre," he said.

Reisman declined for himself and the men. Social dining was not what he had in mind for that morning. "We'll have coffee and K-rations here," he said, "and then we're going to reconnoiter our route of departure as far as the airfield and back. What's the situation this morning?"

"Nothing has changed," Derrieu replied.

He stayed with them while Reisman contacted Philippe on the radio. It was immediately apparent, when Phillipe relayed the newest intelligence from the Resistance network in Hanoi, that things were not as quiet in the rest of the country as they were in Lang Son. Philippe reported that General Aymé, the Commander-in-Chief, was worried about offending the Japanese and had tried to cancel the one alert order by General Sabattier to his regiments. However, Sabattier was already with his troops in the field and they were moving to the west and north. His action had been followed by General Alessandri, who was leading about three thousand of his troops out of a potential trap in their camp in the lowlands west of Hanoi. He was taking them across the Red River and Black River into the mountains toward Laos and China.

"They're dispersing, damn it!" Reisman said, staring at Derrieu indignantly. "They're not getting ready to fight. They're just getting the hell out of the way!"

"If the monkeys attack, there will be no help for us here," muttered Derrieu bitterly.

"Don't you think you ought to go on alert?" Reisman demanded.

"If it were up to me I would do what you proposed last night," Derrieu responded. "I would set charges under the bridge, just in case. I would get every gun out of the artillery park and emplace them close to the levees. I would empty the citadel and outposts—use them only to fall back on—and I would deploy our troops and firepower to cover the approach roads and river."

"Then why don't you?"

"Because I am not the commandant. And he, regrettably, as was made clear to us last night, is under the most stringent orders which he dares not violate."

"Sabattier and Alessandri apparently have."

"Then they will pay for it one way or another."

"Or be proven right."

Derrieu left the barracks to seek out General Lemonnier and relay the intelligence he had learned from the Resistance network as transmitted from Hanoi to Philippe.

Reisman, now wearing his combat fatigues, briefed the men on his plan for their departure. He hung on a wall the Lang Son map Colonel Robert had given him the night before. He showed them all the Japanese and French positions, Madeleine's house, the airfield and the various routes to get there. The best route would take them right past Fort Brière de l'Isle.

"We'll scout as far as the airfield, using the roads and trails this morning," he told them. "But keep in mind, if the shit hits the fan and we have to disperse, you can reach the airfield by stealing a boat on the river and taking it to the east side of this little island. The end of the runway is over the levee and across the paddies. It's about two kilometers from Madame Thibaut's house. We'll stop there this morning briefly and then we'll stage there tonight, if all goes well."

They left the citadel via the southern gate, as if going on a field exercise. Their combat fatigues were similar to those worn by the Colonial Army troops and drew no undue attention from military and civilians they passed. Their weapons were much newer and better, however. Each man carried a heavy amount of firepower—a carbine slung over the shoulder, a .45 and knife at the waist, grenades clipped to pack straps, and an M-3 submachine gun held in the hands, plus a few hundred rounds of ammunition. The load was heavy, but they didn't have far to go. They took turns with the radio and generator. Baw San and Ken Sawyer carried them on the first leg.

Sticking to the roads at first, they headed east toward the river. Theoretically, there were no Japs in that direction. They crossed the bottom of Avenue Clamorgan, passed the military hospital, crossed Boulevard Gallieni, passed the Catholic church, then cut through a patch of woods and came out south of the railroad station on Rue Gouttenègre. The levee was ahead of them and they took a trail through marshland to reach it. The weather was clear and warm, the paddies were wet and muddy from recent rains. When they topped the embankment of the Sông Ky Cung, Reisman stared across the water into the paddies and marshland on the other side. He passed his field glasses to the men so that they too could see the barracks, tents, guns and troops of the Japanese Imperial Army half a mile away.

Reisman could almost feel the anger and tension emanating from Baw San as he stared through the glasses and said, "I wish Ne Tin, San Thau and Ba Chit were here with all of the *hypenlas*. Our friends here would have nothing more to fear. We would take care of those across the river."

It was a wish that Reisman shared. To have with him here the Kachins beside whom he had fought in Burma would make a vast difference against the forces that loomed opposite them. The Kachins would not want to wait. They would want to attack silently and brutally in the night, despite the odds, slitting throats and cutting ears, avenging the ghosts of their murdered tribesmen. The French, playing by the courtesies of European diplomacy and obsolete rules of warfare, were at a terrible disadvantage.

Reisman led his patrol along the levee and then they dropped down onto the path to Madeleine's house. She dashed out from the veranda where she had been watching for them. She took Reisman's hand, but didn't embrace him. The men stared at her admiringly and were introduced. She greeted them warmly in English.

"What is happening?" she asked Reisman anxiously, speaking in French.

He replied in French. "Nothing. The town is very quiet. Do you have news from elsewhere?"

"The Japanese ambassador and other officials will call on Governor General Decoux this afternoon in Hanoi."

Again the alarm went off in Reisman's head. It was what the Japanese ambassador had been doing in Washington on December 7, 1941. "Has it been announced publicly?" he asked.

"I don't know. Philippe is at the radio now. Our agents are watching every move." To the men, in English, Madeleine said graciously, "Come in, please. All of you."

She wanted to prepare food for them, but Reisman told her they could only stay a few minutes. They would return in the evening, if all went well. He went to the room where Philippe was monitoring the radio.

"No general alert yet?" he asked.

"No. Only Sabattier and Alessandri. The Japs are up to something, but nobody knows what. Obviously, it is something at the highest levels."

"And what are the French up to, Philippe?" Reisman asked pointedly. "The two *bataillons* that left from here? The regiments of Sabattier and Alessandri? Are they all running for the hills, as it seems? Or deploying for some secret operation of their own?"

Philippe fiddled with the dials and didn't look at Reisman. "It is as General Lemonnier and Colonel Robert told us last night," he said. "The *bataillons* are engaged in a maneuver ordered from Hanoi. Sabattier and Alessandri are either acting against orders or they are part of those maneuvers too. I do not know, *Jean*."

Reisman did not believe him. "We're going to scout the airfield now and then return to the citadel," he said. "I'll contact Kunming from here tonight. If there is an attack before we return, you must take Madeleine to Fort Brière de l'Isle. We will join you there. Meanwhile, see if you can talk her into flying out with us."

Philippe looked up at him then. "Very well," he said. "I hope that she will go. But she is stubborn."

Madeleine was waiting for Reisman in the hallway. They had only a moment to be alone, to embrace and kiss. He repeated what he had told her brother, but she shook her head. "I will go to the fort . . . shoot a gun if necessary . . . but I will not leave Indochina," she said adamantly.

"Think about it," Reisman told her softly. "*Au revoir* for now."

He rejoined his men, waiting for him awkwardly in the living room, and they left the house. They took a footpath south that ran between the levee and the railroad tracks. In the near distance, west of the tracks and across a road, Reisman saw the lush wooded mound of the Văn Miêu Rocks rising out of the paddies around Fort Brière de l'Isle, and beyond it more paddies, stands of nipa and mangrove and the land beginning to climb again to wooded highlands. They crossed the tracks and road to scout the eastern perimeter of the defensive outerworks, then returned to the paths closer to the levee and continued south.

Looking back, Reisman caught sight of the walls of the citadel half a mile away. There was very little traffic of any sort on the road and few people about. They avoided settlements and saw only an occasional peasant and bullock working in the fields.

"Seems quiet enough, Major," Sergeant Bowren observed, "but I don't like the feel of it. There ought to be more activity. It's like everybody knows something we don't know."

When they rounded the deep bend of the Sông Ky Cung they saw ahead of them the four small buildings of the airfield, the control tower and the radio shack, and the dirt-and-grass landing strip. There was one small liaison plane tied down near a shed, and no sign of personnel or activity. It was a lonely-looking place. They moved along the levee of what was now the eastern bank of the meandering river and Reisman pointed out where the airplane had come in last time to take him out. Then he showed them the little island in the river opposite the end of the runway, just in case they had to come there by boat.

"If it stays quiet like this for another day," he said, "by tomorrow this time we should be in Kunming."

It was what he wanted to do. But he was also disturbed by a

gnawing thought. If there was a battle here, would he feel as if he had run away?

They hiked back via the same trails as far as the Văn Miêu Rocks, then cut directly west behind Fort Brière de l'Isle and north around its western flank on footpaths through the paddies. Between Fort Négrier and the citadel they paused in the woods. Sawyer cranked the generator and Reisman contacted Philippe on the voice radio. There was nothing new.

They marched on to the citadel, but instead of entering it at the southern gate, Reisman led his men all around the exterior so that they would be thoroughly familiar with all routes of approach and departure. Halfway along the western wall they passed between the military cemetery and the *Mā Qủi* gate, which in Tonkinese means *ghost.* Reisman surveyed the emptiness of the surrounding area. Rice paddies edged up to rising tiers of wooded hills on the west, and it was the same on the south, below the route they had patrolled. He had come down through here in the darkness with Sergeant Filmore and Philippe Belfontaine four months earlier.

"That's probably the best way to get out of the fort fast if we have to," he told the men, pointing to the closed *Mā Qủi* gate.

They turned the northwest corner of the citadel and hiked east beside the northern wall, moving back into town. Nobody hailed them from the rampart, but there were guards at the northern gate with whom they exchanged greetings. Reisman looked north for a moment, wondering what might be happening in the rooms of the Hotel Taiwa and on the Rue des Japonaises, but he did not want to tempt fate by taking the men in that direction. He led them instead across Avenue Clamorgan, through a side street past the artillery park and market place, onto Boulevard Gallieni, then south past the Hotel of the Three Marshals, the Foreign Legion headquarters, the Customs House, the Catholic church, and then west again around the military hospital, across Avenue Clamorgan to the southern gate.

The town was quiet. Not empty, but surely less populated with people going about their business as usual. The entire round trip had taken about two hours. They had covered a little more than four miles and made a careful reconnaissance of routes of departure.

Chapter 37

The first alarm was the sound of a horse galloping across the interior compound from the southern gate. It was 1600 hours when Reisman heard it. He, Baw San, Bowren and Wladislaw were walking along a road back to their barracks, where Sawyer was monitoring the radio. They had been looking over the defensive strongpoints within the citadel and had just left General Lemonnier's unofficial command post at the southeast bastion.

In the near distance, they saw the horseman, heard the shouting of orders and saw squads of soldiers dashing through the compound carrying weapons to their positions. The horseman veered his course and bore down on them. He brought his mount to a halt and Reisman recognized the thin, mustached officer in khaki work uniform, blue garrison cap and riding boots. It was Captain Paul Vernières of the Tonkin *Tirailleurs,* whom he had met at the briefing the night before.

"The Japs are out there maneuvering," he called out with remarkable calm.

His brown stallion pawed the ground, snorted and bobbed its head as if it had picked up a greater urgency of events. Reisman grabbed a strap of the harness to keep man and beast from galloping off.

"Where are they?" he asked anxiously.

"All over the place," answered the captain.

He related that he had been riding his horse through town and was startled to see a Jap infantry platoon positioning themselves near the Residency on Boulevard Gallieni, and then another platoon near the railroad station on Rue Gouttenègre.

"Did they try to stop you? Any hostile action?"

"No. Just taking up positions. However, they don't usually deploy their troops or play their little games on this side of the river."

While riding back to the citadel he had seen yet another Jap platoon maneuvering through a muddy ricefield about two hundred meters south of the wall. "I'm putting my men on alert," he declared. "To hell with the brass in Hanoi."

Reisman let go of the harness. "Better let General Lemonnier know about it."

"I'm on my way to him now," said Vernières, and galloped off.

Reisman hurried to their radio in the barracks, his mind racing with the options of what must be done. He was determined that they would not be trapped there. Their assignment had been to train guerrillas and help plan marauding operations. They had not been sent into Indochina to get caught in a nineteenth-century battle precipitated by political chicanery.

"Lieutenant Belfontaine came on a couple of minutes ago," Ken Sawyer said, making way for Reisman at the transmitter. "Wants you to contact him."

He got through to Philippe immediately. "Any sign of the Japs over there?" Reisman asked anxiously.

"No. Madeleine is watching the roads and the river, and she has seen nothing," Philippe reported.

Reisman told him about the Jap troop movements in the town and near the citadel.

"Are you under attack?" Philippe exclaimed.

"No shooting yet."

"Have there been any contacts? Any demands?"

"Not that I know of," Reisman replied. Captain Vernières apparently had ridden right past them without interference. "But there's that dinner scheduled at the Taiwa in a couple of hours."

"I have other news," Philippe continued. "From our people in

Hanoi. The Japanese ambassador and consul general were observed entering Admiral Decoux's headquarters and then leaving approximately one hour later. There has been no announcement of what was discussed, but the rumors are that the Japs are now demanding full military, administrative and economic control of the country."

Then what was happening there in Lang Son, Reisman realized, was directly related to events in Hanoi. The Japanese Imperial Army was preparing to take over, no matter what the French colonial administration decided.

"You and Madeleine stay put for now," he advised Philippe, "but get ready to evacuate. Pack the basics to take to Fort Brière . . . and don't move without the radio. Madeleine will have to help with the generator."

"We'll move it in the Renault," said Philippe.

Earlier in the day, Reisman had been surprised to learn from Major Derrieu that the only communication between the citadel and the outer forts was by visual semaphore and courier. There was only the main transmitter-receiver in the citadel, which was used to keep in touch with Hanoi and other fortress towns. He considered eavesdropping now on the Japs' radio network, then decided it would be futile. Since only Baw San among them would understand even a little of any voice transmissions they might intercept, it didn't seem worth the effort.

Instead, even though it was much earlier than his usual contact time, he tuned to the proper wavelength and started tapping out his signal to Kunming. It took a few minutes until one of the operators there finally heard him and acknowledged. Reisman reported the urgency of his situation and requested that Sam Kilgore and Burt Webley, the pilot who had flown him out last time, be brought to the radio.

He didn't wait for them, however, but started transmitting in code the full details of his plan. He wanted Webley to come in at night this time, at 0200, in a C-46. If Webley was not checked out in a C-46, he wanted him to get a pilot who was and to guide him in. He wanted them to load aboard parachutes for five jumpers and a bunch of flares. Then he carefully detailed his request for air-to-ground support and tactical air strikes. Using Colonel Robert's map, he gave the grid coordinates of the airfield, the citadel and the outlying forts, and then the Jap positions, with special emphasis on the one closest to the airfield.

Webley came on first, sitting beside the Morse code operator in

Kunming: "I'll do better in L-5. You must light and secure runway."

"L-5 not big enough," Reisman responded. "Need one C-46 or three L-5s."

There was a pause while Webley mulled that over, then responded: "Only two available now. We'll round trip twice. Procedure as before. Stage Ch'ing-Hsi. You signal me to come in. Pray for clear night."

"Affirmative . . . 0200. Split chutes and flares between planes. Sam there?"

Lieutenant Colonel Kilgore came on: "Negative on request for fighter-bomber support for French. You know policy."

"Need cover for us. Repeat. Our guys need air support to get out. Also trade goods."

"Stuff there?"

"Big load."

"Night air strikes very difficult . . . seems unnecessary . . . but will try for it."

They signed off and Reisman briefed the men on the radio exchange.

"What are the chutes and flares for, Major?" Sergeant Bowren asked.

"Just an idea for now."

"Another crazy volunteer job, Major?" Wladislaw asked.

Reisman heard the challenge and cynicism in Wladislaw's voice, but he responded to it without rancor. "Yes . . . it might take only one volunteer, Joe . . . or maybe all of us. We won't know till the time comes . . . if it does." He didn't even try to explain further, for it was, as he had said, just a contingency idea. To Bowren, he said, "You and the men stay here at the radio. I'm going out for another look around."

"What do we do if there's an attack while you're gone, Major?"

"Get over to General Lemonnier's position and help them. I'll join you there."

He strode quickly through the interior compound of the citadel, looking for Colonel Robert, Lieutenant Colonel Gauthier or Major Derrieu. It became apparent to him that only part of the garrison had gone on alert. Many officers and men had not taken heed of Captain Vernières's warning. They had finished their day's duties and were preparing for mess call. Reisman saw soldiers leaving the fort to take their evening pleasures in the town as if nothing was happening. He wondered if maybe this too was part of the French plan at the highest levels: to continue to behave as if nothing was happening—and then maybe nothing would happen. Was it possible that Vernières had overreacted to the Jap maneuvers?

Reisman found Lieutenant Colonel Gauthier about to leave his quarters. He stared at the man in disbelief. Gauthier was dressed in ceremonial uniform: light blue pants with gold stripe, high-collared white jacket with gold epaulets, and on the collar the gold embroidered anchors of the *marsouin*.

"Don't you know what's happening!" Reisman exclaimed.

Gauthier tugged at the neck of his jacket. "Vernières has sounded the alarm. He's put his company on alert. Some of the others have joined them. That's all right."

"How about the rest of you?" Reisman demanded. "Nobody seems to be in charge. Nobody is mounting a coordinated defense. Soldiers are leaving the fort."

"General Lemonnier will act strongly when it is necessary to act," replied Gauthier calmly. "My orders are to dress for dinner and attend. I must leave now."

"Where's Colonel Robert?"

"At his home on Avenue Folie de Joux, I imagine . . . also dressing for dinner. We will meet at the Residency with M. Auphelle and the other officers and go on to the Taiwa together."

"I'm coming with you."

"You can't. You are not invited. An American major dining with Colonel Shizume? What a scandal!" said Gauthier, laughing.

"Just as far as the Residency. I want to see what's happening out there."

Gauthier insisted that, except for his sidearm, Reisman was not to carry his weapons through town now. He himself was unarmed. Reisman left his carbine, M-3 and grenades with the Senegalese sergeant of the guard at the northern gate. He and Gauthier departed the citadel together on foot at about 1800 hours. They looked rather incongruous together—Reisman in his combat fatigues, Gauthier in his ceremonial uniform—strolling along Avenue Clamorgan as the brightness of late afternoon dimmed.

It was quiet. There was no sign of Jap troops, little in the way of civilian traffic. They turned right on Rue Emmerich, and just as they passed the north side of the marketplace and came out on Boulevard Gallieni, Reisman saw the Jap platoon: about fifty riflemen, noncoms and officers just standing around in a loose formation near the Residency.

"Stay back now. Don't come with me," ordered Gauthier. "I don't know what they're up to, but it doesn't look very hostile yet."

Reisman fell back into Rue Emmerich. He stood in the shadow of a marketplace wall and watched Gauthier cross the boulevard and enter the Residency without interference. The Jap troops, fully armed and in combat dress, merely loitered, as if waiting for a signal. Across Rue Emmerich from where Reisman stood was the back of the French headquarters building. The entrance was on Folie de Joux, the next street over. It was obscured from his view, but he assumed that the guards on duty there had been alerted and were observing the Japanese soldiers. He slipped into the empty marketplace and watched the street, the soldiers, the Residency. The late afternoon was darkening but there was still good light.

In about ten minutes he saw Resident Auphelle, Colonel Robert, Lieutenant Colonel Gauthier and two other light colonels leave the Residency and turn north on Boulevard Gallieni to walk the two blocks to the Hotel Taiwa. Except for General Lemonnier, whose presence in the citadel was unknown to the Japs, these were the highest civilian and military officials in Lang Son. The Japanese officers and soldiers in the street paid no attention to the Frenchmen—neither the courtesy of a salute nor any gesture of hostility.

Knowing that they were on the way to the Hotel Taiwa, Reisman wondered if Colonel Kita Shidehara would also be at the formal reception. It seemed logical that he would. Did he know now what his compatriots were up to? Or had he known all along, despite his statements to the contrary, his Hamlet-like moods, his philosophical concerns about survival?

Reisman returned to the citadel via the way he had come. The guards at the north gate were on alert, the detail had been increased, but no extraordinary preparations had been made. He retrieved his weapons from the Senegalese sergeant and headed back to the barracks where his men waited.

In preparing for battle, there always seemed to him to be a logical procession of things to be done. As few oversights and wish-I-hads as possible. One did the best one could with the intelligence, personnel and matériel at hand and that was that. Things didn't always go the way one planned, but he had been lucky as well as careful so far. The unexpected could only be dealt with as it came up. To do nothing was worse than doing the wrong thing.

By the time he entered the barracks he had made his choices. They would split up. He would send Bowren, Wladislaw and Sawyer ahead to Fort Brière de l'Isle. He would ask Philippe and Madeleine to join them there immediately with their radio. He and Baw San would remain a while longer and try to reconnoiter the town again.

Major Derrieu was waiting for him anxiously in the barracks. "Do you know what is happening out there?" he asked. The usual cigarette was dangling from his lips, but his voice was strained.

Reisman told him what he had just observed.

"Poor Gauthier. It is a social engagement I would not care to attend," muttered Derrieu. He had reports now, he said, confirming that there were other Jap platoons maneuvering in the city and out in the rice paddies. "As for what it all means, I still don't know. They haven't come across the bridge in force yet. It's as if they are teasing us . . . testing us to see if we get mad and shoot someone. Maybe they want a provocation to do what they intend to do anyway."

Reisman told him about Philippe's intelligence from Hanoi: that the Japanese ambassador had apparently presented severe demands to Admiral Decoux.

"The Resistance network seems to know more than the army does at the moment," complained Derrieu.

"How are you gathering your intelligence?" Reisman asked.

"We have agents in the city and surrounding area. Annamites. Some across the river near the Jap bases."

"Do they report by radio?"

"You joke, *monsieur!* We have no such luxuries, as you well know. They must report in person or send messengers."

"Can you get me a couple of peasant outfits . . . *cu-naos* and straw hats?" Reisman asked. He pointed to Baw San. "One to fit him and the other me."

Baw San understood immediately and looked very pleased.

Derrieu looked bemused. "Yes, I think so," he answered. "What will you do?"

Dirty work, Reisman said to himself, as recommended by the philosopher Sun Tzu. "See if I can pass for an Annamite in the dark," he answered.

Derrieu looked at him warily.

"I need them right away," Reisman pressed. "Please, Major."

"Yes, of course. There are some of these fellows working around the citadel."

▪ ▪

It was 1915 hours, soon after full darkness, that Reisman and his men left the citadel via the south gate. They were a curious-looking patrol: three heavily armed infantrymen with full field equipment and two *can slua tau* padding along in their midst on a trail directly south from the citadel. They went a hundred meters into the darkness before they stopped, hunkered down in the mud off the footpath and listened. The night was cool. There was no moon. The sky was partly cloudy to the south and west, clear and starlit to the northeast, toward China. Perhaps an omen, thought Reisman. Webley would need decent weather to fly in. But that was later. Time enough to think about it then. Nothing to be done about it now.

There was no sign of the Jap patrol that Captain Vernières had seen maneuvering two hundred meters off to the southwest in the late afternoon. If they were still out there in the paddies, they were holding their positions in the muck and maintaining their silence. Reisman could only hope that he and Baw San would not stir them up when they made their way in that direction, following part of the route they had explored that morning.

There was a last-minute briefing and then Bowren, Wladislaw and Sawyer, moving awkwardly but silently in stooped positions, cut east across a field to pick up the trail to Fort Brière de l'Isle. They knew what they had to do if something prevented Reisman and Baw San from joining them by 2400. They disappeared within half a minute. Then he and Baw San rose up and moved swiftly along a path to the west.

Reisman felt unexpectedly comfortable in the *cu-nao,* conical straw hat and sandals, though the clothes stank of someone else's sweat and dirt. His face was darkened with mud, his feet with the muck he was moving through. Baw San looked quite natural as a *can slua tau.* Beneath his loose jacket, each man carried a sidearm, knife and grenades, and the hope that there would be no need to use them. The field wireless had been left with Major Derrieu to augment temporarily the bigger, stationary equipment in the fort's communications room.

They cut between the citadel and the wooded rise at the southwest corner, then along the footpath between the cemetery and *Mā Qủi* gate and around the north wall in the same way they had reconnoitered that morning. It was peaceful—no sounds of war, no signs of Japanese troops—until they walked east of the fort into the city streets, slipped into the empty marketplace and saw the Jap platoon on Boulevard Gallieni near the Residency. They were deployed in the same way they had been when Reisman had seen them there an hour and a half earlier. Just hanging around. No hostile action against military or civilians going past them. Vehicle and pedestrian traffic on Boulevard Gallieni, as on the other streets, was light and unhurried, perhaps no different from what it was on any other Friday evening.

To avoid the platoon, Reisman and Baw San backtracked along Rue Emmerich. Their eventual intent was to reconnoiter in the area of the Hotel Taiwa. But they had to go there in a roundabout way now. At the corner of Rue Emmerich and Avenue Clamorgan they passed groups of off-duty NCOs and soldiers of the Colonial Army and Foreign Legion piling into Café Lili, oblivious to the tensions and drama being played out short distances away. There were no blackout regulations, so the lights from buildings, vehicles and lampposts dimly illuminated the streets.

They turned north, shuffling along in slumped, weary postures, their shabby exteriors blending with the native pedestrians in the streets. The Kempitai station loomed ahead at the top of Avenue Clamorgan, the sight of it both odious and intimidating. There was no activity at the entrance, nothing unusual happening in Rue des Tailleurs, the street that ran past the southern flank of the building. They turned into Rue des Tailleurs going east, continued one block and stared like country tourists at the bulk of the Hotel Taiwa across the way, partially screened by sidewalk trees, its windows shaded but glowing. They passed another café, loitered along the sidewalk beside the courthouse, then crossed the street to reconnoiter all around the hotel.

Just as they passed the Taiwa's frontage on Boulevard Gallieni and were turning into Rue des Japonaises, two Jap army trucks speeding down from the north braked in front of the hotel and squads of soldiers piled out and formed a skirmish line around the entrance. Reisman grabbed Baw San's arm, they reversed their direction, crossed to the east side of the boulevard and lingered there along the wall of a building.

Within seconds, Reisman saw all the French dinner guests—Auphelle, Robert, Gauthier and the two light colonels—their arms and legs bound with ropes, being dragged from the hotel by soldiers on either side of them and heaved unceremoniously into the beds of the trucks. He felt a surge of rage that made him want to rush forward—but he tensed and remained still. There was nothing he could do in that moment to prevent what was happening. To rush at the trucks and attempt a rescue would be suicidal madness. He watched the trucks make a U-turn and speed off to the north. The Jap troops went into a combat patrol formation and started down the boulevard.

Baw San's hand tightened on Reisman's shoulder. "Look, *Duwa* John," he whispered tensely. "There is Jimmy Lum."

In the moment of seeing him, Reisman was forced to explain the reality in low, quick words of warning: "He's not Jimmy Lum. He's an officer of the Kempitai."

He picked Kita Shidehara out of a group of Jap officers and soldiers who had come out of the hotel. Orders were given and most of the group, weapons at the ready, fanned out to the south and west. Kita stood on the sidewalk in conversation with a short, brawny officer.

Baw San moved his head closer to Reisman. Their deep, face-shadowing palm-leaf hats almost touched. Baw San's eyes narrowed, his expression was confused. "Why did he help us?"

"It's too complicated to explain now," Reisman answered quickly.

He stared across the street at Kita and his companion, then scanned the surrounding area. The boulevard was emptying of traffic and pedestrians, as if cut off at both ends. There were no Europeans in sight. Natives were scurrying out of the way of the soldiers sweeping through the streets. Kita and his companion were alone, the centerpieces of a fearful, growing vacuum that Reisman suddenly realized he might fill. The idea became even more tempting when the other officer bowed stiffly and started to walk back toward the hotel entrance.

"We're going to try to take him with us," Reisman said calmly. "I want to let him recognize us. After that, we improvise. Be wary, Baw San . . . but don't attack first. Let's go."

They started across the boulevard in the stooped, shuffling postures they had assumed with their clothes. Colonel Shidehara saw them coming and shouted at them in French: "*Allez-vous en!* Clear the streets, you two! Go home immediately and stay there!"

Reisman raised his head slightly as he and Baw San kept walking closer. The other Jap officer had halted and turned back to see what the shouting was about.

"*Allez-vous en! Cochons!*" shouted Kita. Then his eyes went wide, he muttered "Oh, shit!", stepped off the curb and darted toward them. "*Allez-vous en! Cochons!*" he repeated.

Kita had recognized them and was now playing to the audience of one Jap officer about fifty feet behind him. All other action had swept away from the immediate vicinity, but now bursts of gunfire could be heard in the distance.

Kita grabbed each of them roughly by the arm, hustled them back across the boulevard and muttered in English, "The game is over, John! They changed the rules on us! Get out of here fast!"

"What's happening?" Reisman spewed out angrily. "Quickly now. No bullshit!"

He resisted the urge to draw his automatic, to start moving Kita back to the citadel, to shoot the other officer if he interfered—and Kita if he resisted.

"They are taking over everything, the damned fools!" Kita answered hurriedly. "The whole damn country. Peacefully if they can—by force if necessary."

It was *they* again, not *we.* Kita Shidehara was distancing himself from the actions of his cohorts.

"That was very peaceful the way you took care of your dinner guests!" Reisman accused.

"They weren't my guests, goddammit, you self-righteous son-of-a-bitch!" Kita exploded at him. "Colonel Shizume is just keeping them out of trouble for a while. He doesn't want any heroics."

"Why didn't you warn me?" Reisman demanded.

"Because I didn't know," Kita answered in quick defense. "I suspected *something,* just as you did, but I didn't know *what* until this morning. I thought you'd be long gone to Kunming. And good riddance. You make things tough for me, Major." He glared at him, then flicked his eyes in a nervous signal. "Is that idiot Sousoki still there behind me?"

Reisman glanced quickly and saw the other Jap officer staring at them. "Yes."

"Do nothing to alarm him," Kita said with remarkable aplomb. "He's the head of the local Kempitai. My subordinate . . . but disapproving and suspicious of my *modus operandi.* You will notice by the contortions of his ape-like face that Captain Sousoki is questioning the nature and intent of our dialogue and that he is getting very angry. If he could hear me speaking American he would wonder why I am using this low-caste tongue which he does not understand."

Reisman had to believe him and trust him one step further. "Come with us now," he urged. "You can get out if you want."

"To Kunming?"

"Yes."

It would be a coup to bring him in, Reisman knew.

"To turn me over to your friends? Don't be ridiculous. I'll play out the game here."

Reisman glanced again toward Captain Sousoki, whose hand had gone to the flap of his pistol holster. "Your friend is getting very nervous. We'd better get out of here," he whispered tensely. "0130 at the airstrip, if you change your mind. Same place as before. Get rid of that uniform first."

There was a guttural shout in Japanese from Captain Sousoki across the quiet, empty boulevard. He started to walk in their direction. Kita turned and shouted something forceful in Japanese that halted the man in his tracks and sent him back to the hotel.

"Go quickly now!" Kita said to Reisman and Baw San. "*Au revoir!* I doubt that I will join you. I shall now be expected, by people like Sousoki, to shoot guns and make loud noises. It is possible that an offended Frenchman may shout back at me—or even shoot! *Bonne chance!* Now get the hell out of here."

Reisman and Baw San padded away quickly toward Rue des Tailleurs. They were about to turn the corner when they heard the roar of truck motors bearing down on them from the north. They hugged the wall of the courthouse and saw Japanese army trucks laden with troops speed past on Boulevard Gallieni. Some turned off into the cross streets, others continued south. There were the screeching sounds of trucks braking, heavy boots running, sporadic gunshots and yelling. Then a more ominous sound from a few blocks north and east: tank engines, treads clanking.

Reisman and Baw San ducked into a short connecting street to Avenue Folie de Joux, dashed west to Avenue Clamorgan, crossed it and ran south. In every street, they saw Jap patrols stopping unarmed soldiers and European civilians, piling them into trucks, herding others along the streets under guard. Civilian natives ran to get out of the way and were allowed through. Despite the sporadic gunfire he had heard, Reisman saw no dead or wounded. Perhaps they too had been heaved into the trucks. Crossing the opening to Rue Emmerich, he stared toward Café Lili and saw the unarmed soldiers being rousted out, hands on their heads.

Scurrying between shadows, the walls of buildings, doorways, trees, bushes, vehicles, anything that momentarily hid them, Reisman and Baw San sped south toward the citadel while from all directions came those other soldiers and European civilians who had also managed to escape the Japanese dragnet.

The walls of the citadel loomed ahead. A new growl of heavy engines in the middle distance rose above the near sounds of running feet and the shouted challenges and responses at the north gate. Reisman looked north to the top of the avenue, then east through the cross street to Boulevard Gallieni. Jap troops had not yet shown themselves there, but he could see the shapes of their slowly moving armor, trucks and artillery caissons passing through the light-stabbed darkness only blocks away.

He and Baw San revealed their identities at the portal, were recognized and passed through at 2030 hours. They ran toward the barracks where they had left their uniforms and weapons and Major Derrieu working their radio. All around them, at last, officers and men were preparing for an attack.

Chapter 38

The crackle of radio static, then Philippe's voice speaking excitedly in French, hit Reisman's ears as he and Baw San sprinted into the barracks:

"Admiral Decoux has been arrested! Generals Aymé and Mordant and their staffs are taken prisoner! All French officials, military and civil, are stripped of authority and arrested!"

Major Derrieu sat at the radio, transfixed by Philippe's voice relaying bulletins from the underground network in Hanoi. A cluster of sub-officers and NCOs, armed and dressed in battle fatigues, paid anxious attention close by. The room looked like a command post. It struck Reisman that, except for General Lemonnier, Derrieu might be one of the highest-ranking officers left in Lang Son.

The major looked up and did a double take before he realized who the dirt-covered Annamites were. He briefed Reisman as he got up from the radio table: "Belfontaine and his sister are at Fort Brière. No attack there yet. Your men are with him."

Reisman took the microphone. "Philippe, this is John Reisman. I've just come in from reconnaissance. It's happening here too."

He related the treachery he had witnessed outside the Taiwa Hotel and the comb-out of soldiers and European civilians under way in the city. Derrieu and his men were also hearing the details for the first time.

"There is no sign of them here yet," Philippe said on the radio. "What will you do?"

"Contact Kunming. Try to move up the time of departure. Then join you as quickly as we can."

Even as he spoke, they heard the first booms of Japanese artillery batteries, the screams of shells coming in and the shattering explosions within the citadel.

It was 2100 hours.

Within moments, the officers and NCOs dispersed to their positions and Major Derrieu rushed to the southeast bastion to relay to General Lemonnier the reports from Reisman and Philippe and to seek orders for the defense of the citadel.

Reisman and Baw San were left alone at the radio. Even as he started tapping out his signal to Kunming, they heard the first answering barrage of the French 60 mm and 81 mm mortars and the deeper boom of the 75 mm cannon located in a trench just opposite the northern gate. The defenders' guns were much too few and antiquated, Reisman knew—there were even some 57 mm navy guns that had been converted into army guns mounted on crinoline gun carriages. They were also at a tactical disadvantage, having to fire a trajectory blindly from behind the walls, while all the enemy had to do to wreak havoc was point their barrels and fire haphazardly into the fort. He hoped that spotters had gotten up on the ramparts and were directing the return fire at the muzzle flashes of the enemy guns and at concentrations of troops and armor revealed by the illumination of the town.

Unaccountably, the electricity from the power station on Rue Gouttenègre had not been cut. Reisman was transmitting his signal to Kunming on the wireless plugged into a socket in the barracks wall. As he encoded his messages and tapped at the Morse key he was torn between wanting to go out to fight and staying at the radio. But there was really no choice. He had to stay, even if the barracks itself was hit.

The operator in Kunming was alert for him this time, and Lieutenant Colonel Kilgore—already there in the radio shack to coordinate the night's work—was receiving and responding to Reisman's messages within minutes.

"We're under Jap attack in Lang Son citadel. Moving out to secondary position, then airfield immediately. Need planes at 2300 instead of 0200."

"Two L-5s already airborne to Ch'ing-Hsi. Contact there in one hour. Same procedure as before. Will not . . . repeat, not fly in if field is not secure."

"Agree. Need help here. Air strikes."

Kilgore responded with a maddening, "See what can do . . . you know policy about helping French."

Reisman wanted to rage at him across the three hundred fifty miles that separated them. It was that very policy that incited in him such angry conflict. Nine months earlier he, Bowren and the Dirty Dozen had dived out of an airplane, ordered to help France. That same night and in the months afterward tens of thousands of Americans had been killed and maimed to help France. And long before then, in the years of the Nazi occupation, there had been mission after mission when he had been ordered in on his own, and had gone gladly.

"It's for us—American troops—and your cargo!" he tapped out angrily on the key.

Except for Kilgore's expectation that he was bringing out a huge cache of opium, Reisman didn't discount the possibility that he might just as soon leave him to his fate with the Japs, knowing what he did about Kilgore's criminal involvement with Tai Li. Reisman believed that the mythical shipment of opium would swing the balance. He knew that the lieutenant colonel had the kind of dirty influence, all the way up to Tai Li, to make things happen that rules and regulations and official policy would otherwise foreclose. He had already demonstrated that he could commandeer aircraft and commit them to devious and murderous tasks.

"Contact me later," Kilgore responded, and he signed off abruptly.

The din of exploding shells and now machine gun and small arms fire filled the fortress compound. Baw San squatted at one of the barracks windows, watching what was happening outside and calmly waiting for Reisman's orders.

Major Derrieu burst in, having dodged his way back across the compound from General Lemmonier's command post. He reported that the first attacks by Jap infantry had been repulsed at the north and south gates, both barred, locked and strung with barbed wire now. There had been no attack against the closed *Mã Qủi* gate in the west wall, but the sounds of battle further to the west revealed that Fort Gallieni and Fort Négrier were also under attack.

"General Lemonnier has personally taken charge of the defense of the southeast bastion of the citadel," Derrieu related. "Captain Vernières has rallied his men to the northwest bastion."

"How about the rest of the country?" Reisman asked.

"As we feared," Derrieu said. "Open broadcasts have been heard in the main communications room. Dong Dang, Ha-Giang and fortress towns on the frontier and throughout the country report that they too are under attack. We must have immediate air support from you Americans. General Lemonnier urges that you radio your people for help."

The concussion of Jap mortar rounds close by sent Reisman, Derrieu and Baw San diving to the floor. Windows shattered, walls cracked and ceiling plaster fell.

"I've just done it!" Reisman shouted, getting up and brushing himself off. "Now we wait and hope. What's your garrison strength right now?"

Derrieu reported that as many as two hundred of the citadel's soldiers might have been captured by the Japs or trapped outside the walls before the attack began. There were now also dead and wounded from the battle, but he had no figures. The enemy was being held back by cannon and mortar rounds lobbed over the battlements, directed by spotters on the ramparts, and by concentrated machine-gun and small-arms fire. The few old tanks, half tracks and Bren gun carriers were dispersed through the interior grounds, ready to counterattack if the gates and walls were breached.

Reisman had to face the fact that there was only the slimmest chance that any support at all would be sent from Allied forces in China. It seemed to him that now was the right moment to broach the plan he had been nurturing for many weeks.

"Will you accept help from the Viet-Namese?" he blurted out.

Derrieu looked at him in confusion. "Of course. There are many in the Colonial Army."

"A guerrilla group," Reisman hurried on to explain. "Irregulars . . . Viet Minh . . . men and women who would like to see you leave as well as the Japs."

He knew that Ho Chi Minh's thousand and more guerrillas were ready, though Ho was still protesting that he could not commit them to any real action. In addition, Reisman believed that there were thousands more of the Viet Minh dispersed elsewhere, even if they were ill equipped—maybe hundreds of them in and around Lang Son. If they rose as allies now, how could the French later deny them their rightful say in their own land, a share bought with their own blood against the Japanese?

Derrieu's response was spoken against the background explosions of sporadic shelling, the crackle of machine guns and small arms fire. The confusion on his face was supplanted by an expression of almost amused comprehension. "I always thought that was what you were doing up in the hills," he said amiably. "Can you reach them by radio?"

"I'll try."

"Then do it. I would accept help from the devil himself now—and bargain with him later. I will be with the general. Please come there and let us know."

He left and Reisman tuned to the Pac Bo wavelength. The short range allowed him to use the voice microphone.

"Bring Ho or Giap to the radio immediately," he told the girl on duty.

A few minutes later, Nguyen Thi Mai came on. She said that neither Ho nor Giap was available. Her voice was calm, as if she had no knowledge of what was happening. Reisman told her that the Japs had attacked the French at Lang Son and elsewhere, that he and his men might have a difficult time getting out, and that he wanted help from the Viet Minh.

"Is anything happening in your area?" he asked.

"No. It is very quiet," Mai responded, sounding curiously aloof from the catastrophe he had described to her.

"I want you to bring Ho or Giap to the radio right away," Reisman demanded. "It's time for action, to repay all we've done for you. A Viet Minh attack against the Japs would relieve the pressure and give us time to get out."

But were the logistics feasible, he wondered. If a thousand trained Viets from Pac Bo force-marched the seventy-five miles down their secret trails, it would take as long as two days, maybe a day and a half at best. Any who could beg, borrow or steal trucks would arrive in a few hours. But if Ho signaled his cadre in the Lang Son area, they could begin to harass the Japs from the rear immediately.

"They cannot come to the radio," Mai repeated. "They are not in camp."

"Who's in charge?" He didn't wait for an answer, but rushed on to outline the paths of action he wanted the Viet Minh to take, starting with raising the Lang Son cadres to infiltrate and attack the Japs—people like those who had lit the flares and provided the security for him and Filmore when they had flown out of the air strip almost four months ago. "We've got no time to waste. You hear the guns, don't you? They're shelling the citadel and they've got troops ready to storm the walls."

"Yes, I hear. I am sorry."

"Who's in charge?"

"Only Uncle Ho and General Giap for such matters."

"Where are they? Can you get to them?"

"No. I cannot. They are away on a mission of great importance."

"Nothing is as important as this, goddammit!" Reisman raged.

That they would do nothing at all was a possibility that had not occurred to him. He softened his voice. Any action at all would be appreciated, he told her, and he would see to it that they were substantially rewarded afterward with more arms and supplies.

"I am truly sorry, John," Mai replied through the static and the noise of battle. "I will try to find Uncle Ho. Goodbye."

He called to her to speak again, but there was no response either from her or from the Viet radio operator on duty. Yet they had not signed off. From the sounds he heard when he switched back and forth to the receive position he could tell that they were still tuned to him.

Now Reisman was assailed by a thought that he previously had put out of his mind. *What was happening was not fresh news to the Viet Minh.* Ho Chi Minh and Vo Nguyen Giap might have been standing right there next to Nguyen Thi Mai even as Reisman pleaded for help.

Ho must have known what would happen. He must have known because his spies and agents were everywhere, as he had demonstrated in the past whenever it had been to his advantage to do so. He must have known about the coming Japanese attack for days if not weeks, surely before the day that Reisman, his men and Colonel Shidehara had left Pac Bo for Lang Son. He must have known—even if Kita had not—because the Viet Minh spy network was as ubiquitous as Tai Li's. They were everywhere!

A great rage began to grow in him—against Ho Chi Minh, against Giap and Mai and the Viet Minh and all they stood for. But he could not stay there any longer, raging or begging. He turned off the set, pulled the plug and reeled in the antenna.

"We've got to move out now, Baw San . . . join the others," he called out.

They took off the *cu-naos,* hats and sandals and changed into their own uniforms. They bundled the Viet clothes and tied them to their packs, in case they might be needed again. Carrying all their weapons and gear, plus the radio and generator strapped into rucksacks, they made their way across the interior grounds through the gunfire to General Lemonnier's command post.

Just as they reached it, the Japanese barrage lifted. All firing from outside the citadel ceased, then the return fire from the French. The night was suddenly still and it left the men with General Lemonnier in the southeast bastion uncertain of how to proceed. The general himself continued to direct the process of digging in for a fight and the deployment of guns and troops. It occurred to Reisman, as he searched out Major Derrieu, that the Japs might not really want to destroy the fort, for then they might have to rebuild it for themselves. It seemed more likely that they merely wanted to harass the defenders into giving up.

He located Derrieu in the communications room. He was leaning over a telephone switchboard where a soldier was trying futilely to make contact with any one of the few phones located in various military and civilian offices elsewhere in Lang Son.

"It is useless," said Derrieu, looking up at Reisman. "They have left the electricity alone, because they also need it. But they have cut even the few phones we had."

Reisman took him aside and told Derrieu of his futile attempt to reach the man he described only as a "guerrilla leader."

Derrieu looked at him impatiently. "Which one is it?" he demanded. "Nguyen Ai-Quôc?"

Reisman found himself torn with conflicting loyalties and promises. Finally, he answered, "This one calls himself Ho Chi Minh."

It registered no recognition at all with the intelligence officer. "I didn't think they would come," he muttered. "They make their own deals with the Japs . . . the treacherous bastards."

"I will try again later," Reisman said apologetically. "From Fort Brière de l'Isle. I've got to get my men out, and Madeleine Thibaut if I can convince her to leave with us. There are two L-5s that will try to pick us up at your field."

Derrieu looked at him with great concern. "Your chances there, *mon ami,* are about as good as ours here in the citadel," he said, shaking his head. "Come . . . first a word to the general . . . then I will go with you to the *Mā Qúi* gate. It will be the best way for you to try to slip away now."

But as they approached General Lemonnier, a runner came dashing into the command post to report to him and they too heard his message:

"There is a Jap officer at the north gate, sir, under a flag of truce. He demands the surrender of the citadel."

"Did he ask for me by name?" asked Lemonnier.

"No, sir. Just whoever the ranking officer is."

The general looked around, spotted Derrieu and asked, "Would you care to deal with it, Major?"

"Of course. What shall I tell him, sir?"

"I think a simple no will suffice." Then, looking at Reisman, "Can we expect help soon from your people in China, Major?"

"I have asked my base repeatedly during these last two days, General. I have given them all the grid coordinates of Japanese and French positions. My last contact was approximately half an hour ago. But I still do not know what they will do."

"I thank you for trying," said Lemmonier.

"I will continue to try," Reisman told him. And then, startling himself with a rare expression of his own anger and frustration, he said, "If we make it to Kunming later tonight I will do all I can from there, even if I have to put a gun to someone's head."

The general looked startled himself at that, but then his expression softened to admiration and he laughed. "It seems to be in fashion these days," he said. *"Bonne chance!"*

To find out at first hand what was happening, Reisman and Baw San temporarily put off their departure from the citadel and accompanied Major Derrieu to the north gate. They left their radio, generator and packs in the southeast bastion.

The time was 2145, three quarters of an hour since the Japanese attack had begun.

Derrieu refused to let them go through the gate with him, so they climbed to a place on the parapet from where they could watch the scene outside the walls.

It was a stark and bitter tableau they saw in the headlights of enemy trucks and armored cars. Derrieu was halted by a Jap officer speaking poor French through a mobile loudspeaker system mounted on a truck behind him. In the light beams, Reisman recognized Captain Sousoki of the Kempitai. His imperious voice filled the air and rebounded off the citadel walls. A moment later, Resident Auphelle and Colonel Robert, still tied with ropes, were brought forward into the light.

"Your commanding officers will now order you to surrender!" Sousoki proclaimed.

Auphelle and Robert stood silent and defenseless in the glare of the lights while Captain Sousoki made his demand twice more.

Finally, the tall, slender, white-haired Resident raised his head and shouted, *"Vive la France!"*

Colonel Robert, still dressed in the disheveled splendor of his ceremonial uniform, yelled toward Major Derrieu and beyond him to the men at the portal and high on the battlements:

"Stand fast! *Vive la Coloniale!*"

At that, the two Frenchmen were roughly hauled back and driven away. Derrieu, his features contorted with rage, turned slowly and went back into the citadel, his back stiffened as if he expected to receive a fusillade at any moment. The gate was slammed shut and locked behind him by the soldiers on duty there. Reisman and Baw San joined him as he made his way quickly across the dark interior grounds to report to General Lemonnier in the southeast bastion.

There was never any thought of surrender. Five minutes later the Japanese guns opened fire again.

From the parapet atop the western wall above the *Mā Qủi* gate, Major Derrieu pointed their way out.

To the west there were distant flashes and sounds of battle at the small outposts of Fort Négrier and Fort Gallieni, but there were no Jap troops attacking the citadel on this side. The enemy was concentrating its attacks along the northern flank and the southeastern strongpoint. They were aiming artillery rounds to blast open the gates and breach the walls. Mortar rounds were being lobbed into the interior grounds to explode upon any blind target they chanced to hit—clusters of soldiers; civilian men, women and children; barracks, sheds, vehicles, gun emplacements. Colonial soldiers and Legionnaires defending the battlements on the north, east and south were being killed and wounded by shellfire and bursts of machine guns and rifle fire out of the darkness.

Reisman knew that it was ultimately a hopeless fight. It was only a matter of time before the gates and walls were breached. Yet here on the western side of the citadel, the enemy was more than a quarter of a mile away and facing in the opposite direction, attacking Fort Négrier and Fort Gallieni. There was a narrow corridor of hills, woods, rice paddies and the military cemetery separating the Japs from the quiet ground outside the *Má Qủi* gate. Reisman and Baw San had to use the battle itself to cover their escape from the citadel and make their rendezvous at Fort Brière de l'Isle and the airfield.

"You must go now!" said Major Derrieu, leading the way down to the gate.

They shook hands while soldiers unlocked the tall iron bars. They stared at each other with that terrible feeling of not knowing what the next moment would bring, not knowing if they would see each other again.

"I thank you for all your help, *Jean,*" Derrieu blurted out finally. "Go now, quickly! You too, Corporal!"

"*Au revoir,* Raoul," Reisman said. "I will do all within my power to send help. We shall not forget any of you here."

Reisman and Baw San slipped away through the barely opened gate, which was then locked again behind them. They were watched over for less than a minute by riflemen on the battlement, then they were screened from the enemy by the distractions of the fighting. They headed south on the familiar footpaths through the paddies, always alert that others might also be using them. As they approached Fort Brière de l'Isle they heard new sounds of battle and saw that it too was now under attack. Reisman realized that enemy forces must have bypassed the citadel through the easternmost streets of Lang Son and then come down unopposed on the road parallel to the railroad and river. They were fanning out through the dry land north and east of Fort Brière de l'Isle, but staying out of the paddies on the west through which he and Baw San were making their way.

A burst of machine gun fire dug into the footpath ahead, sliced into the wet paddies on either side of them and sent them diving into the muck. They were within a hundred yards of the nearest concrete outerwork and its flanking heavy machine guns. Major Boery obviously had his western flank prepared for infiltrators. Hugging an embankment, Baw San turned the generator and Reisman radioed ahead to Philippe to tell the soldiers on the west flank to hold their fire and let them through.

They were inside the defensive emplacements by 2300.

Reisman found Philippe and his wireless in Major Boery's bunker. The radio was still operating off the mains, and Reisman wondered again at the paradox of power and lights still working, the latter masked by hasty blackout coverings at windows and doorways.

Madeleine was in the aid station, Philippe told him, helping with the wounded. Sergeant Bowren, Joe Wladislaw and Ken Sawyer had gone up to help at a forward firing position on the northern flank. Reisman sent Baw San to call them in, and to stop in the aid station to tell Madeleine they were there and were preparing to move out soon.

"Will she come with me?" he asked Philippe.

"I don't know," he answered, turning away from his wireless for a moment. "She says she does not want special treatment, that there are many other French women here, as there are in the town and the citadel. God knows what the Japs will do to them."

Reisman felt a terrible moment of anguish, but then quickly thrust himself into what he had to do. Before he saw her again, he needed some way to convince her that she had to try to leave with them—though there was no assurance that any of them would be able to get out.

It was already past the time he had intended to contact Burt Webley at Ch'ing-Hsi. He could not ask him to fly in until he knew for certain that the airstrip was still open. Though enemy attacks appeared to be concentrated only against French strongpoints, he was concerned that Jap troops might also start ranging toward the flying field, and he had to go there himself to find out.

But first he set up his own radio to contact Kunming again, while Philippe continued to monitor the Resistance network from Hanoi. The garrison there was now also fighting off an assault, and there were many open broadcasts from other fortress towns under attack throughout the country, each pouring out its desperate condition to anyone listening, and pleading for help.

A refrain had begun that was to be repeated over and over again in the next hours: "Air support! Where are the Americans?"

The crackle of Philippe's open receiver mixed with the tapping of Reisman's Morse key, and each was on a sub-level of sound against the booms and explosions of the opposing artillery and the chattering gunfire of battle.

As Reisman tapped out his signal to Kunming, Major Boery and two aides reentered the command post after inspecting his forward positions. The husky young commander was grimy with the smoke and dirt of battle, but he exuded strength and confidence, even exhilaration.

He strode up close, waited for a break in Reisman's transmitting, and said, "Please tell your base what is happening here."

Reisman tapped out, "Stand by . . . ," and held his hand poised above the key while Boery spoke on as if he were briefing and trying to influence the military and political hierarchy that he himself could not reach, conveying to them the most salient details of his own observations: that his soldiers were fighting bravely and strongly, though heavily outnumbered and outgunned; that the morale of the men and women within Fort Brière de l'Isle remained high; that his battery of 90 mm guns and well-placed machine guns were making the enemy pay heavily with dead and wounded for their frontal attacks.

Reisman listened closely to Boery's words, then began sending out in English as much as he could of it, not even bothering to encode it. The commander concluded with, "We're holding them back for the moment, but they outnumber us tremendously. We must have help from your American air force in China. Tactical strikes now . . . supplies later."

Lieutenant Colonel Kilgore, through his operator in the Kunming airfield radio shack, chose to respond in code: "Use cipher goddammit. Use cipher. Your request for tactical air strikes is being considered by higher authorities. I haven't the power to call them in myself."

When Reisman read the message to Major Boery, the commander gave a weary shrug, his eyes looked heavenward and he murmured bitterly to the crackling wireless, *"Merci, monsieur . . . merci."* But, with genuine gratitude, he said to Reisman, "You have tried, *Jean. Merci.*"

Seething with anger and frustration, but using the cipher again, Reisman signaled to Kilgore, "I don't believe you! You're going to lose your trade goods!"

Kilgore answered: "Counting on you. Webley waiting. Contact. Procedure and orders as before."

Reisman changed the wavelength and found Burt Webley waiting for his contact at the Ch'ing-Hsi airfield. Webley reported that he and the other pilot were ready to fly the two L-5s across the frontier as soon as Reisman radioed from the Lang Son airfield that they could land safely.

"We're leaving for there now," signaled Reisman. "Listen for contact in one hour."

It was Philippe who figured out a way to make Madeleine leave willingly with Reisman and his men. He, Reisman and Major Boery were ready for her when she finally came into the command post. Baw San had already returned with Bowren, Sawyer and Wladislaw, and the escort platoon was being made up under Philippe's command.

Madeleine saw Reisman across the room, packing up the radio. She started toward him and he held his arms out to her, but the stocky figure of Major Boery stepped between them and shunted her aside.

"Madame Thibaut . . . Madeleine . . . there is little time," he said solemnly. "I have a mission of the utmost importance for you to undertake."

Madeleine looked at him startled, but answered, "Of course."

"It is very dangerous," Boery continued in an anxious voice.

"What is it?"

"I must ask you to fly out with the Americans to China."

Madeleine started to protest, but he stopped her.

"I must order you to do it, Madame. You are not in the army, of course, but you have been for some years active in the Resistance and you are accustomed to being given difficult orders and following them without question. You must do this for us." Boery nodded toward Reisman and his men. "They, after all, are Americans—but you are a Frenchwoman. We need someone like you to report in person to the French mission in Kunming to relate the full story of what is happening here in Lang Son and all over Indochina. Perhaps you personally will be able to sway our Allies to send help."

Madeleine stared at him uncertainly a few moments, then looked toward Reisman, who managed to be busy doing something else at that moment. "Very well, *mon commandant,*" she finally said. "I will do as you ask."

Major Boery gripped her shoulders affectionately and said, "Good. You must go now. Get your things. There is no time to lose." He called out to Reisman, "Major, you must take Madame Thibaut with you."

"Yes, of course. As you wish," Reisman concurred with a straight face. "We're ready to scout out the airfield."

"I have only one valise," said Madeleine. "May I take it?"

"Of course."

She left them to retrieve her leather case, and Boery briefed Reisman on the best way out. "All the Jap forces seem to be concentrated against our northern and eastern flanks," he said. "When you leave here you must first go west, then south and around them to reach the field."

A few minutes later, under cover of the battle and the night, Reisman, his four men, Madeleine, Philippe and an escort of twenty soldiers left Fort Brière de l'Isle, walking to the west. They quickly turned south on footpaths through the paddies, went around the back of the Văn Miêu Rocks, then east to the levee of the Sông Ky Cung. They could hear and see the battle raging to the north of them, but it was quiet where they were.

At the river, they stole two rowboats. Reisman, Madeleine and Baw San got into one; Bowren, Sawyer and Wladislaw into the other, and they pushed both boats out into the dark, quiet river and rowed toward the island near the north end of the runway. Philippe and his soldiers moved along the levee to cover them, though neither section could see the other. Each carried a radio and generator to talk to the other, but they were to break silence only in the direst circumstances.

Philippe's soldiers were prepared to light the flares to mark the north end of the runway when the L-5s came in and would provide covering fire if necessary. The two separate sections had arranged a whistle signal and the password *"marsouin"* so that they would not shoot each other in the dark.

It was past 2400 hours when the two boats drew together in the narrow channel between the island and the airstrip side of the river. Philippe came down over the levee and gave the recognition signal. The boats were rowed in close. He reported that the airfield was abandoned. The battle had apparently drawn all personnel elsewhere.

They left the boats and went over the levee onto the flying field side, where everyone crouched down close to the embankment. The distant sounds and flashes of battle reached them from Fort Brière de l'Isle and the citadel, but the immediate vicinity of the flying field was silent and deserted, as Philippe had said.

Reisman set up the wireless, Sawyer cranked the generator, and Reisman radioed to Burt Webley in Ch'ing-Hsi to take off. The procedure was to be the same as last time. Reisman would start using a homing signal on the radio in half an hour and then switch to voice communication when the two L-5s approached the field. Estimated time of arrival was less than an hour.

"Sounds too easy!" muttered Joe Wladislaw when the transmission was completed.

"I have a favor to ask," Reisman said, confirming Wladislaw's suspicion. He glanced at Madeleine reassuringly, then back to the men. "Madeleine and I will not fly out on the first trip. We'll wait for one of the planes to come back for us."

He looked toward her again, saw that she was watching him expectantly, waiting for the explanation. The men waited with expressions of wariness and uncertainty. He began to tell them why he had asked for parachute packs and flares to be placed aboard the planes . . . and then hesitated, looking toward Madeleine, realizing that he was about to reveal something that he still would have preferred to keep from her. Yet it couldn't be helped now. There was no more time or room left for shadings of purpose and subtle deception.

He turned to Sergeant Bowren. "Clyde, I want you and Baw San to board one L-5, Wladislaw and Sawyer the other. Instead of flying across the frontier to Ch'ing-Hsi, I want you to jump into the Viet Minh camp at Pac Bo and bring the guerrillas to the relief of Lang Son—even if you have to put a gun to Ho Chi Minh's head."

"I'll be a son-of-a—" Wladislaw started to protest, then glanced at Madeleine and stopped in mid-phrase.

But Madeleine was not even aware that Wladislaw had started to mouth an obscenity. She had been caught by the words *Viet Minh* and *guerrillas,* as Reisman had thought she might. "What do you have to do with those people?" she asked softly, staring at him.

"We have made contact with them," he answered vaguely. "It is possible they can help us, or be forced to, if necessary. Major Derrieu and I spoke about it. Now we must try."

"Oh . . . I see," she murmured.

But the look of puzzlement, even injury, on her face, meant to Reisman that even if she did understand she still reserved approval. He turned back to the men and continued his instructions: "I'll give the pilots the compass coordinates and tell them how to signal the Viet Minh radio operators as they approach Pac Bo. Then they will light the drop zone with the flares and you guys bail out."

"That's one hell of a shot in the dark, isn't it, Major?" Sergeant Bowren challenged unexpectedly.

"Less difficult than our little affair at Rennes last year," Reisman declared.

"What about you, Major?" Sawyer demanded.

"I'll follow you when one of the planes returns," Reisman continued. "I'll jump into Pac Bo after you, and Madeleine will fly on to Ch'ing-Hsi, then Kunming. Our chances with the Viets will be a lot better than if we're stuck here."

"They'd be better still in China," muttered Wladislaw.

"Is this one of those volunteer assignments, Major?" Sawyer asked cynically.

"Of course," Reisman answered with equal cynicism.

"I will do it, *Duwa* John!" Baw San spoke up eagerly.

Reisman waited for the others. It *was* a volunteer job, just like coming to China had been, and he would never fault them for turning him down cold.

"Okay," said Bowren. "I don't think anything is going to help the French here, Major, but I'm willing to try."

Reisman peered hard through the darkness at Wladislaw and Sawyer. "If you two don't want to do it, one of you will have to give up your flight reservation to the lady and wait here with me for a couple of hours."

"Shit, Major, I ain't been nothing but a volunteer since I set eyes on you," Sawyer spoke up. "Might as well keep going."

Wladislaw looked around, shrugged and said, "Okay . . . I'm in."

With a catch in his voice, Reisman said, "Thank you. Now all we need are airplanes."

He used his field glasses to scan the full compass range around them through the darkness and up into the sky. The weather was holding; a cool, easy wind from the south that would allow the two L-5s to land on the best heading; clouds drifting very slowly across a starlit sky, clearer to the north and east. But the aircraft would also be visible to the Japs, just as Webley's plane had been four months earlier when it had landed and taken off without interference.

Reisman stared for a few minutes toward the Jap position less than half a mile away on the other side of the Sông Ky Cung. There were some lights visible there, but that was all. He hoped that the troops who had been stationed there were now occupied in the attacks elsewhere.

Going over details in the next minutes, trying to cover everything—even the possibility of Kita Shidehara turning up—he asked Baw San to give Madeleine his Viet-Namese costume. Baw San could get another one in Pac Bo if he needed it. Reisman still had the costume he had worn earlier.

When it was time to send the homing signal to the L-5s in flight, he asked Madeleine to turn the generator. It was she who would have to do it later when they were alone together, and she demonstrated now that she was quite capable of doing the tiring work. Reisman did not dare let himself think of her as anything more than a member of the evacuation party, equal to the others in his concerns.

The minutes dragged anxiously. Ten of Philippe's soldiers disappeared into the darkness to take up positions on either side of the landing strip, ready to light flares to guide the pilots down. The other ten—some equipped with the recently acquired Sten and M-3 submachine guns, the rest with their standard short-barreled Lebel rifles, and each carrying hand grenades—set up a defense perimeter centered on the one machine gun they had been able to take with them from Fort Brière de l'Isle.

They heard the two planes before they saw them, their engines grinding above the intermittent sounds of the fighting closer to Lang Son. Reisman switched to voice transmission and there was a hurried exchange between him and Burt Webley. The second pilot listened, followed instructions, but did not intrude on the transmissions. Philippe dashed across the landing strip and gave his men the order to light the flares.

Everything went swiftly. When the L-5s touched down, and even as they coninued to roll out their landing and turn around, Reisman ran after them with his four men. Webley had the door open when he reached his plane. Bowren and Baw San scrambled in as Reisman gave the remarkably calm pilot the new instructions to fly the men to Pac Bo. He understood the purpose immediately and agreed.

"If it's still secure here, one of you fly back for me!" Reisman shouted. "If we don't make radio contact, don't come back! I'll get out some other way!"

He glanced over to the other plane and saw Sawyer and Wladislaw clamber aboard. The door closed and the aircraft began its takeoff run. He shouted once more to Webley: "We need air-ground support here. Bombing and strafing! Tell them in Kunming!"

Webley gave him the thumbs-up sign. Reisman closed the door, darted out of the way and watched the plane race down the strip and rise into the air to join the other one. He watched the two silhouettes of moving darkness a few seconds, then turned away and ran to the levee, where Madeleine was waiting with the radio. He felt exhilarated that the men had gotten off, that the operation had gone this well so far.

Behind him, along the runway, the *marsouins* smothered the flares. He heard Philippe call to them and to those on the defense perimeter to fall back to the levee. He wondered if the little island in the stream would be a better place for them all to wait the next long hour till one of the planes returned. Should they ferry across on the boats? Or stay where they were?

Just as he reached Madeleine he heard the pom-pom-pom sounds of an antiaircraft battery across the river and then the chatter of machine guns. Fear clutched at his guts. He looked at the sky and saw tracers stabbing like fiery daggers, reaching for the almost invisible climbing silhouettes. Then one of the aircraft exploded into a flaming mass. Transfixed in horror, Reisman watched it arc through the darkness and crash into the marshland northeast of the Jap position, while the other L-5 dipped and turned in evasive action, climbed higher and disappeared into the night.

He had no time to grieve, only a moment to wonder who he had sent to their deaths—which two of his men, which pilot? He felt the tight grasp of Madeleine's hand on his arm and turned to look at her. Her face was filled with anguish. He thrust away the thought that she might have been aboard the funeral pyre. Then there was a burst of gunfire from east of the runway. He pushed Madeleine to the ground and turned as *marsouins* crumpled on the runway, while others dashed across the narrow road that paralleled it and splashed into the paddies that separated them from the levee.

A Jap patrol must have crossed the Sông Ky Cung northeast of them, Reisman realized, to come around on the flank of the main battles and occupy the deserted airfield. He heard Philippe rallying his men into a new defense perimeter just off the north end of the road and ran toward them over the muddy ground. Heavy return fire from the French machine gun, Stens and M-3s kept the unseen attackers from crossing the runway. Philippe was close to the machine gun, directing its fire. The soldiers carrying his radio and generator were crouched next to him, aiming their submachine guns into the darkness. Then the gunfire from the other side ceased, its sources still hidden.

The possibility that Kita Shidehara might have betrayed them crossed Reisman's mind, but he rejected it instantly. Kita could have taken him easily or killed him hours ago in front of the Hotel Taiwa.

"Vite, allez!" Philippe called hoarsely to Reisman in the sudden silence. "Get Madeleine away from here! Try to make it back to Fort Brière!"

Unwilling to run from yet another battle, Reisman hesitated. Yet he knew that Philippe was right. Even if they were not under attack, there was no reason to stay there any longer. He could not ask the surviving pilot to bring his plane in again.

Philippe repeated the order. It was now more a plea. "*Vite, allez!* Do not stay here with us, *Jean.* We will cover for you and Madeleine and then fall back."

Reisman stared at him another moment, torn with conflict. But he had to agree. "*D'accord!* We will go on the river. Don't risk too much here."

He turned away, not wanting even to say *au revoir,* and he ran back to where Madeleine was waiting alone, crouched against the levee with his radio and generator and her valise. She had stuffed the *cu-nao* from Baw San into the case on top of her few things. The deep conical hat covered her blonde hair. Reisman's peasant costume was still tied to his knapsack. With an ache in his heart, he wondered if it was Baw San's plane that had been shot down.

"We must move," he said to Madeleine. "Philippe will come after us." Any moment he expected the firefight to begin again. Even now he knew the Jap soldiers were maneuvering silently for better positions.

"Where?" she asked, tugging the radio rucksack up onto her back.

The wireless seemed almost superfluous now, but Reisman was reluctant to abandon it. He heaved the generator onto his back above his knapsack. "To the boat. Fort Brière if we can reach it."

They climbed over the levee, got down to the boat and unloaded their gear into it. Reisman pushed off into the stream. He handed her his carbine, keeping his M-3 close, and began to row back in the direction they had come earlier.

"I should have embraced Philippe," Madeleine murmured.

Behind them, hidden by the levee, they heard the firefight begin again, joining the sounds of battle at Fort Brière de l'Isle, the citadel in Lang Son and the outposts of Fort Négrier and Fort Gallieni.

Chapter 39

They beached the boat against the embankment 150 yards east of Fort Brière de l'Isle. The sounds of battle filled the night. Reisman looked cautiously over the levee and found himself staring through the blacked-out silhouettes of native huts close to the shoreline and large bungalows like Madeleine's further back, lit by gun flashes and the explosions of incoming rounds from the French 90 mm guns. Beyond the houses he saw the dim silhouettes of Jap soldiers firing artillery, mortars, machine guns and rifles into the French fortifications.

He was separated from the Japs by fifty yards. Their heavy guns and mortars were ranged along the railroad right of way and the parallel north-south road. Their infantry was probing through the fields closer to the fort, moving up, falling back, scurrying off in all directions to seek a way through the French defenses. Return fire from the fort was very strong. Reisman and Madeleine were cut off from them in this direction. To the north, stretched through the dry flats off the road, he saw more muzzle flashes, heard the guns and mortars, the chatter of machine guns and small arms facing Fort Brière. Their approach to the fort was cut off there too. He realized that he and Madeleine were more likely to be hit by the French fire coming their way than by Japanese fire.

Possibilities raced through his mind. They could take the boat south of the battle again, then try to make their way around the back of the Văn Miêu Rocks in the same way they had come out to the airfield. But they would risk getting caught by the enemy forces they had left fighting Philippe and his men. To try to break through to Fort Brière de l'Isle from any direction now seemed both pointless and suicidal. Yet he and Madeleine could not attack the Jap rear alone. They could not fight where they were. They had to escape.

North on the river through the remaining darkness? A possibility—but where? To hide in the familiar pagoda north of the city where he had been with Kita and Ho? Too close to the main Jap base. Or further north, to where Kita had left his motorcycle in the brush off the road near the village of Na Tuot? They could take it and speed up Route 4 into the jungled highlands of Tonkin. But that was impossible, of course. The Japs were attacking at Dong Dang and elsewhere along the frontier. They would be on the roads everywhere, unconcerned about air strikes, in control of the terrain, no need even to worry about the two-faced Viet Minh. Unless his men could get through to them and force them to join the fight.

But which two of his men were still alive? he wondered again in anguish. And if the survivors reached Pac Bo, would the Viet Minh kill them there or come out of the hills to help?

They had to get away from this place. To stay was futile. They returned to the boat, rowed upstream and beached again near Madeleine's house. Reisman left her in the boat and went to scout the area. He moved cautiously down the path to her house, which was a little apart from the other houses visible through trees and brush in the European enclave. At first all seemed quiet there, the din of war coming from a distance, but then Reisman began to see signs that Jap troops had rampaged through the area not long before him. The windows and doors of Madeleine's house were smashed, the walls riddled with bullet holes, and the interior had been ransacked. But not until he went into some of the other houses did he see the full horror of what was happening in Lang Son. He found the corpses of officers caught unarmed in their homes and murdered, their women raped and bayoneted to death, their children slaughtered.

Reisman felt a terrible rage, but there was no action he could take to vent his fury. He was no longer a participant in these events, merely a witness. He was determined to save Madeleine and not perish himself. He was no longer the warrior, sure of himself no matter the odds; he was the victim pursued, the noncombatant who had to get out of the way.

He went back to the boat and told Madeleine what he had seen. Knowing that the Japs had been there already, it seemed the best place to hole up. They carried their things up from the river. "No lights!" he warned when they entered the bungalow. But he plugged in the radio, turned it on, and was amazed again that the electricity was still functioning.

"They didn't think you people would fight," he whispered to Madeleine. "They thought you would capitulate after the first few shots."

The distant sounds of battle still reached them. Through the remaining few hours of night one of them dozed while the other remained on guard, staring out across the veranda into the dark approaches, and monitoring the receiver, its volume turned very low. Reisman stayed off the air himself. No one would come to their help. To be silent and unseen was their only salvation for the time being. The pleas of other dying fortresses were heard in open broadcasts, begging for help. The Lang Son citadel, half a mile from them, reported that the enemy had broken through. There were heavy casualties on both sides and house-to-house fighting was continuing through the interior grounds. The northwest strongpoint under Captain Vernières and the southeast bastion under General Lemonnier continued to hold. There was no word from Fort Brière de l'Isle, Fort Négrier or Fort Gallieni, which had no radio equipment.

At daylight they still heard the sounds of fighting at the citadel and Fort Brière de l'Isle. The shape of their immediate surroundings became visible and they watched the outside for a while. No one passed on the narrow dirt road. Their view of the river was blocked by the high embankment.

"What shall we do?" Madeleine asked.

"Stay here till after the shooting stops," Reisman answered, and in saying it he felt guilt and shame. But there was no other way. "Maybe till night. Then try to work our way past the Japs and up into the hills. There are natives there who will help us."

He was thinking of the Nung, not the Viet Minh. If he and Madeleine stayed off the main road, stuck to footpaths, paddies and brush, they could make it to one of the Nung villages in the night—

maybe the hamlet where he had picked up the downed airman months before.

"I must find Philippe," Madeleine said in a plaintive voice.

"We will bring you to a safe place, as he wanted," Reisman told her. "There is nothing else we can do."

They waited and listened and hardly spoke. He wondered if she would come to hate him now, for doing nothing.

At mid-morning, they heard the last transmission from General Lemonnier: "Still holding three-fourths of citadel . . . No water . . . Request air support and supply drops . . . Where are the Americans?"

At 1300, all noise of battle from the citadel ceased. But from the south, the sounds of fighting at Fort Brière de l'Isle continued.

They ate K-rations from Reisman's pack. Madeleine went to the kitchen to heat water to dissolve the little packets of powdered coffee. She heard noises outside and saw two Viet-Namese civilian men on the road pulling a loaded wagon. They stopped outside her house and she ran to warn Reisman.

He watched them come up the path and realized they were looters scavenging the empty homes of Europeans. He and Madeleine hid, let the Viets come in and surprised them at gunpoint.

"Đứng lại. Đừng sợ. Chúng tôi là bạn," Reisman called out. *Halt. Don't be afraid. We are friends.*

The two men stood still, frightened. Madeleine looked at Reisman, surprised that he could speak any Viet-Namese. He frisked the men, found they were unarmed, and asked them in a pidgin of French and Viet-Namese what was happening outside. The Viets' voices and faces betrayed their fear, but they appeared to be telling the truth. Except for Fort Brière de l'Isle, all the French military posts had been captured. The Japs were executing some captured officers, enlisted men and civilians and letting others live, apparently according to whim. They had gone on a rampage, reported the two men fearfully, butchering soldiers and civilians alike, raping and killing European women, murdering children.

"Il fait terrible! . . . Les Japonaises sont bêtes! . . . Sauvages!" they babbled, seeking Reisman's favor. Many soldiers—Indochinese, Senegalese, Indians and Foreign Legionnaires—had also been killed, wounded or taken prisoner. Others had escaped, they told him.

"Êtes-vous déserteurs?" Reisman demanded. When they looked at him in puzzlement, he repeated the question in Viet-Namese. *"Ong lính dào ngũ?"*

"No, no, monsieur!" one shouted. *"Civil!"*

Reisman asked if there were Jap soldiers nearby. The Viets said the soldiers had been there earlier but had gone away into the city and to the forts. He told them to clear out and go home. Though he didn't trust them and thought they were quite likely to betray him and Madeleine to the first Jap troops they saw, he could not bring himself to shoot them. The men backed out of the house and turned and fled, grabbing their loaded wagon on the run and pulling it after them.

Madeleine stared at Reisman strangely. In a suspicious voice, she asked, "Where did you learn to speak Viet-Namese?"

"Up in the hills."

"Are they your friends . . . your allies . . . the Annamites?"

"My job," he answered abruptly.

She was silent after that, perhaps suspecting a bit more about his job in Tonkin than she had known before—more, certainly, than he had wanted her to know, but still not enough to damn him for it.

An hour later, Reisman spotted a Jap NCO and two riflemen coming down the road from the direction the two Viet-Namese had taken. They passed all the other houses and headed for Madeleine's, confirming his suspicion about the two Viets. Reisman called out a quiet warning to Madeleine, and she came up close to him at the window. She tensed, but not with fear. It was like he himself felt, tired of running and hiding, almost glad that there would be some action. They watched the Japs through the front windows, tracked their movements and prepared for them. When Reisman saw them affix bayonets to their rifles, he knew that they were preparing for some extra fun and he felt his flesh crawl. Belatedly, they started to play Indian through the trees and brush as they came closer.

Reisman took the carbine from Madeleine that he had given her earlier, checked it and handed it back. "You know how to use it?" he asked.

She glanced down at the weapon, saw the safety was still on, and released it. "I have been preparing for a long time," she answered coldly.

"You must shoot to kill," he told her harshly. "Not a moment's hesitation."

"Yes," she answered, just as harshly. "I will not let them take me."

She did not even look at him. There was a tension within her that he had never seen before, as if everything in her life up to now had been preparation for these moments. Her eyes narrowed, staring through the window and beyond across the veranda, following the paths of her intended prey with the ferine ardor of a hunter.

"They are splitting up," she said. "One to the back."

Reisman knew what had to be done. He and Madeleine could not stay together in the front room and meet a frontal attack with their combined firepower. They could not let the flanking soldier have the advantage of coming at them from behind.

"We have to separate," he said in a muted voice.

"I will go," she answered. "You have the big gun—for two. I will take care of the other one. I know my house better than you do."

He did not want to let her go, yet he knew he had to. She could track the one Jap through the side windows, listen for him at the rear, lie in wait in a place of her own choosing. She had the carbine—sufficient for the one. He had the submachine gun—better for the two.

Madeleine started away, but Reisman reached out and touched her arm. When she turned to him, he kissed her lips quickly and said, *"Fais attention. Je t'aime."*

"Moi aussi . . . de tout mon coeur."

Then he turned back to watch the two Japs, who were now at the edge of the raised veranda. Madeleine moved out of the living room behind him to track the other one. He squeezed her out of his mind, did not listen for her movements, concentrated instead on the two coming toward him. When he saw one with a grenade in his hand, crouching low halfway to the door, and the other one reversing his rifle to use the stock as a club, he anticipated what would happen and leaped behind the protection of a heavy couch furthest from the door.

The smashing of glass and wood came a moment later, then the seconds of silence as the unseen grenade was thrown in, the thud of its landing, the explosion. The noise was horrendous. The couch tilted against him but stopped the shards of metal. He waited another three seconds, then rose and sprayed the entryway with a burst from the M-3 just as the two soldiers came through. The fusillade of bullets flung them upward and back, their arms and legs splayed out, their bayoneted rifles flying loose. They dropped to the floor, torn and bleeding. Reisman leaped over the couch and fired one more burst into each crumpled form. Then he heard Madeleine's scream from the rear of the house and two quick shots, and, heart bursting, ran down the hallway toward the sound.

He saw the Jap first, sprawled motionless on top of Madeleine just inside the doorway of her bedroom, but could not fire his gun for fear of hitting her. He sprang into the room with a terrible cry of rage, raised his weapon and brought it smashing down on the man's head.

Only then, as the body rolled off Madeleine's legs, did he see the blood pouring out of the soldier's face and chest and hear Madeleine's voice saying weakly, "It's all right, *Jean.*"

She was sitting slumped against the wall, her carbine still in her hands. But the more fearful sight to Reisman was that of the Jap bayonet rammed into the wall beside her and the bloodstain spreading through the fabric of her jacket from a wound in her upper right arm. She had pulled the trigger twice at pointblank range just as the Jap NCO had discovered her and lunged to impale her on his bayonet. The sharp edge had sliced her arm instead.

Reisman yanked the bayonet from the wall and saw her wince as the steel grazed her flesh again. He threw the rifle aside and knelt beside her. Madeleine's face was white with the emotional and physical shock. Yet there was anger in her voice when she kicked her foot at the dead Jap and muttered, "*Cochon!* No French soldier would do a thing like that to a woman!"

Pulling away the fabric, Reisman saw that the wound was not as severe as he had thought. He eased her arm from the sleeve and removed her jacket, sweater and blouse. Then he got the first-aid kit from his pack, poured sulfa powder on her wound, placed a compress on it and bandaged it.

"You are a man of many talents," she said, watching him doctor her.

"Does it hurt?"

"A little," she lied.

"Do you think you can travel now? We can't stay here. Others may come."

Madeleine insisted that she was all right, though she looked a little shaky. Nevertheless, it was a greater risk to stay there. He explained to her what they must do.

They put on the peasant clothes and conical straw hats they had carried with them, but kept their own sturdy shoes and boots. If anyone got that close to them it wouldn't make any difference anyway. Reisman's object was to deceive others from the distance and to keep moving.

"We'll go south again on the river to Fort Brière de l'Isle and see for ourselves what's happening," he told her.

The sounds of battle could still be heard from there. Perhaps there would be a way to slip through the Jap lines and join the French forces. For them to have held out this long was in itself encouraging.

In the kitchen, Reisman got two burlap sacks. Madeleine carried one over her shoulder with the carbine and ammo in it and a few items from her suitcase. She insisted that she could manage, though her wound throbbed painfully. Her blond hair was pinned up under the deep conical hat. Reisman carried his M-3, ammo, grenades, field glasses, first-aid kit, water canteen and K-rations in the other sack. His pistol and knife were hidden under his *cu-nao* jacket. The wireless, clothes and other gear were abandoned.

Straw hats pulled low, stooped over like peasants with the sacks on their backs, they scurried from the house to the Sông Ky Cung. There they darkened their faces and hands with mud and climbed into the small boat. Reisman rowed south.

The middle of the river seemed a good place to be. Many small boats and sampans filled with natives in clothes like theirs moved on the stream in both directions, either oblivious to the battle still raging not far from them or fleeing it, not knowing which way to go. There were no Jap troops visible on either shore, or any in boats on the river.

It was twilight when they beached near Fort Brière de l'Isle. Before they had climbed the levee, the sounds of gunfire suddenly ceased. Taking their gunny sacks with them, Reisman and Madeleine peered over the top of the enbankment. She sank into the dirt with a moan and he knew that she was suffering despite her brave front. There were pain pills in the first-aid kit, but he was reluctant to give her any until he was certain she needed them. He wanted her to remain alert, not doped up. Their lives might depend on it.

Silent now, the Jap artillery and mortars on the railroad right of way and the parallel road seemed at first glimpse abandoned. In the dimming light, Reisman could see only a few soldiers guarding the guns, staring intently toward the French fortifications into which unopposed Jap infantry were now moving from all sides, no longer firing their weapons. The fields outside the fort were strewn with hundreds of Jap dead.

All along the river embankment now, and in the nearby marshland, Reisman saw mushroom hats and peasant clothes rise from concealment and stare toward the suddenly quiet battleground. Were any of them Viet Minh, he wondered? None of the Jap soldiers were moving toward the river or looking behind them in that direction.

They obviously believed no French personnel could possibly be there. They believed themselves in that moment to be invincible. Enemies would flee, not stay.

In a few minutes, as the twilight deepened, Reisman became aware of some activity near one of the fort's concrete outerworks and saw disarmed French officers and troops being taken from the fort under heavy guard and lined up against the wall. Some were severely wounded and were being carried by their comrades.

A new awareness, then horror and rage, seized Reisman. Machine guns were being aimed at the defenseless survivors of the garrison. He wanted to scream out, to charge the monstrous scene—but he stopped before he had opened his mouth or moved. His whole body trembled. He was a man who understood battle, too often relished it—but he rejected, even as it was happening, the terrible reality of what he was witnessing.

Then he heard singing. The martial passion of *La Marseillaise* rose like a sacrament from the mouths of the prisoners. Moments later it became a funeral dirge sung by the dead as the prisoners were slaughtered by bullets spewing from the Japanese machine guns.

Reisman turned to look at Madeleine. She was staring transfixed by what she had just seen. She murmured the name of her brother. Yet they could not know if Philippe was among the victims, or had been captured or killed earlier, or had managed to get away. Reisman saw his own rage and despair mirrored in Madeleine's face. But he would not let either of them give in to that despair. Better to have died charging the Jap executioners. They had to move now, to lose themselves in furious effort, even if at random. He took Madeleine's hand and drew her after him back to the boat. She moved as if in shock, oblivious even to the pain of her wound.

Chapter 40

In the night they were propelled by actions, hopes and fears through the dimly seen surreal landscape of the Lang Son battleground, seeking moment by moment sanctuary. Reason told Reisman they had to go north into the hills, but reality made the route circuitous. First south a quarter of a mile on the dark river. Then west on foot through the paddies behind the Văn Miêu Rocks, where there had been no battle. Then north on familiar footpaths that ultimately would take them, if they could stay on them, to that bend of the Sông Ky Cung outside the city where he first had crossed with Ho Chi Minh and Kita Shidehara.

Reisman was driven by his obsession to bring Madeleine to safety and by his instinct to survive—to fight and triumph another day. He had a haunting feeling of *déjà vu,* as if he had done this before—and he remembered that he had: nine months earlier, behind Nazi lines in France, he had been obsessed with saving the critically wounded

Clyde Bowren. He had succeeded. Thinking of Bowren, Baw San, Wladislaw and Sawyer, he was assailed by the guilt of having sent two of them to their deaths—and the pain of not knowing which two to mourn.

The great noise of battle no longer filled the air. There was only the sound of sporadic shooting. Perhaps isolated pockets of resistance; or trapped fugitives like Madeleine and him—or the monstrous specter of more executions?

Events and illusions forced them from their intended route, chased them far east again through rice paddies and woods. Reisman guided Madeleine with whispered commands and touches, holding her hand or grasping the fabric of her *cu-nao.* She staggered along like a limp puppet, but kept her pierced right arm stiffly against her side and clutched her gunny sack tightly over her left shoulder.

In the dark night on a footpath two hundred yards south of the citadel they came head to head with two Jap soldiers trotting their way. Reisman forced Madeleine off the path with him to let the soldiers pass. He bowed and scraped and mumbled apologies in Viet-Namese as they went by, then yanked Madeleine after him to keep moving. They had gone only a few feet when he heard an angry command from one of the Japs behind them. They kept moving and the command was repeated. He pushed Madeleine to the ground and started to fall after her, pulling his pistol at the same time—then heard the first rifle shot and felt the bullet smack his left thigh. He twisted and turned, aimed his .45 and fired two rounds into each Jap soldier. Then there was silence.

Holding his pistol in front of him, Reisman slid painfully through the wet earth toward the crumpled forms. They were both dead. He dragged them off the pathway into the paddy, then limped back to Madeleine and fell beside her.

They had to keep moving, but he was in pain now, felt weak and dizzy, and let himself flow with it a few moments. Then he heard Madeleine at his ear, whispering his name urgently, pulling him out of his torpor. The realization that he had been hit had galvanized her out of her own numbness. She pulled away the bloody cloth at his thigh, helped him treat and bandage the wound. The bullet had gouged a chunk out of his flesh but had not become imbedded. Despite the shock of the impact, the blood loss and pain, he was sure it was only a minor flesh wound. But when they started moving again, he knew he would not be able to go far because of it. The sulfa and tight compress would do for a while and lessen the chance of infection, but the simple act of walking was making it bleed and throb with pain.

They kept moving, crossed narrow dirt roads in the empty spaces between shadows and forms, passed outlying huts and buildings without lights or life—and then, to his chagrin, Reisman realized they had come unwittingly to the southeastern approach to the city. Nearby, unseen yet in the dark, was the main north-south road that became Rue Gouttenègre and Rue Unal as it entered Lang Son. Either street would take them north to the bridge across the Sông Ky Cung—but first enmesh them in the middle of the Japanese army.

Reisman had a giddy moment thinking he might just go right on up Rue Gouttenègre and blow the power station now that the Japs had captured the town; and then he had the tantalizing thought that respite, if not safety, might lie in going to where the maelstrom of battle had been and gone.

He led Madeleine to a place of concealment beside the road. He felt hobbled in his movements, slowing down physically, getting fuzzy in his head. They glimpsed Jap trucks, armor and artillery passing north, coming back from Fort Brière de l'Isle. He drew Madeleine against him and held her protectively, careful not to touch her wound. Often during these last hours he had felt psychically the shock and pain of the bayonet that had pierced her. In the flashes of passing headlights he stared into her mud-blackened face. She wore her pain and exhaustion stoically, perhaps better than he did his own.

When the road was empty they darted across it unseen, traversed the railway tracks and ducked into a shed near the station. Now Reisman wondered numbly if maybe they ought to keep going to the levee and river again. It had been on the waterway that they had been safest. Maybe that was where they should try to make their escape.

A few moments later he was bewildered to hear singing—once again *La Marseillaise,* and shouts of *"Vive la Coloniale!"* and *"Vive la Légion!"*, followed by other shouts, the screams of men and women, voices of command and volleys of gunfire. He wondered if he was delirious, reliving again the terrible executions at the walls of Fort Brière de l'Isle. They stalked from hiding place to hiding place, drawn toward the source of the sounds even as they resisted going there.

From concealment, they viewed a place illuminated by the headlamps of parked vehicles, a large open lot across Rue Gouttenègre from the train station. In the moment of seeing it they recoiled from it. The bodies of soldiers and civilians, men and women, were strewn on the ground and filled a long trench. Some had been decapitated by sword, others shot by rifles and machine guns, their bodies afterward impaled by bayonets.

Madeleine turned away from the scene, her fist pressed into her mouth to keep from screaming. Her eyes looked glazed with shock. She pressed her head fiercely against Reisman's shoulder. He started to draw her away from their tenuous hiding place, then caught sight of Japanese and Viet-Namese blocking the way behind them and to either side. Only ahead of them was there an opening—and that was the execution ground. There was nothing they could do now except stay where they were—stay and watch and listen and force themselves to numbness as more processions of executions took place during the night.

Dawn came.

With his new awareness of beginning daylight, Reisman was roused by the sounds of aircraft, then bombs exploding, coming closer, then the staccato of aerial cannons and machine guns. He looked to the north and saw two flights of American P-51s and P-40s diving low. Beyond them were attack bombers hitting the Jap installations close to Lang Son.

But he felt no elation. It was too late. Three P-51s flew low down the length of Rue Gouttenègre, picked out clusters of Jap vehicles and troops and strafed them. As the planes passed close over the railway station and the execution ground, Jap soldiers and civilian Viet-Namese dispersed in all directions—and suddenly Reisman saw a glimmer of hope.

He pulled Madeleine after him the moment they were no longer in the line of fire. Weak, dazed and in pain, they staggered toward the levee, still carrying their gun-filled sacks over their shoulders. But as they ran, a second flight of strafing planes followed the first and roared toward them. Blind impulse took over. Reisman flung his gunny sack to the ground, pulled Madeleine's from her shoulder and, taking her hand, they staggered desperately toward the only place he saw to take cover—the ditch of the dead.

They forced themselves down into the obscenity of the abattoir, while the American planes swooped low over the area twice more, firing cannons and machine guns at everything on the ground. Then there was silence. Reisman hadn't the strength or will to move.

In a little while he heard orders shouted in Japanese. He heard vehicles starting up. He thought he heard the Japanese leaving, abandoning the area to the dead. But he wasn't sure. He was afraid to rise up and be counted among the living. Horror, rage and frustration had dulled his senses and now he felt lassitude. His mind had become as surreal as those battlegrounds through which he and Madeleine had been driven to come to rest here. He lay there for what seemed a long time, mired in the corporeal reality and stink of death. He passed in and out of, if not unconsciousness, then a deep and merciful loss of contact with reality. In moments when he was aware of where he was and what was happening, he risked the opening of an eye, the slight raising of his head among the dead. He thought he saw some rise and crawl away, bleeding from their wounds. He touched Madeleine, uncertain if she was dead or alive, perceived the coursing of her blood, the beating of her heart, felt the return pressure of her hand.

Time passed and he became aware of men and women in dark peasant clothes and conical straw hats like he and Madeleine wore. They walked along the edge of the trench, jumped down into it, searched among the corpses. He heard voices of concern that spoke in languages he understood, and then he felt tender hands lifting him from the abattoir.

"*Duwa* John!" said a voice for which he had been mourning.

Then another voice . . . "It's okay now, Major."

Reisman focused his eyes, saw Baw San and recognized Sergeant Bowren's mud-blackened face between the dark *cu-nao* and straw conical hat leaning over him. He was placed on one litter, Madeleine on another, and they were carried away by men of the Nung, faces he thought he recognized from the long first trek when he had come south across the frontier at Lao Cai.

Sergeant Bowren walked beside his litter and related the things that had happened to bring him there.

Hours later, Reisman heard temple bells . . . perhaps the pagoda north of Lang Son . . . but how could that be? He was no longer certain what he had seen and done himself or had been told by others . . . nor of where he was and where he had been.

But out of the jumble came an awareness, the reality that it had been Joe Wladislaw and Ken Sawyer who had been killed in the shooting down of their small plane. Clyde Bowren and Baw San had jumped to Pac Bo. Clyde had told him that. But the Viet Minh had rejected his plea to fight. They had preferred to leave the satiated conquerors of Lang Son to wallow in their triumph, then abandon the devastated forts and rotting bodies. Only afterward, when it had been safe again to move, had the Viet Minh brought Bowren and Baw San with them to learn his fate.

"Have you been in touch with Kunming?" Reisman whispered to Bowren during a moment of lucidity.

"Yeah. I got Kilgore on the radio from Pac Bo and told him what happened down here . . . told him we were going out to look for you and the girl."

"What did he say?"

"He was worried about something he called his trade goods. I didn't know what the hell he was talking about . . . and he wouldn't explain. 'Secret stuff,' he said."

Reisman lifted his head from the litter. From somewhere deep down in his being, he started to laugh, and as the bile of it sought to bypass the anguish and pain he felt, the bitter sound choked in his throat and he coughed. It was such a pathetically small victory: the lieutenant colonel yearning for his trade goods that never had existed. He would tell Kilgore, if he ever saw him again, that the opium had gone down in the plane with Sawyer and Wladislaw.

To exact vengeance for what Sam had done to Linc Bradford and his Kachins, and to the many others he must have hurt or killed at second hand through his dealings with Tai Li, Reisman knew that there were means to use other than overt violence. Sam was no better or worse than others who had devised schemes to turn war into business. And the good guys didn't always win. He would let Kilgore's own greed consume him. It seemed to Reisman as if that might be all the victory there could be for him now.

His head dropped back again on the litter and his mind wandered to thoughts of Philippe Belfontaine. Was he dead? Massacred with the other prisoners? Or had he managed to get away? Madeleine would be desperate to find out. But there was no way to do that now. Perhaps not for months, not until this dirty distant war was finished and the participants called to account for their actions.

Reisman's litter was placed on the ground. The afternoon sun was pleasantly warm on his face, but the odors he still smelled, like the scenes in his mind, conjured nightmares. He eased himself up onto his elbows and saw Madeleine on a litter beside him. She looked dazed, her eyes staring whitely from the thick, stinking grime of her clothes and skin. Reisman looked around, saw monks in saffron robes, recognized the courtyard. He tried to get to his feet. Sergeant Bowren and Baw San bent down to help him.

The group of Nung and Viet Minh close to them parted to let someone through. Reisman saw who it was and what energy he still possessed rose in fury to his throat.

"I owe you, you treacherous bastard!" he screamed at Ho Chi Minh.

Ho did not flinch. "It is over now, *Jean,*" he said calmly.

"No, it is not!" Reisman raged at him. "I owe you for bugging out on us when you knew . . . when you could have warned us or helped!"

"I did not know," Ho protested.

"I don't believe you!" Reisman flung back at him. "You self-righteous son-of-a-bitch! I owe you for your betrayal of friendship!" He stopped short . . . as if he had said words like that recently . . . and he remembered that he had—to Sam Kilgore. And Kita Shidehara had said them to *him.*

Ho Chi Minh shook his head slowly. "It is not true."

"Why didn't you order Giap's forces into action? Why didn't you send your guerrillas when I first radioed you for help? You were there when I talked to Mai! I know it!"

"Very well. I was there," Ho acknowledged.

"Coward!" Reisman spit out at him. And in saying the word he realized he was raging at himself, too, detesting himself for the fear and despair that had enervated him, for taking shelter among the dead instead of fighting to the death.

Madeleine too was now struggling to her feet. Reisman went to help her and she leaned against him, trying to understand why he was raging at this old Annamite.

"I did not come to help," Ho explained, "because we were tending to matters which were more important."

Reisman stared at him in astonishment at so pale an argument. During these past three days, how could anything have been more important? "I'd kill you with my bare hands now if I thought it would accomplish what I want it to," he said icily.

"I did not come to help you," said Ho, oblivious to the threat, "because the French were about to attack us at Pac Bo."

"Liar!"

"It was their intention to wipe out the Viet Minh in one big campaign," Ho continued, now with growing anger and bitterness. "Instead of being down here with you defending Lang Son, there were thousands of them moving on Pac Bo at the very time the Japs were preparing to attack everywhere else. Is that not amusing, *mon ami?*" Ho observed without laughter. "There were even two *bataillons* of *Tirailleurs* from Lang Son."

Reisman's rage choked in his throat. He turned to look at Madeleine, a grotesque sight bobbing her head in what was either dazed miscomprehension or acknowledgment of the truth of the words spoken by the old peasant.

"We had, as you see, our own concerns," Ho stated simply.

"But the French did *not* attack you," Reisman contended.

"No, they did not. You are right, of course," Ho agreed, as if talking to a child. "At the last moment they fled instead . . . toward Laos, Cambodia and China—and the Japanese are still in pursuit. For us here, it is over."

Reisman turned to Sergeant Bowren and Baw San. "Is he telling the truth?" he asked.

"I think so, sir," Bowren answered. "But like you told us in China before we came down here—we don't have any real friends. There ain't none of them playing it straight."

"Allons!" muttered Ho impatiently. "While the sons of Nippon are resting from their labors, let us get away from this place. I told you long ago that I did not like Lang Son. You and your lady friend are not well. We will travel pleasantly by truck. Colonel Shidehara is waiting. He will escort us to Pac Bo safely."

If that was so, Reisman reassured himself, then it seemed corroboration of what he had believed already, that Kita had not betrayed them at the airstrip. The attack there against Philippe and his *marsouins* and the shooting down of the L-5 had been the chance fortunes of war. For if Kita had betrayed them, he would not be waiting now to drive them to Pac Bo. He knew that Reisman would kill him if he had been responsible for the deaths of Wladislaw and Sawyer.

Yet, there was another taunting ambiguity that had been troubling Reisman these past three days. "Did Shidehara know that his Japs were about to attack us here?" he demanded of Ho.

"No, he did not," Ho answered emphatically. "Not until it was actually happening. I believe him on this. Nor did he know the plans of the French to attack us at Pac Bo."

It seemed to Reisman, then, that the Kempitai colonel—whose cleverness and extraordinary fount of military intelligence had both irritated him and made him somewhat envious—was himself fallible. Though that brought only a feeling of small and cynical satisfaction to Reisman. He and Kita were each men of the same peculiar makeup and honor, and each had been made pawns of forces beyond their control.

The sound of Ho Chi Minh's voice still speaking brought him back from his reverie. "When you have rested a few days," said Ho, "and your wounds are healed . . . I think maybe it will be time for you to go home to Chicago, *Jean.* It is over for you here."

Reisman braced at the man's condescending tone. Baw San stepped closer to him and Reisman placed a hand for support on the young Kachin's shoulder. With his other arm he gently encircled Madeleine's waist. She tried to smile for him, but failed.

"Est-ce que c'est fini?" she whispered hoarsely.

Reisman smiled at her reassuringly. Then he turned his gaze strongly to Ho Chi Minh and spoke slowly, with reasoned calm.

"No, *monsieur,* it is not over. It has only just begun. You will deal with her and her people . . . and then you will deal with me and my people. And it will not be over . . ."

AFTERWORD AND ACKNOWLEDGMENTS

The idea for a story set in the time and places of this novel first occurred to me many years ago when I read some of the books of Dr. Bernard B. Fall, particularly his *Last Reflections on a War,* a collection of articles published after he was killed in Viet-Nam in 1967. I didn't know Dr. Fall. I wish I had.

I was lucky later to meet Charles G. Wilbourn—painter, teacher, sometimes military intelligence officer (now Major, USA/MI, Ret.). He had been on duty in Viet-Nam in times more recent than the people of my story, but he knew Indochinese and Chinese history and politics, was conversant with both *Quốc Ngữ* and French, wrote military intelligence papers for the Pentagon and knew immediately what I was talking about when I told him I wanted to write a novel about things that had happened in Indochina during the last year of World War II. Books and studies came pouring out of his own library and I picked his brains for research from his years of experience in the field and his teaching.

I am grateful also to Colonel Denny Lane, who suggested people to talk to and research material to read and who enabled me to obtain excellent maps of many areas where my fictional and historical characters were operating. Then he put me in touch with two men who were enormously helpful: Major Jean Pichon of the French army and his father, Robert Pichon (Staff Sergeant, Ret.), a veteran of the French Colonial Army who had been a witness to and participant in events in Indochina during the time of my story.

Robert Pichon had been a member of the intelligence section of the Lang Son garrison, but had been transferred to Hanoi just a few weeks before the Japanese *coup de force* in March 1945. After the Japanese surrender in August he was freed from imprisonment and assigned to collect information about what had happened in the Lang Son area in March. Forty years later, in response to my many questions, Robert Pichon summoned up his memories of those days and drew maps and diagrams that helped me greatly, and he and Major Pichon undertook difficult research among other veterans of *La Coloniale* and in the French Military Archives. Their contributions to my research were magnificent and invaluable.

I am also indebted to Colonel Aaron Bank, USA (Ret.), for sharing with me some of his experiences in the OSS, particularly those in Kunming and later in French Indochina in the fall of 1945, when his missions just after the end of the war brought him to personal meetings with Ho Chi Minh. During his long, illustrious military career, Colonel Bank later was to form the 10th Special Forces Group, the Green Berets.

There were others who helped because they knew something of Burma, China or French Indochina at the time of my story, or had knowledge and experience in ground and air operations and supplemented my research, caught technical errors and gave good advice.

Also, it is perhaps less traditional in the writing of fiction to acknowledge a bibliography—but I do. I devoured dozens of reports, articles, histories, memoirs and biographies written before, during and after the time of my story. The novel would have been the poorer if I had not had recourse to the factual accounts of the people and events of those times written by a long list of men and women.

Only I, however, am responsible for the choices of characters and events, for the way the *dramatis personae* have been woven into the history of those days and for the fictional interpretations that I made of what happened.

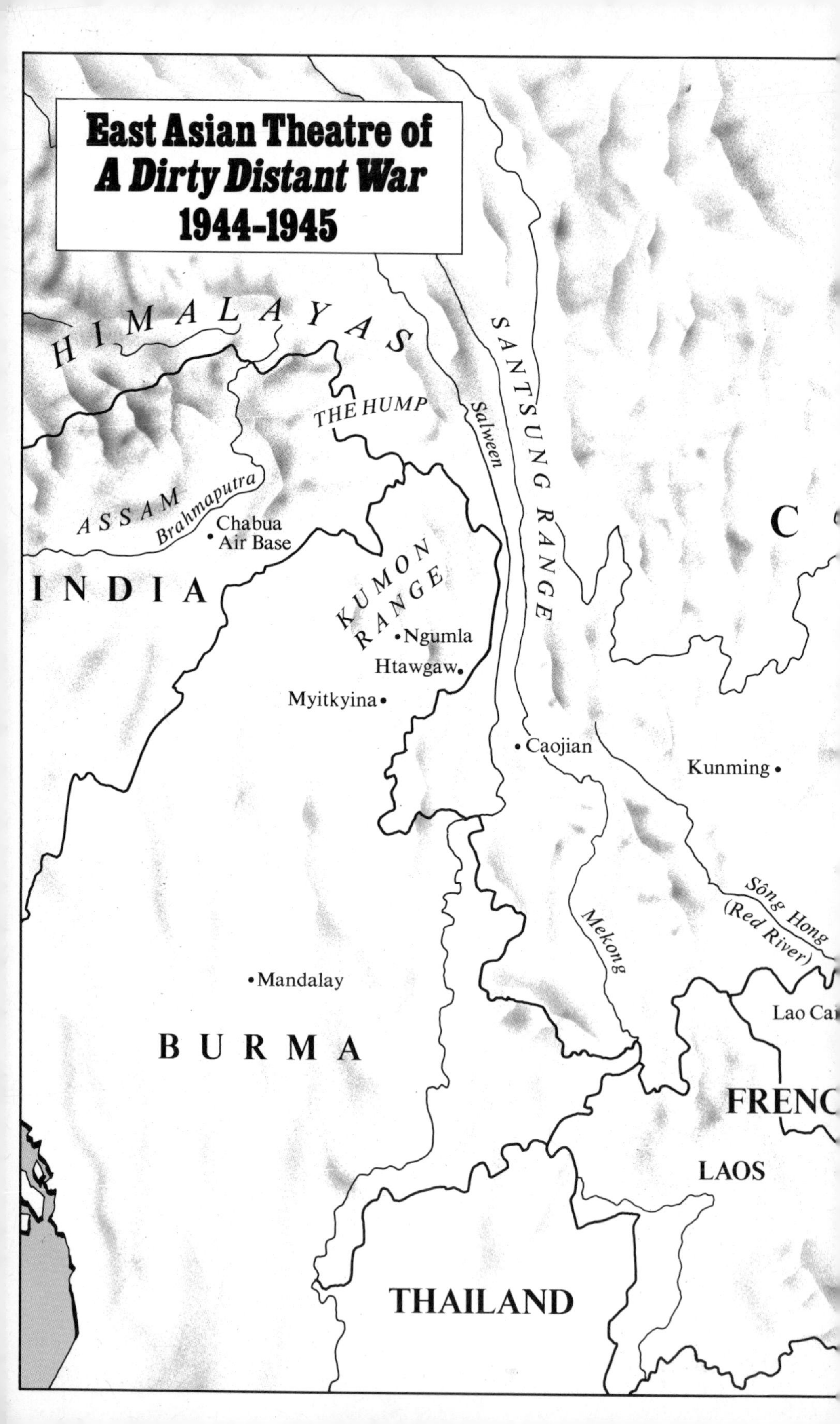
East Asian Theatre of
A Dirty Distant War
1944-1945
HIMALAYAS
THE HUMP
SANTSUNG RANGE
Salween
ASSAM
Brahmaputra
Chabua Air Base
INDIA
KUMON RANGE
Ngumla
Htawgaw
Myitkyina
Caojian
Kunming
Sông Hong (Red River)
Mekong
Mandalay
BURMA
Lao Ca
FRENC
LAOS
THAILAND
C